MASTIFF

BEKA COOPER

BOOK THREE

MASTIFF

TAMORA PIERCE

RANDOM HOUSE 🏠 NEW YORK

Text copyright © 2011 by Tamora Pierce
Jacket photograph copyright © 2011 by Jonathan Barkat

Visit us on the Web! randomhouse.com/teens

Educators and librarians, for a variety of teaching tools, visit us at randomhouse.com/teachers

Library of Congress Cataloging-in-Publication Data
Pierce, Tamora.
Mastiff / Tamora Pierce. — 1st ed.
p.   cm. — (Beka Cooper ; bk. 3)
Summary: Beka, having just lost her fiance in a slaver's raid, is able to distract herself by going with her team on an important hunt at the queen's request, unaware that the throne of Tortall depends on their success.
ISBN 978-0-375-81470-9 (trade) — ISBN 978-0-375-91470-6 (lib. bdg.) — ISBN 978-0-375-89328-5 (ebook)
[1. Kidnapping—Fiction.   2. Police—Fiction.   3. Kings, queens, rulers, etc.—Fiction.   4. Fantasy.]   I. Title.
PZ7.P61464Mas 2011   [Fic]—dc23   2011024152

Printed in the United States of America

10 9 8 7 6 5 4 3 2 1

First Edition

Random House Children's Books supports the First Amendment and celebrates the right to read.

Whether it's for debt, for work, for sex:
For the slaves,
in the hope that one day your freedom comes not through
purchase, illness, or death,
but because slavery and the slavers have been sought out and
stamped out in every home, business, warehouse, ship, quarry,
bar, factory, and nest they inhabit.

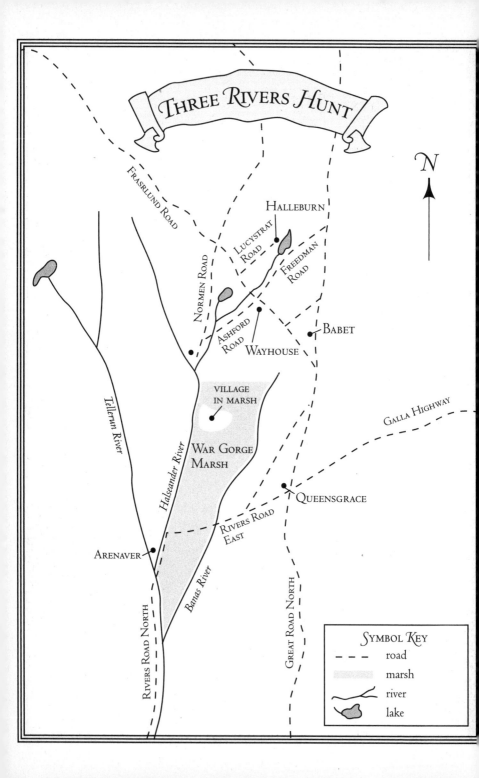

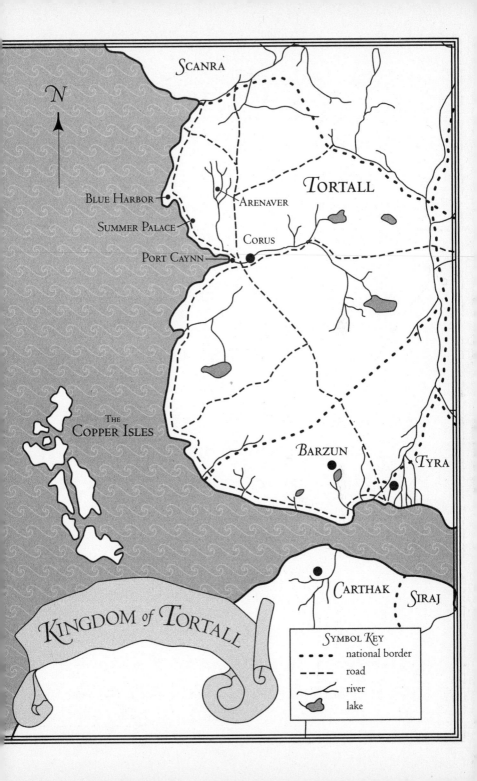

Wednesday, June 6, 249 H.E.

Mistress Trout's Lodgings
Nipcopper Close, Corus
Ten of the evening.
We buried Holborn today.

The burying ground has no trees in it, no shade for us Lower City Dogs. Because most of us work in the dark, we want our bodies to lie in the sun. Stones decorate the graves, stones placed there for remembrance. Some graves are piled waist-high with them, signs that the Dogs who lie beneath were loved by family and guards both.

There were plenty of folk for Holborn. Rosto, Kora, Aniki, and Phelan had come from the Court of the Rogue. Even Rosto had learned to like Holborn this last year, for all that he was green jealous that Holborn was my betrothed. Kora and Aniki wept for me. My eyes were as dry as the ground of the boneyard. Everyone believed I'd wept so hard I had no tears left.

Holborn's family came. The men left my shoulders damp with tears, my belly filled with razors of guilt because I had none to shed with them. They told me how sorrowed they were that I'd never become their daughter, their sister. They also tried to keep his mother back. Only when they turned to go did she break from them to come at me.

I saw her slap coming, but I did naught to stop it. Only when she went for a second blow did I grab her wrist.

"You cold, Cesspit trull!" she screamed. "My poor lad was forever trying to impress you. He wouldn't be here if he hadn't been trying to prove himself as good as you, and you led him to his death!"

My partner, Tunstall, took her and gently put her in the hands of her men. "He made a mistake, mistress," he said gently in his hillman's rumble. "Beka had naught to do with it."

"She was *there*," Holborn's mother cried.

"She was not." My sergeant, Goodwin, had come over. "Had she been there, she would have stopped him from running into a nest of slave guards all on his own. Your son got himself killed."

The men of the family were all Dogs and knew that Tunstall and Goodwin were right. "Forgive her," Holborn's father whispered in my ear while his sons drew their mother out of the boneyard. "It is her grief talking." He looked shamefaced as he followed his family.

Other Dogs were present, to stand for Holborn and for me. Holborn was a leather badge, a five-year Dog who'd transferred to Jane Street last year. His old friends and partner from Flash District attended, as well as the Jane Street folk. Goodwin, her man, Tunstall, and his lady, Sabine, were there, as well as my Jane Street friends. Standing with the cityfolk were my brothers, sisters, grandmother, as well as my merchant friend Tansy and her family. Beside them was my foster family from the days when I had lived at Provost's House.

My informants among the city's pigeons attended, to my surprise. None landed on the grave. Holborn's ghost wasn't riding among them, waiting to say farewell to me. Many a soul that's been murdered rode a pigeon until he, or she, could settle old business, but not Holborn. In his last hours he'd only given my hand one more squeeze before he left me for the Peaceful Realms of the Black God of Death.

I listened to the folk murmur to each other as they waited for the priest and Lord Gershom to arrive. One mot was telling those around her that Holborn had saved her oldest lad when a game of dice went bad. The Dogs from his old district shared the tale that Holborn was known to jump on tables and stand on his hands when he'd had one cup too many. A dancer whose full purse he'd saved from rushers was there. It was she who set a cube of incense by the headstone.

A priest of the Black God said some words once Holborn went into the ground. So did Lord Gershom, before he gave Holborn's medal to his father. Then came the placing of the stones, as all who chose to leave a token did so. Most of them who'd come went on to the Jane Street Guardhouse after that. There Holborn's Day Watch fellows had laid out a funeral feast. Those closest to me stayed for a while. Eventually they came to tell me goodbye. I stood by the headstone as they approached.

My oldest friend, Tansy, clung to me and wept on my uniform, and left three chunks of crystal by the headstone. That done, her man Herun took her and the babies home. Then my lord Gershom and my district commander, Sir Acton of Fenrigh, said their farewells. I collected myself to bow to them. Others followed. Granny Fern, clinging to my youngest brother's arm, my other brother, and my sisters all looked more broken than me. They had loved Holborn, who had wheedled until I was on good terms with my sister Dorine again. My foster aunt Mya, my foster uncle, and my other family from Provost's House left with them. The hardest Dogs of Jane Street kennel, who had gone through so many street battles with me, trickled away, two and three at a time. I embraced my fellow Dogs, knowing they would not think me weak for doing so at a time like this.

Now and then Pounce, my cat, would rub up against my boots, or my hound, Achoo, would lick my hand. I'd give them a scratch to reassure them, until they settled again.

My remaining human friends took counsel of each other as we remained in the sun. Finally Aniki said, "She'll come when she's ready." Most of them went on their way. They never would have left me entirely alone, not with the enemies I've made since I was a Puppy. I didn't care. I was listening to the winds, in case they carried a scrap of Holborn's voice, and to the talk of the pigeons, for the sheer comfort of their coos and chuckles. More and more birds assembled on the rooftops and the fence.

The shadows got longer. The warm early-summer air turned cool. Far off I heard a distant roll of thunder. If I meant to pay respects to Kaasa, the dust spinner by the gate, I would have to do so now, before she went wherever they go when rain falls.

Kaasa had already picked up speed as the storm breezes poured into her. She had risen to the height of my head, spinning graveyard dust, twigs, bits of flowers from offerings, and who knew what else. I took out the packet of dirt I'd brought her special for this day, gathered from the Temple District and the great temple of the Black God, who claims us all, and poured it into Kaasa's twirling body. As she accepted it, I stepped into her heart.

The first bit of talk she released into my ears was familiar enough. "—embrace you and guide you—" It was a mot's voice, reciting the Mithran prayer for the dead. I ignored her. Usually I heard everyday talk gleaned from the district around us.

"Why do they put down *rocks*?" That was a little one. Hard to tell if they were lad or gixie at that age. "Are they too poor for flowers?"

"Dogs are different, sweet," came a mot's reply. "You'll understand—"

"—when you're older," I whispered, though the mother's voice had gone out of Kaasa's reach. I'd had ambitions to say such things to Holborn's child, once.

"—ever stop *nagging*?" That cove's voice was a knife in my heart, not the kindly voice I'd hoped for from his ghost. "You're such an old woman, Beka! Stiff and strict—I feel like a nursling when we're together!" We'd had this quarrel weeks ago, after the burial of his old training master.

"You *act* like a nursling!" That tight whisper was me, may the god save me. I'd been shamed beyond bearing because he was shouting at me. "Can we have this talk at *home*?"

Kaasa lost the rest, but I knew Holborn's reply. "It's not a home, it's a cage!" I had gone to my rooms alone that day. That night he'd come back with me after watch, as cheerful as if we'd never fought. And he'd teased me about being so grim.

Kaasa and I said our farewells. I stepped out of her hold and looked up to see a fork of lightning in a sky that had gone gray-black. The pigeons took off all at once, headed for their night's shelter. Storm winds whipped my clothes and hair about. It was time to leave. Pounce and Achoo deserved better than a soaking.

Long, scarred hands put a shawl around me. "I was starting to think I'd have to sling you over my shoulder and carry you home," Rosto the Piper told me. "Our folk went to the Dove for supper if you'd like to come."

I tried a smile on Rosto and shook my head. I wasn't up to seeing people. I clutched the ends of the shawl as the wind blew harder and colder.

"Thought so," Rosto said as he put his arm around me. I leaned against him. I didn't mind taking a bit of comfort. Rosto knew that it was just comfort, nothing more. He had better manners in some ways than the fine nobles I saw at my lord Gershom's house when I was growing up. "We had supper laid out in your rooms, Beka. I'm staying to make sure you eat it. Don't think you can throw it out the window."

I turned my face into the first scattered raindrops that blew our way. It was the end to a hot, dry week of misery. I'd spent the last three days as half a ghost myself. With the cold rain driving into our faces, I felt like I was rousing from sleep.

It's about time, Pounce said, walking between us. *I almost asked you if you wanted us to bury you with him.*

Rosto looked down. "I know you're a cat, but you don't have to be cruel," he said. "It's easy if you're a god, I suppose. You don't ever lose people."

I am a constellation, not a god, Pounce said in correction, for perhaps the hundredth time that I knew of. *I have lost people I loved, and mourned them. Turning into a gravestone yourself does very little good. Holborn was driving Beka mad.*

"That time together was still worth some grief," Rosto said. "And the guilt is still heavy, even if your love has turned to hate or dislike."

His words sounded true in my heart. I was not surprised. Rosto had plenty of experience at burying former friends, clawing his way up to the throne of the city's Rats. He had been the first of my circle to notice things weren't right with Holborn and me, and to get me to talk about it.

Pounce looked away from the blond Rogue. *Beka, Achoo has found a puddle to roll in.*

That brought me around. Achoo, who weighs more than forty pounds, has a thick coat of curling white fur and is a disaster when she finds a mud puddle. Rosto and I fetched her out and washed her with fountain and rainwater. Once we reached home, I ordered her to stay on the ground-floor landing until we could dry her off. Then we dried Pounce, to his disgust. I loaned Rosto some of Holborn's clothes, but I did not stay to see him put them on. I had not slept in the rooms I'd shared with Holborn, rooms that once had been Rosto's, since Holborn's death. Kora, who still lived across the hall, had offered me her place, and moved upstairs with Aniki for the time being. I called Achoo up to me when I unlocked Kora's door.

Rosto found me staring out the open shutters at the pouring rain. The promised supper was in covered bowls on the table. I hadn't lit the fire on the hearth or more than two of the lamps. I was remembering that fight trapped in the dust spinner, and others. Holborn and I had so many, these last three months.

Rosto lit a spill from one lamp and used it to set the rest to burning. He laid a fire in the hearth and got that going, a small one, enough to heat water for tea and take the sudden chill off the room. He had to step over and around Achoo to do it. At the first sight of the flame my hound had curled up before the hearth.

Seeing Rosto in Holborn's clothes wasn't the shock I expected. Unlike the men I usually preferred, Holborn had been stocky, solid across his chest and belly. His shirt draped like a robe on Rosto. My friend had been forced to tie a scarf around his waist to hold the breeches in place, though at least their length was right.

I smiled to see proud, fair-haired Rosto dressed so badly. Then I swallowed it. The smile was another thing to make me feel guilty. Shame on me for smiling when Holborn was dead.

"Stop it," ordered Rosto. "You're alive—enjoy that. You're alive and you have friends and family who love you. *And* you were smart enough not to follow Holborn into a room without backup."

I dished up the food. "I didn't know he meant to do it," I murmured.

"Of course you didn't," said Rosto flatly. "He was trying to best you and gather more glory for himself by going alone, straight into half a dozen slave guards. It was a Puppy's trick, and he paid the last price."

We were quiet after that because I didn't want to admit Holborn was jealous of my standing among Dogs. Instead we ate. I don't recall what I had, only that I was hungry and devoured all that he set before me. He enjoyed his fair share, too. There was even chopped meat for Achoo and Pounce.

Once we cleaned up, out of habit we gave our blades a check, in case they needed a smith's work. I had a spare sharpstone, so we honed our daggers to the Smith God's standard. The thunder rolled off while we were still working. Rosto talked a bit about the doings of the Court of the Rogue. He'd had a serious rebellion two winters back, after the bad harvest of 247, but these days few cityfolk balked at his rule. Most of his problems now came from hard coves who entered Corus thinking to challenge its Rogue.

"I'll have to start making examples, Beka, you watch," he told me after an account of several duels. "I don't have the time to sort out every new Tom that comes swaggering into the Dancing Dove." He looked at me. "You're tired. Think you'll sleep tonight?"

I finished yawning. "Aniki told you." Aniki and Kora had switched off nights, watching over me.

"Did you think they wouldn't?" He tucked his last dagger into a hidden sheath at the back of his waist and collected the basket where he'd placed the dishes. "I'll return the clothes—"

I shook my head. "Give them to someone that needs them. I'll send the rest to the Goddess's temple." When I can face the chore, I thought. It was one thing to see Holborn's clothes draped and bunched on Rosto, another to fold them, breathe their scent, and tuck them into a basket to give them away.

"All right, then," he said. "Aniki will be in later. You get her if you need anything." His black eyes were fierce as he looked at me. "I mean it, Beka."

I went to him and kissed his cheek. "Thank you, Rosto. You're a good friend."

He left me then. I finished cleaning up. I took it in mind to write in this journal afterward. It seems to be one of those things I should do to prove to myself that I did not crawl into the grave with Holborn today.

Saturday, June 9, 249

Pounce roused me in the dark. Though it was just his paw on my eye, I came as wide awake as though he'd bitten me. *It's time to wake up, Beka,* he said.

"What's going on?" I asked him, tossing my blankets aside. "I was having my first sleep in near a week—"

Achoo started to bark.

Diamlah, Pounce told her. Achoo went silent right off. Pounce told me, *You can sleep on the ship.*

I was about to ask "What ship?" when I heard the sound that had set Achoo to barking. Someone was coming up my stairs. He was known to Aniki, Kora, or me, or the guards never would have allowed him to pass. Whoever it was, he banged on the door of the rooms where I normally slept. I looked about for my baton, only to remember it was in the rooms I had shared with Holborn. I took up two of my daggers and went to the door, clad only in my nightgown.

I undid the locks and opened it a crack. "What's your business?" I demanded of the stranger's back. "Speak up! And if you wake my neighbors—"

He turned and I fell silent. It was my lord Gershom, clad in a dripping oilcloth cloak over a blue tunic and black breeches. He held a wide-brimmed rain hat in one hand. His face was grim. "Let me in."

I stood aside. He shut the door as I lit a pair of lamps. By that bit of light I could see Achoo and Pounce sitting by the bed, watching my lord. "Forgive me, Beka, but you're my best choice," he told me softly. "Dress and pack what you would need for a woods Hunt and a stay of three days. Bring Achoo. Pounce may come if he cares to. I'm leaving a horse tied in the shed in back. Take it to Peregrine Dock as soon as you can. Tell no one where you're bound or who the summons came from, understood?"

"Yes, my lord," I whispered. Nothing good came from orders in the night.

He put the hat on his head. It and the cloak turned him into no one in particular. He was out my door and gone before I could move to open it for him.

"Everythin' all righ', Beka?" Aniki asked drowsily from the landing above. I looked up. She half dangled over the rail, her long gold hair and her sword hanging from one drooping hand. Her eyes were swollen with sleep.

"Go to bed," I told her. "Something's come up." I remembered my pigeons. "Will you feed my birds till I come back? I'll leave coin for the food on Kora's table."

Aniki saluted me with her blade and stumbled back to her room. I closed my own door and rushed to dress and to pack. I put on my uniform and my hidden knives. My lord had not said I was to wear cityfolk clothes. Into my heavy pack I stuffed pads, underclothes, my extra uniform, tooth sticks, warm stockings, my comb, and other everyday gear. Into my shoulder pack I put the gear I needed for my work. Most of it was already there—my piece of spelled mirror, the special gloves that make it possible for me to handle things while leaving no magical traces, the clay that can turn so hard as to make a lock useless, insect-banning balm, lock picks, healing salves, Achoo's brushes and medicines, packets of dried meat strips I use to reward her, my sharp-stone and blade-cleaning gear, my gorget and arm guards, and other bits and pieces. My leg guards and round helm went into my larger bag. My baton, sap, purse, and water flask went on my belt. I shrugged on my shoulder pack, then covered it with my cloak. I put the coin on the table so Aniki and Kora could feed the pigeons while I was gone. At last I donned my hat, hoisted my larger bag, and walked out the door.

"Achoo, *tumit,*" I said. She came, eager for whatever excitement Lord Gershom's strange visit had promised. She was an old hand at late knocks on the door. This made our thirteenth night call since we became partners in 247, Achoo's services being much in demand throughout Corus and even in Torhelm and Groten.

Pounce stuck his head out of an opening in my larger bag. I had not seen him get into it, but that was not new. "If you walked, you would be less weight for me to carry," I told him as I set the bag down to lock my door.

I would also get wetter than I will be already, he replied.

The horse was where Lord Gershom told me he would be, a fine sturdy gelding who looked no happier to be out in the rain than I was. Still, he let me strap the larger pack behind his saddle with no fuss at all. At least all the riding I've had to do in recent years meant that, tired as I was, I could do it properly.

The horse and Achoo sniffed each other nose to nose as I worked, until I was in the saddle. Then we were off, trotting as fast as I dared through the dark streets. There was scant light to go by, only a lantern hung over the door of the odd eating house or drinking den. I stayed on the dark streets, keeping my lord's orders in mind.

The ride gave me a chance to think. The things that went through my mind made me nervous and shivery with eagerness. My lord had come for me himself. That meant whatever he called me to, it was big. He'd said himself I was his best choice and asked for Achoo, so I suspected the one who mattered was Achoo. Every one of the scent-hound handlers I've met, from our chief here in Corus on down, has said she's the best they know.

My lord Gershom stood watch with some Palace Guards. One of the guards took my horse, while a sailor wearing the navy's white-trimmed blue tunic took my heavy bag. I kept my shoulder pack. Lord Gershom led Achoo and me down the dock. If the sailor noticed the purple-eyed black cat sticking his head out of my bag, he gave no sign of it.

Now I was alert. Some part of me had wondered if mayhap Lord Gershom had come for me as a way of apologizing for calling me out the night I'd buried my man. Now I saw it was no such thing. It was big, with my lord meeting me at the dock and walking me to a ship. That was going far for comfort. Then the ship came in view at the end of the long dock, and I blinked, to make certain the water was not fooling me.

A peregrine ship waited for us. It might pass for an ordinary ship at a quick glance, but for the bird's wings painted along its sides. They showed in the lantern light from the ship's prow. I swallowed. I'd never been on a peregrine ship. Few had. They were the Crown's most precious vessels, saved for important messages and the greatest emergencies. And now I was going to travel on one.

Suddenly I wanted to turn and run for home.

Lord Gershom rested a hand on my shoulder. I didn't realize I had stopped. "Easy, girl," he said in that slow voice that always steadies me. "If I can ride one of these curst bounce-buckets, so can you."

I took a deep breath and followed him up the gangplank. To the mot in oilcloth who waited for us he said, "We're all present." Two sailors who'd been standing to the side trotted off the ship and began to slip the mooring ropes off their cleats. My lord pointed to a shelter at the rear of the deck. The sailor who'd taken my bag was already returning from there without it. He got to work on the sails. My lord cupped my elbow in his hand and steered me to the shelter, while Achoo galloped inside. The mot climbed stairs to a deck halfway up behind the shelter and stood there beside the pilot, one hand held out flat before her. With her index finger she drew a circle on one palm, her lips moving. I felt the wind pick up. It filled the sails as the sailors who had slipped the mooring ropes jumped aboard and pulled up the gangplank. Then I stepped into the shelter.

My partner Tunstall was there already, stretched out on a long, cushioned bunk along one side wall. He grinned and put his feet on the floor, but my lord said, "Don't stand, Mattes. You'll bang your head." He removed his hat and cloak, taking the other side bench. Achoo lay on the deck, panting.

Tunstall reached up and hugged me, dripping wet as I was. "Are you all right, Cooper?"

I hadn't thought if I was all right or no since my lord's knock had brought me to my door. "I'm up and about," I replied, looking around. Our baggage was tucked and secured under the bunks, which were covered with fleeces. Straps hung off their sides and from the hull beside them. I'd heard the passengers on these ships traveled under magical sleep, strapped onto their bunks to keep from flying off of them. I gulped and hung up my cloak and hat, then set my shoulder pack on the bunk for use as a pillow and backrest.

Tunstall nodded. "A Hunt will do you good," he said as I worked. He looked at Lord Gershom, who had taken a silk bag off a hook on the wall and was rooting through it. "Do you know what *manner* of Hunt we're about, my lord?"

Lord Gershom fished out three leather bracelets and hung the silk bag on the hook once again. He tossed one of the bracelets to Tunstall and another to me before he fit the third on his own bony wrist. "I've no idea of anything, and I'll not hazard a guess, Mattes," he said. "The news I had called for utter secrecy and the best and smallest team with a scent hound I could assemble."

Tunstall nodded, the wise old owl. "With Elmwood off to Naxen, that leaves Beka."

I looked at Achoo. "You must tire of dragging me along as deadweight," I told her. I didn't mean it, not really. I've proved myself plenty of times to those who said our capture of Pearl Skinner three years back was a lucky start. Of Lord Gershom I asked, "What are the bangles for?" I held up my leather strap. I could see letters writ on it and dyed, but they were in mage script.

"Slumber and seasickness," my lord replied, his eyes twinkling. "It's not such a problem here on the river, but trust me, you two, if you're not wearing these when we strike the open ocean, you'll be puking up everything you ate for the last week. Better to sleep out the trip."

Tunstall and I looked at each other and hurriedly fastened the bands about our wrists. "But we've gone to sea now and then," Tunstall said. "I puked a bit the first time, but the other times went well enough. Cooper took to it like one of those pelicans."

"You weren't on peregrine ships," my lord replied. "These things go so fast—they're blown by mage-winds, you know—they fly so fast that they don't sail over the waves, they bounce off of them. And since we're on emergency orders, the ship's mages have instructions to take us as fast as the ship can bear." He stretched out on the bunk he'd chosen, looking as comfortable as could be for all his earlier complaints.

Tunstall was already stretched out on his bunk, hands

folded neatly over his belly. "Better them than me," he murmured.

Three sailors came in, bringing a cool breeze and rain at their heels. "You're good and settled," one of them, a mot, said. "We'll finish up." She looked at Pounce and Achoo. "Can they be put together? We can strap them under the bunks."

"They're old friends," I replied. I watched as they opened out a net of straps secured to the deck under an unused bunk. Once they'd put a fleece on top of it, I gave Achoo the order to lie down. Once she was settled, Pounce curled up with her. Two of the sailors did up the straps above and below them, tucking them into a space that had enough room for them to sleep comfortably.

I will ensure that we sleep, Pounce told us. The sailors did not seem to hear. *I don't enjoy travel like this, either.*

Thank you, I thought to him. I didn't want these sea folk to think any Dogs were cracked in the nob because I spoke when no one had spoken to me.

"'Twill be a curst uncomfortable ride," Tunstall remarked as the youngest sailor tucked a flat pillow beneath his head.

The mot who had spoken first grinned at him. "You won't notice, my lad. Once we tell the passengers' mage you're all snug, he'll be putting you and them of the crew that ain't needed right off to sleep. You can dream of me, if y'like." She patted Tunstall's cheek and left us, her cackling laugh trailing behind. The other two followed her, their grins wide enough to show what teeth they were missing.

"You don't know my woman!" Tunstall called after her. "She don't let me stray!"

I blinked my filling eyes. Holborn didn't stray, either. I wish he had. It would have been easier to explain to my friends than he thought me a nag and a cold fish who was forever worrying about the future.

Happily, the spell took us all before I could sink too far into my regrets.

When I opened my eyes, the youngest of the three sailors was undoing my straps. I looked for the leather bracelet, and the cove grinned. "Took that off to end the sleep first thing, mistress," he told me. "We've wake-up tea on deck. Your hound and cat is already out there with your captain. We'll be at dock soon."

I blinked at him saying *captain,* until I realized he meant Lord Gershom. What could be so secret that my lord would not even use his proper rank?

As the sailor turned to free Tunstall, I asked, "What hour is it? Where are we?"

"'Tis nearabout noon," the sailor replied, helping my partner to sit up. "We be in Blue Harbor."

"Blue Harbor near noon on *Friday*?" I asked. I still hadn't quite put together all that had happened to me since my lord had knocked on my door.

"Naw," he said, undoing the straps on our baggage. "'Tis Thursday. Wouldn't be worth our salt as a peregrine ship was we to be taking a whole day to get from Corus to Blue Harbor! Mind, we could've been here three hours afore this—we've done the trip in that time—but there was a nasty storm at Port Caynn. Threw us off. The mage lady were spittin' like a cat."

I noticed that he didn't use her name, or give his own. "How do you sailors manage?" I asked. "If we're buckled down in here—"

"Oh, we tie up to the mast," the cove told me. "Each of

us has one, see, and she eases off if we need to trim the sails. It's narsty work, but we're paid in gold, and swapped back to the reg'lar navy every three months. Out you go, now, both of yez. They'll be needin' me to dock."

Tunstall and I walked onto the deck. The sails were puffed out with a steady wind that was carrying us between the twin lighthouses of Blue Harbor.

Tunstall leaned down to mutter in my ear, "I feel like I've been hammered, Cooper."

I had to admit, I was stiff and sore all over. Achoo was running up and down the deck, her plumed tail wagging. If she was sore, she hid it well. Pounce sat at Lord Gershom's feet while he drank from a heavy mug of tea. One of the sailors brought a mug each for Tunstall and me before he got back to work on the sails. The ship was turning, the obedient wind following the changing sails as the vessel angled for the docks on the northwestern side of the harbor.

From curiosity, I set my tea on the deck between my feet and reached into my belt purse for my mirror, the one that shows me when there's magic in use. I angled the mirror so I would see our former shelter and the wheel over my shoulder. When I looked at the surface, the blaze of light from the magic nearabout blinded me. It had not occurred to me that not only would the magic be extremely strong, but it would be worked through every splinter and fiber of the ship.

I hurriedly thrust the mirror into my purse and waited for my poor eyes to recover. I reminded myself that the blessing of the mirror was that it seemed to show me all manner of magics, whatever they were for and no matter what their strength. That was scant comfort when my eyes were watering fiercely.

"I always swear I'll never take one of these ships again," I heard Lord Gershom say. "This is my third peregrine trip this year. I'm bruised all over."

"It could be worse, my lord," Tunstall replied. "You could be one of these sailors."

My eyes were clear enough that I could see that Pounce was seated by my feet. I bent down and picked up my mug of tea. "Did you enjoy *your* nap?" I asked him sourly before I took a swallow of my tea. It was well enough, but I prefer more spices, and less of whatever the bitter herb in it was.

Pounce looked up at me and blinked. *I went to the Realms of the Gods once Achoo was under the sleep spell,* he informed me. *Why should I remain for such an abysmal voyage if I don't have to?*

Tunstall and Lord Gershom both heard, because they choked on their tea. I drank my tea down to hide my own smile. I was glad that Pounce had come along.

The sails were going slack over our heads. We glided smoothly in toward the last of the docks, one that was isolated from the others by a wooden fence in the water. Seeing that we'd be going ashore soon, I went back to the cabin for my belongings. Tunstall followed. We strapped our rain things to our own packs and gathered up Lord Gershom's things while we were at it. I was shocked when he took one bag from my hand and another from Tunstall, but he shook his head when we would have protested. Both of us took his warning and said nothing.

All this secrecy was starting to give me the itch. Never had I been on a Hunt when we kept our names from those who conveyed us. Never had I been on a Hunt when we had no notion of the manner of crime at issue, the Dog Districts involved, or the local nobles. Lord Gershom had mentioned the king, but surely we were here as a favor to someone the king wished to help. The king had better Hunters than the likes of us. There were the royal spies, the Ferrets, to seek out any offenders against the king's majesty or that of the royal family. The most powerful mages in the realm served the Crown, as did knights who were sworn to bring anyone singled out by the Ferrets to justice. The king himself would have no need for a Dog pair and a scent hound. Why then the silence, and the expensive night journey all the way to Blue Harbor?

The ship eased between the fence and the dock. Two sailors jumped down to secure the ship to cleats. My lord went to the prow, plainly looking for someone. Then he nodded. He'd seen whoever he was looking for.

"Have you ever been on a Hunt like this?" I murmured to Tunstall.

"Never. But, do you know, Beka, I wish already that we were not," he replied. "Once folk start to fool with a good, plain Hunt, it never goes well in the long run."

"We can sacrifice some flowers to your luck god, first chance we get," I promised him. "That might turn it about for us."

He was shaking his head. "It will have to be fruit. Flowers won't be enough, I can tell already."

The sailors were placing the gangplank so that we might leave the ship. My lord nodded to them, then motioned for us to follow. Achoo and Pounce beat Tunstall and me, but then, they weren't carrying bags. I felt like I brought up the end of a somberly clad parade, with Tunstall and me in uniform and my lord in black.

Three coves waited for us at the end of the dock. Two of them were from the king's personal bodyguard, the King's Own, marked out by their silvery chain mail and their bright blue tunics. They had horses with them, six with saddles and three for packs. Without a word they came and took our things. They strapped our belongings on the packhorses, which already had some baggage. The oldest stopped only for a moment to talk with Lord Gershom, a moment that left my lord white-faced and staring out to sea.

The third man was not from the King's Own. He was a big cove, six feet and three inches tall, clean-shaven, with brown hair cut short, just over his ears. His eyes were large, set a little shallow in their sockets, and their color was hard to name, partway between pale green and pale blue. He had an easy smile on a mouth that looked as if it smiled often. He dressed in a Dog's uniform with the silver hem and sleeve trim of a Provost's mage.

Tunstall and I followed Lord Gershom as my lord walked up to the brown-haired cove. My thoughts raced. I've done five Hunts with a mage as part of our group. They are a very mixed lot. The one that was a graduate of the university in Carthak was impossible to manage—Achoo even bit her. The one from the City of the Gods barely spoke to us, but he saved all of our lives when we came under attack. The one lent to us by the Duke of Naxen was a kind fellow but of little use, while the two wander mages were decent sorts. This one, at least, dressed like a normal Dog, without strange bits and pieces clanking from his neck and belt, and he bore himself like a normal cove, without any airs.

My lord and the mage clasped hands. "Well met, Farmer," my lord said. "There was no problem in getting your release from your district commander?"

Master Farmer, if that was his true name, smiled. It gave him the look of a boy. I guessed him to be twenty-five. "She was quite pleased to let me go," he replied. "She has a mage nephew she has been wanting to use in my place to see how he manages. Have you more information since you sent your orders? All I had was to meet you here today and tell no one." He nodded to Tunstall and me.

I sucked on the inside of my cheek. So he was a kennel mage? Those weren't the cream of the crop.

"I've little information myself," my lord said. "Master Farmer Cape, meet Matthias Tunstall and Rebakah Cooper, from Corus." Achoo whimpered, indignant at being over-looked, and Lord Gershom laughed. "And Achoo, the very fine scent hound who works with them. You will be working together. For now, we're not wasting any time. Cooper, Achoo will have to ride. We're leaving at the gallop."

He was serious about that. The older guardsman gave my lord, Master Farmer, and Tunstall horses while the younger guardsman helped me to place Achoo atop a packhorse. At my direction we settled her between bags and secured her with the straps I carried for those times we both had to go on horseback. That done, Pounce tucked into my shoulder pack, I mounted the horse set aside for me.

Without another word Lord Gershom led the way at the trot through the gate at the end of the dock enclosure and past the naval guards outside. The older of the two men of the King's Own rode beside him, while Master Farmer rode with Tunstall. Each of them led a packhorse. The other guardsman and I shared the rear while I led Achoo and her mount.

The older guardsman led us down a private route through the naval yards, one that quickly brought us to the city gates. There he showed the guards a medallion he took from his pocket. It had to be official, because the guardsmen let us go as if we'd been Their Majesties themselves.

Our path soon joined a broad road that led south. There

was plenty of traffic to slow us down for ten miles or so, until we came to a wall and gate at a side road. Gate and road were manned by fully armored men of the King's Own. They opened the gate without even stopping us for questions. By then I was sure of our destination. The Summer Palace was close by, set on the peninsula southeast of Blue Harbor and west of the Ware River. Only nine days ago Their Majesties had left the capital for the seaside palace. Whatever we were there for, it had been commanded by the king, I was sure of it. My tripes were one solid knot. I'm no good with nobles.

Once the gate was closed behind us, my lord opened up our speed and we began to gallop for true. We kept to my lord's pace, resting briefly in between gallops and trots.

I have been in many woods since partnering with Achoo, and this was the strangest I had seen. The trees were spaced wide apart and much of the ground cover seemed to be moss, not grass. The streams had bridges that were as much ornament as structure needed for water crossing. They even had gilding for decoration, which was plain wasteful. Folk in the Lower City starve every day, yet out here where few can see it, the very bridges have gilding. It vexed me.

After our third stop for water, the road turned to follow a smooth white limestone wall. Men guarded the height, the sun glinting off their helms and crossbows. The older guardsman took out a whistle much like the ones carried by street Dogs and blew a series of notes as a signal. The wall guards aimed their crossbows at us and I took a deep breath of air. There is nothing so discomforting as the sight of crossbows aimed at your company. Then we heard another set of whistles. The guards lowered their bows.

On we rode. The guards farther down must have heard

the whistled signal, for no more weapons were pointed our way. Now, behind the soldiers, I could see green land planted with trees rising well above the height of the wall.

"It's a summer palace, Cooper," Tunstall reminded me. "They have to catch the breezes."

"How close is it to the ocean?" I asked him.

Tunstall knew I worried that someone might attack the palace on the other side. These walls looked too pretty to hold off a real attack. "There's a wall all the way round, you Fretting Franza," he teased. "And all sorts of mage work you're not seeing. You think they'd let Their Majesties and His Highness anywhere near a place that wasn't protected, ground to crown?"

I wanted to ask him that, if this was true, why were we here, but we had come to another gate, guarded again by men of the King's Own. My skin was starting to itch. I was no expert on palace matters, unlike my brother Nilo. He was a palace courier and knew all sorts of things about royalty. Still, as I remembered it, the Palace Guard was supposed to protect the monarchs' homes, the King's Own their persons. If that was so, why did I see no red-and-tan uniforms on the walls? Everyone who stood up there wore blue and silver.

This time our guards from the King's Own had to come forward, and Lord Gershom had to show his signet ring. I did not like the look of these guards at all. Even the darkest-skinned of them was ashen. Some of them had sweat marks on their pretty tunics. Some of them had hands that shook as they held their weapons.

I looked at Tunstall, who was already eyeing me. He scratched his scruffy beard. I nodded. Something very bad had taken place here.

As our two guides went ahead with the packhorses to

lead us on the road that climbed away from the main gate, I promised myself I would never pack my bit of spelled mirror away again. I was very curious to know if the men who'd just let us enter were magicked like our guides not to talk about whatever had frightened them so badly.

We did not gallop, but we went at a good trot, always uphill, always curving left through trees. These were a bit wilder than the ones by the road below, a proper setting for streams that formed little waterfalls over heaps of rocks. I caught glimpses of a large building atop the high ground. First I saw a long hall open on one side with outside pillars to support the upper story. Next came balconies that stood out from a wall, draped with flowering vines.

Then we came into view of the sea. I had to admire it as it shone there, gold in the afternoon sun. Straight below us lay stone heights, and then a stone wall where a handful of men from the King's Own stood guard. Below the wall were more stone cliffs. If there was a beach, I did not see it.

Brace yourselves, Pounce said from behind my ear. Tunstall looked our way, so he'd heard. Neither Lord Gershom nor the mage so much as twitched. They had not overheard.

"For what, *hestaka*?" Tunstall asked Pounce. It meant "wise one" in Tunstall's original Hurdik.

Pounce always got full of himself when Tunstall called him that, but not this time. *You'll see,* he replied.

The Summer Palace appeared through the trees on my left, a long building with another open corridor on this side. There were balconies and turrets that must have been pretty white stone once. Now soot streaks marred everything. Part of this wing had collapsed into the cellars. Some of the remains stood open to the air. Others sported a single shutter, or half-burned ones. Tatters of burned draperies and furniture had been thrust from the windows to lie haphazard below. A chill ran clean down my spine and up into my skull. This was fearful business.

Achoo whimpered and scrabbled against the ties that held her to the packhorse. Something was frightening her.

"Would you release her?" I called to the men of the King's Own. "She needs to get down." The younger one rode to Achoo's horse to do as I asked while I looked around.

Between the palace and our road were gardens. Mayhap they'd been pretty, too, but not now. Bodies lay among the flowers. Here were the missing Palace Guards, as well as men of the King's Own, and the Black God knew how many servants, all burned, sword hacked, or stabbed.

Lord Gershom swore. "Tunstall?"

Tunstall rode up to the older man of the King's Own. "Once this was discovered, how many people have ridden this track before us?" he asked.

Achoo jumped to the ground. She ran over to my horse, her tail between her legs. She was nearabout spooked out of her fur.

The cove began to reply, cleared his throat, and spoke. "Our party, that was away in Blue Harbor, rode this way to come home after midnight. Guards and couriers have come and gone on this road since. And it is not this for which you are called. Come."

"Not this?" Lord Gershom demanded, but he set his horse in motion. The mage and I followed. Tunstall fell in with me as we passed. We heard my lord mutter, "What in Mithros's name can be worse?"

That same question worried Tunstall and me, for certain. I could not read Master Farmer's face yet.

"Is this what you meant?" I asked Pounce in a whisper.

It's the beginning, he replied.

Master Farmer looked at me. "So your cat talks," he remarked, as easy as if he rode by dead folk every day. "Doesn't it unsettle you?"

Easy, Beka, Pounce said in my mind, when I would have given the mage a tart answer. *He's frightened, too, for all he doesn't act it.*

"He's talked to me for years," I said. "I'm used to it."

"Oh, good," Master Farmer replied, turning to face forward on his mount. "I wouldn't want you to put a good face on it for me."

We rode past sight of the flower gardens, but the landscape of the dead continued. They had fought in the trees here. Tunstall pointed to the far side of our road. There were footprints on a wide path that led down toward the sea. I nodded. Had the enemy come from there, or had people tried to escape taking that path? If Tunstall, Achoo, and I were supposed to make sense of this raid, we were sadly overmatched. I'd put at least five pairs on sommat as big as this, and more than one mage.

Thinking of mages, I wondered, shouldn't that seaward path be magicked to the hilt? Wouldn't that wall down below be magicked just the same? Royalty came here for the summer. Surely those who kept them safe wouldn't leave their protection to a couple of walls and some guards.

We halted in a wide circle where Their Majesties' guests left their chairs, horses, or wagons. This had been cleared of the dead. That there *had* been dead was plain from the blood splashes on the ground. Men of the King's Own silently took our horses. I called Achoo to heel—she was sniffing the blood—and followed Tunstall, Master Farmer, and my lord inside.

Our guides did not come with us. Possibly they did not want to face the soot-streaked, blood-splashed entry hall. We were met by a fleshy, white-haired cove. Mayhap he'd been very well satisfied with his life a few days ago. Now I had to wonder if he would live out the month, for all that he wore rich silks and hose and a great gray pearl earring.

"Your people may wait in there, Gershom." He pointed to a side room well fitted with chairs and small tables. "*You* will come with me."

My lord gave us the nod and we did as we were told. The room had escaped both fire and murder. There were pretty mosaics bordering the walls at top and bottom, as well as inlaid at the window ledges. The shutters were well-carved cedar, open to the air outside. I made note because my friends would surely want to know what the inside of a palace, even a summer one, was like. There were silk cushions with tassels everywhere. Pounce went over to one and idly batted a tassel. Achoo showed no interest in the furnishings. She went to the open door and whined.

"*Kemari,* Achoo," I told her. *"Dukduk."* She looked at me and hesitated. I pointed to a spot next to the chair I meant to take and repeated my commands.

"What language is that?" Master Farmer asked. "It sounds like Kyprish, but it's mangled. Doesn't she respond to commands in Common?"

I'd placed his accent by the time he was done. He'd come from the roughest part of Whitethorn City, off east on the River Olorun.

Tunstall had listened to him with eyebrows raised. "Now, would you go about giving away all your mage secrets to some stranger who asked?" he wanted to know. "Cooper has secrets for the handling of a hound. It's the same thing."

I ducked my head to hide a grin and pretended to be tucking my breech leg more properly into my boot. Tunstall wanted to test the mage a little.

"What kind of mage are you?" he asked Master Farmer. "The scummer-don't-stink kind, or the pisses-wine kind?"

Master Farmer scratched his head. "The I-just-like-to-be-friendly kind. Ma always told me I was forever trying to make new friends." He had changed from the cove who'd greeted my lord to a bit of a country lad. I thought it was to pull Tunstall's tail, but kept my mouth closed. Tunstall was full grown and able to take care of himself.

My partner advanced until he was but three inches from the mage. He was half a head taller than Master Farmer, heavier in the shoulders, chest, and legs. In his Dog's uniform he was overpowering. "Don't play the lovable lout with us. We're Lower City Dogs from Corus. We've seen it all, we've heard it all, and we've hobbled it all. What kind of name is Farmer, anyway?"

Master Farmer grinned. He looked like a very looby. "It's my mage name."

Tunstall was about to spit on the beautiful rug when I cleared my throat. He caught my glare. I don't care where he spits normally, but not in a palace. He coughed instead. "Mithros's spear, what kind of cracknob picks a mage name like Farmer?"

The mage shrugged. "Most of the mages that taught me would say I acted like I had my feet in the furrows and my head in the hayloft. I thought maybe there was something powerful, them thinking the same thing, so I took Farmer as a mage name." He looked at me. "I've been wondering lately, though, do you think mayhap they were making fun of me?"

I scratched Achoo's ears. Why would Lord Gershom

summon such a playactor to so important a Hunt as this one boded to be?

Tunstall shrugged as if he settled his tunic more comfortably on his shoulders and stepped back. "Don't ask us," he said. "We're city Dogs."

"I'm a city Dog, too," Master Farmer said cheerfully. "I never had pets. At home we ate them." He crouched next to Achoo and me. This close, he smelled a little of spices and fresh air. "Is that why you bring your pets along? So no one will eat them?"

I am not edible, Pounce said. I couldn't tell if Master Farmer heard. I didn't think so, not when he didn't even blink.

Achoo was thumping her tail just a bit, telling me she wanted to make friends with the dozy jabbernob. Pounce sauntered over to him and looked up into his face. Master Farmer stared at him for a moment. Then he said, his tone less ignorant and silly, "Now there's something new. You don't often see a purple-eyed cat." He held out a hand. Pounce sniffed it for a moment, then bit one of his fingers. "And that's a lesson to me," said the mage, grinning. "Have you a name, Ebon Cat of the Amethyst Eyes?"

Once again he was speaking like a cove of sense. "I don't know what that means, but his name is Pounce," I said, frowning at the cat. "And he's not normally so rude." To make up for Pounce's bad manners, I said, "You should greet Achoo, since you're to work with us. *Bau,* Achoo." Since Achoo kept wagging her tail as she smelled Master Farmer's fingers, I said reluctantly, *"Kawan."* He seemed harmless enough. Lord Gershom trusted him. That had to be enough for me.

Achoo had rolled over so Master Farmer could scratch her belly when we heard a mot's voice raised outside. "Gershom is here and he told us he brought his Hunters!"

A lower voice answered. I couldn't make out the words.

The mot cried, "Pox take ceremony! I'll see them now! I *need* to see them now!"

The quieter voice spoke again.

The mot snapped, "These people serve the law. I don't think I need a chaperone in their company!"

We all stepped back hurriedly as the door opened. A lovely, delicate mot came in and closed the door behind her. She had masses of brown curls that hung down to her waist. A few jeweled pins hung from them. Her maids were lax, letting her go about with her hair undone like that. She had large, golden brown eyes, a delicate nose, a soft mouth, and perfect skin. Her under tunic was white linen so fine it was almost sheer, her over tunic a light shade of amber with gold threads shot through it. Strips of gold embroidery were sewn to the front and the left side of the tunic, vines twining around signs for peace and fertility. Golden pearls hung from her ears, around her neck and wrists, and in a belt with a picture locket at the hanging end. Pearls were sewn to her gold slippers. Gold rings with emeralds and pearls were on her fingers, save for the heavy plain gold band on the ring finger of her left hand.

I write all this, remembering her beauty purely, though she was smutched with soot from top to toe. Even her face and hands were marked.

Tunstall had seen her before this at a closer distance than I, but we all guessed her identity. We were kneeling before the door was closed. "Your Majesty," the coves said. My throat would not work.

"Oh, please, please, get up," she said, her voice softer now. "I can't stand ceremony at a time like this. Please. Look, I'm sitting down." It was true, she'd settled in one of the chairs. A smile flitted on and off her mouth, which trembled whatever she did.

Pounce walked over and jumped into her lap. The queen flinched and then stroked him. I'd been about to call him back, but I waited, watching. Pounce turned around and coiled himself, not letting her see his strange eyes. As she petted him her shoulders and back straightened. Her trembling eased. "I'd thought all the animals had fled, or been . . ." She looked down for a moment, then turned her gaze to Achoo. "A scent hound? Is he yours?"

I looked at the men, but they, great loobies that they were, stood there dumbstruck. Tunstall flapped his hand at me. He wanted *me* to talk to Her Majesty! But one of us had to, and Achoo was staring at me with pleading eyes, her tail wagging. *She* knew the pretty lady wanted to admire her.

"*Pengantar,* Achoo," I said. I turned to Her Majesty, without rising from my knees. From talking to folk who'd been broken by something terrible, I knew I would be more of a comfort to her if I sat below her eye level. Having Achoo come over made it reasonable for me to stay where I was. As the queen offered her hand for Achoo to smell, I explained quietly, "Achoo's a female, Your Majesty. We've been partners three years now."

The queen looked at me, and at the men. "Partners?"

I pointed to Tunstall, then at my uniform. "Achoo, Tunstall, and me, we belong to the Provost's Guard. Senior Guardsman Matthias Tunstall, I should say. I'm Guardswoman Rebakah Cooper. And this is Master—"

He bowed. "Farmer Cape. I am a Provost's mage from Blue Harbor."

The queen frowned. "Surely we need a court mage for this?" she whispered. "I know His Majesty and the Chancellor of Mages fight over the plan to tax mages, but surely at a time like this, duty to the realm is more important." She looked at Master Farmer. "I mean no offense, but I am used to depend on court mages."

I thought Master Farmer would take offense, having known too many prickly mages, but instead he only smiled at the queen. "Court mages are all very well, Your Majesty, but they do not often work in the cities and the wilderness. I have done both, as Lord Gershom knows. And he may well replace me with a court mage. I imagine he would like more information before he makes such decisions."

"That seems most sensible," Her Majesty replied. "I had not thought of it that way." She returned her attention to Achoo. She'd not stopped stroking Pounce, either. "I've only met the scent hounds we use to hunt. How does one partner a Provost's Guard?" she asked.

I hoped she knew the answer when she felt better, since the purpose of a Provost's scent hound seemed obvious to me. Seemingly she wasn't thinking straight just now. Her eyes were far too wide, as if she'd seen things, unbearable things. Remembering the bodies in the garden, I doubted that our pretty queen had ever encountered anything of the like. "When someone is missing, or something's been stolen, we give Achoo a scent of it," I explained. "Then she goes off and finds it. I run with her to keep her on the scent and to summon help, should she need it. Tunstall guards us."

The queen leaned forward and gripped my arm hard. There was more strength, or desperation, in her fingers than I expected. "It's true, then? You are the ones who must find my son?"

I sat back on my heels, trying not to let my shock show itself on my face. Tunstall looked down. Master Farmer turned away entirely. Now we knew why my lord had fetched us. In all this mess, His Highness Prince Gareth, the sole heir to the throne, was missing.

I collected myself. "Your Majesty, we've yet to hear our orders. It would help if you were to tell us what happened here. We only came a short time ago, and we've been told nothing. When did all this happen?" I emboldened myself and took her hand as if she were one of my sisters. "It looks fresh—the marks of burning, and the dead."

She looked at the men. "Please take your seats. If you find my baby, you may ask anything you wish of me, so please, sit." She smiled at me. "These two animals, they're proof you have a tender heart. My little prince, cruel strangers have him. . . ." Tears spilled down her face.

I always carry a score of cheap handkerchiefs on my person, in my breech pockets and a pocket I've stitched inside the front of my tunic. I fished one of them out now. I was shamed by its rough quality, but I saw no handkerchiefs on her person. She would not leave off scratching Pounce, so I dabbed the tears and not a little soot from her lovely cheeks.

"Oh—oh, Goddess, I'm being so foolish," she whispered, and took the handkerchief from me. Pounce glared at me. She dried her eyes and wiped her nose, then tucked the cloth behind Pounce and began to stroke him again. The two coves, watching her graceful hand caress the cat's gleaming fur, sighed. Now it was my turn to glare at them, beauty-dazed cracknobs that they were.

"My lord the governor of Blue Harbor invited His Majesty and me to a party in our honor yesterday," Queen Jessamine began. "It started around noon. There were nobles from Blue Harbor, the fiefs around Port Caynn, even Arenaver. It was the usual welcome to us that they give every year when we return to the Summer Palace. Roger—His Majesty had a wonderful time. I did, too, of course," she hurried to say, which led me to think that the king liked big parties more than did the queen. "But I was a little unwell. His Majesty was good enough to return home with me at midnight."

"Who went with you to this party, Your Majesty?" I asked quietly.

"My maids. Our personal mages. Half of the King's Own," she replied. "The other half always stays—" She choked at that point and seized the handkerchief, weeping into it.

I straightened, looking around for a pitcher of water or tea, something to give her to drink. Master Farmer fumbled at his belt and unhooked a flask, then handed it to me. "I'll be right back," he said quietly, and left us. I uncorked the bottle and sniffed the contents. It was wine. I hesitated, but reminded myself again that Lord Gershom must have trusted the cove entirely, to bring him when things were dire.

"Have a bit of this, Your Majesty," I said, putting the flask to her lips. "You must catch hold, you know. You've got to tell us the tale if we're to go about finding His Highness."

Tunstall got down on his knees beside her chair, too. "Cooper's right, Your Majesty," he said, his deep voice soft. "It's hard to Hunt when we don't know what happened."

"I understand," she said, and took a swallow. "Have—have you worked with Master Farmer long?"

Tunstall and I looked at each other. "We just met," I said. "Lord Gershom chose him. I've known my lord a long time, and I think he would have brought a mage he knew well for this."

The queen took another swallow from the flask. "If Lord Gershom vouches for him, then I will trust in his skill," she said quietly. "After all, neither Ironwood, that's His Majesty's mage, nor Orielle claim the skills to hunt raiders. Orielle is my own mage," she explained. "Perhaps they do not teach tracking skills to mages in the University of Carthak or the City of the Gods. I know their oath of duty calls for Orielle and Ironwood never to stray a hundred yards from my lord king or me, but surely this is different?"

"I wouldn't know," Tunstall said. "We have no understanding of the skills learned by such important folk." I waited for him to say, "And our mages are scummer," but he did not. Perhaps he didn't want the queen to know most Provost's mages weren't very good. I doubted very much that my lord chose a scummer mage for a royally ordered Hunt.

To change the subject, I asked, "Your Majesty, have you a picture of His Highness?"

The queen's lips quivered. She took a deep breath, blinked several times, and picked up the oval locket that swung at the end of her pearl belt. "Here. We just had it done a month ago for his fourth birthday."

Tunstall and I leaned closer. The portrait was of a solemn-eyed boy with reddish-brown hair and skin as pale as the queen's. He had his mother's eyes and mouth, and the king's hair and beaky nose.

The door opened. In came Master Farmer with a flagon and some cups. "Here we go," he said cheerfully, placing them on a table at Her Majesty's elbow. "It's lemon water, which I thought might do Your Majesty more good than wine just now." He poured her a cup and handed it to her. Then he poured cups for the rest of us and passed them around. I sipped the contents carefully. I'd had lemon water only once before. Holborn had insisted on buying some for me last summer.

The memory bit me deep in the belly. I thrust it out of my mind and savored the drink. Master Farmer took a chair as

Her Majesty and I set our cups aside. I gave her a fresh hand-kerchief and nodded to see if she would pick up the thread of her tale.

"We knew there was trouble when we found no one at the gate on the main road. Captain Elfed wanted to leave us there, but His Majesty said that our mages might be needed. The mages refused to leave us—I told you, they are forbidden to do so. In the end, we all came. We saw the fire soon after that. The mages put it out, but Captain Elfed says everyone must have been dead before the fire started. I went straight to the nursery. I promised Gareth . . ." She took a drink of her lemon water, then made herself go on. "It's where the fire started. The mages say Lunedda is not there—his nurse. If she is gone, I won't believe anything's happened to him. But his mage—Mistress Fea was *melted.*" The queen's lips trembled. "I only knew her by her—her hair, and the seeing glass she wore around her neck, and her rings. The rest was . . . ooze."

"Forgive me, but was everyone melted?" Master Farmer asked while Tunstall and I drew the Sign against evil on our chests.

The queen shook her head. "Only Fea and the head cook. He was a mage, too. The rest were blasted, or killed with or-dinary weapons, or burned in the fire, even the animals. I had two of the sweetest little dogs. . . ." She wiped her overflowing eyes on the back of her wrist, like a child. "Not bold warrior girls like Mistress Achoo." Achoo knew she was being praised and wagged her tail. When the queen lowered her hand, Achoo licked it.

There was noise at the door. Men came in. The first was King Roger, a handsome, tan cove in his early forties with gray eyes. Like the queen's, the king's eyes were red and swollen, though they were dry now. His reddish-brown hair flipped up around the sides of his head in runaway curls. I spotted a few gray hairs, mostly at the sides. His black silk hose and blue silk tunic were streaked with ash. He'd washed his hands, but his nails were dirty and there was soot in the creases yet, as if he'd been digging in fire-blackened ruins. There was a broad streak of ash on his cheek. I'd seen him in parades. Like the queen, he had an air about him that made him the center of the room.

Master Farmer slid straight from his chair to his knees.

"Achoo, *turun,*" I whispered. Achoo lay flat on her belly, her head down between her forepaws.

Only the queen and Pounce stayed where they were. Her Majesty offered him her hand. "My love, I have been telling them what happened," she explained. "How we found . . . things, when we came home last night."

His Majesty looked at the three of us. "Rise, please. There isn't room enough in here for kneeling." His voice was pleasant to hear, musical in a way. I did not look at him as I got to my feet. All I could think as I stood there was the jokes from the days before his second marriage. "Randy Roger," "Roger the Rigid," stories of merchants' daughters, soldiers' daughters, noble daughters, Player queens, courtesans, and trollops. Tunstall's lover, the knight Sabine, had earned herself a spell of patrol in the gods-forsaken eastern hills when she offered her king physical violence if he didn't keep his hands to himself. Her late Majesty, Queen Alysy, had lived with all his canoodling by turning a blind eye and a deaf ear. Word was that since his marriage to Queen Jessamine, he had yet to stray. From the look he had given her before I lowered my eyes, I could tell the word was true. The king loved his young queen.

"His Majesty has also been telling me what was found." That was my lord Gershom's comfortable drawl. I glanced up at him. I'd never seen my lord afraid before, but he was frightened now. "It seems to me that we are best served if my team can set about finding where the raiding party came from, and where they went to."

"It is perfectly obvious." That third voice was coming from the plump, white-haired fellow I guessed to be the king's personal mage, the one who had met us at the door. Like any mage in service directly to the Crown, he would have been trained at the City of the Gods or, rarely, the Carthaki university. I suppose that being acknowledged to be at the height of your craft would put a smug set on your face, but I didn't like this fellow all the same. I would have broken the vows he'd made to go hunting for the missing child the moment he was gone, not told Their Majesties my vows forbade me to do it.

"*Perfectly* obvious," he repeated. I was looking up by then. Lord Gershom was staring at the mage. His Majesty had an arm around the queen's shoulders. Both he and the queen gazed at the mage with no expression at all. "It was a raiding party from the north, or the Copper Isles. We must get word to our brethren at the palace—"

"That the raiders may have the heir to the throne in their hands?" Lord Gershom asked, his voice harsh. "Are you a born hoddy-dod, or was it your learning that brought you to a crawl?"

"I will not trust the palace mages!" snapped the king. "With the row they've put up over the new mage laws and taxes, you'd think I'd attacked them! They will be happy to gain power over our Gareth!"

Tunstall cleared his throat. Everyone looked at him. "Since we lose daylight as we talk, I propose that the three of us begin our Hunt," he said. "That *is* why you brought us here?"

My lord Gershom hurriedly introduced us to the king. Then Master Farmer, Tunstall, and I, bowing a great deal, got ourselves out of that room. Pounce and Achoo raced away around our feet, beating us into the hall.

"That was a splendid escape," Master Farmer said when the door closed behind us. "Do you know where we should start?"

"Are you the investigators Lord Gershom brought to us?" A lady approached us. She was exactly my height, with white skin and blond hair that she had pinned back under a white veil. Her eyes were wide-spaced and blue, attentive, set over a short nose and broad, thin-lipped mouth. Like the queen she wore a very light under tunic and over tunic, but her over tunic was plain gray cotton, with small, sober blue embroideries at the cuffs. I saw no magical designs there. She wore a plain gold chain for a necklace, a black stone on one index finger, and a piece of blue lapis lazuli on the other. There were plain gold hoops in her earlobes. Like the queen's, her eyes were red and swollen with weeping. "Is Queen Jessamine in there?" she asked.

I glared at Tunstall. I was curst if he would saddle me with talking to every mot we encountered.

He smiled at the lady. "She is there, with the king, and a white-haired cove who has vexed my lord Gershom."

The lady smiled a little. "He's Ironwood of Sinthya, His Majesty's personal mage. He vexes everyone, sooner or later. Actually, sooner. If you want a guide—I couldn't help but hear what you were saying—I'll take you to whatever you need to see. Her Majesty has no need of me if she's with the king."

Master Farmer offered his hand. "I'm Farmer Cape, handling magecraft for the Hunt. I serve the Provost's office in Blue Harbor."

The lady raised her eyebrows. "I expected one of the mage chancellor's people. Someone educated in the City of the Gods, as I was, and Ironwood was."

Master Farmer shrugged. "Doubtless someone like that is on the way. I'm just here to get the Hunt started." He said it evenly, as a simple fact.

The lady must have thought he'd taken offense. She sighed and shook her head. "Forgive me. I meant no insult. I'm sure you're good at what you do, or Lord Gershom would not have brought you here. And I'm not always so unmannerly. I'm Her Majesty's personal mage, Orielle Clavynger. Is this a scent hound?" She offered her fingers for Achoo to smell. "She doesn't look like those we Hunt with."

"Her name's Achoo," I said. "She *is* a scent hound. I'm hoping to put her to work."

When Mistress Orielle looked up at me, I saw iron in those mild blue eyes. She might seem to be sweet and approachable, but she belonged to the court, and expected things to be done in a certain way. Reminded to improve my manners, I introduced us properly. "I'm Rebakah Cooper, guardswoman and handler for Achoo. This is my partner, Senior Guardsman Matthias Tunstall. And you have met Master Farmer."

"The day is trickling away," Tunstall said politely. "We would like to get to work, lady mage."

"Oh, of course," Mistress Orielle replied. "Where would you like to start?"

"The nursery," Tunstall and Master Farmer said at the same time. Tunstall glared at the mage, but Master Farmer only gave Tunstall a bland, dozy smile. Mistress Orielle tucked her arm through Master Farmer's and pulled him along, explaining that there would be little to see. The fire had started in the nursery from what her spells had told her.

I wanted to tell Tunstall to back off of Master Farmer, but I was distracted by looking for Pounce. He'd vanished somewhere before I could introduce him to Mistress Orielle. I knew he would be all right. A cat who roamed the stars would hardly lose me here. Still, he sometimes chose to get into mischief that I had to handle later. I liked to have him under my eye.

The damage from the fire got worse as we climbed the stairs and entered what Mistress Orielle said was the north wing. The roof there was burned away, as were parts of the inner and outer walls and chunks of the floors. Finally we had to stop. All that lay before us was a gaping hole from roof to cellar where the north wing had collapsed. I took out my mirror. Magic like cobwebs glowed in the shadows. It was this that held what remained of the floors and the walls. I put the mirror away. It was almost more frightening to see how scant the protective magic was than to know the wing itself was close to coming down.

"Her Majesty said the body of the prince's mage was found in the nursery," Tunstall remarked, staring down into the mass of charred beams and flagstones. "Is it still there?"

Mistress Orielle fluttered. "Well, no," she explained in reply to Tunstall's question. "All of the bodies, including Fea's, were brought out right away. Fea of Seabeth," she added, as if that helped us any.

"So there are no dead actually here," Tunstall said.

"We could hardly *leave* them in the cellar. We *were* searching for His Highness," Mistress Orielle said, lips trembling.

It was my turn to move in. "Tunstall, she's been through a bad time," I scolded, keeping my voice soft. Tunstall and I worked this manner of questioning all of the time. I took her by the arm and gently turned her away from the men. Achoo did her part by looking sad as she nudged Mistress Orielle's elbow in a comforting way. "Do any of his belongings remain down there, Mistress Orielle?" I asked, trying to speak as if we'd been educated at the same school. "Could you tell if they were taken, or destroyed in the fire?"

"Oh, no, they were burned as far as I could tell," she said. "The gold rattle from Prince Baird, the crystal orb from my lady of Cavall—or was it my lady of Coa's Wood?—all of the expensive things were taken, but his clothespresses burned, and his everyday toys." Tears rolled down her cheeks. "I don't understand how this could happen," she said as she took out a better handkerchief than I could offer. "This place has been magicked and remagicked against all kinds of disaster. The Chancellor of Mages renewed the spells before Her Majesty brought Prince Gareth here at the beginning of May!"

Master Farmer had taken a lens that hung on a chain around his neck and was using it to view the ruins. "I hope you didn't pay him good coin," he said. "Or even bad coin."

"What do you mean?" Mistress Orielle asked sharply.

Master Farmer tucked the lens inside the front of his tunic. Gone was his foolery when he spoke. "The spells all around us are shredded, Mistress Clavynger—apply your own spell if you doubt me. If the Lord Chancellor did anything while he was here, it was damage, not strengthening. If the attackers came up from the seacoast, it was because he destroyed the concealment spells on the cliffs, the paths, and the gates."

She stared at him, jaw agape. Was she vexed because he had dared to criticize a mage of much higher rank? Or did she see, as I had, that he'd just accused the realm's chief mage of the worst kind of treason? Master Farmer shrugged. "It stands to reason you have secret paths down to the beaches," he said. "Why have a seaside palace if you never go down to bathe?"

"Blessed mother defend us, the king must be told!" Mistress Orielle turned and raced down the hall.

"Since you've put the cat in with the pigeons, you'd best go explain to Their Majesties how it got there," Tunstall told Master Farmer. "*We're* not speaking for you. *We* didn't say that their big mage left them open to murder. For all you know, she's going to say that you're a fool and don't belong in this Hunt."

"Mayhap that fancy education in Carthak and the City of the Gods needs some additions. A class for not killing folk, and another on holding to your vows." Master Farmer shook his head and followed Mistress Orielle.

It takes a real sack to accuse a great lord and mage before another great mage, don't you think? I heard Pounce ask. He walked toward us over the gap, balancing easily on a charred beam.

"If he did, *hestaka*," Tunstall replied, "why didn't he also say Ironwood and Orielle should have seen the damage themselves? It's one thing to accuse a cove who's far off, and another to rightly say the mages nearby were too smug or too lazy to do their proper work."

Tunstall was in his crotchety mood when it came to the new mage. I knew it would do no good to remain and let him continue to find fault. He would come to like or simply to work with the new mage when he felt like it. "Well, *I'm* off to find the laundry, if it isn't under all that," I said to him, pointing to the two-story hole. My heart was pounding. I feared that somewhere in all this charred wood and ashy cloth there was a dead four-year-old lad with reddish-brown curls, and Achoo and I might find him, once we had sommat to give Achoo the scent. Then I would have to tell that beautiful girl that her baby was gone, and my king that he was childless again. When I thought of all the prayers that had gone up from the entire realm, begging for an heir of our king and queen, it made me want to weep. Everyone liked the king's brother and former heir, Prince Baird, well enough, but he was childless himself, and cared little for government.

"Then let's find the laundry," Tunstall said. "Mayhap after, we'll eye the dead and see if the raiders took off with anyone. I wouldn't mind a look at the bodies of any raiders, myself."

We walked back into the more solid section of the palace, checking each room we passed for someone who could tell us where we might find the laundry. At last we nearabout ran into a maid with both arms full of sheets. She gave me instructions while Tunstall took her sheets so he could carry them for her.

"I don't suppose a sharp mot like you would know where they've been laying out the dead?" he asked her as they wandered down the hall. He turned his head and gave me a nod. He'd catch up with me.

I nodded and told Achoo, *"Tumit."* Split up, Tunstall and I could learn more after we'd dallied so long with folk who didn't seem to know that time was the main point in matters like these. The longer we spent bowing or listening to royalty or the likes of an Orielle, the colder the trail got. I tried to do my figuring as Achoo and I ran down a narrow servant's stair in part of the building that had escaped the fire. Her Majesty said the king's party had left Blue Harbor at about midnight. Even if they'd kept a good pace, and the absence of the guards at the main gate had spurred them on, they would have reached here after one—call it two of the clock. How far the raiders would get depended on whether they had fled by ship or by land. I don't know what His Majesty or my lord thought we could do if they'd taken ship. The Rats could be on their way to Carthak.

And why the secrecy? I wondered as we reached the basement level. I turned right, as the maid had directed me, following the lingering scent of soapy steam. Why had the king not summoned the navy right off, and the army? Why were all the fine mages of the chancellery not having their own little peregrine voyages right now, ready to put their fancy training and tools into the search? I knew there'd been a lot of angry mages when the king proposed that they be licensed and taxed like ordinary folk, but surely *all* of the palace mages weren't rotten.

The laundry was far bigger even than the one at Provost's House. It was a downhearted place, with no maids at work, beating shirts and tunics, dying new batches of clothes, telling jokes and gossiping above the noise of it all. Achoo and I walked in, looking at indoor lines hung with drying clothes and the baskets of dry stuff, waiting for hot irons. The fires were out, their fuel all burned to ashes. When I dipped my hand into the water tubs, I found them all cold. Several times I had to walk around puddles of blood. Either the raiders had killed anyone here and dragged them out, or those collecting the dead had taken them away.

"Black God take you gentle," I whispered, in case their ghosts were lingering. "Find the Peaceful Realms and rest." The more death I know, the more I feel like I must say something, working for the Black God as I do. I wondered if there were pigeons outside who might be carrying any ghosts. If there were, the ghosts might tell me of how the attack had unfolded.

My steps and Achoo's claws echoed on the stone floors. I looked at the baskets, wondering where I could start, when

I saw the second laundry room, connected to the big one. The baskets in there held clothes that were finer than these by far.

This other room was smaller, but better equipped. The flatirons were polished smooth to leave no marks on fine linen, lace, or silk. The starches were the finest ground possible, for a queen's delicate skin, and the soap was filled with expensive scent.

I saw a pair of good-sized baskets. One held small pressed tunics neatly folded and ready for transport upstairs. The other held tunics streaked with berry traces, hose stained with mud, and loincloths marked by a child who was still learning to master the chamber pot. That touched me. I remember one time when my brother Nilo got lost at Provost's House, just after we'd moved there. He'd cried himself into hiccups in one of the cellars, thinking he'd never see any of us again. The poor little prince must be so frightened, out there with strangers. He'd been surrounded by them that loved him all his life.

When I knelt by the basket of dirty laundry, Achoo plunged her nose into it. She began to sneeze right away, having gotten the prince's scent full on. I moved the basket away before she could sneeze into it. If things got ugly, other scent hounds might need these dirty clothes.

A basket was too unwieldy. I looked around and spotted a laundry bag. I slid it over one end of the basket and tilted it so the clothes fell inside. I kept two dirty loincloths, sliding them in a leather outer pocket on my shoulder pack. Then I tied off the top of the bag. Now the scent-rich clothes would be protected from my smell. If we did not find His Highness dead somewhere close, more scent hound teams, the veteran teams, would be placed on this Hunt. They would need these garments.

I looked around this smaller laundry room. Pounce had

returned. He sat on the edge of one of the tubs, staring back at me. Achoo was at my feet, whining because I had taken the strong smells away.

"Where have you been?" I asked Pounce, though this wasn't the idea that was chief of those in my brain.

Pounce answered my spoken question anyway. *Out and about.*

I barely attended to that. Instead I spoke the thing that had been itching at my brain for some time. The itch had gotten almost unbearable since Master Farmer said what he had about the protection spells.

"It was an inside job, wasn't it?" I asked Pounce. "It's not just a matter of the magic being shredded to bits, like Master Farmer said. That hill below the gardens is *steep.* Then we have two outer walls and cliffs down to the sea, as well as those dead soldiers we saw in the garden. For raiders to get by all that, someone helped the kidnappers. Someone opened gates and told them where to find the hidden trails and the prince."

Is that what you think? he asked. Pounce hardly ever tells me things, even when he knows them. He says he doesn't want me to depend on him. Since the last time I expected him to warn me of danger and I got my head cracked instead, I don't argue.

"What I *think* is that if someone got the jump on our little prince last night, they might well try again, on Their Majesties. It's not enough to take the heir. Her Majesty's young, and it's plain they're still in love. Mayhap she's not gotten pregnant again yet because she wanted to spend time with the prince. The first thing they ought to do is get about the business of more heirs, unless their enemies stop them."

Pounce looked up at the ceiling. *Let someone else protect*

them. You're needed to Hunt for the prince, he said. *We're needed.*

I lifted the bag in my arms and walked out through the bigger laundry room. "At least with this stuff Achoo and I have sommat to start with. It's a grand life we have, when excitement comes from dirty loincloths," I told Pounce.

As we climbed the stairs to the main floor, I heard shouting in the distance. I couldn't be sure, but the loudest voice sounded like the king's. When we rounded the turn and came in view of the top stair, there sat Mistress Orielle, weeping into her hands. Tunstall perched beside her, one arm around her shoulders. Master Farmer leaned against the wall behind them, his hands in his breeches pockets.

His face brightened when he saw me. "Is it washing day?" he asked. Tunstall shot him a glare, but Master Farmer didn't seem to even notice it.

"Why is the king shouting?" I asked them. His Majesty's voice came from down one of the halls.

Mistress Orielle found her handkerchief and blew her nose. "The Lord Chancellor of Mages was found at dawn in his office, murdered," she said. "It's disastrous at such a time."

I stared at her. "How did you find out—oh. Magic."

"Ironwood spoke to the Corus palace when I told him what Farmer had seen," Orielle told me. "Everything there is all upended."

"He didn't tell the palace folk what has happened here?" Tunstall asked, alarmed. So was I.

"No, of course not!" Orielle replied, outraged. "No word is to leave this place until decisions are made. His Majesty has placed Lord Gershom in charge of everything, and Lord Gershom has been . . . quite firm about that."

"Everything? He hasn't sent for the Knight Commander of the King's Own? The Prime Minister?" Master Farmer asked. Tunstall glanced at me and raised his brows. This *was* a shocker. Why would His Majesty do such a thing? Then I had a thought. Mayhap the king *already* believed the raiders had inside help. Maybe he's not trusting anyone at either palace just now, except my lord.

I knew Lord Gershom and the king were friends from the king's wilder days. My lord had saved the king's life on many an occasion, and he'd hidden many a mistress from the knowledge of Queen Alysy. Now I wondered what other things my lord might have done for him, that the king would place all responsibility for this mess as it stood in Lord Gershom's hands.

Lady Orielle was clearing her throat to get my attention. "What did you find?" she asked me.

"His Highness's dirty clothes. They're important," I told her when she frowned. "The scent hounds will need them. They must be kept separate and untouched." I offered her the bag, but chose not to mention the two pieces I'd put in my shoulder pack. If the king didn't trust the palace folk, neither would I. "This must be sealed and put aside, in case we don't find the prince here." Mistress Orielle flinched, but she took the bag from me. I looked at Tunstall. "Any word of the kidnappers?"

Tunstall leaned over, about to spit, then thought the better of it. He took his arm from Mistress Orielle's shoulders instead. "None of them among the dead. Every body is someone known by the folk here. The melted ones were known by jewelry, amulets, and so on. They've not found any dead younger than twenty. And all the fairest young mots and coves are gone, too. Twenty-eight missing, total."

Mistress Orielle buried her face in her hands. Tunstall looked at us, having said all he meant to say.

"Perhaps it's time to let Achoo go to work?" Master Farmer asked. "Set her to track the prince, now that she has something to give her the scent?"

Mistress Orielle got to her feet with Tunstall's help and let Pounce and me squeeze by as he climbed the last step to stand with Master Farmer. "I'll take good care of the clothes, don't you worry," she told me, patting the bag. She looked beyond us. Master Ironwood was approaching. I'd thought he looked bad when he greeted my lord at the front door. Now he looked worse. "We have the prince's dirty clothes to care for," she told him.

"What do I care for dirty clothes, you idiot female?" he snapped at her as he passed us by. I bristled and stepped onto the ground floor. Achoo came with me, growling, her head down.

Mistress Orielle set her hand on my arm. "I'm used to it," she said, her soft voice matter-of-fact. "It doesn't bother me."

I would have said, "It bothers *me*," but it wasn't my place. If this quiet little mot was the queen's personal mage, she was far better able to defend herself than I could.

I knelt beside Achoo, telling her, *"Mudah."* Achoo looked at me, as if to ask if I was sure, then relaxed. Master Ironwood was gone down the hall in any event. Tunstall and Master Farmer were waiting. I held a stained and smelly loincloth under Achoo's nose. She gave it a good sniff before she began to sneeze. *"Maji,"* I said. Get to work. I looked around for Pounce, but he had disappeared again. I hoped he was going to drop a wall on Master Ironwood for his meanness, but knew it wasn't likely. He would call it interference and tell me to drop the wall on the mage myself.

Off went Achoo. I cleared my thoughts and followed. In the years I have been running with her, I have found that I make my own contributions, keeping my eyes and ears open as I follow. Up the stairs she took me, stopping often to turn, sniffing. On she would go. I was fairly certain that she smelled the raiders as they carried the lad back along the hall from the nursery, but Achoo had to work in her own way. She could be chasing the prince as he came in from play, sweating and leaving his scent in the air where a hound with an uncanny nose would find it hours, even days, after. She had to breathe in all of the scents and then unravel them.

Achoo halted at last, thwarted by the end of the wooden floor and the gaping hole where the roof, attic, nursery, and whatever lay below had dropped into the cellars. Three charred boards, held by whatever remained of the magic that reinforced this wing of the palace, jutted out over that gaping pit. I had the strange fancy the hole was a giant's mouth, the boards rotted teeth.

"Achoo," I called softly. I didn't want to command her when she had the scent, but she was making me very nervous. She circled on those boards, blowing smoke and the scents of charred wood, paint, and flesh out of her nose. The spells were lace. What if the threads that held those boards up snapped under her?

I offered the loincloth silently, about to call her a second time, when she straightened and trotted back past me, her plumed tail in the air. She was on the move again. I followed her back down the hallway. We passed the waiting stairwell. Achoo ignored it. The prince's captors had not taken him downstairs here. We passed an open linen closet where a noble lady sobbed into a pile of folded sheets and a maidservant awkwardly patted her on the back. The maid glanced at us, but the noblewoman never looked up. Next I looked into a room where Master Ironwood sat in a window, a bowl between his hands. He stared into its contents as a lilac glow shone on its surface.

Then Achoo found a stairwell she liked. She ran swiftly down, but I had to go more carefully. Pooled blood made the marble steps hazardous. Someone had fought like a centaur for this passageway. At the end of it lay a dead man, as I had expected. Gods all witness it, he was chopped meat in chain mail and the tunic of the King's Own, his head still barely attached. From the state of the landing, he'd made the invaders pay for every gouge on his poor body.

I ~~cruich~~ crouched down beside him. Achoo, in the open door to the ~~gardi~~ garden, whined.

"Diamlah," I told her. "Pox rot it, you know what I must do here."

Achoo gave her near silent "wuf," as much of a ~~rebelion~~ rebellion when I'd told her *diamlah* as she would give. She waited as i closed the big cove's open eyes with my fingers and set two copers from my purs on them. Them collecting the ~~ded~~ dead had not found him. Id hav to let them know he was here. "Black God take you gentle, brave ~~defefe~~ defender," I whispered. "The living will cary your duty now. Find the Peeceful Realms and rest."

"what's this?" I heard Master Farmer say nearby. I knew he and Tunstall had followed us but I hadnt wanted to attend upon them. I was working with Achoo

"Quiet, kraknob!" Tunstall whispered. "Shes as close to being a priest of the Black God as ~~mmakes~~ no difrence in a temple so keep your gob buttoned!"

I must stop. I am to tired to rite mor untl Ive had a proper sleep.

Saturday, June 9, 249

The Summer Palace

Now I am better for a bit of sleep and a decent meal. I always forget how much a Hunt takes out of me, until the next time I am on one.

When I stood beside the dead soldier of the King's Own, Achoo was ready to leap out of her skin, she was so anxious to keep on. Anyone might have thought I'd cost her hours instead of a minute at the most. I stepped out into the garden with her and gave her the order to Hunt. Master Farmer and Tunstall followed us.

Off she went, tracking the scent into the night. A vast glow grew behind us, throwing our shadows over the garden paths. I glanced back to see it came from all around Master Farmer. He was lighting our way. The dead had been cleared off, so there was naught to hinder Achoo as she trotted downhill. She leaped the garden wall handily. It was more of an ungraceful scramble for us humans, but she made sure I was over before she went on, across the road we had taken not so long ago to reach the front door of the Summer Palace. The young prince's captors had not even bothered to conceal themselves at that point. They had followed the road straight down to a walled gate that overlooked the sea, knowing they had left everyone in the Summer Palace dead. Were they laughing as they passed through?

I kept to the roadside as Achoo and I continued on. I knew Tunstall would pause to inspect the footprints at the gate, to see who came and who left. Achoo led me down a broad path that wound into the rock formations below the wall. I could see where the path split off twice, to rise toward other parts of the palace. I wasn't certain if it was Master Farmer's pearly light that made my vision of those paths waver, or the remnants of the spells that had once hidden them. In any event, Achoo had no interest in anything but this route. She followed it all the way to a long, narrow shingle of beach. There she ran to and fro between the waves and the stone cliffs that sheltered it, barking furiously at the Emerald Ocean. Seemingly she wanted it to give up the prince she was seeking.

"Tide's still high," Master Farmer said as he came up behind me, still casting light around us. "Doubtless it's washed away all traces of the ships' landing spot."

I saw sommat on the waves. Hurriedly I stripped off my boots and weapons belt and waded in after it while Achoo set up a yelping I was sure they could hear atop the cliffs. The riptide dragged on my knees and ankles, trying to tug me out to sea. No wonder the coast folk talk of mermen and merwomen grabbing hold of someone from under the water—it almost felt like hands about my legs, when no one's seen any of the sea people in two hundred years!

Achoo set up a mourning howl as I grabbed the thing I had seen. It was the body of a cat. Other bodies floated by me—dead rats of the four-legged, pink-tailed kind. I grabbed one of the rats' bodies, and a floating whip. Then a strong arm wrapped around my waist and Tunstall towed me back to shore.

"A little cold for a sea bath, isn't it?" he growled in my ear. "And what was that smokehead thinking, to let you wade in?" He dumped me on the sand.

I glared up at him. "I'd have liked to see him stop me." I dropped my findings on the wet sand before him and Master Farmer while Achoo whined and sniffed me all over anxiously, licking my face and arms.

Pounce had caught up with us again. He looked at that poor dead cat, his tail lashing, then said, *Achoo tells you that while she may be silly,* she *knows better than to go into the angry waters.*

"Achoo only has a name for being silly because she gets bored easy, she's so clever," I told Pounce. The two coves were still staring at the things I had fetched from the waves. Seemingly they hadn't got their import yet. I went on telling Pounce, "When she gets bored, she'll do anything to keep from being bored, even if it means just chasing butterflies or leaves. *I* had to get those things because they tell us sommat that's very, very important." I looked at the coves. "What manner of fleeing raiders take time to throw their cats and rats into the sea? What manner of slavers toss their whips overboard?" I pointed to the cargo of rope, rats, and whatnot that floated on the sea at the outermost edge of Master Farmer's light. "There's more coming in with the tide."

"The beasts weren't tossed," said Tunstall. "They drowned."

Master Farmer crouched on the wet sand, scooping a bit up in his hands. He let it fall and took out that lens of his, putting it to one eye. "Ach," he murmured. "We need more light." He released the lens, tucked it away, then got up and went to a tall stone that thrust out of the sand. He laid both hands on it for a moment. Suddenly it blazed all over, but only in spots, those spots giving enough pure light to cover the beach.

"You put light in the rock?" Tunstall asked. I half hid behind my partner. I'm not at my best with mages in the first place. It was one thing to speak with Master Farmer if he was a Hunter like Tunstall and me, but I couldn't do that if he was going to make lanterns of things that don't hold fire.

"Not the rock," Master Farmer said cheerfully. "But there

are quartz crystals in the rock. Their nature makes it possible for them to hold light for quite some time." *Now* he sounded like a mage, and a clever one at that. Why play the fool, then?

He sat cross-legged at the edge of the wet sand. "I have mage work to do here, if you will excuse me. It may take some time."

Tunstall sighed. "Mages. They're like cats, forever walking their own path. Why don't you search the north end of this beach for anything that might tell us about our raiders, and I'll search south. Oh, wait."

He ambled over to the glowing rock. There he bent down and picked up two smaller stones that had gotten caught in Master Farmer's light spell along with the main boulder. Pounce trotted over to rub against Tunstall's calves. Then the cat leaped up to a flat space on top of the big stone. Tunstall gave him a quick scratch around the ears. As Pounce curled up for a nap, Tunstall tossed one of the glowing stones to me. "Nice to have stone lamps," he said, and walked south.

Achoo came galloping to me, sensing we were about to do actual work. With her at my side, I took my fireless stone lamp along the northern end of the beach, using it to inspect the sand from the waves' edges to the bottom of the cliffs. I found a child's wooden dog, a toy meant to be pulled on a cord, and a woman's scarf. They may have been left behind after an afternoon by the water. Achoo sniffed them and turned away—they did not come from the prince, or his scent had washed clean. Mayhap the toy belonged to one of the other missing children? Given the coating of sand on both, I misbelieved they had been left by the captives.

I had reached the rocky foot of land that walled off the north side of the beach. Even an adventurous holidaymaker would be hard put to it to climb over this high, stony spur of the cliffs to see if there was a beach on the other side. I was about to turn back when the light from the crystals in my rock sparked an answering gleam at the base of the stone. I knelt to see what it was, setting the toy and the scarf aside.

I picked up a bronze pendant or ornament. It hung from a thin leather strap that had been worn through at the end. Did the owner even know it was missing? It was nearly flat and round with a raised edge. At the center, also raised, was a design of four lance blade leaves, laid with the narrow tips meeting in the middle.

I turned the dangle over in my hand, wondering who had brought it to this far corner of the beach. Holding up my stone lamp, I inspected the sand around me and then the cliffs. Here I found one more trail, half blurred by the spells that still remained on it.

Achoo and I climbed that trail a little way. I stopped and raised my bright stone to examine my surroundings. Stone steps were planted in the steep hillside. They led to the Summer Palace. The walls on the trail were slabs of the same rock as the cliffs, rising high above my head. Defenders could pour anything from arrows to boiling oil on anyone who came this way, and they would have no room to hide.

Turning to climb down, I saw light on the sea at the edge of the cove. I shoved my fireless stone lamp under my tunic in case more raiders had come. As I stared, though, the lights traced fiery lines as they flowed to the center of the cove and stopped. There they continued to move, shaping figures in the air. Slowly the shapes became familiar—curved sides, flat-faced sterns, masts, sails. Two ships drawn in fire floated over the middle of the cove.

I snatched up the toy and the scarf I'd found in addition to the brass dangle, then raced with Achoo back to Master Farmer.

I kept an eye on those ghost ships. More details appeared to fill in the ships' outlines, until I could even glimpse the pilot's wheel on one. When I halted next to the mage, he didn't even look at me. His gaze was intent on the ghost vessels.

Tunstall reached Master Farmer just after I did and dumped the things he had found on the sand. "Trickster's blue pearls, what's this?" he demanded as I added the toy and the cloth to the pile of findings.

Master Farmer looked up at us. "There are reasons Gershom called on me," he said. "I can raise the image of something that's buried, under the ground or underwater." He held up his lens. "Once I noticed the traces of magic on the surface out there, I used my lens to see if there was more power under the water. The raiders never left the cove. They sank." When we stared at him, he shrugged. "Many folk carry magic with them. I found the crew's charms and amulets and the magics that went into the ships when they were built." He pointed at the ghost vessels. "With all that, I could draw images of what's there. The closest ship is two hundred feet off. Oh, and the magic that blasted the bottoms out of them and kept anyone from escaping, that's there, too. It's a complex mix of powers, curse it all. Even if I knew the mages who did it, and that's not likely, I wouldn't be able to tell if they'd had a hand in this."

"That's mad," I said. "Two ships, crew, and captives? Why go to all this trouble, only to destroy the profits? It must have taken a lot of power to attack the palace, then flat-out sink the ships so fast that none could escape. That's *seriously* big magic, right? Surely the realm doesn't have that many great mages that could do this."

"She's the thinker," Tunstall said. "I'm the beauty."

Master Farmer smiled at him, then looked at me. "There

are plenty of powerful mages in the realm these days, and lots of them are angry. You know about the licenses and the taxes on mages, don't you?"

"Only a fool Dog doesn't attend to what's going on," Tunstall said irritably.

Master Farmer shrugged. "I meant no offense. The Dogs I work with concern themselves with keeping the peace, not politics. I tend to stay to myself, but even I've heard other mages say the realm has no business interfering in what we do. Some of the loudest protest comes from the great mages— some of the quietest whispers, too, I wager. It would only take one or two great mages to do something like this."

"All that effort and power just to drown the prince?" Tunstall asked. "That doesn't play out. And we see no signs of any other group but the one that attacked the palace."

"Nor a second enemy that came just in time to sink them," I added. "We're missing a piece."

Hearing the sound of folk approaching, I looked back at the steps to the palace. Mistress Orielle and Master Ironwood were coming to join us. For company they had two of the King's Own as torchbearers and a pair of servants. One carried a flask and two cups while the other had what looked to be cloaks over one arm.

"I reached through my mirror to let them know what I'd found," I heard Master Farmer say. "They might help. And it will be interesting if they refuse, or if any help they give goes awry and destroys what we've found."

I turned to gaze at him, impressed. Tunstall also had an expression of approval on his face. There was more to Master Farmer than the plain package that he came in.

The great mages halted near the water's edge and stared

at Master Farmer's creations. Master Ironwood sniffed. "Very pretty," he said. "You summoned us to show pictures?"

Master Farmer looked at him with dull cow eyes. "Naw," he drawled. "I'm showin' you where two ships are sunk along with crew and slaves."

"Sunk?" Mistress Orielle repeated. "These ships are on the bottom of the cove?"

"If you'd looked down here, you mighta seen 'em yourself," Master Farmer replied. "But you've both been that busy, I know."

"Doubtless those vessels have been down for years," Master Ironwood snapped.

Mistress Orielle stretched out a hand, letting her Gift roll down into the sea. After a moment, she said, "No. They are almost whole. The trash that rises from them is fresh. They've been here a day, perhaps less."

Master Farmer nodded. His light ships were coming closer to the beach. "I learned this spell from a teacher that worked in fishin' villages all the time. When my images are close enough, we'll see anything about them that's touched with magic." He'd dropped his yokel's accent some. He'd been mocking the royal mages, I realized. I shook my head. What manner of looby tried to pull a bear's tail? In truth, I'd sooner meddle with that bear than a mage, for mages are far more touchy. Then I saw Master Farmer scratch his head. He wasn't done tweaking these two high-and-mighty folk. He said, "A course, we'd see even the non-magicked stuff if we could raise the ships from the bottom, but I can't do that."

"Of course *you* cannot," Master Ironwood said. If he had noticed Master Farmer's nonsense, it did not show. Even

Mistress Orielle did not seem to suspect. "What manner of Provost's mage studies with fishing mages?" he asked.

"One that studies with any mage that will take him," Master Farmer replied. "I wasn't good enough for the City of the Gods or Carthak, nor had I the coin for it. And Master Seabreeze was good for other things. He could call winds, seek out schools of fish, make dyes from sea urchins—"

"Quiet!" Ironwood said. "I am sorry I asked. Mistress Orielle and I can do work that is far more useful than your gleanings from the ocean bottom."

"I have a grip on one," Mistress Orielle told him coolly. "Will you take the other?" She smiled at Master Farmer. "You may help, if we have need. We have stores of power at hand, should we require any, but you might also learn a new trick or two."

Master Farmer nodded, grinning. His bright ships began to fade. "That's an honor for me," he said eagerly.

"Excuse me for asking, but are you not supposed to guard Their Majesties?" Tunstall wanted to know. "Meaning no offense."

"We placed them in their chambers under layers of protection spells so they might sleep," Master Ironwood replied, his eyes already fixed on the cove. "They are exhausted and will not wake for hours." Yellow fire flowed from him like a river to mingle with the waves.

I frowned. It did not seem proper for Ironwood and Orielle to lock their charges in their rooms, but that was not supposed to be my concern. Finding the prince was. Mayhap these sunken ships would give us more clues, but we could do nothing about that until the ships were above the water. In the meantime, I needed sommat to keep me busy.

Tunstall beckoned me over to the pile of things he had

found on the southern half of the beach. Seemingly that area was more popular with the palace folk than the northern half. We inspected all of it. Nothing seemed important: a wooden comb, a straw basket, a leather ball, a pale blue blanket, and a small fan made of feathers, together with my toy dog and scarf. The brass dangle was too small to be left there, where it might be lost. I kept that safe in my pocket. Tunstall and I looked at our collection with my spelled mirror, but these things showed no magic whatsoever.

"We're wasting time here, standing about with our thumbs up our asses," Tunstall said at last. "I've a mind to take Achoo up to the woods and cast about to see if any other strangers have been near. We don't have to wait for day, now we've got these lamps. Someone sank those ships. I doubt he went down with them. Like as not he sailed off on his own, but just in case he didn't . . ."

I showed him the bronze piece. "I found it up there," I said, and pointed. "Right next to another path to the heights."

Tunstall looked it over. "I don't know the insignia. Might've been there for who knows how long, though it's not scratched up." He flipped it in the air, caught it, and handed it back to me. "Could be something, could be naught. Let's have a stroll, Cooper."

I looked at the mages. Mistress Orielle stood straight, her small shoulders square. Ironwood swayed a little. Masts were poking out of the rolling water, masts and a figurehead in the shape of a vulture. The first ship, drawn by Mistress Orielle, was coming in. Master Farmer was still seated, but his hands were busy. I looked closer. To my startlement, he was stitching on a length of broad ribbon. He was embroidering, and doing so without looking at the ribbon! He got stranger every moment I was in his company.

There was no point to interrupting, so Tunstall and I set off down the beach without farewells. Achoo found a stick and brought it to Tunstall, who threw it for her.

Good Hunting, Pounce called as we passed him on his rock.

At the end of the beach I let Achoo sniff the brass medallion and its leather strap, but they gave her nothing. She circled and circled, sniffing, going to the path, then down the beach. Finally I felt sorry for her and said, "*Berhenti,* Achoo." Mayhap the owner's scent had worn off by now, and this dangle had naught to do with the raiders. I gave Achoo a bit of dried meat, because she had tried so hard.

"Up we go, then," Tunstall said cheerfully, squinting at the half-magicked path. He found his way onto it by feeling ahead with his feet, hands, and baton. Once we were on it, we could see perfectly well using our stone lamps. It was getting past the first spells that was tricky.

As we climbed, Tunstall said, "I tell you, Cooper, this Hunt is shaping to be a true pile of scummer and snakes. Us lowly folk better mind how we go, else we'll be crushed. We've no business dealing with nobles and great mages." He made the Sign against evil and spat to the side of the trail. "Even lesser mages. Did you see what that Farmer was doing? He was *sewing!*"

"Embroidering, actually," I replied. "Mayhap he does trims with magical signs and sells them for pocket money. It's not like he gets a share of the weekly Happy Bag, if he's a kennel mage. They only get coin from the Bag where they've helped to hobble the Rats. And the pay is no royal sum."

"Embroidery," Tunstall said, and spat again. "Sewing and doing your mending, that's manly enough. But fancy work?

And playing with string while those other mages were pulling up whole ships, if they weren't belching braggarts."

Tunstall's view of what men could and couldn't do was sometimes odd. Our old partner Goodwin and I agreed that there was no manly or unwomanly, only what you chose to do. But I didn't argue with Tunstall about it as we often did, when we were unsettled and wanted to think of sommat else. We had reached the top of the bluff.

We stepped onto the road that wound around the Summer Palace, where we'd been that afternoon, on the turn just before we saw the garden full of the dead. Without another word Tunstall and I raised our shining rocks so they cast their light around us for about four feet. We spread just six feet apart. Achoo, knowing her role, went about four feet to my left, a little ahead. Then we began walking forward at a sharp angle through that very clean woodland at a slow pace, inspecting the ground before us. Tunstall would signal, and we'd move ahead in the reverse direction, walking a letter Z among the trees.

"I see it!" Tunstall said when we'd gone about a quarter of a mile. "They groom even the woods like the garden. They get rid of all the brush and little trees and vines so everyone can trot their horses through without getting tangled."

Looking at the neat forest around me, I sighed. Tunstall was right. It meant that there were precious few places for animals to hide. There were no vines to trip me up, and the trees were neatly trimmed well above my head. It also made the woodland seem false, somehow. It was not the way the Goddess made the forests.

"Cheer up, Cooper," Tunstall said. He could read me like a proclamation. "I'll wager the forest where they hunt is messier by far. This is for the ladies. See here." He pointed to his right. I came closer to look and winced. A perfect mossy bank led to a stream. Willows grew there, and flowers. It was so tidy it could have been painted.

Then Achoo charged down to the water and slurped loudly as she drank from the stream, a commoner hound with leaves in her curls and sand in her paws. Tunstall and I chuckled and returned to our inspection of the ground.

We kept close to the cliffs, straying no more than a hundred yards east of them, moving back and forth in our narrow Z, always headed north. It wasn't the best of search patterns, but it was the best that two Dogs and a lone hound could manage. At least we remained in hearing of the little stream, so we could all drink as we got dry. Palace streams, we agreed, should be safe to drink from.

I will say this of Master Farmer's glowing rocks. They did not go out. By their light we covered about three miles of ground, dismaying all manner of bats, owls, and small burrowing creatures that had escaped the humans that had groomed all the interest from the woods. I was about to say we should turn back when Achoo raced to the cliff's edge and began to circle, huffing to herself.

Tunstall and I froze. Here the wood opened on a clearing some five hundred yards or so across, a place where folk might have games and contests. That was not Achoo's concern, though. She looked up at me and whined. She had the prince's scent again!

I went to her. Tunstall followed in my footsteps. After two year of working with Achoo, we knew to keep our own scents to as thin a path as we could, that we might not interfere with what had caught her attention. There, in the bare earth where yet another half-magicked trail faded in and out of sight over the edge of the land, we found the footprints of horses.

Tunstall walked along the cliff another hundred feet and came back as Achoo followed her drift of scent thirty feet inland. "Someone waited with mounts back there," Tunstall said when he reached me. His voice was tense, but he spoke calmly. Achoo did better if she didn't think we were worked up. "On the grass. Hard to tell how many riders and how many horses without mounts there. Is it worthwhile to look down by the water?"

Achoo was moving in circles. She sniffed the air and glanced at us, as she did when she was on the track. I ground my teeth. We dared not let that trail get colder, but we needed all the evidence we could get, too.

"I think we'd better keep on the land trail," I told him. "We know they took to the sea back at the palace. Now we know they came ashore and met someone here, then rode east. We'll have to send someone to look at that beach—there's only two of us now, and if they have a crew and we're caught, we might never get word to the others that the prince is alive."

"Right, then," Tunstall replied. Hurriedly he set up a trail sign to let other searchers find the landing point below.

I produced one of the prince's loincloths and let Achoo smell. She gave me a look as if to say, "Do you *really* think I need a reminder in such a short time?" She gave it the barest of sniffs, looked scornfully at me again, then trotted off across the grass. We followed, crossing the clearing to enter the trees. This was the forest that was left natural for hunters and game. *Now* there was brush and tree branches to dodge, and vines to flay us like whips. I went flat on my face twice, once on dry ground, once as I crossed the stream that was a play area for ladies further south. Half of me got soaked as the other half struck the bank on the far side. Tunstall called softly, "Cooper? This is no time for a bath."

I told him what he might do with himself and his bath. The sorry old guttersnake's by-blow only laughed at me and offered me one of his large handkerchiefs. As quietly as I could I escaped the stream and wiped the mud off. Tunstall offered me the small bottle of mead he always carries in case someone needs warming up, but I shook my head. I don't like to drink at all when I'm on duty, even when it might warm me. Tunstall put the bottle away as I told Achoo to move on.

It was the trotting to keep up with her that warmed my poor sodden legs and helped to dry my breeches out some. We were two miles past the stream when we came to the wall that enclosed the grounds for the Summer Palace. We halted to stare, Tunstall whistling low with admiration. We raised both of our stone lamps to view it.

The hole the enemy's mage had blown through it was about five horses wide. Seemingly the kidnappers didn't worry about anyone catching them by then.

Achoo didn't want to wait even for the scant time we would have taken to survey the broken wall. The prince's scent must have been stronger than ever. She dashed across the road north and into the woods on its far side. Tunstall and I followed, spotting horse tracks that cut across the beaten earth of the main road in the same direction. We halted briefly inside the trees to get our bearings.

I knew his thinking. One lamp would be enough to see the trail while two might draw attention if the enemy was near. I also saw him grimace and rub his knees. They were hurting him, then. He looked tired, though I knew he'd deny it if I asked. I pretended not to see as he took a drink from the flask. The mead would ease any pain in bones that had been broken and healed too often for healing to really work anymore. "How far to the river?" Tunstall asked as he tucked his stone lamp away.

I can never tell if he is testing me or if he doesn't know. If he is testing me, I wish he would stop. I have not been a Puppy, nor he my training Dog, for four years. I called the map to my memory. I knew it because Achoo and I had been Hunting a gem thief between Blue Harbor and Arenaver last winter. "A mile and a half to the Ware," I said.

We covered the next mile in silence. We didn't talk, but even without consulting about it, we slowed to a walk at the same time, while I whistled Achoo back to me. Then I wrapped all but a thumb's length of my stone lamp in the hem of my tunic. The three of us approached the river as quietly as we could manage. We had no idea of how far behind the enemy we were. If they were on the riverbank, awaiting a boat or ferry, we wanted our arrival to be a surprise. If they outnumbered us, it would be even better if they didn't see us split up, one to watch and the other to go for help.

At last we came out of the trees. We stood near the Ware River on an open slope cleared by Crown foresters so bandits couldn't hide close to the water. We looked up and down our side of the river. No one, riders or ferries, was visible in the half-moon's light. We heard only the river's constant rush as it flowed down to the Tellerun. As far as we could tell, there were no humans but us about.

Still, we made our way down to the water slowly. The glimmer of light from my shrouded lamp revealed only a couple of feet ahead of us. Suddenly Achoo whined and butted in between Tunstall and me, her way of telling us something bad was near. Then the smell hit my nose, bringing me up short. It was a tripe-wringing mix of burned meat, scorched leather, and hot metal.

Achoo began to growl, hackles up. *"Diamlah,"* I whispered as Tunstall drew his baton. We moved forward slowly until we discovered a large, stinking pile, or puddle. "Let's have some light, Cooper," said Tunstall. "Any Rat is long gone from here. Any witnesses, too, I'll wager."

We both raised our lamps so we could better see the nastiness that was before us. It was a great soup that lay on the grass, trickling slowly into the river. I stared at it, fascinated. I recognized pieces of metal from horses' tack, metal amulets and jewelry, and swords and daggers, but naught that was leather, cloth, or skin.

"Mistress Fea was *melted*," the queen had said.

Tunstall ran back to the trees. He returned to shove a long, leafless branch at me. He carried one of his own. "Keep the evidence out of the river, Cooper!" he ordered.

I set my rock on the ground, as Tunstall did his, and began to drag the solid pieces from the mess with my stick. The swords might be recognized, not to mention the jewelry. I swallowed my gorge, which was trying to come up, and thrust the sludge aside to find anything that might be under it.

Tunstall was cursing under his breath. "Chaos take the mage that did this, Cooper," he said. He coughed, and went on, "No decent burial for these cracked mumpers."

I stood away from the mess. It was beginning to eat at my branch. "Tunstall," I said, holding the length of wood up for him to see.

He looked at his own half-melted stick. "Gods help us if that poor lad's in this," he said.

"Take heart," I told him. "Look at Achoo." She was going back and forth along the bank a few feet away, sniffing the ground and the air, whining. "Seemingly whoever did this took His Highness on another boat."

"Check upstream for riders to be sure," Tunstall ordered. "Give it a mile."

"Some of us think I can walk to the Realms of the Gods and back," I grumbled. "What will you be doing?"

Tunstall took another drink from his flask, then emptied it onto the ground and walked over to the river, upstream from the mess. Stooping with a soft grunt, he dunked the flask in the water and rinsed it. "I'm going to wash the evil off of what we've retrieved, in case it just takes longer for it to eat through metal."

I rolled my eyes, impatient with myself. "I never thought of that," I confessed. "Don't tell me. This is why you're senior partner."

He chuckled softly as he stood, the flask now full of water. "You think of plenty of other things, Cooper. Now, *maji*!"

I gave him my shoddy imitation of Achoo's soft bark, watching as he returned to the pile of metal we'd made. Using his half branch, he spread the pieces apart. I saw from his movements that he was in pain, two gulps of mead or no. Usually he rides and leads the horse I ride when I'm not running with Achoo. Tonight we had tried his body too far. That's why I hadn't whined when he ordered me to run up the river. When I do complain, he mentions me getting a younger partner, and I don't like that at all. It's my fault we're out running all over the countryside, mine and Achoo's. Without us he'd be walking through the Lower City, a life that would be easier on his legs.

"Achoo, *kemari*," I ordered her. She came to me, her tail between her legs, whining her objections. She wanted to find her quarry, but once more he had vanished over water. *"Bau,"*

I said, offering the prince's loincloth for her to smell. She looked at me with reproach, as if she said, "I *know* the smell, I just want to *find* him!"

"*Maji,*" I said, pointing upstream.

She whined at me again. She didn't want to go beside the water, she complained, or so I believed. I knew she also wondered why we didn't have a way to go *on* the water.

"Pox and murrain, Achoo, I'm too tired to fuss over it. *Maji,* right now!" I ordered.

Supposedly we should only use our hound's name and the words of the exact order, but Achoo and I understood each other far better than the scent-hound handlers' stiff-necked rules took into consideration. Just then, she knew I was a fingertip away from shouting, something neither of us liked. Sullen, head and tail down, Achoo circled the ugly soup and headed upstream. I scooped up my stone lamp and followed her.

We actually went over a mile to see if there was a ferry or anyone who might have seen a strange boat. We found no witnesses nearby, though I knew they could have been there earlier. I was relieved to see there were no ferries as far as we ran. Achoo and I returned to Tunstall, our eagerness and worry over having found the mess completely worn off. My neck was stiff and sore from staring at the ground, but I knew I would have to do a search of the riverbank downstream as well as up. I was sorry I hadn't had a drink of that mead before Tunstall dumped it out.

We found him weaving a rough basket out of willow withes. "To carry our gleanings," he explained. Apparently he'd forgotten he had named Master Farmer unmanly for doing embroidery. Beside Tunstall the metal pile, rinsed clean, gleamed in the light of his stone lamp. When I told him

I would take the downriver search as well, he nodded. Achoo drank from the water above the black patch that was the mess while I took a quick rest with Tunstall by the trees.

"You'll need to do more than check downriver, Cooper," he told me wearily. "We need a mage to look at the evil, and my lord has to be told sooner before later. My legs are giving me Chaos. I would have sworn the night would be clear, but my bones grieve me like it means to rain."

"Let me have a look," I said. He turned over on his belly. We'd done this before, ever since both of his legs were broken in a market brawl. Kora, who knows sommat of healing even though it's not through her Gift, taught me magicless things to help my partner. Tunstall and I both knew that if he'd gone to the Dogs' healers and they understood how much his old wounds troubled him, they'd put him to soft work, not the tough Rat-catching he loves.

First I felt his calf and thigh muscles. They were as hard as stone. I leaned into the muscles with my knuckled fists, like Kora had shown me, working from the narrow part up into the big. I put my whole back behind it, twisting my fists into the knots I could feel. When they started to loosen up, I switched to the heels of my palms and long, looser strokes up through the muscles. I knew it had to hurt like sharp razors, but except for a grunt or two, Tunstall hardly let on.

Such pains are the price of years of Dog work. I'm starting to collect a few of my own, in the arm bone that was broke when a horse threw me two years back and again last year, in the fingers I broke while stupidly punching a Rat in the jaw.

"Tell my lord we need more folk to search these woods for aught we've missed," Tunstall said when I was nearly done. "Hunters will be good, surely. He needs the warriors to protect Their Majesties. If those mages did bring the ships up, they'll have to be searched, too. That's you and me—none of these nobles or their servants will know what to look for or how to look for it. Mage Farmer, too, mayhap, if he knows how to do a sarden search."

"Yes, indeed, but not tonight," I told him, getting to my feet. "And Achoo stays here with you."

"She needs to sniff the riverbank," Tunstall said. "We'll feel like right loobies if it turns out later they swam the river on horseback, or came back on land after they broke this trail we've been following."

"I hate it when you're right," I said. "Achoo, *tumit.*"

Achoo began to smell around us, but her heart was not in it. She had plainly given up on finding the scent in this place. We went to the riverbank and followed it south.

For two miles or so there was naught of use. I would have to ask where boats docked at night, if they docked, and where the trading caravans that followed the road stopped to rest. I suspected no one was allowed to spend the night anywhere near the Summer Palace, but I had to be sure. In the meantime, Achoo and I had ourselves a quiet, boring, disappointing walk. Achoo hates searching places where there's not so much as a hint of the scent that she's after. She droops from top to toe. Once I was certain we'd covered the two miles, we swung back toward the main road, bordered here by the wall of the Summer Palace. We hadn't gone more than a mile before I heard riders approach. Achoo and I went into the trees, not knowing who was out so late.

They came with a jingle of chain mail and torches to light their way. Lord Gershom was in the lead, an armsman of the King's Own riding on his left, Master Farmer on his right. Five of the King's Own were behind them. They led two rider-less horses.

"My lord!" I shouted, taking the stone lamp from my tunic as Achoo and I walked out of the brush. The men of the King's Own had bows pointed at me before we got our feet on the road.

"Stand down!" my lord barked, dismounting. The archers lowered their bows. "Cooper, Mithros spear us all, what are you doing out here?"

I stood up straight. "Begging Your Lordship's pardon, but Tunstall and I went for a walk," I explained. "You know us. There was naught left for us to do on the beach."

Lord Gershom walked over to me and offered me his water bottle.

"I thank you, but no," I said. "My own is half full yet." And I was very glad I'd filled it at the stream inside the royal walls, not at the river downstream from the melted dead folk. "But we did find some things that my lord will wish to hear of and see."

My lord looked at me. Something in my face must have told him. "He's *alive*?" he whispered. "But the ships . . ."

"Achoo picked up his scent north along the coast," I replied, just as quiet. "We lost it again, but not because he was killed. Though we've got another of those melted people messes, like the one back at the Summer Palace. Tunstall's keeping watch over this one. How do you come to be here, my lord?"

Lord Gershom nodded to Master Farmer, who dismounted and led his horse over to us. "Farmer said you three had gone off hunting something. He tracked you with traces from the evidence you and Tunstall had found on the beach."

"Always glad to be of use," the mage said. "It was the prints of your and your partner's hands, Guardswoman Cooper. I picked them up as I examined the things you and Tunstall found. Good thing I got the traces before they went stale."

"Stale?" I asked. How could a magical trace go stale?

"We all leave oil from our skin when we handle things," Master Farmer explained. "You see it best on bright metal, glass, and glossy stone. A mage with the training can draw it off when it's fresh and use it to find the one who left it behind."

"You *are* going to teach it to the other Provost's mages." Lord Gershom's words lined up like a question, but it was actually a command.

Master Farmer shrugged. "If they can, or will, learn it from me, I am glad to teach it," he replied. "Not all of us have the ability."

"And you're all contrary as cats," Lord Gershom retorted. He glanced back at the guards. "Bring a spare horse," he commanded. A man of the Own trotted over on his horse, towing another that was already saddled. I should not have been surprised that Pounce was riding on its saddle.

"Nice of you to join me," I told the cat as I accepted the reins from the soldier.

There is only so much squabbling between two arrogant mages that I am ready to watch before the boredom grows intolerable, Pounce replied, jumping to the ground. *Besides, the beach is cold.*

It was plain everyone heard Pounce. Lord Gershom and Master Farmer were grinning, as were those who did not flinch at the sound of Pounce's voice. "I am sorry your life is such a trial," I grumbled to the cat. Then I attempted to mount the horse. My legs, which had done so well over the miles of walking, trotting, and running, chose to cramp for that. To my shame, Lord Gershom boosted me into the saddle.

Achoo whined. She was worn out, too. "If someone can hand her up to me?" I asked. "I'm sorry she's dirty—"

"I'll take her, if she doesn't mind," Master Farmer said as he mounted his own horse. "Forgive me, Guardswoman, but you look as weary as she does. Carrying her while you ride won't rest you any."

Lord Gershom cocked an eyebrow at me. I argued with myself about telling Achoo a near stranger was that close a friend, but the mage was right. I was weary. Lord Gershom picked Achoo up gently. She licked his face. He was the only one there she would have permitted to handle her. Then he offered her to Master Farmer.

"Achoo, *santai, kawan,*" I told her. As the mage took Achoo in his arms and settled her over his lap, I told myself that I could always rename him as her enemy if I had to.

Lord Gershom brushed off his tunic and accepted the reins of his own mount. When he was on his horse, he even took the reins of mine. He let Pounce jump onto the saddle in front of him, stroking the cat as Pounce settled. "Now tell me what happened," he ordered me, gesturing for the soldier who had ridden on his left before to fall back. "Softly." We rode a little way ahead of the men, my lord beckoning Master Farmer to join us. I told both of them all that Achoo, Tunstall, and I had done since reaching the beach below the Summer Palace.

"Alive," my lord whispered when I was done. "The prince is alive."

"Mithros grace us," Master Farmer added.

"As best as Achoo and I can tell he's alive," I said. "We only went two miles up and two down the river. We should have scent hounds five miles up and down on *both* sides of the river, and mayhap a ship to take us up or down, to see if Achoo can get another whiff of him."

Lord Gershom reached over and patted me on the shoulder. "Cooper, you, Tunstall, and Achoo have done far more than I could have hoped for. We might have lost him entirely, were it not for you three."

Achoo knew when she was getting compliments. She wagged her tail, beating Master Farmer with it. He grinned and scratched her ears.

"So tell me, did he really make torches from rocks?" Lord Gershom asked me.

I passed my lamp to him. "He lit up an outcropping. Forgive me. He lit up the *quartz crystals* in the outcropping. And there were a couple of smaller stones fallen from the main rock, the same kind of stone, so we helped ourselves. His charms stick."

"When it's a charm I can work," Master Farmer said. "Don't confuse me with Orielle and Ironwood."

"Who taught you this one?" my lord asked him.

"Cassine, naturally," Master Farmer replied. "See, Cooper, we hadn't much coin, so I did chores and so on for any mage I found who would teach me something. Then I met Master Cassine, and she took me for her student. She taught me where the spells I knew had things in common or could be put to fresh uses, as well as whatever else I could learn. She's a great mage."

Lord Gershom turned the glowing rock over in one gloved hand. "Who keeps to herself for the most part, the Goddess be thanked. I'd be pleased to know when this lamp fades, just for curiosity, Cooper." He returned the lamp to me.

We all fell silent for a time. I dozed. My lord woke me by asking, "Cooper, how close are we to Tunstall?"

Pounce looked up at him. *Close,* he said.

"And I can find him, with my lord's permission," I

replied. I halted my horse and dismounted. I didn't have to ask Master Farmer for Achoo's return. As soon as she saw me touch down, she wriggled out of the mage's hold and leaped to the ground. We trotted ahead of Lord Gershom and his guards, with me holding the stone lamp up. I'd gone about a quarter mile and my arm was sore when I heard a pigeon's call. I halted and waited for Tunstall to come out of the brush. He stood with Achoo and me, watching as the others rode up to us.

"I said to get some help, but did you have to bring the whole nursery?" he asked me quietly as the jingling men of the King's Own came close.

"You know how it is with boys," I replied. Any Rats that might have been nearby were long gone, alerted by the sounds of a good-sized party of folk on horses. "My lord went for a ride, and he just *couldn't* say no, not when they begged all pathetic like."

Lord Gershom drew up and dismounted. "Mattes," he said, clasping Tunstall on the shoulder. "Let's see what you have."

One of the men from the Own came to take charge of my lord's horse, Master Farmer's, and mine. Rather than follow the others, I tucked my lamp in my tunic and ordered Achoo to *dukduk*. Once I found some thick bushes away from the men, she was quite willing to sit in the cool grass behind them and wait for me.

I was tidying my clothes after relieving myself when I heard several folk walking not too far from my refuge. Cursing silently, I beckoned Achoo to come with me. We hid in another clump of brush a couple of feet away. I meant to work my way around them to rejoin my lord when I heard sommat that kept me still.

"—a disgrace, to see these matters handled by Dirty Gershom and those disgusting commoners of his." With my stone lamp hidden in my tunic, I couldn't tell who it was that spoke, though I dearly wished I could. "I pity his lady and his children. *They* never fail to uphold their name."

"Gershom of Haryse is an original, for certain," one of the others said. "And I wouldn't let that mage hear you. Even hedgewitches can bite."

"But why bring Gershom and his *Dogs?*" a third demanded. "Why not get the Ferrets? At least they know how to treat royalty, and nobility. They keep a proper distance."

"Haven't you noticed he doesn't get along with the master of Ferrets any longer?" replied the one who'd called my lord an original, whatever that meant. "Not to mention the Lord of the Exchequer and the Lord High Magistrate. With what happened here, the murder of the Lord Chancellor and perhaps even His Highness, I wouldn't trust anyone at court."

"He's also made the lords and the mages furious with the new taxes," said the one who wanted our job turned over to the Ferrets. "I wouldn't pay a copper cole for His Majesty's life these days."

"You talk treason," the first speaker said harshly.

"I didn't say I *wanted* it," the Ferret-lover replied. "But do you think half of us would be greeting the Black God right now if His Majesty was still his old, lazy self?"

The voices moved out of my hearing, headed back toward the river. I crouched for a moment longer, clenching my fists over and over. Mayhap the split-tongued canker bums would stop for a drink from the water, below the pile that was melted corpses.

I stood finally and snapped my fingers for Achoo. Everyone knew His Majesty was at odds with his nobles as well as his mages. I found it very hard to feel sorry for the nobles or the wealthy great mages. The king had nearabout beggared the treasury to feed the poor over the winter of 247. What was unreasonable about asking those that had the coin to build the kingdom up again? They made enough riches off of us.

Today wasn't the first treasonous bit of speaking I'd heard, either. Every time someone had a complaint about the realm, they whined about the "good old days," when King Roger sported high and low and his younger brother Baird ruled the Privy Council and the Council of Nobles. Prince Baird was happy to oblige the nobility and tax the merchant class and the poor folk. I know what *I* think of their precious "good old days." The number of them living in the Lower City had doubled as farmers lost their land to taxes and came to the cities for work that wasn't there.

Talk of treason made my belly roll. The hungry winter of 247 and the food and wood riots of those days had given me all the taste of rebellion I could want. The only good thing that had come from it was the night I met Holborn at the Mantel and Pullet.

I stopped near the picketed horses. There. Mourning. For the first time in hours I had remembered Holborn. I wished passionately that I'd get to remain on this Hunt even when my lord Gershom did send the Ferrets out to hunt down the prince. Worrying about trails and tripping over bodies, meeting Their Majesties, I hadn't once thought of my loss.

I went over to a tree and leaned there until I could breathe proper again. Only when I was sure of myself did I go on down to the water. I'd thought for a moment that hurt like a dagger's stab that Holborn would have wanted to know what I had seen, what I had heard, and what Lord Gershom had said.

I spotted Master Farmer, Tunstall, and Lord Gershom.

Tunstall nodded, and my lord turned so he could see me. "Cooper, why don't you, Tunstall, and Achoo catch some rest? The lads will wrap what you and Tunstall salvaged from the remains while Farmer takes care of that pile of rot. They can get their hands dirty. You two have done enough."

I wasn't about to argue. No more was Tunstall. Still, I had questions I didn't want "the lads" to overhear. I beckoned the three coves aside, away from the remains. "My lord, might this be some plot by the king's own nobles?" I asked. I'd made sure we stood in the open by the river, with the water's sound to cover what we said, and no nearby brush to hide any eavesdroppers like I had been. "Is that why you're keeping this close to your chest?"

Tunstall groaned. "Not politics, Cooper," he said quietly. "We're Dogs, not useless natterers."

Lord Gershom looked at me for so long that I began to fear I had angered him. Finally he said, "That is the problem with encouraging a promising young one to learn all she can of Dog work. There will come a time when she learns the things you would prefer stayed hidden. Cooper, His Majesty has enemies, some of whom think they are more fit to govern than he is. It may be that they have chosen this way to attack him."

"Wouldn't it be simpler to do away with Their Majesties?" I asked.

"Not if you want to make certain His Majesty does as he is told," Master Farmer said, his voice soft. "Think how much easier it would be, Cooper, to have a pet king."

"But His Majesty doesn't do whatever he likes," I pointed out. "The Council of Nobles and the Council of Mages make it curst hard for him."

"Us worrying over such matters won't get our evidence

packed up or the prince found," my lord said. "The political problems are mine, Cooper. Don't forget, this kidnapping could be the work of someone else entirely, using a rough time at court to set us on another trail. Keep your mind open."

"Yes, my lord," I whispered.

"Of course, my lord," Tunstall said, giving me a gentle elbow in the ribs.

"Now rest," my lord ordered. "I'll rouse you when you're needed. Nond!" he called to one of the men. "Let's have two of the blankets for Tunstall and Cooper here!"

Master Farmer saluted us. "Enjoy your nap," he said.

Tunstall looked at him. "My lord said you went over the things we found on the beach. Did you find anything besides whatever led you to us?"

Master Farmer shook his head. "All of them had been washed by the tide. I found nothing but your traces."

Tunstall cursed under his breath as one of the Own's men trotted off toward the horse lines. The soldier returned with a pair of saddle blankets in his arms. My lord Gershom had gone by then. I could see him a few yards up the bank, near the mess, talking with other men. They'd brought oiled cloth to gather up the pieces we thought we could identify. Master Farmer stood over the mess. If he was using his Gift, I couldn't see it.

"Here you are," the soldier called Nond said as he gave Tunstall and me each a blanket. "Gods all be thanked for the two of you," he whispered. "I know we wouldn't be out here if you hadn't found his trail. You needn't say anything," he said hurriedly when Tunstall opened his mouth to deny it. "I know it's all secret. I'm just grateful for the bit of hope, you see. I've been giving young Gareth rides on my horse for a year. I don't know what I'd—well, never mind. I'll make sacrifice to Great Mithros in your names, in hopes he'll keep guiding you." He left us, his head bowed.

"Here I thought it was Achoo guiding us," Tunstall whispered when Nond was well out of earshot.

I punched Tunstall's arm. "Don't blaspheme," I said. "You know very well what he meant." Tunstall worshipped the hill gods, Keirnun and his two wives, Morni and Danya. He liked to poke fun at the gods of the rest of Tortall, though he did so only lightly, and never at quiet Death.

Tunstall shrugged. "I think the god would say Achoo has earned her praise this night."

I couldn't argue with that, so I found one of the trees with a broad spread of limbs and leaves. I wrapped myself in my blanket. "Achoo, *turun*," I said quietly. She was still pacing to and fro along the riverbank, trying to get the scent back. She looked at me. I pointed to the ground at my side. "*Turun*. We can't do any more just now, so get some sleep, girl."

She walked over to me and together we lay down, Achoo grumbling in her throat. She wanted to be on the Hunt again.

"I don't like it, either," I told her, "but when we have a boat, mayhap we can pick the lad's scent up. We just need to cast around for a bit. I'm betting upstream. Downstream takes them straight to Blue Harbor. They have to think the Deputy Provost has been alerted."

Achoo sighed.

"I know," I said, scratching her ears. "Sometimes we just have to wait." I nodded to Tunstall as he found a spot under our tree. I think I was asleep before he'd spread his blanket.

The boom of distant thunder roused me. At first I thought I'd been dreaming. As it came closer, I prayed Master Farmer could send the storm off. Then I heard him bellow, "I can't *work* with weather, all right, Tunstall? Some things I do, and plenty of things I can't!"

I got up, not wanting to get soaked where I lay. Achoo was not beside me. I found her sitting with Master Farmer, who stood on the riverbank, hands dug deep in his pockets. Tunstall was walking away from him as I approached. "Aren't you the one forever telling me not to tweak a mage's tail?" I whispered to my partner.

He grinned at me. "How could I know he's sensitive, Cooper?"

"If we're to Hunt together, you'd best find a way to get along with him," I replied.

"Oh, he's all right," Tunstall assured me. "We had a talk, and now I know he's not one of those poxy mages who will treat us like scummer. Not once did he threaten me with magicking, and I wasn't sweet to him."

"Have you done that with the other mages we've dealt with?" I asked, my arms going all over goose bumps. The thought that he'd risked his hide, or mine, testing some of the mages we've had to deal with was a chilling thing.

He patted me on the shoulder. "Some mages are easier to read than others," he murmured. "This one took a little more work." He walked over to where the men of the Own were preparing the horses so we could leave.

I joined Master Farmer by the water. There was no point in trying to find shelter. I'd be soaked by the time we reached the road. "Can you at least conjure hats, Master Farmer?" I asked. "I have a good one, but it's at home."

He smiled at me. "I can weave hats, with my own two hands. I can't conjure them." He ran his fingers through his hair. "Besides, don't you women like to wash your hair in the sweet summer rain?"

"I don't have time, usually," I said.

But he was gone again, vanished into a world of mage vexation. "They think, because you can do some big things, you can do all manner of big things," he grumbled. "I killed the molten remains before too much got into the river, didn't I?" He glanced at me. "You were asleep."

I took a deep breath, relieved beyond saying. I had not liked that stuff. "You're sure?" I asked.

"Not a trace of it left," Master Farmer said. "And I cleaned what you and Tunstall took from it, so we'll have evidence to look at when we get back."

Another burst of thunder struck so near I felt my teeth rattle. "Was it *supposed* to rain tonight?" I asked when it died away.

"Not for the rest of the week," Master Farmer replied. "A lot of weather-seers will have some fast talking in the morning. No, I'd say whoever's working on this plot brought the storm down on us. Look."

He raised his left hand palm up to the sky. Almost instantly I saw lines like bluish-purple fire ripple across the clouds like dozens of thread-width lightning branches. "That's magic in the clouds, stirring up the rain," Master Farmer told me. "Whoever did it must have pulled the storm down from the north. That's why it's getting so cold. How much rain must fall before your pup loses the scent?"

"It varies," I told him. "Part of it's the strength of the scent to start, and then how much rain there is. What worries me is that Achoo's been following a scent in the air. These Rats are carrying the lad. If he's not touching anything, it makes it harder to track him. We need him to be on the ground." The first spits of rain struck my face. "Oh, pox," I said, and sighed.

The clouds opened up and soaked us all three. I whistled

for Achoo to come as we raced for the horses and the shelter of the trees. After we collected our mounts, we found Lord Gershom. Pounce sat on his saddle before him.

Finally, my cat greeted us. He glared up at the shelter of trees they had found. Rain was starting to drip through the leaves. A few drops fell onto Pounce's face. *I only waited to tell you that I will meet you at the palace,* he said, his mind voice grouchy. *Just because Achoo likes to be wet does not mean I have to endure this. You are on your own.*

He vanished. Lord Gershom looked at the spot where Pounce had been. "If I weren't tired to the bone, that would have startled me," he commented. "Anything new, Farmer?"

"We're at a standstill," Master Farmer grumbled as Tunstall rode over to join us.

"We are not," I said. "We know there are mages at work who are powerful enough to call up a rainstorm, sink two ships whilst holding those who are in them down, and kill the Chancellor of Mages, all in a bit over one day. Their Majesties' mages ought to be able to guess who is most likely to combine for work like this. And those two have to give us something, or they should be clever enough to know that if they don't, my lord might be inclined to suspect them."

Master Farmer watched me, his eyebrows raised. "Very true."

Tunstall raised his voice to be heard over the rain. "What foreigners could have gotten so close to the Mage Chancellor, or gotten their paws on Their Majesties' schedule? It's our own folk, Tortallans, who know the court, *and* who know our tides and beaches on this coastline, *and* can make their way through the forest after dark."

"Moreover, there's all manner of upset among the nobles and mages, as I understand it," I said as Lord Gershom made the sign for our group to ride out. This time the men of the King's Own went first, to make sure the road was safe. Keeping a distance behind them, I went on talking to my lord and Master Farmer. "The bigger the gang, the more tongues to tattle," I said. "I think these Rats are home bred, murrain take them and their ratlings."

The rain came down harder as we left the shelter of the trees. "Well thought out, both of you," Lord Gershom shouted as we reached the road. The rain immediately doused our torches. Master Farmer instantly cast a bright globe of light that revealed everything for a hundred yards before and after us. "What do you say, Farmer?" my lord asked.

"She makes a good case," Master Farmer called. "You're going to need more Hunters."

After that we fell silent, in part because the rain made it curst hard to talk, and in part because we didn't want our guards to hear. Instead we kept our heads down and prayed each time the sky turned white with lightning. I soon noticed Achoo was miserable, so I whistled her up into the saddle before me. The soldiers cheered her leap and the horse was steady as Achoo landed in my lap. The hound poked her head over my shoulder so she could thank the men with a short bark. Then she let me cuddle her close, for her warmth and mine.

Tired as I was, I still had it in me to feel sorry for the men my lord left to guard the gaping hole the kidnappers had blown in the wall. True, someone had to keep folk from entering the palace grounds that way, but it was a scummer detail. The rain showed no sign of letting up as we reached the palace, gave our horses over to the men who would stable them, and went inside.

Master Farmer went straight to the room prepared for

him, saying he had to examine the cloth-wrapped metal remains we had brought in Tunstall's basket. Tunstall insisted
that we tell Their Majesties the prince was yet alive. I wanted
naught to do with it, soaked as I was. Achoo had to be dried
off and fed. I wanted to let my lord speak to Their Majesties, as
he offered to do, but the look in Tunstall's eyes was such that
I agreed. Unhappily. I felt bad about our state. Our clothes
were drenched, even our boots, belts, and packs. At least Their
Majesties would know we had not lazed about.

Achoo looked far worse than me. With every curl flat
against her skin, she looked like she'd lost a third of her
weight. One of Her Majesty's ladies offered to take her to the
room that was set up for me and see to it she was dried and
fed. I ordered Achoo to go with the mot. She had no reason to
curry favor with royalty, or to help a friend do it. My hound refused at first. In the end I had to quickly lead her to the room.
Pounce was already inside, looking dry and smug.

"Tell Achoo to let this lady help her," I told Pounce. "No
arguments." As the lady gawped at me I raced back to join
Lord Gershom and Tunstall outside Their Majesties' chambers. The moment I reached my companions, a manservant
opened the door to the royal sitting room.

Their Majesties were dressed for sleep, I think, in jewel-
colored robes over silk and lace, but they did not have the look
of people who'd been roused from their beds. They waited in
wide-bottomed chairs on either side of a table where a flagon
and wine cups sat.

Lord Gershom, Tunstall, and I bowed. Their Majesties
nodded in welcome and the king said something gracious. I
barely remember what it was. My lord replied while I studied
the mud splotches on my boots and the beautiful tiles on
the floor.

My lord poked me in the arm. "Cooper." To Their Majesties he said, "They are exhausted. They found everything on foot."

I looked at my lord. "Forgive me." My voice sounded blurry to my ears. "What was the question?"

The king looked the three of us over. "Gershom said you have good news?"

I glared at Tunstall. *He* could tell them!

"Cooper's scent hound tells us His Highness is alive, Your Majesties," Tunstall explained, bowing. "While Master Farmer found the ships and looked at what we'd found on the shore, we thought we'd search the palace grounds. We expected to find more clues as to how the enemy got in, if they'd let others onto the grounds after they came by sea . . . We had all manner of questions to answer. There is a small beach several miles up the coast. That was where Cooper's hound got His Highness's scent again."

The queen lunged forward and grabbed my arm. "Are you certain?" she begged, gripping me hard with both hands. "How can you know?"

I took a step closer so she wouldn't fall from her chair. It was hard to think of her as royalty, the folk who often stepped on our purses and our lives, when she acted like so many young mothers I'd known when they feared for a child. She needed to weep on her mother's shoulder, or a friend's. Her mother was in Barzun, I remembered. Did Her Majesty have any true friends she could trust for a proper cry? I hesitated, then patted her shoulder, half expecting the king to order me to take my hands off his queen. He said naught, to my surprise. Mayhap he felt like ordinary commoner fathers whose children were missing? Or did he feel worse, because his child would be safe if his father had not made powerful enemies?

"Your Majesty, I found His Highness's dirty laundry," I explained, loud enough so the king might hear, too. "I kept some for myself to give Achoo his scent. Once she had it, she tracked where it led. She won't follow another scent by mistake. We followed it to the River Ware. We think they caught a boat there, because that's when we lost it."

She stared at me, her hold so tight I'd have bruises on my arm later. "What if they killed him there?" she whispered.

I answered her as if she were one of my younger sisters, or my friend Tansy, who tends a bit to the nervous side. "Majesty, they had plenty of chances to kill him. Here. On the beach. In the ships they sank. When they escaped those ships and rowed up the coast. When they ditched that boat and climbed up the cliffs to join whoever waited there with horses. They didn't keep him alive through all that just to kill him at the Ware." I patted her hands. "You do him no good to fret like this. The gods are watching over you, and they're watching over him. My lord Gershom will tell you, it's not killing they mean for him by now."

The queen didn't let go of my arm, though she eased up on her grip. She sat back, drawing me with her. I signaled Tunstall with my eyes, begging him to do something, but he stood there with one hand over his mouth so he'd look like he was thinking deep thoughts, not smirking like the wicked mumper he is.

"Is this true, my lord?" the queen asked Lord Gershom, changing her grip so she held my hand with both of hers. "Is this what you believe?"

My lord sighed and ran his hand back through his soaked steel-gray hair. "I do, Your Majesty. Though I would prefer not to raise the possibility that there is a future game unrevealed as yet."

"We pray that no one is listening, but surely the word will spread soon enough," the king replied quietly. "Face it, Gershom, our court will be a shambles then."

"Which is why I wish to work it so that very little gets out," replied my lord. "Allow these scoundrels to show what game they wish to play. We have plans to make, if you will trust me."

"I am trusting you with everything," the king replied. "I can rely on no one else."

I looked at my lord, suddenly frightened. It sounded like an honor to have a king place all his confidence in him, but kings, especially this one, are fickle. I remembered Lady Sabine, exiled to the hill country for offending King Roger. Others who had offended him had not escaped with their lives. What if one of my lord's enemies convinced His Majesty that Lord Gershom was in on the kidnapping, or that he could not find Prince Gareth?

"Tunstall, Cooper, I have your promise for your silence," my lord said. It wasn't a question. We nodded. He could have just told the mages to magic us into silence.

Lord Gershom was also dismissing us. I hesitated, then risked my life and gave Her Majesty a hug, as if she were one of my friends or sisters. Only then did she let go of my hand. Her arms went around me. "I'll begin work on more heirs," she whispered in my ear. I jumped a little, not expecting such an important confidence from someone so far above me in station. "I've been selfish, wanting more time with Gareth alone. But I know you'll find my baby. You'll bring him back to me." She released me at last.

Tunstall bowed to Lord Gershom and to Their Majesties. The king nodded to us, his face a blank mask.

I managed to bow and back out of the room along with Tunstall and Pounce. One of the queen's ladies waited for us there. "We've made up rooms, and we found nightclothes for you both. If you will place your uniforms outside your doors, we'll have them dried by the morning."

"How do you manage?" Tunstall asked as we accompanied her downstairs. "Have you brought servants in from Blue Harbor?"

The mot looked up at him, eyes wide. "Oh, no, Guardsman. Lord Gershom forbade it. No one is to leave the palace grounds without his express permission. Those of us ladies and gentlemen of Their Majesties' households, those that were in their company last night—" Her lips quivered for a moment and her bright brown eyes filled with tears. She forced a smile to her face and went on, "We must do everything. It's been a good distraction, finding where the servants keep whatever is necessary! I'm afraid the food is not at all up to palace standard, none of us being able to cook—"

Tunstall rested a hand on her arm, his face sober and sympathetic. He has rendered the hardest mots of the Lower City into puddles of tears and information with that look, and his deep voice speaking kind words. "You lost friends last night. You have our sorrow, Cooper's and mine. Would you care to tell me what happened?"

Which was how I ended in my chamber with Pounce and Achoo, alone, while the lady sat in Tunstall's room, telling him her story. He'd waved me off. I was glad of the permission. I was tired, and I needed time alone. I picked up bowls of food for my hound and cat and fed them immediately. Next I opened up my pack and laid out its contents, including the glowing stone, on the worktable. Then I turned the empty pack inside out and set it beside one of the two braziers that warmed the room.

The room itself must have belonged to an upper servant. The bed was big enough for two, which left a bit of room for me beside the hound and cat, who were there already. The clothes in the press were all far too large for me, but I helped myself to a clean loincloth and a nightdress. I knew well the owner would not be returning or they would not have put me here. I murmured a prayer as I put on the dry clothes.

From the looks of the dishes on the floor, both of my four-legged friends were now full. When I rested my hand on Achoo's freshly combed fur, she blinked at me and gave me her shy "bruff" of greeting. She was good and dry.

Fruit, cheese, bread, and a pitcher of wine waited for me on a bedside table. I decided the wine was light enough that a cup wouldn't addle me too badly, if I had some of the bread and cheese first. I combed out my soaking hair between bites, then braided it once more. That was all the supper I managed before I blew out the lamp and crawled under the blanket.·

Achoo whined at me and shoved her nose under my arm. I knew this conversation, which we often had. Rest is very good, she was telling me, but we didn't find the boy.

"We'll find the boy," I promised. I tucked myself against the hound and the cat and slept.

I have no notion if it was before or after twelve of the clock on Thursday, June 7, being that the palace clocks had been destroyed by the raiders. I choose to finish the events of this day as part of the events of June 7, to save myself fuss. It is not as if anyone but me will ever be able to read this journal, which is why I write it in a cipher that is part Dog cipher and more my own creation. I will need this book, to keep my head clear and my thoughts straight. I see dark times coming. In this book I will write the truth, when I can, not the canker-licking half-truths I will have to submit later, for the public record.

Gods all aid me and my Hunting team, I beg.

Sunday, June 10, 249

Ladyshearth Lodgings
Coates Lane
Port Caynn
being an account of the events of Friday, June 8,
at the Summer Palace
beginning at dawn on that day

Achoo woke me, having natural errands to run. I was at a loss at first. My window looked out over rose vines, which would have hurt my poor hound dreadfully. It also looked out into pouring rain. I spat into it and closed the shutter. Seemingly these vile mages wished to ensure that we never got Prince Gareth's trail again.

Happily my uniform, clean and dry, was folded and stacked before my door. It took me but a moment to put it on and to find a pair of the room's last resident's sturdy shoes. They did not fit. I had to put on my own boots, which were nearly as wet as when I'd taken them off.

Pounce remained abed. Achoo led me through the smoky-smelling halls, trusting her nose to guide her outside. We ended in the kitchens. There I came to a halt while Achoo raced through an open outer door into the rain. Tunstall stood before the hearth, a pan in one hand and a spoon in the other. He spoke to an audience of ladies, gentlemen, and soldiers of the King's Own who gathered around the great worktables. Two of the ladies were placing utensils on trays. A third was trimming flowers to fit prettily in a pair of thin vases. Master Farmer was in the kitchen as well, gutting and cleaning some fine, fat trout with the speed of a practiced cook.

"Now, see, my mother never held with Bazhir seasonings,"

Tunstall was saying. The mot with the curling red hair who had gone off with him the night before assisted him, passing him what he needed. "But my lady has a taste for dishes with cumin, and she got me to like it, too."

"You're in service to a lady, Tunstall?" asked one of the men in the King's Own. "How can you manage that and yet be a Dog?"

Tunstall looked down at his chickpeas and took a breath. This was always a difficult moment when we dealt with the nobility. "I mean my lady Sabine of Cahill, the knight. We are good friends."

From the deep silence, I knew they all realized how close that friendship was. I sucked up my courage, because speaking before these folk was not to my taste, and said, "*Cooking? You've got a mage and a Dog cooking?*"

Tunstall and Master Farmer both looked at me like my brothers caught stealing sweets.

"What's most magecraft, if not cooking?" Master Farmer asked. "As for this, if you want a meal that's not stale or raw, then we cook, or you do, Cooper. Our poor friends here don't know how."

It seemed our circumstances, living in the half-destroyed palace, lacking servants, with few high officials keeping an eye on everyone, led to a relaxation of the rules. Certainly I felt comfortable enough to say, "All these folk and none of you know anything? Not so much as how to boil an egg?"

One lady held up a bandaged hand. "I got this cutting the bread."

"Goddess save us all," I said. What a menagerie had assembled in that kitchen, between the nobles and we Hunters. "Has anyone collected eggs today?"

My sole answer came from a number of pairs of blinking

eyes. I didn't dare ask about milk. Someone must have done the milking, or we'd have heard the cows, but that someone was not in the kitchen.

I went over to Master Farmer. "As soon as you can, please tell my lord Gershom that servants must be brought in," I whispered. "We can't look after an entire palace." I saw a stack of baskets and pointed to three ladies. "You will come collect eggs, for Their Majesties," I told them. I found pails and chose two mots and two coves who had something intelligent and humorous about their faces. "You may learn to milk cows, also for the sake of the realm."

I walked out of the kitchen into the rain, not entirely sure they would follow. They did. They knew where the farm buildings were, nicely hidden behind hedges and trees. The nobles used the barns for canoodling, from what I heard.

I showed the ladies how to deal with the hens, with results of a mixed kind, including a number of scratches and smashed eggs. Our luck was better in the cowsheds. Some hostlers who had gone with the royal party to Blue Harbor the night of the attack had milked cows as servant lads. They were already seeing to that work. They were happy to let the gentlemen carry the buckets to the kitchen.

I did not return with them. Sooner or later Tunstall would remember that I knew how to make pasties. He would set me to baking for everyone. We all would be far better off if the nobles went crying to Lord Gershom for servants he could trust. As long as Master Farmer, Tunstall, and I were the only Dogs present, we should be about Dog work. Right now, with the curst rain washing away His Highness's scent, it seemed to me the closest Dog work lay in the ships that had been raised from the ocean floor last night.

Achoo found me in the garden. Together we walked

down through the gardens along paths that had turned to small streams. At least the area was now cleared of the dead. The gardens were being washed clean as the crushed flowers and bushes recovered from their injuries. No one was silly enough to be out in the wet like me. Even the guards at the gate that overlooked the sea cliffs kept to their shelter. They stuck their heads out, ready to object to my departure, but saw my uniform and opened half of the gate for me. Achoo raced through. I followed at a more clumping pace, thanks to my shoes.

Using my spelled mirror, I saw that even the shreds of the path spells were gone this morning. I hoped they got some more mages and soldiers here soon, as well as servants. I didn't like having this beach and these paths open. Summer is prime raiding season for the fearsome ships from Scanra and the Copper Isles. Even the Yamanis sometimes reach this far south in their attacks.

When I prepared to descend in Achoo's wake, I saw that any raiders might think twice before they tried to come up. The heavy rains had turned the path into a rushing stream.

"Achoo!" I called. "Achoo, where have you gone?" She had vanished.

I heard a yelp from below. I reached out to grab a rock at the side of the path, hoping to climb it to see where my empty-headed hound had gone. My boots slid on the mud under the water, pulling me into the current. Now I knew what had happened to Achoo. The tumbling water thrust me down the steep hill, ramming me into stones and gravel. I broke all of my nails as I tried to grab for a hold on the rocks. I had nothing cushioning my back, and only a thin summer-weight tunic and breeches between me and a ten-squad of bruises.

The stream dumped me at the foot of the cliff and sank

into the sand as I cursed the cod-kickers who had called the rain. Achoo ran to me, whining as she licked my hands and arms. After the water, her tongue was startling in its warmth.

"I'll live, girl," I told her as I struggled to my feet. My poor friend was covered in mud. I ran my hands over her body and limbs to be sure she had taken no hurt. Once I was certain that her bones were unbroken, I looked around us. "I daresay neither of us will be happy about it for a day or two, but we'll both of us live."

Achoo gave me her encouraging "roof," the sound that usually meant "We'll do fine."

The tide had come in. The pair of ships that had been raised by Master Ironwood and Mistress Orielle from the bottom were now moored fast to the very stones of the cliffs by heavy ropes. They were half afloat, tugging at their ties to the land, but moving very little. Rope ladders hung from the bow of each vessel. Someone had gone aboard after the mages brought the ships up.

I wiped my muddy face on my muddy arm. Achoo whined as the sea winds blew rain, spray, and the darker scent of bad things done into our faces.

"*Tunggu,* Achoo," I told her. "There's no way you can get aboard one of these." Even my girl couldn't climb a rope ladder.

Achoo whined louder and yipped, her way of arguing. She even tucked her tail between her legs, which always made me feel like a brute.

"It's for your own good, so stop that," I said gently. I know how it feels to be left behind when I want to Hunt. "If you think of a way to climb up, you're welcome. Go find some-place out of the rain."

I looked up around the rocks at the foot of the cliff until I found a stone that ought to be out of the water if the tide came all the way up to the rocks. There I left my boots and stockings. Achoo slunk up and lay down beside the stone, the very picture of misery and abandonment.

I walked down to the closest ship, the *Lash,* and gripped the rope ladder that hung from her prow. Swiftly I clambered up. At the deck I discovered that each vessel had a flat canvas top from rail to rail, with the naked masts poking through the cloth. I was suspicious right off. Checking the canvas with the mirror in my pocket, I saw that it glowed with the same magic as the rest of the ship, part of the trap that had kept the dead from floating to shore. I wondered if we ever would have found the vessels had it not been for Master Farmer. Somehow Ironwood and Orielle did not seem like the type to investigate the cove.

I put my mirror in my pocket and dropped through the opening at the prow onto the deck. My feet went clean out from under me, sending me on a skid across the slanting deck until I struck a barricade. It gave in a way that made me scramble back from it. In the dim light that came through the holes around the edges and masts, where the canvas met wood, I squinted at what lay before me. I'd hit the bodies of two rowers bowed over their oar. Shaking, I made the Sign against evil on my chest. Only when I'd caught my breath did I inch closer for a better look. There was sommat strange about the way they sat, bent over, arms stretched out, thrusting on their oars, as if they'd been frozen in the middle of their work.

I moved closer still. Mithros witness it, the oar had grown *up and over their hands,* holding them there.

For a moment I waited, trembling, trying to work up my courage for what must be done. I scolded myself for a coward, and numbered all the corpses I'd handled. Wasn't it me that washed Holborn and laid him out for his burial, without a tear? I'd dug bodies out of scummer and sewer water with little more than a kerchief over my mouth for the smell, so there was no good reason for me to falter.

I slid over until my legs dangled in the gap in the wood where the oarsmen sat. Then, carefully, begging the dead mumper's pardon like he had the ears or the soul to hear me, I reached down to take anything that might be in his pockets.

Sparks leaped up to shock me. I yelped and flinched, brushing the dead oarsman's arm. Bigger sparks jumped to me, stinging harder.

"Pox and murrain, protection spells!" I snapped. I tried to wriggle away on the ship's deck. I touched the cove accidentally with my foot and got spark-bit one more time. "Ow! Plague take all mages who won't lay a protection spell that doesn't hurt!" At last I thought to use my head. I took my mirror out again and looked about me for magic. Spells of a deep purple color, almost black, coated the ship's wood and the captive dead. More spells, dull bronze in color, were fixed to the canvas overhead.

"Spells to keep any from picking the pockets of the dead, and spells to keep the ship and the dead from rotting, I'll wager," I said to myself. "And never a thought taken for a poor Dog who needs to collect evidence."

Vexed, I sat back and thought. I needed to explore the rest of the ship. I hadn't brought a lamp, not knowing the sails covered the deck. I chose to deal with that first, returning to the prow, where I had boarded. There I drew my long knife. Someone had started a cut in the canvas already—last night, mayhap, when folk were looking to see how the ships went down. It even could have been Master Ironwood or Mistress Orielle who had sealed them this way.

Starting at the cut, I dragged my razor-sharp knife through the canvas, down the spine of the ship, admitting what light there was along with the rain. I had to step around a cove who was collapsed facedown on the walkway that ran between the rowers' benches. From the whip that still lay in his fist, I could tell he was the overseer. It was the deck that held him. It had grown around his feet, and then his hands. I shuddered when I saw it had also grown up around his face. I wasn't about to try to examine the contents of *his* pockets. Some other poor mumper could have that chore.

At last I reached the ship's stern. The wheel gripped the pilot's wrists in its wood. The rail had wrapped a cove and a mot in its wooden embrace. They leaned forward, pressed down by the sail. When I cut the heavy cloth entirely in half and flung it off of them, they remained bent over, their bodies stuck in that position. From long nights with the healers who worked with the dead to tell Tunstall and me what they'd died of, I knew all of these corpses would remain in their final positions for at least one more day, mayhap two. The priests called it Death's rigor. I thought it was a curst sad way to be stuck after dying, and prayed that when my end came, I would get caught flat, in my bed.

I poked them, and the pilot, with my baton, with no results. Feeling bolder, I reached out to search the woman's pockets, if she had them. The moment I touched her skirts, the protection spells sparked out at me, leaving a blister on one of my fingers. I cursed myself blue, for all the good that it did.

Back down the walkway I went, throwing the leaves of sail to either side to lay the deck partially bare. I knew rain would not wash the powerful spells away and I wanted to see the deck more clearly.

At the stern rail I leaned over to see if Achoo had come

to sit at the foot of the ladder and stare woefully at me. Instead I looked straight down into Tunstall's face as he climbed the ladder, his glowing rock shining through his tunic.

"Cooper, you hurt my feelings, running off," Tunstall called as he swung onto the deck. "Just for that, no chickpeas with eggs and cheese for *your* breakfast." He slipped to fall on his back.

"It's slippery," I told him, trying not to smile. I have been in some bad places where I have thought that Mattes Tunstall looked like the handsome young god in the stories. This was not quite that bad. Still, I could have kissed him. The place had me well spooked.

Tunstall grunted and sat up. "Now that you warn me, it *is* slippery." He set about pulling off his boots and stockings. He tucked his stockings inside his boots and threaded the boot tops through his belt. "What have you found so far?" Tunstall asked, rubbing his knees. Of course they pained him on a day like this.

"Protection spells. Nasty ones that bite." I showed him the red spots on my hand. "As for the crew, the ship grew up around them on deck, and the sails came down, sealing them underneath," I said, helping him to his feet. "They were trapped."

He took his glowing rock from his tunic. I went around to the rail and found a point where the sail had been threaded through an oar hole. Tunstall helped me to pull the cut canvas back so we could see how it was fastened. The cloth came out in a neat strip from the mainsail, went through the oar hole, and wove itself back into the sail, without a seam showing. It made me think of how the wood of the oar, the wheel, and the rail had all come out and around their victims, then returned to the main piece, as if it was their nature to grow around human flesh.

"*Beghan,*" Tunstall whispered. It was a word in his native Hurdik that meant something like "so bad I want nothing to do with it."

"We don't get a choice, remember?" I asked. "We have to follow this trail to its end."

"I'm hoping the prince's trail doesn't stink so bad," Tunstall muttered as he looked at the oarsmen closest to us. With the sail pulled back he could see the neat bands of wood that locked their hands to the oar. "My skin is creeping. Let's see what's below, Cooper. They're not paying us by the hour." He walked carefully toward the big hatch at the stern of the ship.

"So far we've not been paid at all," I reminded him, following. "And I can't say much for the food, either."

"You *could* have had my chickpea dish." Tunstall knelt by the hatch cover and lifted it away to reveal the hold. By the light of his stone lamp we could see what lay below. There were stairs, or a sloping ladder with wide steps, all stained with old blood. Water gleamed at the bottom.

Tunstall turned and began to descend, the lamp lighting his way. Once he was down, I sucked up my courage and followed him.

Tunstall made room for me at the foot of the ladder and held the glowing rock up to reveal the contents of the ship's hold. A large gap in the keel lay half in, half out of the sea-water that rocked the ship gently. This vessel was not fitted for long travel, but I already knew that, because it was a small galley. There were a few crates, barrels, and sacks placed in the stern and in the shadows of the bow, just touched by the light. Six people lay in bunks fixed to the hull, three on each side.

All of them were chained to their bunks. I could see those in the middle and bottom bunks. A hand dangled from one top bunk. The occupant of the opposite one had half crawled out of hers before she had drowned. Seawater had soaked everything down there, clean up to the underside of the top deck.

There was no telling how many others had been aboard. They could have been swept out to sea through the gap in the center of the keel. The hole itself was near twenty feet long and twelve feet wide. I wondered how long the ship had stayed afloat with so much of its keel missing.

I took out my spelled mirror and used it to look around the hull. There was magic laid over everything. "I'll try to check for anything they might carry, or what's in the bags, if you insist," I said to Tunstall. "But it's spelled. You'll have to put up with me yelping and whimpering if you do."

"Hmpf." Like most of the senior Dogs, Tunstall had learned a lot about magic over the years. "Let me try." He left the ladder and waded around me, bending down to peer at the body in the middle bunk on my left. He held the stone lamp up so we could both see everything clear.

"A lass, perhaps twelve or thirteen, blond, just blooming," he said, and reached into the boxlike bed, for her arm, I suspected. "Ach!" he cried as sparks bounced off his arm and chest.

"Hurts, doesn't it?" I asked him. I aimed the mirror at the broken wood in the keel, but it showed me only the thin purple sheet of the protection spell.

"Both ships are alike, Master Farmer told me this morning, except for this one being set up to carry slaves," said Tunstall. "They had a big enough mage, or mages, to do that thing with the sails and the wood, to trap the crew on deck, then sink the ships, all at once. But we knew that."

I sighed. "It's more complicated work than slavers usually pay for." I shifted Tunstall's arm so the flameless lamp lit the chain that secured the lass to her bunk. Then I moved his arm up and down so we could see the chains that ran into the top and bottom bunks as well.

"I'll take that back now, if it's all the same to you," my partner told me as he tugged out of my grip. "Where's your stone lamp?"

"Back in my room. I hadn't planned to go exploring today," I replied. "This is a slave ship, Tunstall."

"Seriously?" he asked me, his eyes wandering over the hold. "I thought it was one of the Carthaki emperor's pleasure boats."

I elbowed him. "Did Master Farmer know if the other one is a slave ship?"

He shook his head. "Looked like a plain raiding vessel, he told me. He just knows what he learned from Mistress Orielle." He looked at my face and sighed, tucking the stone in his tunic. "Let's go have a look, then, or you'll pester me to death."

"I didn't say a word!" I cried as I followed him up the ladder.

"You don't have to, Cooper. I know that look on your face. I ought to, by now."

We stepped onto the deck. Of course, since I'd cut the canvas all the way down, the rain fell onto us without hindrance. Tunstall held his hand over his eyes. "It's raining harder, isn't it?"

From his mouth to the gods' ears, the rainfall poured, sounding like drumrolls where it hit the canvas. We scrambled for the rope ladder, slipping and sliding all the way. Tunstall didn't even bother to put his boots back on. Through it all the stone lamp kept glowing. Curious, I looked north along the beach as we descended the ladder. It was hard to tell, the rain streaming down as it was, but I will swear on my mother's grave I could see the great boulder shining even through that.

Achoo leaped at me as soon as I touched my feet to the sand, yipping with glee. Eagerly she washed my face, even though the rain was doing that for her. At least in this downpour the fresh mud had been washed from her fur.

"I'm sorry, I'm sorry," I told her, rubbing her ears. "You wouldn't have liked it up there, I swear it." She was shivering dreadfully as I hugged her. Gently I moved her away so she would stand on her own four feet. "We need shelter," I said to Tunstall. "She's freezing."

"Poor girl," Tunstall said. He bent and lifted my poor Achoo into his arms. "What wicked thing did your ancestors do, that you should get a sarden detail like this, eh?" He looked at me. "Why in the storm gods' names didn't you leave her in your room?"

I glared at him. "She slid down the cliff first. Had I known, I would have stopped her. Speaking of which, how did *you* get here?"

He raised his eyebrows. "I climbed down the rocks. I wasn't going to risk breaking my neck. There's a bit of a cave next to the path. Let's put her there before she drowns."

He was right. I cursed myself for not thinking of it before, but then, I hadn't turned that way once the stream, now a waterfall, had dumped me on the beach. We took Achoo to Tunstall's cave, so she at least would be out of that poxy wet. Before we stepped inside, I used my mirror to look at the sky. The heavy gray clouds were woven through with threads of magic that were the same color as those in the storm last night. I promised myself that if I ever encountered the mage who sent this downpour on us all, I'd go sea fishing with him, or her, as shark bait.

I retrieved my shoes and stockings from their rock and placed them on a ledge in the cave. Tunstall left his boots there as well, while I gave Achoo very strict orders to remain. She was so cold that I believed she would stay put this time.

Back into the mess we went, almost running into the *Lash* before we realized we'd reached the water's edge. We made our way south, squinting, until we found the second ship, the *Rover*. Up the ladder we went. When we stepped into the small open area in the prow, clear of the interlocked sails that covered the deck, I drew my knife to cut a path for us.

Tunstall stopped me. "I'd rather crawl under there than be drenched anymore."

I sheathed my blade, thinking it would take a while to oil it and dry out the sheath when we were done. "You first," I invited him.

He pulled his stone lamp from his pocket. "Follow me, then."

"Tunstall? How long do you think those things will shine?" I asked as we ducked under the canvas. "Kora's lights don't last more than an hour—two, if she remembers to refresh the spell."

"I don't know," Tunstall said, kneeling beside the first pair of rowers. "Ask Master Farmer. They're his stones."

I grimaced at the bad joke. "Why can't you? I've talked with enough people of late."

Tunstall shook his head. "One day you won't have me to take up any extra chatter for you. Then what? You'll have to do it all yourself." He raised the lamp so I could see that these rowers, too, were gripped to the oar by the wood. "Master Farmer doesn't seem that bad."

"He was decent about the cooking," I agreed. "And he didn't whine in all the rain last night. I do wish I knew more about him—my lord never said anything of him to me."

"Folk usually only talk about great mages," Tunstall replied. "And how often do you get to sit down and talk the work with my lord these days?"

"True enough," I said. My life was far busier since Achoo had come to me, and it wasn't fit for me to be seen often with Lord Gershom. Folk might think I was his Birdie, reporting to him on our kennel's goings-on. When I did visit, he and I usually talked about crime in Corus.

Tunstall turned and went on to the stern of the ship, down the middle. I followed him close enough to hear him say, over the pounding of rain on canvas, "If we stay on this Hunt together, let's pray he knows enough to keep us alive!"

When he reached the hatch to the hold, he pulled it off and descended the ladder one-handed, the lamp held out so it would light the area below him. I waited for him to halt before I went down, listening as I strained my eyes to see what lay there.

The *Rover* was no slave ship. There was no setup for narrow bunks with chains attached to the foot. Like the *Lash*, the *Rover* sported a great hole punched through the center of the keel. My mirror revealed the magic that had made that hole, the same mix of colors that painted the upper deck to trap the crew. There were protective spells of a deep crimson shade different from that destructive power. Amulets, spells cut into the wood around us, and charms twinkled white in the mirror. I wondered how long they would last now, with no one to renew them.

From the ladder we could see a crate or two remaining in the prow and the stern, and a wine jar afloat in the water that had come in through the hole. Some cutlasses, daggers, and small shields still hung from nails on the keel. Blankets floated on the water. The rest of the hold was empty as near as we could tell.

We had to search what was there, or we had to try. Tunstall stung his hands on the magic on the cargo. I picked up another blister trying to see what was in the pockets of those who stood on deck around the wheel. That was enough. We were happy to get off that ship.

We found the foot of the cliffs, where I retrieved my footgear, and used them to guide us to the cave where we had left Achoo. We had to dodge a hundred tiny waterfalls that poured off the heights, all produced by the steady, hammering rain. I threw another curse toward the unseen mage, or mages. I wanted to hang them upside down on these same cliffs in their own storm, a kind of natural version of the torture called the Drink. See how they liked it.

Achoo greeted us with dancing and a wagging tail when we found her. We were in no hurry to leave the shelter of the cave once we reached it. Sitting on a rock, I watched my partner and rubbed Achoo's wet fur, wondering what was going through Tunstall's mind. I'd respected him from before my Puppy year—he was a legend in the Lower City, him and our former partner, Goodwin. Being his only partner over the last two years, I had learned there was plenty that went on in his fuzzy nob that most folk didn't expect. He played the part of lolloping barbarian so well that it never occurred to many that he'd have died young if he was who he seemed to be.

"These Rats have deep pockets, Beka," Tunstall said at last. "Deeper than my old mother's loincloth." He always swore his mother had birthed twelve children and had a bottom as big as a bridge. "Deep enough to throw away two ships, their crews, and nearabout thirty slaves—if they did drown all of the slaves. I think they did. The group we followed to the river was a small one."

I nodded. That all matched what I was thinking. I was proud of myself for following Tunstall so far.

"Magic that big is never cheap. Whoever Hunts these Rats will need plenty of mages of their own, and who's to say they can be trusted?" Tunstall rubbed the top of his skull. "Curse it, I hate handling mages, you know I do. But this Hunt is lousy with them already." Tunstall looked at the ceiling of the cave and blew out a huge breath. "I'd like Goodwin on this, so I would. No insult to you. You're the best new Dog I've ever worked with."

I looked at the sandy floor, hoping he couldn't see the color in my cheeks. I knew he liked me. We're still partners, after all! But this was serious praise, coming from an old-timer like him!

"Still, we could use Goodwin," he said. "Too bad she's gotten to like going home with her skin in one piece." He was very quiet for a long moment. At last he got to his feet. "It's not getting drier out there."

I nodded and stood. "We've faced rough Hunts before," I reminded him. "It's the royalty that itches me. I don't want to fail Her Majesty."

"We won't, then," Tunstall said. "We've got Achoo, right, girl? And Achoo hasn't lost a lass or lad yet."

She knew he was complimenting her. She bruffed and wagged her tail, ramming Tunstall in the side with her head.

He'd cheered me up, too, because he was right. Achoo had found every little one we'd been set to find. Surely a prince was just a little lad with better clothes than most.

"Goddess, thank you for our hound," I said as I threaded

my boots and stockings through my belt. Squinting, I plunged into the rain. Tunstall and Achoo ran out past me.

The flooded trail that had swept me down before was even deeper and faster after all of the morning's extra rain. Achoo couldn't even keep her footing. We backed off and checked the other paths, but they were no better. Tunstall slung Achoo over his shoulders and went first, barefooted still, gripping the slabs of rock on the right side of the path with hands and feet to make the climb. I clambered up a foot on the left side and did the same, though not so ably. I slipped and slid, bruising and scraping my poor bare feet.

And what does my cracked partner do, partway up that small river channeled by the rock walls? He halted, turned his head back, and shouted over the roar of rain and storm-stream, "Why did the looby go into that back room alone anyway?"

I stared at him. I couldn't believe it. Then I could, because it was Tunstall. When he had a question, he'd ask it, and wait for the answer, no matter what. "What are you doing? Go!" I cried. "Before we drown!"

"Why did Holborn do it?" he demanded. He shifted himself so Achoo could sit better on his shoulders. She looked at me and whined.

"Goddess save me," I whispered. "I want a partner who doesn't need to be locked up and fed caudles!" I leaned my face against the rock for a moment, then looked at him again. "Holborn didn't think!" I shouted. "He was always looking for a chance to bag more Rats and claim to be the best Dog. He didn't think! His partner, Ahern? He said that's why he was glad Jane Street and Flash District paired up for that raid." My voice caught. I had to clear my throat. "Ahern said Holborn was always like that, charging on in, and he thought having me there would slow him down. But it didn't, and the slavers had guards waiting for somebody to do just what Holborn did." I wiped the water out of my face with my shoulder. It figured. Just when I cried a little, the stupid rain was easing.

It made me feel better to see that Tunstall was looking at the sky, not at me. "Letting up," he said. "Stopping maybe."

I heard a whipping sort of noise and cursed our positions. We were out in the open. The only way we could get to our weapons was by letting go of the rock. That meant dropping into the hard current of water in the path, which could well knock us off our feet and sweep us back down to the ocean.

Tunstall was braced with his feet as well as his arms. He was groping for his baton when we both saw what made the sound. A pair of climbing ropes dropped along the sides of the path. In another moment two coves of the King's Own swung down on them, bouncing off the stone like dancers. With great leaps they soared over Tunstall and me, then halted just behind us.

"My lord Gershom's calling all over for you two," one of them said. "Mistress Orielle looked in her glass and found you for us. You're lucky my cousin and I are climbers."

"We could wait. The rain's stopping." Tunstall wasn't the best of rope climbers. "The water will go down fast enough."

The other was grinning. "Of course, Guardsman. We'll go back and tell that to my lord Gershom, right off."

I reached over and seized the rope. "I'm going," I said. "I'll take Achoo."

Tunstall sighed. "No." He got the rope behind himself and my hound so that he gripped it in each hand, leaning against it with his bum. I'd positioned my rope in the same way around me. Tunstall had learned to climb rocks in the eastern hills, while I had learned it only last year, chasing murderers with Achoo in the Royal Forest. It was amazing how useful I found the skill among the warehouses along the river.

We were two-thirds of the way up the cliff when the rain, which had looked good to stop completely, began to pour again.

A handful of ladies-in-waiting watched for us from the kitchen doorway. As soon as they got a look at us they started to grab drying cloths. I looked around for Master Farmer. He stood by the largest hearth, stirring a pot of something that smelled very good.

He looked at us. "You're wet."

Tunstall scratched at his whiskers. "With those powers of observation, I'll wager the army and the City of the Gods were fighting over you," he said.

"Naw," Master Farmer replied with his three-cornered grin. "The army found out I don't know my left foot from my right. It's a problem. Would you like to be dry, then? I can do that much for you."

"Five days staked in the blazing sun won't dry us off, but you're welcome to try," said Tunstall.

Master Farmer looked at me. "Cooper? Have you objections? I can dry your hound off, too."

I ground my teeth. I hate it when magic's put on me, but we were summoned before Lord Gershom. It was bad enough that I wore a muddy uniform. It would be so much worse to have it wet into the bargain. I nodded, keeping my eyes on the floor. "Thank you, Master Farmer."

"Are you sure?" he asked. "You don't seem eager. I won't force you." It was funny, that he truly seemed to want to know.

I nodded at the floor again. "I dislike being soaked a little worse than I dislike being magicked," I explained. "But there's no sense in being foolish about it when Achoo's shivering and we have to attend upon Lord Gershom."

For a moment everything around my legs and Achoo turned dark blue. Then they took on their normal colors. Achoo's curls were even straight. My breeches hung without a wrinkle. So too did my tunic. Touching the boots and stockings I'd tucked into my belt, I found they were dry as well. I sat on a bench to put them on as I inspected Tunstall. He looked as if maids had pressed his uniform and shined his boots.

One of the gentlemen who attended the king ran into the chamber. He halted when he saw us. "My lord Gershom wants to know where—" He stopped. I would have wagered a week's pay that the words Lord Gershom had actually used were not those the gentleman said. "Where in the gods' names have the three Hunters gotten to, Scanra? He requested their appearance some time ago."

We looked at Master Farmer. He shrugged. "I wasn't going to see him without you. It didn't seem fitting."

We followed the messenger. Achoo remained in the kitchen, curled up by a warm hearth. Since I felt she'd had enough excitement for the morning, I let her stay. I looked around for Pounce, but he was nowhere in sight. I suspected he was still cozy in bed.

The messenger led us to an open door, but he did not follow us into the room beyond. He closed the door behind us. My lord sat at a desk, his long hair falling forward into his face as he scribbled on a parchment. He'd secured a study for his work, one that was lined with maps like his study at home. There were five chairs besides the one that he used. There were books and scrolls in shelves along the walls. Master Farmer wandered over to look at them.

My lord finished what he was writing and scattered sand

over it to dry the ink. "Where were you?" he demanded, glaring at us. "There's work to be done!"

Growing up in my lord's house, I was no match for that growl, which always meant some servant was in trouble. I wanted to run. Luckily, Master Farmer and Tunstall were made of sterner stuff. Master Farmer looked over his shoulder and said, "I was cooking breakfast with Tunstall's help. You need servants, Gershom. The nobles can't cook, they upset the hens, and they're helpless with cows. Unless you want Tunstall, Cooper, and me to do all of the chores while everyone continues to eat cheese and raw vegetables. The bread's getting stale, you know."

My lord glared him into silence. Master Farmer took a chair, leaned back, and crossed his legs at the ankle. He looked prepared to lounge there all day.

Tunstall explained, "Me and Cooper did some nosing about after us lads finished cooking breakfast, my lord." His owl eyes were perfectly calm. "We had us a look at the raiders' ships, since they're above water."

"But it's pouring outside!" my lord protested. "How did you even get down there?"

"We climbed it," Tunstall replied. "It was a sarden holiday to manage, too."

My lord leaned back and put his hands behind his head. "Take a chair, you two," he ordered. As we obeyed, he said to Tunstall, "Go on. What did you find?"

"Not as much as we hoped," Tunstall replied. "Protection spells kept us from searching the cargo or the bodies. Most of the goods were washed out of the holes in the keels of the ships, along with anyone who was belowdecks. Those who were chained down in the *Lash* are still there, along with the deck crew."

"The mage or mages used the ship to trap the ones on deck," I said. "The sails were woven together. Then they wove themselves through the holes made for the oars, to make a flat cover over most of the deck. The wood—the oars, the wheel, the rail—grew up over the hands of those who touched it. They couldn't have freed themselves."

My lord and Master Farmer made the Sign.

Tunstall reported, "The *Lash* is a slave ship. I believe once the six bodies are taken from the bunks on the *Lash,* you'll have six of the missing folk from this palace. The other ship is a cargo vessel built for speed. Most of the warriors would have come on that."

"They disguised themselves as slave transports to get past Blue Harbor and Port Caynn, perhaps," Master Farmer said.

"To pass unnoticed by nearly anyone," my lord said. "Who would pay attention to slave traders moving up and down the coast at this time of year? Everyone's taking cargoes north and south."

"We'll learn more if we can search the bodies and the cargoes," Tunstall said. "Where they came from, if they are branded slaves—"

"That's as may be, but you and Cooper won't be the ones to do the search," my lord replied, sitting up straight. "Master Farmer can do it. Are the protection spells yours?" he asked the mage.

Master Farmer shook his head. "Ironwood and Orielle took care of that, to keep what was on the ships from rotting faster. I can ask them to undo the spell work."

"What's his Dog experience?" Tunstall protested. "What does he know of searches?"

"I've done private Hunts for Lord Gershom in past years," Master Farmer said, his eyes half lidded. "And I've served three years at the Kraken Street kennel in Blue Harbor. I've lost count of the searches I've done there. I don't know what the Jane Street kennel has in the way of mages, but I work on handling of the victims of crimes, inspection of evidence, handling mages, and the detection of poisons and spells. That's in addition to five country Hunts out of Blue Harbor as well as street Hunts. None as big as this, but have you done so great a Hunt yourselves?"

"Enough," Lord Gershom snapped. "Tunstall, I've worked with Farmer off and on for four years and he's a good man. I hope that is enough for you."

My lord is a strict judge of coves and mots. If he says they are worthwhile, then it is so. When my lord glanced at me, to see if I would argue, I busied myself with picking Achoo fluff from my tunic.

"Tunstall and Cooper are to take the ship that is now at the palace dock on the Ware River," my lord announced. "They are to carry a packet of messages that I have spent most of the night writing." He shoved the packet, wrapped in oiled cloth over leather, at us. Tunstall carefully picked it up and handed it to me. "Here are your orders." He gave us one document each. "Show that to any who question you. Cooper, is there any chance that Achoo can pick up the boy's scent if you were to go up and down the river?"

I shook my head. "After this kind of rain all last night and all today? None, my lord. Had your ship come earlier this morning, mayhap, but . . ." I thought it over, remembering the powerful stream that had sent me thumping and bumping down to the foot of the cliffs. "No. It was too heavy even then, and it rains still."

"Very well, then," Lord Gershom said with a nod. "Tunstall, you and Cooper will take that packet to Sir Tullus at Port

Caynn and hand it to him *only,* then wait in the city for his orders. Tell no one else what you have seen here. Part of his instructions will be to set you on the greater Hunt, so don't worry about being cut out. Farmer will bring you whatever he learns from the ships. Cooper, one thing—write up the investigation so far, but do your best to keep Farmer's name, Tunstall's name, your name, and Achoo's name out of it. I want all of the information, but in a pinch, I want no one to know which Dogs, and which hound, were on this Hunt, do you understand?"

I wanted to scratch my head like the men did when they were confused, but Lord Gershom's lady had beaten the habit out of me when I was small. "I don't know if I can do it, my lord, but I'll try."

"That's good enough for me, Cooper," he said. I felt my insides warm up, like they always did when he praised me. Until they did, I didn't know how cold they were.

My lord looked at Tunstall. "Questions?"

"Which boat do we take to Port Caynn, my lord?" Tunstall asked.

"She's called the *Malia.* She's one of the few ships permitted to wait at the royal dock on the Ware River. All of the peregrine ships are in use, so it's a slower trip than our last one. Anything else?" my lord asked, raising his brows.

I had a question—"why can't we pick up the Hunt from here?"—but I also knew the signal of those raised brows. He might *ask,* but truth to tell, he *wanted* no more questions. Instead I pulled the brass medallion with its strange insignia from my pocket. "My lord, this goes with the evidence to be examined. I found it on the northern end of the beach last night, along with other things we left in a pile there. This was too small to leave."

"I'll take it," Master Farmer said, holding out his hand. My lord gave me the nod. I passed the medallion over to the mage. He took out the lens he used for seeing magic. "There's no magic in it," Master Farmer said, turning the medallion over in his fingers. "And I don't recognize the insignia."

"We'll have someone render it on paper and send it around," Lord Gershom replied. Looking at Tunstall and me, he said, "Very well, then. Get your things and go. Master Farmer, stay with me." He wet his pen with ink again and began to scribble. Tunstall and I left the room.

Pounce awaited me in my chamber, along with my pack. It was dry, gods be thanked. "You missed all the falling down and getting bruised and talking about it with my lord," I told him as I stuffed everything into my pack.

No, I didn't, Pounce replied, stretching out to his full length with a yawn. *I heard everything.*

I glared at him. "You couldn't have helped when I was tumbling down the cliffside?"

The toughening up will do you good, he said, the dreadful moralizing beast. *Achoo was there to look after you.*

"I nearly landed on Achoo!" I snapped, checking to see I had forgotten nothing.

You will feel better when you've had a hot bath and a belly full of proper hot food, Pounce said wisely. *You're always scratchy when you're uncomfortable.*

I walked out of the room. I can never argue with him. I don't know why I try.

Achoo sat before my door, thumping it with her tail in her eagerness to get moving. Tunstall met us at the center corridor. Mistress Orielle stood with him. "I'll show you out," she said, matter-of-fact. She wore pale blue today, and pearls in her ears. She had also thrust a handkerchief in her sleeve, as if she expected to cry some more. "No one can object if you use the front entry when I am with you. Besides, I bear a message from Her Majesty." She guided us back down the open hall where we'd first encountered her, past the sitting room where we'd met the king and queen. A soldier in the King's Own opened the front door for her and retreated down the hall when she waved her fingers at him.

When the soldier had turned his back to us, Mistress Orielle reached into a hidden pocket inside her overdress and drew out two small purses. She gave one to Tunstall and one to me. "For expenses," she told us quietly. "Her Majesty does not want you to find yourselves coin-pinched while you seek her baby. She has every faith in you both."

"That faith could be misplaced," Tunstall replied, keeping his voice down. "His Highness may be beyond our ability to find."

"She only asks you to do your best," Mistress Orielle told us firmly. "And I wish you luck, as much as it is in my poor power to bestow."

We thanked her. In saying farewell, Tunstall asked her to give the queen our promises to try everything we knew and sent our message of hope for success to the queen.

Outside, two men of the King's Own waited for us with the horses we had ridden here. Everyone looked surly in the rain, except my chestnut mare. She touched noses with Pounce and Achoo, then watched as Pounce leaped to my shoulder. I mounted, careful not to dislodge my friend.

As we rode I did some thinking while I watched Achoo get covered in mud all over again. Normally I wouldn't have minded the chance to see Sir Tullus of King's Reach. I've missed him at the Magistrate's Court ever since he took up the post of Deputy Provost of Port Caynn two years back. The new magistrate we have is well enough, but once I recovered from being scared of Sir Tullus, I thought he was a bit funny. The new magistrate is too humorless for me. The only thing about him that I like is the fact that he would rather Tunstall give evidence of our hobblings, even if I was the Dog that did the work. He has no patience for my stutterings in front of a crowd. If he can avoid calling on me, he will do so, every time.

It was knowing that Tullus would see us in uniforms we had worn through weather and muck that disheartened me. I liked to look my best going before him. Just now I felt like an unmade bed, while the sky continued to piss on me.

The boat landing lay some eight miles on the other side of the main road, across from the palace gate. That was why we hadn't seen it the night before. We'd been at least four miles upriver.

At the dock rode a tidy craft, a normal ship, with a crew that wore the blue tunics and white breeches of our navy. Seeing our approach, they ran out a gangplank. A mot with the silver sleeve and hem embroideries of a naval mage stood at the foot of the gangplank. Only when she had traded passwords with our guides and checked our orders did she allow Tunstall and me to board. We left the horses behind.

Tunstall, the animals, and I napped for part of the journey. We shared bread and cheese with the crew for lunch. Afterward I worked on my reports while Tunstall played cards with the sailors. It was a quiet and welcome time until we reached the docks at Port Caynn. I enjoyed it as long as I forced myself to concentrate on my report and not on taking the road to Hunt for Rats.

The ship entered the ocean harbor at Port Caynn around mid-afternoon. I found it strange to come at the city this way. Every other time I had seen the place, it had been from the land, from the high ridges or from the rooftops. It was a pretty town, if you didn't look too close at the streets, and you didn't venture into the wrong districts. The Ridge Gardens were plain beautiful, and I'd never had better food at so many eating houses.

But we weren't there to eat. As soon as we docked, Tunstall, Achoo, Pounce, and I were on our way uphill to Guards House. Sir Tullus had sent an escort and horses for our packs. At first my battered legs complained, but the pace uphill soon warmed them up. We stopped for broiled lamb on skewers and fresh cherry juice, the lamb being for Achoo and Pounce as well as us humans. Between the food and a proper walk, my spirits improved despite the rain.

"Folk here must have good legs," Tunstall remarked as we neared the top of the ridge. "Going up and down all day."

I grinned at him. Certainly my legs had improved in the short time that Goodwin and I had Hunted colemongers in Port Caynn. It had prepared me for my future with Achoo. "The locals need them, to work off all the seafood they eat," I said.

Tunstall made the most horrendous face. I had known he would. "Seagoing bugs and snails," he said. "Give me a man's food." Tunstall had not tasted seafood until he'd been a Dog five years. From what I'd heard, he'd gotten angry at having to pay for something he insisted was a joke, not food. He would eat fish, though he preferred freshwater, just as he preferred freshwater eels. Anyone who put seafood on his plate risked a drubbing.

Guards House loomed above us, safe behind its gray stone wall. Our escort took our packs inside while Tunstall showed our orders to the guard at the gate. He sniffed at our soaked, crumpled uniforms and the animals who bore us company. I let Tunstall go ahead of me into the courtyard, then asked the guard who hadn't sniffed, "Is Sergeant Axman on duty?"

"He is, and he'll be none too happy about the condition of yon hound," the guard told me, just as stiff-rumped as his friend. "Why didn't you clean up afore you came in?"

"Because our orders said we weren't to loiter about like a pair of fat-assed gate-sitters," Tunstall said. He'd turned to see why I was gabbing with the guards. "We don't have time to make ourselves pretty for the riffraff. Cooper, there's work to do."

Pounce leaped to the ground as we crossed the courtyard. Without me telling her, Achoo fell in step one foot off my left heel. Following our packs, we climbed the steps and passed into Guards House.

The guard had told us the truth. Sergeant Axman, who had saved my skin three years ago, was indeed on duty. He raised his eyebrows at both of us as Tunstall showed him the packet with the Provost's seal and asked for a meeting with Sir Tullus.

"Welcome back, all of you," Axman said, hopping down from his tall chair. Achoo was flailing Tunstall and me with her tail. "How long has it been since our last meetin'? Five months since a Hunt brought you my way?" He clasped arms with Tunstall.

"Indeed—we were on the trail of boat thieves," Tunstall replied.

"I need not ask if you found them," Axman said with a smile. "You always do with this fine lass." He did not speak of me, but of Achoo, who was sniffing Axman's pockets already. The sergeant was a hound breeder and there were always treats to be found on his person. He was one of Achoo's greatest admirers. I never had to remind her that he was her friend.

"Achoo," I said in complaint. "I taught you better manners."

"But she knows there are exceptions for old friends, doesn't she?" The sergeant lowered himself to one knee to pet my girl.

"Norham, take the desk," the sergeant called to a guardsman who was polishing the metal cressets set around the room. "I'll guide these messengers to Sir Tullus." He fed Achoo treats that he makes up himself. He'll give me bags of them when I visit Port Caynn, but never the recipe, and four-legged dogs go mad for them.

Norham came to the desk as Axman rose and dusted his hands. He took us to the door to the inner offices at Guards House. "Even the creatures, Sergeant?" Norham asked.

Axman pointed a blunt finger at Norham. "Don't you go callin' Achoo Curlypaws a creature," he said firmly, his eyes like steel. "She's one of the finest hounds that ever picked up a scent. And you argue with the cat at your own risk."

Norham sputtered. "I don't argue with *cats*," he protested. By then we were through the door and out of earshot.

Tunstall was chuckling. "You like to keep them on their toes, Sergeant Axman?"

"These second-year Dogs, they think they know it all," Axman replied. "If their desk sergeants notice the signs before they get themselves killed, they send the lads—you never see the lasses get their heads swelled up like that—the sergeants send the lads up to me." The sarge came to a halt before a door I recognized as being the one to the Deputy Provost's office. "You can't tell me what Hunt you're about this time, can you? The nobles' mages are stirred up. They've told Sir Tullus somethin's gone amiss at both palaces, but no one's sendin' word out. Our peregrine ships have been called out of port.

And the messenger bird just came with word that the *Malia,* a Crown messenger ship, is docked in our harbor, and you were aboard."

Tunstall looked at me, since I know the sergeant better. I put my hand on Axman's rock-hard arm. "I'm sorry," I told him softly. "We've got orders to keep it quiet."

Axman made the Sign on his chest. "Then I'll not hinder you." He rapped on the door.

A voice I knew well shouted, "Chaos is in it, I was trying to *nap!*"

Axman opened the door. "Sir Knight, I've two weary Dogs here with sealed orders from my Lord Provost." He nodded for us to go in.

The office had changed some since I'd first seen it three years ago. The beautiful wood of the walls, ceiling, and moldings was still well cared for. The former Deputy Provost had allowed only maps of each Guard District and maps of the surrounding countryside districts on the walls. Sir Tullus had beautifully woven tapestries on the walls as well, showing scenes from the legends of the Great Gods. I would have loved to take a closer look at them, but I have never been able to relax around the man who used to be the magistrate for Jane Street's Evening Watch. I had spent too much time hearing him say, "Tell it slowly, Cooper," or "While we *live,* Cooper," to be at ease with both of us in so small a room.

He had changed Sir Lionel's plain, depressing furnishings, too. The big desk had a couple of carved stone figures and a beautiful ebony bowl on it. There were tapestry-work cushions on the chairs in front of the desk, and bright Carthaki rugs on the flagstones of the floor. The horn in the old windows had been replaced with glass. I'd heard that Sir Tullus had inherited a bit of money on the death of a great-uncle.

Clearly he liked to spend it on comfort. Sir Lionel's old single bookcase had been replaced by five, all stuffed full. After two years of sitting in Sir Tullus's courtroom, hearing him deliver judgments, I figured he'd read them all.

Sir Tullus himself got to his feet the moment he saw who we were. "Tunstall and Cooper, Mithros save me. And on a Hunt, from the look of you."

He'd not changed since he'd left the Jane Street court. He still had that single eyebrow across his forehead, and his cheeks were still ruddy. He dressed like a noble with money and sense, in a tunic of a dark brownish red that suited him, with golden-colored embroideries at the hems and collar. He wore the Deputy Provost's signet ring on his right hand, a wedding band on his left. His black hair was cut in a short, military style, and if he used the perfumed oil in it that was the noble fashion, I could not smell it.

Tunstall and I bowed. Behind us we heard the door close as Sergeant Axman left. I took the packet of documents from Lord Gershom and set them before Sir Tullus with another bow, then gave him my own orders. Tunstall passed me his to set before Sir Tullus.

"Very good," Sir Tullus said, taking the seat behind his desk. "Sit down, both of you. From the look of this, I may need a little time." He went over our orders first and set them aside. Then he sliced the seal clean off the packet and cut the ties with a small, sharp dagger. Sir Tullus opened the wrapping and selected the first document.

He hadn't read the entire page before he said, "Mithros and Goddess save us!" He turned and yanked at a bellpull behind him so hard that it snapped. "Parrot pox," he grumbled. "I do that once a month at least. You'd think they'd make the sarden things tougher."

The door opened. A lass of fourteen, a message runner, stuck her head into the room. "Sir Knight?" She frowned as Sir Tullus held up the rope pull. "You broke it again, sir." I don't believe she was close enough to see that Tullus's hand was trembling with vexation.

"When will you trade for chain, like I keep asking?" Sir Tullus demanded. "Wine, three cups, some pasties. At the run, lass!"

"Aye, Sir Knight." The runner left us, closing the door.

Sir Tullus looked at Tunstall and me. "You were there?"

"Not when it happened, Sir Knight," Tunstall replied. "Lord Gershom in Corus got word that something was amiss and collected Cooper and me for the early Hunt. And a mage, Farmer Cape."

Sir Tullus grunted and returned to reading his document. As he read, he swore under his breath and made the Sign twice before the wine and food arrived. The runner came back then, setting the pitcher and plates at the front of Sir Tullus's desk so we might serve ourselves. It seemed the Deputy Provost preferred such informality. Once she'd poured the wine, the lass left us alone together in the room once more.

Tunstall and I tried not to gobble the pasties as Sir Tullus read the first document three times over. It was hard. Until Sir Tullus had mentioned food, I had forgotten that I'd had scant food all day. The pasties sat well on my belly. From the way Achoo gulped the one I passed along, it sat fine with her, too. Pounce was apparently uninterested, since he had curled up in a patch of sunlight and gone to sleep.

Sir Tullus put the document down at last and knocked back the contents of his wine cup, which he had not yet touched. He went to the door and opened it. "Good idea, to stay there," he said to someone outside.

We heard his runner say pertly, "You did break the bell-pull again, Sir Knight."

"None of your sauce. Another round of those pasties, and the fritters I like," he told her.

"Sir Knight, might she also bring twilsey or barley water?" Tunstall called. "Cooper's not what you would call one for spirits."

"Thank you," I told my partner quietly. I'd never have had the sack to ask for myself.

"And some nice cold twilsey or barley water," Sir Tullus said. "Off you go." He closed the door.

We turned in our chairs to look at him. All of his normal ruddiness was gone. He'd spoken cheerfully enough to his runner, but the look on his face now was that of a cove who'd taken a hard shock. He came back to his desk and poured himself another cup of wine.

"Gershom's orders are, for me to send a number of messages out and wait on replies," he told us, staring at the cup. "I'll need to keep the two of you at hand for a couple of days. There's a lodging house we use for out-of-town Dogs, Ladyshearth Lodgings."

"I know it, Sir Knight," I said. "Goodwin and I stayed there when we had our Hunt in '47." I glanced at Tunstall. "We didn't have time when we were here the last couple of times, but you'll like the place."

"Good," Sir Tullus said. He opened a drawer in the side of his desk. "You'll need coin for a change of clothes." I heard metal clink. At last Sir Tullus held up a small leather bag and tossed it to Tunstall. My partner weighed it in his hand, nodding with approval. "Account for every coin, remember," Tullus said. "I'll try to get you back to Corus for a day at least, to pack." He sighed, rubbing his face with his hands. "I knew certain factions at court were getting restless, but I never thought they would be such idiots. Folk will lose their heads for this, and families their titles."

"They should, if they had a hand in what we saw," Tunstall replied, his eyes hard. "More than a hundred and thirty dead, with the King's Own, the guard on the main gate, and the servants. That's not counting their own people that they drowned or melted. They deserve not a whit of mercy."

Sir Tullus nodded. "I don't see why Gershom picked you two. Was there no one else?" I was starting to feel vexed and hurt when he looked at me and said, "It's because of your loss, Guardswoman Cooper. Surely you would be happier at home."

Here again was sympathy for my grief, grief I didn't feel for a man I didn't love anymore. I looked down, unable to bear the kindness in Sir Tullus's eyes. I felt like a liar before him.

"She will not be happier at home," Tunstall told him. "She has been good, Hunting with me, haven't you, Cooper?" I nodded, and Tunstall continued, "And Jewel and Yoav are too old for this."

"Jewel is, at any road," I made myself remark. It was better to speak than to listen to them talk about me. To Sir Tullus I said, "I thank you for your condolences, but truly, I am easier at work. I will not say that I am the best Provost's Guard for this, but Tunstall is, and Achoo is. Even Nyler Jewel does not come with my hound."

Achoo, hearing her name, sat up and whuffed softly. She seldom talks loudly if she doesn't have to. She is the quietest hound in all Corus, as far as I have been able to tell. Sir Tullus got up and came around his desk to greet her. As I told her to treat him as a friend, he saw Pounce in his patch of sunlight. Pounce blinked at him.

"Master Pounce, good day to you," he said gravely, scratching Achoo behind the ears. "I apologize for not greeting you earlier, but you did not go to any effort to make yourself seen."

You had other things on your mind, Sir Tullus, Pounce replied. *We have all been thrown into a storm of fate. We can forgive old friends if the amenities are let slip.*

"A storm of fate?" Tullus asked with a crooked smile. "I would have called it an unholy mess. Though it's been coming, with all the loose talk that's been going around. I just never expected the attack to take this form, the craven swine! To threaten a child for their ends—Mithros's spear, that takes gems the size of the palace."

"You'll get no arguments here, Sir Knight," Tunstall replied.

"Pardon, Sir Tullus," I said, rubbing my temples. My head was beginning to ache. "You expected this?" I felt as if everyone had done so except me.

There was a tap on the door. It opened and the runner entered, a big tray laden with food and a pitcher in her hands. Sir Tullus lifted away pitcher and cup and poured, handing the cup to me. As his runner placed the tray on a table, he frowned. "Chopped meat?"

"Sergeant Axman sent it for the creatures," the runner said, placing the plates on the floor. "Beef and egg for the hound, and chicken and egg for the cat. And we apologize for those not being ready earlier, the cook not understanding that Sergeant Axman meant Cook was to make them up right off." She grinned at Sir Tullus, picked up the tray with the empty plates, and left the room.

Sir Tullus sat by the table instead of behind the desk.

I gulped down the raspberry twilsey, a boon to my parched throat, and poured myself another cup while Sir Tullus selected a couple of fritters and Tunstall a cheese pasty.

"Anyone with eyes and ears on the Council of Lords has expected some trouble for the last two years, Cooper," Sir Tullus said, once he'd chewed and swallowed his first mouthful. "Mages, particularly great ones, are a haughty crew, the nobles are feeling ill-treated, and His Majesty is no longer prepared to let things pass. He has grown up and the treasury is very low." He noted our alarmed faces and smiled. "I have this place spelled against eavesdropping once a week. That was yesterday. My young friend there can't hear me bellow with the door open."

I whistled in spite of being a bit uncomfortable around him still. I'd been in his courtroom when he bellowed. That was a very good sound-stopping spell.

"I wouldn't work in here without such magic," Sir Tullus said. "That was part of my predecessor's difficulty. People who did not have his best interests at heart spied on him."

I swallowed a snort. That was the mildest way of putting the last Deputy Provost's troubles.

"I don't see how His Majesty can be growing up at the age of forty-three," Tunstall remarked. "Isn't it a bit late?"

"It gives the rest of us old fools hope," Sir Tullus replied. "It's been going on since his marriage to Queen Jessamine. That mother of hers raised her to take an interest in the running of the realm. Once Jessamine and Roger were married, she began to ask questions. Well, no man likes to look a fool to an adoring young woman. He asked his ministers to tell him what they've been up to. He started reading his reports to her. They talk about the kingdom's affairs."

"I begin to see the problem," Tunstall said quietly, polishing off a third pasty. I was picking at one, having eaten enough for a time with the first plate. I think Tunstall's legs are hollow.

"You do indeed. For years Prince Baird and the rest of the Council of Lords handled the realm as they liked." Sir Tullus dunked a fritter in his wine and ate it. "Then His Majesty wanted to know what they did. Next he started to change things. Some of the nobles don't like that. Remember the winter of 247—the Bread Riots in Corus until Midwinter. His Majesty overruled his councillors and opened the royal smokehouses and granaries. He even let commoners hunt in parts of the Crown forest lands."

"Why was that a problem?" I asked. Living in the city, I have little experience of life on noble estates.

Sir Tullus rubbed his chin. "Nobles are a proud lot, Cooper. They feel that if the king grants permission to hunt the Crown lands, it must be to nobles only."

"And in years gone by, the king allowed only nobles to buy from the royal granaries and smokehouses in hard times. The nobles sell the goods to their people for much more than they paid," Tunstall added. "Or they trade for a promise of labor on the nobles' lands, or for someone's children as slaves. You know what folk will do when they are hungry."

I do know.

"You heard of none of this about the council uproar in '47, Cooper?" Sir Tullus asked.

"That winter wasn't a time for us to sit and collect the gossip, Sir Knight," Tunstall explained. "We were busier than fleas on a hot griddle, with folk rioting and stealing food. Mithros bless the king, he made certain the Dogs were fed in the kennels, that we might keep working."

And Rosto shared what the Court of the Rogue had with his friends, I thought.

Sir Tullus, done with the fritters, stood and went back to his desk. He wiped his fingers on a cloth that lay there, and began to look at the other sealed documents that had been in the packet. "Well, with luck there will be no hard winter this year," he said, almost to himself. "The seers are predicting a good harvest, if the trouble they see in our future does not interfere with it. I'd wager the attack and kidnapping is the trouble they've been seeing." He looked at us. "I need to get to work on this. Why don't you two—you four," he said with a nod to Pounce and Achoo, "go on to Ladyshearth Lodgings and settle in. I doubt I'll have anything to tell you at least until tomorrow noon."

We stood and bowed, then left him. His runner bowed to us, then entered his office while we headed on down the hall. In the main waiting room, Sergeant Axman was seated behind his desk once more, perched on his tall chair. He pointed to a pair of bulging packs that lay on a bench.

"I guessed at your sizes, but I've a good eye for such things," he said. "I'd a feeling those packs of yours don't have extra uniforms, stockin's, and the like. There's combs and other useful things, too."

Tunstall grinned and offered Axman his arm to clasp. "Mithros loves a good sergeant, Lord Gershom always says. My thanks, Sergeant Axman."

I smiled up at him. "Thanks," I said. "I know I'll feel like a new mot in a fresh uniform."

"I've had my night calls, too," Axman replied. "And not from a bordel, either! Get on with the two of you. I sent word ahead to Serenity. She'll have your rooms and supper waitin'."

135

He was as good as his word. Not only did Serenity have rooms prepared for us, but there were tubs of hot water inside them. She even had food bowls waiting outside her kitchen door for Pounce and Achoo. They couldn't say they ever starved, working with me.

When Tunstall and I were clean and dressed in fresh uniforms, we found a good supper put on the dining room table. We spoke little, mostly because five other Dogs who were staying at the house at the same time had come off watch and were there to eat with us. They were closemouthed, too, doubtless being weary after their day's work. I thought back on all I had learned about the current mess and how it might have led to a royal kidnapping.

"I *said,* Cooper, mayhap you should go to bed." I looked up. Tunstall was leaning over the table to stare at my face. None of the other diners remained with us. Even their dishes had been cleared away. Only Tunstall and Serenity were left.

Achoo was curled up at my feet, Pounce on the chair beside me. *He's right,* Pounce said. *Only this morning you slid down a cliff and burned yourself trying to search magicked ships.* He looked at Tunstall. *Sleep wouldn't hurt* you *either.*

I got to my feet. "I think you're both right," I admitted. "We should get rest while we can." I knew that once we had our own orders, chances for a good night's sleep might come rarely.

In my room, I tried to work on my journal more, but I am tired. I'll catch up in the morning. Who knows how long we will be here, after all?

Sunday, June 10, 249

Ladyshearth Lodgings
Coates Lane
Port Caynn
One of the afternoon.
being an account of the events of Saturday, June 9,
beginning at dawn on that day

Achoo woke me at dawn yesterday, of course. We went out, nodding to the busy cook and cook maid, and returned, to go to bed once more. I roused again as the city's clocks struck nine and cleaned myself up, then visited the kitchen to beg breakfast for my two friends. The crosspatch maid who had been here during my last Port Caynn visit was having her morning meal in the kitchen. She remembered us.

"Don't you go feedin' them nasty pigeons on your windowsill, like you done last time!" she said, pointing a finger at me. "This is a decent house, and why Serenity lets you in with all your livestock—"

"Enough," the cook snapped. "You cross old mud turtle, leave the Dog alone. These two creatures are as neat and well trained as them that live here. Neater than some I could name. So just stop yer gob." She grinned down at Pounce, who was bumping against her shins. "Some folk just don't appreciate a gentleman like you, Master Pounce." She looked at me. "Now, Guardswoman Cooper, what will you have for your breakfast?"

My belly happily full, I returned to my room. There I opened my shutters to a bright, sunny day and a soft breeze. It was a pleasure to set my soggy laundry outside for the maids to wash. I hoped the crosspatch maid got the task. Then I sat down to my table and this journal. First I recorded what had taken place beginning on Thursday the seventh. I finished that and began the other report that Lord Gershom had requested, the one which did not mention Tunstall, Achoo, or me, all in official Dog cipher. I was just finishing when Tunstall hammered on my door at the end of the noon hour.

"Cooper, it's a beautiful day, and I'm cursed if I'll waste much more of it!" he bellowed. "Come out of there!"

I opened my door, rubbing my cramped writing hand. "You're a cracked lad with the manners of a Cesspool bumwasher, you know that?" I asked him.

Tunstall leaned on the doorframe, taking no offense at all. He never did. Goodwin once told me I might bash him with an oaken club, to see if that might make a dent, but it seemed to be hardly worth the trouble.

"Is the report done?" Tunstall asked. When I nodded, he said, "Then you've no excuse. Pounce and me are bored." He wasn't storying me. Pounce sat at his feet, yawning at us. "Send it to Tullus and let's amble," Tunstall ordered. "You know I can't stay put, not while awaiting orders. Mistress Serenity says she can use her Gift to find us if aught happens— that's why they keep folk like us here."

He had a point. Neither of us waits well. I wasn't sure what would occupy his restless mind until I bethought myself of his flowers. He has a name for himself in Corus for the miniature blooms he grows. Doubtless he'd like to see the flowers in Port Caynn, if I could learn where fine ones were.

Serenity was in the dining room, going over her accounts. "That's easy," she said when I asked her. "You've been there, Cooper, though it was in the fall. Ridge Gardens. The lower levels on the north side, they've got the best flowers." She looked at me, raising a brow. "Strange. I never took you for the flower sort."

"Oh, that would be me," Tunstall said. "I grow them at home."

Serenity dropped her pen. "You're *that* Tunstall! But nobody ever said you were a man! Or a Dog! You're not pulling my skirts, are you? The same Tunstall that grows the Goddess Glory, the rose that's no bigger than my thumbnail?"

Tunstall bobbed his head, rubbing his hair nervously.

"Maiden save me, you here and me having no notion!" Serenity looked at me. I was leaning on one of her chairs, waiting for her to finish flower talk with Tunstall. "We can talk more tonight. Enjoy the sun and the garden," she said, picking up her pen again.

I held out my sealed report and a coin. "Do you have a runner to take this to Sir Tullus as soon as may be?" I asked her. "He's waiting for it."

Serenity took the paper and drew a sign on it in fire that was almost blood-colored. Immediately she looked to be holding a basket of flowers. "I'll take care of it right away," she replied. "Ginmaree!" she called. Instantly a gixie in boys' trousers raced in from the kitchen.

With the report matter settled, Pounce and Achoo bounded out of the door ahead of us. We caught up with the animals in Coates Lane and wove through the traffic, taking the streets pretty much northeast.

We walked in silence for a time before Tunstall remarked, "I hope we're kept on this Hunt. That ghost-eyed glare of yours is as good a weapon as Achoo, especially with Rats who know they've crossed the gods by taking the heir. The way your eyes go all pale and burning like winter ice, they see the Crone in you. They always give up more than they want to when they catch your eye."

I shook my head. I'd have called him a superstitious hillman, but I'd seen it happen often enough that I had to believe it. Even Holborn stepped back when we fought. He'd said it was my eyes, too. I think they are simply a pale gray or blue, but I've never seen my face when I'm angry. "You spook me when you talk that way," I told Tunstall.

"I'm not spooked," my partner told me. "What with your eyes, your pigeons, your dust-demons, and Achoo, you're the most valuable partner in the Lower City, mayhap all Corus. On a Hunt like this, I think we have the best chance to find our boy with what the two of us can do together."

I halted to stare at him as a blush crept over my face. Tunstall's compliments were rare. I knew I would treasure this one. I was too shy to say as much, so I just gave him a gentle punch on the shoulder.

The Ridge Gardens were slightly crowded, but not badly so. Children played on the wide areas of grass, watched by nursemaids and parents. Nobles walked along, eyeing each other's fashions and gossiping. The governor's guard marched along in pairs, dressed in their maroon and black uniforms, carrying spears and batons. They were trained to pay no attention to deliberate distractions, like the little group of lads who trooped behind them, making faces.

Tunstall and I walked toward the north end of the gardens where the wealthy showed off their summer clothes. Tunstall was so fascinated by the flowerbeds there that at length Pounce, Achoo, and I found a bench in the sun where we could laze. For a time I watched my partner as he inspected one flower after another as he might eye a piece of evidence.

I was leaning back with my eyes closed, imagining Tunstall

questioning a flower for its crimes, when I heard the familiar whir of pigeon wings. I did not bother to open my eyes to see if I was right. I have known that sound since I was a child.

Several landed on the ground before me. I always carry pigeon and dust spinner food, so I scattered a handful of cracked corn among the birds. They went after it as the voices of ghosts rose in the air.

"—tell her it wasn't me," an old mot's voice said.

"I am saying, my lord is up to something. Or didn't you notice he's buying weapons?" That was a young cove talking.

"What is your lord's name?" I asked the spirit.

"No!" he replied, panicked. "He'll kill me if I tell you!"

"Lad," I said gently, "he already has."

At that, the spirit sighed. "He did," he said. "I remember now." And he was gone.

"You know I'll love you forever. I would never betray you!" A young mot this time, terrified.

"No, halt!" another, older cove said. "That thing will fall right over!"

I tossed out more corn. One of the pigeons hopped up onto the bench and looked me over. This was the most ordinary of pigeons, blue-black all over, with white rings around its eyes. Its back feathers were ruffled and it trembled as if it were weary to the bone.

I murmured a blessing to them, wishing them peace from their lives' fears and safe passage to the Peaceful Realms. That was enough for most of them. I could feel the spirits leave their birds, the ghosts having said what they needed to say. The black one on the bench stayed where it was.

"Have you something important to say?" I asked the bird.

"Speak with respect," a cove's voice snarled. "You're no better than those treacherous, lying curs at the palace!" My body crawled with gooseflesh. Did this one know sommat useful? "They'll wish they had kept me soon enough. After all I did for them, they murdered me in my bed!"

My throat seized up for a moment. "So you're one of the cleaning folk, then?" I asked, my voice as innocent as a well-off child's. "In the way of knowing the little passages and halls where the servants go—"

"Slut!" the ghost snarled. "Doxy! How dare you speak so to the Lord High Chancellor of Mages!"

I crossed my legs at the ankle easily, turning my face up to the sun. "*Any* old bogle might say the same, and me with no way to prove it. I can't see you, after all. Tell me sommat you've done recently that I might know of."

Lazamon of Buckglen wasted time calling me the kind of names given to some of my friends in the Lower City. Finally, when he ran out of terms for *whore,* I said, "If you want vengeance on your killers, I'm your only chance to get it, traitor."

He was silent for a moment. I gave his poor bird of burden some more corn. At last he said, "What gives a guttersnipe like you the right to call me anything, let alone 'traitor'?"

"I've just come from the Summer Palace," I said. "Very nice work, undoing all those spells with no one seeing you at it. And yet your partners decided they could do without you even after that."

"Spare me your jumped-up moralizing," he muttered. "You understand nothing of the stakes." He added bitterly, "*Your king* wants to regulate mage work! He says we *owe* a debt of service to the Crown! Well, he'll soon learn I won't do as some randy bastard with a title bids. He'll rue the day he crossed my friends and me!"

I yawned, despite the hammering of my heart when Lazamon spoke of his fellow conspirators. Then I said, "Your friends didn't value you so high, did they?" I eyed a broken fingernail as if I'd naught better to do. My luck still held. No one had looked to see a Dog conversing with a pigeon. "Give me their names. It will be a fine vengeance on them. You could greet them in the Peaceful Realms once they've taken the king's justice."

"I'll not give you names," the ghost snarled. "*You* can tell him the misery I have left for him to die on!"

"I *thought* your talk of vengeance was all smoke," I replied. "You must be a mage—you're not enough of a man to avenge your own death."

"I hate your swiving, childish king more," Lazamon retorted. "He'll pay now, and his brood mare. For every lash and blow the child receives, his parents will weaken. Every meal the child does without, the parents will go hungry. It is my finest work, and it cannot be undone, because the maker of it is dead." He sounded so pleased that I would have killed him myself, had he been alive in front of me then.

"Then you made your own death, snake pizzle," I whispered. "No wonder they killed you."

"The problem's easily enough solved, Guardswoman." There was a sneering tone in his voice. "Only find the prince and keep him in good condition." His voice was beginning to fade. "That shouldn't be so hard, should it?" And he was gone.

"It's a good thing the Black God has a kinder heart than I have," I told the spirit as his pigeon took flight. "Shame on you, punishing the child for the deeds of the father!"

The Black God forgives all, it's said. That's why he's a god, I suppose, and why I'm a Dog. I don't have to try to forgive a lousy, sarden canker blossom like the Chancellor of Mages.

We had to get word of the painful connection between the prince and his parents to Sir Tullus, and Lord Gershom, right away. I looked around for Tunstall and Achoo. They were on the grass, Tunstall having bought a ring toy for her to play with.

"A Birdie, Cooper?" Tunstall asked, throwing the ring for Achoo down the open green. My partner had seen me talk with the pigeon. "Any useful information?"

"Maybe so," I replied. Keeping in mind that we had to be sure no one was eavesdropping, I added, "A ghost from Corus found me here." There was a marvel in itself, that he'd found me. "We need to get word to Sir Tullus right off."

"My arm grows weary in any case," Tunstall said. When Achoo returned with the ring, he towed her along as she hung on to her half. Pounce chose to walk just ahead, as if to tell passersby he did not know us and did not wish to be associated with us. Tunstall asked, "Did you know they have some types of lavender here that I can't grow in Corus? And clematis?"

"Did you pick some, so you can plant it when we go home?" I asked.

Tunstall looked as if I had just asked him to take Her Majesty's favorite pearls. "It's a public garden, Cooper! If everyone did that, there would be no flowers left!"

I rolled my eyes at him. "I had no idea I was such a vile rusher."

Tunstall grimaced at me. "You don't understand gardeners, Cooper, don't try to deny it. What I'm thinking is that Serenity may be able to get me seeds or clippings. *Without* stealing."

"If your tribe's headman could hear you now," I told him. "All civilized and proper! Without stealing, indeed!"

"What he doesn't know won't give him the gripes." Tunstall let Achoo have the wooden ring.

When we came to Guards House, the sergeant on desk duty told us Sir Tullus had someone with him. Tunstall hauled his orders out of his inner tunic pocket and pointed to the seals. The sergeant grumbled, but he sent a runner to inquire of Sir Tullus. To his surprise, the lad returned with orders that we were to come to the Deputy Provost right away.

Farmer Cape sat before a small table in front of the desk, wolfing a large plate of food. Seeing us, he raised a hand and waved. Sir Tullus gave the new runner orders for more food and drink not just for Tunstall and me, but for Achoo and Pounce as well. Once the lad had gone, closing the door after him, Sir Tullus said, "I know what brings Master Farmer here, but I thought you were resting up."

"We were, but Beka took a visit from one of her Birdies," Tunstall said, taking a seat when Tullus motioned to it. "One that came all the way from Corus."

"How would Beka's informants know to look for her here?" Master Farmer asked, wiping his mouth on his handkerchief.

"She doesn't have the usual sort of Birdie," Tullus explained. "Beka talks to ghosts, the restless ones that ride pigeon-back."

I squirmed on my own seat. I didn't know what to make of the look in Master Farmer's blue-gray eyes. "I've read of such things," he said at last. "I'd never thought I would meet anyone with such a Gift, though. You have your surprises, don't you, Guardswoman Cooper?"

"And you don't, Master Farmer?" I asked. He grinned at me.

Sir Tullus cleared his throat. "So who was this ghost, did it say?"

"He said, right enough," I replied. Here was the part I'd

not told Tunstall, not out in the street. "It was Lazamon of Buckglen." As they stared at me, horrified to hear the name of the murdered Chancellor of Mages, I told them the rest of it, including the spell that passed the child's pain and weakness on to his parents.

For a moment after I finished there was silence. Then Master Farmer got to his feet and started feeling inside his belt buckle. Before any of us could ask what in any god's name he was doing, we heard a click. He brought his hand up. In it was a round mirror the size of his belt buckle. The click must have been the catch that held it to the metal. "Sir Tullus, I need the most magic-proof room you have," he said. "Lord Gershom has to know right away."

Sir Tullus led Master Farmer from the room. Tunstall went to Master Farmer's plate and picked in a bowl of olives beside it. He was saved from scavenging from the plate itself when Tullus's runner brought a tankard of ale for Tunstall, raspberry twilsey for me, and egg tarts for both of us. We'd eaten half when Sir Tullus returned. He closed his door and poured himself a glass of wine from the bottle he'd been sharing with Master Farmer, but he did not take his chair. Instead he rested against the edge of his desk before us, staring into his wine.

"What's happening to the realm?" he asked softly, though he didn't seem to expect an answer. After a moment he looked at us. "Farmer has orders for you from Gershom." He sorted through his papers one-handed until he produced a sealed document. He gave it to Tunstall, who opened it and began to read. Sir Tullus continued to speak. "He wants you, Beka, and Master Farmer to wait here while Tunstall goes on to Corus. Tunstall will carry a letter for one of your friends in which you will tell her what to pack for a long Hunt." I nodded. We'd done this before. Tullus went on, "Tunstall will go on to Corus with your requirements and orders for Sabine of Macayhill to join you. Gershom wants you here because if word comes of the reappearance of those who attacked the palace, he wants you able to pursue instantly, by peregrine ship if need be. Lady Sabine will be useful in the event—in the probability, particularly considering Lazamon's statement—that you have to deal with the nobility."

Tunstall handed me the letter, grinning broadly. Of course he would be happy if Lady Sabine was to be with us.

My lord Gershom also wrote that he'd sent messages to the cities and towns on the great rivers that flowed east of the Summer Palace. The Deputy Provost in each was to report any party that included children or slaves under the age of ten to Lord Gershom by magic or fast courier, even pigeons if they had birds for the Summer Palace. We were to go where such parties were reported and Hunt them down. Sir Tullus was to go to Corus to gather other Hunters.

Sir Tullus cleared a place on his desk and set out a sheet of parchment, a reed, and a bottle of ink. "Write your friend," he ordered me. "I want Tunstall in Corus before dark."

I wrote to Kora and Aniki. I needed the cuirass that had been too big to pack last time, my weighted gauntlets and baton, and my personal kit of medicines. I had enough uniforms and stockings now for a long Hunt, thanks to Sergeant Axman, but I added three more breast bands and loincloths each to my list.

Master Farmer returned as Sir Tullus was sealing our letters. "I got word to Gershom." He poured himself ale from the pitcher and settled into his chair once more. "Beka can guess what he said first."

I had to laugh at that. I knew well the kind of words my lord would use to greet bleak news like this.

"He says he'll alert Their Majesties, though he feels telling their mages at this point is a bad idea," Master Farmer continued.

"Does he think their personal mages might be in the plot?" Sir Tullus asked. "Or would Lazamon distrust them, since they give their service to the Crown directly?"

I'd thought of that, and if I'd thought of it, I knew Tunstall had. Master Farmer grimaced. "Gershom understands the problem. He has approved a plan of mine, which I've put in motion. I called to my master."

"Bringing in a stranger?" Sir Tullus asked with a frown. "What if this master is part of the plot?"

Master Farmer picked up what looked to be a tansy cake and rolled it up. He smiled. "Mistress Catfoot is a recluse. She teaches only rarely, and she chooses her own students. I do not believe a conspiracy conducted at the palace level has touched her."

"Recluse?" Tunstall asked. "Is she any good?"

"She is very good," Master Farmer replied. "The imperial university rates her as a black robe, one of twelve now living." He looked at Sir Tullus. "She cares nothing for money or status. She would never take part in a plot that has led to so much danger for the realm."

"If she cares nothing for money or status, why would she help Their Majesties?" Sir Tullus inquired.

"She loves children," Master Farmer said with a shrug. "And she likes me. She says I'm not hopeless, at least. She wouldn't have come if His Majesty were one of those warlike kings, or if civil war were not a possible outcome of all of this." He stuck the tansy cake in his mouth and chewed vigorously.

When he caught me staring, he pointed at his stomach and said, his mouth full, "'Ongry." Once his mouth was empty, he said, "She can protect Their Majesties, as well as they can be protected against such a spell. Better, she can do it without Ironwood and Clavynger being aware she does it."

"She can't ward them completely?" Sir Tullus asked, frowning. My belly clenched.

Master Farmer looked at him and at us with something like pity. He could tell we didn't want to hear that. "The boy is their blood and bone," he said gently. "Down to the finest vein and last bit of marrow, in every hair and pore, he is both of them. There are countless doors into their bodies through that little one. No mage can block such a spell completely. Lazamon was very skilled."

"We're swived," Tunstall said gloomily.

"No, we're *not*," I said fiercely. If I let Tunstall get into one of his bleak moods, it would take a dreadful great amount of spirits and a dreadful big, furniture-breaking, wall-smashing fight to cheer him up. "Lord Gershom will get word, and we'll put Achoo on the prince's trail, and we'll find the lad and them that took him. We'll take a lunch to their execution and give Achoo a whole roast for the work she's done, my word on it."

Pounce leaped into Tunstall's lap and slipped a little. From the scream Tunstall let out, I knew Pounce had used his claws to hang on. *That's better,* Pounce said so only Tunstall and I could hear. *No sulks. I cannot see what lies ahead very far, but you will get your Hunt. Satisfied?*

Tunstall sat up immediately. "If you speak so, *hestaka,* then I am content." To Sir Tullus and Master Farmer he explained, "We get our Hunt."

Sir Tullus grinned. "I don't suppose you will say where to look?" Pounce washed a paw, and the nobleman sighed. "No, you never do," he remarked. "Very well. Tunstall, you go to Corus, now. The ship's being held for you. Hurry back as soon as you can with Lady Sabine and all she will need. They will hold a fast ship at the docks for your return."

Tullus handed the letters to Tunstall. My partner got to his feet and bowed to the Deputy Provost. He looked at me and hesitated, as if he wanted to say something more, then shook his head and left.

Sir Tullus waited for the door to close behind him before he looked at Master Farmer and me. "Cooper, see Master Farmer to your lodgings. His room should be ready by now—I sent a messenger to tell them. Master Farmer, do you need to send word for additional gear of your own?"

Master Farmer stood, grabbing another couple of tansy cakes. "I thank you, no. My lodging is in Blue Harbor, so I had the opportunity to pack more than did Tunstall and Cooper."

"I know Cooper, but I don't know you, Master Farmer," Sir Tullus said, his black eyes serious. "You mages learn to keep secrets, it's true, but this is a very big one. Don't get drunk. Don't fall in love with one of the women of the town and babble. In fact, you should go to bed nice and early. Virtue is a splendid thing."

Master Farmer saluted Sir Tullus and gave him that idiot's grin that tasked Tunstall so. I bowed and towed him out of Tullus's presence before he said aught to annoy the peppery knight.

While Tunstall and I had walked up from the docks the day before, Master Farmer had been granted the courtesy of a wagon. He, Pounce, Achoo, and I climbed in for the ride to Serenity's. It was quiet, with only Achoo's challenges, or greetings, I've never learned which they were, to other dogs along the way.

Master Farmer stretched out in the bed of the wagon and finished his cakes. "Is there a place where we can get a good meal tonight?" he asked. "I haven't been here without being too busy to try the eating houses."

I frowned at him. "Do you ever think of anything but eating?" I asked, feeling cranky.

"I can stop," he replied, and gave me that silly grin—upside down, because I sat beside the carter. "After I've eaten." He waved at his long body. "Look how much of me there is to feed. My poor old ma had to sell two of my brothers to manage it."

"She never," I told him.

"Oh, right. I didn't have brothers. But she would have, I was that big of an eater," Master Farmer assured me.

"Cracknob," I muttered, turning to face forward again. Out of the corner of my eye I saw the carter grinning.

Quiet was what I needed when we got to Serenity's. After I introduced Master Farmer to her, I told him I needed to work on my own records and to sleep for a time. He agreed that a rest would do both of us good. Looking at him one last time before Serenity took him upstairs, I realized he was tired. How much magic had he done since I saw him last?

I stepped into the kitchen and released Pounce and Achoo into the rear yard to laze, then went upstairs. I had found a book of maps in Serenity's sitting room and wanted to study it. That kept me occupied until I took Achoo for a short run. Then we returned for a nap.

I woke when someone rapped on the door. "Who is it?" I called, rubbing my eyes.

"Farmer," he replied. "We have a supper invitation. They say they're friends of yours."

I got up and opened the door. Master Farmer looked

better rested than he had earlier. He smiled at me and handed over a slate with writing on it. Reading it, I had to smile. "I know Nestor and Okha from other times I've been here," I explained. "And supper at the Landlubber's Rest will suit us both." Then I remembered Tunstall's dislike of seafood. "Unless you don't like seafood?"

"I love it," Master Farmer replied.

"Then we'll—oh, pox." I looked up at him. "I didn't bring . . . dresses. I'm on a Hunt, I didn't think I'd need them."

He'd been standing with a length of blue wool in a deep blue color over his arm. He offered it to me. "Serenity sent it, with a shift. She says she keeps such things for women Dogs stuck in the same situation." Under the dress were a few sheets of paper. "And my findings from the folk who died on the ships. Tullus forgot to show them to you and Tunstall."

With the dress and shift over my shoulder, I looked the documents over. "You get anything from the coins?" I was careful not to mention any particulars about where the coins had been or what he looked for. Safe enough to house Dogs who visited Port Caynn Serenity may be, but no one must have any suspicion of what we were doing there, all the same.

He shook his head. "Between the sea and the magic, very little information was left. Most of the holders were mercenaries. Some were slave traders. None of them expected what happened to them."

"But nothing from the amulets?" I asked, surprised he could learn from one and naught from the other.

Master Farmer shook his head. "Not the amulets. Not any of them. The few times I tried were—bad. My teacher, Cassine Catfoot—she says it's because I'm so irreverent. I think I'm just not that good with magic that touches gods."

I saw names he *had* gathered from the personal items,

a few combs, eating sticks, knives. I placed the names in my memory palace, the one I had created in my mind for this Hunt, and went on to read his notes about magic. If there were to be more mages to face, I needed to know all I could about them.

Master Farmer made note of the power he and the royal mages had placed upon the ships. That was to keep the dead from rotting before they could be looked at. The way he wrote it, such spells were like a skin that could be peeled off the body. Then he described the spells and magics that had made the crime possible. All the usual ship magics Master Farmer had thought to see—spells against dry rot and barnacles, charms for fair winds—were missing, as if the power to sink the ship and them on it had scoured those things away. The magic that had forced the ship's deadwood to grow, he noted, was a muddy color that came about when more than two magics were combined. They blended until it was very hard to separate them. Master Farmer meant to leave that for Their Majesties' mages and his teacher Cassine.

When I finished I returned the notes to Master Farmer. "Give me a few moments to clean up for supper," I told him. Pounce and Achoo slipped past me into the hall. "And don't you think you're going with us!" I told them.

Absolutely not, Pounce replied. *Cook has promised fish for me and chopped meat for Achoo. And you know I cannot abide those loud, busy places you visit with Nestor and Okha. Give them my regards.*

"They know he talks?" Master Farmer asked as I began to close the door to my room.

"He's not shy about telling folk," I said. "But he does hate eating houses and gambling places." With a nod, I closed the door.

I had only boots to wear, as so often is the case when I visit Port Caynn. I did have my Sirajit opal necklace with me, which was a bit of pretty. I stared into it for a moment, looking at its many fires, and allowing myself to relax. Then I left the room and joined Master Farmer downstairs.

Outside Serenity's gate, we turned right on Coates Lane. I watched a string of dark blue fire flow out of Farmer's chest and vanish. "What did you just do?" I asked Master Farmer. "Won't other mages know what you're about?"

"My Gift is now spread too thin for anyone who isn't looking to notice," he explained. "I don't need much to keep people from eavesdropping on us. I weave my power in with all the unused bits of charms and spells around us, and any mages that try to listen hear only street chatter. At the same time I take in all the unused scraps and keep them for myself."

I stared at him. "Scraps? Scraps of the *Gift*?"

Master Farmer smiled. "Any settled place is covered with bits of magic from old spells." He swept his arm before us as if he revealed the street, and he did, in a way. Patches of multicolored light, layered over the cobbles, buildings, carts, animals, and even the people themselves, gleamed like opals, then faded. "They're a fish-swiving beast to clean up, but if you know how to work with the stuff, there's plenty you can do with it."

"Useful," I said, impressed. "Clever. I've never heard of such a thing."

Master Farmer shrugged. "I worked it out when I studied with Cassine. Not many people realize how easy it is to collect other mages' Gifts and the scraps of power that no one ever cleans up. And this way I save most of my own Gift for other things. So tell me about you and Tunstall. How did you become partners?"

As we walked through the city I explained how Goodwin and Tunstall had me to train for my Puppy year and about Goodwin's decision to leave off being my partner to take up desk duty as our sergeant. Then I set out to learn how he'd become a mage.

"Ma was an embroiderer," he said after I'd teased him enough about it. "With two girls before me and two more after me. Pa was a riverman, gone for long times, so she sewed for rich folk that could afford really good work. They had the idea that Ma's designs had a little more to them than the plain embroiderers' work did. Not enough that she could charge mage prices, but enough that we had meat twice a week. Is that gem you wear an opal?"

"Sirajit. There's all kinds . . ." I stopped my tongue, seeing the grin he gave me. "But you'd know that, being a mage." I took it off and let him look at the stone by torchlight. He examined it as I would, angling so he found the fires that were tucked away in different parts of the stone. "I thought you were a farmer, or you let them think you were a farmer," I said.

He gave me the chain to put on once again and we continued our walk. "Well, eventually Ma purchased a farm and I worked there sometimes. But you don't learn magic that way. One day a new customer arrived to the shop. She brought her mage uncle along. I was eleven or so, not long after I'd taught myself some control over light, and I was watching my younger sisters. They were bored at their sewing, so I switched their threads for colored streaks of light. They'd sew like that for an hour at least before they got bored again, and their sewing got better. Then I could do my own embroidery with them occupied. Master Looseknot caught me making the threads for my sisters."

"What did your mama say about the streaks of light?" I asked him as we skirted a brawl in front of a drinking house.

He shrugged and suddenly I could see him as a lad, already growing big and clumsy with it, his power itching him like fleas. "I never let her catch me. She'd want me to get lessons. We couldn't really afford them. And I was already in school all morning."

"Lazy lad," I said jokingly.

"Ah, you sound like my mother," he replied, amused. "As if I didn't chop and haul wood, and mind the cow and the geese and the chicken, and work in the garden, and carry ribbon and trim and thread upstairs and down! *And* embroider for the shop when I was good enough!"

"I can see you suffered," I told him gravely. "With meat on the table only twice a week." We only had meat once or twice a month, if that, when we lived on Mutt Piddle Lane.

"Exactly!" he said, knowing I joked. "At least, I thought I suffered. I didn't know the meaning of the word. Master Looseknot, the customer's uncle, caught me that day. He talked Ma into letting me come for afternoon lessons, free of charge. He knew I would repay him."

"And you have," I said.

Master Farmer nodded. "He said there was no more he could teach me after four years, and that last year he sent me to mages all around town to trade chores for lessons. I began to travel after that, learning from whoever would teach me. By then I'd earned enough working with weapons charms and grain molds and such that Ma could hire a lad to do my work, *and* dower my sisters."

"And where did the farm come from?" I asked. I could see the Landlubber's Rest up ahead.

"That was when I found thieves who'd stolen temple

offerings. They rewarded me well and told Mistress Cass-ine about me. My reward purchased Ma's farm." He sighed. "Please tell me food is in the offing somewhere. Otherwise I'm going back to that butcher's shop, the one with the whole roasted pig in the window. It was only half an illusion."

I waved to Nestor and Okha, who stood before the Rest. Nestor grinned broadly, while Okha waved a painted fan. Since the evening was a little chilly, I was certain Okha had only brought the fan to make me envious. He always has the most interesting things.

Okha hugged me, his perfume filling the air. Both of them kissed me on the cheek and murmured their consolations about Holborn's death. The reminder shoved a spear of guilt into my heart. Truth to tell, I *enjoy* forgetting about Holborn. I enjoy being *able* to forget about him. That had to be wrong, with him barely cold in the ground. But this is my own book and I can freely say, I feel light enough to float without the worry of the last few months, about watching each word from my mouth for fear I will upset him in some way or that it will get back to him. That he will learn I was out and about with Tunstall and my friends or he'd seen me making merry with them, when he always said I never did with him.

I thanked Nestor and Okha. Their wishes came from a care for me, like those of my friends in Corus. My guilt was my own, no one else's.

Nestor had heard we were in town, of course, through the Dogs' grapevine of gossip, but he knew naught of our busi-ness. He accepted that we were bound to silence, though his raised brows and Okha's told me they were deeply curious. Gods bless them, they did not pry.

Instead they drew out Master Farmer over a splendid supper that they insisted on paying for. We traded gossip of the doings of friends in the city. Okha got Master Farmer to talk about Mistress Cassine, since Okha had heard of her. Master Farmer was an engaging cove at this sort of gathering. He was no ordinary cityman, ignorant of Dog slang or business. He even knew some Port Caynn Dogs, having worked there on loan from Blue Harbor several times. He got Nestor and Okha to laughing and they talked with Master Farmer about folk whose names I'd only heard.

I did as well as I could, since all of me itched for an end to waiting. I want the real Hunt to start. I was glad to be here with good folk like Okha and Nestor, but I *hate* waiting. Somewhere that poor prince had been pitchforked into a monstrous world, the likes of which he'd never dreamed.

After supper, we went to the gambling house where Okha sings. I was glad to hear him and to see him all done up as a lady. Master Farmer didn't as much as blink to see his supper companion transformed this way for the performance. When Okha finished his song in that deep, sorrowing mot's voice of his, Master Farmer was the first on his feet, applauding.

We set off toward Serenity's with Nestor only for company. Okha had hours yet before he would finish for the night. The coves were talking about how Okha and Nestor met and I was idling behind, listening. I was the first to hear Dog whistles off to the north, and then the brass clang of fire bells. I touched Nestor's back and stepped away in case he forgot where he was, and swung on me. He turned fast, but his fist was only half raised. (He has more control than I do, but I'm only a four-year Guard, and he's a sergeant.) He heard the noise then. We saw the source at the same time. Three blocks away a building had caught fire.

Nestor sighed. "They'll need me. I'm sorry. It was a pleasure, if I don't see you again."

"I'll go with you," I said, wanting *something* to do.

He pointed at me. "Not you, not Master Farmer. I know your orders came in under Crown seal. With that, and your not talking about them—your first duty is the Hunt." He thought for a moment and then looked at Master Farmer. "Unless . . . Master Farmer, the fire. Might you—?"

Master Farmer's shoulders slouched the moment Nestor said *unless*. The look that Achoo gives me when she's messed on the floor was in his eyes. "I wish to Mithros I could, Nestor, but I can't touch a fire. Start one, yes. Put it out, no."

Nestor looked at him thoughtfully for a moment, then rested his hand on Master Farmer's shoulder. "Sorry to press a soft spot. And we don't need healers," he said as Master Farmer took a breath. "There's plenty of them in that part of town. Gods go with you both, and Tunstall." He strode off down the street toward the fire, catching up to a pair of Dogs who'd turned into the street from an alley.

Master Farmer and I walked on in silence. It was Master Farmer who broke it. "Gershom knows I'm bad with fire."

"That's not what I was thinking," I replied.

He looked sideways at me, one eyebrow raised. "Oh? What *were* you thinking, then?"

"You can start them, but you can't put them out," I explained.

"Candle, campfire, brazier fire. It's as if once the fire gets strong enough, it doesn't *want* to be put out. Its power opposes something in my own power," he told me. "Most of the people I studied with could at least pull the strength from a fire, enough that it was easily doused with water. I can't even do that."

"It must be maddening," I said. "I'm sure they told you about it, too."

"Yes, they did. Are you thinking I'll be a weak link in the Hunt?" he asked. "I can't move weather, can't put out a fire—"

"Can see a ship on the ocean's bottom, take a person's essence from the things they've owned, sew," I told him tartly. "Tunstall can't sew. I think we'll struggle along, Master Farmer. And you cook. I mostly run with the hound, and Tunstall's cooking is, well, limited. You'll do fine with us."

He was silent for a long moment. Then he said, "It's not just that I have pretty eyes?"

I couldn't help it. I shoved him. "None of that talk, not even in fun," I warned him. "We're serious about our work."

"I'm serious, too," Master Farmer told me earnestly. "Very, very serious. Look. I'm making a serious face right now." He thrust out his lower lip. I laughed in spite of myself and rushed him along back to Serenity's. I wasn't going to let a silly man or tension about the Hunt keep me from another good night's sleep in a fine bed. Once we began, the real beds would come rarely, if I went by my past Hunts.

Monday, June 11, 249

Ladyshearth Lodgings
Coates Lane
Port Caynn
Morning.

Though I knew I had to sleep, my body was not so willing. After enough flipping and flopping that even Achoo complained and joined Pounce on the rug, I got up. I tended my weapons, sharpening my long dagger and a handful of the thin knives that served as shield, ribs, and protection in my arm guards. I gave my leather sap an oiling and checked the waterproofing on the envelope in which I keep my journal. I could hear a distant city clock strike three as, my eyes heavy at last, I blew out the candle and went back to bed.

I woke near ten of the clock by the angle of the sun. When I opened my door, I found that someone had hung a slate from the latch. The plain writing read:

> I have gone to make some purchases.
> I can use your Dog tag to reach you if
> news comes; Serenity can reach me.
> Why not go out and enjoy yourself?
> (Cook fed Pounce and Achoo.
> Pounce said they could get back
> into your room again?!)
>   Farmer

"You could have told Master Farmer how you two come and go from my room," I said to Pounce.

Where is the wonder in the world if I tell all of my secrets? the curst creature replied.

I stuck my tongue out at him, but he ignored me. I would go out, then, but my enjoyment would be of a far different kind than that Master Farmer envisioned, I was certain. I donned loose breeches and a loose shirt only, no tunic. I coiled my braid around the back of my head and pinned it securely.

Pounce, seeing what I was about, jumped up on the bed and disposed himself to sleep. Achoo, also understanding why I dressed as I did, stood by the door, her tail waving frantically.

We had not taken a real run, a tracking run, since the morning of Holborn's funeral. It was bad to let much time go by between practices. If I did, the next time I had to do the kind of running that a big Hunt required, it would be agony and I would be slow. In Corus it was my habit to run outside the city walls. Here we could run inside the city walls, which had no palace to interrupt our path.

It was a beautiful summer morning, promising to be warm. Achoo and I followed the Courier's Road up along the side of the bay. Soon all that was on my mind was Achoo, running ahead but always in my view, the thump of my feet on the ground, and the sun on my head and back. Now and then Achoo would look back at me and grin, her jaws open, her tongue hanging out. Running was her favorite thing to do, always. Our only stops were at places where she could get a drink of water. Waiting for her, I could feed Corus dirt to the dust spinners I had met on other visits and free them of their burden of city talk. I refilled my small pouches with Port Caynn dirt for any new spinners I might meet on the road after I'd done so. Dust spinners are always grateful for a taste of foreign soil, something new, and they often give me fine gleanings of information in return.

We went back to Serenity's as the city clocks struck one, not having heard from Master Farmer or Serenity. I found them eating a midday meal. "Any word?" I asked as, with my agreement, Achoo went to get the bone Cook was waving for her.

Master Farmer was gawping at me. It was Serenity who replied, "Naught."

"Then I'm off to the bathhouse," I said. "As soon as I collect a change of clothes." Since Master Farmer was still gawping, I demanded, "*Why* do you stare at me like a countryman at the fair?"

"You ran *all that time*?" he asked, plainly gobsmacked.

"Why do you think Tunstall is the cook?" I asked him. "I'm the one keeps up with the scent hound. Mostly that's on foot, to see the things she doesn't care about, like trail signs, hoof marks, or suchlike." I ran upstairs and fetched my belongings.

When I returned from bathing, things were very different. A cart loaded with leather packs sat in the courtyard. A cove, who I supposed was the carter, was carrying two of them into the house. Out came Tunstall, looking like a happy lad indeed.

"Cooper! Did you miss me?" he bellowed.

I grinned at him. "Why should I? I knew you'd be back."

The sound of our voices, or mayhap his voice, brought Lady Sabine of Macayhill around the side of the house. "Beka!" she said cheerfully. "Goddess bless your heart and Maiden keep your arm true!" She clasped arms with me in a soldier's hard grip. Just the sight of her made my heart feel light. She was dressed for the road in a brown cotton tunic over matching wide-legged breeches. Strips of gold embroidery decorated the collar and hems of the tunic. Like me today she wore her long brown hair braided and coiled, but the pins that held it in place were spiked steel, useful as weapons. Her riding gloves were tucked into her belt and she wore comfortable old boots. At her waist hung her longsword and dagger in their well-used sheaths, on a battered leather belt. She was one of those lady knights who believed in the work of a knight, not the glory of it. It was perfectly reasonable that she and Tunstall had met at a barroom brawl. I had tucked my fears for this Hunt well back, but I had not forgotten them. With my lady here, looking ready to fight and ride, several of them vanished.

"I was settling Drummer and Steady in the stable out back," she explained. "Isn't this a fine thing, getting to work with you and Tunstall? Who would have dreamed it?"

"I'm glad of the chance, though not the cause," I replied.

"No, nor would any sane person be throwing flowers over it," she told me. "But we will do our duty by the realm, and if the gods are merciful, we shall see our way clear."

"Are you going to gossip, woman, or help get all this inside?" Tunstall called cheerfully. "I'm not paying you to laze about!"

She went toward him with her long-legged stride. "You aren't paying me a copper shaving, remember?" she replied. "Impudent hill crawler!" She slung one pack over her shoulder and carried another by its strap. Tunstall had three. I gathered up what looked like a case for a bow as well as other, smaller packs. I wasn't about to say anything to the others, but the addition of Drummer, my lady's destrier, and Steady, her riding mount, was not a welcome one to me. They were a size down from the great horses bred for male knights, but they were nearabout as slow. We would have to go at their pace as much as at Achoo's. The advantage of having an armored knight with noble connections, longsword, and bow was set off sommat by the speed her horses would cost us.

We finished unloading the cart. Serenity greeted Sabine as if she had a noble at her house every day, while Cook turned out a second lunch that would have pleased anyone, let alone a lady knight. There was enough for Tunstall and me as well—more than enough for me, and just enough for Tunstall. Master Farmer joined us, too, but for talk, not food.

"What of the capital?" Serenity asked when Lady Sabine had eaten enough to lean back and take a breath. "I've heard from the great temple there that the Chancellor of Mages has been murdered and the king will not allow a replacement to be appointed."

Lady Sabine nodded. "That's only just changed this morning. For now the First Priest of the Mithrans and the Eldest Daughter are dealing with things of magic. Hereward of Genlith has taken command of the palace. The Mithrans confirm it and documents under the king's seal arrived with the orders. All those presently living in the palace are forbidden to leave it. Those who have left in the days since Gershom summoned these three"—she nodded to Tunstall, Master Farmer, and me—"are ordered to return and remain, under penalty of arrest. And the city is . . . under guard. Nobles and mages are not permitted to enter, and those who try to leave are turned back. Those who do leave are closely examined by soldiers and mages, to keep anyone who is disguised. Even the herds are being searched as they come in through the Forest Gate."

"The nobles are furious," Tunstall said.

Master Farmer rested his chin on his hand and favored us with his fool's grin. "So will the mages be."

I did not care about what went on in Corus, unless the kidnappers had taken our lad there. It was possible. What better place to hide him than in one of the country's biggest slave markets? But, were I Lord Gershom, I'd have had trusted Dogs search the prince's palace rooms and then take their scent hounds to the docks and the slave markets right off to see if the kidnapped prince was there.

The others talked, but I only listened. I was relieved when Sabine asked me to guide her to the bathhouse. When she invited me to bear her company, I did so, sitting on a bench rather than bathe twice in one day. We talked of weapons and fashions. She told me she'd seen Aniki two nights before, called out on challenge by a Rat who thought he had the right to rule her district. Sabine was proud because Aniki was putting to use the sword lessons Sabine gave her. It was one of my lady's special cuts that my friend had used to end the fight and her challenger.

Those Gentle Mother worshippers could learn a great deal from Lady Sabine and Aniki.

On our return, we found we'd been invited to a second dinner with Okha and Nestor. The good news was that there were no deaths in the fire that had called Nestor away the night before. Master Farmer had straightened when Nestor told us that. Until then I hadn't realized he'd been slouching a little, burdened by his failure to stop the fire.

Back at Serenity's, I took Achoo for a run down along the harbor and back, enjoying the sea air and the smells of fish, salt water, and tar. A couple of coves thought I looked interesting, but Achoo's instant, growling arrival at my side convinced them I was not worth the trouble.

"I can defend myself," I told her as I always do. She whuffed at me and ran at my side from then on. She doesn't believe me, though she's seen me do it thousands of times.

Once home I lingered in the backyard for a time, playing

with Achoo under Pounce's supervision. Then I sat by the little stream, listening to the sounds it made. I didn't know I had nodded off until Serenity came to wake me.

Why did you do that? Pounce complained to her. *Do you know how hard it's been to get her to sleep?*

"She'll catch her death out here, Master Cat," Serenity insisted. "You have fur, she does not. Come in or not, as you like, but she needs her bed."

All three of us returned to my room. I was awake enough to note down today's events, but now I am sleepy once more.

Please, Great Mithros, god of Dogs and the law, *please* take us back to the Hunt soon. Can't you hear that lad crying for his mother?

Tuesday, June 12, 249

begun at Ladyshearth Lodgings
Coates Lane
Port Caynn

I woke with the dawn, dreading another useless day. Cleaned up and dressed, I was feeding grain to the pigeons on my window ledge just to vex the cross-grained maid when Tunstall hammered like thunder on my door. "No lazy day for us, Cooper!" he bellowed. "We're leaving!"

I yanked the door open. Tunstall was in uniform, a heavy-looking leather package in his hands. "Orders?" I asked, my heart pounding.

"Arenaver," he said, his voice scarcely audible. "The ship waits. Breakfast and then we go." He gave me a heavy black leather pouch that clinked. "You look after the money, as usual." He drew out a thin packet made of parchment. *Cooper* was written on the front in Lord Gershom's dashing hand. "Your copy of our orders." I took it. The packet bulged with the shapes of wax seals. "And maps that my lord says are better than what you have. You may keep them after." Those came in a leather envelope, small enough to fit into the big one. I grinned at Tunstall. Everyone who knew me also knew my love of maps. Tunstall tweaked my nose. "Hurry up, then!" he ordered, and went into his own room.

Achoo and Pounce raced out the door. I knew Pounce would arrange for their meal in the kitchen. It had taken a few visits for Cook to get used to a talking cat, but now they were the best of friends.

I hurried to put away what few things lay out, then donned my tunic over my shirt. I checked my belt for all the items I needed to carry on it, then buckled that around my waist. Grabbing my shoulder pack and the lightest of my longer packs, I rushed downstairs.

A cart in the courtyard was already half loaded. Master Farmer came to it just behind me, carrying a shoulder pack and two long packs. "Would you like help with yours?" he asked me. "I've brought all of mine down."

"No, thanks," I said. "I've but the one more. Achoo and Pounce pack themselves."

He grinned at me. "See you over breakfast." He looked up at the sky, stretching. "*Gods,* it's good to be moving at last!"

Lady Sabine came around us to lay a covered bow and a pack that clanked of armor in the bed of the cart. Riding saddles and war saddles were already there. "So mote it be," she said reverently. "I've been having too much quiet of late!"

When we had everything in the cart, we had our last good breakfast at Serenity's for the time being. She kissed all of us farewell on both cheeks.

Lady Sabine had put Drummer and Steady on long reins and a riding saddle on Steady. She rode near the head of the cart while Tunstall lolled on the packs, Master Farmer sat by the carter, and I walked alongside with Achoo. Pounce rode on Tunstall's lap, flicking his tail at mere street cats.

At the naval yards we found our new peregrine ship, the *Osprey.* It was the biggest of the four at the dock, with a fierce sea eagle painted at the prow and a tall, raised afterdeck. Sailors looked down at us and spat into the water.

Dogs came from the guardhouse in front of the dock. They checked the orders that had come with the wad of documents that Tunstall received at dawn. Once the Dogs had accepted our right to sail, they stepped out of the way and let the carter drive onto the dock itself. When we reached the ship, sailors came down to help us collect our gear from the cart. Master Farmer and Tunstall were ahead of me, Master Farmer warning the crew away from his own things. I'd already put the pouch with the coin and my orders and maps in my smallest pack. I slung it onto one shoulder.

"Gods defend me," Master Farmer muttered under his breath as we walked toward the ship. One of the folk on the afterdeck, dressed in a long, pale blue tunic under a deeper blue cloak pinned at the shoulder, was waving to him. Master Farmer raised a hand burdened with the straps of three bags.

"Someone you know?" Tunstall asked quietly. The finely dressed cove was at enough distance that he wouldn't hear.

"Iceblade Regengar," Master Farmer told us, his voice soft. "Graduate of Carthak University and a snob. He bores the bones out of me."

"Good thing you'll be asleep through the voyage, then," Tunstall said cheerfully. "What does he do?"

"Besides talk about his skill as a lover and his last woman? His specialties are wind and weather magic," Master Farmer replied. "His family builds peregrine ships."

We went up the broad gangplank and climbed narrow steps that led to the deck. Lady Sabine came behind us, coaxing an unhappy Drummer into the hold. "What happens to the horses?" Master Farmer asked the sailors who led us to the passengers' cabin under the afterdeck.

"One of the mages handles them," the youngest sailor replied as he thrust our bags under the bunks secured to the walls. "She gets them to sleep layin' down. They're strapped in soft. Nothin' too good for a noble's horses in His Majesty's navy!"

We walked outside again in time to see Lady Sabine lead Steady below. Tunstall and I followed them. A small Yamani mot stood with Drummer in a stall with a straw-covered floor, keeping her hands on his side. Fleece-lined straps already circled his barrel to hold him at the middle of the stall. Pink fire shone around the Yamani as she and the warhorse knelt. When he lay on his side, she kept her hands on him. Lady Sabine shifted uneasily and Tunstall went to her, putting an arm around her shoulders for her comfort. Moving like they'd done this a hundred times before, the sailors who waited nearby fitted more fleece-lined straps around the gelding's muzzle and legs. When they were ready, the mage raised Drummer's great body some inches above the straw so that the coves could place straps along his length, under his tail and around his chest. Once the sailors finished, the mage settled Drummer again and wrote a symbol on his side. It shone in pink light while the sailors began to secure the straps on the stall and the side of the ship. Tunstall watched it all, tugging his short beard. I wondered what he was thinking about.

The mage went to Lady Sabine and bowed. "He has a big heart, that one," she said. "He will sleep well. I will stay with both your mounts, to keep them from harm." She turned to go to another stall, where other coves had begun to put the straps around Steady.

My lady looked at her two horses. "Couldn't I stay here with them?" she asked wistfully. "Just to be sure?"

"You will be in your own slumber. We cannot keep you safely here," the mage replied over her shoulder. She was already patting Steady's neck and nose.

I went above. Master Farmer was there ahead of me and had fallen into the clutches of the well-dressed blond mage he'd named Iceblade. "—nice, firm peaches," Iceblade was saying, his hands shaping the womanfruit he meant. "No pestiferous husband in the way, either—I made certain of that, this time!" The mage's eyes lit on me. He straightened, and smoothed his shoulder-length hair away from his face. To me he said, "The Gentle Mother weeps to see so beautiful a flower in the coarse gear of a Provost's Guard."

I stared at him. A worshipper of the Goddess as Gentle Mother. Did such flummery appeal to any mot of sense?

His smile faltered a little at my glare. Most folk don't like it when I'm cross with them. As Tunstall keeps telling me, the superstitious ones think I have ghost eyes, or curse eyes, because the color is so pale. Surely a mage ought to know better.

"Forgive me, fair Guardswoman, I did not mean to vex," Iceblade said.

"I should hope not," I told him. "Master Farmer, I'll be in our quarters, if Tunstall asks." Tunstall was still below with Lady Sabine.

"I'll come along," he said, too eagerly for politeness where it concerned Iceblade. "We should see what's in that bag m'lord give yeh." He sounded like an Olorun Valley farm lad now, fresh from the furrows. What was he about? "Mebbe they's messages and all innit, eh?"

Iceblade produced a great, false-sounding laugh from somewhere around his belly. "Still moving your lips when you read, Farmer?" he asked, putting a sting into it.

Master Farmer shook his head, grinning like an utter looby. "Naw, I hardly has to do that anymore," he replied. "I've got that good with the reading, these last years. Folk expect it, you know, when you do mage work. Even the Provost's Guards like to see me readin' now and then."

I thought Master Farmer wasted his time, tweaking this strutting popinjay, so I went back to the cabin. Master Farmer caught the door before it smashed shut. He held it open for

Pounce and Achoo, who trotted in past him, then closed it. "What was that?" I asked.

"I don't like him," Master Farmer replied mildly, sounding like his normal self. "He nearly cost the life of a girl lost in the swamp, telling her parents he could find her and I could not. I play the dolt to vex him, because he couldn't bear it that a seamstress's unschooled brat found the child."

"Why care what that mumper thinks?" I wanted to know.

He gave me a crooked smile. "People will do nearly anything to bring a good mage into their service. Powerful mages are happy to bind and sell their rivals and lesser mages to such persons," he explained. "For a reward Master Iceblade lets mage sellers know where unprotected mages are. I am very happy to play the fool for Iceblade, and everyone knows the Provost's Guard can't afford to hire good mages. I'm left alone." Master Farmer shrugged.

The cabin door opened, but it wasn't Tunstall and Lady Sabine who entered. Two young sailor lads had come, one with a couple of fleece pads rolled up and slung over his shoulder, the other with coils of rope.

"We're here to secure your animals," the redhead of the pair explained to me. "So they'll be comfortable, like."

I didn't wish to discuss such vile things anymore, so I turned my attention to the new problem. "The cat," I said. "If you could put him together with the hound?"

"He'll stand for it?" asked the redheaded lad, happily surprised. "We're going to bundle them up, mistress. He might not like it."

"They're friends," I explained. "They'll do fine." Achoo wagged her tail and tried to wash Pounce's face.

The redhead pointed to the other lad. "*He's* my best

friend, and I wouldn't share a bunk with him," he told us as he and his friend covered the bunk with fleeces. "He snores. And farts." The older boy gave him a sharp elbow to the ribs. The redhead patted the fleece. "If the hound and the cat will come up?"

"*Bangkit,* Achoo," I said. Up she leaped, Pounce following her onto the bunk. Soon the lads had secured them with straps.

As they were finishing, Tunstall and Lady Sabine came in. Tunstall gave each lad two coppers. "We'll strap ourselves in," he told them with a wink. "Why don't you come check us before we set sail, so you know we did it right and can tell your captain so? We need a bit of privacy just now."

The talkative redhead touched two fingers to his forehead in a salute. "Aye, Guardsman. Actually, we're only raisin' anchor now. You've a little more time to settle and buckle in before they put the sleep on folk—got to clear the harbor traffic first. Safe voyage to us!" His friend gave us the same salute. Once they left, I took off my shoulder pack and tucked it between me and the wall.

Tunstall looked at Master Farmer and tapped his ear, raising an eyebrow. The mage smiled and looked at the floor. I didn't see the color of Master Farmer's Gift, though I felt it. The air in the room relaxed suddenly; my skin stopped prickling. Over our heads I heard a cove's voice—Iceblade's?—raised in startlement and anger.

Master Farmer looked up. "If he were wise, he would ask himself how I could do that," he said. "Instead I'll wager any amount you care to name he's telling the others one of you must be a mage as well."

Tunstall took the leather pouch from his pack and opened

it. "Each of us gets our own copy of our orders," he said as he gave theirs to Master Farmer and my lady. "My lord wants to be certain none of us risk ourselves while on this Hunt. We each hold true Crown documents in case we are separated."

I opened my envelope of maps as the others read through their papers. Each covered a section of the realm in the finest detail I had ever seen. One set showed rivers and lakes marked out in blue, cities and large towns labeled clearly. The other set was of noble and temple fiefdoms and Crown lands, the owners of the realm. I know Lord Gershom had not meant these for birthday or Midwinter presents, but this was like a lifetime's worth of gifts all at once.

I like maps very much.

"Lord Gershom sent word to those Deputy Provosts he could trust in the Three Rivers Province and along the coast between the Summer Palace and Frasrlund, telling them we seek any party coming from Blue Harbor or thereabouts with a child aged about four. He gave them the date of the disappearance," Tunstall said as all of us got comfortable on our fleeces and bunks. He looked at a paper he'd taken from the leather pouch. "Two days after we left Lord Gershom," he continued, "my lord had word from the District Commander in Eversoul. Just such a party came to town along the Ware River in the north. The party numbered two mages, one a mot, one a cove, three other women, and five small children. He says—" Tunstall read, "*All of the children were less than six years of age. I sent orders that they were to be detained if possible, followed if not. It was too late to catch them in Eversoul. By the time they got my orders, all of the children had been taken on ships on the Arenaver. At dawn on the eleventh I had word from the Deputy Provost in Arenaver that four groups answering my description,* two of them small slave trains, had come from the south, three by land, one by ship. The District Commander there sent two Dogs to track them, but he has not heard from the trackers.

"Proceed to Arenaver. Take up the most likely trail if the Deputy Provost is unable to detain all of those suspected. Master Farmer will sort out false clues and confessions. If you lose the trail, proceed on your own. I will get information to Master Farmer as often as it is available." Tunstall looked up. "There's an emotional bit at the end." He cleared his throat. "You four are the best possible team I can field. You have my faith and that of Their Majesties."

"But we can't be the only ones!" Lady Sabine said, shocked. "We can't possibly cover the entire realm, and who knows how many people are in this vicious scheme?"

Tunstall opened the last fold of his document. "Oh, yes. He writes, I am assembling other teams and have been doing so since the day after we arrived here. You won't be in the field alone! Better, my dear?"

"Gods be thanked." Lady Sabine lay back on her bunk with a sigh. "What do we Hunt? From what I read in the papers Gershom sent to me, these swine have left us precious little to start from."

Master Farmer was toying with a stone globe the size of a walnut, producing tiny sparks of fire with it. "I'd been thinking we ought to look at slaves—" he began, just as Tunstall said, "It's the slave trading that has my eye." They stared at each other.

Since the lads were startled that both of them had come to the same conclusion, I explained, "These Rats came in disguised as a slave-raiding party, took captives like they were taking slaves, and brought at least one slave trader ship. Why do such things when they destroyed the evidence at the palace?"

"Because the slave items were the materials some of the raiders had at hand?" Lady Sabine asked. "Perhaps some of those still alive have ties to slavery?"

"We think mayhap so," Tunstall said with a nod to her. "They took every caution, but they knew there was a chance that evidence would be found. Slave trade is big enough and messy enough that we might get tangled up just tracking the ships or the chains."

Master Farmer locked his hands behind his head. "From that idea, what easier way to hide the lad than in a slave train roaming the countryside? It's summer. Dozens of traders are on the roads and rivers."

"But now we've got this information to follow," Tunstall went on. "We'll look at the evidence in Arenaver. If these travelers don't give us something to chase, we'll follow the slave ship builders."

The ship was moving out into the river, swaying gently under us. I'd seen no oars when we boarded. I suppose the mages filled the sails with wind they had summoned and directed the ship as they willed. "They'll change the lad's appearance, no doubt," I said to my comrades. We seemed to have silently agreed to refer to Prince Gareth only as "the lad," which I thought was a good idea. There was less chance of letting his true name slip that way. "Darker is my guess, since he's fair-haired and fair-skinned. And there are plenty of brown-haired, hazel-eyed four-year-olds out there."

"It will take them time to toughen him up," Tunstall said. "His hands and feet will be soft, his skin white."

"There are stains for his skin," Lady Sabine replied with a grimace. "Walnut juice, properly applied, takes *months* to fade. I know."

"Are they clever enough to avoid using magic on him?"

Master Farmer wondered aloud. "That will be the first thing I look for. A child who's magicked will stand out in any group." He was digging in his shoulder pack.

"They've been evil clever so far," Tunstall said. "I don't see them getting cracknob pox so late in the game."

"Does Gershom mention a ransom note, or a threat?" Lady Sabine asked. "Surely these people want something from Their Majesties. They must have sent their terms by now."

Tunstall riffled through the rest of the papers. "Letter of credit—copies of our orders for each of us—no other notes, my dear."

"Lazamon didn't mention ransom," I reminded them. "He wants Their Majesties to die. My lady, did you hear of my conversation with him?"

Lady Sabine nodded. "Tunstall has told me all of the information you have." She began to do up her straps, but Master Farmer raised his hand.

"One more quick matter of business," he said. He was holding something. "On your feet, please." Tunstall and my lady stood. I joined them as Master Farmer gave us each a round piece of smooth obsidian secured at one edge with a silver clasp. I recognized them as the magic devices called Dog tags. Goodwin and I had used them in Port Caynn three years ago. These looked the same: one side plain, the other with a compass cross cut into its surface and painted white. An *S* was engraved at the end opposite the clasp, to indicate south.

"Each of us must take the stone in our right hands and pile our fists together," Master Farmer instructed. He extended his own right hand turned up, the obsidian gleaming between his fingers. Lady Sabine laid her hand atop his, palm down. He did not correct her, so Tunstall set his right hand palm down atop the lady's, and I completed the stack.

"Now," Master Farmer said, "each of us must choose a color—bright, to stand against the stone."

"Crimson," said my lady.

"Green," Tunstall announced.

"White," I said, thinking of the greatest contrast to the obsidian.

"And bright blue for me," Master Farmer said. "Close your eyes. Think of each of us, carefully, one after another, as we know each other, even if it's just been for a short time. Be sure to consider all four of us, so the tag will show us together."

I had done this imagining with Goodwin. Tunstall was quickest in my thoughts, my big old owl of a partner, who loved flowers, and went mad in a fight, throwing furniture to take down two and three Rats at a time.

Lady Sabine I'd seen too in fights, back to back with Tunstall, control to his fury, her brown eyes intent as she dealt out punishment. But she was elegant in private. Dressed for home, or for one of her family's many obligations, she took my breath away. She had cool humor and a kind heart for the street children who waited for her behind Tunstall's lodgings, feeding them leftovers from meals, letting them into the cellar on cold winter nights where they'd find blankets, a fire, and hot soup.

Master Farmer for me was all questions, grim attention, or folly. It was interesting that he kept his power hidden from his fellows. I wondered if he was like me, not wanting too much attention from those who were stupid, arrogant, or simply bad. He seemed very strong for someone who had not studied at the great schools. Master Farmer was so casual with the little magics. And he was quick with humor.

"There," he said, and I opened my eyes. We all checked our tags. Each had four glowing dots at the center of the cross. I quickly unclasped the chain on which I wore my Dog's insignia—leather only for one more year!—and threaded the tag onto it, then hung both around my neck. The others did the same, Lady Sabine with the chain upon which she wore amulets for Mithros and the Maiden as warriors, and Master Farmer with the chain on which he wore his lens.

Overhead we heard footsteps approach. As I fetched the bag with the bracelets charmed against seasickness from its hook, someone banged on the cabin door.

"Open up!" Iceblade shouted. "Open—" The door swung wide. He flailed and caught himself before he went face-first into the floor. Tunstall snorted. Lady Sabine, always well bred, turned away to hide a grin. I picked leather brace-lets from the bag and gave them to my companions.

"That wasn't funny!" Iceblade snapped, glaring at all of us equally. "Who's working magic down here? We're going to place *our* spells at half of the hour!"

Lady Sabine drew herself up like a queen. "Master Mage, have you a reason for interrupting us? Or do you interfere strictly to make a nuisance of yourself? We are engaged upon *serious* matters."

Iceblade's skin paled under its tan. He even seemed to shrink a little under my lady's imperious stare. "I came to say *all* spellworkings must end. The horn marks the beginning of our speed *and* of the sleep spell!"

My lady raised her chin. "So you have informed us. You may go."

Dismissed, he had no choice but to walk out in a hurry. He didn't bother to close the door. Slowly, as if mocking his hasty exit, the door closed itself. The bolt slid into its socket, shining with blue fire. More such magic collected in the corners of the room and stayed there, glimmering. We all looked at our mage.

Master Farmer shrugged when I glanced at him. "I would hate it if any of the crew went through our packs while we slept," he explained. When my lady and Tunstall raised their eyebrows at him, he added, "I'm not saying they would. I just don't want to invite them to an occasion of bad behavior."

"We all need to be more watchful than we've ever been before," Tunstall said as I donned my bracelet. He buckled himself into his bunk. "Assume as of now that we cannot trust anyone but ourselves with our business." He grinned at Lady Sabine as I got onto my bunk and did up my own straps. "What brought on your wrath with Master Iceblade, my lady?"

"He is the kind of bully who gets the serving girls in corners and roughs them up," she replied as she buckled in. "I don't want to be asleep with someone like that able to enter my room." She smiled at Master Farmer. "Thank you very much, Master Cape."

Without the straps, I would have jumped high enough to smack the ceiling of the cabin when that curst great horn bellowed loud enough to deafen us all. Achoo fought her bindings. Her shrieking bark told me that she was frightened half to death. "Achoo!" I shouted. *"Diamlah!"* I tried to undo my straps so I could go to her. *"Diam—"* The poxy horn blasted again. I dropped, half hanging out of the bunk.

I have Achoo. I could not tell if Pounce's voice was in my head or in the cabin, as my ears still rang. My hound settled, wriggling down into the fleece. Pounce lay against her shoulders, one forepaw around her neck, his chin on her head.

I pulled myself back into the bunk and hurried to do up the straps. It was near impossible—the sleep spells had begun. My hands felt little better than sausages, so clumsy they were. Then I saw dark blue fire. My head cleared. I finished the straps and looked at Master Farmer. "Though I don't like being magicked, I'll forgive you for it this once," I said. "Thank you."

He smiled drowsily at me and closed his eyes. A moment later, I did the same.

Tuesday, June 12, 249

Arenaver and points east

When the sleep dropped from us, I pulled a back muscle fighting to escape the straps, the bunk, and the cabin to reach the ship's rail to puke. If Master Farmer had not woken and raised his spell that kept the door locked and the bolt frozen, there's no telling what sort of mess I might have made in there. Of a certainty my belly threw every meal I'd had in some days out into the Tellerun's waters, and mayhap even my hopes for future meals. At last I could heave no more. By then my cabinmates were being sick in their turn over other parts of the rail.

"Here yez go." It was the dark-haired ship's lad, the one who'd said not a word before. He stood at my elbow, offering me a thick mug. I was almost afraid to touch it, in case my heaves might begin again, but the scent that came from it was one of gentle herbs, a tea that meant well by my poor tripes. One sip, and I felt my belly settle.

"I don't understand," I said once I'd drunk a bit more. "This didn't happen the last time we took a peregrine ship. Those leather bands are supposed to keep this from happening!"

"Oh, they stop ye from pukin' in yer sleep," he told me. "Didja eat afore ye came aboard last time?"

"No," I said, thinking that it would be a dreadful thing if Pounce and Achoo were vomiting in their fleece. "I came to that ship in the middle of the night." I turned to go back, but here they came, Achoo dancing with pleasure at being outside.

I let us out, Pounce said. *Since you were busy.*

"Well, that's the explanation," the lad said, plainly not

hearing the cat. "Ye had a full belly, and ye was under the sleep and the ship at full speed for nigh twelve hours. Anyone pukes with that."

I stared at him. "And the rich folk *like* to travel this way?" I asked.

He gave me a cheeky grin. "Ye think they go like ye done? Four hours under the sleep, and we wake 'em, let 'em walk the decks a bit, then back to the cabin they go. Four more hours, we put in, rouse 'em, rub they feet, bow and scrape, then back to sleep they go. And when they get where they're goin', they say how wearied they are."

I finished the tea and returned the mug to him. "You're a saucebox, laddybuck," I told him.

He laughed and ran back down into the hold with the mug. He left me smiling. My brother Willes is much like him, so I have a soft spot for cheeky lads.

He returned with the other boy to offer the tea to my friends while I gave Pounce and Achoo a good petting. I judged my human companions were not ready for talk. The ship was being towed stern forward to dock by two smaller craft, now that it was too close to land for the mages to thrust it against the Tellerun's current. I leaned against the rail, Pounce on my shoulder. My duties had never called me to Arenaver before. I looked at the city that rose on the point above the joining of the Tellerun and the Halseander Rivers.

Arenaver is not so big as even Blue Harbor, let alone Port Caynn or Corus. It's a port for lumber and mining, so there were plenty of barges tied up at the docks on both sides of the point as we passed it on the right. The dying sunlight gilded them and the old gray stone walls of the city on the height. The docks lay outside the walls' protection. The locals did not trust their trading partners to visit peacefully from the river, it seemed.

Great forests grew on either side of the rivers, rising on the slopes of tall hills. Despite the season, they kept the air cool and comfortable. The sun was already halfway below the horizon, and the voices of tiny frogs and big ones filled the air under the noise of the docks.

Hammering footsteps came up from below. Iceblade stepped onto the deck, his hair uncombed and his clothes rumpled. "Master Farmer!" he snapped. "Farmer Cape! You are going to tell me how in Mithros's name you managed to put a blocking spell like that on your cabin—a spell none of us could budge!"

I watched him approach Master Farmer, who was finishing off his tea. Did all the mages who worked these ships concern themselves with what took place in their passengers' cabins? Might they be Ferrets, or might there be Ferrets among the crew?

Iceblade seized Master Farmer by the shoulder. "Answer me, clodhopper! How did you do it, a dolt like you?"

Pounce leaped down from my shoulder and trotted over to Iceblade. Now what? I wondered, but I said naught.

As slow as a tortoise in autumn, Master Farmer looked at the hand on his shoulder, then along Iceblade's arm, and up to his face. At last he gave Iceblade a large, silly grin. "I practiced," he said.

"Practiced?" the mage snapped, his face crimson. "You could no more do work like that with *practice*—"

Pounce rose on his hindquarters, forepaws up. Gently he laid them on Iceblade's thigh and began to knead, digging his claws into the mage's silk robe. Iceblade yelled and spun, striking out at Pounce. The cat leaped straight up and hooked himself into Iceblade's chest with all four paws. When Iceblade seized him and yanked him away, Pounce left four holes in the gold embroidery there.

"I'll *strangle* you," Iceblade threatened the cat. That was when Pounce vanished clean out of the mage's grip.

Master Farmer made it back into the passengers' cabin, but the whole ship heard his bellows of laughter. Lady Sabine, who'd been cleaning her face with a cloth fetched for her by the redheaded ship's lad, used it to hide her grin. Tunstall didn't bother to conceal his. Iceblade glared at everyone, even the laughing sailors and his amused fellow mages, and returned to wherever he'd stayed below.

"The count's castle is north of his walled city, where the peninsula narrows." Master Farmer had left the cabin again. He pointed over my shoulder, past the walls. "Count *and* governor of the district. He's fair, but strict. His lady's one of those iron-spined sorts. The heir's a nasty bit of work. When he inherits, I mean to stay out of the area."

I glanced up at him. He was ready to go, his packs hanging from his arms. From the way they drooped, they were heavy, but he gave no sign that their weight distressed him. "You seem to know him well."

"I got some work here when I was studying with twin mages in the city," he explained. "I worked for the count and his lady for two months." Master Farmer shook his head. "Rabbits in the gardens, mold in the grain, damp in the linens. Small things that make people irritable in winter or during a siege. I got it sorted out—I have a knack for house and garden magic. My lady made sure I had warm clothes and boots that fit, for a while." He smiled at me. "I was growing again."

"How shall we do this?" Lady Sabine asked from behind

us. We turned to look at her and Tunstall. The ship was coming into dock on the bank of the Halseander, sailors leaping down to tie her off as others lowered the anchors. Once the ship was steady, the horses' gangplank was set out, and the great horses were led safely to land.

"We need mounts and packhorses, and we must check in with the Deputy Provost," Tunstall explained, watching my lady as she took charge of Drummer and Steady. "We'll need the latest reports from her trackers. Supplies, too."

I saw movement at the warehouse that stood open nearby. Three Dogs in uniform walked out of it leading horses, three with riding saddles, seven with pack saddles. Two of the packhorses were already laden—supplies, I was near certain.

Tunstall smiled. "We're expected." Picking up as many of Lady Sabine's packs as he could lift in addition to his own, he went to meet the local Dogs. Master Farmer gathered the rest of the packs as I tucked Pounce into the top of my shoulder kit. I had given up putting Achoo on a leash years ago. She never strayed from her position just off my left side when we were in a new place, just as now.

As Master Farmer and I settled our packs on the mounts that would carry them and chose riding horses, I listened to the local Dogs report to Tunstall.

"—didn't get the rain folk that's come upriver complain of," the corporal said. "Been dry, so the farmers are tellin' us. They're sellin' off children to pay the tax."

"Not getting much for them, either," one of the others, a mot, said. "The littles are bone skinny, half dead."

"There's a crazy hedgewitch, gets drunk off Market Circle," said one, a Senior Dog. "She told any that would listen all our rain was stolen by a southern mage. She said she'd put a blood curse on 'im. We escorted her home—" He interrupted himself to say, "Now *that's* a fine piece of horseflesh, there. Who's the noble?"

Tunstall started to frown, so I kicked him in the ankle. Lady Sabine could handle disrespect if she felt she needed to.

"The destrier is called Drummer," Farmer told the Senior Dog. "The palfrey's Steady. And that is my lady Sabine of Macayhill, who's well beyond loose-tongued folk!" Any other cove might have gotten the back of the Senior Dog's hand for that, but the cheerfulness in Master Farmer's eye and the Dog insignia hanging on his chest just made these tough woods Dogs grin or nudge him. They bowed as Sabine approached.

"Good evening to you," she said, letting Tunstall hold Steady, who was saddled for riding. "Now, if one of these fine packhorses is for my things—oh, splendid, she's all ready! I just need to put her on a string with my Drummer, here."

While the Dogs eagerly offered their help, I noticed familiar signs in Achoo. I motioned for Tunstall's attention and pointed to a corner a little way down the street in the long shadows to let him know we were moving back. He nodded, familiar with our routine. Away my hound and I trotted, staying clear of those who were ending their day's labors.

Achoo took care of her business. Then she sniffed around, learning about everyone else who had favored that spot, or so I supposed. I looked back at our welcoming party. Everyone was chatting, building good will with the locals. When I turned back to Achoo, I found she had moved away from me. She was casting, sniffing back and forth an inch above the ground. She trotted a yard down the street, then another.

"Achoo?" I called quietly.

She replied with a near-silent whuff, one that meant "Don't bother me, I'm busy."

"Achoo!" I said a little louder.

She sneezed. Her tail began to wag furiously. Then she sneezed twice more. She was on a track, her nose right at her own height, on a proper scent. There was only one scent that she was supposed to be chasing right now, and she had it.

"Achoo, *berhenti*!" I cried. She halted and looked back at me, whining her protest. She wanted to chase that scent *now*.

"Tunstall!" I shouted. *"Tunstall!"* He faced me. I pointed to Achoo. Even in that light I could see Tunstall's eyebrows go up. He ran to me, Master Farmer and the lady at his heels. I reached into the side pocket on my shoulder pack and brought out the sealed bag with the prince's sample in it.

"She has a scent?" Tunstall asked when he reached us. "She has *that* scent?" He tapped a finger against his lips to warn me to speak carefully.

I held the cloth lure to Achoo, who sniffed it and danced, panting eagerly. She sneezed again. I put the lure in my pack. This way I didn't have to say anything to Tunstall. Achoo had done so for me.

Now came the local Dogs with the horses. "How shall we manage this?" Lady Sabine asked. "We must still report to the Deputy Provost to find out if her people are already on this path and whether or not more information has come from the capital."

Master Farmer was doing something with the horses. He said nothing.

"The Deputy Provost did say you was to report to her as soon as you docked." The corporal's voice was apologetic, but firm.

Tunstall took a deep breath. "Cooper, Farmer, you're on the scent. Now's the time to learn if your tags work, Farmer."

"I'm hurt that you'd think they'd fail. Hurt," Master Farmer told Tunstall, sorrow in his voice and eyes. He brought the horses forward. Now I saw what he'd been doing. He'd been tying his packhorse and mine into a string. "Cooper, will you ride?" he asked.

I shook my head. "I'd like to stay on the ground with her, for a while, anyway." I took off my shoulder pack, which I'd donned before leaving the ship, and retrieved my stone lamp. The bits of white crystal speckled throughout the gray stone burned as brightly as they had when Master Farmer first lit the rock up. I tucked it in my pocket and put my pack back on as Tunstall murmured to someone behind me.

A local Dog went over to a nearby ship and talked with one of the officers. Coins changed hands as Lady Sabine and Tunstall spoke quietly together.

Set me on one of the packhorses, Pounce ordered. *You know I hate it when you run.* I transferred my entire pack to the horse who looked to be the calmer of the two. Pounce was usually good with horses, but I liked to be careful, for the sakes of the horse and of my friend.

The Dog who'd done business at the ship returned with a burning lantern. "He won't get in trouble with his captain?" my lady asked.

The Dog grinned. "He *is* the captain, my lady," he replied. "And I paid him twice what this is worth, fresh filled and all." Master Farmer took the lantern as Tunstall tied my own saddled mount into Master Farmer's string. All this while Achoo had been whining, half out of her nob with eagerness.

"Go," Tunstall ordered. "We've got the Dog tags. We'll catch up."

I didn't wait to hear any more. "*Maji, maji,* Achoo!" I said. Off she went, sniffing the air that carried the prince's scent. I followed her, steadying into a run. She turned down a long street beside the heights that guarded the town. She took no turns that would lead to the gates of Arenaver. Whoever had the prince, they had not entered the city.

The road began to climb the riverbank and the sky got darker. We finally passed the great gates, running parallel to the road between the city and the count's castle. About a mile past the city walls Achoo led me off the dock road. Here was a grassy area that had been torn up by a multitude of wagons. Plenty of animal dung was smashed there by feet and wheels. Beyond this hitching place Achoo sniffed her way across grass that was pressed flat and covered with fruit and vegetable husks, gnawed bones, ends of ribbon and scraps of cloth, tags of leather, heaps of wood shavings, and patches of grease. She was circling a place that had been well pissed and shit on.

"It was a fair, don't you think?" Master Farmer had halted the mounts just inside the range of my stone lamp. The light from his lantern doubled the area I could see.

"Two days ago," I said as Achoo sneezed and moved away from the spot where several people were kept for hours with no privy at hand. "The piss is dry, the dung mostly so."

"A country matter," he said. I looked up. The air around him sparkled. "Small charms, amulets, talismans were being sold, potions and herbs." The sparkles brightened. I looked away to keep my sight from being affected even more than it was already by our lanterns. "Hah!" Master Farmer said, satisfaction in his voice. "There's the great Gift, or Gifts. Two powerful mages stood here." He pointed. "Looking at the slave area. Hmm." He looked at the patch of grass and dirt that had caught Achoo's attention.

Now my hound ran onto the road. "Is something wrong?" I asked Master Farmer as I kept an eye on her.

"Thought-provoking, not wrong. Do you need a horse yet?" he asked.

"No—I can run for hours," I replied. Achoo had almost reached the trees.

"Go!" he ordered. "I'll catch up. This will be but a moment and some magic. The mages who travel with the slaves—I can gather samples of their Gifts."

I would have liked to hear more, but Achoo was off. I left him there and raced to get her in view. We continued for two miles down the riverside road, where we found a ferry landing. Achoo ran onto the dock where a flat-bottomed boat lay at anchor, and whined, sniffing it over. Seeing a ferry parked on the other side of the dock, she jumped onto it.

"Hey!" a man yelled. "If she pisses in there, you'll pay for the cleaning of it!" A broad fellow stood in the door of the ferryman's house, a club in his hand.

I trotted up to the ferry, wondering if he'd charged his loads of goats, horses, chickens, and pigs for cleaning, too. From the odor, mayhap he had. The planks smelled of strong soap, though the scrubbing could not do away entirely with the animal reek.

"Moonhead! Chase! Brushtail!" The ferryman, or guard, put two fingers to his mouth and blew a whistle that hurt my ears. Three hounds scrambled into view, big ones, ready to fight for their master.

I held up my stone lamp and pulled out my insignia. "Ferryman, if you'd used your eyes, you'd've seen I wear the uniform of the Provost's Guard. That's a scent hound in your ferry, and we're on a Hunt."

The ferryman walked forward. I released my insignia and gripped my baton in case the cove decided to dance a set with me. Instead he halted two feet back and squinted at my insignia. Achoo, noting that a stranger had come too close to me, raced to my side and waited there, hackles up.

"If you're a Dog, what're you doin' out here by yourself?" the cove asked. I could smell ale on his breath.

"Following my hound. The rest of my Hunt's catching up," I said. "We're following a party with a small boy, four years or so."

He snorted. "Good luck to you. Between the families and the fair merchants and the slave caravans that've crossed these last six days, you've a lot of folk to speak with! We just had the Strawberry Fair. Folk come for miles to buy and sell. I have to hire extra asides my boys and me."

I looked about for his "boys," not liking the thought that they might be stealing up behind me.

"Not here," the ferryman said as if he knew my mind. "They have work in the city, they told me. 'Work!' says I. 'Public houses, like as not!' But they labored hard on the barges, so I don't begrudge them."

I had his measure by then. After four years of Dog work, I'd learned to weigh folk and judge how much harm they had in them. This cove would be a hard customer if I tried to take advantage of him, but he'd prove no trouble if I was honest. "Achoo, *bau,*" I ordered.

She hesitated, but she went to sniff the second boat she'd inspected. The ferryman's hounds watched, but they did not interfere or move from his side. Once Achoo had gone over the ferry again, she sneezed heartily. Our quarry had crossed the Halseander in that one.

"I'll need you to take me over," I told the cove.

He looked down at me. "No more will I, till others come!" he said, cross as a wayward rooster. "Take a bit of a wench like you across, and no one else? You'll wait for more passengers, mistress, even if it takes till dawn! I'm not a lad. I'm a father with a bad back!"

I did understand, but I wouldn't delay, at least, not after Master Farmer came. "I expect my partner shortly," I said. "And our horses. *And* we'll pay, though by law we don't have to. You needn't have kittens over it."

The ferryman spat on the ground. "*If* you've a partner and horses. Why couldn't you have come earlier, when there were more folk crossing?"

I glared at him. "Because I wasn't *here* then. And they say we mots complain!"

I saw a lantern's approach, above the ground. *Pounce?* I called silently, so as not to bother the nervous cove. *Is that you?*

Me, and Farmer, the horses, and some fleas. Pounce's voice came back to me. *You seem to be enjoying yourself.*

I snorted and went to the side of the road, where I saw a number of stones. I began to put down a trail sign that would let Tunstall know we had crossed the river on the ferry. I was almost done when Master Farmer and the horses drew up. "Trail sign?" he asked. "You don't trust my Dog tags. My feelings are shattered. Just . . . shattered."

I crossed my arms over my chest. "What a folly lad you are," I told him. "If I *don't* leave it, even with Dog tags, Tunstall will worry that something's happened to me—and to you, for that matter."

"That's so lovely of him," Master Farmer told me as he slid from his horse. "And I was thinking he didn't like me." Sounding much more official, he turned to the local cove. "Ferryman, we need to cross sooner rather than later, I think." Master Farmer looked at me. "I take it the scent brought Achoo to the ferry?"

"She even chose a boat," I said, pointing. I went over to Pounce, enthroned on horseback, and scratched his ears.

"Well, let's go," the ferryman said. "I'd like my sleep yet tonight."

He grumbled, of course, when we chose not the boat that was ready, but the one that held Achoo. I thought we would have to listen to him all the way across the river, but Master Farmer slipped him a silver coin. Seemingly that was all the cove wanted, because he fell silent.

The ferryman was not exactly honest about his help. Mayhap his sons were in town, but a blast on a horn brought his wife and two daughters to help row us and our horses across. All the mots had good strong arms and were far more cheerful than their man.

While they worked, I took out my map of the district around Arenaver, studying it carefully. It looked like there were very few notable roads between here and the Banas River, since none were indicated on the map. Mapmakers usually only noted roads that would take heavy wagons. There was a marsh, a sizeable one, but someone had gone to the trouble to build a bridge across it. Hills were lightly marked in several areas along the road. There were no goodsized towns between here and the Banas, either. As with roads that couldn't take big wagons, mapmakers ignored anything smaller than a town of two thousand.

The moment we touched shore Achoo cast around only briefly before she sneezed and ran down the road.

"Achoo, *tunggu*!" I cried, looking about for stones.

Master Farmer, helping the ferryman's daughters to lead the horses off the boat, saw me collecting rocks. "Trail sign? I'll do it," he said as a young mot fluttered her lashes at him. "I *have* done country Hunts before."

I waved my consent and took off after my hound, easing into my run and holding my fastest speed until I could see

Achoo clearly once more. Then I settled back into the trot I could hold for hours, if need be. I thought of our early days together, when I'd believed a couple of hours at the run was hard work, and smiled at myself. The years behind Achoo had toughened me!

I looked back. Master Farmer was gone beyond sight. He'd been keeping the horses to a walk, so I wasn't surprised. He would catch up.

The deep woods surrounded us, filling the chilly air with the scent of pine. It was impossible to accept it was June out here. I was glad that my running would keep me warm. I held my lamp down by my hip to light the road ahead. Achoo's coat was a pale spot in the dark. I tried to keep to the hard places in the road so I would make less noise. The odds were against any bandits out there on a night that did not follow a holiday or market day, but I preferred to give them as little warning of my approach as I could.

All that met my ears were the sounds that I expected, the ones made by owls and small creatures in the undergrowth. A doe and her fawns startled Achoo and me alike, running across the road in front of us. A raccoon, sitting on a tree limb just over my head, gave us his opinion without niceties.

My lamp did not only show me rocks and ruts in the beaten earth. On its edges I noticed traces of unshod feet and the occasional wheel track where a wagon had swerved. Now and then the smells of scummer and piss struck my nose where folk had done their business to the side of the track. I'd bet a week's wages these leavings were those of the slave train. I stopped a couple of times to pick up bits of leather and cloth. I might need them someday, to track the slavers if we lost the trail of the prince.

I caught up with Achoo when she stopped at a stream for

water. I was about to scramble down to join her when I heard several horses. I tucked my lamp in my tunic and thought to hide in the brush when I saw the light and recognized the horses.

"Wait," Master Farmer called.

I waited, as much to tell him, "Don't shout out here!" as to find out what was so important I couldn't have a drink first.

He dismounted while I scolded. "You're right. Next time I'll wave like this." He waved his arm broadly twice. I eyed him, not sure if he was mocking me or not, as he went to the horse that was laden with packs I didn't recognize. "I think," he said, undoing a set of ties, "that these contain water. And I gave it a touch as we rode, so it's clean." He handed a water bottle to me.

I removed the cork and was about to drink when I had a silly thought. Or it may have been silly if I was on an ordinary Hunt, but was it silly now?

"When I gave it that touch, I also checked for poisons," Master Farmer said quietly as if he heard my thoughts. "I expected you would ask me to."

I grimaced at the bottle in my hands. It was discomfiting to have my mind known so well by someone who was a stranger. "Good thinking," I replied carefully. He was four years older by my near-certain guess, and I did not want to give offense by grumbling.

"Yes, it was," he said with such good cheer that I suspected he knew exactly what was on my mind again. I glared at him, but he was staring up at the trees, innocence in every line of his body.

I snorted, and took two deep swallows of the water. It was very good. I would have hated to slow us down while I shit my tripes out because someone had dumped offal upstream—or while I died of poison or spells. I wiped my mouth on my arm. Achoo was already on the roadbed, tail wagging. I slung my pack around and took out a couple of strips of dried meat. "Pounce, do you want any?" I asked as I fed her.

I thank you, no, he replied from his seat atop the light-colored packhorse. Everything had happened so fast I didn't even know the horses' names. *I am enjoying my ride.*

"I'm wondering if we ought to wait here for Tunstall and my lady," I said to Master Farmer.

"Let's go on if Achoo's up to it," Master Farmer said. I couldn't tell if he really meant was *I* up to it, but said Achoo so I wouldn't snap his nose off. "Arenaver's Deputy Provost is a stickler for procedure. She'll want to go over everything. And the destrier will slow them down."

"I'd forgotten about Drummer. Pox and murrain," I grumbled.

Master Farmer shrugged. "It can't be helped. Let's hope he and Steady are worth the extra trouble. In the meantime, I think we should keep going. Tunstall and the lady will catch up with us eventually."

"So they will," I replied. It was no use grousing. We had to go forward.

I don't know how long we followed that rolling stretch in and out of the trees. At least an hour later we passed through an open part with a big pond on one side of the road. The air smelled of damp earth and greens, while frogs and owls held their nightly gossips. Luckily for us it was too chilly for the biting insects to be out and about. I saw a few lights at the far end and guessed it was a village. Master Farmer put a shadow over his lantern so that it gave out just enough light for him to see the road while I covered all but a spot on my stone lamp.

Neither of us wanted anyone who might be up to see who was on the road so late at night.

When the ground began to rise, I decided there was no point in trying to show Master Farmer how tough I was. The muscle I had pulled before the boat landed was making my back hurt. It was time to ride. I think I disturbed the horse saddled for me. He snorted and shook his head as I took his reins from the string with the three packhorses. "Sorry to wake you," I said, tipping his face up. "Did you think you were on holiday?" I stroked his neck, then blew carefully into his nostrils to make his acquaintance.

Treat her well, peasant, or you will deal with me, Pounce called from his throne.

The horse very carefully turned until his rump faced Pounce, raised his tail, and let fall a great pile of manure. He stopped, waited for a moment, then did the same again, as deliberately as Pounce would have done himself.

Insolent mortal, Pounce grumbled.

Master Farmer was laughing into the crook of his arm to keep the noise from carrying. I thought he might strangle at first. Finally he raised his head and wiped his streaming eyes. "I didn't think . . . gods or . . . horses . . . had a sense of humor," he said, gasping for air as he spoke.

"He's a constellation, not a god," I said as I gripped the saddle horn. The horse looked at me. "With your permission, good sir," I told him, bowing. He snorted. I took that as a yes and mounted up.

Achoo whuffed impatiently, not liking the pause. She thought we had taken enough time for a change of transport. She didn't understand that when the work was so dire, it helped to have a laugh now and then. "Coming," I said, and nudged the gelding forward.

On we went as the road continued to rise. I put my stone lamp away, happy to rely on Master Farmer's lantern. He'd picked up a long tree limb somewhere. He hung his lamp from one end and held it out well in front of him to show the way. It revealed hoofprints and cart tracks in the road as well as the normal bumps.

"Why don't you just magic up a light?" I asked him, trying not to shiver. Now that I wasn't running, the cold was starting to nibble at my skin. "It'd be easier."

"Mayhap so, but not as wise," Master Farmer replied, his eyes focused on the edges of the road. "We'd be in a fine pickle if I wasted strength on keeping a light in midair, only to need plenty of my Gift further along. Your lamp is different. I didn't have to keep using my power once it was made. If I find a big enough piece of crystal or rock mixed with it, I'll make another, but there's no sense wasting this lantern."

It was a little comforting to know he didn't have so much power that he could use it on all of his chores.

"Cooper, are you sure we're on the proper trail?" he asked. "What if they've dropped a lure for Achoo?"

"She got a strong scent," I told Master Farmer. "If it was a lure, the scent would fade. The real one stays strong. Our lad gives it off all of the time. Besides, there's signs from the slave caravan all along the road." I pointed out the middens and the resting places on the roadside as we followed Achoo through the high point of a small pass cut through hills. I was guessing that they were hills. They were marked as such on my map of the district, where they ran between Arenaver and the Halseander River. We never could have told their height then, the dark being so thick and the stars being blocked by clouds.

"So these bits of piss and scummer help Achoo, even

200

though they're more than a day or two old?" Master Farmer asked.

"Very much so. That strong smell hangs on long past scent in the air, and the drops of liquid stick to the ground and the ground cover." I smiled. "I hate the stuff most of the time, but when I'm out with Achoo, it makes my life so much easier."

He fell silent. We both did as we rode on and up. Over the top of the pass, the breeze rose, plucking at my sleeves and making me shiver. I turned and grubbed in the packs on my mount. I hoped that my coat was here and not among my things on one of the other horses.

Master Farmer settled the branch on which he carried the lamp between his knee and his stirrup, and opened one of his own packs. "Here," he said, holding out something bulky and dark. "This will keep you warm."

I accepted what he offered, shaking out the folds. "A *shawl*?" I asked, startled. I hadn't worn one since I got my Dog's coat.

"I like shawls," Master Farmer said. He sounded a little defensive to me. "I hate having a draft on my neck, and I hate having my arms hampered. I tie a shawl right and my neck and back are warm while my hands and arms can move as I need."

The shawl was a big one. I wrapped it around me and draped one end over my back to hold it in place as we continued to ride down. New smells reached my nose from the folds: spices and musk, burned wood, wax. I remember thinking that this must be what mages smell like, before I raised my face to look ahead. New scents were coming on the breeze that flowed through the pass, too, odors I commonly think of as green ones. They are those of broken and rotting greenery and wood, the water in which those things rot, and soggy earth. The scent was heavy enough to worry me. I nudged my mount into a quicker walk, almost a trot. He picked up his pace without complaint. Master Farmer took his cue. I still kept an eye out for leavings from the slaves. They must have entered a clearing to one side. Crushed grass and footprints leading to and from the road told me that a large group had stopped there. Were they moving slowly enough that we might catch up with them in the next day or two?

The road was steeper than it was on the way up. The forest was shrinking, opening on both sides. Then we heard Achoo give a mournful howl, her sign that something had gone amiss. Master Farmer and I urged our horses into a trot. "Is she hurt?" Master Farmer called to me.

"No. Something's mucked up her Hunt," I replied.

When we reached Achoo, I found the source of the newest smells. A marsh lay on both sides of the roadbed, which had been built up a little ways into it. Achoo stood at the end of the road. Beside her was the beginning of what must have been a good bridge at one time. It thrust no more than a foot away from the land before it ended in blackened timbers.

I slid out of the saddle and went to look at the swine-swiving mess. Behind me the lantern light brightened until I could see clearly out into the marsh for a good way, which was part of the issue—it *was* a good way, yet Master Farmer's mage-light did not touch the far side. What it did show was smoke-marked stone piers that crossed the marsh, some with a few bits of charred wood stuck to them yet. I crouched beside the ruins on the road and broke off a piece of wood. Achoo whimpered and paced back and forth, stopping twice to nudge me in the back as if she said, "Can't you *do* something?"

"Master Farmer, we don't need so much light," I reminded him.

The light shrank until it reached just a foot beyond me.

The smoke drifted in the air around us. The thick boards that remained within reach were cool, so it had been more than a day since the fire, but not much more. The smoke would have been entirely gone in that case. I swiveled on my toes to check to either side. There was a well-used footpath leading away on my right. On my left was a small road that led north, skirting the marsh. If there was a village or town nearby, it would be that way. I heard nothing but the cheep of crickets and frogs and the sounds made by calm horses.

I lifted the bit of wood close to my nose and sniffed. Under the odor of burned wood was another smell, one I knew. I took the piece away, snorted to clear my nose, then brought the wood up again. I knew that scent. Tunstall and I have worked enough burnings-for-hire for me to recognize magefire when I smell it.

I rose and carried the piece of wood back to Master Farmer. He smelled it and said, "Magefire."

"Craven canker-licking sarden arseworms," I said. I wanted to break a few kidnappers' heads just to relieve my feelings.

"I think you're being too kind," Master Farmer replied, turning the wood over in his fingers as if it might talk to him. "What's the matter with Achoo?"

"She's poxy mad with frustration," I snapped, "aren't you?" Then I looked at her afresh. She had run a yard down the footpath, away from the road, then back to the bridge. She turned back and forth for a moment, her movement saying as clear as Common that she was torn between two problems. Then she trotted down the footpath that short distance, only to return. Something that bothered her lay not far down that path, close enough for her to smell. It also gave off an odor she recognized as one she would follow while on duty. Only another official business smell would distract her on a Hunt.

I took my baton from its straps and drew my horse's reins over his head, leaving them to drag on the ground so he would not stray. Master Farmer had dismounted and let the reins to his own horse hang. He lifted his lamp from the long stick in his right hand and nodded for me to take the lead.

"*Dukduk,* Achoo," I ordered her quietly. If the problem was close by, I would not need her skills. I also did not want to risk falling over her if we ventured into the tall reeds that bordered the path on both sides.

As we went forward, the closest frogs fell silent. Nearby I heard a splash. We had frightened one into the water. The crickets were undaunted, and continued their calls.

We had not walked more than two yards along the path when Master Farmer halted, covering his nose with his free arm. I nodded and tugged him along. Now the smell was as obvious to us as it had been to my hound back on the road. No wonder Achoo had been worrying her poor head over which scent to follow. She knew she was supposed to pursue the prince *now,* but we have Hunted for corpses so often that she may have thought she had to get both.

The Dog lay half in the water, half out, just ten feet from the road. Animals had been at her legs. When we pulled her from the water, we saw fishes had been at the rest of her. Her tunic was untouched in the front, no holes or slashes. There were no strangler's marks that I could see on her throat, but they could have been destroyed. Her insignia, brass, hung on a chain around her neck. I took it in my hand and turned it over. Her name was carved there—*Palisa Vintor.* Her district, *Arenaver.* Her years as a brass badge, four strokes cut into the metal. She would have gotten her silver badge next April.

I told Master Farmer all these things, hearing my voice as if I stood away from my body. I sounded polite and quiet. I'd retreated into myself as I always do when it's a woman, a child, or another Dog. I don't want to show weakness. I let myself be another mot who knows how to look at the dead without making a looby of herself. "Would you help me turn her, please?" I asked.

"Are you all right?" he inquired as he gently set Vintor on her right side.

"It's my work, Master Farmer," I replied. I held my stone lamp close to the body. No slashes or holes on Vintor's back that I could make out, either. "Curst if I know how she died, unless she was strangled and the signs are hid under the damage. You can put her back now."

"These Rats are profligate with their magic," he said, making the Sign on his chest. I did the same. "They've got so much they spend it like water. Good. They leave more for me. Cooper. They smothered her at a distance—probably from the bridge—and sent the slaves to hide her. They left too much magic on the Guardswoman, and the slaves' hands left their marks. I suspect guardswoman Vintor here is one of the Dogs sent to follow the new arrivals by the Deputy Provost."

Her purse flapped open and limp on her belt. I checked and found it empty of anything, coin or orders. Next I took off her boots to see if she'd hidden orders there. They were empty, though Vintor had slender pockets in both for just such a purpose. Had she stitched them there herself? I wondered.

I had to look inside her tunic, but cutting it open would take even more dignity from her. Instead I cut the cloth along the side seam and reached in that way. No documents. If the Deputy Provost had given her written orders, the slavers would know there was a Hunt for them, or someone like them.

"May I do *my* examination?" Master Farmer asked me when I rocked back on my heels and sighed. "I was asked to do more than carry a lantern and mind the horses, you know."

"I thought, all you told me before, you'd done your examination," I said.

"That was just what I knew after casting a general spell," he replied. "I've yet to *truly* examine her, which means you and all those charms you carry—my tag, the spelled mirror in your belt pouch, the Goddess and Mithros charms on your belt—need to get back. That magic will interfere."

My irritation broke the idea of being somewhere else that I used to keep myself strong. I glared at Master Farmer, thinking, Forgive me for being needed in the Hunt at all! But I backed up to the edge of the reeds on the far side of the path from the marsh. He told me when to halt. *Mind my tail,* Pounce said. I hadn't seen him arrive. *I want to watch.*

"I'll try not to disappoint," Master Farmer replied, rubbing his hands together. "But this won't be anything complicated. Just something basic I created for Dog work." His eyes were intent as sparkling fire spilled from his hands to Vintor. It spread over her like honey, coating her from top to toe. As it filled in the spaces where the fish and the animals had gotten to her, I saw her body take shape under it—eyes, calves, nose, throat. When she seemed whole again, the fire vanished, leaving only a corpse untouched by anything. The effect was not one of solid flesh, but more like a painting that was a little sheer. It was solid enough to show no sign of scarf, belt, or cord around this Dog's neck.

The illusion soon faded away. I bowed my head and made my prayer to the Black God.

"So mote it be," whispered Master Farmer when I was done.

"What now?" I asked. "We cannot go forward." It was one thing to follow Achoo. It was another to sit in the middle of no familiar place, our lad's scent in midair with no way to follow it, a dead Dog on our hands, and no Tunstall to make decisions.

"I want to seal this poor mot off from more damage," Master Farmer said. "If you and Pounce will move well back again?"

As we obeyed, the sparkling fire that Master Farmer had used to blanket Vintor once reappeared, as if it had only seemed to vanish before. The bits of white fire grew thicker, until the entire corpse shone. They faded. Now Palisa Vintor looked to be sheathed in glass.

"I don't know our next step," I admitted to Master Farmer. "On my own I'd go find the nearest village. We need to cross this marsh, and word must be sent to the Deputy Provost that one of her people is dead here."

"Then let's pitch camp—maybe on the other side of the road, for all our sakes—and wait for Tunstall and the lady," Master Farmer suggested. "I don't suppose Achoo will be happy, but she won't like it when we take her around the marsh, either. Unless you mean to take her straight across somehow?"

I was grinding my teeth. "Cod-kicking craven churls," I muttered to myself. "Bad enough they've put us off, but they've bum-swived every last local and traveler, burning that festering bridge." I went to the road and considered the marsh. If I cut a long pole to test the bottom in front of me . . . Achoo could swim the water and walk the reed islands to follow the scent in the air. She'd done it before. I could swim the deep spaces, but not with the gear I needed for a long Hunt. Going alone was a risk, but gods rot these mewling, snake-hearted villains, they put even more sarden ground between us as we stood yattering there, and they were already a day or two ahead.

Camp, Beka, Pounce said. *When you're reduced to swearing and grinding your teeth, you're too tired to choose well. I can feel at least one ten-foot drop-off within six feet of that bridge. There's one that's not just twenty feet deep, but thirty foot wide beyond those first two hummocks there.* He wound around my legs, purring. My eyelids felt heavy. I barely noticed when he began to lean against my calves, nudging me toward the small road that led north. Achoo ran ahead of us, though she often looked at the marsh and whined. Master Farmer came behind us with the horses.

We found an area back from the northern road, screened by the trees, yet still within hearing of the main way. One thing I can say about camping by a marsh, the grass was thick and green. Without talking, Master Farmer and I cared for the horses and picketed them where they could graze. We were about to settle ourselves when I noticed that Achoo stared toward the road, her ears up, her eyes alert. I hand-signaled Master Farmer to look at her. Then we heard the sounds of approaching riders. Lantern light shone just over the brush that screened us from the road.

I was drawing my baton when Achoo whuffed, her tail wagging. Then I heard Tunstall's familiar voice say, "Mithros's balls, where's the boar-buggering bridge?!"

"Put out another bowl, Mother, we've company for supper," Master Farmer murmured. We both walked out to the road, Achoo racing to meet our companions.

Tunstall was at the remains of the bridge, dismounting from his horse. Holding a lantern of his own up high, he was cursing our prey steadily, not repeating a single word. I still do not have Tunstall's skill in swearing.

Lady Sabine waited on Steady three horse lengths to Tunstall's rear, Drummer off the horse string at her side. The lady must have thrust the pole from which her own lantern dangled between the branches of a nearby tree, because there it was where none had hung earlier. She had a small round shield on her right arm and her sword in her left hand as she waited for us to come into view. Had we walked straight into the main road to attack Tunstall as bandits, the lady knight and the warhorse would have been on us in an instant, Drummer and Steady smashing us with their hooves while Lady Sabine cut us up.

Now, seeing Achoo, and then Master Farmer and me, she grinned and sheathed her blade. Drummer snorted and did some quick turns in the roadway to relax as Steady and Achoo watched. "Don't mind my fellow, there," Lady Sabine told us. "If he can't fight, he needs to cool down a little."

"Cooper," Tunstall said, still looking at what was left of the bridge, "report."

"The scent goes that way," I replied. "And we can't. There's a raw Dog over there that Master Farmer preserved in glass or sommat." Folk that aren't Dogs exclaim sometimes when they hear one of us report the death of one of our own. Do they expect us to go down weeping? There's the work to finish. Tearing clothes and sobbing won't help a lost Dog. Vintor would be avenged only when her killers were hung.

"We're betting that this Dog, Palisa Vintor, was sent by the Deputy Provost to chase one of the two slave trains that came to Arenaver in the last few days," Master Farmer explained. "She had the misfortune to find the people who have our lad. They have two very nasty mages with them."

Tunstall nodded, tugging his beard with his free hand. "The Deputy Provost told us Palisa Vintor went after the smaller caravan, and she had not reported in," he said. "The other three tracking Dogs came back with reports that ruled out the remaining targets."

"These slavers have him, we know that," I said, offended anyone might think otherwise. "Achoo's never wrong."

Tunstall looked back at me and smiled. "The Deputy Provost doesn't know Achoo. *Hestaka,* it's good to see you." Pounce jumped up onto his shoulder. "Cooper, finish your report."

I told all the night's events to him and the lady as they'd happened. When I finished, Farmer added what he had learned.

Tunstall sighed and spat on the road. Then he said, "Take me to Vintor."

"You don't need me for this," Lady Sabine reminded us. "Where are the other horses picketed? Mine could use a rest from the saddle."

"One moment, my lady. I'll go with you," Master Farmer said. He raised his hand, palm out, in the direction of Vintor's body. For a moment he closed his eyes. Then he opened them and nodded. "You'll be able to examine her now, Tunstall. I'll enclose her again when you're finished. My lady?"

My partner and I set off down the path, Pounce still riding Tunstall's shoulders. Achoo thought that she ought to come, but I sent her back to Lady Sabine. It was silly to let my hound be upset all over again by the encounter with a dead human.

The glasslike covering that Master Farmer had placed around Vintor was indeed gone. Tunstall examined her as I answered his questions.

Pounce stayed on Tunstall, balancing easily as he shifted. "Have you an opinion, *hestaka*?" Tunstall asked him.

You are all weary, the cat said. *You need rest, for the horses if you will not take it for yourselves. You are lucky it was but a bridge destroyed, and not fighters left to take you. They do not think much of you at the moment.*

"Swive what they think of us," I said.

Tunstall patted my shoulder. "Pounce is right. As for this poor mot . . ." He sighed. "We must get word to the Deputy Provost, the first chance we have. She can send people to take Guardswoman Vintor home."

We walked back across the road and along the lesser track in silence. Pounce jumped down from Tunstall when we reached our campsite, and trotted into the woods. I was about to tell him to stay close when I realized my folly. Pounce has never gotten himself into trouble that I know of, while my own record is not so clean.

Master Farmer and I had stumbled across a favored travelers' site when we'd left the horses there. He or Lady Sabine had cleared out a stone-lined fire pit that others had built near the edge of the trees. They had a pile of dried wood nearby and a fire already blazing where the lady, Master Farmer, and Achoo now sat. The pit was so well set in the ground that it was only when we came into the cleared area that we saw the fire. No one on the main road or across the marsh would see the flames, and the dead, dry wood ensured that the fire gave off little smoke. The scent of cooking sausages was another matter. My belly growled. I remembered that I'd thrown up my last meal.

Lady Sabine had unpacked a small basket onto a spread cloth. "The Deputy Provost gave us this in addition to the supplies already packed," she explained. "There's Galla pasties, parsnip fritters, lamb cakes, and nice, dark bread rolls. Ale for those who want it, raspberry twilsey for the rest. Chopped meat for Achoo and Pounce. Achoo has already eaten her share." Lady Sabine pointed to a space behind Achoo where Pounce was eating a small pile of food. There were signs that another such pile had been next to his, but only a few bits of meat, small enough for Achoo to miss in the grass, were left. Achoo now busied herself with a bone.

I took out one of my many handkerchiefs and folded it over, then chose what I would eat. When I sat between Lady Sabine and Master Farmer, she passed a cup of the twilsey to me. Tunstall had yet to sit. He'd wandered over to the edge of the marsh to think.

"You made good time catching up, better than we expected," I said to my lady.

She laughed. "Master Farmer here said the same thing. My family has been breeding ladyhorses for generations. They may not have liked my choice, but Father said he was cursed if a Macayhill, *any* Macayhill, would serve the Crown poorly mounted. Drummer and Steady are faster than any other knights' horses I've known."

"I still wouldn't put any coin on them at the races," Tunstall said, returning from his thinking spasm.

My lady smiled up at him with just her eyes. It was an interesting trick. I wondered if she was trying to be proper and not let the love between them creep into our Hunt. It still showed. It put a needle in my heart. Had I ever looked at Holborn that way, even in the beginning? I didn't believe I had.

Pounce rammed himself under my right elbow. I ran my fingers into his thick, soft fur and let it warm my fingers. *Thank you,* I thought to him as hard as I could.

He butted my thigh with his head. *Stop hating yourself because of him,* he ordered me. *Holborn wasn't good enough.*

You didn't even like him, not at first, not by the end. You just loved him for a short while.

"What are your orders, then?" Master Farmer asked Tunstall. "Since you're in charge."

Tunstall tugged his beard. "This road is traveled enough. There are always villages in marsh country—the living's good. We'll follow this road north and see if there is a village where we can get someone to take a message to the Deputy Provost about her missing Dog. We need a ferry across the marsh"— he looked at the horses—"or another bridge. What about it, Cooper? Are villages or bridges on one of your maps?"

"This bridge was on the map, but no others," I said, recalling the district map from memory. "And no towns are marked hereabouts, either. Or villages, but they never mark villages."

"From the path here, I'd say there's a village," Tunstall said. "Cattle tracks, sheep tracks. If we don't have a village or ferry, we're swived, and we'll have to go all the way around the curst thing."

I fetched my pack and found the waterproofed leather envelope with its precious documents. I gave it a more thorough search than I had on the ferry and discovered a second map of the area, labeled *The Tellerun Valley to the Great Road North.* It had more details than the district map. I spread it open and found the land between the Tellerun and the Halseander Rivers. There was an area colored blue. Written small over it was the name War Gorge Marsh. I used the first joint of my thumb, which was almost exactly an inch of length, and placed it along and across the area marked as the marsh. I checked it twice, to be sure, muttering "Pox" to myself when it came out the same both times.

"If I've worked the change from inches to miles right,

this festering slice of mud is near forty miles long, with us right in the middle," I told the others. "It's eight miles wide at the widest part and six at the thinnest. There's no road of any kind marked either on the far side of the marsh or on this side of the bridge going to the southern end of the marsh. The only village is in that direction on this side." I looked up to see that Master Farmer was staring at me. "What?" I asked.

"I don't think I've heard you say so many words in the entire time I've known you," he replied. "Is it because you're tired? Is there something in the lamb cakes, or the marsh air?"

Tunstall grinned, the mumper. "Cooper likes maps."

"She talks enough, when you know her," Lady Sabine added.

I scowled at the document before me. I was going to ignore Master Farmer. What could I say, after all? Just because I'm no jaw clacker doesn't mean there should be a ruction put up whenever I have sommat to say. "There *is* a village, seven miles down this road," I told them. "I don't see marks for any other bridges but the one that got burned."

Tunstall sighed. "We'll go around if we must, then, but if our luck's in, the village will have a ferry. They can't manage with only one bridge. Very well. It's an hour, mayhap two, after midnight. We'll take a four-hour rest now. I'll have a one-hour watch. Sabine the second, Cooper the third, Master Farmer the last."

I wondered if Master Farmer would know when to rouse us, then realized that he must. Good mages learn to track the sun and moon whether they can see them or not, so they work their spells properly. Kora can do it, and she never pretends to be any greater than a hedgewitch with bite.

Lady Sabine and Master Farmer did not wait for Tunstall to change his mind. They wrapped themselves in blankets and lay down. My lady used her saddle for a bolster. Leaning against it, she seemed to plan to sleep sitting up. When she saw me looking at her, she smiled. "If I sleep flat after a meal, it comes right up. Annoying, but better this than puking on the good bed linens."

I had it in mind to write in this journal for an hour before I slept, but Tunstall would have none of that. "You can write in the saddle, I've seen you do it," he told me sternly, taking my shoulder pack from my hands. "Bank the fire and sleep, Cooper."

I did as ordered. Achoo and Pounce curled up with me, which was a comfort. I slept.

Wednesday, June 13, 249

The valley of the vile, poxy, sarden marsh

The sun was not quite up when Master Farmer made us a hot herbal tea that definitely roused us. "It's wake-up tea," he said when Tunstall eyed him blurrily. "It's herbs I've gathered from different places. Surely you can taste the ginger and cinnamon."

"I don't want anything that might addle me," Tunstall told him as he slowly drank.

"I wouldn't dare," Master Farmer replied. "Cooper would crack my head with her baton. I shudder to think what your lady might do."

"It's fine stuff," I said, drinking all of mine.

"Have a second cup of this, Mattes," Lady Sabine told him, her voice gravelly. "It's the smoothest such tea I've ever had. Ye gods, I think every mosquito and midge in the swamp found me last night." She scratched the back of her neck.

Master Farmer looked from her to Tunstall. They were scratching necks, hands, foreheads—every bit of skin left uncovered for the appetites of the local bugs. I shrugged when he glanced at me. Since making friends with Kora, I'd not suffered so much as a fleabite. Her balm's also been splendid for winter skin. Heavy though it was, I had a jar of it as big as both my fists in one of my packs. Had I not been so tired, I would have remembered to offer some to my companions.

Master Farmer looked sheepish. "I should have thought. I have a little rune. If you don't mind, I'll put it on the three of you. It's good for four months. There isn't an insect that will bite you while it lasts."

Tunstall stuck out one of his ham-sized fists. "If you sold it, you'd be a rich man."

Master Farmer etched a design on the back of Tunstall's hand. It sparkled briefly and faded as Master Farmer murmured something to himself. Then he said, "I do sell it, in a few shops that sell creams and scents. I fix it to a honey balm a friend makes, and we give it a wicked price. The wealthy pay, and her children have decent lives."

He did Lady Sabine's hand next, then turned to me. I thought about refusing, then scolded myself silently for being a looby. I put my hand out and thanked him in advance. Master Farmer began, then stopped. He raised his eyebrows at me. "It's very nice, that cream you have on. Clever. Not your magic, though."

"My friend's," I explained.

"Will you introduce us?" he asked. "She's got a wicked sense of humor tucked in there."

I nodded, though how he guessed that from a charm in some cream I had no idea. I hoped he didn't have notions about Kora. I would have to mention casually, somehow, that she was taken.

Once I'd had my tea, I was awake enough to realize I had slept in Master Farmer's shawl. I shook it out and folded it, then returned it to him. "I'm sorry."

He put it in one of his saddlebags. "It holds up well," he said. "It's gone through worse than sleeping on the ground. Did it keep you warm?"

I nodded. "Thank you for the loan of it."

"Anytime you want it, ask. I have three packed away." When I looked at him, he grinned. "I like to be prepared."

"And I hate fellows like you who are cheerful before dawn," Lady Sabine grumbled.

We all had two cups each of that excellent tea, then cleaned the camp and resupplied the woodpile. Only when the campsite was as clean as we'd found it did we fit out the pack-horses and saddle our mounts. I fed my riding horse an apple from the supply I'd put in my packs, and checked the pommel of his saddle. There was a name etched there. I squinted to see it. This dark brown fellow was called Saucebox.

Remembering his smelly remarks to Pounce last night, I told him, "You're well named." The gelding looked back at me and snorted.

"Let's mount up," Tunstall called. "It's going to be a long day."

Pounce chose to ride seated in front of me, as if he wished to remind Saucebox who was a person and who was a horse. Achoo trailed with the pack animals on my string, whining and halting to look back at the remains of the bridge. Her scent was there. We were riding away from it. She also knew she could not walk across empty air or marsh water.

"You could comfort her, Master Pounce," Lady Sabine said as she dropped back to ride beside me. "We cannot explain things to her, but you can."

I have explained to her, Pounce replied. *Otherwise you might have been forced to bind her feet and tie her to a horse. She is a simple creature, my lady. She only understands so much.*

I sympathized with Achoo. It bit to ride away from the enemy's trail. I did not look forward to going around this entire marsh, either. These villagers must have a ferry, I reasoned. They wouldn't put up with dependence upon a bridge seven miles away.

Yet I remembered other marsh dwellers I have met since pairing up with Achoo. They tend to keep to themselves, marsh people, distrusting anyone who doesn't share their lives between land and water. They like to live well away from the world, and they like to keep their secrets. The ones I had known were not very helpful at all.

Our road turned and twisted along the edge of the marsh. We found other small bridges over streams that cut the road on their way to the shadowed masses of green and open water on our right. Unseen birds were beginning to sing as the sky grew pale. As the sunrise lit the eastern mountains, we halted on one of the longer bridges to stare out over a broad expanse of water, edged all around by islands of reeds. A heron, blue and immense, took flight, trailing his heavy legs. He startled several egrets, who flapped into the air in his wake. I held my breath at a sight so beautiful. The rest of the water, the part they had not disturbed, was as smooth as glass.

Tunstall clucked to his horse and rode off the bridge. The rest of us followed, still in silence. Pounce sat up—he'd been sleeping curled between my legs—and looked out over the water.

You should have seen this three thousand years ago, he said. The others looked at us as he stretched against the edge of the saddle. *This place was not quiet or beautiful. The Searflame dragon family came here to their final battle with the Ianto clan. They belonged to the immortal race called the Ysandir. The Ianto were smiths—makers of fearful weapons. Dragons and Ysandir, they cut deep trenches in this land and tore huge boulders from it to throw at one another. The trenches later filled with water from underground springs. It's called War Gorge Marsh, and the humans don't even remember why it has that name.*

"You tell it as if you were there, *hestaka*," Tunstall said.

I was, Pounce replied. *They wrecked so much of this country that the Great Gods came to put a stop to it. I kept the Goddess company. The Ysandir would not listen. Their offensiveness*

219

began the war with the Great Gods that ended in their defeat. It was the first time that humans fought on behalf of the Great Gods.

"I've read about the Ysandir," Master Farmer said. "Nothing good, but I've read about them." He yawned.

Pounce leaped to the ground. *They had good music. I do miss that.* He trotted off into the reeds.

We rode on quietly. The others talked from time to time. I drifted to the rear and took out my journal. I had to grab every chance that came to me to write in it, or despite the memory exercises I'd learned in training, I would start to forget small details. Even using my own code of symbols I had barely covered the events of the 12th when I heard a rough cove's voice say, "And who might you folk be?"

I hurried to jam my writing gear and my journal into their waterproofed case, taking a glance to see what was up. We had reached the center of the fields around the village the map had promised. A cove with a fishing pole and basket blocked our path forward, as if he alone could stop us. Beyond him I saw lamps burning through open windows. I could smell baking bread and frying bacon. My belly growled.

"You can see our uniforms, Master Fisherman," Tunstall replied. "We are a commission of the Provost's Guard, under orders from the Lord Provost himself. We need to speak with your headman immediately, and we need a messenger to go to Arenaver."

"Do you just?" replied the fisherman. "Well, you may talk to the keeper of our public house, for all the good it will do you. The Sign of the Trout." Without even a word of farewell, the rude mumper walked on past us, past me, without looking up.

Master Farmer sighed. "Rural folk," he said. "They make you want to move right in and take up a collection to beautify the town square. This is why I took work in Blue Harbor."

"A friend of my mother's once told me that a mage who gets in a rut ceases to learn," Lady Sabine told him as we rode on to the village. "Look at the favor we are doing for you."

"I have been looking at it," Master Farmer said. "The writing of that favor begins to look forged to me."

"You're being a baby," Tunstall told him. "There are plenty of mages in the City of the Gods who would be happy for a bit of adventure right now."

We passed through the last fields and found that our road was the village's main street. People had gathered there, mots, coves, and little ones, to stare at us. Seemingly strangers were not common. Tunstall spotted the Sign of the Trout and drew up there. It had rails for horses, an interesting touch for a place that doubtless saw very few riders. We hitched our mounts to them. Pounce and Achoo stayed with the horses. The rest of us walked inside the public house.

I had time to see the place was being cleaned by a mot and a gixie before Tunstall ordered, "Cooper, take the door."

He wasn't comfortable here, either. I drew my baton and turned my back on the room, standing in the open doorway. Anyone who chose to join the conversation from outside would need to come at me, and I would warn the others. I held my baton two-handed, at hip level, and pretended to ignore all the village folk who stared at me. Achoo came to stand at my side. She could tell things were tense, the local people suspicious of us.

"We need to speak with someone of authority," I heard Tunstall say. "We were told to ask here."

"I'm the headwoman," someone replied. It must have been the heavyset mot who'd been scrubbing tabletops. "Tell me what it is you're after, whoever you are."

I heard the crackle of parchment. "I am Senior Corporal Matthias Tunstall of the Provost's Guard. Here is my pass from the Deputy Provost of this district. My companions and I are on a Hunt," Tunstall explained. "First of all, the bridge across the marsh seven miles back has been destroyed."

"We know," I heard the younger mot say.

"Cork it!" the headwoman snapped. "Go on, Guardsman."

Tunstall ignored the headwoman, who did not use his rank. "Have you a ferry? We must get across the marsh as soon as possible."

There was a long silence behind me, so odd it made the skin between my shoulders prickle. Finally the mot said, "Ferries in the marsh? Are you crackbrained, man? There's no waterpath wide enough nor straight enough for a boat that might fit even half of you folk and your livestock."

I glanced back. Lady Sabine had drawn herself up at the insult to Drummer and Steady, but the headwoman wasn't even looking at her.

I looked outside at the gathering villagers as the headwoman went on speaking. "We get about the marsh here as our fathers and mothers did, and their fathers and mothers before them, Master Senior Corporal. They had no bridge to keep their feet dry."

"That one only brings us trouble—it's not close enough to bring us good," a cove said. His voice came from inside. I did not dare turn in case those in front of me tried to attack, but I twitched. Where had this fellow come from? He said, "It's too far for decent folk to walk. Trouble hereabouts comes on horseback. The bridge be gone, you say?"

"Burned down to the stone piers," Tunstall replied. He didn't sound at all worried. Of course, one time I'd thought him dead asleep before his fist lashed out and broke a Rat's jaw. With Tunstall it's sometimes hard to tell.

"Then how do you cross the marsh?" That cheerful, casual voice was Master Farmer's.

"Shank's mare," the cove said. "And you'll need a guide. As you take the north road, seek the last cot on the left, with a shrine to Merscart of the Green on the north side. Ormer will take you on from there."

I heard the shift of clothing. "How do we know this Ormer is trustworthy?" Lady Sabine asked.

"He'll be with you, won't he?" the headwoman demanded, her voice sharp. "He'll be stranded with you if it comes to that. He's odd, but he'll guide you well."

"There's another task we'll require of one of your people," Tunstall said. "I need a courier to take a letter to the Deputy Provost right away. The matter's urgent. Whoever you choose must stop for nothing and no one on the road."

"So I'm to take two of our folk," the headwoman began, plainly furious by now.

"Three," the older cove said, interrupting her. "I'm going with whoever takes that ride. Look at them, Beldeal. Dogs on a Hunt, with a noble riding along? They're trouble, and the trouble might spread."

Tunstall said naught to that. The enemy had no reason to send killers along the way behind us, or even to think to send killers after us, now that they'd destroyed the bridge. They'd have plenty of time to ride off with the prince by the time we got back to the road called the Rivers Road on my map.

In my mind I saw the drowned oarsmen and their officers, their own ships holding them prisoner as they sank.

Where most folk shrank from killing more than necessary, these bloody-handed scuts slaughtered ten as easily as one.

Beldeal snapped, "You lot best pay them—both of them!—well, to make up for them losing the day's work. And a fee for three horses lost for the time—"

I heard the jingle of coins tossed on wood. When she spoke, Lady Sabine did so in a most elegant drawl. Lady Teodorie spoke in such a way. Hearing it in a voice I loved made the hair stand up on the back of my neck.

"What we will *pay* for, woman, is four good breakfasts for my human companions and me, with rubdowns and food for our mounts, and food and water for the cat and the hound who travel with us." The folk in front of me, who could hear that refined voice, were leaving. For people who lived out in marshland, they seemed to know very well what nobles sounded like. A couple of them, younger even than my brothers, stayed and bowed, pointing to the horses. I nodded to them, and they led our mounts and packhorses around the side of the public house.

"Your riders will be paid by the Deputy Provost," I heard Tunstall say. "On delivery of my letter, with the seal intact. Be assured, they'll be fairly rewarded. I'll want them to go as soon as I write the letter."

"Leave it to me," the deep-voiced cove said. "I might slow us down, big as I am, but all will be done as you need it done."

"We'd prefer you got there alive over getting there a couple of hours earlier," Tunstall replied. "Cooper, stand down," he called.

I holstered my baton and went back into the room. Tunstall had taken his writing things from his pack and was working on his report. Master Farmer was talking to a young, plump maidservant, who he soon had in giggles. My lady had left the room. Since I could hear Beldeal's voice shouting for someone to chop and someone else to bring a ham, I knew breakfast was not coming right away. I found my own table, brought out my journal, and wrote more on our journey so far.

I looked up when my lady returned—she had gotten one of the maids to bring water to a room so she could wash a bit—and when Tunstall gave his letter to a youth of 15 or so and a big man who had the deep voice I'd heard. I went back to work on my journal, having no wish to listen to their orders. The youth looked strong for his age, all rawhide muscle, and the older cove had the air and very short haircut of a former soldier. They would do well if they had decent horses. So would the other messenger they chose. One of them at least would surely reach Arenaver.

I put my work away when Beldeal came in with a loaded tray and joined the others at a large table. For a while all was silent as we ate. Beldeal had sent the two younger mots out of the room once we were served, doubtless not wanting any danger from us to light on them, but she had stayed. The more food that went into our mouths, the more relaxed she got. Seemingly she took pride in her cookery, and the men and Lady Sabine in particular made it plain that they liked it. I ate enough, but I was more worried about Achoo. She paced, huffing like, looking out the open door as if the bridge might turn up out there, with her scent on it. Finally I took my plate and sat on the floor, then called her to me, wheedling her to take bites of my food. Once she tasted the egg pie with herbs, I didn't have to coax her anymore.

"You treat that creature like she's a human. Wasting good coin to feed people food to an animal!" Beldeal said.

I'd heard it before. No matter how many times it happens, I always feel ashamed that folk would think I waste money of any kind. I shifted around so Master Farmer was between me and Beldeal's sharp brown eyes.

"Achoo is a scent hound," Master Farmer said innocently. "She has more rank in the Provost's Guard than I do."

Seemingly Beldeal was one of those mots who had a very narrow view of what was and wasn't right in the world. "An ordinary cur is of more value than a man?"

I started to bristle when she called Achoo an ordinary cur. Lady Sabine, who'd been seated on one side of me, reached down to rest a hand on my shoulder. I tried to relax. I would not disgrace myself before the lady if I could help it.

Beldeal, like most folk who think theirs is the only way of looking at things, was still gifting us with her opinion. "We have hunting hounds, but they're nothing special. We can always train another. You dry worlders are a strange lot."

"Dry worlders?" Tunstall asked.

"You're going to find out," Beldeal said. "There's only one way to reach the eastern end of what the likes of you call the Rivers Road. You'll be taking the ways through the marsh. Merscart of the Green grants us solid pieces of land out there, but sometimes he takes a few of them back. He's not inclined to tell us which, or when."

"Is there a better way around the south end of the marsh?" Lady Sabine asked.

Beldeal cackled. "Oh, no, my lady. There Merscart has married two goddesses, them of the Halseander and the Banas. All three twine together where they meet in water and green."

Once we'd packed up and were riding south on our way out of the village, Master Farmer remarked, "She's a splendid cook, but what a disagreeable female!"

Tunstall chuckled. "Pray you never meet my mother, then, if you think Beldeal is no rose. My mother is *armed*."

"Perhaps we'll just fight over you, then, in a civilized manner," Lady Sabine remarked. "No awkward questions about who sits where at the wedding, should one ever come. Just clean and simple swordswomanship."

"That would terrify me, a battle as a wedding," Master Farmer said. He looked back at me. "Wouldn't it terrify you, Cooper?"

I stared out at the marsh, ignoring him. I was starting to get a very bad feeling, based in part on the fact that I could not see the trees or hills that marked the far side. I was certain Tunstall and the lady at least had made note of it, too, but were far wiser than me and chose not to worry about it yet. After all, there was naught we could do. Without a ferry at the road, this was the only way to pass. I hope Tunstall's report to the Deputy Provost urged her to start rebuilding the old bridge.

We did not have to ride much further before we found an open-fronted shrine roofed and floored in fresh marsh grasses. Birds and creatures fled it as we approached. Lady Sabine dismounted, letting Drummer's reins trail, and approached the shrine, her hands held prayer-fashion before her.

The three of us still a-horse looked at the simple cot set back against the woods between the village and the shrine. Chickens pecked in the dirt before the house while a goat kept the grass nipped near to the roots at one side. On the other side, far from the tethered goat's attentions, was a small vegetable garden.

As the most junior Dog, I have always had the job of knocking on the door. I slid down from Saucebox's saddle and walked up the beaten earth path. I was about to knock when two four-footed dogs, golden brown with white ruffs and pointed muzzles, raced around the goat's side of the house without a sound, galloping straight at me. I got my baton out, then kept my hands out and away from my sides. I looked down at the newcomers' feet, not into their eyes. If I met their eyes they would think I was challenging and attack.

Achoo raced toward us even as the strange hounds neared me. "Achoo, no!" I cried. There are some Common words my Achoo will obey when I say them sharp enough. She halted, her fur sticking up, her throat rumbling in a growl. *"Tinggal,"* I ordered Achoo. "They think we're trespassing."

I heard the ring of steel being drawn. A glance told me my lady advanced from the shrine, her sword in hand. Tunstall had dismounted and his baton was out. I put up an open hand for them as a signal to halt, wishing they obeyed the same commands that Achoo did. I wanted to know where these hounds' master was.

"I don't like Dogs callin' on me, nor do I care for swords in the fist," a man called from the shadows under the trees. "Tell the mage I'll put an arrow through any of yez gullet if he twitches."

"I'm not deaf," Master Farmer complained from his horse's back. The dark blue sparkling fire around his hands faded, but I was beginning to think that meant naught about Master Farmer's readiness to work. "Do you treat everyone who comes to knock on your door this way?"

"On'y Dogs," called the unseen cove. "What do you want?"

"We need to cross the marsh," Tunstall shouted. "Beldeal at the inn sent us to you."

For far too long, we awaited a reply in silence. Then a tall, skinny young cove walked out of the woods. He was well tanned, with black hair and black eyes. Nature had given him short shrift on his chin, but I doubted the local mots noticed when they saw the muscles in his chest and arms. He wore no shirt, only a pair of breeches and rough old boots. I wondered if he had something for the bugs. They did not bite, but as the air warmed, they made a nuisance of themselves around my eyes and ears.

He carried a longbow and quiver. The bow was unstrung now.

"Call off your hounds," Tunstall said. "It's no way to start a talk of business."

"Is it business you're after?" Ormer wanted to know. "Most ways outsiders in uniforms and armor come here to order us about. It's not business we're offered. It's slavery."

"We'll pay you for your labors," Tunstall replied stiffly. "At the orders of the Lord Provost, Gershom of Haryse."

Ormer snorted. "A few pence for four days of *my* life? Be sure I'll make an offering for your lord to *my* lord, Merscart of the Green."

"Four days?" asked my lady, considerably startled.

"My life. Two days of your'n, if we don't bog down," Ormer replied.

Lady Sabine shook her head. "Do we look like coneys to you? Cooper's map says the distance around this end of the marsh is forty miles back to the Rivers Road. It's a map by the Crown's own cartographers, and by their measure we should be at our destination by nightfall if we don't linger here."

Ormer's full mouth twitched. He didn't move as a large green lizard raced up his leg and chest, though I'd wager its claws were sharp. When the creature was braced on his shoulder, glaring at us with black bead eyes, Ormer said, "A Crown what's-it, you say. Mapmaking cove, he is? And he walked the ground himself in his pretty court slippers?"

Master Farmer, the educated buck, cleared his throat. "Not always. Sorry, Cooper. Some of them copy another map, which may have been copied in its time. . . ."

"When was it done?" Ormer asked, seemingly interested and concerned, now. "We've had that much flooding these last three year. If your map be old, mayhap it's missing as much as thirty square mile of marsh, give or take."

"There's no shorter way to get back to the Rivers Road?" Tunstall asked. "Beldeal said the south end of the marsh is worse."

Ormer nodded. "*We* could manage it," he said, giving the lizard a pat and the dogs a nod. "But horses can't go that way, nor mules nor ponies. These last fifty year, folk take the bridge."

"What did you do before the bridge?" asked Lady Sabine.

Ormer looked at her. "We kept ourselves to ourselves."

"My lady," Tunstall said to correct him. "She is Lady Sabine of Macayhill."

Ormer leaned to the side without a lizard and spat. "We're not much for graces here in Marsh Hollow, Your Ladyship."

Tunstall looked at all of us. He stopped at me. "There's no other way?"

I crossed my arms. "Achoo was still on the scent when we got to the bridge. We won't know if they went somewhere else till she smells the other side of it."

Tunstall inspected Lady Sabine and Master Farmer once more. It was my lady who shrugged and said, "At least we need not worry about insect bites?"

"There's plenty else to bite asides midges, mosquitoes, and the like, Your Ladyship," Ormer said. "Don't expect bows and curtsies from the bears and mountain lions. I'll be paid if I'm to lose four days or—" He went silent when Tunstall held up a gold noble. It had to be more coin than Ormer had seen in all his days, mayhap more gold than all Marsh Hollow had seen.

"You'll have it at our destination," Tunstall said. "Not before. And if you think to lead us into a bog and rob us . . ." He pointed to Master Farmer, who gave Ormer that exceedingly silly grin of his. Solemnly Tunstall explained, "That is a mage."

Ormer pointed to his bright green friend. "This is a marsh lizard. They grow up to six feet long. They're common, and they swim." He whistled to the pair of hounds, who finally moved away from me. "I'll pack up."

Thursday, June 14, till
Monday, June 18, 249

I will not write of the next miserable days. I can never forget
all the biting and burrowing pests that stole food and chewed
leather. All of us discovered there were four different words
for mud, each meaning different things about how thick, wet,
and grainy it might be. We made the acquaintance of grass
and marsh snakes as well as turtles and frogs, and dined every
night on eels and fish. All of the horses, even Drummer and
Steady, became good friends as we hauled them out of bogs
which were not there the last time Ormer had passed that way.
We saw, and let live, a good dozen marsh deer, since no one
felt lively enough to skin, dress, and cook one if we brought it
down. All of us were caked in mud from top to toe.

Once we came closer to the western side of the marsh,
we learned what the map could not tell us, the reason why it
would take us a fourth day at least to reach the road. In spreading, the marsh had gone up to the foot of stony cliffs that rose
three hundred feet into the air. I wanted to scream, but I did
not. How could I, when no one else complained? Pounce
did far worse. After an hour's bumpy ride and a near slide
from a reedy island into the water, he had vanished into the
Divine Realms with a promise to join us at our destination.

The nights we were out were not wonderful. Finding a
dry spot to fit all of us was an interesting chore. Once we were
settled, I worked on the journal, bringing it up to date. That
at least I managed. Then we would set the watches and bed
down, to be up before dawn. We never asked Ormer to take a
watch, but he and his dogs were always up several times a night

anyway, wandering noiselessly through the water and reeds around our camp. Sometimes, while he was out, the member of our team on watch would hear a large creature splashing off into the distance, a big animal that we had not even known was so close.

Monday night we came to dry ground at the base of the cliffs. It was twilight. Master Farmer and Lady Sabine had lanterns lit to guide our steps. It was the promise of solid land under us that had kept us pressing on so late.

Once we'd set up camp and had supper, Ormer said, "You're on the good side of it now. An hour's ride from this place, all dry land, you'll have your road. I've been along here recent, and we've had no rain, so you won't be getting wet. I'd like my pay now, if it's all the same. Like as not, I'll be on my way before dawn. I can be home day after tomorrow if the god wills it." He stroked the lizard, who basked beside the fire.

"Why is it so quick for you?" Master Farmer wanted to know. "Why did you take a longer way with us?"

Ormer smiled. "Because I'm not trailing all manner of horseflesh and packs and armor," he said. "All I got's myself, the hounds, and Summerleaf, here." He tickled the lizard under the chin. "Anyone that's burdened heavy goes island by island as you did if the bridge isn't safe."

Lady Sabine propped her chin on her hand. "And what kind of burdens do those island-by-island travelers carry, Ormer?" she asked gently. "Bad magic? Coin? Weapons? Slaves?"

Ormer shook his head. "Don't nobody take slaves over the marsh save by the bridge, m'lady." He'd gotten much more comfortable with Lady Sabine once he'd heard her swear when the horses got stuck. "Too many slaves go and drown themselves, they get the chance. The rest—well, I won't be talking of you folk to them, and I won't talk of them to you. In the marshes, 'tis always better to mind your own nets."

"What if we must come back over the marsh?" I asked. The others looked at me in horror, and I shrugged. "Just in case it's needful," I explained.

Ormer smiled. "When you reach this end of where the bridge used to be, you'll find a great willow. Camp under it for a night and my cousins will find you. Say you want to visit Summerleaf, and they'll guide you over." The lizard flicked its tongue at us, as if it knew Ormer spoke of it.

Tunstall dug the gold noble from his pocket and handed it to our guide. "No doubt we'd have drowned, or mayhap lost much more time if not for you. Our thanks, Ormer," he said. We all thanked him. If not for Ormer, a great many perils of the marsh might have sent us along to the Peaceful Realms with our work unfinished.

Tuesday, June 19, 249

The Banas River and northeast
When we rose, Ormer was gone, just as he'd promised. I was itching to leave, but Tunstall insisted we all have as sound a breakfast as our supplies would allow. As the others were packing up, I took a quick moment to rinse my spare, mud-caked uniform in a nearby pool. I could let it dry on the back of a packhorse. By the Goddess's grace, the Dogs at Arenaver had chosen the most patient animals I'd ever met to carry our goods. Every night I had tried to show my thanks by giving them all a good combing. Not one of them had kicked or snapped despite slips and bug bites. If we all survive this and even find the prince, I will ask His Majesty to give these horses a fine stable, good food, kind grooms, and easy work for all of their days.

Pounce had yet to return, which was disheartening. Three years back I'd had to do a Hunt without him. It wasn't the same. Having him about, knowing what he was, made nearly anything seem endurable. *He* was still here, wasn't he? All our small human messes were just that, compared to what Pounce had seen.

This was the first Hunt I'd ever had that made me feel as if it might shake even Pounce's home in the Divine Realms. I wanted him here to tell me I was acting like a sheep.

I fixed the leading reins for Saucebox and my packhorse, Breeze, together with those for Master Farmer's packhorses. When Farmer took over the reins and he and the other two mounted up, I called Achoo to me. I offered the scent lure to my hound.

"Time to go to work, girl," I whispered to her. "You won't have to wait much longer. Let's go!"

Achoo smelled the cloth and sneezed, then circled, her nose low. She didn't have the scent here, but I didn't expect her to. We were two miles from the place where we would pick up the Rivers Road, if the map was right. I set off at a good trot, the lure tucked in my belt. Achoo ran at my side, trusting me to start the Hunt again. I was a good couple of hundred yards down the marsh road when I heard my companions nudge their horses forward. They would keep us in view without hampering us.

I was fifty feet or so from the blackened remains of this side of the bridge when Achoo took off. She circled in the roadbed there, sniffing eagerly, then went to the side, her nose an inch off the ground. I caught up to see what had taken her attention. It was a small lump of muck, dried and nasty in its look—vomit, I'd wager. Achoo's tail wagged ferociously. She whuffled over the bit of mess as if it were a choice cut of beef. Her quarry had tossed this up.

"But we know he's not here, girl," I told her. *"Mencari!"*

Achoo sneezed and raced east along the road. I placed one of my spare handkerchiefs over the puke in case Tunstall thought it was worth gathering, and ran after the hound. Mayhap Master Farmer could use it to trace the lad, though had that been true, he'd have done it by then.

Now that we were clear of that poxy marsh, the road began to rise again into tall hills guarded by high cliffs that were sheer faces of stone. The road had been cut through them like a channel. It gave me the shudders. There was no way to know if there were archers tucked in the green brush on those limestone heights, ready to shoot down any strangers in the uniform of the Dogs. Achoo didn't so much as glance up. That is the marvel of her. She did not care at all that the scent she had was days old. To her it was as fresh as if it had been laid down this very morning. No rain had washed even a little of it away, no other riders had laid their scent on top of it. She was free to do the thing she loved best.

While she kept her mind on the scent, I watched the heights and did my best not to trip until I could hear the others closing the distance behind us. After that I relaxed. Master Farmer could handle any archers if they were there.

On we ran as the wind picked up in the ever-deeper cut through the hills. We were over the rise of the pass before Achoo swerved to the side, then back to the road. I checked the area where she had sniffed, but there was no sign other than trampled greenery. The prince must have pissed there, but it was dry by now.

I stopped for a moment to look out over the lands before us. I took a swig of water from my flask and rinsed my mouth before I spat it on the ground. Trees covered the slopes of the hills, but where the land leveled off lay a river. It was the Banas. Another chance of a burned bridge or even a ferry, and more delays. I picked up my run again, gaining on Achoo.

Our riders came up with us as we approached the river near noon. As Master Farmer held Saucebox so I could mount, Tunstall looked ahead. "I thought it was ferries at this crossing, not bridges," he said. "The ferries look like no one's done any harm to them."

"Thank you, gods," Lady Sabine commented. She and I sighed our relief together.

"Cooper, stay with Achoo," Tunstall ordered. "My lady, if you will stay with Cooper? Master Farmer and I will question those who run this place to see if they can describe our quarry for us."

I peeked at my lady to see if she disliked taking orders from a commoner, even if he was her man. To my pleasure, she nodded and lined up with me as if Tunstall had always been her commander.

"Achoo, *tumit,*" I called as we rode closer to the water. She snorted. "I mean it." I pointed to her usual position at my side. "I know you have a scent, and I'll turn you loose on the other side of the river. Don't give me a blasted argument."

"Do you think she really understands you?" Master Farmer asked as Tunstall rode forward to the ferryman's house. A woman who'd stepped out of the building was blowing a horn to summon the ferry's crew.

"She's been with me long enough, she ought to," I said, grubbing in the side pocket of my shoulder pack. Master Farmer grinned and followed Tunstall. I fished out two strips of dried meat and broke them into three pieces each. "Achoo, look here!" I tossed her each piece carefully. She ate them in one gulp, then whuffed. "Patience," I said quietly, keeping an eye on things at the house. "Unless you tell us different, we must take a boat ride. Again."

Three good-sized ferries were tied up on this side of the river. I dismounted. As if she knew my mind, Lady Sabine took Saucebox's reins. Whistling to Achoo, I stuck my hands in my pockets and wandered down to look at the ferries, as innocent as I could be.

Achoo found the scent on the second boat.

"That beast best be trained," called a man who spoke with Tunstall. I looked back. Tunstall and Farmer approached us with the cove who must work the ferry while the mot at the house rang a bell on the porch. The stranger, who'd spoken, pointed to Achoo.

"What is the problem with these folk that they can't tell

a hound that knows her manners from a Corus street cur?" I muttered to Achoo. I turned back and called, "She knows what's allowed and what's not!" I stepped onto the ferry with care, telling Achoo, "If you can keep your water to yourself in the palace of our very own king, you can very well keep it in some worm-rotted old raft, am I right?"

Achoo wagged her tail. I wasn't sure as to her meaning. "You *did* behave yourself in the Summer Palace, didn't you?" I asked. Achoo danced as if teasing me.

My lady joined Master Farmer, Tunstall, and the ferryman, leading our horses. Once they reached me Tunstall asked, "Cooper? Did they cross the river?"

"Achoo says in this very boat," I said, nodding to her. Achoo was whuffing at a corner of the ferry in a way that showed she had the scent.

"I told you people, we took six slave trains one way or t'other that day, at least three of 'em with carts," the ferryman said. "How are we supposed to tell 'em apart five days later? They all paid their coin and went on their way. Now, we'll go faster if two of you get in the one by the dock, the one with the gangplank, and we divide the horses between two boats. Here come my lads to help you board."

His "lads," we learned, logged wood in the forest when they weren't working on the ferry. They had come running at the sound of the bell. They were big men who made little work out of moving the gangplank from one ferry to another once a new set of horses was ready to go. I ended up on the second ferry with Tunstall.

"You're doing all right, Cooper?" he asked me as three of "the lads" pushed us away from the shore.

I smiled up at him. "Of course I am," I assured him. "What did you learn at the house?"

He shrugged. "What you heard the old grumbler say. They had enough folk come through here from three different roads that they don't remember particulars. It's trading season. No one looked off-kilter to these folk."

I nodded. What was the enemy supposed to do, kill everyone at the ferry station? Better to pass unmarked with all the other travelers. I wish they'd at least looked sinister enough that the ferryman had remembered them. Knowing the enemy only by scent was scarcely useful for humans.

I looked for my hound. Achoo stood in the ferry's bow, paws on the rail and her nose in the air. Her eyes were squinted nearly shut, all of her attention placed on what she smelled. I knew *that* look, for certain. Achoo had her scent from the air that passed over the coming riverbank already. She was feasting on it, in her way.

I shrugged out of my shoulder pack and took out the bag of dried meat strips, which I dropped down the front of my tunic. Then I secured my water flask on my belt so it would not bump my hip as I ran. Tunstall took my pack. I often ran with it on, but he and the others were coming right behind me, so there was no need to wear it today. It would be easier if I rode, but this way I could follow Achoo off the road instantly if she chose to leave it. Once the day got truly hot, as it promised, I'd be happy to mount up.

Achoo didn't even wait for the ferry to come up by the dock on the eastern side of the river. When it was just two feet from the pier she leaped across, landing neatly. She raced down the length of the dock and onto the road beyond. I waited until the ferry scraped alongside the dock to jump off. I ran after Achoo, knowing the others would be delayed as they unloaded the horses.

Achoo actually slowed down a little so that she was in

my view when I rounded the curve from the dock road. Here three different roads came together. I quickly halted and placed markers so the others would see that I had taken the northeastern road that led from that intersection.

There was a signpost. I glanced at it quickly to compare it against the map. On the road Achoo had taken, the sign pointed the way to Queensgrace, the Galla Highway, the Great Road North, and Richcaffery. Were the slavers taking their cargo to the lords of the northern mountains, or to Galla? If they stopped to sell, they would lose their lead.

My trail markers set, I began to run again. To my surprise and pleasure, Pounce suddenly appeared, running at my side. "I'm honored," I said, feeling the weight rise from my shoulders. "Out for a little exercise?"

It is a fine day, and I am not likely to wear a coat of mud, he replied. *Did you enjoy yourselves among the eels and the reeds?*

"We dined like princes," I replied. "I think my spine sways more."

Pounce fell back a little, then caught up. *No, your neck is as stiff as ever,* he said. *Not even five days of eely meals could change that aspect of yours. If it were so, I would shake you from my paws and find someone more amusing.*

I could not help it. I seized him and hugged him. There was no one to see me in that hollow area of the road, save for Achoo.

Pounce bore it for a moment, then wriggled until I put him down. On we went again.

It was a beautiful place to run. Trees at regular spots on both sides of the road were marked with the Queensgrace coat of arms, a small crown over prayerful hands. I supposed it was the Count of Queensgrace I had to thank for this nearly flat road. They'd have filled out the ruts made by wagons fairly recently, since the new ones were scarcely cut into the earth. A good road like this would bring more coin to Queensgrace's pocket. Local merchants would prefer this road, and the coin they spent in Queensgrace lands would eventually benefit the count. Tunstall had explained it all to me on our Hunts. Hillmen learn a great deal about why folk take one road and not another, so they know where to rob.

Though with the marsh bridge gone, these people would lose a chunk of their trade coin. This summer was going to be lean, thanks to our prey. It was another reason to bring them down.

The trees were old here, the kind we never see in the Lower City unless we venture to the Temple District. I heard all manner of birds going about their days. We crossed bridges over two lively streams, with Achoo halting only quickly to drink. Pounce did the same when we came to each one, while I stayed prudent and drank from my flask. It had taken but one Hunt to teach me the folly of drinking water that had not been boiled.

I watched the trail for Hunt sign. I noted the tracks of a horse with an off foreleg that had gone this way mayhap two days before, and of five mules in a string only yesterday. Several carts had traveled the ground as well over the last three or four days.

Pounce and I caught up with Achoo as she drank from another stream that crossed the road. Pounce joined her at the water, gulping almost as greedily as she did. The sun was high overhead and we all felt the heat.

"*Pelan,* Achoo," I told her. "Slow march."

She looked at me as if I'd taken a meaty bone from her.

"None of that," I said. "We'll be at this all day. Let's save our strength." Achoo trotted ahead at a slower pace, her shoulders drooping as she followed the scent. Pounce leaped to my shoulders. He'd done a wonderful trick he used on other Hunts, making himself lighter than usual, so as not to wear me down with his weight.

I picked up my own pace to keep closer to Achoo. We'd gone some five hundred yards or so when I smelled cooked meat on a breeze from the northwest. Achoo had stopped. From the look of her, I knew the prince's scent had left the road, leading down into the tall grasses on the left. She stepped onto the slope from the road into the weeds.

"*Tunggu,*" I called, trotting to catch up with her. I didn't like her moving out of my sight. These weeds were up to my chest.

Pounce leaped down when I reached her. I looked about for stones to leave for Tunstall. *Never mind that,* Pounce said. *I'll let him know. Be careful. I don't like the smell of this place.*

"We're always careful," I replied. I looked about us. The weeds were bent back from a thin trail. A bigger group than normal had passed this way, leaving bend marks on the stems and yellowing leaves. I'd wager a good meal that Master Farmer would see magic had been done here to bring the weeds upright again.

Achoo chuffed at me. She never understood my needing to look around so slowly when she had something to follow. "*Pelan,*" I told her. That scent of cooked meat had the skin prickling at the nape of my neck. The stench didn't belong here.

Achoo went ahead, tail drooping, staying no more than a couple of feet in front of me. She might complain, but she never broke the rules on a Hunt. How she could ignore the smell, I don't know, but she managed it.

The weeds opened up. Before us lay a wide, bare strip of ground littered with a few young trees. Further on more and more of them grew until they joined with a forest. Achoo took a couple of steps ahead before I managed to scream, *"Tak! Berhenti,* Achoo, *tak!"*

She turned her head to stare at me, but she moved not a muscle. I thanked Mithros, god of the Sun Dogs, for granting me such a fine hound, and ran up to her to show her the peril.

With trembling hands I scratched her ears and talked to her to calm myself down. "See there, the dead creatures?" I pointed to the charred bodies a scant three yards ahead and babbled on. "I smelled the cooked doe and her fawn—you probably ignored them because you had our lad's scent in your nose, you good girl. But look. There's fried birds all along that stretch of grass, where it's gone yellow, and rabbits, and voles and mice." I groped around me for a stone and tossed it at the image of grass and trees that lay beyond the line of dead things. It turned red hot just as it flew over them and fell to the ground, smoking.

I kept a hand in Achoo's collar and pulled the sample lure with the prince's scent from my belt purse. I offered it to her. She sniffed it, sneezed once, then leaned forward against my pull on her collar. She scrabbled at the dirt with her forepaws, her nose pointed right at that deadly line.

"Sarden mage work," I whispered. "They went to a lot of trouble to keep us from finding whatever's here. Let's meet the others and see what Tunstall says." Back to the road we went.

I'd just finished combing a few burs from Achoo's tail when Tunstall, Lady Sabine, and Master Farmer arrived. They all dismounted to hear my report.

"A pretty trap, and mayhap nothing to do with our search," Tunstall said when I'd finished. "We could find the boundaries and take Achoo around. Or we might send her further up the road to see if the scent resumes there."

"Or our quarry could be beyond that barrier," Master Farmer said. "Let's have a look. Better safe than skinned, my old ma always says."

"What if the local people walk into that thing?" my lady asked. "It may have killed some of them already. We should destroy it if we can."

Tunstall ducked his head. "You've all persuaded me," he replied. "Let's see this cooking illusion."

Back down the path we went, Pounce riding one of the supply horses this time. When we came out of the high weeds into the clearer area, Master Farmer held up a hand and walked forward. "Very nasty," he said, and lowered the hand. A great curtain of sparkles appeared just behind the line of dead animals. "A lot of power went into this. It feels like that of the two mages I picked up at the Arenaver fair." He strode forward, and before I could stop the great bumwipe, he thrust his hand into the magic barrier.

I yelped, Lady Sabine gasped, and Master Farmer yanked his arm free quicker than he'd put it in. From elbow to fingertip it burned with a reddish-purple flame that ate his shirtsleeve and turned his fingernails black. Master Farmer, sweat rolling down his face, sketched a sign in the air with a finger that didn't burn. The sign hung there, a bit of dark blue light. He clutched it with the burning hand and the fire went out.

I offered my water flask to him. He poured its contents all over the arm that had been in flames. The only signs left were his blackened fingernails, flushed skin from his fingers almost to his shoulder, and the missing sleeve. Without a word I went and refilled my flask from one of the spare jars carried by the packhorses.

When I returned, Tunstall was scratching his skull and Lady Sabine was patting her forehead with her handkerchief.

I went over to Master Farmer and shoved him in the chest so hard that he fell onto the grass. He lay there, blinking at me. "Beka, what—?"

"Gapeseed! Claybrained hedge-born sheep biter!" I cried. I looked at Tunstall and my lady. "Aren't mages supposed to be *clever?*" I turned back to Master Farmer. "Half the game in the district is cooked right before you and you stick your hand in there! Sweet Goddess tears, why aren't *you* cooked?"

"Because I wasn't so stupid that I didn't protect myself first?" He asked it instead of telling it. He hadn't tried to get up, which told me he had enough wit left to stay down until he knew for certain I wasn't going to shove him again.

"And it did you so well your arm caught fire!" I pointed out. "Now *there's* a useful plan!"

Master Farmer looked back and up at Tunstall and my lady. "Some help?" he asked with hope in his face.

My partner shook his head. He'd had such ratings from me before and knew what happened to those who tried to get in the way. Lady Sabine was tucking her handkerchief in her belt. "She says nothing I disagree with, and she says it with so much more eloquence," my lady murmured. "Your life is not your own to risk on this mission. Surely that was understood?"

"I understood that I wasn't risking my life," Master Farmer retorted. He looked back at me. "I'm very fond of my body. I never risk it when I don't have to. I'm not burned, you know. Just flushed. My nails turned color with the magic's reaction to the breaking of the spell." He held his arm—the unburned one—out to me. "A hand up?" he asked.

I scowled at him, then grabbed the arm and yanked. I had to step back to keep him from colliding with me. As it was, he nearabout mashed my nose with his collarbone.

"I will try not to anger you again," he told me solemnly.

Tunstall gave his cough of a laugh. "You still don't understand, book lad. She only talks so to those she likes and thinks need correction. You don't want to see her angry." When Master Farmer looked at him and raised his eyebrows in question, Tunstall pointed two fingers at his own eyes. "Ghost eyes. That's how you'll know she's angry. Her eyes go pale with all the dead she's talked to, and she'll look at you with them. You'll feel the god's hand on the nape of your neck, I swear you will."

"Enough!" I said, feeling cross. The magic burning just a few feet away made me uneasy. "We've got scent yet. If Master Farmer can break this thing, I wish he'd get to it. Elsewise me and Pounce and Achoo will go on around it and see if it ends and the prince came out somewhere."

"Very true," Master Farmer said. He walked a little closer to that edging of charred animals.

"It would be a pity if we got so caught up with the magic before us that villains caught us from behind. I'll watch the road and the horses," Lady Sabine offered. She fixed the horses' reins into strings and led them back down the trail.

Master Farmer knelt, took off his pack, and set it before him. Opening it, he surveyed the corked bottles and jars inside. He picked up one, shook his head, replaced it, then chose another. Scowling, he put that back and got to his feet with a squat jar in his hand. Achoo and Pounce backed up until they stood with Tunstall, where the short grass gave way to tall weeds. I didn't move. Master Farmer hadn't indicated that I should, and I didn't want to look as if I was afraid.

He opened the jar, stared at the contents, then corked it and set it in his pack. Next he raised an arm, the unscorched one, then shook his head. I heard him mutter, "That won't work."

"Do you mean to do something or do you not?" Tunstall called. "I finished my Puppy year and won my leather in the time it's taking you to—"

Master Farmer put a black-nailed finger to his lips for silence. Then he pulled something from his right boot—a length of white ribbon embroidered in lively colors. Holding it on his unscorched hand, he murmured over it until an end of thread rose from its surface. Grasping it with two black-nailed fingers, Master Farmer drew the thread out of the embroidered design, somehow without ripping any of the other threads loose.

When he had the length of thread he wished, he spoke to it, and the thread broke. Farmer returned the ribbon to his boot and then wrapped his thread around his burned left hand. Pointing to the barrier with that hand, he let fly a stream of brown-colored magic.

An explosion knocked Master Farmer and me into the grass on the slope and deafened me for several moments.

My hearing returned as Pounce washed first one of my ears, then the other. I yelped because his tongue scratched. *Don't be ungrateful,* he told me in my mind.

I sat up. My hands were covered in soot. If Master Farmer's face was any indication, my face was, too. His hair was blown back to stick out at the sides. He turned to yell at Tunstall, "There, now! Have I made you happy?"

Tunstall halted in the middle of one of his hillman good luck gestures. "Why didn't you do that right off instead of canoodling with jars and bottles?" he demanded.

"Because there's no craft to simply blowing something apart!" bellowed Master Farmer. "There's no artistry! Would you like me to spell *artistry* for you, you lumbering ox? No doubt every mage in the district knows there's a new idiot practicing between here and the Banas River now!"

From the road we heard Lady Sabine cry, "Are you alive in there?"

Tunstall turned and yelled, "Oh, aye." To me he said, "Achoo has scent."

Achoo had crossed the line of dead things and stood two yards inside it, whining and dancing. Tunstall was right. I lunged to my feet.

A black-nailed hand clamped around my arm. "Not alone," Master Farmer said. "If there was one trap, there may be more." He struggled to his feet and grabbed his pack.

"*Maji tak,* Achoo," I ordered her. I took the jar that Master Farmer had forgotten and handed it to him. Achoo went forward, her nose a foot from the ground, with Master Farmer and me close behind.

With the barrier gone, we could see the trail again as it led toward the woods. Achoo kept to that. She halted inside the younger trees that fought for room near the great oaks of the forest proper. An area about three square yards off the path had been cleared of greenery. The ground had been dug up, then put back.

Achoo sniffed all around the piled earth. I ground my teeth, fearful that the prince was dead and our Hunt was done, until I realized that she was scenting around, not on, what had to be a grave. The prince was not under the ground, then, but he'd been present when the dead were buried.

"She'd dig if he was buried here, wouldn't she?" Master Farmer asked.

I nodded.

"We still have to make sure." Tunstall had caught up with us. "Cooper, fetch the digging equipment. It's on the horse with the black socks."

"No need," Master Farmer said. "Don't make me talk to you about artistry again." He strode toward the pile of tumbled earth as Pounce yawned.

Tunstall rolled his eyes at me. "He has artistry," he repeated. "Because that's what it takes to blow things up. And cook his arm."

"He's good at keeping bugs off," I reminded my partner as we followed our mage to the grave. "And I've gotten that fond of his tea."

"You interfere in my dreadful concentration," Master Farmer said without turning around. He made his voice boom like the Players did in their performances. "You lack the proper respect for the wonders to unfold!"

I sighed. I am beginning to think that Lord Gershom has saddled us with the silliest mage in the Eastern Lands. Not the stupidest, not that by far. Only the silliest. I looked at him, his body still now as he eyed the turned earth. Funny. I hadn't noticed before that he's got such broad shoulders.

Master Farmer reached out with his unburned left hand, holding it palm up. "I learned this from Cassine," he said absently. "It's a housecleaning spell that I made bigger." Instantly the tumbled earth of the grave began to quiver, then to shake. The protection sign disappeared into the moving grains of soil. Master Farmer beckoned with his outstretched hand and the earth rose, clods and single grains falling off to the sides.

Higher came a block of dirt, five feet deep, five feet wide, seven feet long, as close as I could measure, the earth falling off onto the sides of the grave. Achoo ran between my legs and quivered there. Tunstall gripped his belt with white-knuckled hands. As the dirt fell away two pairs of bare feet were visible to us.

Master Farmer raised his free hand and pulled it down from the one he'd already extended. The rest of the dirt separated from the dead and settled on one side of the hole. With the other hand, he beckoned the dead forward. When they were but a foot away, he gently let them settle on the grass.

He waved his hand slowly, from side to side, and the wind blew the remaining earth from the naked bodies. There were three, a mot my age with a swaddled babe laid on her breast, and at her side a brown-haired girl child near the age of our prince. The worms and beetles had been at them already. They were black and swollen with rot, their scant ragged clothes cutting into their flesh.

Glittering blue fire dripped from Master Farmer's hand. When it touched the dead, there was a flash so bright my eyesight was filled with spots. Achoo whimpered, and I heard Tunstall cursing in Hurdik.

Master Farmer only said, "A rather good mage has been at work here. Interesting."

"Interesting?" Tunstall asked. He sounded vexed.

"If it had been dangerous, I would have spoken out," Master Farmer told him. "You get too excited over big flashes, Tunstall. Mages rely on that to make you think they have more power than you." He set his pack on the ground, took the corked jar I had returned to him, and opened the jar with a whisper. He tapped a quantity of powder into his left hand. I knelt beside him and picked up the wide cork, gesturing for him to give me the jar. For a moment he blinked, as if he'd forgotten I was there, or as if he'd never considered that a second pair of hands might be useful. Then he passed me the jar.

As I corked it, Master Farmer walked alongside the dead,

letting the wind blow the powder from his hand over the three abandoned corpses. It settled, glittering like tiny stars.

He said nothing, only looked at them, his eyes thoughtful and kind under their heavy lids. Plainly he'd forgotten Pounce, Tunstall, Achoo, and me. All his attention was on the dead. He still kept his hand outstretched, though motionless, as if he used it to welcome something that was to come forth. The sparkles on the swollen, rotting corpses twinkled and seemed to move, until they rose as a blanket. In midair they halted and faded, leaving in their wake the seeming of the dead as they must have looked the moment they were put in the ground.

Master Farmer lowered his hand. "I'll say they've been dead four days. That's given the stage of rot and bloat, and the work of the beetles and worms, all compared to their living bodies," he said quietly. "The babe must have been scarcely three days old when she died. See the cleft in the upper lip goes all the way up into the nose? She may not have been able to nurse. A decent healer could have fixed it."

"Slavers don't heal newborns," Tunstall said, his voice a quiet rumble from his chest. "Only if they're old enough to work."

"I know," Master Farmer replied. "I know. The woman is the mother. The spell does not tell me if she had childbed fever. If the infant is only three days old, it could be the mother was ill with it, but the fever did not kill her."

There was a dark slash under the mot's left ear. Master Farmer was placed wrong to see it. I pointed it out to him. There was no sign of a knife. If she had done it to herself, they'd have buried it with her, a suicide's knife being unlucky. Of course, how would a slave have gotten her ticklers on a blade?

Master Farmer turned his attention to the third corpse.

The brown-haired little girl was unmarked save for a dark stripe all the way around her throat. "Strangled," I said. "Not a rope, or it'd be more scratched up. Whip mark, it looks like."

"Can we get a better look at the backs?" Tunstall asked. "If they're branded, it will be on the blade of the shoulder."

Master Farmer rubbed his lower lip with his thumbs. "I thought only the owners brand, not the slavers."

"The sellers brand if it's a special item they might be carrying around for a time," Tunstall explained, his voice flat. "They use special ointment in the healing and when the item's bought, the slaver just says the word and his brand's gone."

Scowling, Master Farmer reached over the dead. Sparkles fell from his fingers. In a slow and creepy fashion, both the mot and the gixie turned to the right, like they was turning over in bed. The babe stayed on the mot's chest. My tripes surged. I clapped a hand over my mouth to keep my breakfast from coming up. I don't know why. Surely I've seen worse in the last four years. Yet there was sommat dreadful in those open-eyed bodies moving, sommat I wished I could un-see.

Tunstall stepped forward, his baton in his hand, and pointed to the back of the mot's shoulder. It showed no mark. The gixie, though, was fresh branded when she went to the Black God. The flesh around it was red and puffy, new-burnt.

I moved closer. That brand, I'd seen it before.

Master Farmer and Tunstall stepped closer, too. Tunstall brought a piece of parchment from his belt purse. He'd put my drawing of the brass token there. We all compared it to the tattoo. They were the same.

"We need to get word to Gershom that we're on the right track," Master Farmer said quietly. "Perhaps he can get other Hunters into Frasrlund. They can come down the Great Road North. We might catch the enemy between us."

"How do you intend to get word to him?" Tunstall asked. "Split one of us off? I think any of us who rides away will be picked up sooner than I can say Ma's name. A couple of coins will have any farmer or ferryman talking of Dogs Hunting in company with a lady knight."

Master Farmer shook his head and went to his pack. Crouching, he opened it out, removing box after box. At last he produced a small dish and a little box of ebony wood, closed and locked with silver. "Water, one of you?" he asked, sitting on the grass. He sat cross-legged and accepted Tunstall's water flask. He poured a little bit of water into the dish and returned the flask, then set the dish aside. "I may be a little odd after this," he warned us.

"What's 'a little odd'?" I asked.

"Cassine made this powder to extend my hearing and speaking range," he explained. "Also to ensure that only the person I *intend* to hear me does so, while anyone who tries to overhear me or find me does not." He wet a finger, opened the box, and touched his fingertip to the odd, purplish dust inside. Instantly his finger began to glow. Master Farmer closed the box and touched his now-glowing finger to the end of his tongue and both eyelids. They too glowed. He shut his mouth and eyes, grimacing as he did. Then he held out the box, obviously wanting one of us to take it. Tunstall shook his head and made the Sign against evil on his chest. I accepted it. Once the box was in my hand, I closed the tiny locks and set it in Master Farmer's pack. I hoped that's what Master Farmer wanted me to do, because I make it a rule never to eat things that glow. After I returned the box to his pack, I loaded the rest of his things into it.

When I turned back to the men, Tunstall had moved further up on the trail. Achoo stood behind him. Next to me

Master Farmer held the small dish in both hands. He looked into it with his glowing eyes. "Come on," he whispered. "Ironwood, Orielle, one of you, hear me. One of you must be able to hear. You're both supposed to have—"

"Who are you?" Tunstall and I jumped. The voice came from the dead child, but it was that of a grown mot. "Mage! Identify yourself! Why have you pried at my work?"

Master Farmer gave no reply. I stayed where I was, trying not to shiver my way out of my boots.

"Answer me, fool!" ordered the female mage. "Did you think we would not lay a trap for prying idiots? Speak, or I will stop your heart dead!"

Master Farmer looked at the child and opened his mouth. Blue-green fire shot out of it to collide with a gout of pale yellow fire that roared up from the bodies. "Did you think I would not be ready? Tell me *your* name!" he cried, though his mouth didn't move. The unseen mage howled in rage. The two magics clashed and vanished. The dead were burned to the bone.

Master Farmer's eyes still glowed. He emptied the water dish with a trembling hand and set it aside. He straightened one leg at a time as if he'd forgotten how they worked. Then, as slowly as my granny Fern, he began to get to his feet. I watched him fumble, trying to brace his hands on the earth or to lever himself upright with one leg. I glanced at Tunstall. He had fetched a good luck charm from his pocket and was praying over it as he petted the shaking Achoo with his free hand.

He'll be all right, Pounce said. Until that moment I'd forgotten he was with us. *He's not at his best with big magics, remember. This was* quite *big.*

"Why didn't you do something?" I asked.

When Pounce glared at me, I said it along with him, "Because you're not allowed."

Why ask me foolish questions, then, if you know what I will say? Pounce wanted to know.

"Because I want to be surprised," I snapped. Then I looked at Master Farmer, who still sat on the grass. I scolded myself, saying that a servant of the god of death ought to be made of stronger stuff than I was showing, until I finally found the sack to go to the mage. Carefully, not knowing if I was courting a lightning bolt or some such nasty thing, I got both hands under one of his arms and braced one of his outstretched legs with my feet. He looked at me blindly, startled, his eyes alight. He said something, but it was in no language I knew.

"It's all right," I said, talking to him as I had to my brothers and sisters when they were sick. "We'll get you on your feet if you can manage it. My, that trull was a nasty bit of slum stew, wasn't she? Arm around my shoulders—good lad!"

Tunstall got over his bit of religion and came to aid us. Together we helped Master Farmer up and slid him into his shoulder pack. I have to say, that man is one weighty piece of beef.

We were about to try for the road when Master Farmer mumbled, "A little rest and I can bury the bones again." His eyes were shimmering only now. I could see the irises through the odd blue-green veil.

"I'd like a bit more warning, next time," Tunstall said gruffly, looking at the ground. "I was certain Morni the Mad had you."

That explained *his* fit of strangeness. Morni was the hill people's war goddess and mad as a rabid cat. I wouldn't want to be near her, either.

"Sorry," Master Farmer mumbled. "You don't usually find that much power in a hidden grave."

"A trap," Tunstall said. "She knew you were coming."

"She wasn't the only one. There were two magics in that, very strong ones. *Very* strong," he repeated, rubbing his eyes.

I pulled Farmer's hand away. "Stop that," I said. "It's not good to rub your eyes."

Tunstall gave me the oddest look. I glared at him. "It isn't. Don't I tell you the same?"

"You do," he said seriously. "After you'd known me two years."

"The other mage didn't speak at all." Master Farmer was looking at his hand, as if he wondered why I held his wrist. I let it go. "There were two. I tried to put a hook into one of them, but I wasn't prepared to work that kind of magic." He glanced at me, then Tunstall, then Pounce. "It needs preparation, see. And a brazier, and at least two things I'd left in my bag, not thinking I'd need them." The muscles flexed in his cheeks. "I will if we meet again. There's a replacement for the brazier, if I work that ahead of time." He stood with his weight more on his own feet now. His eyes were his own again. He still shook a bit, but mostly he looked like the Master Farmer I was used to. I slid out from under his arm. He stayed upright.

With a nod, I stepped away from them. "A moment," I said quietly. I went to the piles of burned bones. I had no fear of the mages biting at me. It was plain they'd fled Master Farmer, and him but one man. I wondered if he'd noticed that yet.

"Black God take you gentle," I whispered to the poor corpses. "Let his messengers guide you to the Peaceful Realms, where you'll forget what happened here."

The clatter of wings got my attention. I looked up. Three wood pigeons had taken to the air. They must have been in the nearby trees. Were they carrying the spirits of these poor folk? Seemingly neither mot nor gixie had any unfinished business for me. Like other slaves, mayhap they were eager to leave such a hard world.

I stood and nodded to Master Farmer. Hanging on to Tunstall's arm, he raised the bones just enough to move them over to their grave. A mother putting her babes to bed could not have been more gentle as he settled them into the hole. Once they were down, he lifted his right hand and summoned the pile of earth that he'd set aside. It tumbled in swiftly until the grave was full again. At the very last, Master Farmer drew a sign for protection in the dirt. It shone with a steady, bright light. I didn't believe any carrion eaters would be digging these folk up.

Tunstall asked, "Is all the barrier gone?"

Master Farmer nodded. "No one else will die here."

Achoo, seeing that we were done with scary things, moved to a spot in the grass where a dead bird's carcass lay in the middle of another path. Her tail was wagging again. She was sniffing, but not at the dead creature. She circled back to a spot that was spattered with brown drops—old piss—sniffed it, and returned to the dead bird. Then she ran a few feet down the path, halted, and danced.

"They didn't take them back to the road by the path we used," I said. "It's a guess, but Achoo says her trail leads that way. I'll wager that trail either picks up with the main road ahead, or leads to a village."

Tunstall trotted back the way we'd come to get Lady Sabine and the horses.

Master Farmer sat on the grass once more. Achoo, thinking we faced another delay, whined miserably.

"Mudah," I called to her. "We humans need a bit more than our legs and our nose to go along with." I crouched beside Master Farmer.

"I hate the waste of it, the waste of life that criminals leave behind," he said wearily. He fumbled at his belt, trying to undo the ties that held his water flask. I slapped his hand away and freed it, then opened it for him. Master Farmer took it with a nod of thanks. "Each of us has power, a kind of magic," he told me, speaking as if I were a scholar like him. "We spend it somehow as we live, in great and lesser ways. Those three never even had a chance to use theirs." He drank from his water flask and tried to fix it on his belt, but his hands still shook too much.

I took the thing from his grip and secured it to his belt again, then fed Achoo some meat strips. I said nothing, I was thinking about his words. They made sense. That was one of my reasons for doing what I did. I want more folk to make sommat of their lives, instead of losing them to slavery or prison or murder. But I'd never thought of it this way, that we each had a fire of some kind. We could each make a difference.

Tunstall returned with my lady and the horses. As Master Farmer was dragging himself onto his mount, Lady Sabine asked, "How did these mages know you were looking at this? Surely they weren't watching all this time?"

Master Farmer smiled as he hauled himself into the saddle. It was a cold smile, a schoolmaster's smile. "They didn't need to. If I'd laid this trap, I'd have set the barrier with a spell, a 'bee.' In the unlikely event a mage who was powerful enough to break the barrier came along, the bee would go instantly to the casting mage. She wouldn't even need her partner to spring the trap, if she's one of the two who's riding with that slave train."

I dug in one of the packhorse's bags. The mage needed to eat something. I cut a chunk off a ham that was conveniently near the top of one pack and some off the cheese that was its neighbor, and shoved them into Master Farmer's hand. Then I cut more for Tunstall so he wouldn't whine that I favored the mage. When I held up my knife and looked at my lady, she shook her head and raised a hand in thanks. I put away the food and mounted my own horse. Pounce jumped up onto my lap while Achoo pranced and whined on the ground.

"*Maji,* Achoo," I called. I rode first down the trail following her, giving Saucebox the nudge to trot a bit.

"There's another bad thing," I heard Master Farmer say. "She blocked me from reaching any mage close to Gershom. I'm hoping that I'll be able to get through down the road."

If the other two said anything about that, I didn't hear it. I made the Sign on my chest and prayed Master Farmer would reach my lord soon.

The trail led Achoo and the rest of us back to the main road after a couple of miles. Short of it, in a glade by a stream that followed the road for a good ways, we stopped to rest the horses and eat a proper late lunch.

"Let's talk about our story again," Lady Sabine suggested between bites. "We can back peasants down with talk of a Hunt and a wave of papers and seals, but that won't work with nobles. At the level of magic we found back there, we're going to find money. They won't be impressed by our documents."

"She's right," Master Farmer said. Even after ham and cheese by the burial ground, he'd eaten a big chunk of bread, cheese, and more ham as if he was starving. Now he eyed a meat pie that lay broken in its wrappings.

"Eat that," Tunstall said. He lay on his back, staring at the sky and picking his teeth. "It won't last forever. Our story. I've been thinking. A noble's child's been kidnapped, but he's ten, see? That accounts for the four of us. They'd never send another noble and a mage out for a merchant, however rich. All we can say is the noble's from the southeast, and there's added trouble with Tusaine if we fail. We've been sworn to reveal no more, and our Birdies tell us that the kidnappers came this way."

"We'll be pressed for more," my lady said. "If we run into any powerful nobles, they won't settle for that."

"Give it to them bit by bit. Hint it's mayhap a fight between father and mother, the mother being from the northern mountains. The father's from the south." Tunstall dug at a back tooth with the pick. When she'd found out he had this habit, my lady had gotten him a set of ivory ones, all very nicely made. "And no, we'll give no name, no mention of politics or rebel mages. It's a straight kidnapping. Let anyone who's so eager to know pester Lord Gershom for it themselves, if they want it so bad."

I chuckled. My lord was famous for his response when folk came to bother him about things he considered to be none of their business. Anyone who knew him would decide life was better if they left my lord alone. Anyone who didn't know of him beforehand would remember forever after.

Lady Sabine fingered the moon charm she wore about her neck. "It should do," she said at last. "For all that the nobility dislikes Dogs, they know it looks bad if they pry too deep, the way the nation's politics are these days."

"I'd think a mention of Ferrets would back them off as well," Farmer observed. He was sharing the broken meat pie with Pounce and Achoo.

"We don't need farting Ferrets," Tunstall said, his voice a rumble of vexation. "We're worth fearing ourselves, right, Cooper?"

I was on my feet, restless and wanting to be on the move again. "Specially anyone that's seen us work," I said absently. Over the far ridge I saw a hint of what might be chimney smoke. It could be a farm, a charcoal burner's hut, or the first outlier of a village or town. "It's a fine story, Tunstall. You always make up good ones." I could hear them stirring behind me, collecting their gear at last. "And if they don't believe us, I can give them the ghost eyes, you can go all big and threatening, Farmer can do his cracknob simpleton, and my lady can don her nobleness. We'll do all right." They were laughing as I told Achoo to *maji.*

As we moved on the country widened out to show us farms and orchards. Lady Sabine and Farmer got into a discussion of apples, which my lady's family was known for growing. Tunstall listened, mayhap for ideas for his tiny flowers. None of them took their eyes off of our surroundings. Anyone could be in the weeds, trees, or bushes, watching us or following.

As the others kept an eye open for trouble, I kept my hound in view. Achoo never wavered. The scent was plain.

A courier passed us by, riding south. Tunstall halted him and gave him our latest report to Lord Gershom, wrapped and sealed, with a gold coin to inspire the courier. Official messengers are made to sign all manner of vows, which meant they were safer than most when it came to their work. Also Tunstall, like me, writes everything in private Dog codes.

We met a goatherd with his flock and a carter with a

load of chickens in crates. Further on we overtook huntsmen with braces of rabbits from their night's traps. More and more houses lined the road, along with barns and outbuildings, some with walls built of wood or stone. Folk were much in evidence, hanging clothes to dry, spinning in the sun, hoeing, tending flocks, making butter. We could see herds everywhere, sheep, more goats, one of horses. There were small roads that led away from our road to local manors, perhaps, or villages.

On our second rest of the afternoon, Lady Sabine climbed a nearby hill to have a look at what lay ahead. "We're coming up on a small river and village," she said when she returned. "Queensgrace Castle is beyond."

"If we're lucky we'll pass the castle by," Tunstall said.

"I never depend on luck, my dear," the lady said, rooting in one of her long packs. She produced what looked like a three-sectioned staff. She fitted the pieces one atop the other, twisting each until it clicked into place. The whole formed a staff of seven feet in length. From the same pack she brought out a banner and fixed it to the wood. It was her shield device, the green flame above the green hill on a field of black, with the green ring and the black ring to show she was a lady knight. It seemed as though someone had shot a couple of arrows through the banner. My lady looked it over, mumbling about wedging it in the stirrup.

"Let me carry it," Farmer said. He and Tunstall had saddled their mounts as she put her flag together. Farmer was the first to get it all done and mount up. "Beka has to stay with Achoo, and Tunstall has his pride. I don't have any."

"I can manage it," my lady said, looking up at him.

"The house of Queensgrace is said to hold itself very high up. I heard of late they've turned to that new cult of the Gentle Mother," Farmer told her. "They make their women ride mules and forbid them any use of weapons. One daughter was cast off when she refused to leave squire's training."

Tunstall said, "Let us give you all the dignity we can manage."

"This Gentle Mother nonsense is starting to give me a pain in my parsnips," I said as I got ready to run some more. Castles meant villages, which meant possible turns down narrow lanes and into houses and yards. I needed to be afoot. "Are they mad, hoping some cove will always be about to guard them? I'll protect my own self, thank you very nicely. That way I can be certain the job will get done."

Lady Sabine's mouth twisted in a bitter smile. "They would rather their women go pure and gentle to the grave than sully themselves with an enemy's blood," she told me.

I gawped at her like a countryman at the fair.

My lady grimaced. "My family had me attend three of the Gentle Mother's services four years ago. Then I threatened to become a prostitute at the temple of the Mother of Delight. After that, I was left to be ungentle."

"Goddess be thanked," Tunstall said, and spat.

Achoo whined. *"Maji,"* I said, and off she went. I ran behind her. My muscles griped a little, as they always did after a rest, but they soon warmed up. Folk watched us as we passed, but while curious, they kept their distance. No one liked strange Dogs in their districts, just as no one ever felt innocent when a Dog was in view.

When I glimpsed back, I could see that unlike before, when the local folk had passed my friends with a nod and a wave, they now stood at the side of the road, removed their headgear, and bowed or curtsied. That was the change caused by Lady Sabine's banner. Corus folk never did that. If we did, with all the nobles in the city, we'd never get anything done.

Here I had the feeling that them that didn't act respectful saw the wrong end of the count's riding crop, or that of his steward. These locals were just too wary as they watched us pass, even me and the hound. They were too fast to move aside for Lady Sabine and the others behind Achoo and me.

It made me growl under my breath.

As Achoo and I crested a long hill, I saw Queensgrace Castle. It stood on its own steep hill across the valley from us, commanding a river view. The inner wall stood higher than the outer, with three different towers inside that rose above the whole. The flat-topped one that would be the main keep flew three banners, those of the Count of Queensgrace and two noble guests, if my memory for such things was right. Between it and us lay a couple of miles of green land split with a winding river, the Retha on the maps. On its banks was a village with a good stone wall and a number of farms outside, but they were just dabs compared to the castle. This would be the reason for the deference of those on foot in the road. They were used to the count, his family, and their guests expecting hats off and low bows for their greatness.

Achoo led us down into the village. I rattled off fast apologies as I ducked around folk doing business or talking, half tripping over a mot who backed away too soon from the village well. I managed, barely, to keep my feet. Achoo and I thumped across the sturdy river bridge. We annoyed three young coves wearing shiny brass shoulder badges hung with Queensgrace red and gray ribbons. They shouted for me to come back, but I ignored them. My lady could deal with the men of the Queensgrace household.

I prayed for Achoo to take the turning of the road, the one with the sign marked *The Galla Highway, the Great Road North, Richcaffery.* She continued straight, onto the castle way.

I cursed to myself and followed. Carters and riders squalled at us as we ducked around them.

Whatever happened to the quiet life of the country? I asked myself, picking up my pace so I could be closer to Achoo. I could find as much annoyance at any palace gate. Queensgrace was no duchy to give itself airs.

The hill was monstrous long and steep. My poor thighs were quivering when I reached the top, and the lower part of my back throbbed like a bad tooth. Looking around, I saw the castle stood atop a bluff overlooking the small river that ran through the village. There was no moat, but I guessed the steep hill was hard enough on charging horses. Then I was too close to the castle to see around it. The gate ahead was as great as any at the royal palace, with no guard in sight. Times were peaceful this far from all the borders. Seemingly the count had no enemies among the nearby nobles, to leave his gate open and undefended. Of course, there were men-at-arms with crossbows patrolling the wall overhead.

Achoo charged through the gate and I followed after. "Achoo, *berhenti*!" I shouted as we came out of the thick tunnel and into the sunlight of the vast outer bailey. She halted halfway across, looked at me, and turned to run closer to a gateway in the castle's inner wall. *"Berhenti!"* I cried. I was no fool. We might have come this far, but we would never be allowed into the inner bailey without someone to vouch for us. *"Kemari*, Achoo," I said, pointing to the ground beside my foot. "Pox and murrain on it all," I muttered to myself, hating the need to stop.

Achoo and I had been through this before, though never in houses so great. Every noble demanded his amount of bum-kissing before he would allow the king's law to be enforced, *if* he was behaving. They thought, if they delayed us, that it bought them time to rid themselves of evidence. They never realized that they could hide very little from my beautiful hound.

Horses clattered in the tunnel, reminding me to be grateful that I was afoot and not being deafened as I rode in.

"*Tunggu, dukduk,*" I told Achoo, and crouched beside her. She sat and sighed. She knew what this was as well as I did. We had come into other hounds' territory and had to introduce ourselves before we would be permitted to continue. She was accustomed. She did not like it. No more did I. Scents get muddled while we wait for orders to be shown and locals to be appeased. One day I would like it to be so a Dog might flash her insignia anywhere she went and everyone, commoners to lords, would stand away.

The guardsmen, who were so invisible when Achoo and I had seemed to be locals rushing in, came out to greet my lady, Tunstall, and Farmer. The mage held Lady Sabine's flag, the foot of the pole tucked into his left stirrup, as casually as if he were always her bannerman. Tunstall halted at half a horse length to her left, his eyes promising trouble to any who did not treat her with courtesy.

She did not get ill treatment here. As the guards looked at her banner—a chance bit of wind puffed it straight out at that moment—they straightened up and bowed. One of them ran off through the gate to the inner courtyard, dodging geese. Another put two fingers to his lips and whistled up three stable lads, who'd been loitering near the smithy. They bowed to my lady and offered to take the horses. One of them jumped as Pounce leaped down from the packs on Saucebox and trotted over to me. Farmer grabbed my shoulder pack from Saucebox's back before the horses were led to the stable.

One winter's night, over hot cider, Lady Sabine had told

Goodwin, Tunstall, my friends, and me about her family. The Macayhills weren't particularly wealthy, but they were related to nearabout everyone. It came from their house being old enough to be listed in *The Book of Gold* and, my lady said, throwing enough fillies to ensure marriages with everyone who mattered. She'd named Queensgrace that night among the other holdings where she had kin.

Lady Sabine pointed me out now to the guards. I took it as my sign. "Achoo, *tumit,*" I said, and walked over to the group. Farmer handed over my pack when I reached him.

Two of the guards returned to the shadows by the gate after bowing to my lady a second time. She nodded, then turned to watch the boy who had Drummer's and Steady's reins. "You know how to handle a warhorse?" she asked, more lordly than I'd ever heard her speak.

"Don't you worry, my lady," said the guardsman who remained. "Our chief hostler trusts that lad with any horse in the stable. Ah, here comes Niccols. He'll make you comfortable."

From the guard's introduction, I knew the soft-bellied cove who strode toward us from the inner gate was the steward of Queensgrace Castle. His scarlet tunic sported some nice yellow and blue embroideries at the hems, and he could afford a matching small round yellow hat. A ring of keys jingled from his belt.

I ignored the introductions as my lady told the steward, Niccols, who we were. There were banners that hung from a balcony that overlooked the inner courtyard. Chasing Achoo as I'd done, I had not read the flags that flew over the castle. These I could not mistake. One was the blue shield of the Conté house with the royal silver sword-in-crown, topped by a silver crescent with its horns up. Prince Baird was here!

Beside that banner hung another, a red buck deer on

a green field under what looked like a yellow strip that was crenellated and laid upside down. Niccols was leading us to the inner gate, where we would pass straight under the banners. I called Achoo to heel. When I looked to see if Tunstall knew what they meant, I discovered Farmer at my elbow. Tunstall was trying to get within earshot of the steward and Lady Sabine without seeming to do so.

"That's Baron Something-or-other of Aspen Vale," Farmer told me. "The label, the three triangles with a line laid over the points, indicates the older son. The other one, the same flag but with the mark of the second son, belongs to Master Elyot of Aspen Vale." Farmer grimaced. "He is a very powerful mage—the pride of the City of the Gods. And being from Corus, I suppose you already know Prince Baird's coat of arms."

I nodded. "I'm thinking this makes our luck good," I told him, keeping my voice low. "With so many guests about, they'll be too busy to watch us." I grabbed for Achoo's collar as she trotted away from me, but it was too late. She'd picked up the scent again.

She knows as well as I that we can't go where we please in a castle. We must present our papers to the master or mistress first and get their approval, or they will howl the gods' own red murder at the next high court.

I took the lead I always wear clipped to my belt and freed it. "Achoo!" I called softly. "*Berhenti,* you ill-bred wench! Right now, *berhenti,* or I'll make you into a shawl for Farmer!"

Achoo looked back at me. When she saw the lead in my hands, her ears and tail drooped. She slumped as she stood.

"Curst right, you're going on the leash! You know this sarden game better than me, you swine's get, and looking woeful buys you no beans!" I reached her and threaded the lead around her collar as she looked pitiful for any who watched.

"Pretending you don't know how to act in some clench-arsed noble's place, when you've been in more of them than me! Now *tumit,* and no more sauce from you, or you get cold eels and vegetable broth for your supper!" She does not care one bit for cold eel, nor for broth made of anything that is not meat and does not have legs. I had to be sure that she understood. From time to time she deliberately ignores me. It is the nature of four-legged dogs and two-legged Dogs alike, to challenge the leader from time to time. Each such challenge must be met forcefully, or the Dog, hound or human, will not obey other orders.

When I caught up with the others, Niccols was telling my lady, "—understand we are pressed for space with His Highness, the baron, and Master Elyot staying. I'm certain the mistress will find a place for my lady in women's quarters, and proper garb for supper tonight—" I wanted to punch him in the kidneys for the look he gave my lady's riding clothes. He babbled on, "Your, ah, attendants will sleep in the great hall. I will try to ensure they have pallets—"

"Niccols, apparently you did not listen to me before." Lady Sabine's voice was chilly and clipped. "I am not in charge of our company. Senior Corporal Tunstall is in charge. We are not here for last-minute hospitality." She looked at Tunstall.

He stepped forward. "We are on a Hunt," he informed the steward. "I have documents from the Lord Provost, which I will show Count Dewin and his lady. We require an immediate meeting with His Lordship to that end. Depending on what we discover and at what time, we may not remain."

"And if we do, we shall do so together," my lady said firmly. "In a stable loft if necessary."

That put Niccols into a complete fidget. Mating pigeons flutter less. The count and his lady were out hawking with the guests, he said. We must await their permission to search the castle, he told us firmly. He sent one servant to the kitchen and another for maids. Before we knew it we'd been placed in a fine armory off the main hall, among a collection of very good weapons and armor. A cushion was brought for Lady Sabine to sit on at the table in the center of the room, while we commoners made do with our own rumps on the wooden benches. Niccols assured us over and over that he would come for us as soon as the count returned, then skittered away to do other chores.

I must end here. My eyes burn from the scant light, and there is still so much more to write of this very long day. I will take up the report again when chance offers.

the continuation of the events of June 19, 249

Commencing upon our being left to our own devices in a small armory

Queensgrace Castle

We hadn't been sitting long when the door opened and a maid shooed in two lads of eight or nine years and a gixie of ten. Each carried a big, heavy tray laden with food, pitchers, and cups. These they placed on the table with care. The maid bustled around them, setting out her own burden of spoons and napkins. The young ones were not dressed nearly so well as she. They had only undyed linen tunics with short sleeves, pale brown in color and needful of a good wash, perhaps even several good washes. They wore no shoes. Their heads were ill-combed, and an iron ring clasped each child by the left wrist.

"Does my cousin require so many slaves?" Lady Sabine asked the maid.

The young mot ushered the slaves toward the door and curtsied to my lady. "Oh, no. There was a slave train passing through as Prince Baird and the men from Aspen Vale came, if it please you, my lady. They had a lot of green folk. The dealers thought it would be a good thing if they stayed and loaned us some of their stock. To give the slaves a bit of training in a noble house, you see, get them used to the stairs and all. They've been that helpful, with all the men-at-arms and lords that came with His Highness. My lord's going to buy some. Is my lady interested?"

I held very still as Lady Sabine raised her brows. *Our* prince, Prince Gareth, was still here, as a slave. Right here. Farmer's eyes blazed. Tunstall clenched his fists. Yet we dared not utter a word. If Count Dewin's court mage placed listening spells anywhere, it would be in the rooms where he placed his guests.

"I shall consider it," my lady told the maid. "My thanks. You may go." She flipped a copper noble to the maid, who caught it and left with plenty of *thank you*s and *my lady*s.

Tunstall frowned at Lady Sabine. "Is that how you like to be treated?" It was just talk for the benefit of the listening spells, or so I figured. I had my own plans. Even if we were spied upon, Tunstall and I had found a way I could look about.

I took the leash from Achoo's collar, working under the table. Having never done this with my lady or Farmer, I had no notion of how they felt about idling with the chance of being refused the Hunt. I did know how Tunstall and I had managed being tucked away like this in the past. I gave Achoo the hand signal we had worked out, also under the table. When I straightened, Farmer was giving me the fish eye. When I glared back at him, he offered me a cheese waffle with butter.

Achoo went to the open door and pawed at it as I had signaled her to do.

My lady had picked up a turkey leg and was answering Tunstall's question about the treatment she'd received. "Don't be a dolt, Mattes," she told him. "I can't tell them not to. They get in trouble if their lords catch them speaking to me improperly."

I stuffed half of the waffle into my mouth and pointed to Achoo. "She has to go," I mumbled. None of them were paying any heed to me, Farmer's attention having been caught by my lady's words. That was how I liked it.

"Never mind that," Farmer said to her and to Tunstall. "Those slavers are still here. *He* may still be here. They may well give us the slip while we wait."

Achoo and I walked out of the room into the great hall.

There were no guards set to watch us. Maids, menservants, and slaves hurried here and there with loads in their arms. They were too busy preparing for the nobles' return to attend to Achoo and me. Pounce came out with us. It amazes me how he can move so as to seem near invisible. He had jumped down from one of the packhorses and trotted along close to Lady Sabine, but the castle's folk had been too busy watching her to take note of the black cat at her heels. Now he went out the main door to the courtyard.

Despite my excuse for her if she needed one, Achoo was not interested in going outside. She had her nose up in the air. I waited for her, trying not to tap my foot or otherwise distract her. Something had caught her attention and we could not move until she decided what it was. I only feared someone would notice that neither of us belonged there.

She trotted away, bound for the great hearth on the far wall. Easily, hands hooked in my belt as if we took a lazy walk, I strolled after her. She was sniffing around the hearthstones. The scent took her into the opening, where she snuffled around the kindling that had been laid there for the night's fire. Back out she came, to a basket full of shavings and another of twigs for more kindling, then a third for small logs. That last she smelled only once. Then she went back to the shavings and twigs. She gave them a last going-over, and followed her scent away from them, down the corridor that led from hearth and hall. I followed, my back braced for a shout ordering me to halt. No one said a word.

Achoo took us outside, around the back of the keep. There, between the keep and the inner wall, wood for the castle fires was stacked under waxed cloths. Her scent led her to the kindling stacks, then out again, around the side of the keep.

We crossed a short distance. I thought we were bound straight for the kitchen, an old-fashioned one set apart from the keep, but Achoo changed her mind. She halted suddenly, her head turning to and fro, then took us to the closest building, the chicken coop. A manservant rushed up to the hen yard waving his arms as she sniffed among screaming hens at the nest. I whistled her back to me and flipped a copper to the cove. He went silent and pointed for us to go. We left, Achoo hanging her head. If ever a dog looked mortified, it was she.

I gave her a strip of dried beef. When we were out of the man's sight, I said, "It's well enough, girl." We dodged a flock of outdoor hens. "I know plenty of human Dogs that would just have gone clean through the place and back to the keep, not thinking that boys who go into henhouses are either stealing or fetching eggs for a cook. At least you follow what is truly there."

Achoo found the main scent and took it to the kitchen. My thought by then was that they'd put the lad to work as a kitchen slave. That explained his being in the great hall. He'd been ordered to help clean out the hearth at some point, mayhap more than once. It explained as well his presence in the chicken coop. Now, in a large and busy kitchen, I waited to the inside of the door while Achoo did her finest work, her nose to the ground as she sorted through all manner of scents to find the one she wanted. Even with herbs and cheeses hung everywhere, four kinds of meat on the spit, and fresh herbs and young onions being chopped, Achoo could not be fooled. My belly might growl as my nose filled with the smell coming from that whole roasting pig, but Achoo cared nothing for that when she was Hunting. She worked around the feet of cooks and helpers and skirted two pups as they wrestled with a thick rope.

One cook swore at her, but she was too busy to do anything. Another cried, "Get that beast away from me!" but she and the others had too much to do other than aim a kick at the nearest animal. Five other dogs sat before the fire, hoping some meat would fall.

I could see that Achoo had our lad's scent all the time. She finally halted by a small keg that was placed beside the spits of meat.

Of course, I thought, squeezing past two mots who were heaving a good-sized bag of almonds onto a table. Turning the spit is a good task to give a child of four. Everyone can watch him to be sure he doesn't let the meat burn. I'd done such work at Provost's House, but there my aunt Mya had wrapped the turnspits in leather so they wouldn't burn my palms. These turnspits had no such wrappings. Had they given the lad cloths, or had they forced him to turn them with no protection for that soft, noble skin?

The gixie who turned the spit now shrank away from Achoo. She was mayhap six or so and armed with handfuls of rags. If she loosened her grip, they dropped to the floor. As she gathered them, she risked smacking her head on the lower turnspits.

I went to her and helped her pick up the rags. "May I have these for a moment?" I asked her. I found my right glove. "Here. This is big, but it will keep the turnspit from burning you."

She giggled once it was on, since she could barely fit two fingers where they belonged, let alone the others and the thumb. Still, she could use the palm to hold the spits as she rotated the meat. In addition to the pig and chickens, there were five ducks and two haunches of venison to brown. There were also the watching dogs to run off. She had a little broom for that purpose. They were hunting dogs, high tempered and not at all patient with slaves who would not feed them. I saw bite marks on her legs as well as whip weals on the backs of her arms. The bite marks were not bad, but they must have hurt all the same. "*Jaga,* Achoo," I said, and pointed to the spits.

Achoo looked at me with reproach, an owl asked to guard a mouse's nest. She had been walking the circuit of the kitchen, following our lad's steps around the tables as she dodged the cooks' swats and curses. She had also looked down the hall behind the gixie's turnspit. I had to do something first, so I put Achoo to guard work, gave the gixie my last chunk of cheese, and fetched my small sewing kit. I quickly threaded the needle, thanking the gods once again for giving me the wit to put forth the coin for this small collection of needles, pins, and thread tucked into a leather wallet. In simple repairs to my own kit it had paid for itself within a year of its purchase, and it also allowed me to do small favors that were often repaid in information. I began to stitch the rags together, one on top of the other.

The gixie looked over her shoulder at me as she turned the spitted chickens. "What are ye doin'? Ye should not be here, like as no." She was from the Lower City.

"Act the same as you always do, and no one will say a thing," I told her. "This corner is dark, and so's my uniform. Do your work, and we'll be fine." There was a fast exchange of snarls and a whirl of fur. Then the hound who'd tried to steal some of the meat ran yelping from Achoo. The others backed up enough that a cook and a maid noticed they were there, and beat the hounds out of the kitchen with their dishcloths.

The gixie took a quick mouthful of cheese. She ate with

it clutched tight to her chest, her head bowed over it, as if she expected someone to steal it. Someone probably might if they weren't all so busy here: "Is he yours?"

Another young slave lurched by us with a load of sticks for the oven where bread was baking. He didn't even glance our way.

"Achoo is a *she,* and yes, she's mine." Sitting there only barely hidden from view, I had no time to explain about the Dogs and their scent hounds. Besides, she might well lock up tight if she knew I was an official. "Do you always turn the spits?"

"Only since this mornin'," she told me. "No-Skin did it afore me, but he's gone now."

"No-Skin?" I asked, wondering if she joked with me. I'd never known a slave who joked, at least not with someone who wasn't a slave.

"That's what they called him, so everyone 'ud remember not t' beat him so it showed on his skin. They was to use only straps over his clothes, or open hands or fists, and not so nothin' gets broke," the girl explained. "One o' th' gixies punched his face so's she cut his cheek, and there! The Viper, the mage, she did the gixie just like that! And her ma started screamin' 'cos her babe'd just died and now they'd killed her little one, and snap! Dead ma into the dirt with the babe and the gixie. The captain that ran things told the Viper she'd wasted a bearing slave, and the Viper said she had her orders and he had his."

"Viper, you say?" I asked, stitching quickly.

"One of the two mots that rode along with the slave train," the gixie said. Looking around to be certain no one had an eye on us, she whispered, "They's both mages, them two."

I was in the middle of biting off my thread when she said

that, making me freeze for a moment. Farmer had worked it out right. "What happened to No-Skin?" I asked when I knew I could speak calmly. It's important, with folk who frighten as quick as slaves, to keep steady. The minute you get shaky, they will bolt. I put the first padded grip across my knee and started to sew a second one.

"We come here, and the captain offered us for work. He told the high-ups here that the trainin' would be good for us," the gixie said. "Me and No-Skin was teamed up on cleanin' the hearth and fetchin' eggs and turnin' the spits, 'cos I done all them things before my last master went toes up and we was sold."

"Was he any use to you, No-Skin?" I asked, glancing around the kitchen. A few maids had looked our way, but I was tucked well into the shadows, and the gixie kept her eyes on her work, turning first one spit, then another. She struggled with the pig. I longed to help her, but that would bring me into view of the rest of the staff. I would be sent away when we were discovered, and no doubt she would be beaten for chattering, if she did not get worse for talking with a Dog.

The gixie snorted at my question. "His hands was as soft as a babe's!" she told me with scorn. "He got splinters in every finger, and he was scared gormless by the hens. They gave *me* a beating for not doin' that work meself, and five strokes to the cook that sent us to the hens, and her a freewoman! They wrapped his hands in linen to turn spits till they took him away from that." She shook her head. "But he was plucky enough. He tried to do his share, even when it hurt him." Her shoulders slumped. "I don't know what he'll do without me to look after him. I've not seen him since they took him from here."

"Who took him?" I asked as I finished stitching longer cloth strips to the second pad.

"One of the drovers came for him and told the cooks to give me his work," she replied. "Then he just scooped No-Skin up under his arm and carried him off." She looked at me. "What if they done for him like they done for the one that punched him?"

I shook my head. "He's too valuable," I said. "They'll not so much as take him over Breakbone Falls, believe me."

She looked at me as if I'd started to pop golden eggs from my mouth. "*He's* valuable." The way she said it, as if she were years older than six, told me she believed me not a whit.

I smiled a little. "Let's just say them that sold him to your master stole him from the wrong folk. Now see here." I showed her how to place the thick rag pad I'd sewn together against her palm, how to wrap the straps twice to hold it in place, and how to tie the cloth on her wrist one-handed so the knot wouldn't interfere with her grip. I handed the other pad to her, its straps wrapped neatly around it. "For when the other wears out."

She returned my glove to me, unable to speak. I didn't think folk gave her things very often. I was getting to my feet when she looked up at me. "Travel safe, travel well," she whispered.

The blessing is an old, honored one. Not many use it anymore. I gave the traditional answer, "May those who have gone before be always with you." And then, because something urged me to it, I asked, "What's your name?"

She scratched her head. "Linnet Beck, at least till the next master gets a big tarse boil and decides he don't like my name."

"Keep yourself alive, Linnet Beck," I told her quietly. "Don't ever talk about No-Skin again. If you need help and you can manage it, get word to the nearest Provost's Guard that you want Beka Cooper, from Corus Lower City. You have that?"

Linnet didn't seem too convinced of the message's worth, but she repeated, "Beka Cooper, Corus Lower City. The Dogs."

I gave her a smile. "That's it. I can't promise, but if you send for me, I'll do my best to come, or one of my friends will. Achoo, *mencari*."

Achoo, who'd been crouched in the shadows behind me, got to her feet and followed her scent, down the dark hall at Linnet's back. That took us to the servants' privy yard, the place behind it where huge barrels of garbage awaited the carters who would dispose of them, and back into the kitchen. Achoo's nose led us into the pantry and out as the maid who'd been working there screeched at both of us. Down another back hallway we went and then up a servants' stair. The climb was steep and dark, beyond the tall level that houses the great hall and into a newer portion of the keep. I could tell it was so by the lighter-colored stone and the lighter-colored mortar that held it in place. Achoo halted on the third story of this newer structure and scratched at the door on the landing, dancing with impatience. I opened the door onto a long hallway.

Achoo sniffed her way down the hall to one locked door. When she looked at me and whimpered, I glanced around. The place was dead quiet. I drew the Sign on my chest and removed my shoulder pack so I could get my lock picks out. All the time I worked on that lock, I was sweating. The moment I had the door open, Achoo and I slipped inside.

I was thinking a string of prayers to every god I could remember as I closed the door behind us. I called to my favorite ones twice. As soon as I looked around that large chamber I knew I was in dreadful trouble. A tall rack supported a suit of armor. A shield leaned against it, showing the bright silver sword-in-crown with the upended crescent. Our lad, Prince Gareth, had been in his uncle's room.

Achoo showed me he'd been all over those rooms, the main chamber, the bedchamber, and the small chamber for the prince's personal attendants. We were triply lucky that afternoon. No one was inside.

My hound traced the scent to the chairs by the hearth, to the tub that stood in the bedchamber, and back into the main room. As she did, I stood by the door, keeping it open a crack, listening for approaching steps and thinking. They had brought Gareth here, almost certainly to Prince Baird. This was bad news, the worst, and it lay on me like a weight. On feast days we had all seen the young prince with his big uncle. King Roger was wiry and lean, his younger brother of the same height, but heavier with muscle and good living. Prince Baird would raise his laughing nephew high in the air and the crowds would cheer them both.

Achoo gave a small yip from the bedchamber. I quickly glanced outside. Still no one had shown himself. I shut the door, locked it from the inside with my picks, and went to see what Achoo had found.

A red string bracelet, the kind a nursemaid would make for her charge, lay on a bedside table among a heap of jewels worn for dress occasions. Achoo nudged the bracelet with her nose and sneezed.

I unsheathed my dagger and turned the bracelet over with the point of it. The string was done up in nine knots for the Goddess, guardian of children, and the ends were braided for Mithros, whose laws bind the realm. Somewhere the maker had found tiny beads to thread onto it, one each of brown agate for protection, pink quartz for love, and onyx also for protection.

If only it had worked.

Achoo had gone on sniffing, her work taking her back to the front door of the rooms. I left the bracelet as I'd found it and followed her. When I opened the door a crack, I flinched. Pounce was waiting for us.

The count and Prince Baird just rode into the outer court-yard, he told us. *They're back from hunting. Get out of here at once!*

"Achoo, *kemari cepat!*" I ordered. Once she dashed through the open door I hurried to lock it, struggling to control my shaky fingers. As the three of us ran for the stair I muttered, "Bum-swived yattering misborn tarses." I tried to think of a lie for when they caught us, and failed. Instead I whistled for Achoo and Pounce to follow me up the steps rather than down.

No need to go up, Pounce told us. *The servants use this stair. The nobles have a wider one paved in green marble for their use. What were you doing, anyway?*

I signaled Achoo to follow us down. She did, sniffing, still on the track. Walking as if we belonged on that staircase, I explained to Pounce (silently) what we'd done in our time away from our companions.

I have been idling around the slave train, he told me. *The slaves are kept near the goat pens while they supply the extra labor during the prince's visit. They are guarded, so it will be difficult to talk with them unseen.*

"Is it them who are in a trap, or us?" I muttered. Pounce didn't answer. Instead he led us along another turn past the servants' privies and along the large addition to the great hall. It was then that Achoo protested. The scent took her in another direction. I ordered her to heel. We needed to get clear of the newly arrived nobles. I did not want to face them without Tunstall at my side. For now, the Hunt must wait. I got Achoo to follow Pounce and me at last, but I could see she was going to complain of me to the other scent hounds at home.

Behind the new addition, where the original wall had been widened to include it, we found Tunstall, joking with men-at-arms who had pitched camp there. These coves wore royal blue tunics and gray trousers, with the crescent-on-its-back design, meaning the second son, on their chests.

"Well, look at this—my partner, Cooper," Tunstall greeted me, beckoning for me to join them. "Taking the hound for a walk?"

He wished me to be casual. I knew that from his greeting and the wave of his hand. I didn't know how relaxed I could be after those tense moments in the prince's bedroom. Worse, any of these coves in blue and gray could put me in chains for the impertinence of having been there without leave. I stuck my hands in my pockets and whispered to Achoo, *"Gampang."*

She whined at me. She didn't want to meet anyone. She wanted to go back to the Hunt.

"Gampang." I repeated as we drew close to the men. "Don't argue!" I walked up to Tunstall and gave a nod to the coves who sat around him, on kegs, camp stools, or upended buckets, tending equipment and weapons as they relaxed. "Good evenin', sirs," I said in my Lower City accent. I looked up at Tunstall, who was lounging against one of their wagons. "Any word on where we sleep tonight, Tunstall? Here, or are we off on the road?" I would have loved to know what news he'd gathered, if anything, but there was no way to ask him

here. I couldn't even inquire if Farmer had gone nosing about. We all had parts to play, and we wanted to give these strangers no idea whatever that we were Hunting when we'd been ordered not to.

"You don't want to be sleeping in that great hall," one of the men-at-arms, a thin, muscled redhead, told me. "There's fleas in the pallets. The count's too cheap to pay a mage to get them out."

"*He's* not sleeping on them, is he?" asked another cove with the look of a Scanran. "Nor that mage from Aspen Vale. You won't catch him doin' flea-bane spells."

Yet Farmer took care of the swamp bugs without a mutter, I thought. He *insisted* on it.

"We didn't even stay the first night," the redhead went on. "Came out and pitched our tents here, after a dunk in the river to rid us of the cursed fleas."

"Farmer and me have been invited to pitch a tent with these good fellows," Tunstall explained. "If you see Farmer, tell him?" He bent his head, scratching his neck and refusing to meet my eyes. "You and . . . the lady . . . ," he mumbled.

I propped my hands on my hips, put one leg forward, and began to tap my toe, as Kora so often did. It worked better in skirts, but it was still a good way to tell a cove, any cove, that you lose patience. It also makes coves think you're a certain kind of mot, the kind they feel comfortable with.

"Best tell her before she sharpens you up with a broom about your shoulders!" one of the coves shouted.

"I bet she sets the Corus Rats to kissing the mules' arses," another called. "Stricter than their old mams!"

Tunstall pointed to the entry to the castle that was nearby. "You'll find her up one set of stairs, in the ladies' rooms," he said, giving me the guiltiest of looks. "You're to sleep in whatever room they grant her. And you'll have to get a dress there, for supper."

Dress? I mouthed at him. My back was to the men-at-arms so they could not see.

Tunstall shrugged helplessly. "It's how they do things here, Cooper," he said. The other coves laughed at that.

"Our women refused even to enter castle grounds," the Scanran told me, a looking of understanding in his eyes. A few of the other men-at-arms were nodding. "Mithros be thanked, our captain and His Highness are upright men who won't let good soldiers be humiliated."

I wouldn't speak up for myself, but they couldn't go on thinking bad of my partner. "There's naught Tunstall can say about it," I told them. "Everyone thinks they rank Dogs, unless they're dealing with my lord Gershom."

"Everyone *does* rank a Dog," said the redhead with a grin.

Tunstall laid a big, friendly hand on the redhead's shoulder. "Not for long, though, eh, laddybuck?" he asked.

The redhead leaned to that side, doing his best not to grimace or complain about the strength of Tunstall's hold.

I shook my head and walked to the castle door, Achoo and Pounce beside me. The coves didn't need me to play their games.

The wing where the ladies were housed was much different from that of the men. I had to pass two armed guards to enter. One of them told me that if the ladies complained of my hound or my cat, out they would go, but they let me pass.

Once upstairs, I wasn't sure which of the open doors I was to enter. I was looking from one to another when a tiny creature made of flying silk burst through one that was slightly open and raced down the hall. Achoo forgot herself and went tearing after, covering in three bounds what the little thing had done in twenty. Achoo trapped the small animal in the corner and was sniffing it in the crudest way when I heard a mot call, "Snowflake! Snowflake! You stole my ivory ribbons!"

A mot came out of the room where Snowflake, if that was the silky creature's name, had been. She was nearly as pretty as the animal, dressed in an ankle-length tunic of cream-colored linen and a round cap of the same color. Her blond hair hung in two braids to her knees. When she saw her pet's situation, she ran down the hall, crying, "You brute! Get away from Snowflake!"

"Achoo," I said, but then the young mot halted. The bit of fluff was dancing under Achoo, running through her legs, and making it very clear that Achoo was her new best friend. Achoo was doing her best to lick the little thing, wagging her tail to show the affection was given back in full. Instead of screaming for the guards, the lady halted where she was and offered her hands, palms up, for Achoo to smell.

"*Pengantar,* Achoo," I said. Achoo needed permission to greet human beings.

Achoo liked the lady's scent. The mot liked the way Achoo held up her head and closed her eyes to have her ears scratched. "What a splendid hound you are," the lady told Achoo as the hound danced. "You're not like our hunting hounds at all, though of course they are very fine animals in their way." With a glance at me she asked, "What manner of breed is she? I have never seen her like before."

I would not shame Achoo by saying she was a breed only by grace of training. Without her great skill she would have been known only as a common street cur. "She is a scent hound, my lady," I replied. I could feel Pounce leaning against my left boot to give me courage. Pounce knew I did not like to speak with the nobility, but this pretty mot could not be so bad if she liked proper four-legged dogs. "Not for hunting game, if it please you. Achoo and I are both in the service of the Lord Provost of the realm."

She gifted me with a bright smile. "Achoo! What a delightful name!" She had discovered Achoo's favorite behind-the-ear scratch. "I'm Lewyth, and *this* dreadful bit of disobedience"— she scooped up the fluffy creature as it tried to go around her—"is Snowball, the wickedest Butterfly Puppy ever bred." She held the mite up to her face, where it proceeded to lick her cheek while wagging a plume of a tail. "Yes, you're very wicked. Still, between you and me, I wouldn't want a ribbon on top of my head, either. You were wise to run away." She offered the tiny dog to me and I took it without thinking. It had a small, pointed nose, a black mask around two button eyes, and two upright black ears that were far larger than a head that size would normally sport. Except for the black fur on her skull and a saddle of black fur on her back, she was white, with tiny paws and a cheerful puppy smile. She seemed inclined to like everyone, because she started to lick my hands once she got used to being away from the lady.

"Why do you call your hound Achoo?" Lewyth asked.

"She sneezes when she gets a scent," I explained. "My partner thinks she sneezes it out and breathes it back in so her nose is clearer the second time."

"She's a wise hunter, aren't you, then?" Lewyth asked Achoo, giving her one more good scratch with both hands. "Our family breeds hunting hounds and Butterfly Pups, now they're popular. We've never tried scent hounds. Were you and Achoo looking for someone?"

"I was ordered to find my lady Sabine of Macayhill. The men-at-arms told me she was up here," I said. Mistress Snowball, being the trusting sort, had turned herself over in the crook of my arm, inviting me to give her a belly rub. The moment I did so, she began to wriggle gleefully. "This is a very happy-natured creature."

It is a very silly creature, Pounce remarked to me. *I wager its brain pan is also full of fluff.*

"The Butterflies are like that," Lewyth replied, holding her hand down to Pounce. "If you give them kindness, they will love you all your days. Now, I cannot believe this handsome fellow is a scent *cat.*"

I looked down to see Pounce boot her hand just like a true cat. He glanced at me and I saw his eyes were gold. I nodded. "No, Pounce just thinks I'll make a muck of things if I roam without him to watch me."

Lewyth giggled. "I'm not making fun," she hurried to explain. "I have cats, too. You may as well come in with us. Lady Sabine is with the countess. You must be Guardswoman Cooper." We walked into the room that Snowball had left so gleefully.

Achoo sneezed. She raced to the baskets of wood placed in the corner to supply the braziers that heated it. Eagerly she sniffed the wood, turning pieces over with her nose, as a handful of small creatures like Snowball rushed to defend their mistresses, barking most ferociously. Only with their ears raised did they come as tall as Achoo's chest. Several cats with fur as long as the fluffy dogs' started to flee the room, but halted when they saw Pounce. Slowly they formed a circle around him and sat, tails flicking.

"Achoo, *kemari,*" I ordered, but my heart wasn't in it. I knew very well why she was going from the wood baskets to every brazier, to and fro, as if she marked the steps of a child under orders to put fresh wood in each. When I thought we risked a call for guards, I repeated more firmly, "*Kemari,* girl!"

Achoo glanced at me. I saw her ribs rise and fall as she sighed. Then she looked at the little dogs crowding around her and wagged her tail.

Achoo is easy to please, if I have not written it before.

"Ladies, ladies," cried Lewyth. "This is Lady Sabine's companion, Guardswoman Cooper. Achoo is her hound, and Pounce is her cat. She was told to meet her lady here, and our countess told us *we* were to supply her with a gown for supper."

"And a bath, like as not," said one of them, a black-haired lady in a rose-colored tunic. Had no one ever told her that if she continued to screw her face up, it would stick in that position?

A stately blond who had not moved from her chair during the fuss said, "Lady Wyttabyrd, the Gentle Mother adjures us to show grace to those beneath us in rank."

I clasped my hands behind me and planted my feet. So now I was beneath them in rank. Usually talk of animals brings folk together. I'd hoped to ask some questions when things quieted, but that was impossible if I was no better than a servant.

The arrogant blond turned to me and gave me a smile that was no more than a curve of the lips. "What is your name?"

"My lady, I am Provost's Guardswoman Rebakah Cooper, a four-year veteran of the Lower City District in Corus," I replied.

Lewyth put a hand on my shoulder. "Where did this formality come from? Baylisa, there's no need."

If anything, the lady called Baylisa grew even cooler. "Lewyth, the Gentle Mother teaches us that a world in its proper order is a peaceful one."

The other young ladies in the room bowed their heads and whispered, "So mote it be." They retreated to chairs and picked up different kinds of needlework. The small dogs, plainly knowing this signal, came to sit by their mistresses' feet, their faces as forlorn as Achoo's when I called her to heel.

The mot named Baylisa turned her ice blue eyes to Lewyth and me. "We follow the ways of the Gentle Mother here," she explained. "My younger sister Lewyth is still learning to keep a serene heart." Lewyth took her hand from my shoulder. "The Gentle Mother could relieve you of the pain and struggle you face in that uniform, Guardswoman Cooper," Baylisa went on. "There are men to perform such brute work. Your spirit cries out for the touch of a child's hands, the peace of the spindle, and the completion of a family."

I wanted to slap this clapper-jawed dismal-dreaming piece of jouster bait. Folk in the Lower City do not tell each other how to worship, or if they do, it is not for long. I clenched my hands behind me and said as calmly as I could manage, "Begging Your Ladyship's pardon, but I am already in a god's service." I did not say that I knew swiving well what my spirit called for, and it was not a curst cage!

She sat back, her hand splayed delicately over her chest. It is a gesture that never fails to give me the royal itch. "You, in service to a god?"

"What is this?" I was never so glad to hear Lady Sabine's musical voice in my life. "Cooper, is there a problem?"

I did not look away from Lady Baylisa. "We were talking religion, Lady Sabine."

Another mot, older, said behind me, "Lady Baylisa of Disart is an eloquent advocate of the Gentle Mother among the women of our lands. She has brought many to see that the world has changed, the wars of old done with, and we must change with it."

I decided I ought to face the mot who was talking, since

the other mots rose to curtsy to her. I bowed when I faced her and Lady Sabine. She was a grim-faced bit of jerky, wearing her dark hair scraped back, braided, then pinned in coils under a sheer veil and a round cap. Her ankle-length tunic was blue silk, with tiny pearls stitched in patterns along the hems. One large teardrop-shaped pearl hung on a gold chain nearly to her waist. One of the little dogs, seemingly all fuzz, ran to her and barked for attention. She scooped it up and tucked it in the corner of her arm. I had to think some better of her for not worrying if the creature might shed its hair on her costly dress, but only some.

"Guardswoman Rebakah Cooper, this is Countess Aeldra of Queensgrace," Lady Sabine told me. She looked as if she'd come fresh from the bath, her curly hair still showing some droplets of water. There was a silver net over her head. She had put on a long tunic in a shade of light blue that did her no favors. It was trimmed with pale pink braid threaded with a silver ribbon. Given the lack of travel wrinkles in the tunic, I knew it must be a loan from one of the ladies. They had even gotten Lady Sabine into a useless pair of soft, flat shoes. She ignored my obvious surprise at her dress to tell the countess, "My lady, Guardswoman Cooper is one of the Provost's Guards I travel with."

The countess looked me over while I fought the urge to scratch my bum. "Who is that monster?" she asked, nodding her head toward Achoo, who sat at my side.

"My lady, Achoo is a scent hound," Lady Lewyth said, coming up to rub Achoo's ears. "She's the friendliest thing. She hasn't bothered the cats in the least, and the dogs love her. But she's a hound of degree, not a pet."

"Though technically scent hounds, at least this one, are not hounds of degree," the countess said coolly, "since the ones who work with the Provost are chosen on the basis of aptitude. They do not come from a recognized breeder of hounds for the hunt."

If her rump were any stiffer, she'd break it every time she rides, I thought to Pounce.

If she fell on the steps, they would never be able to put her together again, he replied.

Fortunately, I have long practice at keeping my face calm when Pounce makes me laugh inside.

Countess Aeldra raised her voice. "Lady Baylisa, have proper clothes been produced for this person?"

Lady Baylisa nodded to a slave who'd tucked herself behind a cluster of noblewomen. She came forward with three tunics laid over her arms. Two were pink and one was pale yellow. I could see the stitching where one side seam had been repaired. They wouldn't be giving their best to help me to pass muster in the great hall.

"Hold that first gown against you," the countess ordered me. I took a breath. I had been thinking this over since the men had told me that I would be required to wear a dress for supper. I knew curst well they would ask no such thing of Tunstall. This was more of the Gentle Mother business, stripping fighting women of the symbols of their battles.

"Begging my lady's pardon," I said, looking at the ground in order to appear as meek as I could, "but I must wear my uniform at all times."

The room went dead quiet. Even the little dogs seemed to know sommat was up.

"You will do no such thing," the countess replied.

"Forgive me, Your Ladyship, but I must," I repeated. "I am not here on my own. I am on a Hunt. In that respect I am here as a Provost's Guard, which means I am on duty. I cannot go without my uniform." I glanced at Lady Sabine, who gave me the tiniest of nods. "I have cleaner uniforms, wherever my bags ended up."

"Ridiculous!" the countess said. "There is no need for your . . . *work* here! You are our guest, and as our guest, you will abide by the rules of this house!" When I glanced up, she had turned to my lady. "Lady Sabine, you are in charge of your party. Tell her to obey me at once!"

My lady started to scratch her head and stopped, remembering that was a rude, common gesture, I think. She had gotten it from Tunstall. "In fact, Countess Aeldra, I am *not* in charge," she said. "I am employed in the service of the Lord Provost. It is Senior Corporal Matthias Tunstall who is in command of our group. You will easily recognize him at supper. He will be wearing the same uniform as Guardswoman Cooper."

The countess pressed her hands together palm to palm and touched her fingertips under her chin. I was not sure if she was trying to pray or if she was calling on the household gods by imitating the coat of arms of Queensgrace. "It is a *meal,* with Prince Baird, the Baron of Aspen Vale, and his brother, who is a powerful mage, as our guests. You cannot possibly have reason to wear your uniform then or at any other time while you are in women's quarters!" She was beginning to sport a bit of a flush on her cheekbones.

I glanced at Sabine. It seemed Master Niccols had not told his countess why we were here. My lady gave me a little nod to say she was ready to help me.

"My lady countess, I have every reason to wear my uniform here," I told her quietly. "We search for a noble's kidnapped child. My hound found the child's scent in this very room when we entered it. We *are* working in this castle."

The countess gripped my right wrist. I found a bruise there later. "I will have no more of your nonsense," she began.

Sabine rested her own hand on the countess's shoulder. "Cousin, release Cooper immediately. She tells the truth. I informed your steward when we arrived why we were here."

"He said nothing about evidence. I would have known of a kidnapped child," the lady began.

"He is disguised as a slave," I informed her. "He has been working here with other slaves. *Would* you have seen him, my lady?"

We heard a soft growl from below and looked down. Achoo had come over. She looked at Countess Aeldra, her lips peeled back just enough to show her front teeth. I could have told my hound to stop, but I wasn't minded to just then.

"My sitting room, right now," the countess said. "Baylisa, ask my lord if he will grant me the honor of his company as soon as may be!" She released me and led us to the back of the room, where a door stood open.

As Achoo, Pounce, Sabine, and I followed, I murmured to my lady, "So much for Gentle Mothers."

Sabine shook her head. "I fear Aeldra needs to work harder on her peace of heart," she replied just as quietly.

If she tries to handle Beka so roughly again, I will help myself to a piece of her skin, Pounce said.

Once we were inside the room, I closed the door behind us. It was more an office than a sitting room, though a crescent of chairs and chests with cushioned tops was placed near parchment windows. Three more chairs were set before the desk. The countess sat behind it and gestured for Sabine to have a seat, but she offered me no such courtesy. She glared at Achoo and Pounce. "These animals belong out of doors."

"They remain as long as Guardswoman Cooper and I do, Cousin," replied Sabine. "They are both important parts of our investigation."

"A cat!" the countess said. There could not have been more scorn in her voice if she had been drinking it. "Are there Provost's Guard *cats* now?"

Sabine leaned forward, her face white and intent. "We need not explain ourselves here." She reached into her sleeve and drew out a folded paper with a seal on it. "We are under the Provost's orders. You will note he has used the seal of the Great Charter, which all noble houses are required to obey." She placed the paper on the desk.

The countess opened it with her fingertips, as if she thought something in the orders might soil her skin. For a long moment she glared at the writing before she lifted the document to the light of the candles, turning it this way and that to examine it. Then she took a pinch of powder from a dish on the desk and sprinkled it on the seal. There was a flash of light and the scent of burning rope.

"Cousin, you teeter on the edge of insulting me," Lady Sabine told her. She was straight as a baton on her chair. "Were I not a patient woman, you would have fallen over that edge just now. Those documents are not forgeries. By my blood and by my birth, my word as a knight of this realm should be good enough!"

Sommat in her eyes must have shaken the countess. The mot placed Lady Sabine's paper on the desk and tried to smile. "I meant no disrespect to any oaths you have sworn, my dear. But this is an accusation of great weight, come from one common born." Her gaze was frosty as she looked at me.

I burned, but I kept my gob shut.

"It is no accusation, Cousin," my lady said, her voice and

face still furious. "It is a fact. Someone brought that child into this house, into your ladies' very solar." She turned to me. "Where else, Guardswoman Cooper?"

Sabine I would gladly answer. "The great hall, the woodpiles that serve the hearth in the great hall and the kitchen, the henhouse, the kitchen, the hall where the noble guests are staying, the woodpile which serves that hall, and the ladies' solar." I glanced at the countess, who had folded her hands in her lap. "Achoo and I have not yet finished. We have not yet found where he is now." I would give Linnet's information, that a cart and several slaves, including Prince Gareth, had left the castle a day ago, to Sabine later.

"We do not harbor criminals!" the countess snapped.

She was not clever, saying things that were complete nonsense. "Most barrel trappers don't walk the day with their coat of arms flying on a stick, my lady," I said. "Plenty of them don't even look that common."

"Cooper," Sabine murmured as the countess turned purple. "Apologize for being so forward."

"I'm sorry," I said, not trying very hard to sound that way. I even gave it a bit of a wait before I added, "My lady."

Sabine half turned her head to look at me. I saw the corner of her mouth twitch in part of a smile before she looked at the countess again. "A barrel trapper is a kidnapper," she explained. "A legendary kidnapper is said to have kept his captives in barrels until they were ransomed."

The countess glared at me yet again. "Do you see what happens, Cousin?" she asked, her voice crisp. "They grub after these evil creatures so long they begin to look and sound like them."

Someone rapped on the door and opened it. I expected the count, and so did the countess and Sabine. We got Tunstall and Farmer instead. It was as they were bowing and introducing themselves, Farmer showing the countess yet another copy of our orders, that the count arrived and with him Prince Baird.

Then came us kneeling, and being given permission to stand. The prince stepped on Achoo's foot, making her yelp. He tried to apologize to her, offering her a strip of dried meat, but she hid behind me.

The prince looked at me with appeal in his eye. "Are you her handler, guardswoman?" he asked. "Please allow me to make it up with her! I would no more harm her than I would one of my own good hounds."

I dared not say no to the king's brother. "*Makan,* Achoo," I told her quietly. "*Pengantar.*" With permission, she ventured out from behind me and accepted the prince's treat, doubtless one of those he kept for his own hounds.

"Did you call her *Achoo?*" he asked merrily as he ruffled her ears.

Yet again did I explain how she got the scent. I could see the king in Prince Baird's neatly arched brows, brown eyes, slender nose, and long mouth, but the prince was heavier in the jowls. He wore a short-clipped beard and combed his hair back into a gleaming horsetail. Plenty of hours in the sun had put gold streaks in that brown hair. He was more muscular than the king, too, which was to be expected. When the prince wasn't fighting with our armies, he was hunting bandits or deer. His voice crackled as did those of folk who'd spent much time shouting.

Once he'd given Achoo a last treat, he accepted a glass of the wine the count had poured out for the nobles. Then he took a seat arranged in the half circle. When he beckoned, the count and countess sat on either side of him. Tunstall and I stood at review rest, hands clasped behind our backs, legs planted a foot apart. Farmer stood easily, his hands in the pockets of his breeches. That bought him a raised eyebrow from the prince, but no more. Provost's mages were not exactly expected to conduct themselves in the same way as the rest of us. They were often considered cracked by outsiders and most Dogs.

"Your Highness, my lord, pray allow me to introduce the members of our company," Lady Sabine said. When permission was given, she named each of us and we bowed. Farmer took his hands from his pockets for that, at least. Lady Sabine was very exact in telling these nobles that Tunstall was in command. When she finished, the count beckoned for her to sit by the countess. Only when Tunstall nodded his approval did Sabine take the chair.

Tunstall produced our orders. "Your Highness? My lord? If I may?"

The count extended his hand and Tunstall gave the papers to him. Normally we'd have shown our papers to the prince, since he was highest in rank, but as the lord of the castle and fief, the count had precedence. I only know scummer like this because I had to learn it for other Hunts. Nobles are a pain in the bum.

The count read the orders over, then passed them to Prince Baird. He read them, then looked at the count with raised brows as he gave the orders back to Tunstall. The count glared at us. "Do you claim one of us is the subject of your inquiries, Corporal?"

"Is our quarry here now, my lord?" Tunstall asked, his face all innocence.

"You *dare*!" bellowed the count.

Tunstall shrugged. "If he has not been here, and you were unaware of the plot to kidnap him, then our business is not with you."

"Actually, he was," I said. "Achoo tracked his scent all over the castle. I've heard that he may be a part of a group of slaves that left here a day or two ago."

"By Mithros!" The count lunged to his feet. "You searched my *home* without so much as a by-your-leave? I'll have you *whipped* for that!"

Tunstall leaned forward, the orders still in his hand, pointing to the seal and the signature of the Lord Provost. Only the Lord High Magistrate could interfere with Dogs on a Hunt under those orders. Still, I wasn't betting my skin on the count's willingness to obey the law. I knelt by Achoo and hugged her. As always when I hugged too tight, Achoo fought my grip.

"Forgive me, Your Lordship, sir, but you don't know what these hounds are like, once they've got the scent in their sniffers!" I explained, being as Lower City as I could. "I took her to do her business because the carpets and the wood was so nice, and off she went, with me yellin' the proper commands and all, but she was on the track. She knew just where she was goin', did the little circle every time he musta stopped, and every time I tried to grab her she was off again. Not that I'm the bravest about catchin' her, savin' your presence, my lord count, not after that time I tried to grab her when she was excited and she bit me so hard!" I showed him the great double-crescent scar on the back of my hand where Rush the Snapper bit me, the time I caught him with a purse full of coles. "So mayhap I'm not the quickest to hold her, and I could only follow as she led, pleading Your Lordship's understanding. It weren't me, I swear, it were the hound."

"It'd be that." Farmer nodded as he scratched his head.

"She seems sweet enough right now, the hound, but when she gets excited, she goes mad."

"Not *mad*," Tunstall said with a glare at Farmer. "She is hard to restrain." He bowed to the prince and the count. "Her . . . circumstances . . . are such that she only responds, when she does, to Cooper. She is a fine scent hound, my lords, my lady."

"I have told you time and again that the hound is a menace," Lady Sabine said at her noblest. "It is poor handling that has ruined whatever training the creature was given."

Snarl, I heard Pounce say in my mind. Achoo began a volley of barks and snarls that made her sound like the vicious animal we had named her. I calmed her down, seemingly, and we waited for the count to rule for me to be whipped or no.

"How is it, then, that she did not savage anyone in the solar?" the countess asked. I wanted to kick the old croaking corbie. "Lady Lewyth called her the friendliest thing."

"Oh, that," I said, half bowing since I knelt on the floor. "It's the little animals, my lady. They calm her right down. Amazing, it is. That's why we travel with my cat. Pounce keeps her steady. Seeing all them pretty little dogs and cats, she gentled enough that I could get a grip on her." I looked anxiously at the count. "Please, Your Highness, I can't help it that the finest scent hound in the Lower City is a little touchy. She'd've been dog meat if they hadn't *saw* she'd work with me."

"No, girl, curse it, the prince is 'Your Highness.' I am properly addressed as 'my lord,'" the count fussed, with one look at the prince to make sure he didn't take offense at my seeming misstep. "Obviously proper manners is not a thing taught in what training you people receive."

The prince waved it away. "I am sure I can grant slack to those who enforce the law, Dewin," he said.

Over our heads a great bell began to chime. The countess half rose, as if it summoned her, then took her seat again, but she was suddenly restless.

"My lady, is there a problem?" Lady Sabine asked.

"Oh, no, not precisely," Lady Aeldra replied. "Only that is the half-hour bell for the closing of the gates. Supper is in an hour. There are things to be seen to, and we have yet to sort out a sleeping place for you and your . . ." She took a breath, plainly searching for a word.

"Colleagues," Lady Sabine told her.

"People," the count said flatly. "My dear, this can be handled after supper. Sabine, you and the wench must dress. It is the rule of my house."

I felt sick to my gut, but I stood and faced the old canker blossom. "Your Highness, my lord, my lady, I may not," I told them, *trying* not to sound rude. I knew I was courting that whipping the count had spoken of. "I am a Provost's Guard on a Hunt. I eat, I sleep, I do all manner of things, but until I bring down my prey, I am on duty. I wear my uniform."

By the time I was done speaking, Tunstall had moved to stand beside me. Sabine was on her feet at my right, and Farmer was at my back. Achoo sat before me, quiet, acting not at all like the half-broken creature I had painted her.

The other nobles looked at us without a word. It was hard to read their faces. I think it's something they're taught when they're young. Finally the count said, "Enough. We have guests we neglect, and no one is going anywhere tonight. If your kidnapped boy is here we shall find him tomorrow as easily as today. I will give orders to the guard to let no one with a lad or lass of that age leave without my permission. In the morning we shall investigate at a proper count's court, not this rude sniffing at corners."

"My lord, it's the slave dealers—" Tunstall began.

"*Tomorrow,*" Count Dewin said angrily. "My patience has been tried to its limit. Your woman is permitted to wear her uniform at supper, but she is to stay away from our gentle young ladies, lest her violence corrupt them. Lady Sabine, I hope you will respect our beliefs and let no taint of the dark world you live in shadow their protected lives. My lady will provide for your sleeping arrangements and for those of the . . . hound." He looked at Tunstall and Farmer.

Tunstall bowed. "The prince's men-at-arms have invited us to camp with them."

The count grunted. He and the prince left as we bowed. They left the door open so we could see Lady Baylisa and Lady Lewyth were outside, looking anxious. Lewyth held some tunics on one arm.

"She will remain in uniform for supper," the countess snapped. She looked at me. "Have you a clean one, at least?"

"In my packs, my lady, but I—" I began.

The countess was not interested in speech with me. "Have the slaves bring her packs and Lady Sabine's in here." She took a deep breath. "It's not the best choice, but I have no other chambers available where you might have privacy, Sabine. This—*wench*—may wait upon you, if she has any skills." To Lewyth she said, "Have the slaves press the clean uniform." She looked at me. "One of the slaves will show you to the baths. Hurry to wash up. There's less than an hour before supper. A slave will bring food for your beast and show you where to take it to do its business."

She bustled off while I looked at the floor and kept a grip on my temper. She had not asked if I wanted *anyone* to handle my things. I had grown spoiled by my company, who paid me the compliment of letting me do as I wished without orders unless orders were needful. I tried to appreciate Sabine instead of hate Lady Aeldra. These last couple of days, I'd come to think of Sabine as a fellow Hunter rather than a noble.

Tunstall closed the door to the solar before anyone could enter. Farmer flicked his fingers, surrounding the four of us and the two creatures with a whitely shining globe of light. "Quickly," he said. "There are three very good mages in this castle and two of middling range. They will start to pry in a moment, and I would rather they think I am laughable. Speak quietly. The shield will keep anyone outside from hearing us, but there are some tricky listening spells in here."

On the ship I'd felt rather cross that he had wanted to seem foolish before other mages. Here, where every hidden weapon could be an advantage against such powerful nobles, I was grateful he kept up his disguise.

"What have we learned?" Tunstall asked, his voice soft. "Cooper, report."

I told them everything Achoo, Pounce, and I had observed. The most damning evidence, of course, was that of Prince Gareth's scent and bracelet in Prince Baird's rooms. The most discouraging thing I had to say was that my Birdie believed the lad was already gone and they knew that already.

"I managed to find where Prince Baird's men-at-arms are camped," Tunstall said. "They are not well pleased at being here. As Cooper knows, the women soldiers among them have chosen to stay in the village rather than dress according to the count's rules. This household is strict Mithran for the men and Gentle Mother for the women. The lads say the whole Three Rivers area—Tellerun, Halseander, Banas—is going that way. They were visiting Aspen Vale, where the prince likes to hunt, and it was the baron and his mage brother who got the prince to visit the count."

"Elyot of Aspen Vale is a Carthaki-educated mage," Farmer told us. "An orange robe, their second-highest ranking. He likes the elegant life. His brother the baron is Graeme. They have deep pockets—plenty of money to finance a rebellion led by mages and nobles."

Tunstall nodded. "There were interesting gaps in what the lads said. His Highness has been out of their view for hours at a time. They aren't used to it. Seemingly Prince Baird is a big one for riding, hunting, and tumbling the local mots when he's out in the country, not holing up in rooms with 'whispering types.' The lieutenant is unhappy. He thinks Baird gets into trouble if he doesn't stick to what he does best. Folk like the baron and the count take advantage of him."

"I found the slave dealers," Farmer said. "They're angry to be held here by a noble who isn't buying. There's a fair in Konstown in two days where they connect with their partners from Frasrlund and Korpita."

"We need to search that caravan," Sabine murmured.

Farmer shook his head. "It's no good. The boy's gone."

The three of us flinched, as if we were on the same string.

"The new people—that's all the slavers I talked to called them, the new people—left early today. It was clear the captain of the rest of the train thought they were crazy, but the two women insisted, and they had the right to leave. They were in charge of the new people. They took guards and a few slaves with them, including a boy of the right age," Farmer whispered. "They all came from Arenaver."

Another large bell chimed.

"The main gate's closed," Tunstall said.

"Lads, Beka has to get cleaned up," Sabine told them. "She'll attract more attention from our hosts, and we don't want that. We'll talk later."

"Tomorrow," Tunstall said firmly. "They won't let us go once the gate is closed. Tonight will be a chance to ask questions while folk eat and drink."

"There's an herb garden in back of the kitchens," Farmer said. "Let's meet there once the household is at morning prayers." He looked at our faces. "Oh, yes," he said. "Everyone is required to go. Let's meet, and say we didn't know we were expected at their worship."

The men left us then, letting Lewyth into the room. "Hurry, Beka," she said, taking me by the arm. "The maid will bring the uniform down to the bathhouse!"

I ordered Achoo to stay before Lewyth half pushed, half pulled me through the ladies' solar, along the hall, and down yet another stairway. "I can walk on my own, my lady," I said, gently tugging my arm from her hold.

"Oh, forgive me! It's just that you don't know the countess! If any of us are late to a meal, it's ten strokes with the switch on the backs of our legs," she explained. "If we're wrinkled or our hair is mussed, it's another ten strokes. My mother says she trains perfect ladies, but *I* think she just beats the spirit out of us."

The air had gotten hotter and damper as we went further down. The door at the bottom landing was decorated with the familiar image of the Gentle Mother, a woman with her hands outstretched, a veil over her hair, her eye cast downward, her robe strained over a swollen belly. A jar, sheaves of wheat, and clusters of grapes lay around her. Lewyth bowed and opened the door. I bowed, too, since it is always a good idea to show respect to any god.

The steam that flowed over us was perfumed with lavender, which I do not like. Bath attendants came toward me with outstretched hands. "A maid will bring a fresh uniform for her," Lewyth told them. "She has to be in the hall in time for the supper bell!"

The attendants nodded.

"I'll see you at table, Beka!" Lewyth told me. Then she was gone, and the attendants were stripping my clothes and insignia, with its companion Dog tag, away. One of them yelped when she found the spiked strap in my braid. Save for that, they were silent and accomplished. Those women had me, including my hair, soaped and scrubbed and into the cold pool faster than I could have done it myself. At least I managed to climb out on my own as a slave rushed in with my clean uniform, spread it on a bench, and ran off before I could give her a coin. The bath women dried me and slipped my insignia and tag around my neck. One cleaned my nails while two dried much of my hair before they combed it out and rebraided it.

As they worked on me, I asked, "Did any of you deal with the lad called No-Skin?"

Three pairs of hands went still. Then, slowly, one mot, then another, took up the combing again. The other one got back to work on my hands, hesitant at first.

"He may have brought some of the oils and soaps we use on the ladies down here," one of the mots said. She was behind me, dealing with my hair, so I could not see her face. "Quiet lad."

"Very quiet," said the other mot with a comb.

"Not even five," the one who cleaned my nails added.

"What did he look like?" I asked them.

"Big for his age," said the one who knew how old he was. "He said he was four, and he was more than three feet tall, like a lord's son! Brown skin, like one of those southerners from Barzun. Black hair."

"Dyed," said the one who'd spoken first. "I could feel it was dyed."

"Underfed. Scared of everything," the second woman who combed my hair told me. "Everyone knew they were forbidden to whip him—that was enough to get us all talking—but he said there were other things they could do to hurt him."

"Enough. He's gone, and that's all there is to that," the first woman who combed my hair ordered. "We'll never see him again and this one needs to get upstairs." Hurriedly they coiled my damp braid and fixed it to my head with hairpins.

I was allowed to dress myself. Sabine had sent what was needful with that clean uniform, I suspected. I'd donned my loincloth and breast band and was about to pick up my tunic when the laundry maid presented me with a long-sleeved, thin silk shirt.

"For under the tunic, mistress," she said quietly. She had not been one of those talking to me earlier. Now, as I handled the shirt, she and the bath attendants watched me. I wonder if they knew they'd each raised a shoulder, as if they expected me to strike one of them.

I wanted to refuse, but I remembered the tunics of the ladies-in-waiting. Despite the warming weather, all wore long sleeves. "Pox and murrain on these canting god-struck nobles," I muttered, and I slid the silk shirt over my head and arms. Through it I could see the mots smile at each other, as if mayhap they agreed with me. I also stole a glimpse at their ankles. All wore an iron fetter. I did not doubt that they would be punished, just like the ladies, if I resisted the countess's will any further.

How could such a harsh mistress follow any goddess of womanly kindness?

As I donned my clothes, I asked, "Mistresses, how long have you been slaves?"

They looked at one another. Finally the oldest of them said, "Long enough that to hear myself called mistress makes me want to laugh." She was not even smiling. She continued to speak. "My father gave me to the count instead of the tax, the year of the blight on our wheat." I recognized her voice. She had been the one to say how frightened Gareth had been.

"And you?" I asked one of the others.

"You have no business asking these things of us, *Dog*," she said, all scorn. She was that first speaker, the one who'd recognized the hair dye. "And if you are late, it is us that'll get the whip for being too slow. Come visit out in the main court once the music begins. That's when the day's stripes are dealt out."

I said no more, but donned the rest of my clothes and held out my hands for my gear. The attendants had cleaned my leather and metal so the metal shone and the leather gleamed. My boots looked near as good as the day I had bought them.

My knives, my arm guards, my baton, none of them were on my belt, only my pouches. Even the knives hidden in my boots were missing. Only my smallest eating knife remained to me. "Where are my weapons?" I asked. "I had a few of them. And my dirty tunic, I need that."

"Weapons will be sharpened, oiled, and taken to your room with your clothes," the oldest attendant said. "Only nobles may carry weapons to supper. Your blades are safe. Under the count's law, a slave with a killing blade is skinned with it. Your dirty uniform will be cleaned and returned to you before prayers in the morning."

"You're done," the one who told me about the slaves' penalties snapped. "Go."

I confess, I spent a bit of the king's coin giving each of them a copper noble. The king could spare it. Besides, I had saved all that money during those nights in the marsh, with no inns to put up at, and no meals to buy.

At last I ran up the stairs to the ground-floor landing. To my relief, Pounce was there. *It will be more amusing to sit with you,* he said as we passed through the door. *Though Achoo would not think so.*

The cats seemed to like you, I told him as we walked down a short hall lined with expensive tapestries.

They are well enough, Pounce said. *But I wish to stay with you. Your temper is rising.*

I have never been in so noble, or so wealthy, or so nasty a house before, I replied. *I'm not accustomed to the way things are done.*

You are a commoner, Pounce said flatly. *You do not get a choice about being accustomed, and if you are not more careful, you will not be given many more chances to* practice *being accustomed.*

We could see people moving beyond the archway ahead, and tables. We had found the great hall. A wave of noise struck us.

You're right, I admitted, hanging my head. *I will try harder.*

Which is more important, your pride or that boy? Pounce wanted to know.

I will do more than try, I told him crossly. *Leave me be. Can't you tell when I'm downhearted?*

You will never end in the slave cages, Beka, Pounce said as we entered the dining hall. *Not you, not your family. You're safe.*

Yet even the king's son was not. How just was that?

The sight before me made me want to run back to the marsh. Slaves and servants, one fettered and wearing cheap tunics, the other clothed in colored and embroidered fabrics, ran to and fro. They were setting bowls, platters, and pitchers on the long tables that had been placed in rows down the length of the hall. Those who were already seated did not eat. Instead they talked to their neighbors or waited, looking around them. The dais now supported a long table covered in white linen. Branches of candles burned there. Those of us below the dais would make do with the torches on the walls.

Prince Baird's men-at-arms were seated already, their uniform tunics as clean as could be expected for coves, most of whom had been hunting all day. I frowned when I saw Tunstall among them. Farmer sat across from Tunstall and the men-at-arms with an older cove and a younger one. They had the look of scribes or mages.

Wondering how I could fit among them when they were so snugly bracketed by other coves, I gave the hall another look and realized the pain of the night before me. All of the castle's women, from the ladies-in-waiting on down to the lowliest of the serving maids, sat at the line of tables closest to the wall where I was. Half of another table, the next one, was also filling with mots, young and old. The remaining two and a half tables sat only coves.

I took a deep breath. I'd never seen anything like it.

Beka, take it with grace, Pounce told me silently. *All of it. Remember you are here as Gershom's representative. Do him proud.*

He must have known I was about to walk away. I released the breath I was holding. *But, Pounce, this is crackbrained,* I told him in the same manner. *How do they expect folk to understand each other if they're separated when they aren't rushing about their work?*

They aren't expected to understand one another, he replied. *The women will learn to flirt over a friend's shoulder, instead of close. The men will see the women as distant and unknowable. Their friends will be only men. The women will see men as strong and unknowable. Their friends will be only women.*

The thought of Tunstall and Farmer, or Holborn, or Rosto, or even Lord Gershom, as strong and ·unknowable made me choke on a laugh. I held it back somehow. From the corner of my eye I could see Lady Lewyth bustling my way.

"Beka, wonderful, you're here! I'll show you where to sit," she said, leading me along the row of benches closest to the wall. "I'd hoped to put you with your lady, but the countess has placed her on the dais, as a dinner partner for the prince."

Thank you, Goddess, I thought. Surely it *was* the Great Mother Goddess who was in charge of seating arrangements. I loved sitting with my lady, but nothing short of chaining me to a plow dragged by a bull would have gotten me onto that dais.

"You're here," Lewyth said, pointing to an empty seat on a bench. "The countess chose this place for you, not me. I'm sorry." She rushed back to her place among the ladies-in-waiting, up at the head of the table.

I wasn't certain why she had apologized until I had seated myself and inspected my setting. It was for one person only. My trencher was a round of bread, not the length that was set between every pair of diners—all of the other diners. If she had written me a note the countess could not have made her wishes clearer. She did not want me to corrupt her Gentle Mothering household with my talk.

"You may as well come up," I told Pounce, who was under the bench, leaning against my boots. "I'm going to be alone here." He leaped up on the empty length of bench at my right.

The mot a yard away on my right, a skinny thing who smelled of herbs, glanced over her shoulder at Pounce and me, then looked away hurriedly. I wanted to thump the back of her coiled, pinned, and veiled head, but I thought of Lord Gershom and behaved.

No, the truth is that I would never have done any such thing. My shyness has gotten much better since I was a Puppy, but mostly when I'm in uniform and acting as a Dog, or on my home streets. Socially, when there's no work to do, I am as miserable as if I were standing before Sir Tullus on my first day at magistrate's court. Lady Aeldra had done me a favor, making it plain I was out of favor with her. No one would be my supper partner, trying to find something we could talk about while I stammered like a goat, and other folk wouldn't be gathered around as they did at other castles, asking me questions about the capital.

Suddenly everyone was getting to their feet. The nobles were walking to their places on the dais. I noted that the count's chair was no higher than the prince's, though all the others were two inches shorter. Prince Baird sat on his right, and Lady Sabine sat on the prince's right.

On the countess's left was a cove in his mid-thirties, brown-haired and sharp-nosed, with a rounded chin and a thin mouth. He wore a brown tunic with white embroideries and a great gold chain with some kind of yellow gem at intervals between the links. Lady Baylisa sat on his left, dressed in ice blue with a white veil over her hair. Her supper partner would be the other cove. I put his age at thirty, with no reason to think I was wrong, after winning last year's competition at age-guessing in all the Corus districts. Plainly he and the older cove were related. They had the same brown hair combed straight back, the same brown eyes, and the same sharp nose. This one's chin was slightly cleft, and his mouth was even thinner than the other one's. He wore dark green. There was some kind of embroidery on his collar and cuffs, but the thread was dark, so it was impossible to see. He wore a large gem on a gold chain, one I recognized right away. It was a fire opal, smoothed and set still in its native stone. Its colors flashed in the light. When a slave tried to pour wine into his cup, he put his hand over it and shook his head, saying something to her. That's when I saw his ring, another stone set in gold on his index finger. It was too dark for me to tell what it was.

Bloodstone, Pounce said. *A very powerful one. I do not particularly like a mage who boasts of his power by wearing showy stones, do you? That is Elyot of Aspen Vale, the mage. The one with the gold and yellow-sapphire necklace is his brother, Graeme. He is a baron.*

What do I care if he is a baron? I asked as a priest in Mithran orange and a mot in pale pink robes walked in to stand before the dais. *Tortall is lousy with barons. Every time a king wants to thank someone for saving his arse somehow, he names him baron and gives him an acre of rocks.*

Did I raise you to be this cynical? Pounce asked me as we all stood for the Mithran's prayer.

You told me it was "worldly," I replied, looking at the floor so as to seem devout. Pounce and I had entertained each other through prayers at Lord Gershom's for years, and had begun again when our Hunts took us to noble houses. *You said I needed to be worldly.*

The Mithran finished and I was lowering myself to my seat when I caught an elbow in the shoulder from my left-hand neighbor. The one on my left, a mot with the strong arms and flour traces of a baker, had moved closer while I talked with Pounce. Her lips barely moving, she said, "There's the Gentle Mother blessing yet."

I straightened up in a hurry as the priestess began to call for peace and bounty, praising the fief's strong men and calling for love and serenity for its women and children. I stopped listening. There were so many better things I could do with this time.

My belly growled, loud enough that the mot on my right and the mots across the table from me looked up and glared. I glared back. It was hardly my fault that it had been a very long time since our bread and cheese on the road.

Do you want me to claw at the embroidery on their hems until it unravels? Pounce offered. *I am willing to make that sacrifice for you. The needlework is bad, anyway, and the colors are not well chosen. I would be doing them a favor.*

I had to struggle to keep from laughing. At last the priestess called for the Goddess's blessings on the royal family and ended. The count gave us the sign to take our seats. Servants began rushing about with more bowls and platters. They went to each of the nobles and placed food in their trenchers or not, as the pairs of diners agreed. For the rest of us, they dumped the serving dishes at central points and left. We lesser folk were to serve ourselves.

The baker turned to me with a basket of fresh rolls. "Take one, for that growlin' belly. Where are you from, that you don't know the priestess of the Gentle Mother?"

I took one. "Corus. My thanks, mistress."

Her trencher mate leaned out around her to look at me. "And it's true, thirty of you Provost's Guard came here to arrest the count?"

"Has he done anything worth arresting him for?" I asked

as I buttered a piece of the bread. The two women began to laugh.

"Not he," said the one on my neighbor's left. "Doin' aught that ain't writ down in—Fay, what's that book them nobles set such store by?"

"*The Book o' Silver,*" my neighbor, Fay, replied.

"Aye, that'n. If my lord ever thought of doin' aught that wasn't writ down in that *Book o' Silver,* he give it up as soon as he thought of it. Like that there roll, do you?" the mot asked.

I looked at the bread in my hands and discovered I was down to the last bite. "Yes, I do," I replied. "It's very good."

"Iris does the rolls," Fay told me. "I do the bigger loaves, like these." She tapped the side of their trencher. "And your'n." A maidservant brought a large pitcher and set it before Fay. She half rose. "Herb and greens soup," she told me, and poured some into my trencher. I tried to tell her not to give me too much, but I was too late and my trencher was full. It was wonderful soup.

"Listen," I said when I'd had a few spoons full. "Mayhap you shouldn't talk with me. The count and countess aren't so happy to have Dogs in their home, and they're particular vexed with me."

Fay took a heavy gulp from her tankard. "So we heard. You'd look prettier in a proper tunic, you know. All that black makes your eyes ghost-colored. Like you've been witness to things that twist your tripes."

I squirmed at that. These countrywomen who see more than their pots and their gardens, they do that to me. They speak their minds, too, just like my gran. Even Tunstall will fidget if such a mot gives him a looking-over.

Fay patted my back. "Ease your belt, young one. The countess can't see more'n three feet off without it blurrin', nor more'n six at all. I have the Sight. My lord lets me do as I wish."

Iris leaned around Fay. "And Master Niccols has taken his pleasures in my bed." She winked. "We're a wicked pair, Fay and me. Me for doin' what I please, and Fay for Seein' what folk don't like. There's none that'll squeak to us about who we talk with. That's why we sat here, instead of at our regular spot."

"It's not my fault if the gods gave me their Gift," Fay said, and elbowed her friend. "But since I got it, I'll speak it true. There's naught my lady can say to halt me, either, not her nor her flower-mouthed priestess."

They refilled their tankards and emptied them while I decided to take them at their word. Few people will cross any who have the magical Gift of Sight, as Fay claimed, for fear the next time a grim Sight came on the one so touched, she would share it. The notion of plump Iris tumbling the prim and pinched Niccols gave me a squeeze in my imagination. I changed the subject rather than think about that any longer. "Do the count and countess feast like this often?" I asked.

"Until the last year, no," Iris told me. "Their Young Lordships being off at court and Her Young Ladyship being married, it got quiet here."

"You can't say *quiet*," Fay argued. "Not during slave season, it's not."

"During slave season?" I asked between some more spoons of soup. It was the best I'd ever had, even better than Aunt Mya's. Up at the head table I could see Lady Sabine daintily eating hers as the prince talked her ear off.

"Oh, aye, they come through every three-four weeks in summer, bound for Scanra, the Yamanis, or Galla," Iris told me. Fay was scraping the last of their soup from the trencher.

We didn't get as much as the nobles did. "Most make no matter, but one a month stops here for my lord to look over." Fay had moved in some and Iris and me had slid back so she could see me as we talked. She could also see the look of startlement on my face. "Don't you know—no, you're not from here." Iris said it like everyone else was. "They have an investment in a slave tradin' company. The count likes to see where his investment gets him."

The skin on the back of my neck prickled. I wished the others could hear, but I couldn't even see Tunstall or Farmer, hidden behind so many walls of people. I looked about, pretending I was trying to see when the next course would arrive. Casually I said, "So he got lucky, having a clutch of slaves on hand when the prince and the baron came for a visit."

Fay snorted as a slave came up with a plate of jugged hare and dropped slices in the trenchers. I slipped a piece down to Pounce, who ate it and said, *Too tart for you.* Of late I have learned that my stomach does not care for things which are very tart, as jugged sauces tend to be.

Fay waited for the slave to move from earshot before she told me, "It weren't no luck, Mistress Dog! My lord count brung them onto castle grounds as soon as they arrived. And that *before* he'd got the message that the baron was coming to visit!"

I started to reach into a pocket for a handkerchief, then remembered I couldn't show nice ways if I was to convince folk I was an everyday dull Dog. I wiped my mouth on my arm, on that lovely thin silk. "I'll wager they've been plenty of help, with three extra nobles and their folk visiting," I commented, and took a seemingly deep drink from my tankard. It was filled with strong ale. I sipped and let the rest stay where it was. The last thing I needed tonight was a gut full of spirits. At the dais,

Sabine and the prince were toasting each other with goblets of wine, but I had no fear for the lady. Her head is harder than Tunstall's, and there's not a Dog in Corus who will drink against Tunstall.

Iris snorted. She had already refilled her tankard and Fay's. "Not enough help, my eye. They sent some of them away with their keepers before dawn."

"Snatched 'em at their work," Fay told me. "One lass who was kneading bread for me. That bossy slave minder, the one they called Viper behind her back, she grabbed that gixie and took her off with no apology to me."

"Right in the middle of kneading," I repeated for a comment. I nodded yes to a slice of lamb and another of baked fish. When the server moved on I said, "That's bad. But surely you can get other workers. The count should have hundreds of slaves, getting them cheap as he must."

Iris shook her head. "Only the debt ones, as owed his da and grandda. Slaves is expensive. You can't just take your own when you like, my man told me. You have to sell them and pay investors their money back. I'm not one for slaves, anyway. You need three times as many to do the work of one free mot or cove. My man manages the apple farms for the count. He says the only places slave labor really pays off is the big fields like they have in Maren or Carthak."

The mot on Iris's left said something to them, taking their attention from me. I broke the fish up and fed it to Pounce under the table between bites of lamb, wondering if Iris's man was right. It would explain why there were so few slaves in the city who didn't belong to the temple, the palace, or the slave traders themselves.

We got stewed beef, new peas, and stewed greens while the nobles applauded the arrival of venison and the roasted, stuffed pig. Pounce had left me, so I worked on my food alone, watching the crowd. And then a thread of air wrapped around me, carrying voices.

"—six blades with rust. Six! I don't call that satisfact'ry, nor will—" That was a cove, all military-sounding.

"—you'd think I was speakin' Yamani, the way she gawped at me!" A mot, mayhap a bit older than I am.

There was a dust spinner nearby. It had sensed me, and the feel of it raced through the breeze that touched me in that huge chamber.

"—one kiss of your hand, no more. Only let me know I may hope!" A cove, educated and noble, and what a cracknob!

"—I'd say you jest, Niccols, save you have no humor that I know of." I did not recognize this tight-arsed mot's voice, but she was noble, no doubt of it. "Count Dewin would never place slaves in the guest wing. He'd cut off an arm before he'd soil rooms meant for the nobility."

"Far be it from me to argue with my lady's own cousin, but it's true." From his careful way of pronouncing things, Master Niccols sounded as if he might have had a bit more to drink than was wise. "He took them up himself—"

The rest was lost. I wondered if the spinner itself might have more. Where was it? Not inside. They were never inside. What kind of power did a spinner have that would cause it to sense me, and reach me, all the way in here?

The mots around me were well taken up in chatter. The ale pitchers had been replaced twice up and down the table. I tapped Fay on the shoulder and asked her, talking direct into her ear, where I might find a privy I was permitted to use. With her instructions, stooping as I slid between two servants bound for the door, I left the great hall.

Rather than follow the servants, I parted from them and

raced up to the room, where I hoped to find doors unlocked and my packs with Sabine's. I was right twice. The ladies' solar and the countess's office were open, and my packs were there, showing signs of the maids' hunt for my uniform. Achoo greeted me with enthusiasm. She was hungry *and* ready to go outside. I saw a cot had been set up for my lady, and a pallet for me. I hoped that Farmer's bug charm still held as I groped in my things.

With a packet of dust from the Day Market in Corus and another from Serenity's garden in Port Caynn, I went outdoors, Achoo at my side. We walked along the skin of the great hall until we halted between two doors that opened from it to a broad terrace. Here breezes from the spinner found me, passing me strands of talk that flowed from the heated chamber across the terrace and down its steps into a good-sized garden. Torches lit my way and voices reached in my ears. I tucked myself in the shadows by the hedges and went in search of voices and spinner alike. Achoo ran silently at my heels.

"—going over the books and I cannot reconcile these amounts. We should have far more coin in the treasury." That was the mot Niccols had called "my lady's own cousin," the stiff arse.

"Ignore it, Lady Rosewyn." That was the count. "I had use for that coin."

The second thread of conversation drowned out the first. "—well, I can do better than a plate-faced virgin nobody who talks of little but religion." This cove's voice I did not know. "If you like her so much, Graeme, *you* marry her."

I did not hear the answer. Graeme, who was likely the baron of Aspen Vale, must have said something. There was a long pause before my speaker, Elyot, that would be, said, "I've never heard of him, but I'm not concerned. Did you see the way he bolted back the ale? No mage with any great power drinks like that. The risk is too great that our magical Gift will start to leak. Besides—"

His voice was gone. I was forced to listen to an eager cove trying to get his fambles into his giggling sweetheart's clothes until the currents in the air led me to the far side of a stone-lined pond. There, on the middle of the broad path, turned my dust spinner. It was thin, like a narrow tornado, nearly twenty feet tall, and, I sensed, very old. No wonder it had so much power.

"Achoo, either sit or wander, but behave," I told her. The clever thing had learned years ago to recognize when I listened to the air, and never bothered me when I did so. Now she trotted off to investigate an interesting rustle in the bushes.

I bowed to the spinner. She had bent herself almost in two, as if she were looking at me. Certainly she wasn't about to bow to any of the many scuttling mortals that had come her way. "I give you greetings, ancient one," I said and showed her my two packets. "I brought gifts for you, if I may."

She slid forward, opening the packets herself. I hadn't expected it. No spinner had done so before. It was painful as the dust and twigs that made up her base scratched my hands, but I held steady. Somehow she undid the tight knots I used to secure the small bags. Stretching out two thin, spinning fingers, she dipped one into each, sucking up it and its contents.

Fess, her name given to me in that moment, exploded outward, surrounding me and picking me up, lifting me high in the air. I held very still and prayed. I'd never had this reaction from a dust spinner before, but then, I'd never fed a very old, isolated spinner my entire supplies of grit from richly lived-in city districts, either. Not that I'd *chosen* to do so, but it made little difference in the end.

What do you seek? she asked me. *You came in search, what is it you search for?*

Her voice was as much in my skull as my ears. I showed her what I hunted in my mind: the image of the prince on the queen's locket, the four-leafed bronze emblem I had found on the beach, and magefire of muddled colors.

The spinner swayed deep, moving up onto the terrace. Terrified, I began my prayers. If she dropped me now, I would smash like an egg.

Closer to the house she went, with me motionless at her center, until I stared at the open windows on the floor where the important folk stayed. I recognized Prince Baird's rooms through one set of open shutters and murmured, "I was here today. He knows they have stolen his nephew. He's part of it."

The dust spinner leaned to the side. She stretched so far to carry me along the row of windows that I feared I might fall straight through the arm in which she bore me. We passed a large room for meetings, or so I guessed. Tunstall leaned against a table while the count, Master Elyot, the count's mage, and the Mithran priest talked. The spinner did not bring me close enough to hear, but from the way Tunstall was smiling and shaking his head, they were offering him a bribe. They were in for a surprise if they thought he would take it. I was surprised he wasn't striking someone, but he was using his company manners. He'd had to learn them, living with Sabine.

The spinner thrust me along, past an empty set of rooms, until we came to the last of them before the corner. Inside a richly embroidered tunic in the Aspen Vale colors was laid across the bed. A small handful of jewelry was on the stand there. Fess bore me closer so I could examine the things. I could tell these were Master Elyot's rooms. Packs in the corner gave off a red glow, warning the servants not to touch them.

On a table near the corner was a bowl filled with water for scrying. Various bottles and jars, also glowing red, were placed on the top shelf of the wardrobe. More clothes than he would surely need here were on the wardrobe shelves.

None of this would help me. I thanked Fess for her efforts. She was drawing me back when I glimpsed something through the red fire that warned folk away from the packs. I didn't even have to ask my friend to stop. Seeing my mind, she moved forward to place me at the open window. I squinted at the packs.

There it was, stamped into the flap cover of each bag I could see. The four-leafed emblem we had searched for so long. Looking at the jewels again, I saw a token like the one I'd found on the beach half hidden in the pile, a bronze round with the bases of lance-shaped leaves on the edge. The rest was under the jewelry, but since I'd seen nothing else like it in all our searching, I was willing to wager that this was what I'd sought.

The spinner's ancient strength was failing. She'd done quite a lot for me, and I will be forever grateful. I asked if she would mind taking me down.

She bent over. I was horizontal to the ground, that was plain. She began to twirl me in a great circle through the air. My supper churned. Between my belly and my fear that Fess was going to throw me into the upper branches of the trees, I was certain I was going to be sick. I tried to drag my hands to my mouth. The winds twisted about me so fiercely, gripping me so tight, that it took a great deal of my strength to clamp my palms over my lips and swallow back my own supper over and over.

Slowly, very slowly, Fess began to ease off her speed. I felt myself being lowered gently to the ground even as Fess poured any number of pieces of talk into my head. I would never be able to sort it all out. She'd held on to some of it as children hold on to special shells or rocks, because she liked the pretty sound. Whatever words had made them up were worn smooth over ages of her use.

In all of it was her thanks for the most incredible meal of her life. She wished me well as she set me gently on my feet.

"Splendid," I said, feeling it to the bottom of my heart. "That was the most amazing thing." I remembered to bow to her. Then I found a patch in the bushes where I could vomit up every scrap I'd eaten that evening.

Poor Achoo was at my side, whimpering, as we climbed the steps. She hates it when I get sick, even though her own vomits never distress her as they do me. I was reassuring her that I would be fine when Master Niccols and two men-at-arms halted us on the terrace. Master Niccols folded his arms.

"It was believed you understood you were to remain at supper and not go prying," he said. "Where have you been? You look the very slut."

Achoo growled. She knew an insult when she heard one.

I glanced at my clothes. I'd been shaking my tunic and breeches as we walked away from my leavings in the bushes, but odd bits of leaf and grit still clung to them and to the long silk sleeves of my undershirt. I touched my hair and could feel dirt and mussed strands.

Then I grinned at Niccols, showing teeth of my own. "I've been savoring your breezes and riding your dust spinner," I told him. "The little tornado that always blows in the garden? They're alive, you know. Yours is named Fess. She's been here since before the stones were laid for the original keep."

"Nonsense," blustered Niccols, while the two coves at his

back made the Sign on their chests. "I've never heard such a thing."

"Being a Dog, *countryman,* I'm more in the way of hearing things than you are." I leaned closer to him so he got a whiff of my pukey breath. He backed up a step, making his coves back up. Now all three of them were off balance, retreating from a little mot Dog and her hound, showing I had them fearful. "Since I'm ill, I'm turning in for the night. And I'll need food and water for my hound. If you have no objection?"

He'd regained his sack. "My men will take you there, wench," he snapped. "They'll get the food and see to it you do not stray."

My hand went to the spot where my baton usually hung. In Corus I seriously would have considered giving this pompous mumper a nap tap and sending him to the cage Dogs for an afternoon of conversation. He knew more about the business of the slaves, I was certain of it. But I was not in Corus, and there was the Hunt to think on. I said nothing, gave him no polite farewell, but walked off toward the hall with his bully boys at my sides. Achoo led the way back to the ladies' solar and the countess's office.

As soon as we entered the solar, the coves shut the door behind me. I waited until a maid came with Achoo's supper. Then, in the dark, Achoo and I skirted the pallets laid on the floor. I'd had a glimpse in the hall light before the maid closed the door again, enough to show me the path to the office. As we entered the room Sabine and I would share, a light flared in a lamp set on the desk. Pounce sat blinking next to the lamp, letting me know who had done that bit of magic.

"I didn't know you could light things," I said as I put down Achoo's bowl and began to pull off my clothes. I stood in a clear spot where the dirt and twigs would fall on bare floor, not bedding or packs.

It's very bad for your character if I do things for you too often, he replied in that training master way of his. *But I do not see how you will be improved if you fall over a chair in here and break an arm.*

"I'm surprised," I said as I removed the silk shirt that had been so lovely in the baths. Now it had grease stains on the arms, as well as spinner dirt. "Usually you spare my character so little."

You're bitter, Pounce replied smugly. *One day you will thank me. I am very proud of you. I thought you might well give in and crack Niccols's skull for him.*

"I have work to do," I said. I stood there, feeling gritty and tired. "And he's not bad enough for me to return and invite him to the back of the barn."

There is a basin and a pitcher of water in that corner, Pounce told me. *They brought it in a little while ago. You can dump what's dirty in the privy behind the door in the opposite corner.*

It didn't matter to me that the water was cool. I was able to clean the grime from my face, neck, arms, and hands, and pour the dirty leavings down the small privy, leaving a clean basin for Sabine. Then I unpinned my hair, and combed out the bits and pieces that were caught in it. The strands were still wet, which meant that the grit had clung. I resolved to wash it in the morning if I woke before my companions. I put on the nightdress that someone had set out on my pack, then got my journal, ink, pen, and stone lamp. Setting myself up at the desk, beside my two lamps, I looked around for Pounce and Achoo. They had gone to sleep, curled around each other beside the pallet that had been left for me. I smiled at them and got to work. I had to catch up on as much of today as I could manage while I had quiet time.

I was asleep on the open journal when Sabine came in. "It's after midnight, but not by much," she told me when I asked the time. "I'll take Achoo out. Go to bed."

I blinked at her. "Did he try to get under your skirts? The prince?"

Sabine grinned at me. "No. He was with us six years ago when I told the king that if he did not take his hand off me, I would break every bone in it. He even reminded me of that tonight." More quietly she said, "There's something on his mind. Prince Baird will usually flirt with anything in skirts, and he didn't even try. By the way . . ." She reached down the front of her dress and pulled something out. It was a metal stamp. When she showed it to me, I saw it was made in the shape of the four leaves.

"Where?" I whispered.

She pointed to a drawer in the desk and then very quietly replaced it there. She went to a little trouble to place it exactly as it must have been when she'd taken it, and closed the door. I clasped her shoulder, so she knew I approved. She gave me a cheerful wink.

Then she took my ink and put the stopper in the bottle. "Go to bed, my dear. You've had a hard day."

I obeyed Sabine and sought the comfort of the pallet.

Wednesday, June 20, 249

Queensgrace

For all that I've risen at dawn nearly every day of my life, if only to visit the privy or take Achoo to do the same, it is always a source of unhappiness to me. I am used to true wakefulness around eight of the clock, being an Evening Watch Dog who comes off duty at the first stroke after midnight. That brief waking at dawn is the world's and the gods' way of saying they still own me. My body wants relief, my hound wants relief, and one day a week I must report on my hobblings in the magistrate's court beginning at seven in the morning. On this Hunt, of course, we rise at dawn to make use of the daylight. I would be far unhappier about it, I suppose, did I not want to find that poor lad and those Rats that have done this to him and his parents.

When Achoo nudged me awake, I groped for my clothes and belt. I did not bother with stockings, but thrust my bare feet into my boots. I tiptoed around Sabine's cot and opened the door to the solar. "Quietly," I whispered to Achoo.

I heard a rustle and turned. Sabine stared at me, one hand clutching a knife that had not been in view a moment ago. I pointed to Achoo. She blinked, then nodded.

"Take weapons," she mumbled. "Nowhere's safe."

"Boots and belt," I said, wondering if, in her half-sleeping state, she'd remember the nasty things in my belt pouches and the blades in my boots.

Seemingly she did. She slid her blade under her pillow, and was instantly asleep. Pounce moved onto the warm spot I'd left to continue his own slumbers. Even constellation cats like their naps.

Achoo and I slid into the darkened solar. Two lamps, one by our door, one by the main door, offered a bit of light, enough that I could see a path between the ladies on their pallets. Some offered snores to the Dream King Gainel. Others murmured. Their dreams were more peaceable than mine, where Holborn and I had been fighting again. That made dawn rising easier. It put a halt to the sight of his face, red with the fire spirits he'd been drinking, eyes narrow and cruel as he cried that I wrung all the joy out of life.

Carefully I opened the door, fearing to wake a lady and start an outcry, praying the guards outside were asleep. In fact, the guards were no longer there. Mayhap Niccols thought all those ladies were enough to keep me inside. In any case, the broad hall was empty.

We left the castle near the area where Tunstall and Farmer camped with the prince's men. Certainly I couldn't let Achoo ease herself where they walked, but the servants' privy and the chicken coops were close by, and the barrels in which castle garbage was put. Surely no one could object if I took Achoo there.

We hurried past the men's camp. Some of their hounds came to attention, watching us, but they were well trained. They would not make a noise or come for us unless we tried to enter the camp. Even at this little distance I heard men's snores. Shivering a little in the cool morning air, I didn't envy Tunstall and Farmer their night in the open. The warmth of the lady's office had been a welcome change.

The servants were stirring already, but they said naught to me, nor I to them. They looked as sleepy-eyed as I felt as they visited the privy and ran in and out of the guest quarters. The slaves were about, too, carrying heavy loads of wood for the castle fires. They acted strangely, lifting a shoulder and running from me as if I'd hit them. Had I been more awake, I might have stopped one to ask what in the god's great gut ailed them, but I was too busy waiting for Achoo to find a spot.

She did her business in back of the servants' privy, but she was not ready to return to the ladies' quarters. She wandered behind it, among the garbage barrels, until I lost sight of her. At last I got impatient and whistled her up. We were to attend that meeting with our partners while the household was at morning prayers. That had to be soon. The breakfast bread was already done. I could breathe its scent, heavy on the air that came from the kitchens.

My whistle got a reply, of sorts—two sharp barks. I disliked that. Achoo hated to raise her voice. She only did so when she could neither see nor smell me nearby and she'd found sommat she wanted me to look at.

"Achoo?" I called.

Again she called, two barks. This time, after a short wait, she barked twice again, then waited, and barked two times more. She needed me to come to her. I did so. She never called without reason, any more than she would shout. I picked my way through the muck that flowed between the privies and the barrels. The smell was thick as a Port Caynn fog. I breathed shallow with my lips open to spare my nose from truly taking in the stink. Searching among the barrels, I was amazed at how much this great castle could throw away. Everywhere I saw the marks of castle scavengers, looking for extra food or bits and pieces they could put to use.

Achoo stood next to a barrel with her tail tucked under her rump. She looked at me and whimpered. I went to see what she had found.

The gixie Linnet was sprawled naked atop heaped slops from the kitchens. Her face was purple and swollen. One of the pads I'd made so she could turn the spits without burning her hand was the rope used to strangle her, the bands of cloth I'd sewn for straps dug so deep in her neck I could barely see them. I tested one of her outstretched arms. It would not move when I gave it a push, a sign that the rigor of death had set in. That would have begun four to six hours after her murder, so she'd gone to the god at least that long ago. Carefully, with a whispered apology, I used my fingertips to push her up on her side. The blood in her body had flowed down into her back and bum, pooling there, turning that part of her skin purple. She had lain this way since death, as blood goes to the lowest place when we die, and does not move once it sets. They had killed her and dumped her in the garbage. I was certain they'd done it because she had talked to me.

I know I stood there a little time, thinking of prayers and forgetting them halfway through. The garbage scavengers, the human ones, the feathered sort in their spinning flight overhead, and the castle's four-footed rats, none of them dared come near when I looked at them. Or mayhap it was the sure aim I had with the rocks that littered the slimy ground, a childhood skill I had never let rust. I do not think I'd killed more than a rat or two when I heard Farmer say, "Cooper? I was trying to meditate, and I heard Achoo bark."

"You know her bark," I said, letting the stones drop. My hands were filthy.

"It's different enough from the hunting hounds in the camp. They don't bark in signals," Farmer explained. "Why are you here?"

He was behind me. I turned sideways so he could see the barrel and Linnet.

Farmer's mouth went tight. His eyes were flint. "Goddess bless her, and Mithros curse the ones who did this," he murmured, like a prayer. He asked me, "Is this the girl who talked with you yesterday?"

I nodded.

Farmer rubbed his chin, thinking. "I can find where she was killed," he said quietly.

"Do so, if you please," I said. "Anything we can learn . . ."

"It doesn't hurt them, the things I do with the dead," he said, digging in a pocket. "I swear it. I had a dead-speaker, a mage who can talk to them in the Peaceful Realms, ask for me. Those who remembered said the shell doesn't matter once they're done with it." When I looked at him, he shrugged. "I worried that I was hurting them. That they might feel what I was doing to their bodies, and creating a seeming would bring back the pain of their deaths." He produced a handkerchief and passed it to me. "Your face is, um, wet," he explained.

My face? I looked down. The front of my tunic was damp. I'd been weeping without knowing it.

"I want His Majesty to put their heads on pikes over the palace walls," I said to Farmer. I hardly knew my own voice, so dark was it. "I want them to rot up there, the target of every gull and crow in Corus."

"If we recover the prince, I imagine you can request that, and the king will only ask you if you want ordinary pikes, or gold ones," Farmer told me. "Will you wait here and keep onlookers back while I get my things?"

I nodded. He hesitated, then took his handkerchief from my hand and wiped my cheek. "You missed where your skin brushed some—dirt, there," he explained. He gave the linen square back to me and hurried off, winding between the barrels, skidding a little in the muck.

I scrubbed my hands well on the handkerchief before I reached into the pouch for meat strips. I gave some to Achoo and told her that she was a clever hound, finding Linnet even when I wasn't looking for her.

We were left alone until I saw Fay picking a path toward us. She was already well powdered with flour, beads of sweat making paths through it on her cheeks.

"They told me a cracknob in black was settling here like she meant to nest," she told me as she drew close. "Stands to reason it's you." She looked at the body. "Ah—Linnet. Poor thing." She made the Sign against evil on her chest. Then her sharp eyes took me in. "You'll not get permission for a funeral from my lord and my lady. She's a slave. And the house ones won't touch her, not when she's been left this way, as a warning. The outsiders will bury her away from the castle. *You* stay clear of that. My lady will have your hair just for being here. It's unseemly."

"It's *my work*," I replied. "She was murdered."

"So she was," Fay told me with a nod. "And every servant and slave in this house will be taking care that they aren't the next. The sooner you and your friends are gone, the safer all of us will be." She turned and walked away. "I'll send some cloth you can wrap her in, but they'll have to wash it and give it back."

It was between her leaving and Farmer's return that the pigeon came, landing on the barrel next to Linnet's. It was one of the wood pigeons, three times the size of a city bird, gray and pink in their feathers. This one was pale gray on her back, almost gray-pink on her head. She looked at me with an inquiring eye, as if she wasn't sure of me.

Luckily I had my belt on, and a full pouch of corn. "Yes, you're looking for me," I said, offering the bird the corn. "I'm her as speaks with the ghosts." My hand was shaking, I was so upset, and my proper way of speaking had gone straight to Carthak.

"No one saw us talking." Linnet's voice came from the air around the bird. "'Twas the pads. I put 'em on both hands, 'cause they made it so easy to turn spits with the pigs on them."

I heard steps. I turned, but it was Farmer. I put a finger to my lips and turned back to the pigeon. A boiling heat raced from my gut up my throat. "Those kitchen fussocks complained of you over those pads?" I kept my voice soft for all my rage. I've learned not to frighten the dead.

"No," Linnet said. "A stranger come in, wantin' to know if you'd been about and what you was askin'. I kept to me spits, but he saw the pads and asked if I made 'em myself. Boss cook said I'd no sewing nor time to sew."

Farmer moved up beside me. Now the ear of his I could see was glowing a yellowish white. So was his mouth. I glanced at his hands. One forefinger shone the same color. He'd been at his strange powders again.

"They come for me at night, whilst I slept," Linnet said. "They put a hood on me and took me someplace. They kept me hooded the whole time. I never saw their faces. They wanted to know what I said to the Dog." I heard her sob.

I opened my mouth, to tell her she could go, but I closed it again. She had stayed behind because she wanted to. She was not leaving because she had sommat yet to tell me. I wanted her to have her peace, but I wanted anything that would lead us to her killers more.

"How did they speak, Linnet?" Farmer asked. Now I knew what this powder did. It made it possible for him to hear and speak with the ghosts. "What did they sound like? Noblemen? Countrymen?"

"Just one spoke. He was a hard man, a noble," Linnet said. "I said the Dog only talked of the slave train and when they had come. He said I lied. He hurt me with magic. I told him the same thing until he got angry and killed me. The birds said the one who feeds and listens would come if I waited, so that's what I did. And they were right."

"What did you wait to tell me, Linnet?" I asked. I felt the bird peck at my palm. It was empty. I fetched out more corn for her and smoothed the feathers of her breast. "What's so important that you would not leave until you spoke to me?"

"They dyed No-Skin's hair black, and his skin dark brown," she said. Our guesses were right, then. "He's got a tattoo for the master's—the count's—slaving company on his right shoulder. The four leaves in the circle, that tattoo."

Farmer tugged the bronze token from his breeches pocket. He held it in the hand with the glowing finger before the pigeon.

"That be it," Linnet said. "That's the company Master's part owner of. They come by every summer, twice, so my lord and my lady can look over the stock."

"Did No-Skin tell you his real name, or the name of his family?" I asked. "Did he tell you how he came to be a slave?"

"He told me nothin'," Linnet replied. "He was afeared to. He gave me this great farrago of a tale, sayin' if he told anyone anythin', he'd be hurt for it, and any hurt he took, his parents would feel it. They could even die, if he was hurt bad enough. He said one of the mages with the slavers, the one called Viper, she showed him a picture of his ma bleedin' 'cause a girl shoved *him*. Have you ever heard the like? And over a weak slave that could hardly work."

"But you believed him, didn't you?" I asked her quietly. I knew the sound in the voice of one I questioned, the sound of self-doubt and growing belief. "You knew there was sommat not right going on."

"For what good it did me nor No-Skin," Linnet retorted. Her voice was growing faint. "I'll tell you this for free. The mage as hurt me? I heard him tell someone 'they're halfway to Frasrlund' when they wrapped the cord around my throat. That's where you'll find No-Skin. I'm done now, Beka. I'm weary."

"Black God give you peace, and accept my thanks," I whispered to her.

"They was nice pads to use with the spits," Linnet replied. I could barely hear her. "I wish I'd had 'em longer." She was gone. The bird took off, circling her body before it headed out over the wall. A guard on the wall aimed his crossbow at it, likely thinking to shoot his supper from the sky. He did not see the small, blue-glowing stone that flew straight at him. When it hit, he dropped his bow with a cry and knelt on the walkway, clutching his head.

I looked at Farmer, wanting very much to hug him for saving the bird. Luckily for my dignity, he still glowed yellow at ears and mouth, which kept me where I stood. He shrugged and said sheepishly, "It seemed wrong to let him eat one of our Birdies."

I slapped his back, as a fellow Dog would do. "Good work, Farmer," I told him, so he would know I approved. I turned to Linnet's corpse. Having my back to him made it easier to say, "I did not tell her they'd used the strings of the pads I made to kill her."

"I didn't get that part," he admitted. "What were these pads?"

I explained about Linnet and her blisters from turning the spits.

"Seeing that you gave her one good thing on the day she died, forgive yourself, Beka," Farmer advised. "If you hadn't done that for her, and someone had seen her talking with you, her end would have been the same. She wouldn't have had an act of kindness on her last day. Neither of you knew the use to which they'd be put." Farmer unslung his pack and balanced it against the slightest edge of the barrel, that had been occupied by the wood pigeon, to open a front pocket and remove a handkerchief.

"You think Master Elyot was there? Linnet's hard man, mayhap?" I asked.

"I am certain of it." Farmer reached over and touched Linnet's shoulder. His Gift sparked around his fingers and vanished. When it was gone, a glowing orange patch showed up on Linnet's shoulder. It vanished shortly.

"*That's* Elyot's Gift," Farmer explained. "He gripped your Linnet's shoulder." He wetted his handkerchief with water from a flask secured to his shoulder pack, then wiped his mouth, ears, and hands with it. The glowing yellow stuff that had remained on his skin vanished. He took a deep breath. "Do you know, I believe I'd like to sit."

I hesitated. "We were going to learn where Linnet was killed. Track her back from where we found her."

Farmer grimaced. "I'll try it in a moment," he said. "I just need to collect myself."

I remembered seeing a bench along a wall just beyond the first line of barrels. I couldn't imagine why anyone might want to relax and smell the garbage, but I would not mind moving away from the sight of Linnet's body.

"This way," I told him.

"Interesting, to watch you at work," he commented as

he hoisted his pack onto one shoulder. "The birds just started coming to you?"

I nodded. "Ma took me to Granny Fern—my da's mother. It's in that side of the family."

"Why your gran? Your father didn't know how?" He thumped himself onto the bench and leaned back against the tower wall behind it, closing his eyes.

With him not watching me, it was easier to say, "I didn't know him. He died when I was still in swaddling clothes, Ma said. Granny Fern knew what was needed, even if she didn't hear the ghosts herself. Listen, if you don't have to do it, why bother? The dead aren't the best at conversation."

Farmer smiled without opening his eyes. "My da was killed in a market riot. I never had the chance to say goodbye. Learning ways to hear the dead wasn't just useful when I went to work for the Provost's Guard."

"Did you ever talk with him—your da?" I asked, curious.

"You know how they are, when the older dead are raised, don't you?" Farmer asked.

I nodded. A friend in Lord Gershom's service had made me go with her to a mage when she wanted to speak to her gran, dead ten years. Then, because Farmer's eyes were still closed, I said, "Oh, yes."

"At least my father remembered he had a son, even if he was foggy on my name. I continued to practice the skill and study of what could be learned from the dead in other ways. Eventually my district commander wrote Gershom about me." Farmer sighed. "He came to visit. He was the first person who didn't think it was wrong for someone of my talents to be interested in crimes instead of getting rich."

"My lord gets lonesome, too," I said, leaning forward to

scratch Achoo's ears. "None of his family took after the work like he does."

He chuckled. "That's interesting, because he told me he had a foster daughter who learned whatever he had to teach her as if she'd been born to it."

I felt my cheeks turning red. "He did teach me a great deal," I said in a tone that usually discouraged folk from talking.

Not Farmer. "He said she'd ended up with the best training Dogs in the city, and then the best partners," he murmured. He opened his eyes and grinned at me—I was glaring at him by then—and looked over my shoulder. He sat up, the grin vanishing. I turned.

Five slaves, two of them women from the bath, had come. The bath slave who had told me to go yesterday held a length of folded cloth in her arms. "Didn't I tell you?" she demanded of me, her eyes blazing. "Your pack goes nosing about, and poor Linnet ends in the muck. She's there as a warning to the rest of us, *Dog*. Won't any of us talk with you more!"

Farmer got to his feet. "You could be made to talk," he said. I looked up at him and shivered. Were my eyes like that at times? That pale shade of ice? In that moment I knew his silliness was all a sham, and that the true Farmer was deadly.

"And will you kill us then, mage?" one of the older slaves, a cove, demanded. His arms were striped with whip scars. "You may as well, for we'll die if the master finds out we've given his secrets to you."

The bath slave glared at me. "We'll bury Linnet. Our own way, the way we've always done. You'd best run if you're to be clean before prayers."

They turned and walked into the trash yard.

"Why did you say that?" I asked Farmer. "You wouldn't have done it, would you?"

"If it would have advanced the Hunt, yes," he told me. "But I'd have made it secret and painless. They couldn't know that, of course. It's not hard to do, but how many mages go to that trouble for a slave?" He looked down at his shirtfront and grimaced. "Bollocks, we *are* filthy. You'd best run to the baths, or however you mean to clean up. We have to meet Tunstall and Lady Sabine very shortly."

I set off for the baths at the run, Achoo galloping at my side. I did not look back, not at Farmer, not at the slaves who had found Linnet. It is only now, as I write, that I am grateful that Farmer made me leave before they carried her away.

The women's baths were empty. I seized a robe, filled a bucket, and plunged my tunic and breeches into it. I used a cloth and another bucket of water to clean the slime from Achoo. She stood patiently, used to the strange things I do. It did not hurt that she knew I would give her a treat at the end of it. Then I took a quick plunge in the bath myself.

With the robe tight around me and my wrung-out clothes in the now-empty bucket, we ran up the stairs. "You'd think, if they wished to be so careful of their ladies' virtue, they'd build a door straight between the bath and where the ladies are kept," I grumbled to Achoo as we waited for the hall to clear of servants with burdens. Once all were gone, I raced for the ladies' solar.

I closed the door behind us and turned to an interesting sight. The young ladies, gowned in pale colors, their hair veiled for morning prayers, were gathered around a chair. Lady Sabine sat there, dressed for the day in maroon tunic and brown breeches, her face intent as she spoke to them softly.

Those closest to her gripped her shoulders and arms, as if their touch could make her tale clearer.

"She wept," I heard Sabine tell them in a voice filled with intensity. "She seized my hands and her tears bedewed my fingers, her mother's tears. 'You are young and unmarried,' she said to me, 'you cannot know a mother's heart. Still, you are a woman, despite your coarse trade. I know there is tenderness in you. I know you have sweetness in your soul.'" Sabine hung her head.

One or two of the silly gixies gasped. Another sobbed outright.

"How could I deny her?" Sabine asked, her voice throbbing with pain. "'My lady,' I said, 'I will do what I can.' 'No,' she cried, 'swear to me, swear by the Gentle Mother that you will let nothing keep you from your Hunt! Swear that no power in this world will hold you from finding my dear lad! Swear that you will lead your fellow Hunters!'" Sabine looked up at an invisible horizon, her eyes blazing. She was better than any Player I had ever seen. "And I swore it! 'My lady,' I told her, 'there is naught that will keep me! Your lad's name is writ on my heart, and I swear, each noble soul I encounter on the way will know of my search! I vow with all my soul, I will find your young baron and bring him home to you!'"

I fled into the chamber Sabine and I had shared before I ruined it all by laughing. I was not certain why she had enacted this madness for the young ladies, but she plainly had her reasons. She had been careful to keep up the tale that we searched for an older lad, the son of a noble, which was the important thing.

Pounce lounged on the countess's desk, stretched out comfortably. *If being a knight ever wears on her, she can make a living as a Player,* he remarked. *I am sorry about Linnet, Beka.*

My amusement evaporated. "Me, too," I said, putting my bucket on the floor. I searched out one of my spare uniforms from my packs and dressed. "I wish I knew who'd done it. I'd make them sorry, so I would."

You have bigger chores ahead, Pounce told me.

The door opened to admit Sabine. She made certain it was closed before she blew out a chestful of air and said, "Well! I'll soon know if *that* pays off!" She looked into the bucket I'd set on the floor. "I have no idea of how to dry this if we're riding today," she murmured. "I believe the countess will object if we hang it over her chairs." Then she rested a hand on my arm, gently. "Beka, what's wrong? Is it Holborn?" I looked up at her, horrified, and she explained, "It was your face when you came into the outer room. You looked as if you were grieving."

I wondered if the name Holborn would always fill me with guilt. "No, no, my lady. I'll explain later."

She nodded and draped my wet things over the window ledges, remarking that the countess was not likely to come here before prayers and breakfast. I finished cleaning up and the four of us left the room. Only the Butterfly Puppies and the cats remained in the ladies' solar, curled up on chairs and cushions. The little dogs wagged their tails, but only one tried to follow us outside. Pounce turned and said sommat to it. I don't know he said, but I can usually tell when Pounce is speaking by the way he holds his ears and tail. The dog yipped and didn't follow us outside.

"Why did you scare him off?" Sabine asked as we walked down the hall. "He was just being friendly."

He didn't want to follow. He had a warning for us, Pounce said. *He said the men outside the doors last night had bad thoughts about us. That Butterfly Puppy is wasted on these people.*

"We can't bring another animal on a Hunt," I said, alarmed. "Particularly not a special-bred noble one!"

I will think of something, Pounce replied. *You need not worry.*

"That doesn't make me feel better," I told Sabine and Achoo. I've known for years that Pounce has affairs of his own, and I'm always sure that one day I will get caught up in them. I have plenty of work of my own to do.

A gong was struck somewhere on the castle grounds, ringing out three times with a pause, three times with a pause, and three times more. Once we got to the lower levels, people walked by us, mostly servants, headed to the great hall. We slipped into the back hall and around, coming out near the kitchen privies.

By then the yards behind the kitchens were empty, save for chickens pecking in the dust. The herb gardens were on the far side of the coops and privies, so I did not have to see the garbage barrels at all. The gardens were large and well tended, guarded by a rail fence. Tunstall and Farmer were already there, Farmer perched on a seat made from half a barrel, Tunstall on a fence rail. Without a word, Farmer pointed at the ground in front of them. He'd drawn a circle in the dust with some sort of powder. I lifted Achoo over it.

Once all of us were inside—I would have loved to know how Farmer had made the circle around Tunstall and the fence rail with no break in the circle—Farmer whispered a word I did not understand. For a moment all the world around us turned white. Then the whiteness vanished. We could see the gardens clearly.

"Anyone who looks, or listens, will see and hear only the normal sounds," Farmer told us. "They won't see us. I think I got Master Elyot's measure last night to build the spell to keep him out, and Count Dewin's mage. I hope so, since I'm going to need to do so with every spell I use after this until the Hunt is done."

Sabine nudged Farmer with her shoulder so he would share the keg seat with her. Someone had placed a wooden crate for me to use. "You think that Elyot is part of it, then?" Sabine asked.

"Assuredly," replied Farmer. "I got him to show off a little last night for the count's mage and me. I recognized Elyot's magic. It was part of the trap we set off at the graves down the road. And he helped to murder a young slave girl last night, leaving his essence behind."

"Has he recognized your power?" Tunstall asked. He looked worried. I certainly felt worried.

"Not from me showing off," Farmer said with his looby grin. "I was too drunk."

"You weren't—" Tunstall began.

I couldn't help myself. "Of course he wasn't," I interrupted. "Can't you tell when he's acting the crackbrain?" I glared at Farmer. "What did you do, vanish the wine from your cup?"

Farmer's grin grew even bigger. "She's so clever," he told Tunstall as my lady chuckled. "I want to marry her when I grow to be a man." He looked at me, and the grin turned into a proper smile. "I vanished it just as if I drank it. Created the spell myself, when I learned too many fellow mages were not to be trusted. I place the spell just inside my lips, where no one looks for it."

"Elyot's being part of it—if that's so, then Graeme and all Aspen Vale is in it, too," Sabine told us. "Graeme doesn't move without his brother's advice."

"We're getting things all muddled now. Let's go one at a time," Tunstall said, rightfully. "Cooper, you start."

I opened my memory palace for all I'd done yesterday evening and this morning and made my report, though not word for word as I have written it up here. Sabine looked away when I told them of Linnet's fate. Tunstall's face went bleak. They did brighten when I told them, thanks to Linnet's spirit, we knew part of the caravan, with the prince and the mage I called Viper, was on its way to Frasrlund. If we could catch up, if we got word to my lord, it might be we could exact vengeance for Linnet.

Sabine's report came after mine. "I was trapped as Prince Baird's companion throughout supper," she told us. "I'd hoped to slip away after, but Countess Aeldra and her ladies caught me and subjected me to a thorough quizzing on the life of a lady knight. They also pried quite a lot on my travels with the three of you, which they seemed to think—though gods forbid they should say it!—are one long orgy." She saw Tunstall turn his head, and said forcefully, "Mattes, don't spit!"

"Truly, don't spit," Farmer said mildly. "You might blot out part of the circle."

"I turned the discussion a bit when I asked Aeldra how she could soil her hands with slave commerce," Sabine told us, her brown eyes wicked. "She gave me a great deal of scummer about slaves deserving their position or the gods would not have placed them there. She claimed we've been at peace with our eastern, western, and southern neighbors for so long because no one wants to lose the benefits of the current trade—no, Mattes, don't smile, she truly did. She thinks only crude and unmanageable stock comes of war. Seemingly Queensgrace deals only in the most select stock, sold to those who tend their slaves as such expensive property deserves."

Farmer snorted.

"She showed me their account book," Sabine told him

quietly. "They have financial links to some of the noblest families in the realm. Several of them have known resentments with regard to the Crown. I noticed purchases and sales between those houses all taking place this year."

"They use the trade to communicate," Tunstall said as I was thinking it. "To plan."

"Perhaps even to move weapons and fighters closer to the capital," my lady told him. "Groten and Disart made purchases this year, as have Palinet and Blythdin."

"This is supposition," Farmer said, frowning. He caught my look and explained, "Guesswork. From the word *suppose*." He didn't even seem to find me stupid because I didn't know the word. "I could try to talk with the lady privately, but I would not want to be caught. We don't need to draw attention."

"And we can't be diverted from our Hunt," Tunstall said. "We pass this information on to my lord. Was there aught else, my lady?"

Sabine's mouth went thin. "A lot of meaningless noise," she said. "A great many silly hens putting their beaks in dust instead of grain."

"You mean they wanted to know why you were with me," Tunstall said.

"It was naught," Sabine insisted. "The kind of babble women talk when they are out of the center of events." She looked at the plants of the garden, or appeared to. "There is another thing, though you all may think me foolish for bringing it up."

"You are never foolish, Sabine," I told her. "Or if you are, it's over what's there to be foolish about."

She nodded without looking at me. "It's Prince Baird," she said. "He's not himself. I've been to enough engagements

347

with him, social things. I know what he's like. It doesn't matter if you're someone's chaperone with a face to frighten bogles, he will flirt as if he's besotted with you. He laughs, he jokes. There are reasons he's the most popular guest at all the Corus parties. He makes anyone feel lovely and cheerful."

"Not last night, I take it?" asked Farmer.

My lady shook her head. "His attention kept wandering. He was tense, and he drank too much. He mentioned that this country is splendid for hunting, but he's not getting to do nearly enough of that, and far too much talking. He told me it was a relief to have me as his partner at table. A relief to speak of simple things, like hunting, and fighting. And he asked me if I'd seen Their Majesties of late."

"Did he think you'd have been to the Summer Palace?" Tunstall wanted to know.

Sabine shook her head a second time. "He seemed . . . worried." She looked up at us. "Frightened."

Farmer and Tunstall traded looks, but it was Pounce who spoke. *The men who guard the prince are worried for him,* the cat said. *The count and the men from Aspen Vale take him indoors. They allow none of the prince's men to wait on him, but accept trays and pitchers from servants and wait on themselves. Sometimes they admit the countess to these meetings, and other guests who come here, but that's all.* When I glared at him, Pounce stretched gracefully and said, *A cat hears what a cat hears.*

"They're not going to want to let us go," Farmer said quietly.

"We'll think of something," replied Sabine. "Mattes will." She smiled at Tunstall.

He'd taken out his dagger and sharp-stone and gone to

work on his belt knife. "You won't be surprised, then, to know the count tried to bribe me to his service last night."

I said, "I saw you talking with them. A dust spinner lifted me up so I could look in the windows." My hands were shaking. Dogs take bribes all the time, including Tunstall and me. This just seemed like a very bad moment to do so. "I thought you were refusing them."

"What manner of service do they want?" Sabine asked.

"To turn on Their Majesties, of course, though I would not admit we were in search of the prince," Tunstall replied, eyeing the edge of his blade. "I would not admit, nor would they admit they knew who we truly pursued, nor that they knew anything about the kidnapping. It was so civilized I was like to puke."

"You told them no," Farmer said.

Tunstall looked at him as if he'd gone mad. "I told them yes! With that Master Elyot sitting there with small lightings playing from hand to hand? I told them yes in my best Dozy Dog fashion, and I'll thank you to think of a way to protect me, because they took a lock of my hair to ensure I'd be a good lad!" He looked at Farmer and me, his eyes sparkling as always when he'd fooled them that really should know better. "I said they'd best steer clear of you both, being you were Lord Gershom's special pets. Seemingly His Highness had ordered them to leave you out of it, too, my dear. He has a soft spot for you." Tunstall raised his brows. "Is there sommat I should know?"

"I taught him how to trap rabbits when we were children," Sabine retorted, smiling at Tunstall. "We've always been friends. Not so close as grown nobles, with me serving in the field and him at court or off doing the rounds of the kingdom, but we have a liking for each other, and *not that kind,* Master Jackanapes!"

Tunstall looked at his knife and sheathed it. "He's royal, and unwed."

"And wishes to stay so," Sabine told him. "What did they offer you, to report on our movements and keep us from finding the prince?"

"What else do folk like them offer folk like me? Wealth," Tunstall replied. "Wealth and a title from the new king, since I aim higher than my station."

"You do not!" my lady cried. "That is, you do as far as they may be concerned, but I *don't* care!"

Tunstall's smile was sidelong. "I had to tell them something to explain why I'd turn on Gershom, my dear," he told her. "Wanting to marry above myself was what they expected, so that's the excuse I gave." He grimaced. "I can't expect more than a barony, I was told, but should I do what is necessary to make it possible for a new monarch to rise . . ."

"If you kill the prince, Their Majesties will die, and your new masters will be able to place the blood guilt squarely on your shoulders," Farmer said, his voice very soft.

Tunstall smirked. "They seem to believe I am too stupid, or too greedy, to have thought of that."

Farmer nodded his understanding. Then he added, "I'll wager that every spell placed on Their Majesties to find anyone who attempts their murder will soon lead the realm's Ferrets straight to you."

"I heard sommat like that could be done years ago," Tunstall admitted. "I believe they thought I was too stupid to know that, too."

Sabine's hands were fists, her face white with rage. "I should kill all of them now."

"We pass their names to Gershom as soon as we get clear of Elyot's spells," Farmer told her firmly. "We do *not* let them know we are aware of their tricks. As long as they feel Tunstall's their man, that lad is safe. They can watch Their Majesties weaken as the prince is enslaved and know that all is well."

The first servants were emerging from the castle. Tunstall looked at them, rubbing his beard. "Well, leaving will be a trick," he admitted. "They want to keep us here a few days more. To let the slavers with the prince get more distance from us, would be my guess."

"We'll find a way out," Sabine told him. "I have something I'd like to try." She rose and kissed Tunstall on the forehead.

My partner stood and kissed her back. "We must leave here today," he said. "They know we found traces of our lad here. They'll be wondering how much else we know." We all nodded. It was nothing we hadn't already worked out.

Farmer scratched a couple of signs in the dirt, then broke the powder circle by drawing his foot across it. "They'll think we're servants until we're inside," he said. "Let's go to breakfast, then see what the count has in store for us. Or rather, you go ahead. I have something to attend to."

Most of the castle servants had already begun their work, breakfast being whatever they could fit in their pockets. In the hall, Master Niccols made certain that I sat a good distance from the young ladies again, while Tunstall returned to the far side and the company of the mages and the steward. Lady Sabine was given her seat next to Prince Baird once more.

Between the common men and the ladies-in-waiting stretched a wide open space. The area filled with two more rows of tables last night was empty now. Coming from our talk, I felt lonelier for my companions than I'd been the night before. Pounce climbed on the bench at my side again and ate whatever I fed him, leaning against me in a comfortable way. Achoo stayed at my feet. She had company there. The countess's ladies had brought their Butterfly Puppies to breakfast. They were extraordinarily well behaved little creatures. I would not even have known they were present, had they not been frolicking around Achoo under the table. I heard repeated soft finger snaps and whispered names as their mistresses summoned their pets back to them. When they realized what was going on, more than a few of them actually smiled at me. I couldn't help it. I smiled back. It's hard to dislike anyone who loves her creatures as much as these young noblewomen did.

Breakfast was a short meal, happily. I felt an itching in my skin, a knowing that the lad drew further from us each day. I also feared what measures these mighty folk might take to keep us here. Farmer had done a number of tricks that looked good, like returning the seeming of life to the dead, whilst shattering the magical barricade appeared to point to some strength in his budget. Still, there were other mages here. Master Elyot was known to have great power, and the count's own mage ought to be good for sommat. A count bold-faced enough to plot against his king would surely have a strong mage at his back. That left three unknowns, unless Farmer had turned up gossip or better about them.

I was half tempted to take Achoo and see if I might bargain with Fess to set us over the castle wall. We'd be on our way, and the others could catch up. I'd never tried such a thing with a spinner before, but first times tell the tale, Granny Fern always says.

As I laid misty plans, strangers entered the hall, taking seats on the benches at the lower ends of the tables that remained. Servants rushed to clear away the breakfast things. Clerks set books and documents before the count and his lady, while Master Niccols stood behind the count, a tall staff in one hand and a document in the other. The priest and priestess who had done the prayers the night before moved in, the priest to stand at the count's right hand, the priestess at the right hand of the countess.

Tunstall had slipped away at some point while I was dreaming of escape. He returned now with documents of his own, Farmer behind him. I noticed Lady Sabine had risen from her seat beside Prince Baird and was walking around the men's side of the hall. All of them looked grim and determined. My heart lifted. Mayhap we could get out of this den of traitors together. That would be so much better than me going out in a world that seemingly had villains behind every tree, or spending more time here.

"Achoo, *tumit*," I whispered, getting to my feet. With Achoo and Pounce I went to join the others of my Hunt at the side of the hall opposite the prince, the count, and the countess.

A big cove in a tunic trimmed with marten fur stepped around us, glaring our way as he walked by. Master Niccols proclaimed, "Parris Eckard, silk merchant—"

Tunstall strode forward, seized the merchant by one arm, and dragged him back, saying, "No, my buck, your matter can *wait*."

The merchant began to sputter. Farmer tapped him on the back. When Eckard turned to bellow at him, Farmer put a finger to his own lips, as if he said hush, but finger and lips were sparkling blue. The sparkling fire leaped to Eckard's mouth, silencing him completely. When Niccols opened his mouth, no doubt to call the guards on us, Farmer made the same shushing gesture at him. In that moment Farmer's magic appeared at Niccols's mouth, stopping the words before they could emerge.

"Now, see here, Cape," Master Elyot cried from his seat, "you can't go about silencing the count's subjects!"

"I can't?" our mage asked, as innocent as the day. "I'm sorry." The glow on the merchant vanished. "Do you want to speak?" Farmer asked him politely. "I'm very sorry I was rude."

The merchant, frightened by that touch of magic, fled the room.

Farmer turned toward the dais. "I *am* sorry," he explained, "but we must leave here. The more days that pass, the more danger to our quarry."

Tunstall walked up to the dais, Lady Sabine and Pounce at his side. The nobles, prince, countess, and all, were on their feet, the count and countess red with outrage. As Farmer, Achoo, and I went closer to the dais, Farmer whispered in my ear, "Linnet was killed in a wood room not far from the kitchens. Elyot was there."

For a moment I stared at Elyot, wondering how it felt to kill a little girl, or to watch that murder. I doubted he'd done the actual deed, when I'd had a moment to think. He could have managed it with no sign of murder at all, without using the present I had made her. I knew they'd used the pads to strangle Linnet as a warning to anyone who might find her, so it was possible Elyot had killed her like that, but my tripes said no. After four years of dealing with Rats, I'd learned that when mages murder, they prefer to do it with their Gift. It keeps their hands clean of death's stains. They seldom use their hands when their Gift will do for them. I've not shared this idea with Farmer, though.

Elyot struck me as the worst of mages, strong, arrogant, and selfish. Someone else had strangled Linnet as he watched.

Tunstall knelt to the prince. So did the rest of us. Then Tunstall got to his feet again, which drew a gasp of shock from many of those watching. Farmer, Sabine, and I got to our feet, too. We bowed to the count and the countess when Tunstall did, and straightened when he did. He was our leader and he was making it plain that our orders put us outside the usual requirements for rank with these people.

Tunstall said, "Your Highness, my lord count, Farmer has said the truth. Our mission is urgent." When the prince, the count, and the countess waited, Tunstall went on, "We have learned that our quarry has been here and is here no longer. How this came to pass must be investigated at another time, by other officials. We must follow the track of our quarry immediately. We are already a day behind. Thus, we take our leave of you, with thanks for your hospitality."

He bowed, as did the rest of us.

He is wonderful when he talks as if he were gently raised, Pounce remarked from his position by my right foot. *I am always surprised when he does it, and always delighted.*

It is as I always tell you, hestaka, I heard Tunstall think, with Pounce's help, *A good Dog learns all manner of tools.* Farmer and Lady Sabine held their bows a little longer than need be to hide grins. I love it when Pounce makes it possible for others to hear entire conversations this way. It makes me feel that they believe I'm not mad when I talk with him in my mind.

"I differ," the count said.

We all snapped upright.

"I am not easy in my mind about these nebulous orders," he continued. "You have taken them to mean that you may poke into any corner of my home, when the Great Charter expressly states that no officer of the Crown may interfere with the operation of a noble domain."

"We have not interfered in any way," Tunstall said, holding out our documents. "And we operate under orders bearing the seal of the Lord Provost himself." He pointed to the seals. "By that same charter, you are required to grant and give aid to officers of the Provost's Guard when those officers are on an officially designated Hunt."

I was so full of pride in Tunstall I nearabout burst. He was forever telling me how useful it was to listen in the justice court, and there was the proof of it. He spoke like an advocate.

The count leaned back in his chair, linking his fingers before his chin. "As it happens, I question the authenticity of those seals."

I heard a gasp. I'm fairly certain it came from Lady Sabine, who stood in front of me. She stiffened. I saw her right hand go to the hilt of her sword, while armsmen posted behind the dais came alert.

The count went on, "I wish to verify your mission with Lord Gershom. Now, my own mage tells me, and Master Elyot, that for some reason, we are unable to communicate with any mages, even those nearby. Master Farmer, have you tried to do so?"

Farmer hung his head. It was not the Farmer I'd talked with all morning who replied. "It's not my long suit, sir—"

I couldn't help it. He'd sucked me into his silly games. I leaned close and whispered, "My *lord*!" loud enough that others could hear me. Sabine half turned and gave us a scowl while Prince Baird covered a grin with his hand.

"My lord," Farmer said sheepishly as he shrugged at me. "I've not reached anyone I should be able to reach. Mayhap it's like a storm, only in the realms where magic comes from?" He looked at Master Elyot as if that leech's whelp would answer.

Master Elyot shrugged. "I don't understand it, my lord, but these things do happen, and there are times when we never learn why. I am unable to reach His Highness's mage at our home estates, let alone the Chancellor of Mages in Corus."

"Then I will send horse messengers to Corus and to Arenaver," the count said. "Since your documents claim the Deputy Provost there will also confirm your Hunt. It will be but a matter of a few days for word to return from Arenaver."

Not with the marsh bridge down, and you know it, I thought. It was Lady Sabine who cried, "We informed you that the bridge over the marshes has been burned! It will be ten days at least before a courier returns, and who knows what will befall our quarry in that time?"

It was as if she had signaled the young ladies of the countess's solar. They rose to their feet in twos and threes, Lewyth and Baylisa leading them as they rushed over to halt in front of us, facing the prince, the count, and the countess. As one they dropped to their knees and raised clasped hands to the nobles.

"Please, Highness, my lord and my lady, please do not hinder them any longer!" Lewyth said, her voice loud enough for the entire hall to hear. "Forgive our intrusion, we mean no harm or impertinence, but hear our plea!"

Another miss cried, "We know their Hunt! We know a

poor lad of tender blood and rearing has been taken from his mother by villains and poorly used!"

It was Baylisa who begged, "In the name of the Gentle Mother, let them rescue that poor stolen lad!"

"In the name of the Gentle Mother we pray!" said the maidens, bending their heads over their hands.

"We don't understand things like seals and politics." That was another of the young ladies. "But surely a mother's pain must override these worldly considerations. Surely a child's agony must take first place in your hearts!"

I knelt down beside Achoo as if to keep her calm when, truth to tell, I wanted to bray like a mule with laughter. I hid my face in Achoo's fur. *This* was Lady Sabine's plan, the one that had led to that early-morning conversation with the young ladies! How had she known what to say that would work them into such a frenzy of devotion? Surely never in the ordinary course of things would they have spoken out before men, and in defiance of the count!

I glanced up. Farmer's legs were quivering in his boots and his hands were clenched into fists behind his back. Don't laugh, I begged him silently, with a glance at Tunstall. My partner was in the same condition. Whatever you do, don't laugh, or you'll ruin it.

"Mithros's spear, Dewin, let Tunstall and his people go." That was Prince Baird, to my surprise. He lounged in his great chair, a broad grin on his face. Mayhap he found this show in the name of the Gentle Mother nearabout as funny as we did. "I'll vouch for the curst seals. I've known Lady Sabine all my life. She'd never lend her name to anything off center."

"Highness," the count protested, trying to convey what words would say with only a look.

His Highness sat up. "Let them go, I said." All of a sudden

he was royalty, and not used to having his words questioned. "It's bad enough you've got me tied up in conversations here. At least these Dogs can get in a good day's ride."

There was naught the count could do. Prince Baird was his superior in rank, for all that a noble might be near as good as a king in his home domain. Moreover, if he and his friends were trying to talk the prince into being king, it would be a bad idea to offend him. I'd thought Baird was part of it all, when I found No-Skin's trail in his rooms. Now I wondered. Why would Baird let us go, if he was in the conspiracy?

Tunstall dispatched Achoo, Pounce, and me to the stables to have our mounts made ready. Sabine assured me she would have our things packed, even my wet uniform, as soon as she thanked the damsels of the count's household. I wished I could say farewell to Lewyth and the Butterfly Puppies, and to Fess, but thought that it would be easy to slip burs under saddles and easier still to draw cinches too loose. I ran for the stables.

The hostlers greeted me with nods and silence as I asked for our horses. When one lad went to place my riding saddle on Saucebox, I halted him. "Pack it, if you will," I said, slipping him a coin. "I won't be doing much riding today, if any."

His eyes widened. "You walk as th' others *ride*?" he asked. Everyone around us halted work to hear.

I smiled at him. He reminded me of my brothers, one a horse courier and one a hostler in the king's own stables. "I don't walk," I said, and he relaxed a little. I added, "I run, ahead of them, with her." I pointed to Achoo. Not realizing that she was supposed to uphold the dignity of the Provost's Guard at just that moment, she lay on her back, paws in the air, as she wriggled and scratched herself in the dust. "She's a scent hound," I explained.

An older cove laughed and spat in the straw. "Yon's no scent hound," he said. "My lord and His Highness, *they've* got scent hounds for any kind a prey. Yon's a bastard dog. Mebbe she's got some water dog in her, with them curls, but them's no scent hounds, neither."

I shrugged. "Have it as you will," I replied. "What have I to gain from lying?"

They had the horses ready when our men came with their belongings. They were settling the last of the packs when Sabine came with ours. The young ladies had insisted on bearing our old leather packs as if they were a knight's vestments, which touched me. The hostlers accepted them with much bowing and tugging of forelocks, then loaded them on our horses. As I settled Pounce on one of the pack mares led by Tunstall, I noticed that the prince, the count, and the countess had come to see us off.

"Achoo, *kemari*," I called. She came away from the Butter-fly Puppies that had entered the courtyard with their mistresses and trotted over to me, her tail a-wag. She knew we were going back to work again. I slipped Prince Gareth's loincloth from my belt pouch and let her sniff it vigorously. She greeted it with happy sneezes.

Countess Aeldra brought the stirrup cup, a traditional drink of farewell in noble houses. The countess offered it to Farmer, as was traditional when a mage was present, a gesture to the departing guests to let them know the cup wasn't poisoned. With a nod Farmer drew a circle in the air over it. When the circle burned gold, showing there was no poison or magic in the cup, he bowed to her. Then the countess offered the cup to Sabine. I looked away so the nobles wouldn't see me glare. Shouldn't they have given it to Tunstall as our leader? But no, to these folk, blood would always count more than work. I looked back in time to see Sabine take a sip, then pass the cup to Tunstall with a smile. He gave her a smile in return, took a drink, then offered the cup to Farmer. I looked at the count and countess and happily noted the purpling of his face and the stiffening of her back. Farmer drank and offered the cup to me, but I shook my head. I did not need any mead in me so early in the day, and it was almost always mead in a stirrup cup.

"*Mencari,* Achoo," I whispered while the count made a surly-sounding speech about a good end to our Hunt. Achoo began to sniff around for the trail, now a day old. She was bound for the outer courtyard as the count and countess walked back into their great hall without watching us go.

"Swive them," Tunstall muttered. He said sommat else to my lady, but I did not remain to hear. I followed Achoo through the gate into the outer courtyard, across that, and on through the main gate. Halfway down the hill I glanced back. My companions were behind me. As I looked my last at Queensgrace Castle, I saw three coves observed us from the barbican. The tallest was Prince Baird. He was flanked by the brothers from Aspen Vale.

Ill fortune follow you all your days, I thought, then fixed my attention on Achoo. She was moving fast, giddy with the freedom of the road after her frustrating time inside those castle walls. I knew exactly how she felt.

Achoo turned northeast at the sign in the road, with the arrow directing travelers to *The Galla Highway, the Great Road North, Richcaffery.* I settled into my trot as we wove among folk coming to do business thereabouts. Achoo ignored them all, her nose and neck level. I thought of nothing but what I saw ahead of me and to either side. It was some way before we were beyond all sight of that great castle. I did not know how it had weighed on me until it was no longer visible off my left. I heaved a sigh. Never would I think of House Queens-grace without the reminder that my talk with Linnet and my gift of hand protectors had brought her to her death. She had not seemed to blame me, but I could not keep from blaming myself. Only when I saw Master Elyot and whoever did his strangling for him hanging from a gallows would I feel a small bit of relief.

I thrust my bitter thoughts from my mind and watched Achoo. I saw when she first stopped to sniff beside the road and knew she'd found the prince's piss. She looked back at me, wagged her tail, and ran on. I noted the mess of browned grass and a bit of scummer without slowing my run.

I glanced back, but my companions were not within view, there being a ridge in the way. They traveled slower to make things easier for Lady Sabine's horses while they could.

On we ran, Achoo and I, at our own steady pace in the warm early-summer sunshine. Folk in the fields waved as we passed, not knowing our business and not caring, or so I thought. They might ask their friends at night what they made of the woman in black, trotting after an ivory-colored hound, but unless they knew, we would remain an interesting curiosity.

We came to the intersection with the Great Road. Here our quarry had turned, bound due north. I left a trail sign at the nearest and farthest corners for Tunstall, though he could surely follow us with our Dog tags, and continued on my way. Here we kept to the right side of the great width of pressed earth, as those bound south kept to the left. The center of the road, the highest part of its gently curved surface, was reserved for the use of couriers. One of those passed me at the canter, headed south. She gave me a tip of the hat as she went by and I gave her a salute. I wondered if she knew of the mess that was the capital at present.

About four hours after I'd passed the courier, we reached one of the wayhouses kept on the Great Roads for travelers. I called Achoo to me and waited for our companions, who were not far behind us. Tunstall saw us hunkered down by the wall and led the way through the wayhouse gate. Once inside, he bought lunch for us all and a rubdown and bait for the horses.

We ate in silence outside the house, aware of the folk coming and going. Pounce decided I was in need of attention and spent the meal reclined across my shoulders, accepting the occasional tidbit. He complained loudly in cat when we got to our feet, and continued to do so, to other travelers' amusement, until I climbed into Saucebox's saddle. Once he realized that I meant to ride for a time, Pounce was quite willing to slide into the space between my lap and the saddle horn.

Much better, he told me as we followed Achoo out the gate. *There is scant travel on the road ahead for some miles. If Farmer does as he should, you will be able to speak without fear of anyone overhearing.*

"You would think he was in charge, not Tunstall," Farmer remarked.

"I thought he was," Tunstall replied with a grin. "Beka, Achoo is on track?"

"Very much so," I said, loud enough for the other three to hear. "She's picked His Highness's scent up twice where he stopped to pee," I reported. "I don't know why they haven't taken him in the cart and made better time. Seemingly they're still letting the slaves walk."

"They had warning we were still on their track, and they left Queensgrace before we arrived," Sabine replied.

"They don't feel they have to rush. They might now, once they hear the count wasn't able to keep us there."

"So that block on magical communication was only for us?" I asked.

"Not even for us anymore," Tunstall said. "Farmer's been talking with Lord Gershom all morning."

I was almost afraid to ask, but I did so anyway. "Their Majesties?"

"The king shows himself and bluffs that he's hale and angry and wants things done," Farmer told me, his face hard with anger of his own. "Her Majesty is not well. Weary, Gershom says, and losing weight for all that she eats enough. Now that he knows we have Prince Gareth's trail, he's sending other teams to inspect the doings of Prince Baird, the houses of Queensgrace and Aspen Vale, and their known friends. There is already a team on its way to us from Frasrlund."

"I'm glad we're out of such hustle and bustle," Tunstall said flatly. "Assignments and delegations, deciding who to investigate, who to arrest first—better for upcity Dogs to handle that. We're the right team for this task. My lady shone today, Master Farmer has given what we know to Lord Gershom, I supply the ideas, and Cooper gets among those who won't speak with anyone intimidating. Perfect."

Farmer and my lady smiled at Tunstall, plainly flattered as all daylight by his words. I was pleased beyond measure that he'd made them feel good by his recognition of their work. Someday I might lead a team.

"There is one thing," he told us as we prepared to go on. "Before our stay at Queensgrace we could assume no one knew we were on the road for this particular Hunt. Now powerful folk do not like what we did there. Assume we are followed and stay wary."

Sabine nodded gravely.

Farmer said, "Do you wish me to put out feelers? It's risky. They might notice, but—"

Tunstall stopped him with a shake of the head. "We need you at full strength in case something comes up. Save your Gift."

As we rode on, we left what had been mostly farmlands to enter forested country. It was here, in a clearing just off the road, that Farmer worked a spell of protection on Tunstall.

I had been bred to think an enemy with magic could work terrible things with someone's hair, blood, or nail clippings, which was why anyone with sense burned theirs. To see Farmer go at the business of safeguarding Tunstall, you would think he did it only to soothe Tunstall's nerves. A figure drawn in powder at Tunstall's feet, the same figure drawn from the powder and earth on his forehead, and what Farmer had done vanished, on the ground and on Tunstall.

"There," Farmer said, rinsing his hands with water from his flask. "It will be as if they hadn't clipped that lock from your head. That hair will never keep its tie to you again."

"It's that easy?" Tunstall asked, frowning. "I've seen such things done before. They take hours. How do I know you're not working a nimmer here?"

"Working a what?" Farmer asked.

"A swindle," murmured Sabine. "Mattes, be reasonable. If Farmer leaves you open to tracking by these Rats, he leaves all of us open. I doubt Gershom would saddle us with a traitor."

"Unless it's Pounce," I joked. Tunstall has the odd black mood. It's always important to get him out of them in a hurry.

"Maybe I'm just better at this than those other mages," Farmer said. "Now, be nice, or I'll ask for my dirt and powder back." Tunstall clapped his hand over the mark. We left it to Sabine to explain that it was already gone as Farmer mounted up and I settled Pounce on a packhorse.

Achoo led us steadily through the afternoon, her nose keeping us all on the Great Road North. We passed a number of turnoffs to towns, but Achoo kept on. The sun was touching the edge of the mountains to the west when we came upon a second wayhouse. We took supper there, but none of us wanted to remain if we could wring a little more from the day. We were burning with the awareness that the slaves and the mages who guarded them were mayhap three and a half, even three days ahead, or would be by the time we made camp, we'd made such good speed.

Leaving the wayhouse, we took up the running order we'd had back at Arenaver. I followed Achoo on foot. This time Farmer asked for my stone lamp. When he gave it back to me, it shone even brighter than a lantern. With that in my hand, I set out running just behind Achoo, as Farmer rode just behind me. Tunstall and Lady Sabine kept up for a short time, but the need to rest her big horses made them slow down and fall back, out of view. By then we were the only ones on the road, most folk preferring to retire into the protection of way-house walls than travel after dark.

The moon, near full, was rising when we reached a bridge over a small river. We halted while Achoo trotted down the bank to drink. There she stopped, whining. I could smell rot from the road, as could Farmer, from the way he covered his nose with his hands. Holding up my stone lamp, I approached the water. "Achoo, *kemari,*" I called. She was happy to run to me, where she hid behind my legs, quivering.

Here again was the work of the mage I called Viper. Dead skunks, deer, rabbits, squirrels, and other game lined both banks of the river. Dead birds lay among them and dead fish floated atop the water. Even the reeds were dead. I cursed her silently to a doom far beyond the Peaceful Realms, begging the Black God to let her shade wander without rest and forgiveness forevermore. I'd never heard of the god denying his kingdom to any, but I thought if he started with the Viper, he would not be wrong in so doing.

"I'm surprised to see no dead humans," Farmer murmured. He had dismounted and followed me.

I watched the fast-moving water. "Doubtless they've been swept downstream," I replied softly. "And it wasn't so long since they left Queensgrace."

Farmer's mage-light rose from him and spread, revealing everything around us until it reached the trees. I looked at him. "If this isn't the Viper's work, then there are other vicious mages in this area, and they should die," I told him.

"Viper?" Farmer asked.

"One of the two mages that ride in the cart," I explained. "Linnet called her that. She's the one who killed the slave mot and the two little ones."

"Ah," Farmer said. "She would be the one who spoke at their grave, then. The one who made the barrier that killed animals there. The poison in the river carries the same strain of power that was on the dead slaves and in some of the magic." Farmer went up to the road and led the horses to our side, tethering them away from the river. I remembered Achoo's original errand and poured water from my flask into one cupped hand for her to drink. I continued to fill my hand this way until she was done. Finished, she joined Farmer's horses.

I remained where I was, tense as I watched Farmer walk down to the small river. I knew better than to pelt him with questions when he was in this thoughtful mood. He would speak when he was ready.

I walked up to the road and waved my stone lamp over my head three times. In the growing dark to the south I saw an answering spot of light swing three times. I glanced back at Farmer, who had not moved.

Tunstall, Sabine, and the other horses arrived at the trot. "Pounce says you've found trouble," said Tunstall. Pounce sat in front of Sabine again, looking very pleased with his place. Tunstall looked over my shoulder, seeing Farmer at the water's edge, surrounded by his globe of soft light.

I reported what Achoo and I had found. Then I tried to put my stone lamp in my pocket. I'd clutched it so tight in my telling that my fingers had cramped shut around it.

Tunstall spat. "We'll leave word for the local constable— there's a town a mile off, according to the sign a little way back. We can still get in another ten miles—"

"Mattes," Sabine interrupted. "We can't do that. We'll lose time if you go for help in the dark. And if Farmer can mend the river, we'll save lives."

"Let the local hedgewitch see to it," Tunstall replied. "We can make more headway tonight."

"I doubt if any local mage can manage the work," Farmer called. "This creature—let's call her Viper, as Cooper does— this Viper likes spells within spells. There's a spell in this poisoning that will kill any mage who tries to fix it with the usual magics. There is a spell tucked in a level down that, if ignored, will recast the original poisoning spell at the dark of the next moon. And there is the basic viciousness of placing it in a river, which carries it far beyond the original setting point. Every moment we talk, more life dies."

"*Can* you fix it?" Sabine asked.

He took too long to reply for my comfort. At last he said, "Yes. Yes, I can, I will, and I must. By the time another mage of sufficient skill got here, it's possible this poison would reach all the way to the Olorun." He cocked his head at Tunstall. "Don't you think the realm has enough problems without letting this one grow?"

Tunstall said sommat in Hurdik under his breath. "We'd best find a place to camp, then. Do you require help?"

Farmer turned to look at the water. Then he strode up the bank to the horse who carried his extra packs. "Cooper, if she doesn't mind."

"Beka's been running all afternoon," Sabine protested, but I put up my hand.

"I'll be fine," I said. "Will you look after Achoo?"

"Of course," Tunstall replied. "We'll set up watch on the road in case anyone is looking for us. Achoo, *tumit.*"

Achoo looked at me. "It's all right, Achoo," I said. "Go with Tunstall."

She went, her tail a-wag, the hussy. She knew she could get more meat out of Tunstall than she could me.

"Pounce?" I asked as Tunstall and Sabine prepared to turn their mounts.

I prefer to stay at the camp, the cat said. *What Farmer plans to do . . . it is not painful to me, exactly, but in close proximity to it, I will itch. I prefer not to itch.*

"If I could spare Beka, I would," Farmer said, trudging down to the river with his extra pack over his shoulder. "It is sad that human magic and that of the gods do not mix."

I am not a god, I heard Pounce say as Tunstall and Sabine rode off.

"He's a constellation," I murmured to myself. The night seemed to clamp down as the others left. I hurried to get inside

369

the bowl of light cast by Farmer, but it was the first thing to go. Instead he took my stone lamp and tucked it into the crook of a tree. Then he made me take off my belt and boots, assuring me the poison had not entered the ground under our feet. Together we shook out a large cloth that was in the big pack. Laid out on the riverbank, it showed a glittering circle made in golden embroidery, with written signs for Mithros at the east, the Goddess at the south, Gainel in the west, and the Black God in the north. At its heart was the circle of two halves, Father Universe and Mother Flame.

I gasped when I saw the whole of it. "Your stitchery?" I asked Farmer. He bowed to me with a grin.

Then he opened his shoulder pack. He set three jars, a vial, and four boxes on the ground, then set the pack aside. Next he unwound a roll of ribbon of an ugly shade of green embroidered in white and a second roll of cream-colored ribbon embroidered in pale blue.

I'd barely had a chance to inspect the embroideries when he asked, "Beka, will you get some things from the big pack for me?" I took the bag he'd mentioned from one of the horses and awaited his orders. "I'll need my mortar and pestle," he began. "They're in a pocket by your right hand." I retrieved them and started to rise, but Farmer said, "No, wait, please. In the flat outer pouch next to that one, you'll find a map of Tortall in an oiled leather envelope, along with some other envelopes. They're all maps. I just need Tortall."

I couldn't miss the Tortallan map. It flashed silver. I drew it a little ways from the envelope and saw that it was very differently marked from mine. "May I look at this, when there's a moment?" I asked.

"Of course," he said. The flash on the map faded, which made me think he'd gotten it to do so in order for me to find it. "Next, in the pack main, you'll find a fat cloth wallet about as long as my hand. I need that."

I found the wallet, which glowed silver, as the map had done. The glow vanished when I picked the wallet up. "I have it," I said.

"Under it is a leather-sheathed box. It's my sewing kit. I'll have that, and next to the sewing kit is my everyday mirror in a pouch. I want the pouch only, not the mirror. Leave the mirror where you can see it when we pack everything up. Last item, Beka. There's a pouch full of nuts right under the kit and the mirror. I'll take those."

I stacked everything in my hold and carried it all to Farmer. Piece by piece he lifted everything from me, placing it all inside the circle on the cloth. The bag of nuts he kept in his hands, taking out ten or so. He returned the bag to me. From its weight, it was yet half full.

"Will you keep that near you?" he asked. "I may need it again."

I agreed, but I don't believe he was listening. Holding the nuts in his cupped hands, he whispered to them, then rubbed his hands together. The nuts did not fall out of his grip as I expected. Instead, Farmer produced a thin piece of something that looked like rolled dough or paste, which he ate. He stepped onto the cloth and lowered his irreverent arse on the linked symbols for the Father and Mother of the gods.

I looked near the river, where he had left his jars and vials. Had he forgotten them? From what I knew of magic, he would do his great working from within the circle he'd made—or she, if it was my friend Kora. If I had to pass anything to him over the circle, I would break the working as easily as if I had stepped on the powder circle Farmer had made in the garden that morning.

He saw me look. "I don't need those for this part," he said, startling me. "This is the part where I reclaim magic from some of my hiding places so I have enough to do all that needs to be done."

"The magic you've—um—drawn from other people, right?" I asked.

"Some is my own," he replied absently. "Whenever I think it safe, I put away some of my Gift. It grows back."

"It grows *back*?" I asked, plumb bum-clappered at the idea.

"Of course it does," he said calmly. "Otherwise mages could only ever do a few spells and retire."

Once I'd given it thought, I realized it *had* to be true. Still, it gave me goose bumps to think of the Gift growing like a vine inside someone.

"Nuts, too," Farmer told me. "Wonderful storehouses for magic, nuts. Don't let any wild creatures get them, Beka. They'll have a considerable surprise if they do."

He shook out his hair, worked the kinks from his neck with a number of startling popping sounds, then went absolutely still.

The great embroidered circle blazed with light, not slowly, but all at once. One moment Farmer sat on a cloth, the next he was covered by a dome of gold fire. I could not see a thing of what passed inside. Instead I turned outward, keeping my eyes on the road and my ears set for any noise that did not belong to the night. The rush of water beyond the mage was a cruel mockery, tempting any living thing to its death.

At last I heard, "Well, that's better." When I turned around, Farmer was rubbing his eyes. The cloth wallet was open for one fold. It showed embroidered ribbons secured to the fabric. Except for all the threadwork, Farmer looked like a big-built man who most likely spent his days behind the plow or mayhap with herds.

I went to help him fold the cloth. "If you'll put all of these things back?" he asked me with boyish hope in his eyes. Did he expect me to scold him for leaving the fetching, carrying, and packing to me? I waved my hand for him to get to his work and slung the folded cloth over my shoulder. My skin prickled where it touched my neck. I gathered up everything else as he stepped down to the edge of the water.

His voice came from the air by my ear. "You see, the problem's twofold," he explained as if we were talking over supper. "The river must be cleansed, and I want to confine that sarden Viper." He went silent. I looked to be sure he was all right. He was raising his arms.

By the time I'd finished stowing everything as I'd found it, I felt his spell-making. Every hair on my arms and the nape of my neck stood on end. There was not a sound to be heard from the woods. I was willing to bet that any creature that could walk, crawl, slither, or fly had fled or gone to ground. Even the air had gone dead still.

I made myself turn.

Farmer had taken off his boots. He was covered in a sparkling blue sheath of fire from his shaggy hair to his muddy toes. The river itself shone a sickly green in the dark, the green of mold and rot. It was threaded with Farmer's Gift, the magics he had taken from Ironwood and Orielle, a thick gold thread, and three other colors. They surged back and forth, the green trying to overwhelm all else. Farmer held his hands palms up as he spoke in a strange language. The blue sheath that covered him sent power flowing out over the little river to its opposite bank.

An image formed over the water, bright against the dark and the magic. It was that of a woman in dull olive silk, collapsed onto a floor covered with cushions. She leaned against a hanging-covered wall, pressing the heels of her hands into her temples as if she wanted to crush her own head. She'd managed to shove a veil and round cap off hair that was reddish brown with strands of gray. Her heavy-lidded eyes were a cold blue. She had to be the Viper, and I would remember her for when I found her at last. There was no sign of the other female mage who was supposed to be traveling with the cart.

The mixed-color fires rose from the river and flowed into the image of the Viper, swirling around until they swallowed her, forming an egg-shaped bubble. Farmer was whistling now, a soft, breathless tune. I'd have thought it nonsense, save that it called a rope of white fire up and out of the river and sent it into the image. There it wrapped around the bubble, covering what was already there. Now Farmer called back his own power. Like an obedient snake the glittering blue Gift returned to him and vanished into his skin. The Viper was left with only the white fire cocoon that held her inside it. I saw nothing of Farmer's stolen magics beneath the white fire.

The Viper's hands slowly fell from her temples. She breathed in a couple of gasps of air, then started to stand. She was almost on her feet when she fainted.

Farmer waved his hand. The image vanished. Then his own knees buckled and he fell into the river.

I ran down into the water and got him by the arms. I was slipping on the stones of the riverbed when the dozy charm chanter began to scrabble with his legs, getting his feet under him. Even with those signs of wakefulness I did not release my hold, but towed him back and up, onto dry ground. He was coughing and choking. I turned him on his side and thumped his spine to remind him to spit out the water.

"I hope your spells worked, or we're both dead," I snapped in his ear.

He flapped an arm as he spit out a mouthful of water and caught his breath. "Of course they worked," he said. "I'm not some idiot apprentice who can't do a simple working to clean up foul water. This was just a little bigger."

"Keep spitting," I ordered. I got one of his arms under my shoulder and stood him up. "Gods, did you have to eat *everything* set before you at Queensgrace?"

"I practically starved myself there," he argued. "I'm just big-boned. If you weren't such a scrawny scrap of a thing—"

"It's all muscle, mage, all muscle," I replied as we walked away from the water. He was starting to shiver. "Will any of those nuts be of use to you now?"

"Almonds, please," he said. "There's a pouch of the shelled ones in a pocket on the side of my pack, opposite the maps."

I risked letting him go to stand on his own. He managed it. I got the bag of shelled almonds and handed it to him. I was about to get the shawls when he said, "Beka, wait a moment."

I didn't see it, but I felt it. Warmth wrapped me round like a head-to-toe blanket. When it ended, having lasted but a moment, I was dry. I put a hand on Farmer's shoulder. He was dry, too.

"I was really drying myself, but I couldn't control the field as well as usual, so you were caught up in it. Sorry," the bold-faced liar told me.

"And if you hadn't said 'wait a moment,' mayhap I'd believe you," I told him. He was still too pale for my liking. "Mind that magicking of me, that's all I'm saying to you."

"Yes, Mother," he replied, all meekness. I was not fooled. I was also warmed as much inside as out to hear us talking as I had with Tunstall over the years, those times when we were in deep and talked to calm down. It was good, in a Hunt so filled with shadows and menace, to have another Hunter that made me feel so comfortable when we were out on our own, far from any kennel.

I got two of his shawls and draped them around him. "Have you sommat to drink that will brighten you up?" I asked.

"The flask on my pack. Seriously, Beka, I'll be fine with a little rest."

"I'd as soon we did our resting back with Tunstall and Sabine," I explained, going to retrieve his shoulder pack, stockings, and boots. "I wouldn't put it past the Queensgrace Rats to set a hunting party after us tonight."

"They'll have to fix the portcullises on the main and the postern gate," Farmer said, all innocence. "They broke about midday. Strangest thing. Both sets of chains rusted through in several places. Even with the smith working at dead speed, no one's entering or leaving Queensgrace Castle until tomorrow."

I stopped to stare at him. Then I couldn't help it. I laughed until I got the hiccups. In that condition I retrieved my stone lamp as well. By the time that was done, Farmer had donned his socks and boots. I'd stopped laughing and hiccupping both. Farmer's magicked almonds and brew had restored his strength. I took his shoulder pack and he his larger bag as we followed the road to Tunstall and Sabine. Their camp was easy enough to find, because Achoo and Pounce came out of the dark to lead us. I was roaring hungry by the time we reached them.

Although they were watching the road as we approached, they'd made camp and left the horses behind a wall of rock that extended off into the forest. The wall hid the camp and fire from view. They'd thrown ham, lentils, onions, garlic, and water into a pot and let it cook. The wind was in their favor or they never would have made something so wonderfully scented. The minute I caught a whiff of it, I feared I might actually drool.

I let Farmer tell our partners what he'd done while Achoo and I ate. Pounce came out of the dark to sleep by the fire. Plainly he'd taken care of feeding himself, though he did allow me to give him a bite or two of ham.

"But I don't understand," Sabine remarked when Farmer was done. "Did you kill her?"

Farmer looked at his full bowl sadly. "I didn't kill her. I returned the power of the spells she had set to her," he said with a sigh. He picked up his spoon.

"So she can use them again?" Tunstall demanded. "What sort of crackbrained notion is that?"

"She doesn't *know* she has them," Farmer said with his mouth full. "No more than she saw us—I made certain of that—or that I twisted them around her." He swallowed and explained, "She sent her spells out. I sent them back with the power fixed to her. She doesn't know it yet. She might feel a little warm, a little confined right now. Perhaps not. She may not notice any change at all until she casts her next spell." He shoveled another spoonful into his mouth and chewed, smiling.

"What happens then?" Sabine wanted to know. "Farmer, it's not nice to toy with your fellow Hunters!" Tunstall drummed his fingers on his thigh.

Watching Farmer, I thought, He likes it. He likes showing off when he's been particularly clever. Whatever he did to the Viper, that was special, and he wants to brag a little.

I wanted to laugh again and elbow him in the ribs, like I would one of my friends at home. I felt that much at ease with him, for all that I'd known him for less than a month.

Pounce looked up. *Tell us, by the dark between the stars,* he ordered. *You're just dying to.*

Farmer swallowed and coughed. Sabine handed him a cup of tea. Once he'd taken a big swallow, he bowed to Pounce. "A fellow's got a right to enjoy his craft, doesn't he?" he asked. He looked at the rest of us. "The next spell the Viper sends out, it will come back to her. The stronger the spell, the harder it will return. The little ones will go through—if she lights a candle, say, or makes herself look younger. But nothing bigger than that. The poison spells won't kill her, now." The smile on his lips and in his eyes went as cold and sharp as a sword. "I want the Crown to do that for her. But deadly spells will hurt her very badly."

Nobody said anything as Farmer continued to eat. The only sound was the hiss of the fire. When he put down his empty bowl and drained his cup of tea, Tunstall said, "Remind me to stay on your good side."

"Nonsense," Farmer replied cheerfully. "You don't cast poison spells that could end up killing half the countryside. Do you?"

"It seems like a stupid waste of power," Sabine remarked, refilling Farmer's cup.

"She likes to kill," Farmer replied. "She likes to know that people who never heard of her will mourn because they accidentally crossed something she left behind. The river spells were placed to trap or kill some of us, but she enjoyed knowing others would die." He accepted the full cup with a quiet thank-you. "You meet them, sometimes. Mages who like to leave their mark on complete strangers. For good and for ill." He yawned hugely.

I found his bedroll among the packs. Sabine and I opened it up. "I'll tell you, I'm curst grateful you pulled that Viper's fangs," Tunstall said as he helped Farmer into the bedroll. "Any chance she can get out of it?"

"She'd need help," Farmer murmured. And he was asleep.

"We are blessed to have that one," Sabine remarked quietly as she returned to the fire.

"So mote it be," Tunstall murmured.

I think I spoke the same, though I'd begun to yawn as well. Tunstall and Sabine were talking when I fell asleep where I sat. Mayhap it was Pounce who told them I would not be doing first or second watch that night. Sabine got me into my own bedroll, where I had a fine, dreamless sleep.

Thursday, June 21, 249

The Great Road North
writ as I find the chance to do so
It was nearabout dawn when soft, arguing voices woke me. From the sound, my fellow Hunters were off by the ridge of stone that hid us from the road. I don't think they realized the stone reflected their voices so I could hear.

"—should have told us *you* didn't ward the camp!" Tunstall was saying.

"I was bone tired! I thought *you* were wise enough to work it out for yourself," Farmer retorted. "Elyot and the count's mage could find us if I did. Gods alone know who else they've got out here looking. There's too many poxy mages in this mess, and I'd as soon not stand up and yell, 'We're here! Here, tucked out of sight!'"

"Heskaly's drum, what a mess," Tunstall growled. "Too many poxy mages is right. And there's another thing. Stop dragging Cooper into your magics. She does enough, working the hound all day."

"Who will help me?" Farmer demanded, keeping his voice down. "You and all those charms you need to watch me do anything bigger than a hiding spell? You obviously don't want my lady to assist me. I don't have six arms for bigger workings."

"Mattes, Beka has lived with Kora since Beka was a Puppy," Sabine reminded him. "She's comfortable with magic. More comfortable than you. She's volunteered to assist Farmer every time. I'll tell you something else. She's been happier at that—at most of this Hunt—than she's been in months."

"Months!" Tunstall said, only barely remembering to keep

it quiet. "Months? When she had Holborn, and him talking wedding plans?"

"*He* was, you great looby," Sabine told him. "She'd been pulling away. She was *this close* to breaking it off. She likes working with us and Farmer. She likes being on the road, away from people saying how sorry they are he's gone."

I turned over in my roll, as if I still slept, so they would not see me blush red with shame. I thought I'd hidden it so well. But I should have known Sabine's keen eyes would notice more than movement in the brush. I thought, too, it was not so bad if Farmer knew I was not sodden with mourning my dead betrothed. Then I felt guilty, but not as much as before. A Hunt clears a lot of old miseries out of the brain.

I glanced at Farmer's sleeping spot. His bedding was already rolled up and ready to go. Atop it sat the box he used for his embroidery thread and needles, something I'd seen often during those nights in the marsh, and three lengths of crimson ribbon. Two of them were covered with designs in thread. The third was half done, a needle thrust through the cloth to keep the unfinished design from unraveling. I blinked at it. Where had Farmer drawn the magic to fill these ribbons?

"Enough," Tunstall was saying. "Farmer, did you report to Lord Gershom?"

"A bit." Farmer sounded troubled. "But shadows kept passing through the images, and the sound . . ." He hesitated, as if searching his mind. "It *fluttered.* I don't know how much Gershom heard." He paused, then said, "Our enemies are at it again. They don't want us in touch with Gershom."

I sat up, yawning. The others would be thinking as I thought, that Master Ironwood or Mistress Orielle was a traitor. "You let me sleep without taking a watch?" I asked Tunstall.

"Get used to it," he told me. "You run all day with Achoo, or run and ride. The three of us can manage the watches. And if helping Master Cape with his magic is too much for you . . ." He glared at Farmer.

I yawned again, so they'd think I hadn't been awake enough to overhear. "Well, last night you and Sabine set up camp. And at the slaves' burial ground, Sabine watched the road whilst me'n Achoo waited to see where the trail went next. It was only reasonable I aid Farmer. I help Kora some-times, when she does medicine work and such." I got out of my bedclothes. Like the others, I slept in my shirt and breeches. I pulled on stockings and boots. "If you'll excuse me, I need a visit in the bushes."

Sabine went with me. She told me she was the one who'd dug the neat trench in the screen of brush nearby.

"You heard us, didn't you?" she whispered as we were doing our belt buckles up.

"Did you have to mention Holborn?" I murmured.

"Was I wrong?" she asked in her turn.

I shook my head. "Kora and Aniki knew, and Ersken. I just found out Holborn was a boy, and I wanted a man."

"I'm sorry he turned out that way. You need someone who respects you," Sabine remarked. "Not a gloomy fellow, but one who understands why you care about people who've been thrown away." She smiled at me. "That's why I'm so hon-ored to be on this Hunt with you. You care."

I couldn't bear the respect and the affection I felt for her just then, but I made certain that she heard me as I looked at my boots and said, "It is an honor and a comfort to *me,* Lady Sabine, and to Tunstall. We both rejoiced to have you in the Hunt."

"No, you were doing so well with plain 'Sabine,' don't

stop now," she said, and chuckled. "I always knew Mattes was safe with you to watch his back, but I confess, it is *so* much better when it's both of us." Her voice went darker, making me look up as she said, "And we are hemmed with brambles made of swords, risking death with every step."

I nodded. There was little more I could say to that.

We left the privy and cleaned up for the day. Sabine coiled her braid and pinned it up for some reason, while I let mine hang as usual. Then we settled to breakfast: fried ham, slices of bread with cheese melted on them, and Farmer's wake-up tea. Pounce and Achoo feasted on chopped ham. We cleaned our pan and bowls at a nearby pond, then packed up. Today Sabine donned armor, which explained the braiding of her hair. It made her helm fit snugly on her head.

"Why?" Tunstall asked as he helped her to buckle her chest and back armor at her sides. "Why arm up today?"

Sabine looked at him over her shoulder. "Because yesterday it was more important to me that those vermin at Queensgrace thought we weren't aware of how dangerous they are. We took risks yesterday. Today I want to travel as if there are enemies at our backs."

Tunstall winced. "Good point," he said. He and I got what fighting gear we had from our packs.

I donned my cuirass and arm guards, the ones that had many thin blades as ribs and weapons. Next I put on my gorget and gauntlets. I would need to ride since I was armored, but I had the feeling that things would be better this way.

"What gear do you have to wear against weaponry?" Sabine asked Farmer.

He gave her his looby grin. "My charmer's personality," he said.

"Cozening wretch," grumbled Tunstall.

"You're only sad because I said it first, Mattes," Farmer replied. Pounce jumped up into the saddle in front of the mage. "There, you see? A cat understands how to be pleasant in the morning. He doesn't talk."

Sabine grabbed Tunstall by the sleeve. "Help me ready the horses." Over her shoulder she called to Farmer, "And stop needling him, you! As far along as we are, you ought to know he's a grump in the morning!"

"Nobody asks the *wizard* if he's a grump in the morning and would like lovely ladies to be nice to him," Farmer commented, scratching Pounce's chin.

"Nobody dares," I said. "I'm filling the privy. No, don't get down. Gods forbid you should disturb that cat." Grinning at his folly, I went to do the task everyone else had ducked.

The day passed well, save for Farmer's attempts to reach Lord Gershom and his teacher Cassine. He was vexed he could find no trace of her in a mirror he carried in a pocket sewn on his outer garment. That was the strangest piece of clothing I'd ever seen, a jacket-like outer tunic, sleeveless, but with six pockets down the front, and six more sewn inside the front. If I caught a glimpse of his back in just the right light, as did Sabine and Tunstall, we could see flashes of signs embroidered within the dark green wool of the cloth.

Late in the morning Farmer made us halt where a cow track crossed the road. Some herder had lost his sun hat. Either it had gotten caught on the low branch where it presently hung, or someone had left it where the herder might find it. The hat was the poorest of things, wide brimmed and low crowned, the brim bent so hard on one side the straw was cracked. Farmer dismounted and gathered some reeds. He took down the hat and held it under one arm as he wove the green reeds together, his lips moving. I saw a sparkle here and there, but nothing big like the night before.

When he finished, he had an exact copy of the hat in his hands. It was the copy that he left on the branch, and the original he put on his own head. Tunstall rolled his eyes. "You look the very gods' fool in that folderol. There will be folk asking if the Players have come to town."

"My head gets hot in the sun," Farmer said mildly. I glared at Tunstall. He can always be annoying when it comes to mages, but he seemed at his worst with Farmer.

"Then why not take the hat and leave off magicking another?" Tunstall wanted to know as we set off. Achoo, having stopped well ahead to wait for us, turned and ran on. "Why hold us up?"

"For one, the lad who lost it may not be in the way of getting another. If he were, why keep wearing this battered thing?" Farmer asked sensibly. "For another, a magicked hat is easy to spot if you're a mage. I can't tell if you've noticed, but at least four times this morning this area has been examined by mages seeking other mages. I've hidden everything of me but myself, including the Gift I used to make the copy. Now not only am I keeping the sun off my head, but I've tucked enough magic under this hat *not* of my own making to hide me. Until they figure it out, it will be as if I vanished, or I'm napping under that tree back there."

Since I was ahead of her, I could not see Sabine's face when she said, "You must work your magic far more often than we realize." She did sound a little startled.

"A bit here, a bit there," Farmer replied. "When you're dealing with a conspiracy of powerful mages, it's safer to use small magics. They're looking for a great mage, not a normal one."

"I can't decide if you're a powerful mage or simply a thief," Sabine told him.

"A thief, naturally," Farmer replied with a grin. "A thief whose stealing is not considered a crime, hiding out with Dogs."

We halted sometime after noon for a meal at a wayhouse. Here we came in for a bit of luck. The housekeeper told Sabine of a slaver's cart that had stayed several hours the day before, needing repair to a wheel. A hostler told Tunstall of a dark-skinned, dark-haired lad of the proper age who was chained inside the cart. The cove showed us the whip lash on his cheek that the mot who led the slave group had given him for prying. I was confident in Achoo's nose, but it was always good to have confirmation of our quarry from other sources.

We stayed only long enough to eat, feed the animals, and give Sabine's big lads a bit of a rest before we were on the road again. Achoo stayed on the trail, not even hesitating when we came to the divide of the Great Road North and the Frasrlund Road. She took us northwest then, past the royal rest house at the parting of the ways. Signs pointed the way to Babet, a good-sized town three miles north between the roads. We could have laid up at the rest house or Babet for the night. After a short talk we all agreed we'd as soon take advantage of the waning moon and press on, even if it meant a second night on the ground.

Pounce disappeared. He reappeared while we stopped at twilight for supper and a nap as we waited for moonrise. He spoke to none of us that I could tell, but paced along the road, tail whisking back and forth. Tunstall pointed to him and raised his eyebrows. I could only shrug. Pounce would tell us when he felt like it.

When Tunstall roused us at moonrise, I decided to go

afoot for the rest of this day. I could run in pieces of armor, though not nearly as long as I could without it. I used soot from our small fire to dim the shine on my round helm, cuirass, and greaves and wrapped a dark scarf around my gorget. Summer or no, the forest cooled off in a hurry. When all of us were ready, I gave Achoo her signal. Off she went on the right side of the road.

It wasn't much later before we lost the moonlight. The trees here grew high. I fetched out my stone lamp and Achoo and I went on as the others caught up with us. They didn't say so, but they plainly didn't want our group too far apart out here in the dark.

It must have been a couple of hours after midnight when Tunstall called a halt. I didn't mind in the least. The armor weighed me down like boulders. I was glad to strip it off, though I left my gorget and my arm guards on and set my cuirass within reach. I knew from bitter experience I could not sleep in a cuirass and greaves. As I unrolled my bedding I looked for Pounce. He paced at the edge of the fire Tunstall was building, tail all a-twitch again.

"Beka, I'm digging the privy over behind that pine tree," Farmer told me, pointing. I managed to look where he did and fix the spot in my memory. I was so tired I felt giddy, drunk with exhaustion.

"Sleep, Cooper," Tunstall ordered me with a smile. "We'll set up camp and watches."

I would have argued about not doing my share a second night in a row, but I was already falling asleep. I didn't even realize I had not gotten under the blankets. Tunstall always set up camp on our other Hunts, anyway. It was having company along that made me so foolish, when I was in no condition to help.

Achoo's alarm bark—not her usual quiet whuff, but a piercing roar—woke me. Farmer's bellow of rage got me to my feet as I bent to grab my long knife in my left hand and my baton in my right. I lunged in and kicked our banked fire into flames.

Warriors on foot attacked us. They were all in dark clothes. They had swords in their fambles and masks on their faces. I screamed as one hacked at Achoo. She danced out of the way and leaped for his throat, snarling. Pounce went for the eyes of the cove beside that one. I glimpsed Tunstall at Sabine's back, the two of them guarding each other. The lady stood braced, wielding her longsword with both hands, keeping three attackers at bay. Tunstall struck at his Rat, his baton in his left hand and his short sword in his right. He used the baton as a shield.

"Kemari!" I cried, summoning Achoo to me. I was still half kneeling on the ground. A Rat came at me on my right. I swung my baton hard into his knees, hearing bone shatter as he pitched face-first toward the fire. He threw himself to the side, away from the flames, but didn't remember I was still there with my dagger. I killed him and hunkered by his corpse, keeping low. Achoo was with me now, hackles up, her lips skinned back from her teeth. Where was Farmer?

A big sound like *crump* pushed at me. Dirt and small stones rained down as a column of white fire blazed close to the nearby stream. There stood Farmer, searching for his next foe or foes. I think I saw the remains of three pairs of boots. *He* did not see two of the enemy crawling toward him over the ground on his off side, one of them shimmering with red fire. I seized a good-sized rock, rose, and threw it hard at the red-fire mage. Seemingly that cove's magic was not for protection against rocks, for mine struck him square on the skull.

That brought Farmer around with a flare of his own power for the other mage's companion. By the time he'd made sure both were dead, Achoo and I were at his side. Let him take the mages, I thought. We'll cover him for the rest.

We were fighting off a second mage and two of *his* guards when I heard high whistles in a definite rhythm. The shrill neigh of a furious horse, followed by another horse's enraged challenge, sounded from the area where we'd tethered our mounts. Drummer and Steady charged into the light of the fire and of Farmer's white blaze. Drummer reared, lashing at attackers who battled Tunstall. The warhorse knocked one swordsman down with a steel-clad hoof and trampled the other. Steady grabbed one of Sabine's foes by the collar and dragged him back, then dropped and stamped on him.

Still the attackers came, another mage, then two. One stayed back, away from Farmer, while the other came in close, though not so close that I could stick him. They showered Farmer with a blaze of magic. Achoo seized one of them by the wrist, shaking it ferociously. When the mage looked away from Farmer, trying to throw off Achoo, Pounce leaped onto his shoulder from the dark, clawing at the side of his face. He managed one scream before I knifed him. That put him down. Farmer did for his friend, wrapping a blue fire snake around the mage's throat until the cove was dead.

The fighting blurs after that. A bolt of greenish fire came dead at Farmer, and he brought his fiery hands up too slow to counter it. I knocked him down, freeing one of the knife ribs from my arm guard. Onto my knees I went. I threw the knife. The blade struck in the green mage's throat—they are always looking for magic in a fight, not knives. He tried to get off another strike at Farmer and dropped to the ground, green fire still on his hands.

That's when I heard Achoo scream.

One of them had stuck a knife into her side, in her belly. I dragged her to me and crouched over her, protecting her, as I drew another reed-thin blade from my arm guard. I threw it at the Rat that had hurt her. He put up an arm, where it stuck. I threw another, and another. I stopped at seven. He'd fallen with four of them in his face. The paralyzing drug Kora had given me to put on the knives had taken hold. I didn't know that Farmer had knelt beside me. He had a hand on Achoo, pressing the wound to keep it from bleeding more.

They had begun to fall back by then. Killing Achoo was their last sarden act. They tried to take their wounded, but Sabine, Tunstall, and the horses would not let them. Eventually there was only the gasping breath of our group and our animals and the crackling of the fire, which had spread from the fire pit into our woodpile.

"Let me look at her," Farmer told me quietly. "I'll do what I can."

I smoothed Achoo's fur back from her eyes. "Farmer will help you, all right?" I whispered to her. "This is more than I can fix. Don't bite him." Shaking, I got my pack and fetched out Kora's balm and the kit of things to care for Achoo when she was hurt. I gave them to Farmer and went to help the others clean up, ignoring the pains from where I got pounded without knowing it. Achoo yelped once. I looked. Farmer was stitching the wound in her side. I'd done the same and she'd never yelped before, but it had never been so grave before, either. I kept on working, shifting burning wood into the fire pit. Sabine groomed Drummer and Steady, calming them and washing the blood from their hides and hooves. Tunstall collected the dead, dragging them to the western edge of the camp and setting them out in neat lines for examination. I made sure that our regular packs, taken from our supply mounts and set under some brush where they would not be easily seen, were still there. Assured we had them all and that none appeared to have been meddled with, I found Tunstall's pack with the big medical kit and carried a bundle of linen bandages to Farmer. He thanked me with a nod as he smeared some odd brownish goo on Achoo's belly. Her breath came shallow, in soft, short gasps.

I could not watch. Instead I moved out into the woods to search for any bodies, gear, or horses the enemy might have left. They had taken all they had with them, leaving us only those near our fire. When I returned to camp to inspect the Rats I thought might yet live, I found they had swallowed their tongues. I doubted that they had done it apurpose. The plot to kidnap Prince Gareth was riddled with mages who could make them do that.

Tunstall and I went through their pockets, with little satisfaction there, either. They'd left aught that might identify them behind. Even their weapons were unmarked, save for the signs of excellent care. They'd been professional fighters, but we all knew that. They'd chosen a time when we'd be in our deepest sleep, worn out from the day, and our guard in the same condition. Nor did it matter. Whoever had the watch could have been as fresh as April on the ocean, and we would still have been overwhelmed by the numbers of the enemy.

I was shocked by how many were slain, by us, by the horses, by their own hands or a mage's spell. I hoped the enemy's leaders would be shocked at the cost, too. They had sent more than twenty-five warriors to take us, and at least six mages. Later I would look at my companions, and Sabine's horses, with awe. Had there been more witnesses than me, this would have become a battle for songs. As it was, I had run out of things to do, and Achoo turned every bandage that Farmer pressed to her wound crimson.

When I came over to them, Farmer shook his head. "I think she still lives only to say goodbye," he told me softly.

Achoo tried to wag her tail as I knelt beside her. She licked weakly at the hand I used to cup her head. I took the latest bandage from Farmer and pressed it to the stitched-together wound. "Haven't I told you again and again that you are not a fighting hound?" I whispered to her.

She ignored you because she was defending us. Pounce sat next to me, washing a bloody paw. He had some cuts and I'd seen him walking with a limp, but he would heal in a day or two. He said only a killing blow would destroy his present body. *She always ignores you because she wants to defend us.*

"I'm so sorry, Achoo," I whispered. "I wasn't at your side." Her side, Holborn's side . . . I bit my lip. I had my share of death.

Achoo tried to raise her head and failed.

"You'd better go," I told her. "Don't stay here in pain. The Black God is very nice." My throat was closing up. "You'll see."

A pox on your rules, Pounce said. He did not seem to be talking to me. *Punish me as you like.*

I looked at him. He was illuminated in silver and very hard on the eyes, as if his light burned. He took two steps forward. *Take the bandage away, Beka.*

I did as I was told.

Pounce set a forepaw on Achoo's bleeding wound. Achoo shuddered all over and whined, but held still. Pounce kept his paw there a moment longer, then took it away. The bleeding had stopped. Pounce began to wash the long gash. As he licked Achoo's side, Farmer's stitches came away. The wound closed and shrank, until it looked like an old scar Achoo might have carried for a year or two. She stretched out, closed her eyes, and sighed.

For a dreadful moment I thought she was dead. I put my hand before her nostrils and another hand on her ribs. She was breathing the deep, quiet rhythm of sleep.

And I will join her, Pounce declared. *No fussing when we wake up, either. Fussing annoys me.* He curled up against her belly. If he did not go to sleep instantly, he pretended it very well.

"Pounce, won't the gods be angry?" Tunstall asked, his voice soft. "So often you've told us they forbid you to interfere."

Pounce opened one eye. *Let them be angry. It will take them a time to decide what to do. And if it isn't permissible for a good hound like Achoo, it should be.* He closed his eye again.

"The horses," Sabine said. Tunstall, Farmer, and I looked at her. "I'm sorry, Beka. I know we've had our very own miracle, but if the packhorses and the other mounts are gone . . ."

She was right. She and I went to find the mounts while Tunstall and Farmer set about freshening the camp. We found our horses not where we had left them, but across the stream in a small clearing, cropping the grass that was there. They had pulled up the tether stakes and found each other to make a small herd, close to their humans and away from the fire and the noise.

"Mother of Mares, I thank you," Sabine whispered, when we'd counted and seen we had all of them still. We would have been seriously hampered without these brave companions. "Good lads," she told a couple of the geldings who had come to nuzzle her pockets. "Good girls," she told the mares. I wondered in that moment, with the waning moon gilding her dark hair, if she didn't have a little horse goddess in her. Of course, the Mother of Mares sported no black eye.

We cozened and cajoled them into letting us gather their reins and lead them back to camp, bringing them into the side farthest from the dead.

Tunstall, still examining the enemy corpses, looked up at us, grim-faced. "Some of these men Farmer and I met at Queensgrace. They were in service to the count and to the baron of Aspen Vale."

"Are you surprised?" Sabine wanted to know. I went to the coves I'd taken down with the blades from my arm guards and retrieved my weapons.

Tunstall spat in the face of one of the dead men, which set me back. Even for Tunstall, that was hard.

"I suppose that means you are not surprised they served Queensgrace and Aspen Vale," my lady said, unflustered. She looked at the others. "Some of these are Prince Baird's people."

"His Highness is in it, he's not in it," Tunstall said wearily. "I'll leave that for the king and the lords to decide, if the king is triumphant."

My heart skipped a beat. Of course the king would be triumphant. Lord Gershom was at his side like a guardian eagle. The great priest mages of the temples of Mithros and the Goddess would uphold their vows to keep the kingdom in peace and prosperity—wouldn't they? The realm's great lords would come to the rescue of the Crown, surely.

Farmer came over to say, "I've set wards around the camp. Now that you've brought the horses inside, I can call up the power, and we can sleep."

"Before you said you didn't want to ward the camp," I

reminded him. "You didn't want strange mages to know where you were."

Farmer smiled crookedly, but it was Sabine who said, "I think half the kingdom knows where he is now. Am I right, Master Farmer?"

He nodded.

Tunstall thrust himself to his feet and scowled at us. "*Sleep?* Are you mad?"

"I am worn out," Farmer replied, meeting Tunstall's black gaze with his relaxed blue one. "So is Sabine, so is Beka. So, my friend, are you. The horses need to calm down, particularly Drummer and Steady. Horses don't kill and immediately turn into sweet-natured riding beasts again. Tell him, Sabine."

"He's right." She sighed, taking the pins from her braid. "Drummer is a warhorse, and Steady learned bad habits from him. They're as jumpy as you are. I know we can't lose time, but we'll lose more if a horse goes lame or gets the colic, or if Farmer drives himself too hard."

"I can put a hard ward on the camp that will keep any creatures from coming in or going out," Farmer went on. "Look at yourself, Mattes—have you cleaned your wounds yet? What about Beka? Sabine? It will be wonderfully heroic if we drop dead on the road from infection."

Tunstall grumbled, but he was the one to fetch water for heating over the fire. We spent the next hour or so cleaning and stitching each other up, and smearing balm on lumps, while Farmer worked charms that eased aches and purified the open wounds. Sabine required no stitching, but she had some truly magnificent bruises where enemy swords had worked with her own armor to smash her flesh. Tunstall needed three gouges stitched and a score of little ones covered with ointment. He complained ceaselessly until Sabine dumped a mug of healing tea on his head. I would have thought she had remembered Tunstall is a dreadful patient. Worse, Farmer discovered that Tunstall and Sabine have both been magically healed often enough that any spell isn't as good on them as it should be.

I had my sore hand and my back—there was a great gouge on it, though I have no idea how it got there—seen to at last. Farmer used an application of some balm that he said was created by his master and should make me good as new.

"You don't have to give other people credit for what you do," I mumbled as he rubbed the stuff on my hand. "We all know you're a strong mage."

While the men looked the other way, Sabine cut my tunic and shirt to reveal the wound on my lower back. Gods be thanked, it was too shallow for stitches, just badly placed over muscle. The lady set a pad with more ointment on it over the cut, then slid a fresh shirt over my head.

Farmer hunkered down by the fire, his face in his hands. I found the pouch of nuts he'd used before to recover from the poisoned stream and gave them to him. Farmer chewed some and swallowed.

Tunstall passed a cup of tea to Farmer. "Can you still call up your wards?" he asked.

Farmer nodded. "The magic's in them, not me. I only need a touch to wake them. And then I need sleep."

Tunstall rubbed his eyes. "It's near dawn, curse it. We must be on the road by noon. And those bastards will make up the time they lost yesterday."

Everyone nodded and retreated to the bedrolls. Farmer and I said nothing about how Tunstall's and Sabine's bedrolls had merged into one where they lay down together, fenced around by weapons in easy reach in case of a second attack. I banked the fire well and went to my own bed, next to the heavily sleeping Achoo. While Pounce curled up against her belly, I stretched out along her back, resting my hand on her shoulder. She continued to breathe.

From the direction of Farmer's bedroll, a couple of feet from mine, I heard a lonely sigh. I was trying to think of a response when sleep struck me like a rock. I don't even remember Farmer calling his wards to wakefulness.

Friday, June 22, 249

The Great Road North
writ as I find the chance to do so

The others slept till near noon, as far as I could tell. Not so I. I woke when Achoo did, about mid-morning, and sleepily watched as she found the wards. With a sigh, she went among the horses to do the necessary, then came back to Pounce and me. Pounce was eating something with a tail. I did not examine it. Instead I softened meat strips in a cup of water for my hound.

My hands were trembling because my fear for the cat was so great. I finally asked, *Pounce?*

I do not know when the gods will choose to punish me, he replied, knowing my question before I could think it straight at him. *We are at a crossroads in time, with all the possibilities so tightly woven together they may not even learn I have done it yet. Or they may know, and care less, because Achoo is one of the Beast People and not a human, and crossroads are governed by human fate. Or they are swept up in other matters. I believe the Goddess will take my side, since she has affection for me. Great Mithros may well do so, because he has an affection for loyal hounds like Achoo and has mentioned to me how he likes to see her work.*

Mithros knows who Achoo is? I asked, giddy with the thought that my hound had drawn the favorable attention of the chief of the gods.

He is *the patron of four-legged dogs and of the Provost's Guard,* Pounce said.

As I fed the softened meat to Achoo, I asked, *What will they do to you?*

Pounce curled up, having finished his own meal. *What can they do? Bind me to my own stars for a century or two, that's all. It's only because I poke my nose into human affairs that they have any power over me. Now hush. I'm going to nap some more.*

Once Achoo had gulped down her breakfast, she did the same. I found that, while I was no longer so fearful for my friend the cat, I could not go back to sleep. Instead I dressed and cleaned up, then set to bringing this journal up to date.

I also thought. Farmer was on watch last night, and thank the gods for that, or the enemy might have caught us abed, so quiet had they been. But how had they known exactly where we were camped? We had covered our tracks well, coming off the road.

Perhaps one of their mages was a tracker, though I'd never heard of such a thing. Of course, before Farmer, there were plenty of kinds of magic I'd never heard of. Still, Ahuda taught us, back in our Puppy days, "Go thinking everything is done by magic, and you'll end with a knife in the back." Most mages keep to one or two specialties in addition to some general guard, battle, and healing spells all mages are called on to use. The specialties were pretty well known among Dogs. The Viper was an all-around destroyer—a war mage. From things I'd heard at Queensgrace Castle, Elyot was good at defense and strength, while the count's mage was a healer of land and crops as well as human beings.

No, it was far more likely the enemy had a very fine tracker. I need to stop looking for bogles where there are none.

written later

Farmer rose as I was making porridge and tea for our breakfast. He brought the wards down and went to the stream to splash his face and clean his teeth. The noises he made brought Tunstall and Sabine around, both of them sitting up with swords in hand. I covered a grin and pointed to Farmer. Pounce and Achoo had already followed him to the water.

We made a quick meal and packed up. Though Achoo tried to tell us that she was fine, I coaxed her into riding a packhorse today. Pounce jumped up beside her to keep her from fussing. He also addressed a few comments to the horse when the mare seemed inclined to refuse her passengers.

"I don't understand," Sabine said when she saw me tie ropes to hold Achoo in place. "I suppose we can take it for granted they mean to continue on to Frasrlund, but what if they've left the road?"

"I'm Achoo today," I told her. I had found my cuirass and was putting it on. "I run at the side of the road and check for the slave middens we sought out before. When I see one, we have Achoo give it a sniff. She'll tell us if we've got the right scent. We did it once a year ago, when she broke her foreleg in a trap."

Don't look at me because I didn't heal her then, Pounce said. *The stakes weren't so high.*

"When will they punish you?" Farmer asked, his eyes worried. "The Great Gods?"

If Pounce had been human, he might have rolled his eyes. *I could not begin to guess,* he replied. *It could be tonight, or tomorrow, or next year. They do not exactly understand mortal time, and the nature of the crisis confuses their vision of this world right now.*

"Will they let us speak for you?" Tunstall asked. "Explain things?"

Let us worry when it happens, Pounce told him. *If we may cease fussing, please, and go now?*

We finished getting our armor on and bringing out the weapons we preferred to use. I noticed that today Sabine had strapped her longbow and quiver to her saddle, while Tunstall wore his short sword. Farmer had his embroidery hoop and thread ready for work, which made me grind my teeth. Though I can write in the saddle, I cannot sew without plunging the needle into my flesh over and over. It was very annoying.

The day was fine, cool turning to warm, but the road was in shade most of the time. I found the first evidence of several humans' piss before my legs were even well stretched. Achoo told us all that Prince Gareth's scent was there. On we went, the others riding close to my heels to guard Achoo and me. We did not even stop at the next wayhouse. Traffic was light, local folk with carts and two merchant caravans bound south.

By mid-afternoon the brightness was failing. Clouds fat with rain rolled over the trees. Achoo was tired of riding by then. At a stop when we still had a bit of sun in the sky she refused to return to her place atop the mare. I thought she would know if she was up to regular duty, and let her take the lead on foot. She did not waste time, but sniffed the midden, sneezed, and set out down the road. Now Tunstall rode beside us, Sabine and Farmer having dropped back to rest the bigger horses.

We were an hour along and I wanted to stop to make a piss-mark of my own when I began to feel sommat was off. Thunder rolled in the distance. The wind was blowing in the strangest way, first from the east, then the south, whipping the trees madly. Branches tore off and flew through the air. One struck me on the right cheek. Sabine shouted an inquiry and I raised my hand in warning. I was fine, or fine enough, but Achoo was suddenly acting strange.

We were running up the slope of a hill. Near the top she halted, going from middle-air-seek, with her nose at the same level as her shoulder, to madly questing in the air, nose raised, mouth open, turning in the road. She smelled sommat she didn't like. I hand-signaled *trouble* to Tunstall as I drew my baton and called Achoo to heel.

The bandits ran at us from the woods on both sides of the road at the hill's crest. They were armed with crossbows. Achoo and I dove for the protection of a big tree without waiting to see if they meant to shoot or no.

They shot. A wall of Farmer's blue flame ate their first arrows. Then a mage came out, eight feet tall and hooded and robed in fire. I bit my hand rather than scream. The thing wavered, to my relief. It was an image or disguise, not a true creature. It was deadly all the same, returning Farmer's blue Gift with a bronze-colored blaze of its own. The two lines of fire met over the road and meshed, surging back and forth like arm wrestlers. I looked at Farmer. He was sweat-soaked and grim-faced.

Sabine dismounted from Drummer and walked forward, her longbow strung and an arrow already set to the string. She loosed and took a bandit through the throat. Drummer and the other horses save for Farmer's gelding moved back, away from the lady. Sabine continued to shoot, using up the extra arrows she held in her mouth before plucking more from the quiver on her back. She killed three more bandits outright before the others stopped watching the mages and realized their own peril.

Tunstall's saddle was empty, his mount backing up, seeking the safety of the herd of packhorses. Immediately I knew what my partner was up to. He'd gone into the brush and trees on the far side of the road, just as I'd sought the right side. "*Tinggal*, Achoo," I whispered to her. She sat, whimpering. "I don't care how you sarden feel, we are not risking you. We need you to seek, so you curst well *tinggal*."

I left her hidden behind the tree as I went back into the forest. The wind steadied into a blow from the east—the mage had whipped it up before, I would wager, to keep Achoo from smelling the bandits beforetime. The thunder was closer and louder now. Its boom covered any noise I might have made.

I found the bandits' camp and their horses first. Quickly I stripped the animals of their gear and slapped their backsides, scaring them into a flight through the woods. They were scrawny, half-starved things. I asked the Goddess to lead them to better owners if she would.

A bandit fleeing the action on the road discovered I had driven off his means of escape. He came at me with a battle-ax raised high. They always think I'll try to meet such an attack from a longer weapon or blade and a taller foe. They never expect me to come in from the side opposite the weapon, driving my baton up between the rusher's legs. He'd just grabbed my shoulder when my lead-cored weapon hit his loving muscles. That straightened him up. He gripped me still until I seized his hand and smashed the end of my baton up under his chin. That was the last of him for a while. I bound him hand and foot in case I hadn't killed him, and went back the way he had come, looking for his nest mates.

Another coward on the run with a black arrow lodged in his shoulder raced down the trail. He was looking back toward the road and never saw me as I stepped aside and swung my baton right into his middle. Down he went. I bound him with strips torn from his filthy tunic and turned him over so he wasn't jamming that arrow deeper into his flesh. I wasn't sure if I ought to remove it or not, but decided to leave that decision for our mage.

I reached the road just as lightning struck the ground in front of Farmer. The Rats' mage was too busy watching him and paying no attention to aught else. I looked for the solid form inside the wavering illusion and struck as hard as I could. The mage *was* female, as I learned right off. She must have used her protective magic in her battle with Farmer or she had trusted the bandits to guard her. The image vanished. The mage lay in the road, a dent in her head from my blow. I knelt, looking all around me as I checked the mage's throat for a pulse. She was as dead as the first of our kings. Tunstall was pulling his short sword from a bandit's corpse. Two Rats were on the ground before him, one moaning and the other still. Three more lay in the road with arrows in them. They would not be getting up again.

Sabine dismounted to help Farmer to his feet. His horse lay in the road unmoving, killed by the lightning at my guess. Farmer looked dazed, but no part of him was singed or burned.

The local weather god decided to receive the Great Gods' gift of rain. The clouds split to bless the land, if not us, with a blinding downpour.

I started dragging the dead off the road. Tunstall's moaner had gone to the Black God by the time I reached him. I'd moved two raw ones before I remembered Achoo and whistled for her. With my hound's aid I was able to drag three more onto the side of the road closest to the camp.

That was when Sabine and Tunstall appeared out of the downpour, leading the horses. They had gotten Farmer onto Tunstall's horse. He swayed in the saddle, his eyes half open. Even in the rain he smelled of smoke and cooked meat from his horse's death. He looked at the enemy's mage, who still lay in the road, and a slow smile spread across his face.

"I see she met Beka." I barely heard him through the rain.

"It could have been Tunstall who did for her," I called. "Though he'd have done the left side of her skull, then, or mayhap the whole thing."

"Let's get under cover for a bit," Sabine shouted. "We'll search the dead when it lets up some."

I didn't exactly like that, leaving what information those raw ones might hold in the road for passersby to loot, but with so hard a rain it was difficult to see. Quickly I dug in the pockets of the one closest to me, bringing out an amulet and a couple of copper coins. Then I gestured for my partners and their horses to follow me. I collected the prisoner with the arrow in his shoulder while Tunstall grabbed the other cove near the camp.

The gods be thanked, the trees were bigger and heavier here, so we did have some shelter from the drumming rain. We set the prisoners off to the side. Tunstall helped Farmer down from his horse. Once the mage was seated against a tree with enough leaves to keep him from getting wet, we searched the bandits' gear. Their packs were poor things, with rags of clothes and carved wood charms, knives so worn from sharpening they were almost needles, and herb medicines.

"Locals recruited by the enemy," Tunstall said with disgust when he and I had inspected the lot. He held up a leather purse he'd found in the best-quality pack of them all. It was heavy with jingling metal, but when we poured it out, we found only tin coles.

Farmer touched one and grimaced. "The count's mage did this. He put a seeming on the coins, to make them look like silver. Poor men lost their lives for a lie." He gathered up the rest of the pocket gleanings. "I can't do anything with the amulets and charms, but later, when there's time and I have the strength, I'll go over the rest."

"I'm just as grateful these men lost their lives, Farmer, if you don't mind," Sabine said, resting a hand on his shoulder. "Given they wanted to kill us. And there's sad news about our living prisoners." While we'd been examining the bandits' gear, the two coves we'd brought into the camp had decided not to wait for us to question them. They had swallowed their tongues. Like every other enemy we'd taken down this Hunt, they had naught in their pockets. "Pox," my lady said.

She'd put it lightly. I stepped back a little ways in the trees, behind the horses, so I might be sick. Over the years I'd had to harden myself to crushed skulls, gaping and rotting wounds and their stink, cut bellies, the burned dead, and those who'd been gone and left unfound for a day or more. But there's something about a mumper swallowing his tongue, or the magic that forces him to do it, that gives me the heaves.

There was nothing I could do with these poor Rats, so I went to the packhorses. Farmer needed sommat to perk him up. I don't know if he'd had a chance to replenish the Gift in the ribbons he had used at the poisoned river, but he had other ribbons. He'd about done for the shelled almonds, too, but I could crack the ones in the pouch for him to eat.

I found Whitknees, the mare who carried Farmer's gear, and was reaching to undo the straps that secured the bag with his magic things when I saw sommat odd. Dangling from a buckle on top of the pack was a bronze medallion I recognized right off. I reached for it and ran my fingers over that raised design—four leaves, pointed inward. The last time I had opened this bag, it had not been there. What was it doing on anything of ours, hanging out in the open like a signal to follow or to steal these packs and not Sabine's, Tunstall's, or mine?

I was tugging the buckle to the main compartment when Farmer's big hands closed over mine. "I'll do that," he said wearily. He stopped for a moment, as if he was deciding what to say or how to say it. "I've been thinking, maybe I shouldn't ask you to get things. . . . So much in there is dangerous." He wouldn't look at me but he did look, I saw, at that bronze medallion. After another pause he said, "I didn't put that there."

"I never thought you did," I said warily. He wasn't normally a pauser when he spoke to me. "Nor did I."

He looked at me then, hard, asking me with his pale blue eyes if I'd tagged his pack. If I might be a traitor to our Hunt, to our realm. His hands tightened on mine. I held his gaze, trying to say without words that I'd had no part in marking his things with the enemy's sign. It's harder to do with the eyes than it is with words, but that's the trick. It's easy to lie with words. I'm told it is, anyway. I'm not good at it, so I seldom lie, but Farmer did not know me well and could not risk believing any speech of mine. He didn't try to magic me in that moment. Tired as he was, I think he could have done it. He always seemed to have some little bit of Gift tucked away. But he didn't try. He either respected me or wanted to believe I would not lie to him. I hoped for both.

And me? I've met so few folk in the world I trust to the bone. Can I be wrong about Farmer? Because that medallion says I am dead wrong about someone.

He released my hands. "I'll get what I need, and thank you."

I nodded and went to my packhorse Fireball for my helm. It was time to start wearing it.

Freshly helmed, with the rain ringing on the metal, I passed among the pack animals, making sure they were comfortable and promising I would take their burdens off if we were stopping there. I hoped not. I did not like that place. I also checked for other medallions.

As I was saying hello to Saucebox, I noticed that Pounce stood by Drummer and Steady. They were still worked up over the fight, shifting to and fro on their great steel-shod weapons of hooves. Since my eyes were drawn to Pounce on the ground, I also saw that the fighting horses' hooves were bloody and caked with pieces of matter and lengths of hair. When had they killed anything?

I called to Sabine, who was talking intently with Tunstall. She walked over, shaking her head. "He wants to push on," she called to Farmer as he cracked nuts at Whitknees's side. "We'll need a boat if this rain keeps up!" Coming to my side, she looked where I pointed. Then she said quietly, "Beka, let's scout the road." She hand-signaled Tunstall, murmuring to me, "We didn't look behind us in that downpour, we just whistled the horses along."

She drew her longsword and followed me into the tree cover along the thin trail. Achoo wanted to come, but again I made her stay behind. Tunstall vanished into the woods behind the camp. I knew he would be silent and not take foolish risks while he searched in that direction. I also knew I'd feel much better if Farmer were up to strength and able to go with him.

Both of you managed without a pet mage for three years, I scolded myself. You split up all the time and it worked out very well. It's just having Sabine and Farmer and all these animals along that makes you wish for baby minders.

It was easier to see along the road with the rain easing. Sabine and I walked along the place where we'd been attacked. Now we saw two black-clad corpses in the middle of it. They must have been hidden by the downpour when Sabine and Tunstall collected the horses.

"Stormwings," Sabine whispered. "They distracted us to steal the packs."

"I doubt they had a proper chance," I replied, the image of the medallion on Farmer's pack clear in my mind's eye. "I think your horses put paid to that."

Sure enough, when we got close, we saw the marks of heavy steel shoes in the bodies. They'd been sorely trampled.

"I'm thinking that when we give Lord Gershom the accounts for this Hunt, we ought to add Drummer and Steady to the pay roster," I told Sabine as we searched the corpses. "They're as good as two more Dogs, and they're always sober."

She grinned. "You should see them drunk."

My raw one wore only a Mithran emblem at his neck, which I took. His pockets were empty. I stood with a sigh and Sabine too got to her feet. She showed me an earring, a plain amber drop. "These might tell Farmer something, when he has the strength for it."

She tucked the drop in a pocket, bent, and gripped her corpse by the boots. I did the same. Neither of us wanted to touch the soggy mass around their heads and chests again. Together we dragged these two coves to the side of the road.

"I can't help noticing," I said as I tugged, "that Drummer and Steady appear to go out of their way to kick a foe in the head." Looking at the remains of both raw ones with a gulp, I added, "They are truly enthusiastic when it comes to the head, in fact."

"Ah, that," Sabine replied. She dragged her corpse into line with those I had set by the road before. She helped me settle mine. Then she stood for a moment, looking at them in the mud side by side. Finally she said, "Being one of the sisterhood—the lady knights—it isn't always easy. Plenty of men are happy to try to do to one of us what they'd never do to a male knight. Sadly, some of those happy men *are* our fellow knights. It happened to me but once. After that I not only trained Drummer and Steady to fight as all warhorses fight, I trained them to go for a man's face. Once my fellow knights saw it, or talked to someone who had seen it, they left me alone."

"*Good* plan," I whispered in awe.

"I know a number of fine men," Sabine told me. "Your partner is one of them." She sighed. "If only he would give up this notion that he is not good enough for me."

"I tell him you know your own mind when he mentions it," I assured her. "That you're a grown mot who knows what she needs and has."

She gripped my shoulder. "So he says. I thank you. He respects your opinion."

As we returned to the bandit camp, I wondered if he would respect it if I said we might have a traitor among us. But who? Farmer? He was the most likely, being the one we knew the least, but I could not fit my mind around it. Was I a fool to think there was no evil in that broad face, or those placid blue eyes?

I was not a sheltered young thing who could believe no wrong of a cove I liked. Nor was I terrified to face the idea of a turncoat. If we had one and he, or she, went uncaught, then we were as good as dead.

Those two dead men were the professionals, the ragamuffin bandits there simply to distract us. It was the professionals who'd set the bronze tag on Farmer's pack before Drummer and Steady caught them. The count's people had surely had plenty of time to learn what bags belonged to each of us. The threat came from outside our group. The trick would be to escape them without losing our quarry.

Farmer, Tunstall, Achoo, Pounce, and the horses were gathered under the spreading arms of an ancient oak, out of the rain, when we returned to them. "I searched down the other trail," Tunstall said when we were within hearing. He pointed to the path opposite the direction of the road. "No camp. Someone halted within view of us and ran back to others on horses. They all rode south, but I could follow only a little before the storm washed out their tracks."

"Two dead men in the road, attired the same as our attackers from Queensgrace," Sabine replied. "Beka has an amulet from one—"

"Two," I said. "The second is from a bandit. He had some coin as well."

"And I have an amber earring," Sabine continued. "Farmer?"

He was holding a silk bag against his forehead. I thought I'd seen it in his pack, wrapped about something square. "Not yet." He opened the bag and held it out to us. "Put them in here. I'll get to the earring and coins when I've got myself back up to strength. You know I can't manage amulets. The rest— that won't be today. I'll try to get my Gift restored, but it won't be enough for anything big."

Thunder rolled in the distance. The storm was returning. Sabine grimaced. Tunstall ran his fingers through his hair. "Sore-biting lice on this Hunt," he grumbled. "If I'm remembering the last road sign, there's a wayhouse three miles along. Let's stay there tonight. We can leave word of our dead bandits for the army patrols while we're at it."

We collected ourselves and I put my cuirass back on before we returned to the highway. Achoo was the only one in good humor, rolling gleefully in the mud. She did it twice more when she discovered I was too weary and lost in my thoughts to stop her. Sabine rode my Saucebox, giving Drummer and Steady a rest, though Pounce rode Drummer. Pounce gets surly when he's wet, and he never wants to talk with anyone. At least he didn't rub it in by vanishing to the Divine Realms.

I followed Achoo at a trot mixed with a walk. The scent she had was strong yet, thanks to the prince's piss-markers. Another day or two of these hard rains and the scent would be overwhelmed. Only prayer could change that. I finally had to take off my boots and stockings and run barefoot as the mud got slippery under my hobnailed soles. Luckily for us the local folk kept the dirt of the road packed down hard, or we'd have been deep in mud.

The rain continued, growing harder as the storm got worse. I almost overran the wayhouse before I realized the black shape by the road was its wall.

The place was huge, walled all about, four stories tall from ground to attic. It was as big as Provost's House, built to give cover to several caravans at a time as well as anyone that might come alone.

The wayhouse keeper would have put us in a dormitory with twenty or so other travelers, had he not spotted Lady Sabine's shield and the haughty look she gave him as we waited on a long porch out of the downpour. He had but one room left, he told us, and it with two beds. He apologized over and over for the lack, saying his people would dry out our bedrolls in time for the extra two to sleep warm in the stables and we could eat for free, though not drink.

I did not miss the looks of regret Tunstall and Sabine exchanged. "One moment," I told the man. "If you would set your folk to getting the room ready?" Once he had left us alone, I said to the others, "Someone ought to stay with the horses and Achoo, just in case. I'm volunteering. I prefer straw and animal smell to stale inn pallets and too many merchants."

"That's a good idea," Farmer said. "Beka and I can trade off watches in the stable. You two can guard the packs in the room."

"Who would bother the beasts?" Tunstall wanted to know. "Places like this—Sabine!"

She had delivered a hard elbow to his ribs. "Don't be a hoddy-dod," she said with a smile for Farmer and me. "They're giving us a night alone. Let's take the packs to the room. Say thank you while you're about it."

Tunstall blushed a fiery red. He muttered sommat that might have been a thank-you and hoisted some packs on both shoulders. I took charge of the other horses as Sabine brought Drummer and Steady along. The big horses would do naught unless she gave them the special signs and words to obey. I can't help but think that it is like having two more Achoos, both the size of bears. If only they could be taught the craft of scent hounds, they would be the perfect creatures for Dogs.

The stable was bigger than Jane Street kennel. It was oddly built, with two long buildings that housed four rows of horses in each. The buildings were connected by a smaller one at the center. Hostlers raced out of that one to take control of our other mounts, showing Sabine where Drummer and Steady could be lodged. While she saw to them, I chanced a look out of a back door. From there I could see white-painted railings like fences, but regularly broken, about twenty yards behind the stable. Rows of them stood there between building and wall. I was confused, but then, we'd never had cause to stop in a really big wayhouse before this. Normally Tunstall and I preferred to sleep wild on a Hunt.

The hostlers were a cheery group. They were good enough to arrange an area where all of our animals could be near each other. When I explained to the chief hostler that Farmer and I would spend the night with our horses, he fetched out blankets and safe lanterns and kept an open box stall for us to bed down in. He took my coin and my thanks and bowed to Sabine, who had groomed Drummer and Steady as we settled the other horses. When Farmer arrived with his shoulder pack, he helped to groom our remaining animals with me, waving the stable lads and gixies off to their supper with a grin. For a time we all busied ourselves in quiet, looking after our pack animals and riding mounts alike, seeing to it that they got a decent supper when we were done. They had earned it.

I felt better there than I had all day, wrapped in the scent of horses, straw, and the old stone of which the stables were built. It was good simply to work there with Sabine and Farmer at their most silent, comfortable with the tasks of horse care. A couple of stable hounds came to sniff at Achoo as I cleaned her up, wagging their tails and acting like gentlemen. They were friendly folk, ranging in all sizes, down to one curly little thing who could rival the Butterfly Puppies. She and Achoo had quite a talk, nose to nose, before the little pup ran off into the shadows.

At last Sabine climbed the ladder to check the loft for anyone who might be lingering. Farmer and I, understanding what she did, inspected the rest of the place. Once we were certain we were alone, we joined Sabine at the stalls where Drummer and Steady were settled.

"I should have done this before," Sabine told us. "It's needful that you two be able to handle my lads here without trouble, just in case." She took Farmer's hand first and drew him over until he held his hand out, palm up, under Drummer's nose. "Friend, Drummer," she told the big gelding softly. "This is Farmer, and he's a friend. Friend." She pressed a lump of sommat she'd been holding onto Farmer's hand. "Feed it to him, and say *friend* several times," she told the mage. She did the same with me and Steady, then had us switch horses so that we were formally introduced to both. Inside me I had a little shiver. What if I was wrong, and Sabine was introducing her splendid warriors to a traitor? "You've done this with Tunstall?" I asked.

"Of course," the lady replied. "Otherwise Drummer might have killed him the first time he saw us embrace!" She grinned. "Drummer can be *most* protective."

"Remind me to stay on his good side," Farmer said, giving Steady a nervous pat. "I take it what's in these balls isn't just sugar or fruit?"

"You take it rightly," Sabine replied. "It's my own special mixture. They're trained to take ordinary food from stable folk, but any who try to feed them by hand will get an unpleasant surprise. Honest people know better than to get in close with a knight's horses."

"What about mashes?" I asked. "Food in buckets?"

"They know the common poisons by smell," Sabine replied, stroking Drummer's big nose. "If they detect even the tiniest hint, they refuse the meal. They're my good, clever lads."

While Farmer and Sabine talked about horse training,

I ordered Achoo to stay with them. Then I went to cleanse myself of the mud that was splattered all over me. As I rinsed off the mud on the kitchen porch I listened to the help's talk. Mostly it was about sweethearts, hard work, and the busy night ahead with so many travelers in the house. One thing in particular caught my ear. It seemed the local lordling had raised the tax on his people without even waiting to see if the harvest would be good or bad. If it was bad, a great many starving folk would be on the roads this autumn, looking for work and a place to live.

Once I was clean, I went to the taproom. There a serving mot told me where to find the room given to our party. Looking about me as I crossed to the stairs, I saw eaters and drinkers pleased to be out of the rain. None wore only black. They were a mixed lot, farmers on their way to a wedding, merchants and their guards bound south and complaining loudly of the fees lords were charging on the side roads, a knight and his sister, accompanied by their guards and servants. I gathered all this as I crossed to the stairs that would take me to my partners' room.

"Be careful as you travel," the innkeeper advised everyone from his place by the taps. "Bandits and slave takers on the road of late. And the lords are that irritable nowadays. Troublesome times . . ." He shook his head.

I did not like hearing that, either, but none of this bad news was my problem. Wearily I climbed two flights of stairs to reach the room. I could recognize it by the familiar pairs of boots set beside the door to dry.

Somehow Farmer and Sabine had beat me there. Perhaps they had not been eavesdropping downstairs. They and Tunstall were on the thin beds, bowls of soup in their hands and cups of ale on the floor by their feet. I picked up the bowl on the floor next to Sabine. She and I sat directly across from the lads.

"No bread?" I asked, staring into the bowl. It held meat stripped from the bone, turnips, onions, noodles, fresh peas, chunks of this and that, garlic, thyme, and who knew what else. It was a basic bordel stew, left to simmer at the back of the stove and changing as the cook dumped each day's scraps into the pot. The results went one of two ways.

I tasted it, using the spoon I kept in a side pocket of my shoulder pack, and sighed happily. This batch had gone well.

Sabine passed me a chunk of heavy, moist bread and the butter pot. "The choice was cold ham, bordel stew, or wait two hours before the beef they'd just put on to roast was done," she explained. "The innkeeper told me they almost never ran out of mains before in all the days his family's run this place for the Crown."

I nodded and dipped a serious mouthful out with my spoon. "Achoo and Pounce?" I asked before I ate it.

We have been fed, Pounce told me sleepily. *I told Achoo it was all right to do so.* He was curled up on the bed where the men sat, snug against Farmer's heavy thigh. I yanked my eyes away from the discovery that Farmer's legs were very well muscled. *Achoo is under the bed with a bone. She fears someone will take it, though none of us have ever done so.*

Now that Pounce mentioned it, I could hear the sound of Achoo crunching a bone eagerly. Sabine was grinning.

"She pays us the compliment of thinking we are like her, grumpy one," Sabine told Pounce.

It is not a compliment to me, replied Pounce.

I looked at Tunstall, who ate without speaking. It should have occurred to me that his bones would be aching, given the weather.

"Do you need a rub?" I asked.

From the way she sagged against the wall, her face strained, Sabine was too weary to have thought of it. "Donkey puke," she whispered. "Mattes?"

"I do not want nursemaids," Tunstall snapped. "A man pays no heed to pain of any kind, not traitors and their weapons, and not bones. The only pain he should heed is what he serves up for his enemies."

I rolled my eyes and caught Sabine doing the same. The pain must be bad for Tunstall to talk like a hillman.

I glanced at Farmer to see if he could help Tunstall, but he was trying to dig a thread of meat from between his teeth, using his bone pick. Seemingly he was not about to say anything. Before I could swat him for being annoying, he put the pick away.

Farmer, the things you mean to use make my nose itch, Pounce complained.

"I'll need *you* to take your breeches off," Farmer told Tunstall lazily. "And I am sorry, Master Constellation, but my medicines are the easiest solution just now."

Sabine and I looked at each other. "I'll check the animals," I offered just as Sabine said, "I should take a last look at my horses."

"Cowards," Farmer told us as Tunstall glared at him. "Ask the house to send up a small pot of hot water, if you will."

"Hurt me and you're a dead cove, mage," Tunstall announced.

Farmer glared at Tunstall. Now there were sparks in his blue eyes. Tunstall had finally gotten under his skin. "Enough carping, curse it all! I have a headache!" he snapped at Tunstall. "*You* haven't been holding off four or more harmful spells a day along with everything else, you rock-skulled hillman.

We've been under constant assault. If Gershom hadn't been lucky enough to have me at Blue Harbor, you'd be dead by now, do you understand that?"

"Ho, the great mage!" Tunstall cried, rising from his seat on the bed. "So you've halted the rebellion all by yourself, have you? Just you, a stink-assed pig's knuckle from the midlands!"

I began to wonder if they hadn't had enough cold water that day and if I ought to fetch a bucket of it to throw on both of them.

"Chaos take us all, have you a brain that you actually *use*?" Farmer demanded. "Of course not! But I am keeping some enemy mages busy, folk I imagine they thought they'd be putting to better use than keeping one four-Dog Hunt under watch!"

"It's more than the four of us!" Tunstall snapped. "You poxy cityman, what do you know of the way a Hunt's done? There's the Dogs we've requested from Frasrlund—"

"Are there?" Farmer asked. "*Are* there? How would you know? We're cut off from everyone, remember?"

"And the teams in Corus!" Tunstall shouted. "They've met and combined notes and read our reports by now, and they're on the Hunt, too, hobbling these Rats in their dens!"

"Wonderful!" Farmer shouted back. "I'll just go and let one of *those* teams snap at my tail awhile, so *you* may have some rest!" He clenched his fists, took a breath, and looked at Sabine and me. "Now, if I'm to heal this oaf, I need hot water." He glared at Tunstall. "Unless you *like* to suffer?"

Sabine and I hurried out. On our way downstairs, I told her, "There was this fortuneteller we saw once, at a fair in Kleo."

Sabine nodded. "The Bazhir trade there."

"Yes," I replied. "The fortuneteller said to Tunstall

that his was a sunny nature that would bind friends to him."
Sabine's mouth twitched. I added, just between us mots, "I
always wondered what she'd been drinking, and if I should
try it."

Sabine burst into laughter.

I didn't hear our door open or close, but a moment later
Pounce and Achoo caught up with us. "Did you know about
the spell attacks?" Sabine asked Pounce loudly. The sound of
the taproom was drowning out any noise on the stair.

Pounce answered with his mind. *I did. He didn't want you
to know you've all been under spell-siege. I thought you were
clever enough to have thought of it, given the bad luck that's
befallen this Hunt. There's only so much one mage can do, as
good as this one is.*

Sabine cajoled the pot of hot water from one of the cooks.
"I'll take it back to the lads," she told me when she had the pot
in hand. "I trust you to look after the horses." She winked at
me. "We'll see you in the morning."

The cook gave me a gift of berry turnovers before I went
back out into the wet. As I made my way back to the barn,
I wrestled with envy. The best thing about Holborn was our
time in bed. I missed the bedding, though not the man, and I
deeply envied Sabine and Tunstall that night.

Outside I discovered that the rain continued to beat
down as hard as before. At least there was a covered wood
path from the inn to all three parts of the stables. I stayed
mostly dry but for a few wind-driven spits of water. The central building turned out to be a station and residence for the
stablemen. They were gathered in their watch room with an
after-supper drink. They waved to me as I passed through on
my way into our stable building. There were a few lamps for

light, the horses being well asleep, so I found my way easily to the section where we'd been placed. Over the box stall where Farmer and I had set up for the night, I saw the hostlers had hung a good lamp. Achoo and Pounce were curled up in the straw already.

I went back into the shadows where Saucebox dreamed whatever horses dreamed. I slipped her a treat when she roused. Then I hurriedly took off my muddy, damp clothes and put on dry things, keeping to the rear of the enclosure in case anyone came by. The feel of dry cloth was wonderful. I left the wet clothes there to dry, hung on hooks like tack, and returned to my cat and hound. Once seated in the fragrant straw with my back against the wooden wall, I had a turnover and gave a happy sigh.

I was just nodding off in spite of myself when I heard approaching footsteps. I grabbed my baton, which lay within reach, then relaxed as Farmer came into view. He carried a steaming mug in one hand. "Do you want some?" he asked me. "It's herb tea—mint."

"No, thank you," I replied. "It might make me sleepier, and I want the first watch." We said nothing as he put out his bedding and his embroidery work. It was only after he'd settled, his back against the wall, and began to stitch on a length of ribbon that I spoke again. "I thought you didn't have much power left to you."

He smiled at me and winced as he stuck a fingertip. "I have more. And I'm gathering some now."

I squinted at him, but saw no threads of Gift. "I don't understand."

Farmer shrugged. "There's magic lying around everywhere here—scraps of it that have gone unused for decades.

I'm just collecting it." He shook his head. "Mages are wasteful folk, Cooper."

I smiled at that. He sounded like a priest when the collection of coin is not what he hoped for. "I never asked before—I thought mages couldn't use other mages' Gifts."

"They can't," he replied. "But when it's sent out into the world to be worked, *then* those with a talent for it can gather it up for their own use."

"But that's not common." I said it rather than asked, because I was near certain of the answer.

"No, my dear, it's not, any more than talking to the dead as they ride pigeon-back is common. I'd only heard once or twice of such mages, and I *never* heard of mages who could talk with dust spinners."

That made me uncomfortable. "It's not like either one is very useful to any but a Dog."

"And I happen to think that is important enough. I'd like to write about it, one day, if you'll permit me. It might help teachers locate others like you," he explained.

I put my head down, because I could feel myself blushing. "Let's survive this Hunt first."

"So mote it be," he murmured. We were silent again for a little while, until Farmer cleared his throat. "I'm sorry about what happened, back there. I'll apologize to Tunstall in the morning."

I smiled at the way his words mimicked Tunstall's. "Don't talk of sorries to me. You've been under the hammer. It stands to reason you'd need to clear your head."

"I wasn't bragging." He looked up at me then, his eyes intense. "About the other attacks. I wasn't making it up."

I took off my arm guards and fetched a sharp-stone and cloth out of my shoulder pack. "I never thought you were. I wish you'd said sommat earlier, though—we'd have tried to make other things easier for you."

But Farmer was shaking his head. "I don't like special attention."

Now he had me interested. "You learned to hide your spell-working to hide for other reasons, right? It's not just for them that try to sell your folk as special slaves. You were hiding that others attacked you, too. Why? A mage's work is partly to defend against spell-casting."

"It's all of a piece," he explained. "We Dogs have the right way of looking at things. What a person *does* is worthy of respect. Not the social gain that can be had, because there isn't any. Not the power over great lords and governments, because there isn't any. So many strong mages want kings and lords to dance to their tunes, to ask their advice and pay them richly, even seek them for marriages to have their power in the family lines."

"But you can't be bothered with any of that." It wasn't a question on my part. I knew him better.

"It's boring. It's so curst boring. Out here, in the world, there's always something new," he told me. "When I'm at the kennel or on a Hunt, I'm doing work that means a great deal. It sets the balance between order and chaos right, in that one area, anyway. Maybe you think I'm being foolish. . . ."

I smiled at him. "I don't think you're foolish. I don't know about order and chaos, but doing good for them that have no one to speak for them, that's important. The rich have plenty of folk to aid them if trouble comes. They can *hire* all manner of help. But where Tunstall and me work, the people can't do that." I grimaced, feeling like a fool. "I didn't mean to make a speech of it."

Farmer was looking at me very seriously. "You *do* know."

I shrugged, turning my attention to caring for the blades in my arm guards.

"There's so much to *learn*, Beka. So much I haven't seen or tried." I glanced at him as I drew the first of my blades along the sharp-stone. His face was bright and eager, that of a lad who's found a gixie who likes him. Farmer stared off into the shadows as he went on. "There's a tribe in southern Carthak where they work their Gifts with music. I'd love to learn what I can from them. And my master believes there's a kind of magic that isn't worked with spells and charms like the Gift. It comes from living things—animals, or sprites. I think it's in Sabine's family."

Pounce opened his eyes. *Oh, indeed?*

Farmer nodded. "They call it wild magic, my master and those who speak or write of it. It's not taught, though. There are tests for the Gift and for spells, but who can test magic that only works through certain people for specific things? Take the Macayhill line. They've *always* been known for their fine horses. Always, from Kellyne, the first Lady Macayhill. Particular individuals have stood out for the horses they've bred and trained, but the whole family is good at it. And it's known in particular circles that if you have the coin and the correct approach, Lord Norow, his son Martinin, or his youngest daughter Sabine will teach your warhorses special techniques."

"So my lady's a mage?" I asked, keeping my eyes on my work. I wasn't sure about this. Magic no one had heard of?

"Not as the teachers in the City of the Gods or those at the Carthaki university see it," Farmer replied, stretching his long body out with a great sigh. I stole a glance at that body. It was as pleasing to look at as his voice was to hear.

"They think that if magic can't be tested or taught, it's not worth the bother. They haven't even found ways to see it. At the City of the Gods they just told Mistress Cassine that the Council of Mages has no interest in the doings of those with a lesser degree of ability. So I've been digging around, to see what I can learn." He locked his hands behind his head. "Most folk with wild magic don't even know what they have. I've been thinking what *you* have is wild magic, more than the Gift."

I shrugged. "Anything's possible, I suppose," I replied. Survival was even starting to look like a possibility. Achoo and Pounce were yet with us, and we four humans remained healthy and on the trail. Help was on the way from Frasrlund and mayhap closer. I had forgotten those other Dog teams back in Corus. If Nyler Jewel and his partner was put on this Hunt, that would be as good as having an army. As soon as we had regular communication again, I'd see if Farmer could learn who else was out there.

I looked up to tell him so, but he'd fallen asleep with his needlework on his lap. I set my things aside quietly and went to pull a blanket up over him. I was just settling the coarse wool over his shoulders when his eyes popped open and he gripped my arms. I waited for him to recognize me. I'd done more than seize them when folk touched me as I slept.

He froze briefly, then released my arms. "Beka. Sorry," he whispered.

I brushed a lock of hair out of his eyes. "No harm done. Sleep. I'll wake you for your watch."

He gave me the sweetest of smiles and pulled his stitchery out from under his blanket. He stroked my cheek with one hand, then turned on one side and went to sleep.

The hostlers went to their beds. I set aside my arm guards to write in my journal, breaking the work up by walking around the stables. I ran into the head hostler around midnight. We talked a little, then went our different ways, he to his bed and I to continue my watch.

Saturday, June 23, 249

Slavada Gorge Royal Wayhouse
written much later, so my own record will be complete,
from the memory palace I had made for this Hunt

When I judged my watch time coming to an end, I returned to
our stall to wake Farmer. As I shook his shoulder, a ripple of
something exciting went up my arm. I'd felt it before when I
touched him, and always thought it was his Gift. Was it coming back?

I was considering that and rubbing my wrist as Farmer
got to his feet. I say this only because I wish to explain how it
is he caught me by surprise when he leaned down and kissed
me softly. His lips parted from mine gently, he stroked a lock
of my hair away from my face, and then he went to the privies to ready himself for his watch. Trying to calm my galloping heart with slow breathing, I thought it was as if certain
things were already understood between us. That of late we
had been courting while we Hunted. I did try to tell myself he
was wrong about him and me being suited, but I couldn't even
convince myself.

I was setting out my bedding when I smelled that first
whiff of wood smoke. I looked around. Our lamp was just a
bit of light inside its globe. Besides, these lamps burned oil,
not wood.

Farmer returned to find me sniffing the air again. "Beka?"
he asked, worried. "Is something wrong?"

"Do you smell smoke?" I asked him, turning my head as
I sniffed the air. When I encountered a draft from the front of
the building, I smelled it again. "Achoo, *bangkit*. Pounce—"

Awake, he replied.

I went into the broad aisle at the front of the stable, sniffing. I'd walk into drifts of scent, but not enough to lead me to the fire. Behind me I heard Farmer tell someone, "She went toward the front."

Scrabbling at the whistle I wore clipped to my belt, I shoved open one of the small stable doors. The rain had ended. Fire blazed under the wayhouse roof and through the attic windows.

"Mithros!" the chief hostler said behind me, his voice shaking. "You, Master Mage. Take your creatures out the back doors, that way. There's rails you can tether 'em to—"

That was the last thing I heard him say. I put my whistle to my lips as lances of fire suddenly shot through the third-story shutters on either side of the inn, where the staircases would be. Screams came from the attic. I blew my whistle in the Dog's alarm call and ran for the inn. There seemed to be no flames on the second floor or the ground floor. That progression—fire in the attic, followed by fire in the third-floor stairwells, which usually acted like chimneys—kept puzzling me. Then I yanked open the unlocked kitchen door. I had important things to do, more important than wondering where the fire had started.

As I hoped, the maids and cooks slept on the kitchen floor. They scrambled to their feet as I shouted my news. The cook ordered them to form lines to the well as I ran into the taproom where the manservants were, blowing my alarm again and again. I got the men on their feet before I reached the stairs that led to the room shared by Tunstall and Sabine. Screams coming from the upper floors almost drowned out the sound of my whistle. I blew it with all my strength. Folk streamed down that stair and the one on the far side of the taproom, their things bundled in their arms. One mot near me tripped over clothing that trailed from her grip. She went down, forced to the floor by the panicky travelers behind her. I smashed a few with my baton, driving them away from me, and dragged her to her feet.

Upstairs I heard a sound that cut through the roar of screaming cityfolk. It was another Dog whistle blown in the signal that meant "All well—do your duty." There was only one other Dog here. Tunstall was awake.

I replied with the signal for "Fire!" in case he didn't know. Then I heard a shriek from the opposite stair. The steps were stone, like the floors and the walls. The railing was thick, hard wood, but the rush of people frantic to escape was too much for it. I could hear it crack.

In front of me, struggling to keep their feet on their way down the stairs, were two lads. One carried a baby while the other had a little gixie piggyback. They were fighting to stay upright with the press of folk behind them. I worked my way in until I had an arm around each. I kept them on their feet as we reached the floor. There I dragged them out of the flood of travelers, pulling them with me across the taproom. When we reached the door, I shoved them outside.

Next I helped some of the servants jam tables next to the steps. The rail was creaking dangerously—so was that of the other stair, where more folk did the same thing we did. When the railing snapped, those who were driven off the stairs did not fall as far as they might have without those tables. It was a rough drop, but with us to pull them free as they struck, they survived it.

As the crowd on the steps began to thin, I began to tug the ablest servants and guests into a line. Its end reached into the inn yard and to the big well there. Those nearest the well began to pass buckets, huge bowls, and pots. The empty ones went to the well as full ones were passed up the line. I took the first spot, bucket in one hand, baton in the other. Using my baton to keep those who still fled the blaze to the innermost side of the stair, I climbed to the next floor.

A couple of mots ran from door to door there, opening them to see that everyone had gotten out. Except for a fog of black smoke that flowed along the ceiling, I saw no evidence of fire, but I dared not take chances. I led the line down a separate hall, the building having the shape of a rectangle around an inner court. Carefully I felt those doors that were closed, checking them for heat before I hammered on them with my baton. When the door appeared safe, the cove behind me would open it if there was no answer—there were few answers—and check the room. Whether we took out folk too frightened to go or whether we found the room to be empty, he always closed the door afterward.

"Learned it in Port Caynn," he shouted. "Never open a door to a fire!"

I nodded. I knew that, too. There were times when I'd been inside at Corus fires, getting folk out. I learned fast how bad it was to leave a route for the fire.

At last the others who'd followed me up and I had the floor emptied out. The fire had yet to reach this level, which was very strange. Had it started on the next floor? The thought made my heart pound and my throat squeeze thin. Were Tunstall and Sabine still alive? *They* were on the next floor up. I'd heard the whistle off and on, but I'd not heard it recently. Where were they?

I could not go upstairs right off. We still had work to do. Bucket by bucket, or with bowls and pots, we soaked the floor with water and sent each holder back down the line to be filled. Fresh containers of water came up, handed to one of us on every step and along the passages. With more empty buckets sent down and more filled ones in our hands, we returned to our stair and ventured up.

We were closer to the fire. I could hear its roar and the creak of ceiling beams. On the stair we found them that had encountered the blaze or its smoke, coughing fearsomely as they stumbled down past us. There were only a few of them, all marked by the fire.

I gripped the first one, a cove, by the arm. "Did you see a Provost's Guard up there? Or a tall lady with a sword?" I shouted in his ear. The cove shook his head. I passed him, and the mot and gixie who clung to him, on to the folk behind me so they could be helped downstairs. After the family I'd questioned came a pair of Mithran priests. They had not seen Tunstall or Sabine, either.

The third floor was nearabout empty, with too many cursed open doors. A cove, half crazed, ran along the corridor ahead of us, ignoring the heavy black smoke that filled the hall from the ceiling down to the top of my head. "Halt!" I yelled to him, dashing forward. He was looking at room numbers. "Halt, you dolt! Don't—"

He gripped the latch and screamed, pulling his hand away. Before I could shout for him to leave the door alone, he grabbed the latch a second time and yanked. The moment he opened the door, flame roared out to cover him as dragons' fire must have once covered their victims. He was ablaze from head to foot as the fire spread around the door, flowing up and down as it burned. I retreated, waving back the other firefighters. At the stair landing, I looked down the other corridor. There was our room, the door was open. Tunstall's and Sabine's boots, still in front of it, were burning along with that half of the hall.

We looked at the stairs to the attic, but they were filled

with fire. I could hear no voices, but I saw a burning body fallen on the steps. We began to fight the flames on the third floor instead, tossing bucket after bucket of water onto the blaze. Suddenly water began to pour through the landing's window. We backed down the stair, wading through a waterfall that streamed from the attic. Clouds of steam came with it. On the ground floor, I saw a second waterfall that spilled along the other staircase. Curious, I looked out into the front courtyard.

Three people stood by the well. One was the cook. Her hands dripped a bright crimson fire into the well. A cove in his nightgown added a dark bronze Gift to their working, as a little girl whose Gift was shimmery yellow poured her power into it. Somehow their magics combined to draw up water in a great snakelike column that rose all the way to the attic, entering the window on that side of the building. A branch sprouted off to enter the third floor as another ran into the second floor. On the attic and third floors I could see the flames dying.

As I watched, I also looked. Wandering through the crowd, I saw no sign of Sabine or Tunstall. I knew not to blow my whistle again. If I did, I might startle these weeping folk into bolting for the gates. Tunstall knew the same thing. We'd been at the heart of a riot that began with an unwise use of the whistle.

Besides, those two were tougher than me, and I'd heard Tunstall's whistle while I was still downstairs. If he was awake then, he'd have gotten my lady to safety, and she would have done the same for him. I just couldn't find them right off.

Once the fire was out, we went back in to make certain the flames were quenched everywhere and there were no burning coals. The second floor was empty of the dead, but not the third floor. There we brought away twelve poor mumpers. Four had gotten the blessing of the Black God. The smoke had stolen the breath from them, leaving them to look as if they slept. They had not known or had to fear the burning. The others were not so lucky and required what sheets the wayhouse had left before we carried them away.

It was plain to me as I went up and down that the worst of the fire began in the attic and in the wing near Tunstall and Sabine. The rooms on that part of the third floor were destroyed, eleven more dead still inside. Two in separate rooms had gotten to their windows and opened the shutters, blowing the fire into the courtyard instead of into the hall. Perhaps only that had given my partners time to escape. To my relief, there were no bodies in their room. From what I could tell of the ruins, most of our packs and weapons had burned. The arsonist hadn't killed us—the origins of the fire told me we had an arsonist—but he, or she, had hurt us with the destruction of our belongings.

Once the dead were cleared and the flames out, I made sure those that had fought the fire with me were all right or being seen to. Mostly we firefighters had been hurt by smoke and small burns. We all coughed and coughed, spitting black stuff onto the ground.

At last I walked through the stable, where the hands were busy returning horses to their stalls. They told me with pride that the inn hadn't lost a single beast, thanks to my warning. Those who had survived the inn were also bedding down in stalls and up in the loft.

The chief hostler grabbed me by the arm and nearabout got punched for his effort. I was weary top to toe and not as attentive as I should have been. "Your places are safe. I told the lady and your partner," he said.

They were alive and well. Tunstall and the lady had survived and were nearby.

"None will argue with the room that's needed for warhorses and them that care for them, nor for what's granted to any of you," the hostler went on. "You all saved lives this night."

I thought of the stupid mumper who'd opened that door before I could stop him. "Would I could see it that way," I muttered.

"You young 'uns, always counting them you lose, not them that you save," he replied, shaking his head. "You'll learn." He listened to me hack and said, "See that mage of yours. T'warn't enough for him to show the mages we had how to put out the fire. He's got sommat for the smoke cough, Goddess bless 'im." He waved me off.

Farmer was behind the stables, near our small horse herd. They were still tied to the rails. He was mixing sommat in a bowl held by a smoke-streaked mot. Sabine and Tunstall leaned together on a nearby rail, pale spots on their faces showing they'd had a chance to wash. Achoo and Pounce raced over to me, Pounce actually leaping onto my shoulder. I ached from all the carrying I had done, but I had no heart to shift him, not when he was so very soft and his purr shook the pain from my backbone. Achoo flung herself onto my feet and lay there, panting.

"That should last a while," Farmer said to the mot, taking the dagger he'd used to stir out of the bowl. "A small spoonful for each. Two if they continue to cough. If two spoons don't finish the hacking, fetch me." She nodded and carried the bowl away.

Farmer looked up and saw me. His face lit, even in the shadows with only torches on the stable walls for light. He took a step toward me, but Tunstall and Sabine left their resting spot to approach us as well. I felt my tripes clench. Had Farmer meant to kiss me a second time? Of course I'd have to tell him we were on a Hunt and had no right to be canoodling, but I did wish our other partners had been looking the other way for just a moment.

"All well?" Tunstall asked. "Burns?"

"Little ones," I croaked. Of course I began to cough. This one was bad enough that I bent over, bracing myself on my knees to make it easier on my chest.

A big hand settled under my chin and pressed up. As I rose, Farmer put a slender bottle to my lips. At my next gasp he let a trickle of liquid into my mouth. I held my breath so I would not choke on it and swallowed. It tasted like the weariest wine ever pressed from a grape. Even the way it rolled down my throat felt tired. I coughed, then stopped.

"A small sip," Farmer said, putting the bottle to my lips again.

I obeyed. I drank it and straightened all the way.

Had I wanted to bounce up and down, I would have picked a tree branch, Pounce complained. Somehow he had remained on my back. *This is what happens when I spoil you by welcoming you—Uh-oh.*

He leaped away. I had no time to ask him what was wrong when the worst series of coughs struck me, scouring my chest like pieces of glass. A wad of stuff worked its way up my throat. Horrified, I hacked it onto the handkerchief that Farmer held in front of my mouth. I would have accused him of knowing this would happen, but another billow of coughs rammed up my throat, and another. Both carried more black phlegm out of my chest.

When I was finally granted the ease of standing still

to catch my breath, Tunstall squeezed my shoulder. "Nasty, isn't it?"

I looked at Farmer. He passed a water flask to me. I used it to rinse my mouth and spit yet more black into the grass. "Thank you," I squeaked as I handed it back to him. I was thinking, Well, there's the end of that. No cove's going to look at a mot with dreams in his eyes when he's seen her covered in mud and soot and hacking up black nasties. Then Farmer placed a warm hand on the back of my neck and gave it a gentle squeeze. He smiled, and I knew he still cared for me, snot and all.

"You need sleep," Tunstall said. "All of us do." He looked at Pounce and Achoo. "Would you take guard detail for the rest of the night? There isn't much of it left."

Pounce flipped his tail to and fro. *Why not? I can sleep as we ride in the morning. Achoo can sleep now. She will wake if she hears anything.*

Tunstall bowed to him. "Thank you, *hestaka.*"

We were walking toward the stable, our mounts' reins in hand, when the chief hostler came out to meet us.

"A word, if I may?" he asked, looking us over.

Tunstall grumbled deep in his throat, but we all moved out of the way of remaining guests who were taking their horses inside. "I've found it's never good news when country-folk want to talk private after a disaster," Tunstall told the hostler quietly. "I'll remind you that my lady and I were near roasted ourselves, and we've all lost most of our belongings."

"My brother, as runs this place, and I won't ever forget it," the chief hostler said. "Nor will we forget the lives you've saved and the healing your mage friend did. But there's near-about eighty folk as will be sore unhappy and wantin' answers in the mornin'. We've sent to Babet for the Provost's Guard and healers. It won't take them much past dawn to get here. We'd like you four to be gone before that."

"Before that!" protested Sabine. "On next to no sleep? Listen, fellow, we've done you a good job of work. We deserve better treatment than this."

"Another time I'd give it, my lady," the cove replied. "But they'll find out you four was on a Hunt, and they'll blame the fire on trouble you brung down on the inn. They'll say 'twas *your* enemies that did this. We'll have a bad enough time keepin' them here till a proper questioner arrives. If they think 'twas all your fault, they'll demand we let them go. They might even do more than demand. We don't have enough of our own folk to hold 'em."

"And doubtless it will be someone of your folk who lets them know we are here," Tunstall pointed out. "Folk in general lose control of their tongues when they are frightened."

"True enough," the chief hostler said with a grim smile. "But you're Provost's Guards, aren't you, and under Crown orders to boot. We're a Crown wayhouse, with permanent orders to assist you on your task in any way. Do you want to be stuck here whilst your Dog brothers from Babet ask their questions? Write up what you want the local Provost's Guards to know. Dawn comes early, this time o' year."

Sabine, Farmer, the chief hostler, and I settled the horses. Using Dog cipher, Tunstall set out our group's description of what happened. He ended by telling the locals that if the investigators had a problem with our departure, they must take it up with Lord Gershom.

As Tunstall wrote, I asked the hostler, "Has anyone said yet if the fire happened natural, or if it was set?"

He snorted. "In all my days we've not had a fire that got more than two rooms," he told me. "A' course *I* think 'twas set. And I'll be plumb sorry your lot stopped here if 'twas your enemies that set it." I think we all cringed at that.

Once Tunstall had finished his note and sealed it, he had a turn at speaking with the chief hostler, taking him out into the stable aisle. Once we four were alone again, with Achoo and Pounce on watch, Tunstall said, "We'll take only our riding mounts and spares. These people will return the other horses to the Provost's Guard. There's no point in bringing them to carry supplies we no longer have."

"None?" I asked, feeling the skin creep over my spine.

"Sabine and I had no chance to bring aught but our shoulder packs when we escaped our room, and we were busy after," Tunstall said tightly. "It all burned—our big packs, yours, and Farmer's. We heard that whole end of the floor burned."

I nodded. "I saw it."

"It will be curst hard to forget," Sabine added.

With that, we all tried to obey Tunstall's order to grab as much sleep as we could. I lay down and closed my eyes, but I could not relax. For the first time I thought of my large pack, with my changes of uniform, my gorget, my jerkin, my cuirass. That armor was curst expensive, and now I'd be near-about naked in the woods, with Rats shooting at me! I began to choose curses for them that had started the fire, unpleasant curses that might not go where I sent them, but made me feel better to think of them. If it was Prince Baird who led this plot, I wanted to grab him by the throat and shake him like the terrier folk back home called me. All this and the torture of a little boy for a bloody chair and the ability to tell others what to do! Who among the sane would want such a life? Who would want the burden of so many lives and decisions?

With such angry thoughts and the screams of those killed

in the fire rattling in my head, I lay awake. At last I carefully rose and went into the aisle to stand watch with Pounce and Achoo. Only when Pounce demanded that I sit so he might curl up on my lap did I even settle, leaning against my pack. With Pounce in my lap and Achoo at my side, I glared into the shadows. The cat began to purr, demanding that I stroke him. Somewhere between one movement of my hand and the next, I slept after all.

Saturday, June 23, 249

The Frasrlund Road
written much later, from the memory palace
Short of the crack of dawn it was, mostly dark, and us awake
thanks to Pounce. I rose and dressed in the foulest of moods.
I hoped the local Dogs would find the leeching piss-pots who
had set the fire. It would brighten my year if they could leave
those Rats hanging from the wall that guarded the wayhouse.
We'd almost met the God last night, each one of us. I wanted
vengeance for that and for all those who'd burned.

Fire-starters. Canker-licking sewer swine.

While the others took the horses to the gate, a servant
was directed to take Pounce, Achoo, and me to the shed where
those who'd died lay under sheets on hastily built tables. I
asked what he wanted with me and Tunstall had said, "Just go
with the lad, Cooper."

In the shed the servant remained by the door, watching us
with suspicion on his face. Achoo and Pounce sat facing him,
making it as plain as they could that they were not letting
him any closer to me.

I looked around. The place had been cleared of all else
to make it into a holding room for the night's dead. Only
prayer lamps and incense sat on the empty shelves, sending the
lighter's wishes to the Black God for those who had entered
his care. The room was not completely empty of life, though.
Two wood pigeons roosted above inside, heads tucked under
their wings.

"Have you aught to say to me?" I called softly to the
pigeons, my back to the servant. "I'm sorry to wake you,
but they're kicking us out." I found the small bag of feed

in my pack and drew a line on the dirt floor with the grain. The birds fluttered down to eat. Food was food, whatever the hour.

"It started in th' corner of th' attic," the ghost of a mot whispered to me. "It was that cove as bought us all wine downstairs. Merchanty-lookin', he was. Waited till most of the regular custom was in bed or gone home and bought us wine, us in service, for havin' so much work and so little thanks."

"*I* thought it suspicious," a second ghost, a cove, said. "Who buys drink for servants?"

"It never stopped you from havin' your cup or five," the mot replied tartly.

I had an ear straining for the innkeeper, thinking he might come to toss me out at any moment. "'Merchanty-looking,' you said," I interrupted. "Meaning what?"

"Dark wool tunic," said the cove's ghost. "No leggings. Leather shoes with triple-leather soles. Chin beard and combed-back hair with sandalwood-scented oil."

"I heard you sneezin'," the mot's ghost said. "Shoulda known sandalwood was in the house."

"Sneezing's what woke me up," the dead cove said. "He was in the corner of the room where I was . . . sleeping with a guest. I only glimpsed his knife afore he cut me."

"Did you see what he was doing in the corner?" I asked, setting another handful of grain before the pigeons.

"Same as he done in mine in the attic, I'll wager," the mot's ghost said bitterly. "He kilt me before he went to work, pourin' oil over a pile of rags he'd set there. Then he poured it on me, on my bed, since I wasn't goin' t' squeak."

"I didn't wait to watch after he killed the guest I was with," the ghost cove admitted. "I was terrified I'd burn, not knowing I was already gone. I jumped from the window and he acted like he didn't even see. This bird who carries me now, it flew to me, and I landed on its back."

"He opened the shutters in the attic," the mot said. "Then he went down the center, dumpin' oil after him and on the pallets. Lots of us hadn't bothered to come upstairs, gods be thanked. The others was work-sleepin'. He could have rode an ox through there and they'd never stop snorin'."

I watched the birds eat, thinking hard for a moment. "What caravan was he with?" I asked them.

"Well, there's the funny thing," the mot told me. "I don't recall, Canart, do you?"

"I thought they must have come in while I was bringing up a keg," the dead man—Canart—answered. "He didn't seem to drink with anyone. Kept to hisself. But I saw him talking with the caravan folk."

"I never saw him come with a caravan, neither," the mot replied.

"He was tall as me—well, a hand taller than you, young Guard," the cove said. "Thin, but strong and fast. I hope you catch him."

"But don't expect me to do it," the mot said. "I've a yearnin' to move on, now that I've talked with you."

"And I feel the same," the cove added. "I've never liked this place much."

With that, they were gone. I spoke my blessing to the air they had left, just to let them know I was grateful. I glanced at the servant. He'd turned pale and was muttering his own silent prayers. I had a feeling he would have fled if he weren't under orders from the innkeeper. I wasn't certain he'd heard the ghosts. It seemed to vary. From experience I knew he was shaking in his boots either way. I shrugged at him, the best apology I could manage, then turned to the other corpses. My partners could wait for my news for a moment.

I stood with the dead, offering up my prayer and hope that the Black God would take them gently into his home. Then I looked for two in particular. The attic servants were set on one side of the shed, those guests from the third floor on the other. Carefully, keeping my back to my watcher, I examined the few burned bodies from the third floor. The throat cuts were visible even on such charred remains. They belonged to a tall cove and a small one. Canart and his guest? Silently I promised them both that the sandalwood-scented killer would pay for what he'd done. To keep my books even, I found the mot with the cut throat among the attic dead, and promised her the same.

The servant detailed to watch me cleared his throat. He flinched when I glared at him, but it was all for show. I was finished. I went outside to find my companions. Who should I tell? The keeper of the wayhouse? He already knew the fire had been set. Surely the Dogs who came to investigate must be informed, in case this throat cutter was known to them. I stripped a sheet from my journal and wrote the sandalwood-scented man's description in it, saying I had it from one of those burned who died as we bore him out. There was no one who could give me the lie, since I'd carried plenty of victims last night. I closed it with a complicated set of folds since I had no seal with me, and addressed it to the Provost's Guard investigators. The servant and I walked outside.

I stuffed the note in the front of my tunic, one corner scratching the underside of my chin as Pounce and I mounted Saucebox. Achoo, eager to be moving again, danced beside us. The servant left, making the Sign on his chest, as soon as I nudged Saucebox.

Sabine and Farmer were on horseback, holding Tunstall's mount and the spares, near the open gate. The innkeeper and the chief hostler stood with them, their faces angry in the light of the torch held by the lady. Tunstall knelt just beside the gate, holding a lantern high and moving it over the ground.

Sabine rode to me after passing the torch she held to the chief hostler. "The gate was ajar," she said, her voice low. "Since the mud is drying around the open position, it's plain whoever opened it did so last night, while everything was still wet." She nodded toward the brothers. "They are furious, and I can't blame them. There are three horses missing. They can't tell yet who has gone."

"Pox and murrain," I replied. I had a feeling in my gut that the fire-setting killer was one who'd ridden out that gate.

We returned to the brothers and Farmer and watched as Tunstall, walking at the edge of the road through the gate, went outside it. Ten feet away he crouched again, inspecting the road with the lantern held close. Suddenly he rose and paced a big circle around that part in the road, stopping to inspect grass he pulled from the margins. Having made his circle, he knelt and collected a pinch of earth, smelling it before he rubbed it in his fingers.

Despite the early hour, I enjoyed seeing him work. As much as Achoo, Tunstall is a master tracker. People scorn him sometimes because he's a hillman, but everyone who wants to learn the skills of a tracker among the Corus Dogs comes to my partner for lessons.

Tunstall rose and came back to us, handing the lantern to the innkeeper. "One person on one horse," he said, still partway inside that daze of concentration he has when he's been working a complicated set of signs. "He helped himself, or herself, to spares, two of them, but they carried no burdens of any weight. The ground was sloppy, but starting to dry. We were abed by then and you coves were tidying up. Anyone awake was too busy to notice." He sighed and took his gloves from his belt. I was startled to see them, and glanced at his feet, then Sabine's. The innkeeper must have found them gloves and boots that fit somewhere. Most of these places kept stores of goods left behind for one reason or another. "He still had company," Tunstall went on, taking his mount's reins from Farmer. "A party of five horses was waiting where you saw me stop. The riders had been there some little while, long enough for the horses to eat grass. They left when he joined them. Are there any other roads besides the Great One going northwest from here? Their party didn't turn south."

"There's the Ashford Road," the chief hostler replied. I realized what I would be doing and began to strip off my boots. The hostler went on, "That's southwest, just where the bridge is. Closer to us, on your right as you ride to the gorge, they's Freedman Road. That leads northeast, up to Halleburn Lake."

Sabine made the tiniest of grimaces. "I didn't realize we were so close." The men all looked at her. She shrugged. "My father is first cousin to the lord of Halleburn."

"Curst lucky for you," muttered the chief hostler. His brother glared at him. Since I was securing my boots and stockings to my mount's saddle, I could hide my grin. The chief hostler, who seemed to run things here, plainly did not serve as the public face of the inn. Diplomacy did not appear to be one of his skills.

"We'll try to send word back which road they took the first chance we get," Tunstall promised the coves. "May we purchase a torch for Cooper?"

"I don't need one," I reminded him. I reached into my pocket and produced my stone lamp. "See?"

The chief hostler looked at me while the innkeeper stepped back. "Pretty," he said. "Had we enough of those, we'd need never pay for lamps or torches again."

Farmer grinned. "If I ever find enough stones and muster enough power, I'll make you some to help repay you for the losses of the night."

"You've done enough with your cough medicine," the hostler told him. He looked at Tunstall, then at me. "One of you tracks standing and one running?" he asked me. "A sound way to divide the work."

"If we had aught for scent of these Rats, Achoo would do it all," Tunstall said. "My friends, our sorrows for what has happened to you this night—"

I held up my hand. "Your pardon, Tunstall, but I've more news that we all have to know. This is for the Provost's Guard when they come," I told the innkeeper as I passed the note to him. Then I told everyone about the sandalwood-scented fire-setter.

"How did you find this out?" the innkeeper demanded. "You knew this last night and you didn't tell us?"

"I learned it just now, and you might not care for my means of learning this," I said. "Look at my partners. Can't you tell they've just heard it from me?"

"You have my word," Sabine told the innkeeper, in a tone that informed him to accept that and seal his gob.

"Don't go on about our Beka," Farmer said with his biggest looby grin. "You wouldn't ask me how I make up cough medicine, would you? All those sacrificed birds and so on. Magic."

They both made the Sign on their chests and moved away from me. I had my back to them, so I could silently mouth at Farmer, *You're a bad man.*

The cook came running toward us, her uncombed hair

tumbling over her shoulders. She carried a basket. In answer to the innkeeper's glare, she said, "The lady and her man saved my boy's life last night. I'm not letting them ride hungry." She handed it up to Sabine. "Gods all bless you folk. I pray you find what you Hunt," she said.

"You saved more than us, with the water magic," Sabine told her. "But thank you, and Goddess bless."

That made us all remember what had taken place, and sweetened our moods. "I only wish our stay here had been happier for everyone concerned," Sabine told the brothers. She leaned down and clasped hands with both of them. As she did, I saw a flash of gold each time. I hoped that coin would help them to rebuild.

As we rode off, the men closed the gates behind us and locked them.

Tunstall gave me a roll cut in half, with sliced ham and cheese between the pieces of bread. I ate it with appreciation as I ran ahead with Achoo, tracking both our prince and the horses of the inn's horse thief.

The day dawned, if such a shining word might be used. It was chilly for June. Fog lay everywhere, muffling the forest sounds. Before I could see well without my lamp, we had reached the divide in the road and the sign that read *Freedman Road, Halleburn Lake, Castle Halleburn*. When I tried to go that way, following the very early-morning tracks the arsonist had joined, Achoo yelped. She might have had only a little of the scent left after so much rain, but it was enough to tell her that our true path lay on the Great Road. The Rat from the Wayhouse was someone else's problem. Tunstall left a trail sign for the Dogs from Babet, should they come this way. It was all we could do, barring a message from the next stop where we could find someone to carry it.

I tucked my stone lamp away once there was light enough to see by. Now that we were done with the runaway arsonist from the inn, I mounted Saucebox, making Pounce grumble. He liked it very much when he didn't have to share the saddle with me.

I confess, I napped as we rode on. I'd had too little sleep the night before and couldn't help it.

When we halted, Farmer roused me. "Beka, we're at the bridge."

I pried my eyes open. A pair of men-at-arms stood before a small cabin at the side of the most immense bridge I'd ever seen, named on my maps as the Black Griffin Bridge. The men-at-arms wore the maroon and cream of the army, which meant there was a fort somewhere nearby. I watched them with suspicion, wondering if they were part of the lords' and mages' rebellion, with orders to shoot us down.

I was wrong. They took the coin for the toll from Tunstall, speaking with him in quiet voices. Impatient to ride on, I looked around. Achoo danced her own impatience at the foot of the statues that marked the corners of the bridge. These were griffins carved of strong black wood, both of them fifteen feet tall. One had wings halfway extended. The others kept hers neatly folded. They were lovely. I wished I could meet the one who'd made them so splendid, with each feather beautiful in its detail.

While I admired the carvings, Farmer stared into the fog-filled gorge. "I'm surprised she hasn't done something to this bridge. It seems to be her favorite thing. Maybe the spells here are too strong," he said, more to himself than me.

"Spells?" I asked.

He looked down at me. "Layers and layers of them,

placed by more mages than I can count. Even small mages do it, so they can be certain the bridge will always be there."

I ran my hand down the side of the griffin with his lifted wings. He looked as if he would take flight at any moment. I wanted to be on his back if he did. "You wish she'd spring the trap to your spell," I suggested to Farmer.

He sighed. "If she did, it would be one less mage to worry about. Apart from Achoo keeping on the scent, we haven't had a bit of luck on this Hunt."

"Achoo's a lucky dog," I said, tossing her a bit of dried meat. She gobbled it and returned to dancing her impatience on the bridge.

Tunstall rode up to her, his talk with the guards over. "Let's go, everyone," he called.

I dismounted and tied Saucebox's reins to the string of packhorses led by Farmer. With that done, I ran forward. Achoo didn't even wait for me to give the order. She raced down the bridge.

When we were in the middle, Tunstall trotted up to me. "We'll keep close today," he said. "The guards told me the cart went this way two days ago."

Soldiers were also posted on the far side of the bridge, but they just waved us by. I waved to them and Tunstall flipped them a silver coin for friendship's sake. When I looked over my shoulder, surprised by his generosity, he shrugged. "It never hurts to butter the army, Cooper, you should know that."

"Some of my best friends are soldiers," Sabine agreed with a wave to the guards. Seeing Tunstall's look, she grinned. "No, dearest Mattes, not *that* kind of friend."

Nice as it was to have them so close, I wished they would be quiet. I needed to listen to the woods. I also cursed the road. The way was muddy, though more so on the sides than the middle. The first time Achoo stopped for a drink, I stripped off my breeches, which were splattered. I rinsed them in the stream where Achoo drank while the others waited for us. Quickly I draped them over my shoulder pack to dry. If I had to deal with folk in wayhouses and towns, I had no clean extra clothes to change into anymore. My tunic reached to my knees, which was respectable enough for country work, and I cared naught for running barefoot like this. I was so grateful to be directly on the chase that I would have run through sewers again.

The country on this side of the gorge was heavily forested. Far off I saw mountains with snow on their peaks, for all it was near the end of June. Tunstall and I had never gone so far north, and I truly didn't want to do it now. The thought of the length of such a trip and the damage that would befall Their Majesties and their little boy over that time, was a nightmare. Still, they were beautiful, those mountains. They looked peaceful. Of course, they were far away. Everything looks peaceful when it's not on top of you.

For the first time since we had begun to track the Viper and the prince using the small middens with the lad's scent, I could now see clearly how many traveled with them. Once I had crossed the bridge, theirs were among the few tracks left on the right, as caravans had come south on the other side of the road and the travelers going north were scant of late. From the tracks around the cart's wheels, with the guards' feet marked by boots and the slaves' by their bare footprints, I worked it out to be six guards. Two always flanked the cart. Four stayed with the six slaves. The lad must ride in the cart, because there were no footprints in his size. I worked it out on my fingers, which Sabine teased was a habit of the illiterate. Six guards, plus a driver for the wagon, plus the prince, plus at least two mages—the Viper and the other mot said to be in the cart. We would be tracking them for a long time until Lord Gershom could send enough Dogs to arrest them all.

We'd been running two hours off and on since the bridge. We'd encountered no one and heard naught but creatures and birds when Achoo and I stopped for a rest. Our Hunt mates drew up with us.

"*Tunggu,*" I ordered. Achoo found a dry rock in the sun and lay down.

Farmer inched his mount up between Tunstall and me. Carefully, I suspected so Tunstall wouldn't grumble, he held out a hand. I took it without thinking. It was a good hand, warm and comforting.

Farmer cleared his throat. "Beka." I looked up at him. His cheeks were red. "That's . . . I've never seen you . . . Usually you wear breeches with your tunic."

I shrugged and pointed to the top of my pack, fingering my clothes. They were still drying. "I only have one uniform. It's best if my breeches aren't all over mud should I need to be civilized."

"Oh, absolutely!" he said, nodding too hard. "It's just that I've, I've never, well, you look different. Good. Very good," he said quickly, turning redder. "I'm going to shut my gob now."

Now it was my turn to blush and turn away. If I was right, he'd just complimented my legs. Most coves didn't, those times I ran bare-legged. Either they felt they might eat my fist if they did or they were the object of my running.

"How many are we chasing, Cooper?" Tunstall asked. He dismounted and stretched. Sabine did the same.

"Sixteen is my count," I told them, and added how many I thought were riding and how many were afoot.

"And a day or less ahead," Tunstall added as Farmer let go of my hand and dismounted from his own horse. "I'd like to know what happened to those Dogs that were supposed to be coming from Frasrlund, or even if there are closer Dogs we can trust. Farmer, can you reach Lord Gershom yet?"

Farmer shook his head. "I can't get through at all now," he confessed. "Either someone has blocked Cassine, or me. Either one is bad. I do know from what I heard last that they're not sure of the loyalties of the Dog stations between here and there. They were going to see about those that are more toward the northeast."

"Loyalties. I wouldn't trust the loyalties of *anyone* today," Tunstall muttered. "Why do you tell us this only now?"

"When else should I have told you? Before the fire, when you were in the wayhouse and we were in the stable, or after the fire?" inquired Farmer.

"Mattes, enough," Sabine told him, tugging his ear.

Achoo barked at me. She was tired of resting. I told her, "*Maji!*"

She sniffed beside the road, then took off. I raced to catch sight of her before she vanished around a curve. I was too late. She was out of my sight when she let out a howl that almost made me trip over my feet. I recovered from the stumble and ran to find her, rounding a large stone boulder at the roadside as I yanked my baton from its holding strap.

The first thing I saw as I passed the great stone was a wagon-house, a red-painted hut on wheels like moneyed folk took on the summer roads. The roof trim was painted yellow and decorated with signs for protection. More such signs were painted around the shuttered window and the door in the back, and on the yellow-trimmed wheels. It lay on its side, the door hanging open on its leather hinges. I saw no sign of whatever beast or beasts had pulled it. The shafts were empty. Bandits, I thought. They would have taken everything of value to sell and like as not the cart would slow them down.

But Achoo was not howling at the cart. She had halted there, but she stared into the woods, making that dreadful sound. I followed her, whispering, "*Diamlah,* Achoo!" in case the bandits were still nearby. I heard the jingle of reins and looked back, but it was only my partners. Their faces were as horrified as I felt. Achoo sounded more human than hound.

I went to see what had drawn her attention and fear. It was a pile that buzzed. I knew that sound, just as I knew the smell that was carried to me on the breeze. Enough, I thought, even as my feet carried me closer. First last night, and now this. How much can one Dog take?

The flies rose from the corpses as I came near, buzzing like demons chased from their treat. I slid my baton into its loop, knowing it could do no good against flies and it could not help the dead.

"Stop there, Beka," I heard Farmer say. "Don't go any closer. It could be a trap."

A woman of full years lay closest to me. Of them all, she was the only one who had not been killed by a sword. Her face was bloated and black from the time she had lain here in the sun. She crawled with maggots. They all did. Even yesterday's rain had not stopped the flies.

Some of the dead were younger, twenty and less, dressed in simple shifts. Some were blocky with muscle and armed with swords. None were as young as four.

"Is it a trap?" I heard Tunstall ask.

I couldn't speak. My throat was too dry.

"I'll find out. Beka, Achoo, move back," Farmer said.

"What if it's a trap for you?" Sabine wanted to know. "We can't be too careful, Farmer."

I slipped my bit of mirror out of my belt pouch. It showed me no magic, only flies, maggots, and day-old flesh. I let my partners look in their turn. "My mirror isn't as strong as any Farmer could make," I explained, "but if they're rigging spells to catch Farmer, it would show here."

"Will this take too much of your strength?" Tunstall demanded of Farmer. "If it does, you do nothing. We need your Gift for our defense."

Farmer looked at Tunstall and raised his eyebrows. The expression on his face turned him into a mage who would not be ordered about. I fought the urge to step back, knowing this wave of greatness that flooded from him was as much a part of Farmer as his silliness. Any who cared for him must deal with that.

"Strange," Farmer said. "I thought my Gift was needed to help find our lad." He rubbed his hands together, as he had over Vintor's body, back in the swamp. His blue fire spilled from his fingers, sparkling as it went, until it covered that entire dreadful pile completely. Once all of the dead were sealed under that cover, Farmer did something different. He thrust his hands forward, palms down, then raised them. The sparkling cover turned solid, or mostly so, and rose up until it stood before him. By moving his hands, Farmer arranged it so that images of the piled dead were separated, letting us see each of them as clearly as if they'd been painted in bright colors on gauze. They looked as they must have done in their lives. The ones in shifts were comely lads and gixies with cloth-wrapped ropes hobbling their ankles, in order not to leave scars. The blockier ones were hired muscle, guards in dark red tunics with the sign of the four turned-in leaves at their right shoulders. These wore sword belts and weapons. Two carried whips. One, in a maroon tunic with no weapons, must have been the driver of the cart. And the mot was the Viper. I knew her face from the night I'd watched Farmer trap her.

"Stop it," Sabine told our mage, her face white under its tan. "It's too horrible. The youngsters' promise is gone. I don't weep for the guards, but those slaves . . . Please stop."

Farmer closed his hands. The seeming vanished. The flies, scared off by the presence of magic as they often were, returned to their feast.

"We can't get much from this," Tunstall said with disgust. "It would be lovely to think we'd frightened them into getting rid of the extra weight, but for all we know, bandits stopped them and killed anyone they couldn't carry."

"It's the wagon that was described to us," Sabine reminded him.

"That's the Viper," Farmer and I began at once. He looked at me with the tiniest of smiles and went on. "When I cast the cocoon spell at the poisoned stream, we saw the mage who cast it. This woman is the Viper, and no sword touched her body. She was slain by magic. *Strong* magic, to break through the trap I had on her and defeat her own power." Farmer glared down at the mot's maggot-covered corpse. "I wanted to watch her stand trial, by Mithros, I did."

"There are more of them," Sabine reminded him. "The one that killed her, or the ones, and those who lead this rebellion. We shall have the chance to watch *their* trials. They'll pay for all the lives they've ruined."

I walked back toward the wagon. "Do you think there's a shovel in there?"

"Cooper!" Tunstall called. "There's no time! We've got

fourteen dead. That's a poxy deep hole to dig, even with four of us wielding shovels. Another good rain and we're finished— the scent is fading. Whoever did this, *they took the boy!*"

"You'd leave them here?" I asked, turning to face him while I tried not to weep. "To the flies and the beasts?" I knew Tunstall was right, but it seemed to me that when we started to abandon the dead, we became more like the killers. By caring naught for them that were slaughtered, we made it possible for our hearts to care little for the living.

"I can burn them," Farmer suggested.

"And warn any who are watching? Waste your Gift some more?" Tunstall demanded. "Use your common sense!"

Pounce and Achoo walked past us. They had been waiting by the wagon, where we'd left the horses. Now they came to sit a foot from the dead, watching that horrible pile with fixed attention. I opened my mouth to call Achoo, at least, back to me, but closed it again. She seemed to be waiting for sommat.

Farmer was arguing softly with Tunstall. "She's worked herself to a shadow, running her legs off. Give her *something* human, before she starts to break."

"Lads," Sabine told them, her voice soft, "be silent."

By then I could hear what she heard, mayhap what Achoo and Pounce had heard. It was the beating of wings, lots of them. The sky went briefly dark as the wood pigeons flew to the clearing to land all around it in every tree, each branch loaded with as many of the birds as it could take. They settled, fluttered their wings one last time, and folded them. They stared at the pile of the dead. I turned to face it to see what they did.

On the opposite side from me a great shape took form, one that was as big as the tall tree behind it. It was a being in a robe, its face hidden under the folds of a hood. At first the robe seemed black, as it always was in the statues. Then it changed color, turning brown, orange, white, blue, chestnut, yellow, and every other color that might possibly exist.

You need not try to bury them, my finest priestess. I will do so, he told me.

The god I'd been taught to call black reached out hands gloved in ever-changing colors, holding them over the murdered slaves, the guards, and the Viper. Suddenly green tendrils sprouted from the earth, twining around limbs and bodies like so many agile snakes. As they moved they grew, turning thicker and putting out leaves. Buds formed and sprouted until the bodies were covered by a riot of flowers of every shade in the god's robe. They continue to grow solid and fat as the mound beneath them shrank and collapsed. By the time they had stopped, the ground where the dead had lain was sunken. It looked as if their remains had been placed there decades ago and only flowers remained.

I glanced back at my companions. They were on their knees, their heads bent. I wondered if I ought to do the same. Surely I'd have felt the need to bow if the god had expected it of me.

He raised a hand and pushed his hood back from his face. I say *he,* but he could as well have been a she. He didn't correct me, so I continue to think of him as I have always done.

I cannot remember his face, though I do remember his words.

They are safe in my Realm. They shall have a rest, and then another chance. Continue your work, Rebakah Cooper. You are a good servant to me, and a good friend to my messengers.

Thinking of all the times I'd been wing-slapped, pecked, bitten, and splattered with pigeon piss and dung, I could not think the birds agreed with their master, but I bowed my head and nodded.

He was gone, just like that. The pigeons leaped into the air in an explosion of powerful wings, a feathered clap of thunder that made all of us duck.

We dared not let our feelings overwhelm us for too long. We still had a Hunt. The prince had been missing from that ugly pile, and the second mage reported to be with the cart was not there, either. Immediately after we returned to the road, we found horse tracks pressed into the mud, sixteen sets altogether. Could these be the killers who had left with the prince? Important to us, was the mage who had helped the Viper among them? And why had they killed the slaves, the guards, and the Viper here, particularly? Bandits would have kept the slaves—they were worth money. They wouldn't have needed a mage of their own because Farmer's spell would have brought down the Viper the moment she used her Gift to fight bandits. Only another, stronger mage would have left her in that pile.

I was struggling with my questions when Achoo found another midden. She caught the prince's scent off to the side of his companions' piddle. Had he thought to do so himself, to keep his scent from being covered by those who had taken him? I hoped so, but the lad was only four. I could not expect too much.

Shortly after that I saw a road sign ahead. Achoo turned into the road leading away from the one we'd been following. She'd gone but a couple of yards that way when she shrieked and leaped into the air, dropping to the ground like a stone. I screamed and cut across the grassy turf between me and her, running for all I was worth. It was when I reached her that everything went white.

When I roused, I was sitting upright on a horse's back. My head throbbed and my nose ran. I felt in my breeches pocket for a handkerchief and discovered I was hobbled so tight around my waist that I couldn't reach very far. I had to bend over to blow my nose. I could reach my saddle horn, but not the reins. My feet were tied to the stirrups and the mount was being led. I blew my nose and cringed from the pain.

"I know," a mot's voice said. "That spell would rip a monkey's gut out with the monkey on the fly. Try this." A hand gloved in fine gray kid pressed a lump of green jellylike stuff into my hand. "Doesn't taste very grand, but it's good for the aches."

I was tied to a horse—not Saucebox, but one of our spares. I held my hand out and let the lump roll off his withers to the ground.

"Suit yourself," the mot said carelessly. "It's no hair off my head if you want to waste it."

I squinted at her through bright sunlight that made everything sparkle, or mayhap that was just the magic that seemed to float everywhere around us. She rode beside me on a gray mare that matched her gloves and boots. The mot herself was my age, a glorious creature in pink silk leggings and a matching pink silk tunic. She had fine, shining blond hair pinned up in loops around her head, with a frivolous sheer white veil over it. When she turned and smiled, I thought I was looking at the most beautiful lady in the world, even more beautiful than the queen. Her gray eyes glittered.

"What a scruffy thing you are," she told me, her voice soft, pretty, and playful. "I can't believe so much worry and thought has been expended on you. Does Farmer keep you going? I never thought he was so dedicated a Hunter, myself, but I have never had a chance to speak with him at length. Sabine's just a crude brawler, mad for sex and fighting. I can't say much for her latest toy, but maybe he's more clever than he looks."

For a moment rage filled my head over her saying those things about my friends, but suddenly my mood reversed. I wanted her to like me. She was so beautiful and sweet. If *she* didn't like me, why would the friendship of those other three dirty, tattered people matter? I was confused by the change of my own feelings, so I looked around instead.

My fellow Hunters were alive. Like me they rode upright in the saddle, tied to it as I was, their horses each led by a guard. Farmer rode a little way behind me, a small frown on his face, staring into the distance. Sabine and Tunstall were ahead in our line of riders, encircled by rough-looking hunts-men, those behind and on both sides holding crossbows aimed straight at them. Sabine happened to glance back as I was looking at her. She gave me a tiny nod before the guard at her side punched her arm.

The warriors beside and behind Farmer also bore cross-bows. Another row of archers rode farther out, their bows pointed at Farmer as well. Far behind Farmer's guard rode a small group of men, but the light was too bright for me to make out their faces. Either I was not regarded as a threat or no one wished to risk shooting my riding companion, be-cause we only had a cove to lead my horse. Nowhere did I see Pounce or Achoo. I closed my eyes and sent a brief prayer of thanks to the gods. Then I looked at the delightful creature beside me again.

"Who are you, what have you done to Farmer, and where are we going?" I demanded. All those archers told me how they kept Sabine and Tunstall under control. I just couldn't see a mere clutch of archers slowing Farmer, even a double ring of them. I'd had a sense he held more of his power back than he was letting on. Why wasn't he putting it to use?

She simpered. "*I* am Dolsa Silkweb. Farmer is fine, such as he is. Really, is he the best you people could get?"

Part of my mind said, He's better than *you,* while another part said, He certainly isn't as good as you! I didn't know which was real, not entirely. I settled for blandness. "I'm not sure what you mean."

"I know all about your little Hunt," Dolsa told me. "We tried and tried to stop you, but it never pays to use hirelings. My lord said to cut our losses and bring you four straight to him. For days I rode in that stinky little cart with your brat of a prince and that bossy woman! My lord had best remember my sacrifices for this." Her gray eyes slanted sidelong with a glitter like ice. "Or I'll help him remember."

So she *had* been aiding the Viper.

"What have you done to Farmer?" I insisted on asking. It seemed she would only talk at length about herself.

"Oh, he still thinks he's riding along the road after you. He's terrible at illusions, I'm sad to say. Why don't you call in that hound?" She asked it quickly, without warning, her charm gripping me so tight that my mouth instantly opened to call Achoo. I remembered Achoo lying on the ground, the killing wound open in her side, Farmer with his hand on her, and shut my mouth. For good measure, I ground my teeth together.

Dolsa looked at me for a long moment, her slender brows knit. I could feel the need to please her press on me, wrap around me, even seek ways into me through my nose, ears, and eyes. I bit the inside of my cheek until it bled to fight her Gift, forcing myself to see Achoo beg me for scraps, curl up with Pounce, and chase her toy in the park with Tunstall.

At last Dolsa sighed. "I suppose you have some charm or other on you, to fight my spells. Or you're like most common dullards, not imaginative enough for my Gift. We'll have any protective magic off you before nightfall, you know." She tugged her gloves until they sat her hands more neatly. "Truly, the hound isn't necessary. I just thought you'd be more pliable, if we had your animal to work on. Still, the woods aren't kind hereabouts. Something will get her, eventually. Maybe even one of our own hunters."

"Where do you come from, Lady Silkweb?" I asked, letting her spell squeeze the *lady* out of me. "Who do you serve?"

She laughed. It was a musical sound that made a number of the guards turn to smile at her. She snapped her fingers imperiously. Every one of them yelped and flinched, as if that dull snap of the fingers—it didn't work in gloves—had the power to hurt them. I had the feeling it had done just that. "Idiots!" she cried. She'd made her voice louder somehow, so everyone could hear. "*Keep your eyes on your prisoner!* Next time it won't be a bite on the ear!" She looked at me. "That's the punishment," she told me, her voice at its normal loudness for only me to hear. "I took the pain from the time a horse bit me and tucked it into a little spell. I touched each guard on the shoulder as we readied to go, and . . ." She shrugged one shoulder, very pleased with herself.

"Like brats pulling wings off flies," I said, meeting her eyes.

She gave that sparkling, musical laugh again. "You're very brave, aren't you, *Dog*?" Silkweb asked when she stopped laughing. "You think you and your friends have a chance? Lady Sabine will be lucky to live, since she's so entrenched on the king's side. You Dogs? Trash. Farmer? I can dance rings around your Dogs' mage, and I'm not the only one here who can. Tell me, brave *Dog*—"

If she said *Dog* that way again, charm spell or no, I was going to do my best to bite her like that horse she'd mentioned.

She did not hear my thoughts, so instead she finished what she was saying. "Does Farmer's master still give him gifts of power?"

My skin crept. "What are you talking about?"

"Everyone knows," she said and giggled like a gixie telling secrets with her friends. "It's said Cassine tucked power all around him. He *can* draw magic out of things, at least he's not inept *there*. That's why it was so important to burn his packs, so he couldn't use his emergency stores."

"How could you know about that if you were with the cart?" I asked, thinking, No, no, no. I won't believe her.

She rolled her eyes. "That was the plan. Farmer is the biggest threat, so we sent a man in to set the fire. I know because I was in touch with the others through my scrying crystal. Without his little bag of tricks, he's nothing." She glanced back at him. "I had the boys take that shoulder pack and his belt, boots, and necklaces off as soon as we dropped the four of you."

All those dead. Linnet on the garbage barrel, the bandits, the poor mumpers forced to travel with the Viper, the sleepers at the inn. "Is it worth it, what you've done?" I asked her. "Do you know how many you've killed just to 'drop' us four?"

"Is it worth it?" She acted as if she hadn't heard the second question. "You silly thing, don't you know? Your precious king has put *taxes* on mage work. He's taxing items we need badly if we're to create anything of real *meaning*. Now he's demanding that we be licensed—*licensed!*—and in exchange for this precious license, we have to guarantee so many days a year in work for the Crown." There was a blush of rage on her cheeks. "We are *mages,* not piddling jewelers or sellers of greens! We won't submit! We must be free to work as we please!"

"Why don't you go to some other realm?" I asked. Had I seen a bit of cream-colored fur off in the trees?

"Because all the best places in all the realms that matter are held, or there are fifty competitors for them at least. Because this is my home." Her hands trembled as she arranged them prettily on her reins. "Because if Randy Roger gets away with this, the other kings will do the same. Because no one tells a great mage what to do. Not *ever.*"

I heard the jingle of reins behind our group and twisted to see who was coming out of the group at the rear of the train. When he passed Farmer, I recognized him. Farmer gave no sign that he even saw the man, though he rode right before Farmer's eyes.

It was Master Elyot, dressed in a cream-colored tunic and brown breeches and looking too poxy cheerful. The fire opal on his chest blazed as it caught the sun. "Dolsa, my dear, I don't believe you've stopped talking to this poor captive since she came around. Whatever do you have to say to her?"

Dolsa treated him to her simper for a change as he brought his horse up on my opposite side. What a delightful trio are we, I thought, sick with what Dolsa had said about Farmer and her reasons for rebellion. All this because the mages didn't care for work?

"We've been talking of every manner of things," Dolsa told Elyot. "I don't think she knew Cassine used to feed Farmer extra magic."

Elyot frowned at Dolsa. "I didn't see that in him."

Dolsa laughed. "You didn't look at his packs, silly. They

half blinded me! Where else could it have come from if not Cassine? Certainly not from *him*."

"I don't know," Elyot said. "He struck me as well enough. Not on *our* level, but how many mages are?" He looked at me. "I'm glad to have the chance to take a closer look at you, Gershom's pet. I've met Lady Teodorie a few times at court. I'm surprised she actually let you live in her house." He chuckled. "I'm surprised she let you *live*. She never struck me as the sort to let her man keep his child mistress under her roof."

I spat on him. Sadly, it stopped partway to him, halted by his scummer magic, and dropped to the road.

He slapped me hard, rocking my head back on my neck. I growled and threw myself at him, forgetting I was tied in the saddle. One of the guards seized the bridle and Dolsa the back of my tunic as an invisible mask slid over my face, cutting off my air. I fought it as long as I could. Finally, as my sight went black, the mask vanished.

A cruel hand gripped the hair at the back of my head and Dolsa said in my ear, "Mind your manners or we'll drag you the rest of the way to Halleburn. And I have to warn you, Lord Thanen is not as good about keeping his roads as he should be."

I took some deep breaths, then nodded. She pulled me straight in the saddle with one arm, gave my hair an extra twist with the other hand just for meanness, and released me. Too bad she hadn't grabbed me by the braid, but like as not she'd seen the spikes sticking from the strands.

I took inventory of my condition. My scalp ached. I ignored it. My left cheek was swelling, including the side of the eye. A slap from a gem-decorated glove is no joke. I'd wrenched my arms fiercely, trying to yank free of the rope bindings. One of my wrists ached in a dull way I did not like.

To take my mind off the pain, I kept my head down and looked at Elyot under my lashes. "When did you get here?" I demanded. "We left ahead of you."

This time he grabbed my ear and twisted it hard. Again, I bit the inside of my cheek till it bled rather than cry out for this nuncle's tarse. "I don't care who you were in Gershom's house, any more than I care that you're a Provost's Guard," the mage said, breathing garlic into my face. "Gershom is dead when we succeed. And I wouldn't give a cracked kernel for the lives of you and your Hunting party, do you hear? So mind your manners, or I'll kill you in such fashion as they never find your bones." He let go of my ear. "We were only a day behind you, stupid bitch, riding hard. We passed you by night and took the other route to Halleburn. How did your creature track the boy?"

"Elyot, why are you abusing my poor Beka so?" Sabine called from her place in our train of riders. "She's wonderful with hounds and she knows the rules of the Guard, but she doesn't have two thoughts to rub together. Come and tell me why you're mauling her about. This *is* the forest road to Halleburn, isn't it?" To hear her, we were just on a tour of the estate.

Elyot looked at her, then at me. He glanced at Farmer and raised an eyebrow at Dolsa, who shrugged. Then he spat on me and rode up to Sabine.

His spit landed. There was naught I could do but watch it soak into my tunic.

"Elyot's furious because none of the traps he planned for you worked and mine did. He feels it reflects badly on him. I think you're going to die in very unpleasant ways." Dolsa shrugged. "Maybe if you promise to give *me* your blood freely, I can talk him into letting me kill you. I'll do it nicely."

I stared at her. "You truly think I would do that?" I asked, not sure that I'd heard her right.

Dolsa rested a gentle hand on my shoulder. Her glove was scented with some kind of perfume. "If you knew the ways Elyot kills people, you would," she assured me. "Oh, look, there's a rabbit!" She pointed gleefully at the animal, which ran for its life, dashing to and fro as if it knew it was hunted. Something gray and glittery darted from her pointing finger to chase the rabbit, missing just as it made the shelter of the woods.

"See, that's the difference between Elyot and me," Dolsa explained. "I know sometimes you lose. And if you study your losses enough, you get a big, fat, *victory.*" She kicked her pretty mare into a trot, turning to ride with the group in the back.

I looked at Farmer. Never more had I wanted him awake and aware. I could face anything if Farmer rode beside me, talking away. If I hadn't known what was happening to my feelings about him before then, that was the point at which I realized it whole. To keep from thinking about the bad things ahead, I tried to work it out in my mind, how he was different from other men I'd known.

He liked me to help him when he did things. He explained what I didn't know, warned me when to stand aside, *never* told me to get out of his way because he could do it faster, and thanked me for helping. There were moments when he needed me to rescue him, and he never blamed me for it, or got angry about it.

He took nothing seriously, not even—particularly— himself. He was kind to animals. He kept his temper, for the most part. So do I, for the most part. He is not afraid to admit to what he cannot do. He is not afraid to admit when he is weak, even though he hates it.

I wish he would not pinch so at Tunstall, but Tunstall pinches first and back. They're like my brothers in that way. I sometimes think a good fistfight would solve things between Tunstall and Farmer. I wish they would get it over with.

As to Farmer's magic all being given to him by Cassine? Mayhap Dolsa thought that. That claim above all told me she did not know Farmer, but one of the faces that Farmer liked to put on.

My thinking served to keep my mind off our future as we rode along a series of hills, each taller than the last. At the top of the third, I nearly gave myself away when I spotted the black cat standing on a boulder near the crest. I forced myself to remain still and to pretend I saw nothing unusual. He flicked his tail at me and vanished. I sighed with gratitude. Pounce was still with us. I knew he would be, but it was one thing to know, and another to *see*.

Over the crest, I almost gasped at the view. The road down switched back and forth to allow traffic to climb without overworking the humans or animals that used it. The hill was part of a long ridge of solid rock. Forming the valley's northwestern edge, the ridge overlooked all that lay between it and the lake.

About a quarter mile along the cliff to our left sat Halleburn Castle. Built on a spur of rock that thrust out of the cliff, it looked a spear pointed at the lake. The inner curtain wall stood higher than the outer one, while towers crowned the spur's peak. I'd heard that Halleburn had never been taken. Now I could see why.

The road went over a great causeway up the far side of the spur of rock on which the castle sat. On the ridge behind the castle, the ground had been cleared of trees for a mile. At no point were we ever out of view of the towers.

I still was calculating. The rock face on which the place rested was rugged enough for a good climber. A good climber with a four-year-old on her back, or his back? We might have to learn. Then it was a mile, nearly two, to the lake. As a path of escape, the lake gave me no confidence. It was thinner than it was long, with the far shore always in view of anyone on the near shore, from what I could see. Had it been bigger, it might have been possible to lose pursuit, but they could give chase on both sides easy, and have us trapped unless we had Farmer with us.

There was also the small problem of getting out of Halleburn. As we rode through the gates, I saw the thickness of the walls and felt the weight of its age. Far too many men and women-at-arms stood about idle, sharpening weapons and watching us go by. Those who weren't armed were slaves, marked by their plain clothes and an occasional shoulder brand.

"Unfriendly place, isn't it?" a familiar male voice asked. They'd let Farmer draw up beside me. Seemingly, they'd also let the spell on him drop. I tried to keep from grinning at him like a looby who'd just been offered sweets. "I'll bet they hardly get any visitors for the Midwinter holidays. You see that point in the outer curtain wall? Fifteen Halleburns have jumped to their deaths from there." He tried to count them all on his fingers, but like mine, his hands were hobbled at the wrists and bound to his waist.

A guard smacked him on the back with the butt of his crossbow. "None o' yer magickin', you!" he snapped.

I kept myself from reaching for Farmer. I couldn't let these creatures know how I felt about him. They'd use it against me, like they'd have used Pounce or Achoo if they could have caught them.

"If you'd listened to your masters, you would have heard they are keeping me under a magical lock," Farmer told the cove patiently. "I've got no more Gift than you do. Less, if you have one. And wouldn't your poor old mother be ashamed at your lack of courtesy to a guest?"

The guard spat. Without looking at him, I asked Farmer, "Will you please not needle them? They're nasty enough as it is."

"Most likely they're worried about getting paid. *I* would be. Thanen of Halleburn is as tightfisted as a clam." He saw the guard look at him suspiciously and said, all innocence, "It's true. He'd as soon kill someone as pay him. Sooner."

Elyot came riding down the line. "Farmer, what are you up to?" To the soldier he barked, "Get them down. My lord wants to see them right away." He grinned at us both. "You're in for a treat. Lord Thanen doesn't like folk who give him as much trouble as you four have."

"We'd have given him no trouble at all if he hadn't kid—" Elyot went to slap me again, but this time I was ready. I kicked my horse forward, straight into his own mount. Off-balance with his slap, he struggled to stay in the saddle until I hooked my leg, stirrup and all, around his, and shoved myself toward him with all of my strength. He was a bad rider. His horse, scared by sommat—I have my suspicions about who scared him—shook his head and reared a little. Onto the ground went Elyot. As he slid, I spat on him. I'd often had the chance to observe that when mages were confused, they did not always think to employ their Gifts.

The guards, frozen still until that moment, hurried forward. They cut me free of my ropes and yanked me from my mount. Once I stumbled to the ground, I dropped and curled myself up, tucking my head and wrapping my hands around the back of my neck. It was the best I could do before the guards began to beat me. So much fuss over one dumped mage!

"Stop," Dolsa called. "I don't care if she hurt Master Elyot's feelings, my lord wants to see these four meddlers as soon as may be. *All* four."

The blows stopped and I went to straighten, knowing I was going to pay for tweaking the bull's tail. There was a razor's pain in my right side that meant a broken rib. The rest was bad, but bruises at most. The guards might be dressed as rough woodsmen, but they were well-trained professionals.

I looked at Master Elyot. He was shaking off the hands of those who would help him as he stood. The glare he gave me promised nothing that would make me smile. I wondered when he'd last been handled so rudely and was glad I'd chosen to do so, even knowing I'd take a beating. He certainly acted like he'd never had to take a good punch in his life, let alone a deliberate shove from his mount.

A hand wrapped around my shoulder. Almost immediately I felt warmth spill into my body. Muscles and bone eased along with their pain. I breathed a little better, though Farmer couldn't do a true healing in full view of the enemy.

"I'll take charge of these captives, Dolsa." The new speaker was a mot all in brightly polished armor. She was five feet and ten inches, with long, slanting brown eyes and blond hair coiled and pinned at the back of her head. The armor did not hide her generous figure. For all the armor shone as if she never wore it, the sword at her waist had a plain leather grip and sheath, both of which were well battered. So too were her sheathed dagger and the boots on her feet. She might be wearing dress armor, but she was a fighter. "My father wants them before him now."

"I will take them, Nomalla, since I captured them," Dolsa replied pertly.

The knight looked down her long, straight nose at the mage. "It's your method of keeping things in order that makes me question whether all of them will reach my father alive, Dolsa," she said dryly. "Come with me, then, if you're so anxious to receive all the credit. And don't chatter at me." She walked toward Sabine and Tunstall, giving Sabine a nod. "Sabine. As usual, you are in low company."

Sabine looked Nomalla in the eyes. "This time it's *you* who are in low company, Nomalla of Halleburn. Your father is a traitor. All of you who serve him are conspirators. I'd rather break bread with pickpockets."

"And have," Lady Nomalla replied, but her cheeks were red. "My father knows what the realm needs."

"A traitor," Sabine replied agreeably.

Nomalla rested her hand on the hilt of her sword. "Get moving, you and your lover both."

"Dolsa did *not* capture them on her own!" Elyot snapped breathlessly from behind us. "She will not cheat me of the credit for taking them!" He stalked past us, in a hurry to catch up with them. I would have thought all of them had forgotten Farmer and me, except both Elyot and Dolsa shoved a veil of Gift back our way. It turned into a muddy-colored sparkling scarf that wrapped around Farmer, making my skin tingle where his arm lay on my shoulders. He moved his arm away. I wanted to seize it and pull it back into place, but that would give the enemy more information than they needed. They already knew, I supposed, that he'd healed the worst of my beating. Let them think he'd tried and failed to fool them as to what he was doing by putting his arm around me.

I heard Farmer whisper, "From what I've heard of Lady Nomalla, this is not the sort of thing she would do." His lips hadn't moved.

"Can't they hear you?" I replied in a good Dog's whisper, my mouth almost unmoving.

Inside the sparkles he smiled. "Perhaps this spell is without flaw when just one mage works it, but with two mages it is full of holes," he explained. "Neither of them wants the other mage to get a grip on their power and use it. I can use a baby spell called threading the needle to sneak my voice through one of those holes. Beka, I'm so sorry. I should have been looking for more varieties of illusion. She's too cursed good at them."

"Better than you?" I asked.

"Yes," he replied frankly as we were ushered into the keep. "There are ways to trip her up, but my mind was on other things and she jumped me like I was a novice."

We went through one set of doors, then another. Tunstall and Farmer were taken into a chamber on the left by Elyot, ten guards, and a couple of other coves who wore mage-like robes. Lady Nomalla, Dolsa, and two of the female guards went into a similar room on the right with Sabine and me. The room was stone with no hearth or braziers. Standing screens were placed along the rear wall, blurry metal mirrors hung here and there, and the room was furnished with a scattering of chairs and hassocks. It seemed to be a chamber where folk could wait and check their looks before they entered the presence of the lord of Halleburn. My cheeks burned at the impudence of this nobleman, no matter how old his bloodlines, holding court like the king.

"Everything on the floor," Dolsa ordered, stripping off her gloves. "Packs, belts, weapons, boots, clothes, underthings. Take those spikes from your hair, Cooper, and you too if you have them, Sabine."

"I am not disrobing before the likes of you, mage," Sabine replied. "Nor these traitors."

"Sabine, we have never fought one another," Nomalla said, her eyes steady as she spoke. "And we will not here. I will have this mage and these guards drag you down and strip you. Or you can go behind that screen and disrobe with dignity. So may—Cooper, is it?—Cooper, here."

Sabine stared at the lady knight, her brown eyes burning. At last she said, "I never would have imagined you as a traitor, Nomalla. Not here and not in any of the realms."

"I am no traitor," the other knight said calmly. Her cheeks were as crimson as mine felt. "Family comes before all, as does a child's duty to her father. Strip here or use the screen, my lady."

Sabine clenched her hands. Then she turned to me and nodded. We left our packs, boots, leather, and what armor remained to us there with them. She jerked her head toward the carved screens when we were down to our clothes. I found the linked wooden panels were set up to make small alcoves, giving us a little privacy. As I took off my garments and set them down, I heard the women pick apart the contents of our packs. Dolsa found every magicked thing we had, and made certain to tell Nomalla what it was and how pathetic she found it. I wanted so badly to kick her bum straight up between her ears.

Finally, as I stood there naked and a woman soldier inspected my garments, Nomalla sent Dolsa to inform Lord Halleburn that we were nearly ready for questioning. Then she dismissed the guards and told Sabine and me we could dress. I guessed that someone must have inspected Sabine's clothes at the same time that a mot did mine.

When we came out from behind the screens, both of us red-faced and looking for a fight, only Nomalla remained in the room. Sabine strode up to her and slapped her across the face. Nomalla let her do it, to my shock.

"We are caught up in things that are bigger than we are," she told Sabine. "Fate turns. We ride with her or are left behind."

"And what of honor?" demanded Sabine hotly, keeping her voice low. "What of the vows made to king and country? You are a *lady knight,* not some back alley Corus strumpet!" She glanced at me. "Apologies, Beka." She knew lots of my friends went by those names.

I shrugged. "I've seen plenty of great house strumpets," I replied.

"I am my father's daughter and a knight of generations of Halleburn knights," Nomalla replied steadily. "If your family took more of an interest in the realm's politics instead of raising horses, my lady of Macayhill, you would know what I mean."

"If this is what that interest means, I'd as soon be an honest horse breeder," Sabine told her.

The door opened and a man said from outside, "He bids you bring the prisoners, my lady."

Nomalla beckoned for us to leave the room. "I wish you hadn't crossed my father's path, Sabine. I really wish you hadn't."

Following behind her, I told Sabine, "To me, that noble honor is a wonderful thing. I see folk put it on and take it off all the time, and no one ever notices how wrinkled it gets."

Nomalla clenched her hands into fists. Sabine only smiled down at me. "It might seem so to you, Beka." Her mouth curled down bitterly. "In your boots, it would to me as well. But for some of us, it is a garment that is the same as our own skin, impossible to take off and live."

We joined the men as they stood before a fresh pair of closed doors. Tunstall was down to his uniform like me, no belt, no boots. Apparently the folk that had searched us knew of our habit of wearing buckle knives, using the leather of our belts as stranglers' nooses, and of tucking knives or spikes in our boots. The castle flagstones were cold under our feet. Sabine and Farmer were in the same case as we were, bootless and beltless. It was enough to make me think these Halleburn folk didn't trust us.

Elyot was gone, as was Dolsa. Guards in Halleburn tunics of hideous orange and pink thrust the door open and Nomalla led us into the great hall beyond. We had a way to go. They had left a nice, large space for us to cross before we reached a stopping spot in front of an overblown dais. There, in the seat of honor, sat Prince Baird. I supposed he had overcome his qualms about betraying his family. On his right sat an older man of sixty-two with Nomalla's long nose. Unlike her, he had bright blue eyes, deep-set, a mouth with lips so thin they seemed well-nigh invisible, and well-groomed white hair around the sides and back of his bald pate. Unlike His Highness, who fidgeted uneasily in the higher chair, Thanen of Halleburn sat upright and comfortable. Nothing seemed to miss his gaze, unless it was the black cat that had chosen to sit in the shadows between his chair and that of the prince.

My companions tensed around me. Then they forced themselves to relax, just as I did. They had to be asking themselves, as I did, what Pounce could be allowed to do to help us. They would remember that Pounce had said the gods had done nothing when he intervened before because Achoo was an animal, not a human being. My companions might even know, as I did, that minor gods and immortal creatures like dragons had been brought low before by mages, and gods had been hurt by them.

We did not face only two mages, Elyot and Dolsa, who both stood at the shoulders of the prince. Count Dewin of Queensgrace sat on the dais, with his personal mage in attendance. At Thanen's shoulder stood another cove in one of those stupid robes so many of them seemed to think made them look magical. At Prince Baird's side I saw two familiar faces. Master Ironwood and Mistress Orielle, Their Majesties' personal mages and supposed defenders, had come to join the fun.

Tunstall lunged for them. "You!" he cried as some purplish magic froze him in place. "What are you doing here? Were you traitors all along?"

"Where was I to go when *Mistress* Cassine cast me out of the Summer Palace?" whined Master Ironwood. He had lost weight even in the two weeks since I'd last seen him. "Where could I go with the suspicion of treason on me?"

"Stop complaining!" Orielle snapped. "Embrace your future, you fool—you've been a part of this for too long to back out now!" She was greatly changed from her soft, fluttering ways in the Summer Palace. "Why couldn't you beggars have died when you were supposed to?"

"Dreadful sorry, mistress," Farmer said at his most foolish. "Ma always said I was too silly to die."

"Quiet!" Lord Thanen barked. Though Count Dewin and Prince Baird were of higher rank, he clearly was in charge. "There's no reason to bandy words with these underlings!"

"Forgive me, my lord," Orielle said with a pretty half curtsy. "But they eluded every trap set for them. They were nearly on your doorstep when your people gathered them up. Surely it would be interesting to learn why?"

"My lord Gershom knows the route we took," Tunstall said. "Other Provost's Guards are on their way to meet us now. There may yet be time to save your families and lands, though not your own lives."

"You mean those five poor Dogs out of Frasrlund?" Elyot asked. "Dead in the road. And any other help out of the kennels between here and the border will not even leave the towns."

I looked at the floor and asked that glorious, multi-colored creature I had once called the Black God to care for my fellow Dogs. I also asked the God if he, she, might find it in his heart to step on these leeches when they came into the Peaceful Realms, even though that was not his usual policy. The God did not reply, but this time I didn't mind so much. I had seen him once and that was more than enough answer to any prayer.

"Sabine," Lord Thanen said. Everyone on that dais went still. Looking at them all, I knew this was the noble core of the rebellion. Elyot's brother Graeme of Aspen Vale was there. Other lords in armor or silk held the chairs on either side of the prince and Thanen, waiting to hear what he would say. A couple of them leered at Sabine, but changed their minds when Tunstall glared at them.

Sabine had not moved when Lord Thanen called her by name. She waited, legs slightly spread for balance, hands clasped lightly in front of her. She'd made it plain she was pre-pared to fight, with or without weapons.

Then I saw the boy struggling to fill Thanen's wine cup

from a heavy jar. It was stupid. He was little, four by my estimate. He was dark-skinned and dark-haired. . . .

He spilled. Of course he spilled. He was a little boy surrounded by great lords, and he was only four years old. Lord Thanen gave him the back of his hand, knocking the child into the shadows behind the chairs. The wine jug fell to the floor. "Nomalla, tell one of the squires to get out here and serve," he snapped. "See that the slave gets five strokes. And have someone clean this mess up."

Nomalla bowed, but from the way she clenched the hand on the side opposite her father, she did not appreciate being ordered about like a housekeeper. No one else had moved. How many of them knew the identity of the little slave? I was shaking from head to toe. I had gotten my first look at my quarry and, like Achoo, I was ready to launch myself across any ground between me and him. The bruise around his left eye, the long red scrape on his right leg, visible where the thin tunic he wore ended, those only made my need to sweep the lad up and run with him worse. I had often wondered if years of chasing Achoo had made us sommat alike. Now I knew it was true.

The squire was there almost instantly with a jar of wine and fresh cups. He must have been waiting outside the door. He was graceful and quick, coming around behind the chairs, but he could have been as clumsy as a bullock and no one would have noticed. They were all waiting for the lord of Halleburn. How could he keep so many in thrall?

Thanen himself had not taken his eyes off Sabine. When the squire had refilled Prince Baird's cup and given Thanen a new, full one, the old man waved a long white hand at Sabine. "Give the lady knight a cup."

Sabine's deep, rich voice rang out through the hall. "I

would not drink it if you held my nose and dumped it down my throat."

"Sabine, Sabine," Thanen said, trying to look sorrowful. "Is this the way to speak to family?"

"I do not feel like family just now, my lord," Sabine told him. "I feel like a traveler who has been caught by robbers and dragged to their hideaway."

Tunstall cleared his throat. "Beg pardon, lady knight, but that *is* what happened."

"Were you not Sabine's . . . special friend, I'd serve you well for your impudence," Thanen snapped. All of his speech seemed to come from one side of his mouth, as if he were forever sneering. "As it is, count yourself fortunate and hold your tongue. Many here will tell you I am not a patient man."

Everywhere I saw heads bow, as if folk wanted to agree but were afraid to do so even when they had permission. He had to be a *very* nasty bit of work, if these wellborn folk were so skittish around him.

"Sabine, we may be here initially as enemies, but that need not be so," Thanen said in that cozening way. "We could mend our differences. Did you know your grandfather Masbolle has revised his will? He is very old. Should you not die before him, *you* will be very rich."

Sabine's head jerked back. "I did not know of the change to his will, nor do I care. I also did not know that it is suddenly legal for anyone not a member of the family to read a will."

The old barnacle stared into his wine cup. "Accommodations can be reached between friends with mutual interests," he said idly. "Just as they can be reached between great heiresses and kings."

"The king is married," Sabine replied.

Thanen looked up at her, his eyes blue ice. "Don't be a fool, girl. Your grandfather is ailing. Your marriage would bring with it connections to this house, Masbolle, Cavall, Mandash, Queensgrace, and Niede's Jewel. You would be King Baird's queen instead of a vagabond."

I ducked my head. He didn't know Sabine very well, to say that such things would interest her.

She paused for a long moment before she said, "If you think you're just going to wave pretty promises before me, you are wasting your time. I admit, I've considered a change. A woman gets older."

"Sabine!" Tunstall said, horrified.

"Not you, pet." She actually patted his cheek.

I was going cold all over. I've had nightmares, but none like this. I prayed all the gods that this was sheer trickery from Sabine. If only she weren't so convincing!

"I want something more solid to deal on," she told Thanen. She looked at Baird. "And I keep Mattes. I know you. You'll never give up your amusements after we wed. Well, I demand the same."

Prince Baird slowly grinned at her. "Done."

"Hah!" Thanen actually rubbed his hands together. "Then let's retire to someplace more private for proper negotiations." He looked at Farmer and me. "As for these two, ensure he is useless, then toss both of them into the dungeon until I've decided what to do with them." He pointed at us. "You've cost me time and money. I will have some satisfaction before I'm done with you."

I fought, of course, but the mages laid a stillness on us both until guards could come. They took Farmer one way and me another. Down through back stairs in the keep we went, the air getting colder and colder. At last we passed down a long stone corridor marked with doors that held barred windows at face height. The hall ended in a watch room where two guards played at dice on the floor. They took charge of me and walked me back to one of the cells. There they unlocked the door and shoved me in.

The cell wasn't so bad, as cells go. There was torchlight through the window in the door, giving me a decent view. I paced it at ten feet by fifteen feet. Back home it would be considered a four-man place, but we liked our Rats good and annoyed with each other while they were caged.

There were narrow stone benches or beds built into two walls facing each other. There was no window to the outside. Straw and rushes lay on the floor and two sets of shackles were bolted to the rear wall, in case they wanted to keep a prisoner standing. A piss bucket, empty, thanks to the gods, sat in a corner. The stink was bad, but not as bad as it was at Outwalls Prison, say, or even the cells at Jane Street kennel. Thanen must not get many visitors to house down here.

Judging from the narrow cracks in the walls, I knew there'd be rats and mice. I had naught to ward the rats off. I rather like mice, but rats will fight. The cell was cold, too. That might account for there being so little stink. There *were* fleas and lice, but they left me alone. I hoped that was Farmer's spell at work, but who knew how long it might last? I might be the only corpse uneaten by worms sent to the god by these Rats, at least until Farmer and mayhap the others joined me. I had no faith in Thanen of Halleburn's bargain with Sabine and Tunstall, however much she might have believed it. Having cooled off in more ways than one, I was finding it harder and harder to think that she or Tunstall could have turned into the folk I saw in that great hall. On the other hand, I had little trouble at all imagining that they'd done it to gain time to work a way to get themselves and mayhap the prince, Farmer, and me out of this trap.

My inspection of my new home done, I lay on one of the stone benches, hugged my arms around me, and concentrated on the palace in my memory. I would *not* think of Farmer's fate, or Pounce's, Achoo's, Tunstall's, Sabine's, or my own. If I did, I would shake myself to pieces. It was better to do something, even if it was only in my head. I began work on my journal for the time since the fire at the Wayhouse, making sure each event of our arrival there and all that happened thereafter was set exactly where I might find it if I lived. I included what had been said by my companions to have the fullest report I could put together. It seemed unbelievable that I would survive this halt in our travels, but that was no reason to be sloppy in my record keeping.

I dozed off, I believe, as I was trying to fix the god's ever-changing self into a shrine separate from all else, where I might see him again. There was comfort in remembering the beautiful melting colors of his robe and the power of his voice. I knew I was sleeping when I half woke to find a long, thin black body stretched out on mine, giving off warmth like a fire. I hadn't known until then that I'd been shivering.

"What?" I asked.

Hush, Pounce replied. *The guards won't see me, so don't talk aloud to me in front of them. Unless you want them to think you mad, of course.*

"What of Achoo?" I asked fearfully. "Is she dead?"

You underestimate her, Pounce said. *She played at it once she woke from that mage-trap. Once no humans were about, she went into the trees and tracked your captors until I made her stop, before she went on the causeway. She is well and in a better position than you.*

I was too worn out from the scant rest I'd had in the last few days on the road to give him a pert answer. I muttered my thanks for the knowledge and went back to sleep. When I woke again, it was because the guards were rattling the cell door, opening it.

They took me out of there twice. They did not tell me what day it was or how much time had passed, any more than they told me the fate of my Hunting pack. The only things they said when they took me to that other dungeon room were questions and orders. I will not tell of that, not in this journal, not in the official report. I started silent like any tough Rat and ended in such a mixed pottage of whatever lies would please my questioners that I cannot remember what I said. They gave me the Drink, far worse than my training experience of it, but mostly they used their fists. Even I could tell they weren't that interested, or they would have used instruments on me. They showed them to me to frighten me more, as cell Dogs would, but it was only for show. They used none of them, drawing none of my nails, breaking none of my fingers, not even strapping me to the rack. After the second time, they didn't return to my cell.

Pounce told me they were bringing the brown, sloppy stew and the jug of water once a day. He would purr me to sleep and make a pretense of washing my hair that miraculously left it clean and properly braided. It was all he could do for me with the eyes of the Great Gods now fixed on this place and this time. It's funny how much it comforted me, though, to feel my hair clean and neat when the rest of me got filthier by the day. He also told me tales of the Great Gods and heroes of the past to entertain me. I did what exercises I could. That helped, too. Planning my testimony before the Lord High Magistrate, so I would not stammer as I might if I gave it cold, helped as well.

Tuesday, June 26, 249

Halleburn Castle
Still as I record it in memory

On the third day by Pounce's reckoning, we had company. I had waited to see if they would plant someone else with me, in case a spy could get any information from me, so I wasn't surprised by the new arrival.

"I wouldn't be in yer shoes if ye had 'em," one guard said as they heaved a big cove in an undyed linen tunic and breeches into the cell. "Them mages upstairs is all beggin' my lord for yer blood. Seemingly they can do all manner of wicked things wiv it! Still, a last night with your lass—enjoy while ye can!"

"At least till they start bleedin' yez," his partner said.

The shape raised his head. It was Farmer, tangled hair, black eye, bloody nose, bruised face, and all. *He* was a surprise, and a glad one. And they were utter dolts if they thought we would say anything of interest to them.

But how did common jailors know that I cared for Farmer beyond the bonds of a Hunting team?

"Doesn't it matter to you that they want to use those 'manner of wicked things' to kill the king and queen?" Farmer asked the guards.

There was a crack of crude laughter as the guards slammed and locked the door. "If'n it'll get my lord out of the castle and livin' in Corus, they might kill every king and queen wiv our blessin'!" cried the one who'd spoken first. "Anything to take my lord's attention off us!" The other one hushed him and they went chuckling down the hall.

Unwise to beard those creatures, Pounce said from his seat in the cell window. *You're lucky this time they laughed.*

"Luck has nothing to do with it, Pounce," Farmer replied calmly. "They're under orders not to beat me. Their masters believe they have other ways to get at any information I might have."

I believed him, of course, but I still waited until they were out of hearing before I got up from my bench to help Farmer to his feet. I'd meant to get him to the other bench, but his ideas were different from mine. He wrapped both arms around me, but let go swiftly when I yelped. "What have they done to you?" he asked, turning my face this way and that in the light of the cell window.

"Not nearly what they should have done, if they were cell Dogs at Jane Street," I replied, inspecting his face and mauled hands. His fingers weren't broken, but it looked as if they'd had a try at his nails, and lost. "I've been wondering why they haven't done that to me. Not that I'm ungrateful," I added hastily.

Farmer made a face. "I'm not as hurt as I look," he whispered. "I feel bad, but not as bad as I could. If they really try to hurt us with the rack, the ugly parts of the thumbscrews, or the boot, our minds crack first. We lose our hold on our power. Then our brains are useless, so our answers can't be trusted. Magical torture works a little longer, but their powerful mages seem to be very busy. The great mages did strip what Gift of mine they could before they left me to a lesser mage. That one got nothing from me."

"Gods be thanked," I murmured.

"I'd hold my thanks, were I you, sweetheart," he said, pulling me against his chest. "I believe they've put us together so when they try me next, they'll give you what they'd like to give me. That's why they're giving us a night together, to make it worse." He kissed the top of my head. "If they torture you, I doubt I'd even be able to stand the first turn of the rack or the screw. And I've a feeling they'll have a mage with strong truth spells, which ruins any plan to lie I could make."

I tried to laugh. "That sounds unpleasant, I have to say."

"We'll think of something." This time he held me carefully while kissing me in a most satisfying way. I returned the kiss with as much strength as I dared out of consideration for both of our lumps.

When I looked at him again there were tears in his eyes. "I thought they'd taken you off to kill you," he said when we stopped for a breath.

"It's all right," I whispered. "We're alive now. That's what matters."

He rested a finger on my lips. "Beka, dear one, hush. I can't stand it. You are so brave, you're strong—"

"Stop that," I interrupted him, partly because I wondered how it would feel if I gave his lower lip a little nip. I'd managed some of my torture by thinking of the parts of him I wanted to kiss, and now that I had the chance, he wanted to talk!

"And you hate to hear good things about yourself, it drives me mad." He gave me another good, long kiss, and then he said, "I've kept quiet because it's been such a short time, though it seems far, far longer."

"It does," I said, wrapping my legs around him and trying to hoist myself so they were wrapped around his waist. That was too painful for both of us, so he sat on a bench and pulled me onto his lap. Then, with most of him around me, and me around a good bit of him, I was content to hold him. I rested my head on his shoulder and listened to his voice rumble in his chest.

"I know you just buried your betrothed," he began, but I shook my head.

"I should have ended it months ago, when it got ugly," I told him. "You don't shout or hit or throw things, do you?"

"No. None of those. Well, I shout sometimes, but not at lovers. I walk my anger off. Beka, I do love you."

I thought my heart was going to hammer itself clean out of my chest. "You're sure, you're certain?"

He kissed me. "I have never been more sure of anything but my Gift. Do you love me?"

I kissed his ear. "I love you," I said to his shoulder. "Though you're enough to drive a mot mad."

He turned my face up to his with a gentle hand. I looked into his eyes. "But you're like no one I've driven mad before," he said with a smile that made my belly go all warm and liquid. "Either you scold me and it's over, or you roll your eyes. Have you thought that when this is done you'll have nothing more to do with me?"

I had thought so many things, but never that. "Why?" I asked. "I'm feared you'll go back to Blue Harbor and that will be the end of it, but nothing more to do with you? When you make me laugh with your silliness?"

"You hardly ever laugh," he said truthfully.

She has her own way of doing it, inside, Pounce told him. *She laughs with you all the time. Not at you. With you. You have to catch her by surprise to get her to laugh out loud.*

"As you would know better than anyone," Farmer told the cat.

"It's not just the laughing," I explained. "You're kind

even to the lowest folk. You cook supper and shoo away bugs when plenty of mages turn their noses up at such humble stuff. I would hate to leave Corus, but if you ask it, I would." Let's plan for the future, I thought. Right now we still have one.

Farmer kissed me so very softly. "Don't worry. I am not so attached to Blue Harbor. I will come with you." To Pounce he said, "You are a welcome sight, my friend."

I can't spirit any of you out of here, Pounce warned him. *Don't even ask. This place, this time, is the crux. Perhaps you cannot hear all Chaos howling around us, but I can.*

"I don't want to be spirited out, and I'll wager neither does Beka," Farmer said. "We have work yet to do."

"Marry me," I said, his words running like fire in my blood. "If we get out of this, marry me. What you just said, who you are—if we weren't meant to wed, I don't know who is. Marry me."

He kissed me hard and long. "You only needed to ask once," he whispered when he was done. "I was getting tired of waiting to ask myself."

Well, that's done, Pounce said with satisfaction. I made a rude gesture at him.

Farmer grinned. "And no one is going to torture my dear girl again," he said in my ear. "We are going to show them what happens when you defy the law and the gods alike."

I went weak in my knees to hear so bold a statement from my man, but my practical nature had something to say. "You haven't any magic," I protested. "You said they took it when they gave you the Question. Even before that the mages wrapped their spells around you so you couldn't get at any more."

He gave me the warmest, sweetest smile I had ever seen on a man's face, and stood, though we both winced and groaned

490

when he set me back on the cold bench alone. Then he said, "Sweetheart, never listen to what my enemies say. They're very confused people. I know they are because I've spent years making them that way." He undid the closing on his breeches. "One thing niggles at me. Who knew we were getting close, you and I? Close enough that the enemy thought they could torture you to break me?"

"Shh!" I ordered. "We are not canoodling right now, not when the guards can hear!"

He chuckled. "No, no. There is a silencing spell here—not mine."

Mine, Pounce said. *A cat's spell the gods won't even notice. It's little enough, but it's something.*

"My thanks," Farmer told him with a bow. To me Farmer said, "The gods know I want to love you, but when we do, it'll be someplace curst better than this." He glanced at Pounce. "And more private, even with favors given." Pounce washed a paw. "No, Beka," Farmer went on, "I need to retrieve something." He pointed to the piss bucket. "If you want to use that, you'd best do so now. I may take a while." He stripped himself of his breeches.

I'm no gently raised maiden, but the thought of sharing a room while he emptied his bowels nearabout made me cringe. I reminded myself that we'd shared forests when both of us had the same errand. Surely this was not—much—different. I used the bucket while Farmer turned away, then did my own staring at the ceiling when he passed me clad only in his tunic. Even from the corner of my eye I could see huge red and purple bruises on his well-muscled thighs. They looked so bad I couldn't even enjoy the glimpse of his legs.

Had he sommat inside him? "Didn't they look up your bum?" They hadn't done mine, the lazy loobies.

I heard the thump as he settled himself on the bucket. "Nope," he said.

"What about when they gave you the Question? What did you do then?" I asked. It was a matter of professional curiosity now. "You've got sommat tucked away, haven't you?"

"I left it in my cell, on the ceiling. Wrapped it in cobweb like a nursery spider—well, a big one. Folk never look at the ceiling anyway. Did they look in your bum, or in your coyne?" I shook my head. "Sloppy, these conspirators," he said. "You could have a weapon in either place. A strangling cord at the very least."

I flinched at the thought. I *had* tried it. "They tickle. And it's hard to run long distances with things in your soft spots."

Farmer laughed. "And you're dangerous enough on your own. But truly, Beka, how do these people plan to rule a country when they can't even do a rightful search?" There was a wince in his voice. What *did* he have in there? "It's enough to make a cove go off and live in the wilderness like Mistress Cassine."

"If that cove is thinking of being a Dog's lover, he might want to reconsider either the lover or the wilderness," I said.

He grunted and said, "Too many bears and mountain lions out in the wild. Trees rustle all of the time. And you have to walk miles for decent bread or cheese. I can't make—ahh!"

"Farmer?" I asked, alarmed yet afraid to turn around.

"It didn't feel so big before!" he cried. "Ha! Finally!"

I will clean that for you, Pounce said. I heard the sounds of a tiny rainstorm.

"Isn't that still more meddling?" I asked.

Hardly, Pounce replied. *Cats are forever washing things. I have just done a little more than most.*

I heard a happy sigh. Farmer said, "It's fine now, Pounce."

I trust so. For someone who has been known to run through sewers, Beka can be squeamish, Pounce said.

"Rats take to the sewers to escape the Dogs," I snapped, "so that's where we must go to catch them. I don't have to *like* it!"

Farmer walked around me, a white thing in his hand. It looked like a wax turd. Just the thought of retrieving such an item from my arse made my tripes knot. "How long have you—" I asked, waving my hand at it.

"Every day since the raiders attacked our campsite," he told me. "I took it out at night. Always kept it on me, though, until we came here." He set it on a bench and donned his breeches. Once he was clothed, he picked the thing up and patted a spot beside him. "So what's this about sewers?"

I told him about the Hunt that earned me the nickname Bloodhound in Port Caynn and, later, Corus. As I spoke, Farmer began to peel the white wax away from whatever lay inside it. It was backed with muslin strips, so once Farmer had worried a strip away, he could grip the muslin and begin to unwrap the contents of the thing.

Pounce sat in front of us, watching. He was blinking constantly as Farmer revealed something in blue silk.

Blue? the cat asked, leaning forward in interest. *Not red, or orange?*

"For maturity, and stability," Farmer replied. "Beka, go on. This Dale fellow, do you see him anymore?"

I smiled at him. "Only once in a while, and only as friends. Pounce, what is wrong with your eyes?"

You don't see the power in what he has, Pounce said, blinking hard. *It's very strong.*

"You let us believe you had naught!" I said, cross with Farmer.

"Wasn't it better that I did?" he asked, his eyes worried. "We were followed, Beka, at least from Queensgrace. Given that cozy deal Sabine made for her and Tunstall, you have to wonder if one of them left a trail."

I *had* been wondering, and sick at heart over such thoughts. Back and forth I had gone since they had put me down here. Tunstall? Never! But . . . Sabine? I would have sworn before the Goddess that the lady had no turncoat blood in her veins until she accepted Thanen's invitation. Both of them together? Impossible, and yet . . . Here I was, and here was Farmer. Of course, it was not unknown for captors to place a traitor with a captive to winkle information from her, but a turd made of wax and silk? Surely that was going a little far to get information from a common Dog.

Farmer went on, "The traitor could have made the deal at Queensgrace. That's where our troubles got relentless. They knew to tag my pack. Not the pack with my spare clothes, the pack with my magical resources."

He was right. I'd known it since that first night away from Queensgrace, or guessed it, and was certain when Farmer and I both found the slave trader's brass tag on Farmer's pack.

And who? The knight I'd looked up to for four years, fought beside, laughed with? My new love, with his frank, open blue eyes? Or worst, much worst, of all, my partner. The cove who, with Goodwin, had taught me all I could learn as fast as I could learn it. The cove who'd saved my life so many times I could not count. No matter where I looked, there was a possibility that was fit to tear me in two.

I heard soft sounds and turned back to see Farmer open the silk. Pounce leaped up to see as well. Inside the blue cloth was a long, flat roll of ribbon. As Farmer set the wrapping down, I opened the roll a couple of folds. By the back

I knew—barely—that the ribbon itself was red, the color of magical power. It was covered edge to edge with embroideries in all different colors. Looking closer at the front, I realized that each color continued down the ribbon without breaks. It was only in the weaving and curving of the design in tiny bends that it appeared to be tiny bits of color intermingled.

"It's all spelled, isn't it?" I asked Farmer. "I'd've gone blind, doing this kind of stitching, so small and tight."

He picked up the ribbon and opened it out another couple of folds. "I have a spell to make the stitching bigger," he explained. "And I worked on it for a very long time. This makes what went up when my packs burned look like a bucketful compared to a lake." I looked up at his face. It was set, determined. His soft mouth had gone firm. He had plans for those threads, each holding magic from a different mage. I could not wait to see those plans unfold.

He glanced at me and put one arm around me as he stuck the ribbon in the pocket of his breeches. "Whatever happens, get the lad and get out of the castle," he told me. "I'll be right behind you, no matter what."

"But we don't have Dog tags," I reminded him.

"I never needed them," he said quietly. "That was to make the rest of you feel better."

"I don't know the layout here," I told him. "The Gift is all very well, but there are some practical things to be covered, don't you think?"

He kissed me and took his mouth only a little bit away. "Do you mind if I magic you? If I call the castle map into your head and mind while we pretend to nuzzle for the guards?"

It was a good plan. I nodded and whispered, "Do it."

He cupped the back of my head in one hand and wrapped the other arm around me. As he pressed his lips to mine, I felt a vision unfold in my head. It was like my memory houses, only this was a castle, drawn in pen and ink. It built itself from the underground up, dungeons, wine cellars, great hall, kitchens, studies, pantries, armory, and on. It built out, adding floors and towers as it included outbuildings and walls. When the last tower and gate were placed, the vision folded itself up like a map, settling in my mind where I would be sure to find it.

He released the spell, but I continued to show my affection for him a moment longer. I stopped only when the rattle of metal on metal told me that our time alone was done for the moment. The guards who had opened the door after banging on the bars made merry at our expense as they brought in a pitcher of water and two bowls of something.

One of them looked directly at Pounce and didn't see him. "If I knew I had my last hours to spend, I'd like it this way, lovin' up a pretty girl!" he jested. They were different from the guards who had shoved Farmer inside.

I glared at them and they stepped back. "Whoa, wench, warm them eyes before you look at your man again!" said the shorter of the two, holding up his hands. "Elsewise he might only be givin' you cold comfort!" He shivered.

"Her eyes are beautiful," Farmer said, turning my chin so he looked at me.

"Ghost eyes," said the taller guard, and "Ice eyes," said the other.

"Too many mages hereabouts," the short one added. They left us, locking the door behind them.

"I'm no mage," I snapped, and spat on the floor.

"No, sweetheart," Farmer replied, "but that's a glare that tells folk what you will not—that you are a very bad mot to muck with, and you will see them to their graves. There's

power in it that sticks to those you glare at. It makes *me* trem-
ble in my boots. Or it would if I had them." He looked sorrow-
fully at his bare feet.

I gave him a light buffet on the head. "Looby," I told him.

As my reward I got his silliest grin. "Ma allus said—"

"Your ma should have drowned you at birth," I told him
as I picked up one of the bowls. It was the usual brown slop
with a hint of beef and gravy, and something that looked like
a turnip. "I've eaten this all along. Unless it's poisoned today,
it's all right."

"They're not poisoning us," Farmer said, getting to his
feet to stretch. "If they want my blood, they want it pure. No
wonder they need to change kings. Roger would never allow
blood magic to be practiced here. Baird will."

"Why do you say so? Baird is Roger's brother, and it's
their father that forbade blood magic," I said, handing Farmer
his bowl.

"Because Thanen and his mages will make sure that's part
of the bargain, if they haven't already," Farmer replied.

"Sarden maggot-ridden corpse baits," I muttered.

Farmer was inspecting the contents of his bowl. "What
do you suppose *that* is?" he asked, prodding a lump.

"It's better not to know," I said. "Eat it fast. Don't try and
taste it."

Once we'd finished, to help pass the time, Pounce told us
a story of a hero he had befriended; then Farmer and I managed to find a clean spot of floor to nap on with the cat. None
of us spoke of Sabine, who had seemed to turn traitor, or Tunstall, who had gone along like a lamb. None of us spoke of
Achoo, out in the woods.

The jangle of lock and keys brought us all to our feet,
instantly awake. "Get ready," Farmer whispered in my ear.

Don't worry about me, Beka, Pounce added. *If you see me or not, I am with you.*

The door swung wide and a lone jailor came in, a short sword in his hand. Already I was scornful of his worth. No cage Dog ever approached celled Rats alone, weapon or no.

"Back, mage," the empty-headed pig's knuckle said, pointing his sword at Farmer. "We know your magic is tied up. If you don't care for your mot to be the same, you'll stand back. The trull comes wiv me."

I heard a chuckle from the door. *There* was his fellow guard, holding the key ring and a glowing orange globe that I guessed was supposed to keep mages under control. "Don't worry, Master," that one said. "We'll take *fine* care of her."

"No more gab from you," Farmer announced in a loud, official bark. "I don't know what game you're about, mage, but you'll not fool any man of my lord's guard! Over against them shackles on the wall, right quick! You, gabble-monger!" he snapped, pointing to me. "Stop scatchin' yourself and get that wench afore she sneaks off down the hall and the cap'n sees her!"

"What's you talkin' about?" asked the one already in our cell. He sounded even slower than before, dreamy.

"I'm no wench," murmured the other.

Farmer hadn't said that he meant to do magic now, but neither had I needed his brief warning to know we were about to take a chance. He was acting like *we* were the guards, and the guards were us. Seemingly the guards had begun to believe it.

"Here, you!" I ordered, and dashed forward to grab the one with the globe and the key ring. Slipping the ring over the hand I used to hold the globe, I gripped the cove's louse-ridden hair and thrust him into our cell.

He dug his heels in partway. "I'm a . . . guard," he protested, trying to turn in my hold. "A guard in the dungeons . . ."

I hooked his right leg from under him and helped him drop by shoving his head. Once he was down, I set the globe and keys aside and got one of his arms up behind his back. I released his hair to grip his wrist, shoving it up toward his shoulder. With my other hand I shoved his elbow up toward that same shoulder. Nobody likes that hold, particularly when it's pushed hard enough to break bones. He screamed. Suddenly he was shouting, "How dare you treat a Provost's Guard this way! I'll get you hobbled, so I will, and hie you before a magistrate!"

Seeing that Farmer's magic had taken, I let the cove go. We did the pair of them up in the shackles on the rear wall, in case anyone came looking from outside. We used their belt knives to cut gags from their tunics to silence them.

The last thing Farmer did before we left that cell was take up the globe. He held it in his palm, eyeing it calmly, with that look that told me he was examining it from the inside out. Slowly the light began to fade. Once the globe had turned lead gray, he dropped it to the floor. It smashed into hundreds of tiny glass fragments. "I'll take any extra power I can find," he explained.

Since I had the keys, I locked up. There was no one else in the corridor. I beckoned to the other cells with the keys and raised my eyebrows to my partner. Farmer thought on it for a moment, then nodded. "Don't let yourself be seen. I'll silence the keys."

I peered into one of the cells. Four men were inside, looking as unhappy as any caged Rats I had ever seen. I hoped they were not rapists or murderers and went about my work.

As I unlocked each cell, Farmer drew a strange mark on

it that glowed the colors of his Gift. No one left the cells. I was going to open one, but Farmer signaled me to wait.

Next we found the guardroom. No one was there. Farmer twiddled his fingers over a pot of ale that was heating on the fire. Then we looked for the stairs.

"We'll look like guards for half an hour unless a mage sees the spell and breaks it first," he whispered in my ear. The climb was a long one. "I learned that bit of magic from a hedgewitch who normally sold it to wives who were cheating on their husbands. If the husband came home while the lover was still there—"

"That's wicked," I told him sternly, seeing how such a confusion spell would be useful. Then I grinned.

"Meet me by the shrine to the Maiden of Archers if we're split up," he said. I nodded. The shrine was a small one, tucked away near the stables. I had it on the map in my head. "The magic I put on the cells just now opens the doors in an hour. Then this place will be a madhouse. There won't be any jail guards down here to stop them, not if they drink that ale. Do we find Tunstall and Sabine?"

I thought fast. "Our first duty is to the prince," I said. The voice I heard was still that of a mot, though deeper and coarser than my own, and the body I saw was shorter and thicker than mine. "Then we just go. However we can. We've no time to spend testing the others' loyalties."

"Sabine's giving way to them could have been a ruse," Farmer pointed out.

I nodded. "I'd thought of that. And it's better for Tunstall to be with her and free of the cells. But the lad is more important than anything. I'm wagering he's in the kitchen, the slave quarters when it comes toward bedtime, or Prince Baird's rooms."

"The kitchen?" Farmer asked softly. We had reached the room where the servants passed in and out, cleaning up after supper. They didn't look at us.

"He worked there before. It's warm and there's food. If he's avoiding punishment or been set to work again, I'll wager that's where he's to be found," I explained. "He doesn't know the heat and the smoke make him wearier, or that mayhap they're instructed to give him bad food."

"Where do you think I should search?" Farmer asked. He stopped by a tapestry that covered an entry to the great hall, and peeped through a slit. "They've gone to their amusements," he told me softly. "I'll be safer than you will, hunting among the nobles."

"Prince Baird," I whispered. "You stand a chance of getting to his chambers and looking around."

"The stroke of midnight at that shrine, unless we're occupied," Farmer told me. "We'll know something by then."

I nodded. I didn't want to leave him, but the lad had to be found. Farmer kissed his fingers and touched them to my cheek, then slouched and ambled through a break in the tapestry, the picture of a guardsman off duty. I'd walked but two steps toward the stairwell that smelled of kitchen when I heard Elyot's voice from the other side of the cloth.

"I *thought* I felt strange magic. Did you really think such an obvious disguise would get past me, you dolt?"

Back came Farmer's reply. No more was he playing the country lout for this treasonous louse. "Your thoughts and your ability to detect me aren't my concern, Elyot. I have more vital business than you."

I did not wait. I could not wait. Pounce and I trotted down two stairs toward the kitchen smell. When a red and sweaty maid climbed toward us, I stopped her. "Don't go there," I warned her. I sounded gruff, the sort of mot who whipped prisoners and teased the maids for extra food for herself. "Two mages is arguin'. I don't think they mean to keep it to talk."

As if I could foresee things, the tapestry hiding the big hall's entry burned in a flash. Crimson and blue fires replaced it. I gripped the maid under the arm and rushed her back down the stair. She clung to me until we were in the kitchen, then screeched her tale to the servants gathered there. They did not stop to argue, but fled through the several doors that opened onto the huge room.

When they were gone, I waited. I knew the child slaves here had not followed the adults. I hadn't seen them go. They would be tucked in the shadows, niches, and cupboards, or hiding in the open pantries, hoping to steal scraps.

I heard a crash up above. I ground my teeth. I wanted to be there, guarding Farmer as I'd done the night our camp was attacked. Instead I had to follow my duty here, Hunting for a boy who might one day be a liar like his turncoat uncle Baird. Surely I'd be better off helping Farmer!

But duty was duty. I had never failed Lord Gershom. I looked around.

A haunch of pig, half of it already cut away, lay on a table. The cooks must have been preparing it for a baked or stewed dish of some kind. I took up a knife and began to cut slices of my own, stuffing one in my mouth and setting others on a table behind me. I heard them before I saw them, at my back, grabbing the meat I'd set for them. They gave off the telltale jingle of slave chains. When I thought I'd left enough on the other table, I began to set slices on the bare space next to the roast. They had to think about that. It would mean coming into my view. These were the ones who were tucked away behind me.

They knew I'd see them when they came out, but they'd be hungrier than ever after watching the others eat.

Mage-made thunder boomed down the stairs. The first of the hidden kitchen helpers dashed out of a niche between cupboards, seized a handful of scraps, and scrambled back to his hiding place, thinking I would be distracted by the noise. Another came after him in that tight-legged run they had to master with only a short chain between their ankles. Their clothes were but ragged shifts. The curst shackles had cost far more.

When I tired of cutting up meat, I went to the shelves and started to look through the bowls. A huge one near the top provided cherries, fresh ones. So did the bowl next to it. I turned with them in my hands to face six scrawny slave children, the youngest six, the oldest ten. Their faces and hands were smeared with pork fat. Three of them held knives.

I set the bowls down on a worktable. "Greasy as your hands are, it'd be easy work to get them knives from you," I said. "Can you even use those in a fight?" My voice came out differently. I was still in Farmer's disguise.

Nobody spoke. They'd learned the hard way that silence was the better road for the likes of them. Something crashed again on the level above and all of them flinched.

I shrugged. "Cherries here. Fresh picked. I'm havin' some. When was the last time you had cherries?" I scooped a handful from a bowl and moved back, leaning against the shelves. Then I ate my cherries, spitting the pits on the floor. I hoped that any of the kitchen staff who'd put those lash marks and scars on these little ones' arms would slip on one and break his head, or her head.

They waited until they couldn't stand it anymore, then went for the cherries, making a wide path around me. I didn't move. When I finished my fruit, I stuck my hands in my pockets and waited. Pounce walked in and leaped up onto the table with the pig. The little slaves didn't notice that a big slice of meat suddenly turned into a fine-chopped pile before the cat began to dine. Had I known Pounce could mince his own meat, I wouldn't have worn myself out for years doing it for him!

I walked around the kitchen, keeping away from the table with the pork and that with the cherries. To them I seemed only to be idling about. I did set cheeses where they might reach them, as well as a loaf of bread and a jar of honey. I found what I sought at last, a small bundle of wires used to lace up stuffed birds, tucked away above the knives. With a mallet for pounding meat I shaped two of the wires as I needed. As I banged away, the battle did the same, flat, ugly crashes sounding along the stairs.

When I ceased hammering the wires and looked at my companions, they stared at me. The ones that had gotten knives held them tight, their hands white-knuckled on the grips. Their nervousness had not stopped the boldest of them from grabbing the food I'd taken down, I noticed. One of them held Pounce awkwardly in her arms as Pounce gave me his most patient look.

"What?" I asked them. "Why are you still about? It's not like you can't hear them mages battlin' up there."

One of the older ones opened her mouth, only to cringe when a particularly large smashing noise boomed down the stairs. "This old pile be full o' magics," she said when she could be heard. "They done tol' us that. 'Twill never fall. An' you's leavin' a mess o' food. We'd be fools t'let it go."

"Wasn't doin' it for free," I told them. "Everything's got a price."

A small lad with a face like a fist said, "What's yours, then?"

"A slave for food," I said quietly. They moved closer to hear me better. "There's a new one in this place, here only a few days. He was out serving three days ago when they brung in prisoners. He was a little lad, and he fell. My lord cuffed him and sent him away. They call him up to the nobles' rooms, mayhap only a couple of times, mayhap a lot."

"What d'you want 'im for?" asked the gixie who'd spoken first. "What's he to the likes of *you*?"

I took a breath. It was funny, how tense it made me just to say it. "His friend sent me. Linnet."

"Linnet?" I heard a voice say. "You know Linnet?"

"I spoke with her a bit," I replied, deliberately not looking for the speaker. "Another gixie, she called you No-Skin, Gareth."

"They have ordered me not to use that name," the invisible speaker replied. "Gareth."

My heart twisted in my chest. No wonder they had kept him mostly in the cart. All he had to do was speak to let folk know he was not a typical slave. No child bought and sold in the markets spoke so well.

"It's all right, lad," I told him. "I've come to take you home." I looked at the others as I heard someone struggling and scraping near me. Holding up the wires, I said, "I'll take you all if we can find a way out of this place." There were a couple of promising tunnels on the map in my head, but they would trust me more if I needed something important from them. Slaves and the poor trust no one who offers sommat for nothing.

"There's no way," lisped a fair-haired gixie, but the oldest gixie and the oldest lad were trading looks.

"Like we'd get anywheres with these," the fist-faced boy snapped, tugging his ankle chains.

The prince crawled out from under the shelf at the bottom of one of the tables. I took the angry lad and sat him atop the same table fast, before he had time to do more than hit my cheek. I grabbed his arms and said, "Don't hit me again. It makes me cross."

"I'm no toy to be lifted up and about," he told me, but he kept his hands to himself. "An' you don't look like you did when you come in. You're taller. You got a braid, an' you're skinny."

"I had magic on me," I said, "and it wore off. You want to complain? Or do you want the shackles off?" I ignored the other slaves' whispers.

The noises from upstairs were quieter. Who was winning? I looked at the opening to the stair, then ordered myself to keep my mind on business.

Gently I set the prince next to the cross-grained lad. "Were you born so nasty, or did working here make you this way?" I asked the vexing one, going to work on his shackles. Lucky for me these were the expensive kind, that locked with a key. I'm no hand at striking them off, but locks I can pick.

"I was sold," he told me, peering at my work. "What's that you're doing, with the wire?"

"Quiet, and you'll see," I said. My good lock picks were in my shoulder pack, wherever it was. These clumsy ones took more fumbling. "Someone give the lad here some meat."

"You can't get out of here, magic spell or no," the gixie said, the one who did the talking at first. "They'll kill you."

"They're going to be busy for a bit," I replied. There was the click as I turned the second wire. The first shackle popped open. Under it the lad's skin was red and raw. I wanted to kill someone. Instead I turned to the second shackle. It took less time. I kicked it under the table and the lad jumped to the floor.

When I turned to Gareth, I saw he was feasting on a strip of meat that someone had given to him. My change in appearance did not seem to worry him. I started on his shackles. The infection under them was bad, though not old. They could only have put the ankle shackles on recently. He had a wrist infection where another clasp must have been. Seemingly the orders about no marks on him had changed. He'd lost a lot of weight. His rib bones showed stark against his skin through the overlarge armholes of his tunic. His eyes were sunk deep in his skull and surrounded by dark skin. He was ill.

He chose to stay where he was, eating hurriedly, while I turned to the others and held up my picks. They shrank back, behind the oldest girl, who shook her head.

"They'll kill us if they catch us without the chains," she said. "They'll kill us if we try t' run. There's more slaves comin' in every week this time o' year and we're the cheapest sort. You're mad t' take the little lad, and Daeggan there is mad t' go with you."

"I wasn't born t' this," the cross one—Daeggan—said. He must have been all of eight. "They already know I'm bad. How long before they break me?"

I nodded to him. "Do you know a way out, then?" He made a face in a way that told me he did.

"'Tis risky, and none've ever come back t' say if it works. Could be they're still layin' in there, gone to see the Black God," he told me.

"We'll learn soon enough," I replied.

"You'll be in the woods," protested the oldest gixie. "Where can you go after that? You've no horses. They hunt runaways on horses, with hounds! And all the land hereabouts is my lord's. Anyone on it would give you to him. Is your magic enough?"

"The lords will be occupied, I think," I said. "I know how to travel in hostile country. If I'm lucky, I'll have a better mage with me." At the very least Pounce and I could reach the road. With Achoo already in the woods, we would do even better. It wrenched at me to leave these other children behind. I knew they would slow us down. Daeggan at least looked to be in good shape, but most of them were exhausted and starved. They would be frightened in the dark woods and terrified of other people. And we had to hurry to take advantage of the distraction provided by Farmer and Elyot. Still, I had to offer the chance to them. "Think again. I'll take off your shackles. Go with me and Gareth, or stay. You're fed here, I suppose, and warm enough. If we make it away, I can promise you'll be free, and I'll find places for you."

"You're mad," the oldest girl said firmly. "And nobody's lucky here. There's bears and mountain lions and wolves in the forest, and snakes and traps. All this is Lord Thanen's, *all* of it. They'll brand my face and I'll never get anything but hard work again."

One by one they all refused to go with Pounce, Daeggan, the prince, and me. Seemingly dying a slave was better than the forest and the chance of dying or being fetched back for punishment. I thought I'd be relieved, but I wasn't. Daeggan made more sense to me. He wanted to leave before he was broken. It was no wonder, after he'd been working with the broken all of the time.

We bundled up food in a hurry. I made a strip of sacking into a sash where I tucked the food pouch and four good, sharp knives. Then Daeggan led us down a hallway littered with straw and splinters, plainly used for deliveries. I could have done so myself, as the map in my head lined the path to his tunnel in yellow. About five hundred yards along Daeggan took a turn into a lesser hall. We trotted down a set of stairs and along another hall. By then Pounce had disappeared again, gone off on some errand of his own. We were in the stone under the castle now, the air cold and forbidding. I liked it no better than I had liked it in the dungeon.

Gareth was shivering and laboring to keep up with me. I took pity on him. First I set my knives aside so they wouldn't stab me in the gut. Then I knelt, motioning to my back. "Up with you," I told him quietly. "Piggyback, let's go."

"Go *on*," Daeggan urged. "Ye're slowin' us down, honeytongue."

I frowned at him. "The lad's name is Gareth, please." I turned my head to look at the prince, who had frozen in place. Tears ran down his cheeks. "What is it, my boy?" I asked him softly. I swiveled on my feet to wipe his face with my hand. He was no prince to me in that moment. He was just a little fellow who'd gone through a month of ruin with no understanding of why.

"My—friend, Tassilo, that protected me," he whispered. "He—he'd give me rides on his back. He fought right in front of me and they killed him."

They had made him afraid to name his guards and surely his parents and servants. Either that or they'd spelled him. I smoothed his hair, hating Thanen and his fellow traitors myself. I could not let hate distract me. Mine was the task of getting clear of these monstrous conspirators with the boy in one piece.

"You will have justice for your friend," I told him. "Now, come. We'll go faster this way."

He linked his arms around my neck. I grabbed my knives and rose to my feet, sticking the blades in my belt before I gripped his legs with my arms. My bad rib stabbed at me, but I ignored it. I started forward, surprised to find Daeggan had waited for us.

"Thank you," I said when we caught up.

"I'm goin' soft," he replied. "Keep up, now."

We had gone but a hundred yards or so more, past a handful of sets of stairs leading up and away from the corridor, when I heard the approach of running feet. I put Gareth down and sent the lads up a stairway into the shadows. Then I took a torch from a bracket in the wall, waiting to see what nasty surprise the gods had arranged.

Pounce rounded a curve first, with Farmer in his wake. Like me, he looked like himself, not the guard in the cells. It was all I could do not to cry out. The ribbon was gripped in my man's fist, the flesh red and swollen around it. The ribbon itself was unmarked. Farmer was burned on the side of his head and on his chest. Half of his tunic was charred, but he still gave me his looby grin. The moment he embraced me, he sent healing into my body, mending that bad rib at last and getting soot and scorched cloth on me. I struggled, but he wouldn't let me go until he'd kissed me well.

"Take care of your own self, you great cracknob!" I scolded. Luckily for him, I could see his burns slowly healing. "And don't overdo. We've got company. He knows a way out." I looked up into the stairway. "It's all right. He's with us."

Daeggan, knife in hand, came down first, keeping Gareth behind him. He looked Farmer over, then he pointed at Farmer's fist. "Don't that hurt?" he asked.

"Only when I laugh," Farmer replied with a straight face.

He rubbed the swelling with a wince as the red flesh began to shrink. "Did someone mention a way out?"

Gareth hung back on the stairs, eyes wide, his thumb going into his mouth. I took my knives from my belt and set them down, then crouched on the bottom step with my back to him. "Farmer's all right," I said to him. "A little odd, but you know how mages can be. Come here, lad."

I heard a sound and looked back. Gareth had backed up two steps rather than come to me. He pulled his thumb from his lips. "Mages were there," he whispered, his eyes huge. "They let the murderers in. They burned everything." He put his thumb back in his mouth.

Daeggan glared up at me, then at Farmer. "Now see what you done?" he demanded. "We nearabout had him not suckin' his thumb, bein's how my lord and the mages pinch 'im whenever they catch 'im at it. Lookit 'im!" I thought of the ugly round bruises that I'd glimpsed, pinch marks, showing up against Gareth's dyed skin, and bowed my head so no one would see my fury.

Farmer crouched where he was, in full view of the stair. He had to be as on edge as I was now that the crash of the fight was ended. Folk would be moving about soon, mayhap even down here, but Farmer acted as if we had all night. "I wasn't one of them that attacked your friends," he said. "The mages that did that were wrong. We need to catch them. I just came from fighting one. Elyot."

"Tell me you killed him," I said quietly. I knew him, knew what his answer would be, but a mot can dream.

"No," Farmer said, shocked. I sighed and my soft-hearted man told me, "It is not my right to kill him. It's the law's right, and the king's right as wielder of the law. I knocked him half-way to Midwinter and laid a sleep on him."

"Faw," Daeggan said with scorn, and spat on the floor. "All the slaps and pinches I've had from that one, and he only gets a nap?"

I glanced at the prince. Gareth had taken the thumb from his mouth. "The law?" whispered the lad. "You work for the law? The law belongs to my papa."

"It's your papa who sent us, and your mama," I said. "I promised them we'd bring you home."

"We all swore to serve the law and bring you home, and find out who took you," Farmer added. "Come along, lad. We need to hurry."

Gareth trotted down the steps and climbed onto my back.

"*That's* better," Daeggan said as Pounce leaped onto his shoulders. He flinched, but he accepted the cat's weight and looked at Farmer.

"We need to go back a way," Farmer told me. "There's another tunnel. It looks better suited to us than the one you were aiming for."

"Are you certain?" I asked quietly, following him back down the corridor. "I want to get the swive-all pus mouse out of this sarden castle."

"Those are bad words," Gareth said in my ear. "Lunedda spanked me when I said *swive*." I waited for him to weep at the mention of his dead nursemaid, but he only buried his face in my shoulder.

"You have no idea of the bad words Beka knows, my lad," Farmer murmured back. "Once she starts, she nearabout sets my ears on fire. We're very, very lucky she's no mage, or the power of her words would split every lawbreaker she arrests from top to toe." He led us up a flight of stairs. The downward end was the way to the dungeons.

"Stop blathering," I ordered Farmer, as if he'd listen.

Truth to tell, I was grateful for his folly, as the boy seemed to take comfort from it. He was relaxing in my grip. His trembling eased until it was the slightest of quivers. I doubted that he'd stopped shaking since he was yanked from his home.

"You arrest people?" Gareth whispered.

"Farmer and me are Provost's Guards," I explained as we continued to climb. "There's three of us and a lady knight who came here seeking you."

"I want to be a Provost's Guard when I grow up, before I'm . . . you know," he said, stumbling to a halt before *king*, I was sure. "I thought you all had uniforms and batons and boots and badges."

It was good to hear him so eager. "This is my uniform. It's very dirty," I explained. "One day you'll see me properly kitted out." Farmer was hand-signaling for silence. I put my finger on my lips so the boys would understand and the three of us ducked into a hall that opened onto the stair. Farmer did something to the nearest door that made it open partway. The room beyond was dark and smelled of lack of use. Silently we three moved out of the light that shone in through the opening.

Farmer bumped me with his hip and tugged Gareth. Gently he shifted the boy onto his own back. He *would* do so when I couldn't object, not aloud, and not with hand signs that he would see. When I put my hand on Gareth's side, though, he was trembling no more than he had on my own back. I relaxed. Seemingly the chatter between Farmer and me had made him feel better about my man, better enough that Gareth didn't mind riding on Farmer's back instead of mine.

I moved to the crack between the hinges on the door, where I could see the stair. I heard the approach of booted feet and voices. The folk were arguing softly and passionately. I took out two of the knives I'd stolen, just in case. Then I realized that one voice was Sabine's. When they came in view, I nearly gasped. Nomalla of Halleburn walked with Sabine and Tunstall as if they were taking a stroll after supper. Only the fact that all three carried four heavy packs and the belt with my baton put the lie to their appearance. Tunstall was in uniform again, his baton hanging at his waist. He even had boots!

I clicked my tongue twice, in the way Tunstall had taught me, the way hillmen do it. He stopped the two mots. "Cooper, it's all right, I think," he said quietly, with a glare at Lady Nomalla. She'd put her hand on the hilt of her sword the moment he spoke. "The lady has rethought things."

"Go," Farmer's voice whispered beside my ear. "We'll wait."

Pounce left Daeggan to join me. We went out onto the stair, keeping distance between us and the Halleburn knight. Sabine gripped me by the shoulders and looked me intently in the eyes. "We were coming to release you from the dungeon," she explained. "Farmer's gone somewhere—he locked Elyot into a substance like glass and tore the main hall apart." She picked up Pounce and kissed him. He even let her. "Have you seen the boy?" she asked. "We got into Prince Baird's rooms, but there's no sign of him. We just found some of the kitchen servants. They told us they fled when the mage fight began upstairs. We have to find the boy and Farmer before we can get away."

I pointed to Nomalla. "Why are you trusting *her*?"

"She freed us," Tunstall said.

"You wouldn't understand," Nomalla told me. "You're

a Guard, you're for sale to anyone with a sufficient bribe. A knight has her honor."

"That's *enough*," Sabine barked, her eyes fiery. "Nomalla, if you speak so of *these* two Guards again, you'll face my sword. Their honor is every bit as good as yours. Better. They've not turned on the Crown for so much as an hour."

"May we brandish our shields at some better time?" Farmer asked wearily as he stepped from the darkened room with Gareth on his back and Daeggan at his heels. The prince whimpered and struggled to flee when he saw Nomalla, but Farmer hitched Gareth around to sit on his hip and bounced him as if he'd been a mother all his life. "Easy, lad. She's on our side, for now." He looked at Nomalla with eyes that had turned the color of ice. "If she isn't, I'll make her very sad."

"Will you turn her to ice, too?" Daeggan asked. "She's all right, you know, for one of *them*. She made her brother stop whippin' me."

Nomalla backed away from Farmer a step. She put both hands on her weapons, one on her dagger hilt, one on her sword. "You buried Elyot in stone, or ice, or something up to his neck," she whispered, her voice shaking. "He's screaming for someone to let him out."

Farmer's smile had no warmth in it. "Only Cassine Catfoot could free him. Let's be on our way, shall we? You first."

"One moment," Tunstall said. He smiled at Daeggan. "Who's this?"

"This is Daeggan. He's a slave who wants to change his place in life," I said. "He knows a way out."

"So do we," Sabine told us. "Nomalla and I played in the tunnels as girls. I know one that's best for our purposes."

Daeggan looked up at me. I nodded, knowing he was asking if my friend could be trusted.

"I think you'd best make your own way out of here," Tunstall said, resting a hand on Daeggan's shoulder. Gently he told the boy, "If not that, go back to your place and wait for us to return with soldiers to arrest the lord. We have a rough journey ahead. A deadly one. Too risky for a lad, even one as brave as you."

Daeggan gave Tunstall his clenched fist of a scowl. "I'm stayin' wiv *her*," he said, pointing to me. "Her I know better'n you. I go wiv her or I tell my lord ye're down here."

"Clever lad," Farmer remarked.

"Daeggan's my friend," Gareth said.

"That settles that, then," Tunstall said, grouchy. "If we live, I'll find him a good position scrubbing privies. Let's move." He passed my belt and pack to me while Sabine set Pounce down and gave Farmer's shoulder pack to him. I took the kitchen knives from my makeshift belt and put them in my pack before I donned my true belt and felt for my own blades and my baton. Then I checked my pack and nearabout yelped with delight. My arm guards, each with ten thin knives as ribs, lay on top of my other belongings. Hurriedly I slid them on. Though I could manage the ties myself with one hand and my teeth, Farmer did them up for me. As I bent to close my pack, I saw light near the bottom. It was my stone lamp. I slid it into my pocket. A little light is always useful.

Once Farmer and I had our packs in place and Farmer had settled Gareth in his arms, Nomalla and Sabine led the way down the steps. Pounce walked between Tunstall and Farmer, whilst I brought up the rear. Daeggan trotted along with me. I started to feel uneasy as we went deeper. So did

Farmer, from the looks he gave Tunstall, and so did the lad beside me.

Finally Daeggan halted. "She's takin us t' th' cells, she's gonna lock us up and turn us over!" he whispered, clutching my arm. We weren't far from the guards' station. He had a point. All we needed was a cove with a short run to an alarm bell.

Nomalla and Sabine halted on the last landing between us and the dungeons. They turned left and walked three yards down a small corridor there. Farmer followed while Tunstall put his finger to his lips and frowned at Daeggan. Into the hall we went. I paused on the landing, trying to hear any noise from either way on the stairs. All was silent. Wouldn't they come to the dungeons to find me, knowing Farmer was out? Had they tried to find Gareth, or had they gone for Sabine and Tunstall, believing them to be more important just now? I rubbed the back of my neck and caught up with the others.

Sabine and Nomalla had turned to face the left-hand wall. Like the rest of this part of the castle, it was old stone. The rock was not all cut to the same shape, but the pieces were fitted together, round, square, and rectangular. The differences between them were filled in with mortar. Among them one small, reddish stone hardly stood out, though the other ones were gray. The red one was at chest height for Lady Sabine. She set a couple of fingers against it and pushed.

A section of the wall in front of the lady swung in like a door. Gareth, who seemed to know to be silent, gasped and almost clapped his hands with delight, stopping himself just in time. Beyond the door lay a dank tunnel, barely high enough to fit Tunstall and scarcely wide enough to fit him and Farmer walking abreast. It was veiled in cobwebs and thin roots. I checked the map in my head and found this place. The tunnel that opened into that corridor was one of those that led off the edge of the map.

Tunstall grabbed the nearest torch from its bracket.

"I can light the way," Farmer protested. I reached in my pocket for my light stone.

Tunstall grinned and passed the torch around the opening, burning the cobwebs away. "Can your light do that?" he asked.

Farmer shrugged. "You know I can't do fire, remember?" he asked. It was just as well. I had the firm opinion that Farmer should save his strength, physical and magical. We had a long road ahead, all of it on foot, with Farmer, the lads, and me barefoot at that.

Tunstall went first with Pounce beside him, then Nomalla and Sabine. Farmer put Gareth down and shooed him, Daeggan, and me ahead of him. Once we were inside, he shoved the stone door closed. Daeggan, for all his spirit, did not like the dark that filled the air around us. No more did Gareth.

"Keep to the main path," Nomalla told us. "Don't go into any of the side tunnels. It's too easy to get lost down here."

After that the two lads clutched each other tight and flinched at every side tunnel we passed. The torch did very little for those of us behind Tunstall and the ladies. I was taking my stone lamp from my pocket when a cool kind of moonlight filled the tunnel.

"There's no need," I said, showing Farmer my own lamp.

Farmer touched it with one of his glowing hands. The stone shone brighter than before. "Stop worrying," he murmured. "Tunstall appears to have forgotten I do light, if not fire. Light's the easiest thing I do. And it's everywhere."

I let Daeggan hold my stone. Once he realized it wasn't

hot, he clutched it like his life depended on it. I took the lads' hands. We hurried on after the others, poor Farmer bending so he wouldn't bump his head. Tunstall was in the same basket. I noticed that after a time he began to rub the back of his neck. The position and the tunnel's chill damp were making his bones ache. There was a warm balm in his pack, but neither he nor Sabine would take the time to get it out. I think none of us believed that our captors would not discover our absence and work out that we had help from within.

"How many know of these tunnels?" I asked Lady Nomalla.

"My brother, who is not here," she replied over her shoulder. "Perhaps my father and my aunt, who grew up in this place. The castellan, certainly. He is one of my father's byblows. That's all."

"I always preferred him to your brother," Sabine remarked, as calmly as if we were on a daylight stroll. They talked quietly about relatives as we continued on through the depths under Halleburn's causeway, where the tunnel grew wider and higher.

No such daylight walk I'd taken sported blind white lizards moving at the corner of my eye, or pale fish in the stream that ran alongside one section of the tunnel. The side tunnels sometimes showed bigger webs than either of the boys. At one turning some poor mumper had been chained to the rock and left to die, a skeleton in very old-fashioned rags.

Sabine halted and laid a gentle hand on the dead man's skull. "I still say a prayer for you before each fight, Brother Bones," she told him quietly. "I have kept my promise." She noticed we all stared, and explained, "I was lost here when I was very young. I promised Brother Bones that I would pray for him if he would show me the way to the castle, and he did."

"Do you know who he is?" Tunstall asked.

Lady Nomalla replied, "My father does not know and says his father did not know, so the poor man has been here nearly a century at least."

The lads gave the skeleton a wide berth. I looked back as we hurried on. The dead man had naught to say to me. I thought my own prayer for him and sent it to the God, in case Brother Bones's soul still wandered for lack of a pigeon to carry him.

It seemed as if we'd been treading the uneven ground forever when I felt a breeze coming from somewhere in front of me. A moment later Tunstall whispered loudly, "Douse the lights!"

Daeggan handed mine back to me. I stuck it inside my breeches, under the band of my loincloth, rather than risk the light escaping my pocket. Farmer's glow faded slowly, not going out until we could dimly see the end of the tunnel, a mass of ivy. Tunstall passed his torch to Sabine. Holding up one hand in a "halt" signal, he used the other to draw his long knife. Carefully, silently, he eased out through the curtain of vines.

"Are we home?" Gareth whispered.

Daeggan hushed him. I knelt beside him and shook my head. I didn't say it would be one of the gods' great miracles if we made it to the boy's home.

Wednesday, June 27, 249

Halleburn Fiefdom

yet recorded in my memory

At last Tunstall returned to wave us into the open. Once we were outside, Farmer faced the tunnel. He had opened his roll of ribbon to expose two inches of it. His lips moved, shaping silent words.

Lady Nomalla reached out as if to stop him, but Sabine grabbed her by the sleeve. Nobody dared make a sound. Something pressed on me. I shoved Daeggan and Gareth back toward the others but stayed where I was, afraid that Farmer might overdo again.

The feeling moved away. The vines and their heavy wooden trunk were mashed against the stone until trunk and leaves alike flattened. Then, in the light of Farmer's magic, I saw the rock's edges and crevices run together. When the liquid stone had erased all sign of the door to the tunnel, it went still and took on the look of old rock.

A tiny line of smoke rose from the embroidered face of the ribbon. I advanced to look at it. A charred line ran through the face of the embroidery, marking where one color had burned. He looked at the others and shrugged. "Ma always said to close the door behind me," he explained.

We were in the woods, but I saw open ground thirty yards away. Leaving the boys to gawp at Farmer, I advanced into the clearing and beyond, crossing a wide swathe of grass. I reached the edge of the cliff.

The moon was gone, but starlight and the castle torches below were enough to see by. I did not risk my stone lamp. Halleburn lay to my right atop its rock finger. We were on the cliff northwest of the lake and the castle. I wasn't close enough to see the guards' faces as they walked the walls, but I was close enough to see *them*. To my left there was a path about two yards wide, made of tamped, bare earth. It followed the cliff's edge.

The castle was quiet, the guards bunched up to gossip on the walls. The prisoners in the other cells would have gotten free by now. Farmer's battle with Elyot had been a noisy one, sure to draw attention. Someone would have entered the great hall to see the warring mages. Others would have found the guards that drank the drugged ale, or Elyot, or the children who had feared to join us. A servant or guard would have checked Sabine and Tunstall's chambers. Missing them, they might have thought to call Nomalla. The alarm should be out.

Yet the guards returned to their pacing. I heard no sound of the drawbridge as it was lowered to allow pursuers to ride out, and Farmer had said nothing of meddling with the chains this time. It was all wrong.

The traitor among us must have left signs of our escape.

I would know who the traitor was only when the trap was sprung, I realized. By then all we had done and all we'd endured, all Their Majesties had endured, would be wasted.

Up there, the night breezes pushing at my face, I knew that in the end, I could only really trust Gareth, mayhap Daeggan, Pounce, and Achoo. If needful, I would leave everyone, even Farmer, to get the prince away free. It was the only way to be certain I did not have a traitor at my back.

My mind set, I ran back to my companions. They were there, pasting mud and leaves on one another. The boys even helped Nomalla to cover her armor as Sabine pinned the other mot's bright hair in place and coated it. The lady had worn no helm.

"Cooper, darken that skin," Tunstall ordered me. "Let's not stand out more than we already do."

"Do we know where we're going?" Farmer asked.

I pulled a close cap from my pack and drew it over my head, tucking my braid into it until my hair was hidden. Then I smeared all of myself that I could reach. Farmer did the back of my neck. I did his. No one noticed if we took a few extra seconds in touching.

As we worked, Sabine told us, "Mattes and I figured out a plan with Nomalla's help."

Daeggan spat on the ground.

Nomalla glared down her thin nose at him. "I don't normally explain myself to slaves, but you cannot know my father if you believe he will accept me back into his house after this."

"Enough," Tunstall ordered. "We're dead deer if we're caught. Now listen—Nomalla says there's a village a couple miles off. We can steal horses there."

Sabine picked up the tale. "We want to try for King's Reach—their loyalty is unquestioned. We'll steal horses all the way if we must."

Inside, I winced. King's Reach was across the Great Road North at the headwaters of the Halseander. We'd have to steal a lot of horses to get there, unless we found good ones, but what other choices did we have? And all this depended as well on our pursuit. We had to *move*.

We were nearly ready when we heard something crashing in the woods. Tunstall, Sabine, and I grabbed our weapons, putting ourselves between the lads, Farmer, and Nomalla.

You worry overmuch, Pounce told us. I knew everyone could hear it, because the lady knight and the lads turned to stare at the cat. In the darkness of the brush, he was only a pair of gleaming purple eyes. *This time, anyway. I told her to make noise so you'd have warning.*

Farmer was explaining Pounce to the boys when my poor Achoo, her curls tangled, leaves and twigs in her fur, leaped from the undergrowth into my arms. Tunstall grabbed my long dagger before she speared herself on it. I laughed as my hound washed off all the dirt I'd put so carefully on my face. Then I dropped to my knees with her. While she wiggled and whined, I dumped the meat I'd stolen from the kitchens onto the cloth I'd used to carry it. Achoo ate in several big gulps while Sabine, Tunstall, and Farmer petted her and told her what a wonderful creature she was.

I kept her in my mind, Pounce explained, winkling a bit of pork from the pile before Achoo could devour it. *She had her work to do to keep away from the normal hunting parties, but she did it.*

"Is that *your* dog?" asked Gareth.

I turned to look at him. He and Daeggan had inched back to stand with Nomalla, the outsiders at our family welcome. "She is a hound," I explained. Nomalla snorted. I ignored her. "Achoo—that's her name—is a scent hound. She's one of the finest—"

With the smell of pork out of her nose, Achoo looked around. She saw the other three members of the group, but most important of all, she *smelled* one of them, the one that she had tracked for so many miles. She threw herself at the prince, whimpering and wagging her tail as she knocked the boy over and licked his face clean. Nomalla drew her blade in a flash, I think to protect Gareth, but "It's all right," Sabine told her. "Achoo's just enthusiastic."

Gareth, met with real affection for the first time in weeks, wrapped his arms around my hound's neck and wept.

"The king keeps hounds?" I asked him. "Did you have one?"

Gareth looked at me, still hanging on to Achoo. "They killed them. The bad men." There was a hardness in his face that belonged to a man, not a little fellow like him. "I want to kill them."

Tunstall knelt so he was on the same level as Gareth. "That's what we're going to do," he said gravely. "Capture them that hurt your friends and take them for judgment."

Gareth nodded. "Then let us go," he said, a little old man in a child's slave clothes.

Achoo would not leave him. She nuzzled him all over, as if to see if anything was broken, and licked the mud off of one of his arms. Daeggan covered Gareth with more dirt. Achoo smelled Gareth on the older lad and licked him as well, ignoring Daeggan's complaints.

At last Farmer picked up Gareth. We formed a column, Sabine and Nomalla in front, Tunstall behind them, Farmer, Achoo, and the lads next, and me last. At first I thought Tunstall and I would quarrel over that final spot, but he gave over when Sabine hissed, "Mattes! Let's go!"

He followed her. I felt much better about being in that last spot. I was still inclined to trust Farmer of all the other adults because my gut said he was true. Of course, my gut had been wrong before. Still, not everyone of these folk could be false. If I kept worrying, I would fail to listen to the dark, so I turned my attention to listening.

Up to the cliff's edge and northwest we followed the path as quietly as possible, even the lads. That was how we came to startle a doe and her fawns as they grazed by the path. We halted briefly for the rustle and thump of a large creature built low to the ground. I sent up a prayer to the gods that it be a bear and that it stumble across anyone hunting us. I was certain that our scent had frightened it, unless the big thing was simply clumsy. I'd never been with such a quiet group.

The trail turned away from the cliff, down through a ripple in the ground and into the trees. Now we had cover for an enemy ambush on both sides. When we stopped at a spring for Achoo and the others to drink, Tunstall insisted on taking Gareth to give Farmer a rest. It was all done by hand signs. I moved up next to Farmer while Tunstall settled Gareth on his hip—like Farmer, Sabine, and me, Tunstall had a shoulder pack—and took my man's hand.

With everyone's thirst quenched and the dirt replaced on those whose faces had gotten wet, we pressed on. An hour or so later Daeggan began to fall behind. It was amazing he'd kept up until then, kitchen work not preparing him for long marches. He whispered that we should leave him, but no one accepted the offer. Nomalla and Sabine cut two saplings to equal length. Farmer sacrificed his tunic and did a small bit of magic that bound the ends of the side slits together. Once the poles were slid through the armholes and slits, both lads could ride the litter if they lay sideways. Nomalla and Sabine took the first turn carrying it and Tunstall went to the head of our line.

The path continued to lead down. It got steeper, slowing us. It was so hard to see under the trees that I passed my stone lamp up to Tunstall. He used it low to the ground, keeping his hands in a shield over it to limit how much light would show. We followed the path to a stream, then up and down into a second deep cut. We stopped by a spring near the crest of the second cut to rest again and drink. I prayed the water was clear, because we had no other.

"What's that way?" Tunstall asked, pointing northeast.

"The cliffs go all around this side of the valley," Sabine replied. "Another trail leads out of the village where we're bound. Keep on the cliff trail and you reach Prachet town. We want the southwest road out of there."

Farmer crouched by the boys, who had crawled out of the litter. He held each by the hand as they stared at him. Nomalla lay flat on her back, catching her breath and staring at the sky. Such a hike in armor was new to her, I guessed, but she was tough. She'd kept up without complaint.

Sabine went to the hilltop and wriggled through the grass to survey the land beyond. The village should be there. Achoo lay on her belly beside the stream, watching me. I could not see Pounce, but it *was* very dark. After drinking his fill, Tunstall followed Sabine.

Soon, I thought. The traitor would have to move soon.

It was midnight by the stars when Sabine and Tunstall waved us onward. Pounce and Achoo led this time, trotting down the grassy slope toward the small village below. The lads would have run behind them, suddenly full of renewed strength, but we kept them back, Farmer and me. The warriors went next, then the rest. I kept glancing back, but there was no one on the hilltop.

The village dogs, the four-legged sort, did not make a sound, though they came to sniff Achoo and Pounce. The other animals, the cows, goats, sheep, and geese, were also quiet. I couldn't know if this came from Farmer or Pounce, but I was grateful for it. Geese are much harder to silence than dogs.

We were partway through the village when soldiers ran out of several houses into the street, swords bared. Farmer grabbed Daeggan; I, Gareth. We raced into a thin opening between dwellings and out past their gardens. There were no other houses behind these—it was a very small village—only fallow fields where Dolsa, Ironwood, and Orielle stood in a bubble of light. They cast some manner of glittering veil over Farmer.

He blew it apart without appearing to do anything. "Go!" he ordered me as he put Daeggan on the ground. "Tunstall, take the boy!" he cried. He shrugged off his pack and used it to block whatever nastiness Ironwood threw at him then. I'd had no idea the shoulder pack was magical.

I froze, staring at Farmer as he opened up his entire roll of ribbon. It fell to the ground in tumbled loops, gleaming in a multitude of colors.

"Do you think you'll fight us with *embroidery*?" Ironwood cried.

"I think I'll beat you with your own power," Farmer shouted back. Blue fire lashed out from his side, tangling itself around the claw that was flying at Daeggan.

Tunstall popped out of the thin gap we had used. He grabbed Daeggan and pushed Gareth and me toward the barns that lay to our right. "The girls will hold the soldiers—they've backed into a house they can defend," he said, his voice rasping as we raced for the buildings. "Farmer has the mages. Our duty is the prince."

I said nothing. Tunstall was a good Dog, even a great one, but I had always thought that, forced to a choice between Sabine and duty, he would choose Sabine. He had confused me.

He must have guessed what I was thinking, because he glanced at me and laughed. "She said if I didn't go with the prince, she'd never see me again!"

He ran past a couple of sheds and into a horse barn with Daeggan under his arm. I spared a look at Farmer. The length of ribbon that he held blazed in five different colors as thin wisps of smoke wrapped around his face. Ironwood was shrieking spells as Dolsa and Orielle shaped magic with their hands. "Gods, take care of Farmer," I whispered, and ducked into the barn behind Tunstall.

He'd found the place where the mages and soldiers had stashed their mounts while they waited for us. When I lit one of the lanterns, I saw that every mount was saddled and bridled, waiting for its master. I looked among them, trying to spot any who wouldn't mind two complete strangers as riders. I'd learned through bitter experience that not all horses welcome folk they don't know.

"Cooper!" Tunstall called. He'd kept my stone lamp and was waving it to show me his location. He and Daeggan already had two horses by the reins. They submitted to him as if they were those he'd ridden this far on the Hunt.

Quickly I doused my lantern and ran to Daeggan and Tunstall, Gareth right behind me. I mounted the closest horse and let my partner hand up the prince, settling the lad in front of me on the saddle. It might be a little more awkward than having him on my back, but this way I could grip him with my arms if need be. He was too small to ride alone. I wished I had something to wrap around him to bind him against me.

Tunstall mounted the other horse and swung Daeggan up behind. As the lad tossed my stone lamp back to me, Tunstall clucked to the horse and rode to the rear of the barn, where the back doors stood open.

Before we left the building, Tunstall said, "As fast as we can, Cooper, onto the trail leading to Prachet and along the cliffs. Southward takes us right in front of those mages." He glanced at Pounce, who stood in the open doorway. "We may be leaving you behind, old friend."

We'll see, Pounce said. Achoo moved into sight beside him.

Tunstall leaned forward in the saddle and lashed his mount with the ends of his reins. Off he galloped, Daeggan clinging to his back. I nudged my mount, who was all too happy to follow the galloping horse.

In the darkness Tunstall was sound more than sight, though the fires cast by the mages gave us rippling, flashing lights of many colors. Tunstall had a good lead, but my own horse was smaller and faster. We were also a lighter load, Gareth and I. We passed Daeggan and my partner a couple of yards before we reached a streamlet that ran across the road. My mount splashed through it eagerly, but behind us I heard a dreadful sound like a horse's fall.

"Go!" Tunstall shouted as I looked back. He was struggling to get the horse on its feet. I saw no sign of Daeggan. "The animal is fine—we'll catch up!"

I obeyed. I had promised the heartbroken young mother back at the Summer Palace that I would bring her son home.

I glanced at the village. Lamps were being lit in a couple of brave souls' houses. Farmer wove the colors of his enemies' magics as the other mages launched their spells at him. The weaving lit the sky where he battled. We had to get out of view before anyone saw us. Achoo had already trotted several yards ahead and was waiting for us.

Then I heard a scream from the south—not a human scream, but a scream I knew well. I'd heard it on the road, when the warhorse Drummer and his partner Steady protected Sabine. I looked down for Pounce but he was nowhere to be seen in the dark.

No, I did not interfere, he replied from wherever he was. *Those horses killed everyone who tried to stop them and took off.* They *knew their lady was in danger. Those mages down below helped when they left the castle gate open. That Macayhill horse magic is stronger than even Farmer knows.*

Feeling my heart weigh several pounds less, I urged my mount up the next steep part of the trail. When I glanced at the valley again, I saw Drummer and Steady gallop down the southeastern trail past Farmer and into the village. If Sabine was still alive, her horses might turn the fight for her. My man stood in the field before his enemies, a rim of sparkling blue fire around his big body. He held up what looked to be a hoop of stars. It was his embroidered ribbon, pulled tight between his hands.

My horse stumbled. I concentrated on my ride and the ground, pulling the animal upright with an apology. I'd let it drift into the rockier earth at trailside. That was stupid. By the time we reached the height of the cliff's edge, the poor creature had slowed from a gallop to a limping walk. I guided the horse into the grass and dismounted. She—it was a mare—had picked up a stone in her right forehoof. Achoo sniffed the mare's nose as I searched for the hoof pick in a pack on her saddle. She seemed calmer when I started working on the hoof by the light of my lamp, perhaps because Achoo distracted her. The stone came out easily, but we would not be galloping for a long time.

Pounce joined us then. Together we three walked and Gareth rode as we moved on slowly, up along the cliff. I'd found a couple of apples in the horse's pack. I gave her one for being so good about my demands and another to Gareth.

"Are we going to escape?" he asked softly, looking at the apple.

I have never been good at lying to children. "I don't know," I told him. "We have a long road ahead."

"Do you help slaves escape all the time?" he inquired, taking the apple.

"No. I hunt criminals." I shone my light ahead briefly. The trees grew close to the trail here, which was worrisome. I was on my own if there were any bandits fool enough to think they might find someone worth robbing on this stretch. No, not entirely alone. I had Pounce and Achoo.

"When I am—when I am big," the little boy said, still avoiding the words that meant he was a prince who would be king, "I am going to help escaped slaves. And when you take me to my papa, I will ask him to do so."

"Very good, Gareth," I said. They would tell him that he did not understand how the world spun, that slavery had always been with us. How would the work get done without slaves? they would ask, and, he did not want to make the great nobles angry, did he? He would reach manhood believing those things, like all the rich. Let him have his dream of changing the world for now. I wasn't going to be the one to shatter it.

"You don't believe me, but I will do it," he told me. "You'll see."

"I will, I hope," I replied. That was certainly the truth.

We had walked for a short time longer when I heard a lone horse on the trail. Quickly I drew our mare into the trees, Achoo and Pounce following me. I tied the horse far enough from the open that she would not walk out into it by accident. "Stay here, Gareth," I whispered as I helped him down. "Don't come out, no matter *what* happens. Achoo, *jaga*," I ordered. She would keep him in their hiding place.

Then I stepped out of the tree cover. From there I recognized the shape of the rider against the starlit sky.

I gave the double click Tunstall and I used as a signal. When he drew up, he looked around, not seeing me in the shadows by the trees. I unveiled my stone lamp a little so we could look at one another. Daeggan was not behind him on the saddle.

"Where's the boy?" I demanded, coming a step or two closer. Everything about this meeting felt bad to me. Mayhap it was the dark. I couldn't see Tunstall's face well with all the mud on it. His hands were washed clean, visible even with their tan. "Where's Daeggan?"

Tunstall dismounted. "Cooper, I'm sorry. We fell at that stream—"

"I heard you fall," I said.

"The boy." There was sorrow in Tunstall's deep voice as he approached. "He struck his head on a rock. I couldn't bring him around, and then I found the break in his skull. We must get out of here. Where is the prince?"

He knew as well as I that we weren't using the word throughout the Hunt. We did it to keep Gareth's title from slipping out at the wrong moment. "We're a long way from being able to call him that," I reminded my partner. Sometimes he could be careless, but that was usually at the start of a Hunt.

Tunstall scratched his head. "You're right. I fumbled it. Are you surprised, with the night we're having? Look, girl, where is he? We must ride on, before the enemy knows he's not in the village."

"I've got him," I said, rubbing the leather grip of my baton in my nervousness. "My horse went lame."

He swore in Hurdik and slammed his fist into his palm, but it didn't seem right. It sounded and looked playacted. Or mayhap by then there was little he could do that would make me easy in my mind. I was seeing traitors everywhere. "Give him to me. I'll get him to safety. I'll take him to Prachet and work something out from there."

"We were trying for King's Reach," I said. I didn't know why I was so suspicious.

Then I saw the spreading bruise on the web of skin between his right thumb and finger, the mark of a hard stabbing, and I knew. Mayhap I should have seen it back at the barn. I had looked around the first horses we'd met when we entered it, trying to tell which was safe and which was not. Tunstall had gone straight to the back, straight to those two mounts. It was the only slip he'd made apart from that fresh bruise. Even his tries to keep Daeggan from coming with us just looked like he wished to spare the lad a dangerous trip. And I had said to let him come. I had signed Daeggan's death warrant.

"There's a war party between us and King's Reach now," he said rightfully. "Give the boy to me, Cooper. We're wasting time."

"I have a better idea," I said. "Give me your horse. I ride lighter. You can help Sabine. Gareth and I will meet you at King's Reach."

Always before in our Hunts Tunstall had agreed to do what made the most sense. Not this time. "You'll never make it!" he snapped. "Have you forgotten you're but a leather-badge Dog? And Sabine will be fi—" He stopped, staring at me, while I nodded.

"She'll be fine because those guards have orders to keep her safe," I said as I took out my baton. "Nomalla, too? Or did her father wash his hands of her?"

"You've gone mad," he said flatly. "You finally cracked." His hands rested on his belt easily. He'd left his horse to crop grass, its reins hanging so it would not move.

I shook my head. "You killed Daeggan because he was in your way. You couldn't get Farmer's bags stolen on the road—

Drummer and Steady saw to that—so you settled it with your new masters to have the wayhouse and Farmer's extras burned, while you and Sabine got out just in time. Why? You owe me that much." I drew my long knife with my left hand. I also thanked the gods that Tunstall's pretending to be one of us had meant he'd had to bring our weapons when Sabine or Nomalla recovered them. I would have been drowning in scummer without my belt, its weight of weapons, and my arm guards.

"I don't want to kill you, Beka. You're like my daughter," he said quietly. "But don't you see? These people will win. I want to be on the winning side."

"What will you tell Sabine when you—*win*?" I demanded, waiting for an opening.

"I'm *doing* this for Sabine!" he roared suddenly and charged, his baton almost magically in his grip. I dodged and struck sidelong, aiming for his left elbow. I had to go for his joints. He was vulnerable in his joints, where all the years, all his fights, and all the broken bones had added up.

I missed and his left kick took me dead in the right hip, knocking me down. I rolled, my knife held out so I wouldn't cut myself. He lunged in to stomp me with that kicking, booted foot, but I was already lurching to my feet. I'd made it onto the trail.

"What will you say when you come back without me or Gareth?" I demanded, moving sideways, my eyes on the center of his body. I'd see the first twitch of movement there. He had not taught me that, but he'd taught me never to forget it. "Them's your orders, right? Kill me *and* the lad? The lad dies, his parents die, and the lords' hands are clean?"

"I'll say you were riding hard when your horse stumbled,"

he told me. "It was up here, you went off the cliff. I couldn't save you. Beka, don't make me do this!"

"I'm not making you do scummer!" I cried. "It's greed, because it can't be cowardice—"

I knew he'd move if he thought he had me talking. He did, coming at me on the right, his baton in his left hand. He liked to fight left these days, with his right shoulder aching more and more. I blocked his baton with mine, lunged in, and got his knee in my belly. We went hilt to hilt on our knife hands. I collapsed against him with my shoulder up in his armpit and dug in with my bare feet, fighting to keep his knife hand occupied. Inside his right arm as I was, he could do naught with his baton but hammer at me weakly with the butt.

I rammed my baton into the upper half of his belly. Then I jumped back. I wasn't fast enough. His knife came down and cut me from ribs to hip, a long, thin, nasty slice that slashed my clothes, though not my belt.

We backed off, trying to get some air. I cut a strip from my tunic, watching him try to catch his breath. I'd driven my baton as far up into his lungs as I could go. He was wheezing from it, though he still kept knife and baton pointed my way. Clumsily I tied the strip around the upper end of my cut, my shoulder and collarbone. I tried to calculate how long it would be until I'd bled so much I couldn't stand.

"You do this for Sabine? She'll gut you as soon as she finds out!" I snapped.

"She won't know!" Tunstall wheezed. "No one will tell, lest *I* give out they were in a conspiracy to murder royal blood. Soon enough Baird will be king, I Lord Provost." He took up a small flask at his hip and drank, his eyes watching me steadily. It was mead, to numb his pain. He sounded better when he said, "They'll say they were impressed by my work on the Hunt. I'll tell *her* I saved money from old bribes and invested it in trade. I'll be almost good enough for her. We can marry."

"She doesn't want to marry," I reminded him. I reached for a handful of dirt, but he stepped closer with his baton. I had to back up. I needed to think of something, but what? I didn't want to kill him. I couldn't. But he had betrayed the law we served. He had betrayed that little boy, who had done naught to deserve his last days of hunger, cold, and whippings.

"She says she don't want to wed," Tunstall replied. "She says it to spare my feelings. But she would do it if I had a place at court. If I had money." He came straight at me this time. He gave me the high stroke we'd practiced so often in the yards and I countered it. Middle stroke, low stroke. His knife was out to the side, ready to block mine. He struck with all his strength even while he used practice blows. He toyed with me, and I knew it. He knew my ribs were hurting, that I was losing blood. Every time he smacked that baton down on mine, the shoulder ached more. Worse, the contempt of what he did lashed me like the torturers' whips. This was *Tunstall*!

I took a tiny step closer. He had to close his elbow up a little to make his next stroke. "You're getting weak," he told me. "I'll do it quick—"

He was older and tough. I was young and desperate. I rammed him in the sack with my foot, jamming my blade into his knife arm and the top of my head into his chin. He dropped his knife, but he used his leg to sweep my feet from under me while he grabbed my braid. He yelped and let go when the spikes bit into his palm.

The back of my head was on fire. I fell on top of him as he got his baton arm under my chin and yanked my head up.

He meant to choke me or break my neck, but he'd forgotten my arm guards. Rather than take time to pull at the arm around my throat, I let one of my hands fall. With it I drew a long, flat knife from my arm guard and shoved the blade clean through the heavy muscle of his left forearm. Gritting my teeth, I wrenched it all the way around.

He grunted and let me go to yank the knives from his flesh. I scrambled halfway up, but again he grabbed my braid, at the end this time. I lifted myself as high as I could go, raising my arms as I gripped my baton two-handed. With all my strength I slammed my lead-cored baton down on Tunstall's oft-broken knees.

He bellowed in agony and released me, trying to sit up with legs that would not work. To be certain, weeping now, I struck his knees a second time.

I did not dare nap tap him. The healers in Corus had been very clear. Another good blow on his head would kill Tunstall. I fumbled in the pouch on my belt that was supposed to hold hobbles, but found none. I glanced at him and saw that he'd started to roll toward the cliff.

Limping—he had kicked me at some point right on some torturer's lump—I caught him by the back of the tunic and dragged him away from the trail. He fought to reach me over his head until I dropped him and stood on the arm that bled the most. He lay back, tears rolling into his hair and ears, as I stripped off his belt. I winkled his buckle knife out of its hidden sheath and tossed it over the cliff. The strangling cord followed it. I could not trust him not to hang himself. I used my own knife to cut up his tunic, first to tie his hands in front of him, then to bandage the knife wounds in his arms.

"Let me die, Cooper," he ordered as I wiped the tears from his face with a piece of the cloth. "Or kill me." It was only when I saw more drops fall on his skin that I realized I was crying, myself.

I could only stare at him. "I'm not a killer, Tunstall. I'm a Dog—remember? You taught me how to *be* a Dog. We don't kill. We hobble and we let the magistrates decide."

"You know what they'll do," he said, trying to reach the cliff. It must have been agonizing with the pain in his knees, but he would not stop.

"Mattes." The voice was Sabine's, raw and broken. "Is it true?"

He started to roll cliffward, not daring to face her. How could I hate him and pity him at the same time? Feeling dizzy, I went after him and seized the back of his tunic. My right hand lost the grip.

"Here." Nomalla had come out of the shadows on the trail leading a horse. A cut on her forehead had bled on her face and dried, giving her a dark half mask. She took a rope from her saddlebag and looped it around Tunstall's chest, slipping it under his hands and arms, ignoring his face. Fixing it in a knot at his back, she then looped it around her mount's saddle horn and dragged Tunstall to a tree on the far side of the trail. There she tied him, wrapping the rope around him and the tree several times before she secured it with hands that shook.

Then she spat on him.

She looked at me. "We heard most of it. We were afraid to interrupt and risk your getting hurt."

My dizziness was worse. The bandage I had put around my shoulder was soaked with blood. "Just you two?" I asked.

Sabine and Farmer rode forward. Sabine's muddy face showed tear tracks. Farmer's hair was all on end. His tunic was gone. He passed his horse's reins to Sabine and dismounted with a wince, then limped over to me. "She's bleeding," he called to Sabine. "That horse you're riding—it was Dolsa's. There should be medicines in the saddle pack."

"The prince?" Nomalla asked. I glared at her as I leaned on Farmer. I did not trust her any more now than before. Perhaps even less.

Sabine came over with a small pack in one hand, the riding horses, Drummer, and Steady trailing her. "You should have seen Nomalla fight," she told me. "Her father's men cursed her with every swing. You could have learned a word or two. And I too would like to be certain of the boy's well-being."

Farmer picked me up, wincing. "We'll all go together," he said firmly.

This way, Pounce said, a black spot in the grass. *Would you hurry, Farmer? Achoo and I are really quite concerned. It's only because she was ordered to stay with Gareth that Achoo didn't come out to fight herself.*

"Good girl," I whispered. My shoulder hurt. I faded in and out. I remember that Nomalla surrendered a saddle blanket for me to lie on. Sabine gave me a drink of some liquid that set my insides on fire. I slept.

Halleburn Fiefdom

yet recorded in my memory

When I woke in the morning with the sun near ten of the clock, I was surrounded by sleepers. Farmer lay at my side, snoring lightly. Nomalla and Sabine had taken blankets from three more of our stolen horses and slept on them nearby, Sabine with one arm wrapped around Gareth. Pounce and Achoo slept with them.

The horses were picketed nearby. Next to Drummer, who would have announced it if anyone came near who was not Sabine, was Tunstall. He looked gray and old in his bonds. Someone had put wooden splints on both of his legs. I suspected Farmer. Kora always says that mages are selfish at bottom, which made Farmer the exception who proves the rule.

Slowly, clutching the tree near me, I got to my feet. Every move was an ache. Keeping as silent as I could, I hobbled out into the long grass between forest and trail. The dew was still on it, the cool ground a blessing to my poor feet. I was used to running barefoot, not fighting. At the trail, I passed through something like a gauzy curtain. I'd wager that Farmer had found sommat in Dolsa's bags to hide us.

When I turned, the forest looked normal as could be. There was no sign of seven horses or their riders, and no sound of some riders' snores.

I thought I heard thunder, but after a Hunt plagued by rain, there wasn't a cloud in the sky. Slowly I walked to the cliff's edge. By the time I reached it, I realized the boom was too regular to be thunder. It was the steady heartbeat of battle drums.

As I gazed into the valley, I heard someone patter across the trail. I glanced back. Gareth was awake. "Did you tell Lady Sabine where you were going?" I asked. My voice was gravelly, as if I had a cold coming on.

"She said something and went back to sleep," Gareth replied. "I believe she wished me to stay nearby." He tucked his hand into one of mine. "Where must we run to next?" he asked.

"I don't know," I said. "Mayhap things have changed."

We looked down at armies as they circled Halleburn. They were too far distant for me to see their banners.

"Are they for us or against us?" asked the little old man.

"My work is to assume that they are against us until your parents or Lord Gershom order me otherwise," I told him. "We'd best wake the others."

Gareth clung to my hand for a moment. "You will stay with me?"

I knelt and hugged him like I'd hugged my little brothers when they were his size. "Until I give you to your mother like I promised her, I will stay with you," I told him.

By the time I had brought the others to see what was happening in the valley, mages were attacking the walls of Halleburn. Some of their fires only scorched the walls, unless they chanced to hit a window. Then the colored blaze disappeared inside. Some blew chunks from the stone.

Nomalla stood on the cliff, her hands planted on her hips. "I think it's safe to say they aren't on Father's side," she said coldly, as if she did not care about the outcome. She'd taken off her armor last night. Now she looked to be a weary lady of Sabine's years, dressed in a sweat-stained quilted pink tunic and gray breeches. "There's a trail near the tunnel we used. It goes down the cliffside. I could get closer that way, see who's out there."

"I have a better idea." Farmer had stopped to pick up a saddlebag with the letter *D* prettily sewn on it in pearls. He'd opened it up while the rest of us stared wearily at the battlefield. Now he waved a mirror the size of both of my hands, framed in gold. "Dolsa has given us her scrying mirror."

That made me ask, "What did you do with her?"

The two older mots also looked at him. "That's a good question," Sabine murmured. She looked as if the gods had ground her to meal since she'd learned the truth about Tunstall. Her eyes were red from silent weeping.

"I left her in that pasture with the others," Farmer replied, inspecting the mirror back and front.

"Locked up in ice like you did Elyot?" Nomalla asked warily.

"No, no. I improvised with those three," Farmer said. Standing in the sunlight with no tunic on, his chest and back covered with bruises and lash marks, his face cut and swollen in spots, he still looked wonderful to me. "I left them sunk into the pasture up to their chins," Farmer continued between puffs of air as he covered the mirror with steam from his own mouth. "I drained off their power. Orielle seemed concerned that the cows might step on them. I noticed an anthill nearby, but honestly, what can any man do about ants?" He sat cross-legged on the ground and passed his open palm over the mirror. "At least now they can wait to be taken in charge, before enough magic returns to them that they can do more damage."

We all drew near to look on. The mirror went foggy, then cleared to show us a close view of the armies below. Farmer looked first at those on the northwest side of the lake and their banners.

"Korpita, Lisbethan, and Hannalof," Nomalla said, identifying their devices. "They have to have come on at fast march, but how did they know?"

"I reached Cassine while they were taking us to Halleburn," Farmer said quietly. "I used a hole in the power that was supposed to keep me captive." He looked up at me and smiled. "I don't really need a scrying tool to communicate a single word, and that one plainly got through."

"What word?" I asked, curious.

"Halleburn. She was waiting for news of where I was and if I needed help," Farmer explained. "That I sent only one word, when she forever accuses me of chattering, told her I was in trouble."

The image in the mirror shifted to troops on the lake's southwest side. "Those are King's Reach colors on the biggest contingent," Sabine murmured. "Gerry, Fenrigh, Susha. Quicker for some of them, perhaps, because they could use the rivers. Goddess bless us, it's as if the realm has declared war on Halleburn."

Farmer looked up at her. "Halleburn started it. Look at this. It's the King's Reach banner."

The mirror blurred, then cleared. A handsome young squire in gold and purple rode beside an ominous-looking cove all in armor. The squire carried a banner pole with two flags on it. The lower one was that of the Reach, double towers framing an upright sword, both in gold, on a purple field. The upper banner was the silver sword and crown of Tortall on a bright blue field—the flag of the kings of the realm. These warriors had come at the king's request.

The mirror blurred again. "What are you doing?" demanded Nomalla. "I wanted a look at our gates!"

"I want a look at Queensgrace and Aspen Vale," Farmer replied quietly. Nomalla went silent.

An image came into the mirror, a castle in flames, surrounded by the men in the maroon and ivory of the realm's army. "So much for Aspen Vale," Sabine murmured.

"How can you say that?" Nomalla demanded hotly. "They're of our rank, they—"

"Traitors," Sabine told her in a voice like ice. "Or will you sanction child murder now?"

Nomalla looked down and away from Sabine and straight into Gareth's eyes. "I was the one they tried to murder," he told her. "And the wicked man killed Daeggan."

I picked him up and balanced him on my hip, in case Nomalla was actually having second thoughts. I wasn't sure. "They didn't even have the sack to kill this lad clean," I reminded her. "They were killing him day by day, holding off feeding him, then beating him."

Tears overflowed Nomalla's eyes. "I didn't know," she said, and knelt before the prince. "I pledge my blood and service to you in repayment, Your Highness. Whatever you command of me, if you demand my life, I will give it to repay any small measure of the hurt my family has done to you."

"I am a slave," Gareth said, looking at her. "You shoved me once because I was in your way."

"Anyone want a look at Queensgrace?" Farmer asked cheerfully. He broke the ugly tension between my lad and Nomalla. She turned, still on her knees, for a look at the mirror.

I whispered to the prince, "You've learned to hate. Now

you must learn to forgive, or you'll have enemies at your back forever."

He looked me straight in the eyes. "That will be hard."

"The harder the goal, the more important it is," I said, just as I'd told my little brothers that if they wanted to ride the horses, they were going to have to muck out the stables first. "You're a clever lad, aren't you?"

"My tutors say I unnerve them," he replied. "What is Farmer looking at?"

I bent over Farmer's shoulder with Gareth still in my arms. The army, with siege engines, encircled Queensgrace Castle. "Do you remember this place?" I asked Gareth. *I* was remembering the Butterfly Puppies, the cooks Iris and Fay, the lady-in-waiting Lewyth, and even sour-faced Cattran. What would become of them?

"Linnet," Gareth whispered. "And the others. Are they going to die?"

"If the castle surrenders now, the slaves will be taken and sold, I think," I told him quietly. "The servants will work for the new lord, if they wish. Most of the ladies and squires will return to their families, if they had no part in taking you. My lord and lady go to prison, and any who helped them."

"What if the castle doesn't surrender?" Gareth asked.

"Then the army attacks," Nomalla said. "And they attack until the castle *does* surrender."

"Let's hope the castle surrenders," I told the lad. I hugged him close, ignoring my aches, as the mirror blurred again. When it cleared, it showed us the army on the causeway below, armed with a catapult.

"You asked to see the gate," Farmer told Nomalla.

"He's destroyed our house," Nomalla whispered. "Father and his ambition."

We heard a roar below and went to see what had happened. Catapults had struck the wall together, driving gaps near the top, while the one on the road to the castle had been loosed. Whatever the stone was made of, it had smashed through the gate, leaving plenty of room for the knights and soldiers to attack. Sabine put her arm around Nomalla's shoulders as the other lady knight wept.

While everyone watched the fighting in the lands of the three traitorous households, there would be no one to see me weep if I checked on Tunstall. Nobody would call me weak-hearted if I found him something to eat among the packs stolen by Sabine, Farmer, and Nomalla. I should have killed him or let him kill himself the night before. It would have been easy then, when my blood was up and I could only think of the many dead, Rats and innocents, he'd left in our trail. Today I was remembering all that he'd taught me and the way he scratched his head when he was thinking. I was remembering all the good meals we'd had together, and all the Rats we'd hobbled. The thought of taking him to execution was tearing at me.

Farmer had removed the seeming of invisibility from our hiding place. I stepped among the trees and took a deep breath, then sucked up my courage to approach the tree where the horses guarded him. Drummer stepped aside when he saw me. I thought he'd remembered Sabine's instructions at the wayhouse stables, but then I saw Pounce come to put his nose up for Drummer to sniff. It was probably just that I had the constellation along.

In the tree shadows Tunstall looked to be asleep. "Tunstall?" I called softly. "Wake up." He did not stir. "Tunstall?" I walked around the back of the tree to make certain his bonds were still tight, then hunkered down at his side. When I touched him, his head did not move. I tried to lift his arm—his wrists were bound in front of him—but I could not. I could not stir his legs, either. He was fully locked in death.

I heard the flapping of wings. The wood pigeon settled on Tunstall's bound arms. I scrabbled in my pouch, but had naught in the way of pigeon food. In the end Pounce brought me a piece of bread from somewhere.

"You don't have to feed her, you know," Tunstall's voice said from the air. "She will stay until I say what I must."

"Feeding them makes me feel better," I replied, looking down to break up the bread into pigeon-size bites. They can't manage big pieces. "Say what you must, then, will you?"

"I only wanted to be worthy of her," he told me. "By the time I got to understanding that meant betraying you, I was in too deep."

"Me?" I asked bitterly. "What of Lord Gershom? What about Goodwin?"

"One day, lass, you'll be faced with such a choice," he told me. "It won't seem so easy then."

"Who are you lying to now?" I asked him. "Me, or yourself?"

For a moment I thought he'd gone while the bird hopped over to peck at the crumbs. Then he said, "Me. I lie to me."

"When did it happen?" I demanded. "When did they buy you?"

"Cooper, I told you. I told all of you. They took me aside the night of the banquet at Queensgrace," he explained. "Seeing where we sat in that dining hall while she was up above us, knowing they wanted her to marry the prince, all that made me agree when they gave me their offer. I was tired of forever being placed apart from her."

"Don't blame her. She would have married you had you

asked, if she agreed to marry anyone," I snapped. "She adored you, and you betrayed her."

"And you settled the bill, or started me along the path to settling it, Cooper. The chill of the night and the weakness from my hurts, that finished it, but you put me on the path to your god." He sighed. "Tell her I love her and beg her forgiveness, Cooper. And I love you and Goodwin. The pair of you have always been my true sisters."

He was gone for good this time. It helped to know he'd died of the chill and shock, not any direct blow from me. I'd meant to write it up as battle shock and the cold. There's no good to be had from anything else. It was better than a traitor's execution.

It was Farmer and Achoo who came to find me sommat later. Farmer held me as I gave the others the news. Sabine went to see for herself and spent a bit of time there. She had done some thinking when she returned to us.

"The plot is not ended," she announced grimly as we all watched the battle below. "We may be safer, our enemies may be in disarray, but there are still miles between us and the Summer Palace, and there will be soldiers to pass. Lad, you must pretend to be a commoner for now. We'll call you Gary, is that well enough?"

The lad nodded shyly. "As long as I stay with all of you," he said. "Not strangers."

I was kneeling beside him. At this I slung my arm about his shoulder. "We won't leave you until you are safe with your parents," I told him. "Our word on it."

"I'll accompany you," Nomalla said, turning away from the noise and sights below. "You need at least one other warrior between here and there. And I can't watch this." We all knew that she meant the assault on her home.

"I can arrange for friends to meet us between here and there," Farmer added. "Fortunately for me, scrying does not require a great deal of the Gift."

"But we need to get out of here. I want to ensure that these horses do not belong to the villagers," Sabine explained. "If they do, I'll get some from the army, but I'd as soon not call their attention to us."

Farmer looked at me. "I think it's a good idea," I said, my mind on the body in the woods. Farmer nodded to Sabine.

She and I went into the woods to fetch the horses we'd taken from the village. I made a string of them while Sabine knelt by Tunstall's body. She soon came to saddle Steady. As we worked, Nomalla joined her and me, saddling another horse for herself. Once she was mounted, Sabine took the string of borrowed horses in hand. She and Nomalla rode off to the village.

Farmer and I watched them ride away. "I'm going to find Daeggan," Farmer told me. "I'll bring him back here. We'll need to find a way to dig graves. We can't take them with us."

As he strode away, Pounce leaned against my leg. *Leave the graves to Achoo and me,* he said, whacking me with his tail. *You need to rest those bruises and cracked bones.*

"What can you do?" I demanded, following him and Achoo into the tree cover. "Graves must be deep. It's not like Drummer can help, you know. . . ." I stopped talking. Raccoons, pine martens, foxes, wolves, and beavers were busily digging in a clearing near where we'd kept the horses and Tunstall.

Friends, Pounce informed me.

By the time Farmer returned with Daeggan's poor corpse, the animals had finished a grave that would fit the boy and were halfway down a larger one for Tunstall. Before Sabine and Nomalla returned with several more horses than they'd left with, Farmer and I had placed our dead in their graves.

The mots had also brought shovels. After I'd said words over Tunstall and Daeggan, they filled in the graves. Then they thanked the creatures who'd dug them. The animals had waited until the burial was over before leaving. Pounce told us they hadn't been sure that shovels could do a proper job in filling the holes.

Then we prepared to ride out. "I don't understand," Farmer said as he saddled his horse. "They're not too well off in that village, I remember it from last night. I don't understand why they would give you permission to take valuable horses. The owners were criminals—they'll be allowed to keep them."

Nomalla smiled thinly. "They kept more than they gave us, that's why. And before we got there, our enemies hurt some of their people. They thought a few horses was the least they could do."

The villagers wanted no more part of the events of the night before, be it housing the enemy's mounts or keeping custody of the mages trapped in one of their meadows. When we rode back down the path, they stopped us long enough to give us supplies and to ask when we were going to take their enemies away.

I could not believe what I saw in that meadow.

"Get me out of here! There are insects on me!" screeched Orielle, who had once pretended such care and concern for the queen. None of the traitor mages could even move their heads.

Sabine rode over to the fence and looked at her. "I can change that, but you won't like what I change your situation to," she said gently. Orielle went white under the dirt and cow dung that blotched her face. "I thought not," Sabine remarked. "You may wait here until the Earl of King's Reach sends mages to take charge of you. I asked one of the villagers to carry a letter to him. Of course, it will be all day for the messenger to find the earl, since he's busy assaulting Halleburn just now. I hope you don't mind a touch of sunburn." She turned her mount and rode on.

"Don't look at me," Farmer said to them as we passed the mages by. "Sabine's in charge now."

Dolsa screamed, "What did you do with our power, you lowborn cur?!"

Farmer gave her his sweetest smile. "I took it. Every last drop. I'll put it to far better use than you did." He looked at Ironwood. "Have you any blessings to give, before we turn you over to the Crown magistrate?"

Ironwood gave us a brief shake of the head. He was well and truly broken.

Farmer looked at Gareth, who rode on the saddle in front of me. "Lad, have you anything to say to these traitors? You are the one they harmed most." Gareth too shook his head. "You're probably right," said Farmer. "They really aren't worth talking to, are they?" Gareth smiled and shook his head a second time. "Even a four-year-old can see it," Farmer told the air. On we went, leaving Dolsa and Orielle to screech behind us.

The village had seemed tranquil enough, but on the path between it and the Great Road, we were stopped five times by the army's outposts. They delayed us so much that we had to make camp on the northern side of the Black Griffin Bridge. We had a few comforts, thanks to the guards on that side. They showed us to a clearing used often by other travelers. There was a small shed with a good supply of dry wood and kindling.

We even had a stream where we could get water and bathe. The guards shared their ale with Farmer, Sabine, and Nomalla. I feared I would weep if I had spirits, so the lad and I drank water.

Two days later, Farmer shared the news from his evening's scrying. Thanen had surrendered Halleburn Castle. Stripped of his greatest mages, under bombardment by royal mages as well as an army, and knowing his allies had already fallen, he leaped from the tallest height in the castle. The coward left his family and remaining allies to face the royal courts.

In the morning, traveling the gauntlet of outposts along the road to the fallen Queensgrace, I let Prince Gary ride with my companions. With room on my saddle once again, I began the long task of writing out my reports.

Sunday, July 1, 249

Mistress Trout's Lodgings
Nipcopper Close, Corus
We had spent the night of the 30th on the Great Road where it met the way to Queensgrace. We had to decide how we could return to the Summer Palace without having to deal with the marsh. In the morning we were just riding onto the Great Road when we saw the much larger party that was coming toward us. Soldiers in army uniforms encircled an enclosed cart. Their weapons were very good, their clothes and boots expensive. The cart itself was newly painted, with shutters over the side windows. At the head of the party rode a mot in pale blue whose pale blue scarf covered most of her light blond hair.

Seeing us, she turned and rode back to the cart. She stopped beside it and leaned down to talk through the window.

A door popped open on the side and another mot nearly fell to the ground in her rush to get out. The queen steadied herself, then ran through the soldiers, clutching a gold-spangled veil over unruly curls. She even lost the veil as she drew close to us and flung her arms wide.

"Gareth!" the queen shrieked. Nomalla, his riding companion that morning, set the boy on the ground so he could get to his mama. Her Majesty stumbled and dropped to her knees in the dirt, where they clutched each other. The others and I dismounted and stood off at a respectful distance. The queen looked little better than her son. Her face was but skin over bone, and what I could see of her arms told me she'd lost flesh there, too. I wondered how many more days she would have lived if we hadn't found Gareth.

"Cooper?" she said at last, looking at me over Gareth's shoulder. She reached a hand out to me. "Cooper, what happened to you?"

I hand-signaled for Pounce and Achoo to come with me as I walked over to her and Gareth. "Just Dog work, Your Majesty," I said, getting on my knees with a wince. "Farmer and Achoo and Pounce and Lady Sabine—she was brought in after I saw you—and Lady Nomalla, they took a pounding as well."

"What of Tunstall?" she asked. "Was he—is he all right?"

I couldn't answer her, but hung my head in shame. It was Gareth who said, "He betrayed us, Mama."

Achoo whimpered and licked Gareth's hand. My hound had been mourning her old friend, too.

"I am so very sorry," whispered the queen. "That's the problem with royalty, isn't it? The stakes are just too high. People do things for royal stakes they would never dream of at home." She touched my cheek. "Goddess bless you, Cooper, all the days of your life. And you, Pounce, and Achoo." She sighed. "Cooper, would you give me your arm? Gareth, you may introduce me to the lady knights, if you will."

As I scrambled to my feet so I could help the queen, she murmured to me, "The healers were very unhappy with me for coming, but I had to see my lad." She kept hold of one of Gareth's hands. "His Majesty is still too ill to move. Cassine says that when we three are together, she can undo the spell that hurts us so."

I escorted her to Lady Sabine and Lady Nomalla. Farmer was busily talking with the woman who had told the queen of us. Finally the captain in charge of the queen's party asked us if we could retreat to a nearby hilltop to talk, a place where he and his soldiers could see anyone who approached. While Her

Majesty sat on the grass with the lady knights and the prince, Farmer came to collect me. I went, but my knees were unsteady. What if Cassine did not like me? What if she thought the partner of a traitor must surely be a traitor herself? From the way Farmer spoke of her, the great mage was a second mother to him. Her opinion meant a great deal to me.

She watched as we approached. She had removed her veil. The sun shone on silver-gold hair cut ear-length like a man's. She was as tall as me but slender as a willow, with bright blue eyes and a very pretty smile. When she took my hand, her smile broadened until she was chuckling.

Farmer scowled. *"Cassine,"* he said with reproof.

She covered her mouth with a fine-boned hand and turned her chuckle into a cough. When she caught her breath, she squeezed my hand, which she still held. "He's told me for years that girls aren't as interesting as magic. I always said that one day he would find a woman who would be just as interesting. Now he has, and I don't believe either of us conceived of that woman being anyone like you!"

I scowled, unable to help it. "That don't sound good."

"Oh, no," Cassine protested as she hugged me. "It is! If he's going to *insist* on being a Dogs' mage, what better wife than another Dog?" She smelled of lily of the valley, and though I hugged her with care because I thought her fragile, I learned there was steel under her soft skin and her soft voice.

I could feel myself blush. "That was our plan," I mumbled.

Cassine placed a gentle hand on my shoulder. "Very good, my dear," she told me softly. "I couldn't arrange better myself."

Mistress Trout's Lodgings
Nipcopper Close, Corus
With the queen and her prince reunited, I feel no need to write further of our return home. We did indeed have to take a longer route, on down the Great Road to its meeting with the Great Road East, then east to the palace in Corus. His Majesty and Lord Gershom met us there.

I don't know what I would have done without Farmer. He and Cassine were good friends to Sabine and me alike. The lad—Prince Gareth—was a comfort, too. His mother graciously let him ride with me for a bit in the afternoons.

Sabine and I didn't speak to anyone but Farmer about Tunstall. If Gareth spoke to the queen of him, she said naught. That was a great kindness in itself.

The worst on our arrival was having to tell Lord Gershom and Goodwin what Tunstall had done. Even knowing his motive, that he'd wished to be worthy of Lady Sabine, did not make the news easier for my lord and Goodwin.

Sabine's and my friends in Corus held a farewell to Tunstall once we told them he'd died during our Hunt. If anyone had questions, the grief on Sabine's face, the chill in Goodwin's voice, and the shadow over me kept them from asking. The farewell was a lively thing, with many of the city's Rats and Dogs each relating their own story of Tunstall. I laughed and cried, remembering the partner who had taught me so much while I tried to forget his last acts.

Next to be endured were the trials. It was then that we learned two of the Dog teams assembled after we left Corus had found evidence that Aspen Vale, Queensgrace, Halleburn, and several other great families had taken part in the plot. Individual nobles who had supported the conspiracy were named, as were mages, slave traffickers, and shipping companies. All the realm was ever told was that a plot for treason had been unraveled, and that those involved would be revealed in the lists of those to be executed. The Chambers of Law at the palace were closed to visitors.

Witnesses came from all over Tortall to testify. Listening to them, we learned that all information, weapons, and money that had not gone by mage or messenger bird had gone by slave caravan. We heard that over a hundred palace slaves were part of the plot, bribed with freedom or bound with magic. As I had seen, no one cared about slaves, so they could go everywhere.

A mage disguised as Lazamon's own apprentice murdered the Mage Chancellor. It was not done with magic, but with a strangler's cord. Only when Lazamon's real apprentice went to wake him in the morning was the murder discovered.

Slaves and slave traders gave testimony before and after lords and mages. Dogs and soldiers answered the nine judges' questions as mages chosen by the head of the Mithran temple and the temple of the Great Goddess weighed the truth of the witnesses' words. Time and time again Farmer, Sabine, Nomalla, and I were called to tell what we knew.

Even Gareth was called. The poor lad was frightened when his day came. Rather than let him sit in the hold of one of his parents and have a judge claim they told him what to say, they allowed me to stand at his left at his request, so he might hold my hand if he wished it. Achoo stood on his right, while Pounce sat on his lap, his purple eyes veiled to save us all from an accusation of more magecraft. With us to reassure him, Gareth told his tale. It made a number of the great ones who were in attendance blanch as he described the attack on the Summer Palace, his life as a slave, and the murders of the Viper, her slaves, and her guards. His tale took three days, with the judges' questions.

At the end of Gareth's testimony, Farmer, Sabine, Pounce, Achoo, and I were granted the honor of escorting His Highness and the queen back to the palace. We were not needed, of course. A tight guard of the King's Own encircled us all the way to the steps, where we were allowed to kiss the prince's hand in farewell. Looking sad, he hugged Achoo and Pounce. Then he and his mother walked into the palace.

The trials ended. When they did, the executions began. I attended those of the traitors I had helped to capture. Sabine, Nomalla, and Farmer went with me. When the day was done and the dead were left swinging or smoking, depending upon the magistrates' judgment, Rosto, Aniki, Kora, and our other friends of the Court of the Rogue would collect us, take us back to the Dancing Dove, and do all in their power to make us feel less like murderers.

I think most of Corus and half of Port Caynn came to the execution of Prince Baird before the palace gates on the fourteenth. It's not often a king's son is beheaded for treason to the Crown. It had been decided by the king and the Lord High Magistrate that, since Prince Baird had not led the conspiracy based on the evidence, he would not be forced to endure being hanged, drawn, and quartered, as the other nobles had. Once it was done, his head was placed over the main palace gate as a warning to others with ambition.

I did not attend. I was tired of death.

Today we were summoned to the palace at one hour after noon and warned beforetime to dress in our best. Since our arrival in Corus, I had discovered that Farmer liked expensive clothes. He had money with bankers in Corus, Port Caynn, and Frasrlund, and he liked to spend it. When I returned from an early-morning visit to the bathhouse, I found my man dressed in a pale blue silk tunic and breeches, wearing new sandals.

"I'll look like a crow next to you," I said as I took off the clothes I'd worn from the bathhouse.

"I've always noticed how glossy crows are," he said, pointing to the bed. There lay a proper Dog's uniform, but it was all silk, a dress uniform like the richer Dogs and district commanders had. "Don't look at *me* this time," he said when I glared at him. "That came from Lord Gershom. He said to tell you that your sisters made it with pride."

I gazed at it, swallowing a lump in my throat. While my sisters had found a way to live with my choice of work, Diona at least never said she was proud of me before. Yet I knew Lord Gershom. He would not have sent that message unless it was true.

I set about doing my hair up in its usual braid, but Farmer would have none of it. He loved to comb my hair almost as much as he loved taking it out of its braid at night. I thought mayhap it was weak of me to enjoy being waited on in such a way, but it was so soothing. Pounce watched, as he always did, and said, *You would make a good cat, Beka.*

"I don't know," I said. "Folk are forever naming me for dogs, remember?" I smiled at Achoo, who dozed under the window. "At least they haven't found a name for me this time!"

Farmer set down his comb, done with my hair. "Smooth like silk," he told me, kissing the top of my head. "I added a little, if you don't mind." He swung the braid over my shoulder so I could look. He'd replaced my usual spiked strap of leather. I now had a thin silver chain wound in my braid. It was dotted with crystal ovals that flashed a deep blue. "Rainbow moonstones," he said. "Not incredibly expensive, so don't scowl at me."

I loved them. Turn them one way and they were plain white crystal. Turn them another and the blue shot across them. "They'll clash with my fire opal earrings," I told him.

Farmer handed me two earrings, also rainbow moonstones. I struggled to lecture him on spending, and gave up. I couldn't refuse them. They were too lovely. "You're spoiling me," I scolded as I hooked them in my ears.

"Good," he said, taking one of my hands and kissing my palm. I melt when he does that. "I want to spoil you for a very, very long time. And speaking of spending and spoiling, I found a bigger place. It's just on the edge of Upmarket, so you won't have far to walk to Jane Street. Will you look at it with me tomorrow?"

"But why don't you buy it for yourself?" I asked, facing him. "You don't need me to do that."

He sat on the bed next to my chair and took my hands. "But, dear one, I don't want to buy it for myself. I want to marry you and bring you there as my wife." He kissed my palms. "If you're worried that I have no work, Gershom has assigned me to the Waterfront District kennel. I'll bring in a purse of my own."

I realized the important part of what he had said to me. "Y-you want to g-get m-m-married *soon*." My old enemy, my stutter, had come back in force.

"I thought Midwinter would be nice. Or we could do it at All Hallow, and you could invite the god." He looked like Achoo at her most hopeful, his eyes wide and shining. His hands were warm and firm around mine. This was not like Holborn's proposal, when he was giddy with victory after a hard hobbling that we'd shared, and we'd swived together like two wild things in a dark alley. This was so different. I'd thought Farmer had reconsidered after that mad time in the dungeon, since he hadn't spoken of it since. This wasn't the kind of thing that would burn hot and be gone. "I'm no mage," I reminded him.

"But you're calm around mage things, sweetheart," he said, tugging gently on one of my earrings. "And *you* have *your* little oddities. Yesterday you stood in the middle of a dust spinner for half an hour and talked to it. I had to tell folk you were taking a dust bath."

"A dust bath!" I cried. "Like I was a pigeon, by all the gods!"

Farmer grinned. "I was reading a whilst I waited. It was the quickest explanation that would make them go away."

Will you just agree to your wedding? Pounce demanded from his napping place on our pillows. *The gods have summoned me for my punishment by Midwinter, and I want to be there.*

"Your *punishment?*" we both cried at the same time.

I told you they would get to it, sooner or later, Pounce replied, as if the gods were inviting him to a small supper. *It would be far worse had you not saved Gareth's life and—well, other great things will come of it.*

"What other things?" I demanded.

It is forbidden for me to tell, Pounce replied at his smuggest.

I made a rude gesture at him. I would not worry about one of his mysterious hints, not now. "And Sabine or Farmer would have saved Gareth."

"I don't think so," Farmer murmured. "Tunstall would have had him, and killed him, by the time we got there."

With the good to the realm, my punishment has been

reduced to a century away from humans, Pounce said. *And I am being allowed to remain for the wedding. So pick a day for it.*

"All Hallow?" Farmer asked. "In case your god wants to come? So what if he scares all the guests?"

"All Hallow," I said.

He kissed me, then drew a breath. "There is one thing," he said. I waited. With some men it might be a babe born out of wedlock, or debts, or madness in the family. With him I knew better even than to guess. "I don't want you to take my name," he said. "I want to take your name."

"You want to take *my* name," I repeated, to be sure. "I've never heard of such a thing."

"I hate Cape for a last name," he explained. "I took it for a mage name, but it confuses folk and it means nothing, really. Cooper is a good name, even if you aren't a barrel maker."

"If Cape wasn't your last name, what was your real one?" I asked, deathly curious now.

"Ahhhh," he complained. "Pincas Huckleburr."

After waiting and picking me up and throwing a cup of water on me didn't stop my laughter—I could see my big, sleepy-eyed man as one of those burs with the hooks on the end that had to be worked out of clothes—Farmer resorted to wanton kissing. That worked. I am much in favor of wanton kissing and other things.

Eventually, with Pounce to remind us, we finished getting ready for whatever it was we had to do at the palace. When we left Mistress Trout's, we discovered that horsemen had come for us, with spares for us to ride. Lord Gershom led them.

"You two look very fine," he said with approval as we mounted up. Then he eyed Farmer's beaming face and then me, whereupon I blushed and looked down. "Mithros's spear, what happened?"

Farmer looked at me. Plainly he was leaving me to say what I did, "We're to be married, my lord, on All Hallow."

Handshakes would not do for my lord then. We had to dismount, me to be hugged, Farmer to be slapped on the back, then me to be spun around in the air. At last my lord said with alarm, "You're not quitting me, either of you? You're too good to go now!"

Farmer and I reassured him that we meant to continue our work without change, as the head of our escort got us back on our horses and on our way to the palace. "This works out well," Lord Gershom said as we trotted onto the green stretch before the wall. "Farmer will be available for emergencies, and you—"

"Continue in the Lower City, please, my lord," I said. "I belong there. It's my home."

"You could have anything you want," Lord Gershom said. "From me or Their Majesties. Surely you know that."

I shook my head. Farmer sighed. "She likes fire opals and Sirajit opals," he said. "If you are thinking of a gift."

"I did my duty!" I cried. "That's good enough. And you and Sabine and Nomalla and Achoo—" I looked at my lord. "If I could be assured that Achoo's health could be overseen by the city's best houndsman, that would be wonderful," I told him. "And if she could have a suitable mate? She is getting old for a first litter, and I promised her."

Lord Gershom's mustache twitched downward. I knew he was covering a smile. "So we'll grant something for the others of your Hunt and Achoo, but naught for yourself. Luckily you have Farmer and me to watch out for you, Beka. I've arranged palace places for your brothers and sisters. A royal courier's place for Nilo, since he is already a palace rider, and situations for your sisters among the queen's seamstresses. Willes will be a courier for the Lord High Magistrate. And the house that Farmer has looked at thrice already has been purchased in his name. Give the orders for any changes and repairs you wish to my secretary, Farmer. He will see they're done, and he will give you the papers of ownership. The Crown pays for all, as it pays for the four horses you now own."

"You think I'll be doing a lot of riding?" Farmer said wistfully, looking at me.

"You both will be doing a great deal of riding. I've already been presented with three requests for your services and Beka's from lords who have been in attendance at the trials," Lord Gershom said as we rode through the palace gates. "Be grateful it is not more. I told them Beka would not accept it. They will come to you with other offers, Farmer."

I looked up at my lord with gratitude. I had my man, Gareth and Sabine were safe, the conspiracy was overthrown. What more could a mot want?

Our escort led us through the main courtyards to the one before the Hall of Crowns, where stable hands in clean garments decorated with a royal badge took our mounts. I began to get very nervous. After we'd dismounted and straightened our clothes, I asked Lord Gershom, "Does Nomalla get a reward?"

"She gets her life," he said, in that iron way of his that meant she ought to be glad for that much. Given that I'd seen her mother, uncles, aunts, and brothers die for their part in the treason, I thought he might be right. After a moment, he added, "And she gets to work in the service of the Crown, on the Scanran border. She'll redeem herself there, of that I'm certain."

A squire in colors and a badge I didn't recognize came to us and led us through a door in the wing that led to the hall, not into the hall itself. I'd had a glimpse of the hall once, when Gareth was born and named. It was huge, a great chamber terraced in stone for seats, where everyone present could see what took place on the stage. Here our kings were crowned and their children presented to the nobles, mages, religious folk, and guild leaders. Above the seats the doors formed sections of the entire back wall, so they might be folded back and the common folk given a look at the doings of the great. I heard that every time the hall was opened, those whose work it was to guard Their Majesties and their children got headaches.

The squire turned right as we entered the palace. The soldiers standing guard inside the door tried to halt Achoo and Pounce, but Lord Gershom put out his hand. "Where she goes, they go."

They stared at him, then snapped up into their positions, staring blankly ahead.

I frowned at my lord. "Sir, what is going on?"

Gershom smiled at me. "Beka, I have proceeded along the lines that if I told you more, you would panic and flee."

I was starting to get a very bad feeling.

"You see?" asked Lord Gershom as if I had spoken. "The less you know, the happier you are. Just remember, when the time comes, how proud your mama would be."

We entered a room *very* like that where Sabine and I had been stripped, back at Halleburn. There were screens so folk could change garments privately and actual glass mirrors on the walls.

Sabine was already there in new armor polished to a mirror shine of its own. Her curling hair framed her face. It was braided and ornamented with ruby-headed pins instead of her own spiked strap. She wore ruby earrings, too. She looked at us and smiled wryly. "All done up like Midwinter geese, aren't we?"

"Beka said yes to a day," Farmer told her.

The lady's face filled with cheer. She rose from her chair and, despite her armor, insisted on hugging us both. Then she had to give Achoo a treat and Pounce a pet. "Can I come to the wedding?" she asked. "I promise not to clank."

"We wouldn't hold it without you," Farmer said, and I nodded. I wouldn't tell any of them yet, but I hoped the lady would be godsmother to our first child.

The door to the chamber opened again, this time to admit Her Majesty and the prince. We all scrambled to kneel before the queen. She took each of our hands and raised us to stand.

Gareth beamed up at me and beckoned. I knelt before him. I think that no one was more surprised than me when he hugged me about the neck. "I miss you," he whispered in my ear.

I cleared my throat, which tightened up, then returned his clasp. "I miss you," I replied.

The other door in the chamber, the one which had not opened before, did so now. Yet another squire bowed deep to the queen. She made signs to us about the order in which we were to follow her. The queen entered the hall beyond, followed by Sabine, then Farmer.

I looked out and balked. That was the Hall of Crowns, far worse than the Jane Street magistrate's courtroom. By the little I could see from where I was, it was jammed full of persons in silks trimmed in gold, silver, and jewels. These were not my sort of folk at all.

Gareth took my hand. "I know," my little old man told

me. "I don't like it, either. Mama says it helps if I imagine them all in their loincloths."

The thought horrified me. Folk don't look nearly as good unclothed as they think they do. "Does it help?" I asked him.

"No, but I tell Mama it does so she can be happy," he explained.

I couldn't help it, even though he is our prince. I bent and kissed his head. "You're a good lad, Gareth the Strong," I told him.

"You think I'm strong?" he asked.

"I know you are," I said.

"I learned it from you. Let us show them," he replied, trapping me neatly. Together, with Achoo beside me and Pounce ahead of us, we walked out onto the great stone stage to stand with Farmer and Sabine. To do so we had to pass behind the royal thrones where the king and queen now sat, and behind my friends. I thought Gareth would sit with his parents, but he shook his head when I asked. "They told me to stay with you."

Once we had settled in place, the king spoke. "Those of you who attended the recent trials and executions know that a great conspiracy against our throne was uncovered," said His Majesty. "In this dread time, a small handful of people saved the lives of our person, Her Majesty, and our son. Prince Gareth was kidnapped and made a slave."

There were shouts of genuine fear and outrage. People called out, "Gods save Your Majesties!" and "Gods save His Highness!"

"We trusted in our old friend Gershom of Haryse, now Count of Yolen," King Roger continued gravely. "Count Gershom called together a team of Hunters to trail our son's kidnappers and to bring him home. While other faithful teams from the Provost's Guard ranged over the realm, gathering facts and arresting those who plotted against our throne, these Hunters found His Highness and returned him to his proper place. Lady Sabine of Macayhill, come to us."

The lady walked forward as the king stood by his throne and drew his sword. In that great hall there was only silence. "Kneel," ordered the king, and she obeyed. "Sabine of Macayhill, I create thee Lady of Princehold, that was formerly Queensgrace, with ownership of all its lands and grants," the king said, his voice ringing everywhere in the chamber. "These lands and grants, together with the title, go to you and your heirs in evidence of the gratitude held by the house of Conté for your service in this dark time." Sabine looked up at him. I saw her mouth move, but the king only smiled at her. "In addition, I ask you to take charge of the guard assigned to the persons of His Highness Prince Gareth and any other children of the royal family. Will you guard our children, Lord Sabine? Will you protect them as you protected Prince Gareth?"

I heard Gareth whispering, "*Please* say yes, lady, please, *please!*"

I don't know if Sabine heard him, but she nodded to the king. He tapped her shoulders lightly with his sword and said, "Then rise, Sabine of Princehold and Macayhill, Lady Captain of the Household Guard!"

Sabine got to her feet, bowed to the king, then the queen, then Gareth. Shakily, she went to stand at Gareth's back. I thought my heart would burst, I was so glad for her. She had fought long and hard for the Crown. Now at last she had a post where the best healers would look after her knees, her shoulders, and her back, and Gareth would have a friend he could trust in his guard.

"Farmer—" the king began.

"Cooper," my man said firmly, walking over to kneel before the king.

"Farmer Cooper, then," said the king, raising an eyebrow at me. "You did many fine deeds of magic in the Hunt to find our son and keep him alive. You did not accept the post of Chancellor of Mages, which Cassine Catfoot has taken up for the time being. You have accepted only humble work for the Provost's Guard. Will you agree to help the royal mages screen those mages who come to work in Corus, with a proper gift from the treasury for your aid?"

"I will and I thank you, Sire," Farmer said.

"Will you accept, with our thanks, this deed to lands, including the property you have recently purchased, for a city block in Corus? Property always helps a man in the world," the king said, handing Farmer a document with seals on it. "Even more so when he is about to marry."

I swear I saw the king wink at Farmer.

Farmer stood, did his bows, and looked back to join me, but Lord Gershom gestured for him to stand with Sabine.

Then His Majesty picked up a large document edged in gold, dripping gold seals on ribbons, and faced the hall rather than calling me forward. Gareth, to my surprise, wrapped both hands around my arm and hugged it tight. I knelt beside him, wondering what had him so excited. He latched on to my neck in reply as our hounds and Pounce moved closer to us.

"The third member of this group has asked for very little for herself, and we are told she is uncomfortable before crowds," said the king. "But I have read her reports." He took a deep breath. To my shock I realized *he* was shaking. "We read them, and we asked our son, whose life she saved, what he thought she would like. He said that she wanted the same thing that he did. And when he told us what became of other slaves, of their lives, we found ourselves disgusted. This is not the way people should live, in want and fear. No one deserves to be thrown away as refuse. All are equal in the Black God's eyes.

"Throughout this, we have seen one thing over and over," the king told them. "Messages, armed men, and weapons have traveled this land with the slave caravans. Spies disguised as slaves have been found in the great houses of the realm. Our enemies used the slave trade to disguise their activities. Several of those found guilty held shares in the slave trade and used the caravans and their ability to buy and sell slaves to plant enemies everywhere, even here.

"And it was money from the trade that paid for this. The mages came because they had grievances with the Crown. Others came because they were offered the gold that comes from buying and selling men and women. Over and over our son's kidnappers told him that if he was not good, he would be branded. Anyone who was kind to him was sold or murdered. He was whipped like a slave, slapped like a slave, starved like a slave."

The queen had her handkerchief out. The room was deathly silent. Looking around, I suddenly realized there were soldiers all along the walls. Where I could see in the crowd, I suddenly found faces I knew from the Afternoon Shift in nearly every district in Corus. They were planted carefully, like seeds—to spy on the audience should they attack Their Majesties even now?

The king unrolled his document. "As of the first day of

October, all slave traders will leave Tortall. From that time forward, there will be no selling of slaves within our borders unless the sale is to reunite families and has been approved by a Crown magistrate. All slaves may buy their freedom, as has been the custom, or they may remain with their owners until their deaths. No owner may cast a slave out. All slaves who choose to remain slaves must be cared for during their lifetimes. Those families who have made income from the trade may negotiate with the Crown for loans depending on their plans for a new trade. And as of the spring equinox, 250, no child under the age of ten may be a slave. Owners must find a trade for these young slaves to learn or face a visit from the Crown's representatives. In time, as older slaves go to the Black God, we will have no slaves in Tortall." He lowered the document. "Some of you will feel unfairly punished for the misdeeds of others. The Crown is not trying to beggar you. We will do what we can to help. But the *keeping* of slaves beggars many lesser nobles and well-to-do tradesmen. We do not have the great farms of Maren and Carthak where they may work. Many evils take place under the canopy of slavery, including the banditry and piracy that plague our mountains and seas. This trade may go elsewhere. Let other monarchs deal with its mischief. I hope they can protect their children from it. Prince Gareth, and Rebakah Cooper!"

I jumped, I was so startled. Gareth steadied me as I got to my feet. He whispered, "You're far better for me to think of than loincloths."

I bent to straighten my boot and whisper, "Thank you—I *don't* think."

He giggled. He actually giggled.

A squire stood beside the king with a quill pen and an ink

bottle. Another had brought forward a small table to set before him. Next to the queen stood the Lord High Magistrate.

"We sign this proclamation of the end of slavery in this realm," King Roger announced. He dipped the quill in the ink and signed his name at the bottom. "And now Prince Gareth, who is a clever lad and already knows how to write, will sign as witness." He dipped the quill again and offered it to his son. Gravely Gareth took it and signed his name, one letter at a time. I leaned on Achoo, barely able to stand, I was so nervous. I was also awed by Gareth. I didn't know any other four-year-olds who could write. He's going to be something when he is king.

"And for my second witness, Rebakah Cooper," announced the king. He dipped the quill in the ink and offered it to me. "It is she who found His Highness among his kidnappers and brought him out of captivity."

I thought I was going to faint. Then Gareth said, "Loincloths." His father looked at him oddly, but it woke me up. I smiled at him and carefully wrote my name below his.

Then came fiddly parts with wax seals and the Lord High Magistrate wielding the Crown stamp. Gareth and I stepped back with Achoo. Pounce settled on my feet as soon as I was in place. He purred and purred, which kept me from throwing up or falling. I could see scowls on many faces, too many. This wouldn't go down well.

And yet—"We did it, Beka!" Gareth whispered as the king was talking about heralds to ride throughout the land with copies for the lords and the guilds, and copies to be read in the streets. "We did it! We got Papa to end slavery!"

I could have told him that his father couldn't have done it without the outrage from the plot against the royal family. I even could have said his papa had a real fight ahead of him. Nobles didn't give up money so easily. In the Lower City there would be some parents with something to say to me, and it would not be "The Gentle Mother prays for you." How could they make extra coin if they couldn't sell their children?

I felt Farmer's big hands settle on my shoulders, steadying me, as I began to grin. There it was, and I would never forget it. This king, and his son, had stopped the sale of children. That was something for one Dog to be part of, wasn't it?

His Majesty had finished. He and the queen were rising to the reluctant cheers of the crowd. Too many, I'd wager, were counting the cost to their purses.

Then I saw Holborn's old partner stand, his fist in the air. "Cooper the Mastiff!" he cried. "Cooper the Mastiff!"

In pairs and groups the Dogs tucked into the great hall got to their feet. "Mastiff!" they shouted. "Cooper the Mastiff!"

Other people stood, their fists in the air, shouting, "Mastiff! Mastiff!"

Their Majesties glanced at me. "You have a new nickname," His Majesty said with a grin. "And well deserved." I bowed and said nothing. The king knew my nickname!

Gareth came to me and took my hand. Now most of them were chanting the name. Farmer took my free hand and kissed it. "Courage, dearest," he murmured in my ear. "It will die down—in a year or three."

"I hope so," I told Farmer, turning my face up toward his. "Elsewise you'll have one wrinkly wife. Have you ever seen a mastiff?"

The shouting continued even after we'd left that stage. As we returned home, we were surrounded by folk crying the name. Even Rosto used it, jokingly, when all of us came together for supper that evening.

It wasn't until Pounce, Achoo, and I were alone in my room tonight after Farmer went for a walk that I had a chance to finish this journal. I will keep no more after this. Reports I will write, but no private journal. What kind of hobbling could I do that is greater? It is better that I stop now, so my descendants will have only great things to read of me.

And the slaves will be free, all of them, by my grandchildren's time. That is better even than any hobbling.

Epilogue

FROM THE JOURNAL OF
GEORGE COOPER, ROGUE OF TORTALL

January 2, 430 H.E.

The Dancing Dove
Corus, Tortall

Ma patched me up well enough after my fight with old Garsay, though I swear she made the stitching harder than it need be. She brewed the blood-fixing tea good and strong and stood over me while I drank every drop.

"Why didn't you go to one of the better mage-healers?" she asked, folding her arms as she looked at me. "You can afford to do so, now that you're the Rogue. They'll beg for your business."

I slung my unsewn arm around her waist and gave her a squeeze. "Now who's going to look after me better than my old ma?" I asked her. "Family's family, when all's said and done."

"You mean you don't know who you can trust," she told me. "You're the Rogue now, with the old Rogue's blood on your hands. Every young buck that thinks you're weak will be looking to fight you as you did Garsay. And the first folk they'll want to help them are the healers."

I was hurt. "I've folk I'd trust with my life, and they'd trust me with theirs. You don't get to this point alone, Ma. And that reminds me, I was thinking there's a nice little house up on Meadowsweet Way, with plenty of room for a garden—"

"No," she said, her voice flat. "You may call yourself King of the Rogues, and have gold in your pocket, but I'll take none of it. I do well enough on my own. I won't cast you out. We only have each other, after all. But don't expect me to give you my blessing. You've shamed our great ancestress and all she stood for, all *I* stand for."

"Ma, not this again," I complained.

But her eyes had gone black clean through. She seemed

far taller, with long, waving black hair and arms wound with snakes. I wasn't there with my ma anymore. The Goddess, my mother's Great Goddess, was putting her nose in my business. "Do you think it will be easy now? There will come a day when you will wake and sleep with regret and shame over this path you have chosen. Those you thought loyal will betray you. Your entire life will be upended. Your future is nothing you have dreamed, and the fit will not be a comfortable one. I would say you will be miserable until the end, but you are a scamp, and I love your mother. Still, you will have a love that will stick you like pins."

She gave me the chills. The Goddess has only taken Ma twice that I know of. This is the first time I've heard that god-voice turned at me, and I don't like it. The Trickster is god enough for me. Let her god stay out of my life.

When the otherworld look faded from her eyes, I stood, trying not to show how much it cost me with all my cuts and bruises. She sat on a chair with me helping her. "Take care, Mother," I said, and kissed her cheek. I chose not to tell her about the guards I was moving into the lodgings and houses around her. No one would try to make me kneel with threats to my family, as Garsay had made the Rogue before him do.

I stopped at the shrine beside the door. I ignored the Mother Goddess figure. She frowned at me in any case. My business was with the family shrine. All the way at the top was ancestress Rebakah and her black cat. I quickly replaced them with copies I'd had made, and tucked the real ones in my pocket. I meant to put them up where my honored Provost's Guard ancestress could watch her descendant, the Rogue of all Tortall. It is a joke I've been laughing over for years and hope to laugh over for many more.

* * *

Proud of himself, limping only a little from his ferocious battle with the former King of Thieves, George Cooper left his mother's house and sauntered down the street. Two fellows, both carrying swords, joined him on either side. Ahead of him and behind him, other guards took their places, ensuring that no one decided to attack the newest thief-king while he was still recovering from his rise to the throne.

In the shadows of an alley ahead, a purple-eyed black cat watched George Cooper approach.

You are indeed a clever fellow, Pounce—who would one day soon be called Faithful, and had many more names besides—thought as he watched the youngest Rogue in all Tortallan history saunter along. *And your cleverness will be much needed in the time to come. But it does not serve my wishes that you remember that your Beka's counselor was a purple-eyed black cat. You're wary of god-touched people, and the sight of me might scare you away from the one who will upend your life. So—forget the purple eyes, George Cooper. Your ancestress had a black cat that went everywhere with her. No more, no less.*

May 24, 430 H.E.

The Dancing Dove

Corus, Tortall

I write with the figure of the old huntress's cat watching me. I used to think there was something odd about it, something almost magical, but no. It's just a very well-made carving of a black cat. Whoever cut it even made the tiny face look a bit clever. Of late I've gotten in the habit of carrying it with me in my pocket. Ancestress Rebakah has her shelf high over my head, but I don't think she grudges the cat's company to me.

I met the oddest little fellow today, Alan of Trebond. He's come to start as a page at the palace. He's got a tough oak burl for a minder, Coram Smythesson. That one's a smith and former soldier and no fool at all. He warned young Alan I'm a thief. The lad, being full of spirit and sauce, didn't mind that at all. My Sight was all around him, making him glow like fire. There's something about him. . . . I think we might do one another good. I told him so. It's laughable, a little lord like that and me doing good for each other, but my Sight doesn't steer me wrong.

He's a redhead. I hope it's true, about redheads and tempers. He'll need one, the way those pages and squires pick on each other. And he's got purple eyes. I never saw the like.

* * *

On his desk, in the pits that served the cat figure as eyes, twin sparks of purple glowed, then vanished.

Cast of Characters

Rebakah Cooper (Beka)	fourth-year Provost's Guard (Dog), protégée of Lord Gershom of Haryse (the Lord Provost)
Pounce	normally a constellation called the Cat, Beka's advisor and friend for the last eight years
Achoo Curlypaws	scent hound assigned to Beka

AT PROVOST'S HOUSE

Gershom of Haryse	Lord Provost of Tortall, Beka's patron
Teodorie of Haryse	Gershom's lady, patroness of Beka's brothers and sisters
Diona, Lorine, Nilo, Willes	Beka's younger sisters and brothers, all training for work in noble houses
Mya Fane	Beka's foster aunt, cook at Provost's House

PROVOST'S DOGS AND ASSOCIATES IN CORUS

Sergeant Clara Goodwin	Desk Sergeant, Evening Watch, Jane Street kennel, the Lower City Guard District
Sir Acton of Fenrigh	Watch Commander, Evening Watch, Jane Street kennel, the Lower City Guard District

Senior Corporal Nyler Jewel	most senior street Dog, the Lower City Evening Watch, Yoav's partner
Senior Guardswoman Osgyth Yoav	street Dog, Jewel's partner
Senior Guardsman Wulfric Birch	street Dog, Westover's partner
Ersken Westover	street Dog, fourth year, Beka's friend, Kora's lover
Ahern Walker	Holborn's former partner, Flash District
Holborn Shaftstall	five-year Dog, deceased, Beka's betrothed, the Lower City Day Watch

The Hunt

Achoo Curlypaws	
Beka Cooper	
Pounce	
Senior Guardsman Matthias Tunstall	Beka's partner
Farmer Cape	Provost's mage from Blue Harbor
Lady Sabine of Macayhill	lady knight, Tunstall's lover

The Court of the Rogue, Corus

Rosto, called the Piper	Rogue of Corus
Aniki Forfrysning	swordswoman, rusher, chieftain in the Court of the Rogue
Koramin Ingensra	mage, serves the Rogue, Ersken Westover's lover

Residents of Corus

Tansy Lofts — Beka's oldest friend from their slum days, now a respectable wife, mother, and businesswoman

Granny Fern Cooper — Beka's paternal grandmother

Kaasa — dust spinner in Dogs' cemetery

Provost's Guard in Port Caynn

Sir Tullus of King's Reach — knight, Deputy Provost, Port Caynn Provost's Guard

Sergeant Terart Axman — Desk Sergeant at Guards House, hound breeder

Sergeant Nestor Haryse — cousin of Lord Gershom, a Day Watch Sergeant in Deep Harbor District, Okha Soyan's lover

The Royal Family and Their Household

Prince Baird of Conté — King Roger's younger brother

Prince Gareth of Conté — Roger and Jessamine's only child

Queen Jessamine of Conté — Roger's second wife, mother of Gareth

King Roger II of Conté — husband of Jessamine, father of Gareth

Ironwood of Sinthya — King Roger's personal mage

Orielle Clavynger — Queen Jessamine's personal mage

Lunedda — Gareth's nursemaid, murdered

Tassilo	Gareth's King's Own guard, murdered

AT QUEENSGRACE

Aeldra of Queensgrace	countess, wife to Dewin, Sabine's cousin
Baylisa of Disart	lady-in-waiting
Dewin of Queensgrace	count
Elyot of Aspen Vale	master mage, educated in Carthak
Graeme of Aspen Vale	baron, Elyot's older brother
Fay	talkative baker
Fess	very old dust spinner
Iris	talkative baker
Lewyth of Disart	lady-in-waiting
Linnet Beck	six-year-old slave
Niccols	castle steward
Parris Eckard	silk merchant
Rosewyn	noblewoman
Wyttabyrd	lady-in-waiting

AT HALLEBURN

Daeggan	slave boy, tough
Dolsa Silkweb	illusion mage, great mage
Lady Nomalla of Halleburn	lady knight
Lord Thanen of Halleburn	Nomalla's father, Sabine's cousin

OTHERS

Beldeal	irate headwoman, War Gorge Marsh
Ormer	local guide, War Gorge Marsh
Cassine Catfoot	Farmer's Master, female great mage
Looseknot	Farmer's first teacher
Elfed	captain of the King's Own
Iceblade Regengar	peregrine boat mage
Lazamon of Buckglen	lord chancellor of mages
Martinin of Macayhill	Norow's only son, Sabine's brother
Lord Norow of Macayhill	Sabine's father
Palisa Vintor	Dog from Arenaver
Okha Soyan	popular male-dressed-as-female singer/entertainer, Nestor's lover

Glossary

afore: before

aught: anything

bailey: courtyard in a castle

bait: food and water for horses at a rest stop

barbican: fortified gateway

barrel trapper: kidnapper

beard: oppose boldly or impudently

Birdie: informant

blessing: birth control device or charm

bogle: ghost

bolster: long, narrow, stiff pillow or cushion

Book of Gold, The: oldest census of the noble houses of Tortall, dating back to the founding of the realm

boot: metal boot placed on a victim's foot. Wedges are hammered into the inside of the boot, pressing on the lower leg until they break bones. Metal boots can also be heated to burn the victim's leg.

bordel: house of prostitution

budget: pouch or wallet

by-blow: illegitimate child

canoodling: sexual activity

caudles: soothing drinks given to excited or crazy people

cipher: shorthand method used by Dogs, with symbols for entire common words

cole: false coin

colemonger: someone who makes or passes false coins; counterfeiter

Common: language spoken in Tortall, Barzun, Tusaine, Maren, Tyra, and parts of Saraine and Scanra

coney: victim of a theft or any crime; sucker

copper noble: coin equivalent to ten coppers

corbie: raven

cot: small house or cottage

cove: man

coyne: vagina

cozening: cajoling, wheedling

cracknob: madman

craven: cowardly

cresset: metal wall fixture containing wood or oil to be burned for light

cuirass: piece of armor protecting chest and back

dance a set: fight

destrier: warhorse

detail: assignment

Dog: member of the Provost's Guard

dozy: sluggish

Drink: form of torture in which water is poured down the victim's throat and nose to simulate drowning

dust spinner: small dust whirlwind, what our world calls a dust devil

elsewise: otherwise; or else

fambles: hands

Ferrets: street nickname for Crown spies

folderol: nonsense, foolishness

fussock: donkey; old mean woman

gab: speech

Galla pasties: turnovers with beef, cheese, pine nuts, currants, and spices

get bit: be cheated

gixie: girl

gob: mouth

gods' fool: crazy person

gold noble: coin equivalent to ten silver nobles or four gold bits

gormless: gutless

Great Gods: most powerful gods in the pantheon: Mithros; the Great Goddess (three aspects: Maiden, Mother, Crone); the Black God of Death; Oinomi Wavewalker; the Smith God; the Trickster or the Crooked God; Gainel (Master of Dreams); Wind (god of all winds); Pelmry (bird-clawed god of scribes); Apetekus (god of slaves); Wilnedur (goddess of slaves)

ground cover: anything on the ground: grass, trees, bushes, gravel, stones, and crops

Happy Bag: weekly bribes for Provost's office

Heskaly's drum: instrument used by the trickster god of the hills to make people crazy

hoddy-dod: slang for snail; someone who is slow

Hunt: criminal investigation; pursuit of criminals

hunter: hound trained to hunt escaped prisoners and slaves

Hurdik: language of Tunstall's native hill tribes

jabbernob: chatterbox

Jane Street kennel: Tunstall and Beka's home base

jerkin: hip-length sleeveless jacket

jumped-up: raised above one's station

kennel: Provost's watch house; police station

ladyhorse: destrier (warhorse) bred smaller and lighter for lady knights

looby: fool

lure: scent sample used to give Achoo the right scent to follow

mains: main dishes for meals

Master: Mr.; mister; old title of honor for a mage

mayhap: perhaps

mot: woman

mumper: beggar

new Tom: overeager stranger; one who thinks he knows the game

nimmer: swindle

nuncle: pimp

pallet: narrow, straw-filled mattress

pig's knuckle: barely competent worker; major insult

Puppy: trainee in the Provost's Guard

rack: torture device on which the victim is placed with arms and legs spread. Turns of the handle and grips stretch the victim until his or her joints dislocate, then separate. Muscles are also stretched to a point at which they no longer contract. Some racks also have a spiked roller that can do bloody damage when the victim is placed facedown.

randy: always having sex on his or her mind

Rat: captive, civilian, criminal, or prey (to Dogs)

raw one: corpse; body

rushers: thugs

sap: lead-filled six-inch leather cylinder; bone-breaking weapon

sarden: blasted; damned; detestable

scry: watch something magically in water, a crystal, or a mirror

scummer: animal dung

scut: idiot

seek: hunt down a criminal or missing person

Sign: sign against evil; an X intersected by a vertical line to form a star on the chest

sign: in a Hunt, some indication of the prey, such as a footprint or handprint; marks of urine, feces, or vomit; or pieces of clothing

slum stew: liquid garbage

stripes: marks of the whip

swive: vulgar term for having sexual intercourse

tack: harness for a horse, including bridle and saddle

take someone over Breakbone Falls: administer a very severe beating

tarse: piece of meat

thumbscrew: vise that crushes the victim's fingers or toes

ticklers: fingers

tightfisted: cheap

trencher: "plate" cut from a stale loaf of bread, used to hold food

trull: very low-class woman; the dregs

turncoat: traitor

twilsey: refreshing drink made from raspberry or cider vinegar and water

wander mage: mage who travels, picking up work here and there

wench: less-than-respectable woman

ACHOO'S COMMANDS

Come here	*Kemari*	(kehMAHRee)
Down	*Turun*	(tooROON)
Easy	*Mudah*	(MOOdah)
Eat	*Makan*	(mahKAN)
Friend	*Kawan*	(kahWAHN)
Go	*Maji*	(MAHjee)
Go fast	*Cepat*	(SAYpaht)
Greet	*Pengantar*	(pehnGANtahr, *gan* like *can*)
Guard	*Jaga*	(JAHgah)
Heel	*Tumit*	(tooMIHT)
No	*Tak*	(TACK)
Quiet	*Diamlah*	(deeAHMlah)
Relax	*Santai*	(sahnTIE)
Seek	*Mencari*	(mehnKAHRee)
Sit	*Dukduk*	(DOOKdook like *bookbook*)
Slow	*Pelan*	(pehLAHN)
Smell	*Bau*	(BOW, like *cow*)
Stay	*Tinggal*	(tingGAHL)
Steady/easy	*Gampang*	(gamPANG)
Stop	*Berhenti*	(buhrHEHNtee)
Up/rise	*Bangkit*	(bangKEET)
Wait	*Tunggu*	(toonGOO)

Acknowledgments

My heartfelt thanks goes to Dr. Daniel Wnorowski; Daniel DiMartini, P.A.; Cheryl Bryant; Dr. Sami Abdul-Malak; the aides, housekeepers, nurses, and therapists of Menorah Park in Syracuse, New York; and Ted Lambert of Orthopedic Rehabilitation Associates of Syracuse, New York. All of you saw me through my surgery and subsequent therapy with knowledge, kindness, efficiency, and professionalism. Thanks for putting me back on my feet (knees, actually) and back to writing again!

My thanks to my Random House crew: Mallory Loehr, who continues to be wonderful; Lisa Findlay, who edited *Bloodhound;* Schuyler Hooke, old friend and new editor for *Mastiff;* and Chelsea Eberly, who runs interference.

Cheers for my beloved agent, Craig Tenney, and for the foreign rights team at Harold Ober, who keep the lines of publication open and flowing.

Gratitude to Bruce Coville, my reading buddy and fellow Bollywood fan, who swaps notes with me as we read our works-in-progress to each other.

And at home, I say thanks to my beloved Spouse-Creature, Tim, who is an integral part of all of my books, and to my assistants, Sara Alan and Cara Coville, who tolerate my goofy self and help keep me moving forward. It would not be the same without any of you.

I'd also like to thank Freetheslaves.com for their splendid information and work. Wherever we are, the United States or former Soviet socialist republics, Australia or Dubai, Canada or India, there are slaves. Someone may come up with a prettier name, but they are slaves at the core. Please don't forget them.

TAMORA PIERCE captured the imagination of readers more than twenty-five years ago with *Alanna: The First Adventure*. She has written over twenty-five books, including three completed quartets (The Song of the Lioness, The Immortals, and The Protector of the Small), the Trickster duet, and now the Beka Cooper trilogy, set in the fantasy realm of Tortall. She has also written The Circle of Magic and The Circle Opens quartets, as well as two stand-alone titles, *The Will of the Empress* and *Melting Stones*. Her books have been translated into many languages, and some are available on audio from Listening Library and Full Cast Audio. She and her husband, Timothy Liebe, also co-wrote the six-episode comic *White Tiger: A Hero's Compulsion* for Marvel Comics.

Tamora Pierce's fast-paced, suspenseful writing and strong, believable heroines have won her much praise: *Emperor Mage* was a 1996 ALA Best Book for Young Adults, *The Realms of the Gods* was listed as an "outstanding fantasy novel" by *Voice of Youth Advocates* in 1996, *Squire* (Protector of the Small #3) was a 2002 ALA Best Book for Young Adults, and *Lady Knight* (Protector of the Small #4) debuted at number one on the *New York Times* bestseller list. *Trickster's Choice* spent a month on the *New York Times* bestseller list and was a 2003 ALA Best Book for Young Adults. *Trickster's Queen* was also a *New York Times* bestseller.

An avid reader herself, Ms. Pierce graduated from the University of Pennsylvania. She has worked at a variety of jobs and has written everything from novels to radio plays. Along with writer Meg Cabot (The Princess Diaries series), she co-founded SheroesCentral, a discussion board about female heroes; remarkable women in fact, fiction, and history; books; current events; and teen issues. SheroesCentral and

SheroesFans are now independent of her, but she still drops by and welcomes the Sheroes she meets on tour.

Tamora Pierce lives in Syracuse, New York, with her husband, Tim, a writer, Web page designer, and Web administrator, and their eight indoor cats, porch cat, basement cat, two birds, and occasional rescued wildlife.

For more information, visit tamorapierce.com.